# STORM CROW

'So detailed, so accurate in its depiction of terrorist and counter-terrorist activities, that had it been written as a piece of non-fiction, the Government would almost certainly have tried to ban it' *Time Out*

'*Storm Crow* is that rare bird – a meticulously researched thriller with a gripping and ominously plausible plot' Dr Bruce Hoffman, Director of the RAND Corporation's Washington Office

'This rattles along at a fine pace, yet has time for the detail which not only adds authenticity but demonstrates the author's thorough research and sound knowledge of his subject' *Shots*

*Also by Jeff Gulvin*

# JEFF GULVIN

# STORM CROW

ORION

An Orion paperback
First published in Great Britain by Victor Gollancz in 1998
This paperback edition published in 1999 by Orion Books Ltd,
Orion House, 5 Upper St Martin's Lane, London, WC2H 9EA

Fourth impression 2001

A CIP catalogue record for this book is available
from the British Library.

ISBN: 0 75283 457 6

Printed and bound in Great Britain by
Clays Ltd, St Ives plc

*For Humphrey Price*

The author would like to thank:

The Domestic Terrorism Operations Unit
and Fugitive Publicity Office,
FBI Headquarters,
Washington D.C.

without whom this novel could not have been written.

Also:

The people of Hailey, Idaho.

And:

Chief, for pulling me out of the fire.

# GLOSSARY

| | |
|---|---|
| AMIP | area major incident pool |
| ARV | armed-response vehicle |
| ASAC | assistant special agent in charge |
| ATF | Alcohol, Tobacco and Firearms (Bureau of) |
| ATO | ammunitions technical officer |
| BLM | Bureau of Land Management |
| Box 500 | MI5 |
| Box 850 | MI6 |
| CAD | computer-aided dispatch |
| CJIS | Criminal Justice Information Services |
| con-ex | controlled explosion |
| CRO | Criminal Records Office |
| DEROS | date of estimated return from overseas |
| DPG | Diplomatic Protection Group |
| DRA | Defence Research Agency |
| DUI | driving under the influence |
| ESLA | Electro-static lifting apparatus |
| EOD | Explosives Ordnance Disposal |
| Expo | explosives officer |
| FEST | Foreign Emergency Search Team |
| HAC | Honourable Artillery Company |
| IED | improvised explosive device |
| LCD | liquid-crystal display |
| LED | light-emitting diode |
| leg-att | legal attaché (FBI) |
| MOE | method of entry |

| | |
|---|---|
| NBC suit | nuclear, biological and chemical warfare suit |
| NVGs | night-vision glasses |
| OP | observation point |
| PINS | portable isotopic neutron spectroscopy |
| PNC | Police National Computer |
| Prot' | close protection officer |
| RSO | regional security officer |
| RSP | render safe procedure |
| RVP | rendezvous point |
| SFO | specialist firearms officer |
| SIOC | Strategic Intelligence Operations Center |
| SO3 | Scenes of Crime |
| SO11 | Directorate of Intelligence |
| SO12 | Special Branch; also SB |
| SO13 | Antiterrorist Branch |
| SO19 | Tactical Firearms Unit |
| TPU | timing and power unit |
| TSU | Technical Support Unit |
| UCA | undercover agent |

'. . . Militia members believe that the US government is part of a conspiracy to create a new world order . . . existing boundaries will be dissolved and the world will be ruled by the United Nations. Last year some of these militants continued to conduct paramilitary training and stockpile weapons.'

'Terrorism in the United States'
Terrorist Research and Analytical Center,
National Security Division,
Federal Bureau of Investigation

# PROLOGUE

*August 1996*

The Irishman sat on the balcony of the Chart House restaurant overlooking the Potomac River. If he thought about it, he could hear the traffic on Woodrow Wilson Bridge. A wasp hovered over his beer glass and for a moment he watched it, then flicked it away with lazy fingers, FTQ tattooed on his knuckles. He looked briefly at his watch as the *Cherry Blossom* steamer bumped against the jetty. It was white with yellow-piped trim, a riverboat whose massive sun-coloured paddle gleamed in the brilliance of a sky with no cloud. He checked his watch again. One-fifteen. Lifting the glass he drank, the beer crisp and dry at the back of his throat.

Boats shifted with the mud-coloured water that ebbed from the wake of another, passing down the river. The Irishman watched two girls in shorts and T-shirts sitting at the table along from him. He could smell their cigarette smoke and he wrinkled his nose in disgust. He tapped his fingernails on the table top and glanced at the mobile telephone next to the stem of his glass.

Two hours previously he had been sitting in the White Lion bar. It was cramped, slightly run-down, not the sort of place he would normally go. Billy the barman played rugby, read rugby reports from a stool and flexed his muscles. The Irishman sat upstairs on his own, reading the *Washington Post* and listening to the hubbub of students downstairs, and to Billy being accosted by the Coors sales girl with her three kids and no husband. She hung on his arm as he poured glasses of Bud or MGD or Newcastle Brown Ale for the regulars. The Irishman watched Kuhlmann below him. Kuhlmann had no idea he was there.

An hour before that he was in Dean and Deluca's, sitting at a marble-topped table, dipping a bagel into cappuccino, while two men from the FBI sat deep in conversation only a table away. The Hoover building was right around the corner and mini debriefs or private conversations quite often took place in here. The deli was downstairs, below street level. It had a wide chequerboard floor, with mock marble tables and a huge metal counter, and pipes like the tentacles of some metallic monster disappearing into the wall. The Irishman liked to sit there and watch the Feds talking to themselves. He had phoned Kuhlmann from the call box on Pennsylvania Avenue, and that brought a smile to his face.

He sipped more beer and watched the boats lifting again with the swell. Humid August sunshine; he could feel it begin to burn his face. Lifting a booted foot to the vacant chair in front of him, he gazed down river towards the city. He could see the Observatory and the Bolling Air Base from this vantage point. A woman with heavy make-up walked past him. She dropped a half-finished cigarette on to the deck where it slipped between two slats and stuck, the smoke rising to irritate him yet again. He watched her go, oblivious to the hazard she left in her wake. Gold-coloured hair, brushed under her cheeks, white T-shirt over white pants overfilled with sagging, loose buttocks. Leaning forward, he poured beer over the cigarette and in the same moment looked towards the flagpole. Kuhlmann walked up from King Street.

☆

14

Bruno Kuhlmann had been sitting on the grassy square within the confines of the law school, talking to some girls he used to know, when the call came in on his cellphone. He rolled on to his stomach, facing away from them as he answered. 'Yeah?'

'Torpedo Factory Arts Center in Alexandria. D'ye know it?'

'Of course.'

'There's a flagpole just in front of it. In fact, there's two. Stand underneath the one flying the Stars and Stripes at exactly two-fifteen this afternoon. I'll meet you there.'

The phone went dead before he had a chance to say anything else. He switched it off and looked back at the girls. 'You guys wanna beer?'

They had gone to the White Lion where Billy wore T-shirts and mimicked Patrick Swayze, not in the way he spoke but the way he looked, the way he stood. Kuhlmann used to listen to him go on about rugby, the latest imported sport. Contact, more contact than football. He nodded and smiled; said nothing and thought what a sad fuck he was.

He had left the girls in the bar and bought a five-dollar pass for the Metro at Foggy Bottom Station. From there he went down the Blue line and got off at Braddock Road. He could have gone on to King and walked straight down, but today was D-Day and he wanted to be especially careful; so he had bisected the streets from Braddock to Waterfront Park. August Sunday and bikers in leather cruised King Street. Wannabe good old boys with gleaming fifteen-thousand-dollar motorcycles, piss-pot helmets and drooping moustaches. Kuhlmann was clean-shaven, his hair longer now and blond, but that was for a reason. He silently mocked the Harley riders, leather-clad on a Sunday, and lawyers and doctors come Monday.

He came out at King and Royal and looked at his watch. One-twenty. That gave him time enough. He knew the area but he had not been here in a while and he needed to check his exit routes, just in case he needed them.

There were two entrances to the waterfront from King, one through the shopping mall, one slightly nearer the river in front of the Dominion. The guy with the water glasses was there, quite a crowd around him as he dipped his fingers and played tunes on the rims. They were not bad: the guy had talent, you had to say that, more than most of the so-called entertainers who hung out here on a Sunday. From where he stood on King Street he could see the flagpole and the girl who rode the unicycle, entertaining kids. The way out was clear this end. He checked the mall and figured he'd spot anyone who shouldn't have been there. The other side of the Dominion was water, so no exit there. That only left the far end of the park itself, beyond the Chart House restaurant.

From the Chart House balcony, the Irishman sipped a fresh glass of beer and watched Kuhlmann carefully quarter the area. Ex-army, Explosives Ordnance Disposal. He must have done some covert exercises if none of the real thing – by the time EOD got involved, covert wasn't what was wanted.

Kuhlmann marked out the territory, though, and the Irishman silently acknowledged the action. He sat and watched. With long black hair and a red bandana wrapped about his throat like a gypsy, the Irishman wore a leather waistcoat over his T-shirt, fading Levis and cowboy boots. Half a beard and black-lensed Ray-Bans. Kuhlmann walked the length of the boardwalk and disappeared round the other side of the restaurant. Fifteen minutes later, he came back from the mall and stopped under the flagpole. From the breast pocket of his jacket he took cigarettes and cupped his hand to the breeze as he lit one. The Irishman looked at his watch. Not time yet. As if on cue Kuhlmann looked in both directions then sauntered up the steps of the restaurant, walking past him and on into the bar. He reappeared with a bottle of Miller in his hand and leaned on the rail not ten paces from the Irishman's table. The Irishman slipped the phone into his pocket and stared up at the sky.

He could smell Kuhlmann's cigarette. Rob Whiteley. That's what Kuhlmann called himself when he was talking, quite a bit of talk now since all this began. Today would be the day when talking ceased. Kuhlmann looked at his watch, drew stiffly on his cigarette and let go smoke, most of which blew across the Irishman's table. Not once did Kuhlmann look at him.

At precisely fifteen minutes after two, Kuhlmann finished his beer and walked back to the flagpole. The Irishman took the cloned cellphone from his pocket and dialled. He spoke without looking round.

'You're on time.'

'Of course.'

'Murphy's bar on King Street. Ten minutes from now. Order two pints of Guinness and make sure he pours it slow. Guinness takes time to pour. Tell him not to hurl it in like water.'

'Whatever you say.'

'Sit at the back of the bar, to the side of the cigarette machine. I'll make myself known to you.'

He switched off the phone and sat back in the chair. The wind had got up and the river slopped against the jetty. The *Cherry Blossom* moved on her ropes. He allowed two minutes, then rose and looked round. Kuhlmann was gone. He stepped down to the jetty and wandered round the back of the restaurant. A couple arm in arm were having their photograph taken in front of the riverboat. He smiled and nodded and wandered to the steamer, where he inspected the shine on her paintwork. Taking the cellphone from his pocket, he dropped it into the water. He stood a moment longer, pushed a hand through his hair, then walked up past the Arts Center.

Murphy's bar was dimly lit, a lot of people still out to lunch. Most of the tables were taken, but Kuhlmann had secured the correct one just to the side of the cigarette machine. He sat facing him, with a view over the whole room, two tall glasses of blackening Guinness before him. The Irishman moved the length of the bar where every stool was taken, people eating and drinking. He caught snatches of English accents from two men counting coins.

Kuhlmann lifted his eyebrows as the Irishman sat down. 'You were at the Chart House.'

The Irishman sat across from him and looked at the Guinness. He rested both palms flat on the table, head half-cocked like a dog. The beer still had not settled. 'Did ye do like I asked?'

'Slow, right?'

'It doesn't look slow.'

Kuhlmann grinned then. 'Not like in Dublin, eh?'

The Irishman stared at him through the black of his glasses. 'Never been to Dublin.'

'Belfast then.' Kuhlmann had that smug look on his face. 'I had a feeling we'd be talking Irish.'

The Irishman leaned closer to him. 'How do you know we are?'

Kuhlmann stared at his fingers, the tattooed letters in blue. 'Fuck the Queen,' he said.

'Ah, but whose queen?'

Kuhlmann lifted his eyebrows. 'Anyway, I was told *American*.'

'Were you now?'

Kuhlmann sipped the Guinness and made a face. 'I

hate this stuff.' He pushed the glass away and took out his cigarettes. He had half taken one out when the Irishman suddenly leaned over and closed his hand over the pack.

'Don't smoke,' he said. 'I really don't like it, and people are eating in here.'

Kuhlmann stared at him for a moment, then at the crushed pack of Marlboro Lights. His first instinct was to hit him, but the Irishman sat there with his elbows on the table and stared at him through sunglasses. Kuhlmann could not see his eyes.

'OK, let's cut to the chase,' he said. 'My man wants to know – do we have a deal?'

'No.'

Kuhlmann narrowed his eyes. 'What d'you mean – *no*?'

'Exactly what I say. We were paid more than that in Mexico, and that was just a few mortars.'

'Look,' Kuhlmann said. 'I don't make the prices.'

'Then maybe someone else should be sitting here.' The Irishman steepled fingers in front of his face. 'Either way, the price isn't good enough.'

Kuhlmann wiped froth from his lip and leaned his elbows on the table. 'Listen, Mr Irish or whatever your name is, it's a fair price. If you don't want it . . .'

'You'll get somebody else?' The Irishman leaned towards him suddenly, and the chill in his voice made the hairs rise on Kuhlmann's neck. 'I don't think so. The price is the ten million dollars stated. No negotiation. We have plenty of customers and there's no urgency about our business.' He paused then and looked at him. 'But I gather there is for you. It's been forty years already.'

Kuhlmann ran his tongue round the line of his mouth. 'How'm I gonna justify ten million dollars to him?'

The Irishman creased his lips. 'I'll tell you, Bruno. Shall I?'

Kuhlmann stiffened. 'My name's Rob.'

'No it's not. You like people to think it is, but your real name is Bruno. Last name – Kuhlmann. Your father's name was Jens and your mother's Heike. You were born in 1973. August. Your birthday was last Tuesday. Happy birthday, Bruno. You graduated in Dayton, Ohio, and after college you joined the US Army. Explosives Ordnance Disposal. Your last posting was at the Navy EOD school at Indian Head, just down the river there. You worked as an instructor under Sergeant Robert G. Gittings. You got a scholarship to George Washington University to study electronics to Master's level and you graduated last year. No problem – with your EOD background.' He sat back and sipped beer. 'You moved back to Ohio, but got bored, so ye drifted a wee bit. Michigan, Illinois and then Buffalo, Wyoming. You met our mutual friend at a gun show in Twin Falls, Idaho. You like survivalist magazines and you surf the Internet web sites. "Alt. Constitutionalist" and "2nd Amendment" mostly. You once submitted an open letter entitled "America Awake".'

Kuhlmann was staring wide-eyed at him. 'Your girlfriend's name is Susan,' the Irishman went on, 'but she's just Wednesdays and Fridays. You sleep with Jackie on Saturdays and you've got your eye on a wee lassie called Rosanne whenever you come over here. You had a drink with her and a friend of hers – Stacey her name is – today, at the White Lion bar. Diana was there. I don't know if you know Diana, she's the Coors sales girl who hangs around wi' Billy.' He grinned then and rubbed at his tattooed knuckles. 'But that's small fry, isn't it. Shall I tell you what else we know?'

Kuhlmann smarted then, a faint flicker in his eyes.

'You're the John Doe from Atlanta.'

Kuhlmann's face was cold. He did not say anything.

The Irishman drained the rest of his Guinness and pulled Kuhlmann's unwanted glass towards him. 'We know everything there is to know about your man. We know what companies he runs, which ones are dummy and how he uses banks to front him with discretionary trust funds. We know about his interests in the steel industry, and in gold. We know what he does in Paraguay. We know about the hotels in Europe and the mills in Finland. We even know about the licensing problems he's been having with the Finnish government. You see, they like to control their paper industry. It's about all they've got up there.' Again he sipped beer. 'Still, shouldn't cause him too much of a problem, not as if it's a big part of the empire. Last count, Bruno, your man there was worth five billion dollars.' He shook his head and smiled. 'Now, I think you'll agree we're worth the ten million.'

'I thought it was a *him*, not a *we*.'

'*Him, them, us, her.* Who knows, Bruno? Who indeed knows. But I think you understand what I'm saying.' He smiled again and stood up. 'You've got twenty-four hours to think about it. Twenty-four hours to talk to your man. Put the answer in the usual place and somebody'll collect it.' He glanced about the room, then he took a long, slim envelope from inside his waistcoat and dropped it in front of Kuhlmann. 'Give that to your man as a keepsake.'

After he had gone Kuhlmann wiped sweat from his palms on his jeans. He took a cigarette from the crushed pack and noticed that his hand shook as he lit it. He glanced at the envelope, then picked it up. It was light, as if there was nothing inside, but he could feel something. He slid his finger the length of the flap, peered inside and his palms were moist once again. A single black crow's feather.

The Irishman walked the length of King Street, then turned off for the Seaport bar. He went inside with his hands in his pockets. The familiar flagstone floor and dimly lit bar area: he could smell the coffee from the back of the room. The barman nodded to him.

'Gimme an MGD, buddy. Will you? No glass. I'll be right back.'

'You got it.'

The Irishman made his way out to the restaurant area and went into the men's room. He unzipped and urinated, the smile spreading over his face. When he was finished, he washed his hands with soap from the dispenser. Blue ink ran from his fingers. When he dried them, the knuckles were clean.

**I**

---

### June 1997

Jack Swann stood on the cliff and paid out the rope, the hardware clanking on his harness as the breeze came up off the sea. Caroline fought with the travelling rug while her husband, George Webb, struggled with the buckle of his sit harness. Swann glanced over his shoulder at the shingle-strewn beach two hundred feet below him. For a moment the wind seemed to rise and he could taste it cold on his breath. But out of the wind, the sun was hot. Earlier, the week had been iffy, but this weekend was lovely. Caroline got the rug settled and sat down to squeeze Bergasol on her arms. She looked up at Swann, shading her eyes from the sun. He nodded to the rug. 'You sure you want to put that there? We're climbing further down.'

She looked at him again, then the rug, then stared further along the cliff path where it inclined in a steep, sweeping arc. 'It's too windy up there, Jack. I'll catch more sun where I am. Yell when you get to the top and I'll open the wine.'

Webb looked at Swann. 'We're doing Kinky Boots, right?'

Swann shook his head. 'Pink Void.' He pointed. 'Kinky Boots is the other side of that outcrop.' The abseil rope had hit the beach. He let it go and pointed to a jagged gathering of rocks that broke open the path of the sea.

Webb fastened his harness and sat down to pull on rock boots. He moaned about the size, then Swann reminded him that all good climbers wear their boots two sizes or more too small.

'Whoever said I was a good climber?'

'Right. You just wanted to look good in the shop.'

Webb wagged a finger at him. 'There you go again, Flash. Judging everyone by your own piss-poor standards.'

Swann shook his head, feeding the abseil rope through the figure 8 on his harness.

'We climbing on 11 or two 9s?' Webb asked.

Swann indicated the twin coils of rope over his shoulder. 'Steep pitch, Webby. Use the 9s, eh?'

'Whatever. You got the right sticht plate?'

Swann patted his harness, winked at Caroline and stepped backwards to the edge of the cliff. He paused, not looking down, just allowing his weight to come to rest against the figure 8 at his middle. He stood upright, pivoting on the balls of his feet, crammed and buckled into the Asolos. He looked beyond Caroline, beyond George Webb, up the empty clifftop to the sky and beyond that. For a moment he closed his eyes. He could feel Webb watching him, sweat moved against his skin, then he looked between his feet and eased himself backwards.

At the bottom, he waited for Webb and checked the guidebook. When Webb hit the ground, they began to make their way along the short stretch of beach to the foot of the route. The sea broke against the shingle. Swann could smell salt, the damp rancid seaweed that choked the edge of the surf. On the clifftop, Caroline looked down at them and waved.

Swann knew what was going through her mind, what was going through Webb's. He unwound the two 9mm ropes from his shoulder and laid them out carefully. Webb moved up to him, his face dusted by sea spray. Above them, a grey-winged herring gull flew across the path of the sun and cried to them on the wind. Swann felt the need for a cigarette. He had some in his chalk bag and took one out, fighting with the wind to light it.

'Thought you were knocking that on the head,' Webb said to him.

'Pia, Webby. Smokes like a bloody chimney.'

Webb scratched his head and looked for a suitable rock to mount a belay. 'That'll do,' he muttered, then wrapped an eight-foot sling round it and pulled it tight, before clipping in a karabiner. 'Don't want to go yo-yo when you peel off.'

Swann looked up at him. 'I'm leading, then.'

'First pitch, Jack.'

'First pitch, my arse.'

Webb made a face. 'Hard Very Severe, Jack. You want to know how long it's been since I led HVS?'

'You told me you could lead Extreme.'

'I used to be able to dance like a Cossack too, but I'm older now.' Webb made an open-handed gesture.

'And fatter, eh.'

'Shit happens, Jack.'

Swann bent to one knee, resting the length of his arm over his thigh. He looked up at the 320-foot climb that awaited him and dropped his cigarette in the shingle.

Webb stepped back and looked up. Swann tied both ropes to his harness and checked his sling full of runners. He had all the Rocks and three sizes of Friends. He even had a couple of ancient Clogs and Hexentrics. Some of the line was a bit worn now, but the knots were still good. He lowered the sling and felt the weight pull against his middle.

He looked briefly out to sea. The gull called again, then

dived for something in the surf. He did not see it surface, but faced the cliff, which stretched flat and all but vertical above him, grey and brown, looking damp where the sun set the smooth rock gleaming. He dipped each hand in turn in his chalk bag and rubbed them together, then he moved up to the rock.

'First pitch is the hardest.' He looked above his head and to the right. 'Need to make the groove up there.'

Webb was looking at the guidebook. 'Says there's a peg to tie off on.'

'Hundred and twenty feet. See you in a bit.' Swann dusted his hands and felt out the first holds, a thin crack that arced upwards to the main groove sixty feet above his head. 'Climbing,' he muttered and started.

He moved upwards slowly, feeling out the crack, testing each hold with his fingers before placing any weight on them. There were no footholds to speak of, just pressure points where the slick rubber of friction boots would hold you. It was not vertical, but it was high and exposed, with the wind sending sea spray scuttling across the flatness of the rock for the first fifty feet or so. The twin 9mm ropes dragged at him and he put his first piece of protection in at fifteen feet, a small wire runner, clipping both ropes to it through the karabiner. Below him, he could hear Webb whistling as he paid out the line.

Swann's movements were awkward; the smoothness with which his peers would have associated him in the past was gone. Every time he did this he tortured himself in some small way. It should be a bit better now, but it wasn't. He knew that tonight he would dream. At least he would see Pia tomorrow.

He got through the first sixty feet, which were without doubt the hardest, and rested at the groove. He placed a runner and Webb took in the slack. Swann allowed himself a moment or two to catch his breath and adjust the weight of the ropes before going on. At eighty feet it grew steep again and he placed runners at shorter intervals. The sea stretched to his left, calm beyond the initial boil of the surf where restless waves broke against one another. He could see a ship all but stationary along the line of the horizon. He climbed on, gaining in confidence, more sure of the moves. The rock face was warm and firm and polished, the crack thin, and he used his feet for poise and balance while feeding his hands up and over one another. He could see the peg for the belay and the end of the first pitch about twenty feet above his head. The next hold was slim and he reached beyond it, pivoting round on one foot for extra pressure.

His foot slipped and he fell. Ten feet, fifteen, zipping off the rock. The runner popped and he careered fifteen feet more. At the bottom of the route, George Webb hauled the ropes hard across the sticht plate and groaned as he was lifted off his feet. The belay held and Swann dangled above him like a spider.

Webb got his feet firmly on rock again and saw Swann scrabbling for handholds. The second runner had held. He got himself upright and cursed, heart thumping against his ribs, guts aching where the harness had bitten his flesh.

'What you trying to do, Flash, give me a heart attack?' Webb shouted up to him.

Swann said nothing, moisture gathered above his eyes and he was not sure of his voice. He looked down at the rocks and the beach and Webb seventy feet below him, where the surf gained ground on the shingle. He let go a long stiff breath, closed his eyes and for a moment he was back there with the cloud all about him, damp over the cold that gnawed through every ounce of clothing until it chafed his bones. He opened his eyes, twisted his face to the sun and breathed. The gull called again from above him.

'You'll have to climb it all over again now.'

He looked down at Webb, looked in his eyes and even from that height he knew. Webb cupped a hand to his mouth. 'Go on, kidder. You can get there.'

Swann dipped in his chalk bag once more, looked up and wiped the sweat from his eyes with the back of his hand.

'You want to get back on the wall, Flash, only my breakfast is coming up?'

'Climbing,' Swann said, and started.

At 120 feet, he tied off and relaxed. Webb swarmed up after him and clipped into the belay. He laid a hand on Swann's shoulder.

'If you're going to peel off – tell me, eh, so I can prepare myself.' He patted his middle. 'Not as slim as I was.'

Swann wiped his hands on his thighs and saw that they were shaking.

'I'll take the second pitch, yeah?' Webb said.

Swann shook his head. 'No. I'll do it.'

At the top, he wound the ropes about his neck and sat down. Webb was waving across the clifftop to his wife. Swann stared out at the ocean. One man chugged towards the horizon in an open boat, the wake washing out from his inboard in a fan of white ripples. Gulls chased him, calling to one another, their cries as part of the wind. Swann looked at his feet, then wiped the sweat from his palms.

Caroline poured white wine, chill from the cooler, into long-stemmed glasses and handed one to each of them. She had food laid out on a red checked cloth from the hamper.

'God, you're so civilized, Caroline.' Swann sipped the wine and it cooled the burning at the back of his throat.

'Good climb?' she said.

He looked at the soles of his feet, crossed underneath him. 'Peeled off.'

'Did you?'

'Yeah. Just below the first belay, hundred feet or so.'

'I held him.' Webb drank wine and grinned. 'Overstretching himself as usual.'

'You hurt yourself?' Caroline asked him.

Swann shook his head.

He lay back then, resting his glass on a rock, and closed his eyes to the sun. It was warm across the skin of his face and he felt himself relaxing. Caroline offered him food, but he shook his head and sat up. 'In a minute, maybe.'

Webb's pager went off and he cursed. 'You got your phone, Jack?'

Swann took it from his rucksack and tossed it over. 'Tell them it's Saturday and we're in North Devon. They'll have to send someone else.'

Webb walked a little way from them and dialled. Caroline laid a hand on Swann's arm.

'You OK really, Jack?'

He let go a breath. 'Runner popped out. Couldn't have set it properly. Stupid.' He shook his head.

'How far did you fall?'

'Thirty feet or so. Managed to get my feet round, kept me off the wall.'

She looked at him and her eyes were soft with pain.

'I'm OK,' he said.

Webb came back, tossed the phone into Swann's lap and sat down. 'Tania Briggs,' he said. 'Guv'nors are having a meeting with Special Branch and A4 surveillance in the morning, they're going to decide what to do about the target.'

'Hit him?'

'Tania reckons yeah. Probably Tuesday morning. We've got to be in by 0700 on Monday. If the old man decides to scoop him up, SO19'll do their recce then.'

Swann nodded and took a chicken leg from Caroline. 'They'll go for it,' he said.

'Rude not to.'

'So you two'll be busy next week, then.'

Webb patted his wife on the arm. 'Looks that way, love.' He smiled and stroked his moustache. 'Some climbing to do before then, though.' He looked at Swann. 'Kinky Boots next. I do like kinky boots.'

## April 1997

The Northwest Airlines shuttle from Washington D.C. to Detroit reached twenty-nine thousand feet. Two men sat drinking cocktails in the business-class section at the front of the plane. Both of them wore suits and carried leather briefcases. One of them had his lap-top set out on the tray table of the seatback in front of him, and scanned the pages of a report. Next to him, the other yawned and stood up.

'Going to the john. Hold my drink, will you?' He handed his glass across while he eased himself out of the seat, then made his way up the aisle and through the curtain. Economy class was less than half full. He glanced at his watch, twenty minutes before they landed. He made a swift calculation, then he moved back along the line of seats to a vacant one close to the rear section of the plane. Sitting down, he took his wallet from his jacket pocket and an AT&T phone card from the wallet, then he picked up the phone housed in the back of the seat.

He dialled a London number, and a sleep-filled voice answered.

'Wake up. It's morning,' he said.

'Not yet it isn't.'

'What's happening?'

'It's all arranged, cars and drivers. Just like you told me.'

'Good.' He was watching the flight attendant serve a fresh drink to a woman seated further down the plane. 'When it's done, call me on the number we agreed.' He clipped the phone back in the housing and stood up.

☆

Three-thirty in the morning and the dark-skinned man drove the old Ford Cortina in from the East End. It did not run very well, the gears grinding, but it did not have to get him far. On the seat beside him was a home-made cigar box, and on the back seat a travelling rug. He drove with care, not wishing to draw attention to himself. He passed a couple of police cars and ignored them. The second car was following, he could see it in his rear-view mirror, one car between them. He moved on towards the West End, easing the wheel through his fingers; face set, eyes the colour of coal.

Two cars back, the driver of the Vectra tapped his fingers against the steering wheel in time to the music on the radio. He smiled to himself as he saw the Cortina turn up into Soho and he indicated right. Easy money, he thought, blue eyes looking back at him from the rear-view mirror, really easy money.

Billy Williams was washing down the surface of the American Diner on the junction of Moor and Old Compton Street in Soho. Quiet now, busy till about three-thirty, but tailing off after that. Dark outside, much of the neon burning only dimly. Out in the back, the two remaining waitresses were smoking cigarettes and drinking coffee. The door opened and Jack the Hat stood there looking hopeful. You could set your watch by him, this old man who lived over one of the video shops on the edge of Chinatown. The first time Billy had seen him, he thought he was a well-dressed if ageing businessman, in a blue three-piece suit and a grey fedora hat. But on closer examination, the suit was rumpled and dusty and his twill checked shirt frayed at the collar and cuffs. He carried a cane and tap-danced down Shaftesbury Avenue. His voice was weak and his eyes the liquid blue of his age. His neck hung in folds and when he took off his hat, his hair was white and sparse across the broken veins of his scalp.

Billy smiled at him and poured a mug of hot, frothy coffee. Jack made his way to the metal counter and pressed his thin frame on to a stool.

'There you go.' Billy slid the coffee across to him. 'No sleep again?'

'Bad dreams, son.'

'Again?' Billy leaned with his arms across the counter. Jack sipped noisily at the coffee. Outside, one of the girls from the strip club screeched at her boyfriend, who revved the engine of his car in response. Billy and Jack watched, as she belted the side door with her handbag before finally tottering away on heels that ended in needle points.

'Tell me something, Jack,' Billy said, 'what d'you do before you go to bed?'

Jack hunched his shoulders.

'What d'you eat?'

'Chocolate. I always have a bar before I go to bed. My treat for the day.' He half closed his eyes, holding the coffee cup with both hands, and started humming to himself.

Gone, Billy thought. Never took him very long. When he landed again, he would tell him about the chocolate. He glanced behind him to the kitchen where the girls were still gassing. He shook his head, collected a cloth from the counter and began polishing the tables.

A car pulled up outside. Billy glanced at it – Mark II Cortina, looked in quite good condition. A figure in shadow stepped out from the driver's side, away from the pavement, back to the window. Almost immediately a second car pulled up, much newer – a Vectra. Billy watched as the first man climbed into the passenger seat and the car sped off up the road. He glimpsed the final three letters of the number plate. RAH. Behind him, Jack's singing had grown louder and the girls were beginning to complain.

Billy went back to the counter and tapped Jack on the shoulder. 'You've got to be quiet, mate. Or I'll have to chuck you out.'

Jack stared at him, blinking a little sheepishly. 'Can I have some more coffee?' he said.

Billy poured it for him, but all the time he was looking at the car outside. He glanced at the clock on the wall behind him. Four-twenty. Funny time to park a car and piss off again. He passed the coffee to Jack and moved round the counter once more, then he went outside to look at the car.

He shivered. It was windy, the pavement still damp from yesterday's rain. The metal of the car's bodywork pinged as it contracted. Across the road, outside the Prince Edward Theatre, a drunk was trying to throw out a sleeping bag to lie on. Two women were talking together at the junction with Charing Cross Road.

Billy had a look at the car, green or blue, he couldn't tell. Not bad condition. Not an E but a GT. The tyres looked pretty bald. Light from the Diner shone on the dashboard and he had a quick look to see if it was plastic or wood. He bent, framing his hand round the line of his eyes. Plastic. Then he saw something on the floor, poking out from under the seat. It looked like a small wooden box.

Back inside the Diner, he shut the door and lit a cigarette. Then he sat again, and watched Jack the Hat mumbling to himself. Cheryl came through from the back, filched one of his cigarettes and asked if she could go early. Billy was still looking at the car.

'Yeah,' he muttered. 'Go now if you want to. Nothing's happening, is it.' Again he looked at the car and Cheryl cocked her head at him.

'What's up with you?'

'Nothing. Just that car. Somebody parked it there a few minutes ago.'

'So?'

'So nothing. They got out and got in another one, that's all.'

Cheryl shook her head at him and went back to the kitchen for her coat. Billy sat on his stool, smoking and thinking. Jack was up in the ether somewhere. Billy looked at the car, then at the phone fixed on the wall behind him. Four-thirty now. He was off at six. Again he looked at the car, then he moved off the stool and wandered over to the window. Two lads walked past on their way up Old Compton Street. Billy stood with his hands in his pockets, nose pressed to the glass. 'Not right,' he muttered, then turned back to the counter and picked up the phone.

The 999 call came into the central command complex in Scotland Yard. 'This is Billy Williams. I'm night manager at the American Diner on Moor Street. Look, it's probably nothing, but right now I've got a car parked outside my restaurant. Someone drove up quarter of an hour ago, parked it and got out. He was picked up in a second car straight away.'

'Right,' the operator said. 'Can you give me an exact location, sir?'

Billy gave the full address. 'I'm probably being stupid,' he said. 'One thing, though. There's some kind of box on the floor.'

'Box?'

'Yeah. Well, it looks like a box, poking out from under the driver's seat.'

The operator took his number and Billy hung up. He lit another cigarette and looked across the counter at Jack. He was asleep with his head across his arms.

☆

Detective Sergeant Jack Swann was duty officer in the combined Antiterrorist/Special Branch operations room on the sixteenth floor of Scotland Yard. The white phone linking them directly with the communications room rang on the desk in front of him and the computer-aided dispatch started printing. He glanced at Christine Harris from Special Branch, who sat at another desk, reading the newspaper.

'Swann. SO13.'

'We've just had a 999 from Moor Street in Soho. Suspicious vehicle parked outside the American Diner. Been there since four-fifteen.'

'Anything else?'

'Caller said there's some kind of box on the floor by the driver's seat. But we haven't received a codeword.'

Swann pushed out his cheek with his tongue. 'Hold on.' He laid down the phone and dialled Superintendent Colson, the operational commander and senior duty officer downstairs. Colson was quiet for a moment, then said, 'What time was the car parked?'

'About four-fifteen.'

'We've had no coded warning, Jack. The box could be anything. Standard response. It's a West End Central decision. Let them make an assessment.'

The West End Central duty inspector was a Welshman called Wilson, with thirty years in the job. He looked at the clock on his office wall and phoned Jack Swann. 'Inspector Wilson, Swann,' he said. 'Savile Row. Just letting you know – I've sent a car to Moor Street. I have to say though, I'm not happy.'

Swann rested on one elbow. 'Fair enough, sir. We've logged it as standard response. But it's your decision.'

'I don't like small boxes in cars, Swann. They have a habit of being PIRA timing and power units.'

'We've received no accredited codeword, sir.'

'Not yet, anyway. I'll be back to you shortly, Swann. What time was the vehicle first spotted?'

'Four-fifteen.'

'So if it is dodgy, we've maybe got some time.'

Swann nodded to himself. 'Maybe, sir,' he said.

Five minutes later Wilson phoned him again. 'Yes, sir,' Swann said as he answered.

'I'm not happy, Swann. There is a timing and power unit in that car. I'm evacuating. And I want an explosives officer here right away.'

'OK, sir. Red response it is. I'll task the Expos immediately. Cordons at two hundred metres.'

'I know the drill, Swann.'

'I'm sure you do, sir.'

Swann put down the phone and immediately lifted the black one, a direct link to the explosives officer's suite in Cannon Row. It rang without him having to dial, then Phil Cregan's voice sounded in his ear. 'Cregan.'

'Put your boots on, Phil. I think we've got a live one.'

36

# 2

Cregan scribbled notes as he listened to all that Swann had to tell him, cigarette smoke eddying from the ashtray at his elbow. He wanted to know everything: time, location and the full assessment from West End Central. 'Where's the rendezvous point?' he asked.

'Brewer Street.'

'Is it clear?'

'They're searching it now.'

Cregan put the phone down, picked up his boots from where they lay by the chair and extinguished his cigarette. The fifth floor was quiet; night duty and only the one team working. Nicholson, his driver, was already in the corridor looking at the huge map on the wall and plotting the journey in his head. Cregan put his boots on in the lift going down to the car park.

He tied the laces quickly, bent to one knee. The last thing he needed was to be tying them when Nicholson was flinging the van through the streets. Slightly built, Cregan stood five foot nine. He was originally from Perth, and had been a Met explosives officer for five years now, a veteran of many IRA mainland attacks. Before that, he was Explosives Ordnance Disposal, part of the Royal Logistical Corps based in Didcot.

In the car park downstairs, the four Range Rovers were parked in readiness, each with an individual officer's equipment inside. Normally it would be the two duty teams' vehicles in front, ready for the turn around when the relief changed. Tonight, however, the big van was parked in front. One officer on duty only – there was no one to back him up with additional kit if he needed it, so everything was in the van.

Nicholson got the van started and they were rolling, blue lights flashing and siren on the yowl. It was 4.51 exactly. Cregan hung on to the Jesus bar on the dashboard as they raced through the empty streets. By 4.55, they were parked between the inner and outer cordons at the rendezvous point. West End Central controlled the perimeter, and everyone had been evacuated within the two-hundred-metre zone. Nicholson was already at the back of the van beginning to assemble the gear.

'You want the heavy or lightweight suit, Phil?' he asked.

Cregan made a calming motion with the palm of his hand. Nicholson was new and very keen. 'Just hold on, Tom,' he said. 'Things to sort first.'

Webb and Swann waited for Cregan at the inner cordon line, facing north-east along Brewer Street. Cregan arrived, took a cigarette from Swann and cupped his hands to the match. 'RVP clear?' he asked.

'Yes.' Webb nodded to where Nicholson was still holding the bomb-suit bags.

'Bit keen, isn't he?'

Cregan spoke without looking at him. 'JFD, Webby. Just a fucking driver, and a new one at that.' He sucked cigarette smoke with a hiss and shivered. 'Tell me the story again, Jack.'

'The call came in at four-thirty. Car was parked about four-fifteen, no later than four-twenty. The caller knows the time because one of his regular night owls had just turned up for his cocoa.'

Cregan looked at his watch, a maximum of forty minutes. He pushed out his lips. The first twenty-five to thirty-five minutes after a device has been laid is known to be the most dangerous in PIRA incidents. After that, it was the twenty-minute period between one hour fifty and two hours ten. He looked down the length of Brewer Street. The target vehicle was well out of sight. Everything was very quiet, frost on the pavements glistening in the fall of light from the streetlamps. 'No warning?'

'No.'

'Still none?'

Swann shook his head. 'Decision was the local's, Phil. PC reckons he's seen a Provo TPU before and this is definitely one of them.'

Cregan made a face. 'I wasn't doing anything, anyway.'

The duty officer from Savile Row came over to them from where he had been talking to some of his officers, ensuring that the outer cordon was not breached. He was a smallish man, not much bigger than Cregan. They shook hands and Wilson introduced himself.

'What're we going to do?' he said.

Cregan looked at his watch. 'Nothing for the moment.'

The inspector squinted at him. 'You want to stand off?'

'Aye.' Again Cregan looked at his watch. 'If it is a TPU, it'll either be a Mk 15 or 17 that'll have a Memo-park safety-arming switch and maybe a kitchen timer, with a one- to two-hour wind-down from when he pulled out the dowel. It's now almost five o'clock. We reckon the car was parked at four-fifteen. That gives us at least another fifteen minutes to see if it goes bang.'

'And after that?' The inspector was looking back at the roadblocks.

'Soak for another hour at least.'

'Why another hour?'

Cregan looked him in the eye. 'Like I said, there could be a secondary timer.'

'That'll make it six-fifteen, then.'

Cregan nodded. 'About that, yeah. In the meantime, any chance of some coffee?'

He sat with Webb and Swann in the back of Swann's car. Swann took a call on his mobile from Superintendent Colson.

'Soak period, Guv'nor,' Swann told him.

'Who's the Expo?'

'Phil.'

'OK. Listen, I need you to get back over here, Jack. We've run a check on the vehicle and it's a ringer. I want you working on it.'

'Right, sir. I'll be with you in a few minutes.' Swann put the phone down. He glanced at Cregan who sat in the back looking at the street plan and considering his approach path. 'The car's a ringer, Phil,' Swann said. 'So it may well be a live one.'

Cregan waited the full two hours, then went round to the back of the van and opened the armoured door. The Wheelbarrow robot squatted on its tracks in the darkness. The driver switched on the rear light and Cregan climbed into the back. Attached to the nearside wall was the TV monitor for the drive and attack cameras fitted to the upper hamper of the Wheelbarrow. He wiped the thin layer of dust that had gathered on the screen, then took down his cases, two of them, black, about the size of ordinary briefcases but made of hard plastic and deeper. One contained his tool kit and the other the various pulleys and ropes he required if a device had to be moved before the render safe procedure could be conducted. Carefully, he checked his tools, then glanced at his watch. It was beginning to get light, tendrils of grey working into the shadows that marked the edge of the night. It was very cold now, and quiet. They were some distance from the outer western cordon and he was only vaguely aware of the traffic.

Cregan hummed as he checked his equipment. This was his first call-out in nearly two weeks and sometimes the boredom got to him. He ought to be used to it after twenty-odd years dealing with improvised explosive devices. But you never did get used to it. You got better hopefully and more careful, but you never got used to it. The last call-out had been the first for his new driver. In Whitehall – an undercar booby trap left in a telephone box. He could almost see it from their floor at Cannon Row. Red response, accredited coded warning and exact location. The cordons were in and the area evacuated. Cregan had got 'suited and booted' behind the cordons, then walked as far as the Cenotaph for a better look. Initial reactions had been to 'pig-stick' it, but he could see how far the Memopark had wound down when he looked through a set of binoculars. He was watching when Nicholson spoke in his ear through the radio. Cregan nearly jumped out of his skin. Rule one broken. Radio contact is for the Expo to speak to his second – not the other way round. The last thing any EOD man needed was a voice in his ear just as he was about to render something safe.

'What does it look like?' Nicholson had said.

'It's about seven feet tall and grey with a telephone inside. Have you never seen a phone box, Tom?' After that Cregan had wandered down and disarmed it manually. Fifteen minutes left on the timer.

The duty officer called through to Webb and Webb relayed the message to Cregan. 'Wants to know what you're going to do, Phil.'

Cregan looked at his watch. 'I'll send in the Wheelbarrow and have a look.'

Webb moved back to the cordon, leaving Cregan alone

with his driver. Swann had already gone back to the Yard to start work on identifying the car. Nicholson set up the hydraulic ramp and then Cregan lifted the handheld control set, activated the robot, and drove it as far as the cordon tapes. Here, he paused. Alvis, the manufacturer, always recommended radio control as the best form of operation – which was probably true given the constraints of cable. But the last time he'd used this particular Mark 8, the radio signal was weaker than it ought to have been and the thing kept stopping and starting. He had two other options, the regular or fibre-optic cabling. 'Use the normal cabling, Tom,' he said, and moved into the back of the van. Nicholson set up the linkage and climbed in behind him. The ramp was up and the doors closed. Above their heads, the roof was reinforced with Kevlar and anticrush bars in case any buildings fell on top of them.

Cregan squatted in front of the TV monitor as the robot rolled along Brewer Street. The drive camera lens was wide-angle and gave a reasonable view of the road ahead. The Wheelbarrow came to the intersection with Old Compton Street. Fifty metres further on, the front of the car came into view. Cregan slowed it a fraction and scanned the area. He had the attack camera engaged now and the sawn-off shotgun set up underneath the modular weapons mounting system, which had three fixings for disrupters. The Expos had rigged up the shotgun as an addition. They used it to fire No. 6 shot from four feet. It had the force of a single slug at that distance, but there was no danger of overpenetration. It meant you could take out the doorlock without using one of your disrupters. That was what he intended to do now, take out the passenger door and have a good look round inside. The shotgun would remove the lock and then he could wrench it open using the hooley bar.

The Wheelbarrow was all but alongside the car now and Cregan studied the monitor as he guided the robot around it. He needed to be careful the cable didn't snag against obstacles in the road, though the limited vision sometimes meant that was easier said than done. Using the actuators to lift and lower the teleboom, he checked for any sign of booby traps. Then he raised the boom so he could look in the window from the passenger side. He could see a bulky travelling rug partially covering the back seat, and something on the floor sticking out from under the driver's. He screwed up his eyes and looked closer; definitely a wooden box. He had seen the type before.

He decided to take the driver's door out instead of the passenger side. Reversing the robot back along the pavement, he brought it round in front and then out into the road. The shotgun was loaded with No. 6 and ready for firing. Cregan squared the Wheelbarrow to the driver's door and lowered the attack camera so he could see the doorlock clearly. He paused and licked his lips. Critical moment; the shock and sudden rocking of the car could knock out a mercury tilt switch and set the device off. He looked again at the lock, then sent the electronic charge to the firing connectors underneath the weapons mounting system. The shotgun smashed the lock. No explosion. Once the smoke and dust was clear, Cregan focused on the damage and then applied the hooley bar to the hole.

This was the second critical moment; the car rocking badly as the robot hauled the door open. Nothing. No blast. Next to him, Nicholson watched intently as he guided the Wheelbarrow back over to the now open and accessible car. The drive camera showed them the hole where the door had been but little else. In close, Cregan tilted the boom so the attack camera was covering the floor. He focused in on the timing and power unit and saw the hole where the dowel had been.

'Definitely a live one,' he said, and tapped the video screen. 'Mk 15, Tom. Remember the components?'

Nicholson nodded. 'Memopark with a nail soldered on to it, another nail or screw as a contact, couple of batteries and the microswitch held in place with a dowel.'

'Good lad.' Cregan scratched his head. 'Fortunately this one's not working, though, is it. One-hour timer only, should have gone off by now.' He then spoke into the radio to Wilson. 'We have a TPU,' he said. 'I'm going to perform a controlled explosion. Stand by.'

He settled himself over the control panel once more and guided the Wheelbarrow back, then forwards again, lifting the boom. He got the weapons mount positioned over the box and selected the central disrupter: a high-pressure jet of water to literally blow the box apart, ruin the electrical circuitry and remove the power source from the detonator. A tiny bit of sweat gathered on his brow as it always did and he could feel the moisture under his arms. It was warm in the van with the engine running and the back doors closed and sealed. He tensed, screwed up his eyes and fired.

For a moment afterwards he sat there and considered: the TPU was smashed to pieces, bits littering the inside of the car. Next to him Nicholson was smiling. 'Got it, Phil,' he said.

Cregan arched his brows. 'Looks like it, doesn't it.' He called the con-ex in to the uniforms, then eased the robot back into the road and guided it round to the back of the car.

Selecting the second disrupter, he smashed the lock and the boot popped open. Set squarely over the petrol tank was a green and black sports bag, with the word *Jaguar* written on the side. It was bulky, clearly quite full, with the sides bulging slightly. He moved the boom up and down and from left to right. Two wires extended from the bag to the back of the rear seats and disappeared beyond. He spoke to Webb on the radio. 'There's explosives in the boot, Webby, or at least a sports bag with wires sticking out of it.'

'Don't normally come like that, do they, Phil.'

Cregan grimaced. 'The one I bought my son didn't, no.'

'What's happening now?'

'Soak for another hour, then I'll take a look manually.'

'OK. But don't forget the famous SO13 battle cry.'

'What's that, then?' Cregan said.

'If in doubt – run away.'

Cregan sat for another hour and drank coffee. When he was ready, he told Nicholson to get the bomb-gear bags. He held up the blue one and Cregan nodded. This was the lightweight suit – modular body armour with a vest, detachable sleeves and trousers. It had been tested against eighty-pound mortars and experienced minimal fragmentation damage. Kevlar-lined, with acrylic to avoid blunt trauma internal organ damage.

'You don't want the heavy one, do you?' Nicholson said.

Cregan shook his head. 'Just give me the vest and trousers.'

Nicholson passed them across and Cregan got into them. Then Nicholson held the bomb helmet, as he squatted and screwed his head up into it.

Cregan started to move along Brewer Street, vaguely aware of the eyes on him from the gathering the other side of the cordons. He walked slowly, the trousers gripping his legs like motorcycle leathers, only heavier and that bit more cumbersome. He walked past the sex shops and the video stores and the revue bar. Then he stopped. A one-hour Memopark timer winding all the way down.

Mk 15 TPU. Single safety-arming switch with the dowel-held microswitch as the final precaution. In his mind's eye he revisited the images on the screen in the back of the van. The flat wooden box on the floor, back seat covered with a rug. No trace of the wiring. Hidden. Deliberately hidden. He stood where he was for a long moment and then turned back towards the cordon. Maybe he should get the big suit after all. If you went to all that trouble to hide the wiring, why leave your TPU sticking out? You wanted the bomb to go off, because you didn't telephone a warning.

He paused for a moment, looked again towards Old Compton Street, then turned back for the cordon. A rush of air hit him and then the blast and the booming sound that blocked his ears. The sudden force of the pressure wave lifted him off his feet and sent him crashing against a lamppost. Glass flew on the wind, the windows of the buildings exploding in thousands of pieces as they were sucked from their housings. It shattered all around him, bouncing off the pavements and the parked cars, littering his head, chest and legs.

When it was over, he sat on his backside with the wind knocked out of him, hundreds of little rips in the cloth of his vest. He studied his arms, shook his head and let go a breath. There was not a mark on him. The police officers standing on the other side of the cordon could see him. They shouted. He waved and sat there for a moment longer, before getting to his feet and checking again for cuts. George Webb came over to him, already suited in a nylon coverall with overboots and sterile rubber gloves. 'You OK, Phil?'

'What was that battle cry again?' Cregan glanced at his watch. 'Shit, I'm not even on overtime.'

☆

Jack Swann was in the squad room on the fifteenth floor of the Yard when the blast ripped through Soho. He looked up from his desk as Superintendent Colson came in.

'It's gone,' Swann said.

Colson lifted his eyebrows. 'It certainly sounds like it, Jack.'

Swann got up and went over to the window. He could see Parliament from here and beyond it, the City. Down the corridor, the bomb-data team and exhibits officers who would aid George Webb were making their way to the lift.

The door to the squad room was open and John Garrod came in. Garrod had just assumed overall command of the security group as deputy assistant commissioner, giving him direct responsibility over SO13, the Antiterrorist Branch, and SO12, Special Branch. The move was a good one and had been welcomed by the troops. Although the day-to-day running of the Branch was handled by DSU Colson as operational commander, Garrod carried overall responsibility; and unlike his predecessors he had argued against close protection officers being assigned to him. His house was guarded but he did not carry a sidearm.

Swann had literally bumped into Colson just over a year ago. His first day had been when the IRA ceasefire ended abruptly with the massive lorry bomb at South Quay. He had gone up to the fifteenth floor as soon as the coded warning came in. Swann and Webb met him as they walked out of the lift, on their way to Canary Wharf. Welcome to the Branch, sir, they told him. Later, they had talked him through what had happened. An explosion, Webb had explained, was a solid becoming a gas instantaneously. It comprised three elements: heat, blast and fragmentation. Various videos later, he understood what they meant.

Colson folded his arms and looked at Garrod. 'We never received a codeword, John.'

'That's strange.'

'Very,' Swann put in. 'They've not done that since the first Harrods bang.'

Garrod looked at him then. 'We'll have to see what develops. Who's crime-scene manager over there?'

'George Webb, sir.'

Garrod nodded and turned to Colson again. 'Let me know when you get the video from the explosives officer, Bill. I'd like to have a look.'

☆

The dark-skinned man with close-cut hair and black eyes watched the early morning television news in a large house in West London. He sat with one leg draped over the arm of the chair and the remote-control set in his hand. On the small table next to him was a book on the life of Geronimo.

Slowly, he crunched his way through a Granny Smith apple. The newscaster was detailing the bomb scene in Soho. It was literally within the last hour and the TV crews had not yet been allowed access. The details were scant, but the man sat and listened and bit into his apple, tasting the juice as it squirted over his tongue. When the broadcast was over, he got up and switched off the set. At the window, he leaned with his forehead against the glass and watched the dustbin men taking away the rubbish.

He could see the man who owned the garage at the end of the street, where black taxis were repaired. He was in his blue overalls as usual, a roll-up cigarette stuck to his lip as he sat in the car and fiddled with the doorlock. The dark-skinned man moved back from the window and caught a glimpse of himself in the mirror. Then he went into the hall, collected his coat and bag from the banister and left the house. He stopped at a phone booth on the Broadway, dialled a mobile number and waited. After a few rings, the phone was answered by a woman.

'Yes?' she said.

'You've seen the news.'

'Just now.'

'Pass it on.'

He put the phone down, then turned and walked into the tube station. He rode into the West End and got out at Piccadilly Circus, crossed beyond the statue of Eros and paused at the foot of Shaftesbury Avenue. Halfway along, it was cordoned off by police tape. He could see that some of the buildings up by Romilly Street had shards of glass hanging from where their windows had been. He took a camera and press ID from the bag, hung the ID about his neck on its chain and then walked up to the police officer guarding the cordon.

'When're we allowed in?' He indicated the press pass.

'Not been called yet. Be about twenty minutes. Soon as the buildings have been inspected for safety.' The officer turned then and pointed up the street. 'You need to go to the cordon on Brewer Street. It's where they're all assembling.'

George Webb was in control of the chaos now, bomb-scene management his speciality. He and Phil Cregan had taken a look at the seat of the explosion, now a sizeable hole in the ground, beside the ruined shell of the American Diner. The car was unrecognizable. Bits of it would be everywhere. There had to have been a second TPU. The video from the Wheelbarrow showed the complete disintegration of the one under the seat, so there had to have been another, possibly on the floor between the front and back seats, or maybe covered by the travelling rug on the back seat itself. Disturbing thoughts were already occurring to him. Why have two TPUs? The first was obviously a decoy. There had been no coded warning, yet the TPU on the pictures looked exactly like the box used to house a PIRA Mk 15. PIRA had not blown anything up without a warning since the first Harrods bomb. Whoever planted the bomb knew that they would do a controlled explosion on the TPU and render the device safe. That had been accomplished; and if Phil Cregan had not had second thoughts about bomb suits, there would have been at least one casualty.

Cregan was looking at the bent frame of the Alvis Wheelbarrow. The platform chassis was intact, as, amazingly, was the stance gearbox. The upper hamper, complete with teleboom and weapons mounting system, had been ripped off by the force of the blast.

Webb had swept an approach path to the scene up Old Compton Street and was busy zoning the area for evidence. He had ordered six brand-new lorry skips and the sterile equipment had arrived from the Yard. He wondered how many tarpaulins they would need to package the car for the Defence Research Agency in Kent. Control swabs for explosive contamination were being taken while the make-safe checks on the buildings were going on. Give it five more minutes and the press would be allowed in.

The dark-skinned man gathered with his 'colleagues' behind the cordon tape and waited patiently until they were called. The word came that the area was deemed safe enough for photographs and they moved forward along the approach path, all of them wearing yellow hard hats. The dark-skinned man could see that window fragmentation damage had reached as far as the 150-metre mark along the cordon path. After that, there was significant structural damage. He could see impact and pressure marks on the walls of restaurants and strip clubs along the route. The gay bar, in particular, was shattered. They came to the main area of impact, which was directly around the site where the car had been parked. Here the buildings were very badly damaged. The Diner was all but gone, as was the video shop and adult entertainment centre alongside it. The Prince Edward Theatre had lost all its windows and suffered serious impact and pressure damage. It would not be showing *Martin Guerre* for a while: the sign advertising the musical dangled at a pitiful angle.

He took photographs and listened to the short account of the damage given to them by the unnamed man in the blue coverall suit. He was stocky with a moustache and blue eyes and the dark-skinned man would remember him.

Webb allowed the press to take their pictures and confirmed for them that it was a car bomb with a substantial amount of high explosive. He said nothing about the lack of an accredited warning or the fact that there had clearly been two timing and power units, one of which was a dummy. When they were all done, he got the uniformed local officers to escort them back to the cordons, and returned to the job in hand.

He zoned the areas for evidence, zone one being the seat of the blast, the area immediately surrounding the remnants of the car and the crater left in the road. The other areas were the streets leading off the intersection. They swept and sifted and sought the wreckage of the car. The minutiae of detail, the maximalist approach to forensic evidence gathering. Everyone knew that assuming they caught the bomber they would have to prove the explosion and link him to it. Control swabs for cross-contamination were vital. That was always the main thrust of the defence lawyers, that and whether the exhibits team had done their jobs properly. The defence would have access to the press photographs and video footage, which was largely why they were no longer allowed to film the antiterrorist officers working. Webb organized it all. The large bits of car were located and brought back to zone one and the seat of the explosion, where they were prepared in sterile packaging and freighted to Kent on the low-loader.

Every building within the cordon area was checked and, slowly, parts of the car were recovered. The mangled bonnet, along with part of the windscreen struts, was retrieved from the roof of the pub halfway along Old Compton Street. Webb wanted the engine, intact hopefully, with the engine number accessible so they could begin to trace it.

He started work on the ruined American Diner, easing himself inside, squeezing past the melted metal chairs still half fixed to the floor. The floor itself was broken up and uneven, and the metal counter had buckled into itself and most of it was pushed up against the back wall, which was now half inside the kitchen. Thank God they had got everyone out.

He wanted some part of the timing mechanism. The others could concentrate on the bigger items and were already piling everything into the skips, leaving aside glass and stone. Wood they kept for impact marks. Webb knew from many years of experience that the spring on the timing mechanism would be intact. It had still to be found, but it would be intact. It was made of high tensile steel and light, so it was not generally thrown that far away. The seat of the explosion had been on the north side of the Diner, so the immediate vicinity of that stretch of Old Compton Street was prime. If he found the spring from the Memopark, he could probably match it with exhibits taken at other scenes. He moved aside a fallen chair inside the Diner and made out what he thought must once have been the till, smashed in pieces with all its innards ripped open. Then he saw a small dog, scruffy-looking thing, the sort you see with beggars on the Underground. It was tugging at something under the fallen counter.

Webb moved over to the dog. 'How the hell did you get in here?' he said. 'You're not supposed to be here.' The dog looked up at him, ducked to pick something up, and Webb made a grab for its scruff. The dog yelped and slipped his grip, then made off, leaving behind whatever it had been after. Webb shone his torch into the recesses of the hole under the counter and saw what looked like a severed foot. He stood up, scratched his head and looked again. It had been a foot, shoe and sock burned off by the blast along with most of the skin. What he could see was a reddened lump of meat with part of the ankle bone sticking out at the top.

Outside, he phoned the Yard and asked to speak to Superintendent Colson.

'Colson here, George. How's it going?'

'Fatality, sir.'

For a moment Colson was quiet. 'I thought West End Central told us they got everyone out.'

'Apparently not.'

'What have you found exactly, George?'

'A foot.' Webb looked at the distance between the seat of the blast and the counter in the Diner. Fifteen feet at best. 'I'm not going to get much else. A few bits and pieces maybe, jawbone, that kind of thing.'

'Do we know if anyone's unaccounted for?'

'Not as far as I know.'

'OK, George. We'll check the evacuees.'

☆

Swann phoned Pia at her flat when he knew she would be up, to tell her that he wasn't going to make it. He had been on nights and often went to her flat before she left for work in the morning. 'Hi, darling. It's me.'

'Jack. Are you coming over? I don't have a meeting till eleven.'

Swann blew out his cheeks, sorely tempted. Already, the fatigue dripped in his eyes and he imagined the warmth of Pia's naked flesh against his own.

'I can't, love. A bomb's gone off in Soho.'

'Oh God. Was anybody hurt?'

'Not sure yet. You haven't seen the news?'

'I've only just got up.' She sighed then. 'Bed's warm, Jack. Can't you spare half an hour?'

Swann groaned. 'Oh, don't.' He shook his head. 'No. I really can't. I'm up to my neck here.'

'All right. I want to see you later though, before I go away. We haven't talked for ages.'

'OK, love. Don't worry. We'll sort something out.'

Swann hung up. The description of the car was an old Mark II Cortina. The E suffix in the index number matched correctly with the possible year of manufacture, but the number plate was from a Hillman Imp. The second vehicle was a Vauxhall Vectra and he had the last three letters of its number: RAH, it had stuck in the night manager's mind. Swann discovered that the RAH suffix was used to register vehicles in parts of East Anglia. He checked with the manufacturers and got confirmation that they first introduced the model in October 1995. The prefix letter must either be an N or a P.

They had already dubbed the operation Ding Dong after the ringed car, and Colson had requested the video tapes from traffic cameras in and around the area, together with those from any shop which ran street-surveillance tapes all night. They needed to try to ascertain the exact route the car had taken before being parked and the explosive device primed.

Swann phoned the Vehicle Licensing Centre in Swansea. Colson walked into the squad room as he was finishing the call. 'How're you getting on with the car, Jack?'

'RAH is a Lowestoft/Norwich suffix,' Swann told him. 'The car can only be an N or a P, so I've asked for a list of registered cars, from Swansea. Should be over here tomorrow.'

Colson nodded. 'Webb's just been on the line from the crime scene. It appears there was a fatality after all.'

'Who?'

'We don't know yet. We're getting West End Central to do a check, find out who was missing.'

Swann sat down. 'Where did he find the body?'

'It's only a foot so far. Apparently, a dog was chewing it inside the Diner, so it's likely to be one of the employees. Either that, or a customer who didn't come out when he should have.'

Swann nodded. 'Any other witnesses come forward yet?'

'No. The commander's giving a press conference in an hour. He'll make an appeal for calls on the 0800 number. Hopefully, we'll get something from the public. I'm going over to the scene now with DI Clements if you want to come along.'

The three of them went to Soho in Clements' car. 'Why would PIRA suddenly stop using coded warnings?' Colson said to no one in particular.

'What about the intended target?' Swann leaned between the two front seats. 'What's there to hit in Soho at four in the morning, except a bunch of knackered old farts in long raincoats?'

Clements squinted at him in the mirror. 'That's what I've been wondering.'

Swann sat back again. 'We don't know it was PIRA, do we?'

'It was their Mk 15,' Colson said. 'The election's coming up; who knows what they're up to.'

They pulled up in Windmill Street and got out of the car. Swann could see Webb placing evidence in nylon bags. He had his head down and did not see them approach.

'Hey, Webby,' Swann called.

'One minute.'

Swann looked at the evidence bags: a few of them were red and sweating. He sifted through them and found the foot that the dog had inadvertently alerted them to.

'Got half a jawbone as well,' Webb said, looking up for the first time. 'Might get an ID from that.' He picked up another bag. 'Also recovered this.'

Clements looked closely at it.

'Spring from the Memopark,' Webb told him.

Swann took the bag from him and stared at the bent piece of metal. Webb looked at Colson. 'Definitely PIRA, sir. No question about that. My guess is there were two of them. The one that Phil Cregan disrupted was a decoy – not attached to anything.'

'Cunning. Cunning and very nasty.'

'Could've been. Phil was on his way in when it went up.'

Colson nodded. 'He wasn't hurt though, was he?'

'Take more than that to hurt Cregan,' Swann said. 'If he fell off El Cap, he'd bounce on his head and get up.' The climbing reference made them all look briefly at him. 'It's all right,' he added. 'I can still make jokes.' Cregan was a climber too, never got involved with snow and ice, but a great rock man. He had climbed El Capitan in Yosemite in only three days.

'What else've you got, Webby?' Clements asked him.

Webb pointed to a large piece of tarpaulin. 'Found the engine halfway up Greek Street,' he said. 'I'll get someone from the funny car squad to take a look at it. It's bent but pretty much intact, except of course for the usual.'

Swann looked at him then. 'Engine number's missing.'

☆

The dark-skinned man ate lunch while the photographs he had taken were developing. Upstairs in his darkroom afterwards, he closed the door and dipped the remaining negatives. Large black and whites, he watched as one in particular came into focus. He had taken it from waist height, guessing at the angle of the subject. He had guessed right. Slowly but surely the face of the fat detective materialized under his yellow hard hat. The dark-skinned man took the picture from the tray and hung it up on the line. When he was finished, he had a roll of twenty-four developed, selective shots of the damage. The camera imprinted the date on the bottom corner of each picture.

☆

In the betting shop on Croydon High Street, Tommy Cairns squatted on a stool with a rolled up copy of the *Sporting Life* in his hand. He tapped it lightly on the counter as his third winner of the day romped home at 5–1. He laughed to himself, showing the punter next to him his broken front tooth, which had got punched out in a scrap with some Asians while he was on remand three years ago. Not the whole tooth, just the inside section, which effectively gave him an arch above his bottom teeth when he didn't put the crown in. He pushed long, blond hair out of his eyes and thought about his winnings. He had got up late today, no work on the site. He didn't need to work as hard as the others. The job was more of a cover than anything else and he liked easy days like this when he could get up at midday, shag the girlfriend and spend the afternoon in the bookie's. He went up to the counter and collected his winnings. As he took the money, his mobile phone rang. He moved away from the counter and put it to his ear.

'Hello?'

'Tom?'

'What d'you want, Charlie?'

'Haven't you seen the news?'

'I've only just got up. Scratched my arse and headed straight for the bookie's.'

'Listen, Tom. I need to talk to you.'

'When?'

'Soon as possible. I can't believe what's happened.'

Cairns frowned then, his mouth twisting down at the corners. 'You been nicked or something?'

'No. Nothing like that.'

Cairns sat down on a stool and looked at his watch. 'Meet me in the pub. I'm going there now.'

He got there well before Oxley: one of the team, a foot soldier and not a bad one. He could mix it up with the best of them, notwithstanding his lack of stature. He was five foot six tops, and his build was nothing to write home about. But what he lacked in physique, he made up for in bottle. He had more guts than a lot of so-called hardmen twice his size. If he ever needed a reliable back-up man, it would be Charlie Oxley. He sat at the bar, drank a pint of lager and watched a fat man playing on the fruit machine. Charlie was not fazed easily – something must have happened.

He waited the half-hour, and then another fifteen minutes, and drank a second pint. Oxley came in five minutes later, white dust in his cropped hair, wearing faded Levis, desert boots and a green nylon bomber jacket. His face was chipped red from the wind, blue eyes smarting. Cairns ordered beer and they moved to a quiet corner.

'So what's up?' Cairns said, elbows resting on the table.

Oxley sipped his pint and gave a quick glance about the bar. 'They blew the fucking car up.'

Cairns sat very still. 'You what?'

'The fucking Cortina. The ringer you got for them. The black geezer drove it to Old Compton Street and I picked him up. It went bang a couple of hours later. It's all over the news.'

Cairns picked up his drink and sipped at it, staring over the top of the glass. The woman, Joanne Taylor, or whatever her name was, had phoned him and said Ingram had put her on to him. They wanted a car, any car so long as it couldn't be traced. No problem with his contacts: car, driving licence, sawn-off, whatever the hell you wanted. The car had been stuck together in a hurry and then delivered. Hire car to pick them up in. He had said they'd nick one, but she had insisted and given them a false driving licence to use. They had also bought four sheets of armoured glass and stored it. She'd paid for the car and the glass and another five thousand pounds as a fee. Easier than betting on horses.

Oxley was watching him. 'You told me this was a driving job, Tommy.'

'Well it fucking was, wasn't it.'

'You know what I mean.'

Cairns made a calming motion with his palm. He couldn't think with Oxley prattling away in his ear. 'Relax, Charlie. You've got nothing to worry about.'

'Tom, I drove him away.'

'So what. You think they're going to trace you?'

'I don't know.'

'You weren't there, Charlie.' Cairns looked stiffly at him. 'You know the form. So they blew up a car. Big deal. Direct action, Charlie. It's what we fucking do.'

# 3

Swann left the Yard at nine o'clock that night. The clear-up operation had not yet been fully completed, although Webb's team had recovered as much of the car as was possible and it had been packaged with sterile tarpaulin and freighted to DRA. They had identified the engine found in Greek Street as a two-litre V4 from an old Ford Corsair. So now thay had the body of a Mark II Cortina with a Corsair's engine and a number plate from a Hillman Imp.

Swann got the tube home, a couple of stops along the District line and then one down to Waterloo. He did not bother to sit down, just stood by the doors and held the rail, watching the faces of those around him. He had been in the job almost seventeen years now, uniform for most of that time. He had taken his detective's course five years previously and then joined the Antiterrorist Branch as a DC, on George Webb's recommendation, before passing his sergeant's board. Six teams in the Branch, seven if you counted bomb data, four investigation and two exhibits. It had been a strange situation in the early days; everyone knew his past and he knew his psychological condition had been scrutinized pretty closely. But he believed he was tough enough, both mentally and physically, and he knew respect for him was growing. SO13 was unlike any other department he had worked in and he knew that anything less now would be small fry. He had worked on murder squads and suchlike before, but nothing prepared him for the Branch. Access to anything, every fatality dealt with as priority one, full-time liaison at DRA, with the Expos at Cannon Row, Special Branch and – since the end of the cold war – MI5 on tap.

The train arrived at Waterloo. It was still very busy and he made his way past the off-licence and W.H. Smith's, then out of exit 2 on Waterloo Road. As he got to his flat in Pearman Street, he checked his car as he always did and then climbed the stairs to the top two floors. He had been lucky with this place after Rachael left him for the Australian. He had got it fairly cheaply considering, and it came with a roof garden which was great in the summer. Two bedrooms and a bathroom on the lower of the two floors, then a living room-cum-kitchen with stairs up to the roof.

He checked his answerphone and got a message from Pia telling him that she had had to go to Paris early. It soured his mood, no chance of getting together now. Some of her clothes were on his unmade bed and her make-up and stuff littered the chest of drawers. Stupid having two places really, they all but lived together. He listened to his second message; Rachael wanted him to phone her.

He rewound the tape and then plugged in the kettle. It was cold but he still wandered up to the roof terrace as he always did. The sky was clear tonight, though the stars were dulled by the polluted light from the city. He took his coffee with him and stood on the secondary part of the roof watching the silent emptiness of the old MI5 building, rising from the corner in darkness. His breath came as steam. For a second he closed his eyes and saw again white walls of ice and the darkness of rock where the crusting was weakest. He opened his eyes, sipped coffee, then went back downstairs.

He picked up the telephone and dialled Rachael in Muswell Hill. 'Hi,' he said, when she answered. 'You wanted me.'

'Where've you been, Jack? I've been trying to get you for ages.'

'Bomb went off in Soho this morning. Didn't you hear about it?'

'I've been busy.'

'Right.'

'Don't say it like that. You're not the only one who works, you know.'

'No.' He sat down on the arm of the chair. 'Anyway, what's up?'

He heard her sigh and knew he was in for a long phone call. He scraped a cigarette out of the packet on the table and fiddled in his pocket for his lighter.

'It's the children, Jack.'

'What about them – they're not ill or anything, are they?'

'No. They're fine. It's me.'

'What about you?'

'I just don't see how I can get this teaching thing off the ground and look after them properly. Not only that, there's Peter.'

Swann grimaced. 'I tell you what, Rach,' he said. 'This sounds like something we need to talk about face to face. I've been at the Yard for the last eighteen hours and I can't think about it now.'

'All right. Can you come over?'

'I'll try tomorrow for an hour or so. I'm going to be busy, though.'

'Make it when the children get home from school, if you can.'

'Yeah. Right. Tomorrow then. See you.' Swann put down the phone.

He lay awake long into the night. They had been married for twelve years if you counted the period of separation before the actual divorce. To be fair to her she had not gone off with the Australian in the *affair* sense of the word. She'd said, and he believed her, that they had not slept together until she told him about it. He respected her for that, and considering the early days of hating and fighting, they got on pretty reasonably now. She still didn't live with the Australian and, as far as he could see, she had merely swapped one workaholic for another. He rolled over and looked at the clock by the bedside. Three a.m. He might as well get up and go back to the Yard. He showered, dressed and made fresh coffee, then he drove into Victoria and parked.

There was no one in the squad room, so he walked the length of the corridor to Webb's office. Tania Briggs was there, first call-out if anything went bang. She was a dark-haired woman in her thirties, an exhibits officer like Webb. 'All quiet?' he said.

Tania nodded. 'You heard?'

'Heard what?'

'PIRA have denied responsibility.'

Swann furrowed his brow. 'It was a Mk 15 TPU.'

'I know. That's what makes it interesting.'

Webb came in at seven and brought Swann some coffee. 'Got in early for a parking space did you, Flash?' he said as he placed the plastic cup beside him.

'Couldn't sleep, Webby. Rachael phoned me about the kids.'

'What's happening?'

'Don't know yet. I'm going to nip over for an hour later today to see what the problem is.'

'You seen Pia?'

Swann shook his head. 'Tried to. Didn't work out.

She's gone to Paris on business. Coming back at the weekend.'

Webb sat down on the edge of the desk and sipped coffee. He smoothed fingers over his moustache and looked out of the window. 'Hear about the statement?'

'Tania told me.'

Webb nodded. 'If it *was* a PIRA cell – we don't know which one. All our surveillance is intact. Box 500 have had no losses, neither have SB.'

'Sleeper, maybe. Someone we don't know about.'

'Possibly.' Webb shifted off the desk. 'I found something else yesterday, though, Jack. Nobody knows yet.'

Swann looked quizzically at him. 'What?'

'Part of the other timing and power unit.'

'Another Mk 15?'

Webb shook his head. 'No. I recovered a piece of printed circuit board. Zone five of all places. Come and have a look.'

They walked down to the 'sharp end', so called because that was where the things that went bang were dealt with. Webb went through to his evidence cage and pulled out a transparent nylon bag. He laid it on his desk. 'Printed circuit,' he said. 'Veroboard. You can't tell very much from it.'

Swann turned it over in his hands. 'Has Phil Cregan looked at it?'

'Not yet. He's due at the briefing this morning. I'll show it to him then.'

'Is he bringing the video with him? Be nice to get a look at the car.'

Webb nodded, then looked again at the veroboard. 'This isn't PIRA, Jack. I don't know who it is, but I don't think it's PIRA.'

☆

The woman sat in a car parked across the road from the converted flats in Crouch End. Black leather gloves and dark glasses, long blonde hair over high-boned features and an Indian headscarf pulled tightly round her face. In the rear-view mirror she saw the postman gradually making his way up the street in his red van; stopping, running up steps to communal entrances and running down again. Ten minutes and he would be there. She started the engine and pulled away from the kerb, then drove up towards Alexandra Park where she stopped again and watched people walking their dogs. Fifteen minutes later, she turned the car round and headed back. The postman had got to the next street. She could see the van as she drove towards the address. She drove beyond it, well beyond it, and parked around the corner in somebody else's permit zone. Then she walked back to the flats. For a moment, she paused on the top step while she sought her keys. Number 43 – flats A to E. She opened the door and stepped inside. The mail was in a heap on the floor; the occupants would sort through it and take what was addressed to them. There was only one for her, a large bulky envelope sealed with clear tape, Flat 43F scrawled on the front of it.

Back in the car, she opened the package and carefully leafed through the pictures of the bomb scene in Soho, pausing briefly at the one of the police officer in coveralls and hard hat. An elderly man pulling a shopping trolley walked past the car, his head hunched against the wind which bent the branches of the trees like elastic. The woman stowed the pictures back in the envelope and placed it inside her briefcase.

☆

Phil Cregan set up his video in the conference room on the sixteenth floor. The SO13 officers who had been tasked were all gathered. DI Clements was at the front talking to Colson. Webb had just shown Cregan the piece of veroboard from the second timing and power unit. Two operatives from MI5 had been summoned and they were talking to Christine Harris and the other Special Branch officers. The beginnings of an Annacappa chart had been started on one section of the wall, which described the who/how/where/when and what of an investigation. Swann looked at it from where he sat. All they had so far. The vehicles, the time and date, the fatality and the information from the night manager at the Diner. Clements called them to sit down. 'OK, girls and boys,' he said. 'Let's get on, shall we. Apart from our colleagues from Box, you all know what happened.' He looked at the two MI5 men. 'Julian, David – you're not up to speed on this?'

Julian Moore, a specialist from the A4 surveillance team, shook his head. 'If you're not clear on anything after the briefing, speak up,' Clements told him. He looked at the rest of the gathering then. 'Phil Cregan's going to take us through the video and anyone can ask questions as and when they want. I know Webby's got something to share with us and,' he looked over at Swann, 'Flash has done some work on the car.'

Cregan took them through the video from the Wheelbarrow up to the point when the screen went fuzzy as the upper hamper was ripped off, taking with it the attack camera. Swann was able to get a good look at the car for the first time and it was certainly the body of an old Mark II Cortina. Cregan finished by describing the second timing and power unit scenario. 'Nasty,' he said. 'PIRA have done it before.'

'Only this time it wasn't PIRA.' Swann shifted his position in his seat.

Colson looked across the room at him. 'We don't know

that, Jack. Not for certain, anyway. At this stage, every-thing is still very much cōnjecture.'

Swann sat back again and dusted the leg of his suit. Webb winked at him and stood up. 'The second TPU,' he said. 'Forensic examination of the scene is just about complete. We've interrogated the crater and done a fin-gertip search of zones one and two. The vehicle's at DRA. We decided in the end to dig up the hole as well and ship it to them in its entirety. They should be able to give us a clue on explosive traces shortly. I imagine it was Semtex, but we won't know till later. We've got substan-tial structural damage around the scene and I'd estimate about a couple of kilos.' He paused then and looked at the chart on the wall. 'We've got most of the driver's seat. It's vinyl and, as far as I can tell, it wasn't covered. No melted bin liners or anything, so we might get some fibres. We know from Phil's video there was a rug in the back of the car and we've recovered a little bit of it that wasn't too badly burnt.'

'Anything from the timer?' Julian Moore asked him.

'First TPU was a PIRA Mk 15. You can tell from the video before Phil did the con-ex. Christ knows, we've handled enough. Not only that, but we've got the contact nail and the spring from a standard Memopark. Only PIRA use them.'

'What about a splinter – INLA, maybe?' Christine Harris suggested.

Clements leaned his elbows on the table. 'It's possible, Chrissie.'

'There is one thing.' Webb picked up an evidence bag from the box beside him. 'What I think is a piece of the second TPU.' He passed the bag back for everyone to have a closer look at. 'I haven't had time to check if we've seen it before or not,' he said. 'All I can tell you is that it certainly isn't PIRA.'

For a few moments the room was silent as the small piece of veroboard was passed between them. Webb leaned on the desk. 'One fatality,' he said. 'The only person unaccounted for is a tramp called Jack the Hat. Always went into the Diner early in the morning because he couldn't sleep. He had a place round the corner, but he often slept rough. We know from the witness to the car parking that he was there just before the evacuation. Maybe he dropped off somewhere, maybe he just didn't want to go. Anyway, I found a dog chewing his ankle.'

Webb sat down and Clements went back to the front of the room. 'Not too much, but when do we get very much.' He looked at Swann. 'What about the car, Jack?'

Swann told them what he had. 'RAH is an East Anglian suffix,' he said. 'We've got two hundred and twenty-three Vauxhall Vectras sold with that suffix. There's about half a dozen dealers up there, so I got the research team to do the leg work. We'll do the London ones ourselves and send the rest out to the counties.'

He was about to sit down again, when David Whitman, the second man from MI5, spoke. 'Do we have anything on the driver of the second car?'

Swann shook his head. 'The commander made the appeal yesterday, but I checked what's come in so far and there's nothing I can see that we don't know already.'

'What about the colour of the car?'

'Dark, is all the witness can tell us.'

'Videos?' Christine said. 'Street cameras and that.'

'We're still looking at them,' Clements told her. 'There aren't any in Old Compton Street, so we can't see it being parked. There's a porn shop along there with one, but it faces the other way. We've got a car going past, but you can't tell anything from it.'

'Approach path and exit route?' she said.

'We're trying to work it out.'

The briefing broke up then and Swann went back to the squad room. Webb took the veroboard circuit back to his cage and then came through himself. Swann was scouring the list of Vauxhall Vectras. He had separated out those registered to London addresses and was nodding. 'Might get a result here, Webby. Look.' He showed Webb the listing and pointed to a group of ten cars at the bottom. 'Hire company in Heathrow. They must buy them from all over the place. I'm going to take a drive out there now. You coming?'

'Sure.'

'I'll drop you back here, then go up and see the crab.'

'Crab?'

'My ex. You know – shuffles from side to side and every now and then snaps her claws at you.'

Webb shook his head. 'God, you're a cynical bastard. You ought to thank her, mate. Look at you.' He touched the lapel of Swann's suit jacket. 'Four-button Armani? Bird like Pia Grava. What've you got to moan about?'

They located the hire company at Terminal 4, close to the long-stay car park. Swann parked in a visitor's space and they entered the Portakabin office. A young woman was sitting at a desk behind the counter. She was on the phone and lifted a hand to them. Swann looked round the office: nothing to it other than a couple of cloth chairs and a coffee table with *Autocar* magazines stacked on top of it. Webb stood by the window and looked out over the car park. He motioned to Swann who came over. Webb pointed to the rows of new cars. There were two Vectras among them, both were dark in colour. 'I'll go and take a look,' Webb said.

While he was outside, the receptionist finished her phone call. She stood up and smiled at Swann. Attractive, with tawny-coloured hair and green eyes.

'Morning,' she said. 'What can I do for you?'

Swann showed her his warrant card. 'Detective Sergeant Swann,' he said. 'Scotland Yard. I want to know if you've rented any of your RAH-suffixed Vectras in the past few days.'

'If you hang on a moment, I'll check the system.' She smiled and sat down again behind the desk. Swann moved back to the window and saw Webb looking closely at the two cars.

'Here we are.'

Swann turned again and she stood up, moving over to the printer. The machine whirred and she picked up two hire contracts.

'We've rented them both. Vectras are very popular.'

Swann took the contracts and sat down on one of the seats to read them. Webb came back inside and Swann handed the second one to him. The one Swann looked at had been rented for twenty-four hours on Tuesday at 3 p.m. He looked up at the receptionist.

'P770RAH,' he said. 'How many miles did this last hirer do?'

She checked the computer again. 'Seventy-two,' she said.

Swann glanced at Webb, then stood up and walked over to the counter. 'Who was working when the car was taken?'

'I'll have a look.' She moved to the back of the office and checked a duty roster taped up on the wall. She ran her finger across the dates and nodded. 'Sally Barnes,' she said.

'Is she here?'

'No.'

'Can you contact her for us?'

The girl looked doubtful. 'It's her day off.'

'Try.'

'OK.'

'I'm going to need a copy of the hirer's driving licence.' He looked down at the form. 'Edward Davies.'

The girl suddenly looked flustered. 'I think I better just get the manager. He's over at the terminal having lunch. I can page him for you.'

'That'd be good,' Swann said.

The manager arrived looking more than a little put out at having his lunch interrupted. He was a squat Italian of about forty. The receptionist had tried to get hold of the Barnes girl, but with no luck. The manager took Swann and Webb to his office in the Portakabin next door, and sat down behind his desk. 'What's this all about?'

'The Vectra outside,' Swann said. 'P770RAH. I think we're going to need it.'

'But it's going out in ten minutes.'

'I'm afraid it can't go out,' Webb told him.

A sudden redness burned in the manager's cheeks. 'But the customer has already landed.'

Swann made an open-handed gesture. 'You'll have to find him another car.'

The manager looked at him and his face sallowed. 'You can't just walk in here and ruin my day,' he said.

'I'm afraid we can.' Swann leaned on the desk. 'We're from the Antiterrorist Branch and we ruin a lot of people's days.' He smiled at him then. 'Now, we can seize the car or you can just let us have it.'

The man sat very still after that. 'OK,' he said. 'Whatever. I'll find another car.'

'Good.' Webb sat forward. 'Now, we need to get hold of Sally Barnes, the employee who was working when the car was rented. Your girl has tried but got no answer. We're going to need her address and a full copy of the driving licence the hirer used.' He paused. 'The car's been valeted since?'

'Yesterday.'

'By whom?'

'We subcontract. Clean-up 2, they're called. They pick the cars up and take them over to Uxbridge.'

'OK. Can you get them on the phone, please?'

☆

The address on the driving licence was Queen's House Mews in Hammersmith. Swann left Webb at Heathrow and drove over. He rang the bell of number 4, but got no reply. He phoned Webb from the car. 'There's no answer at the address, Webby,' he said. 'I'm going up to see Rachael, find out what's going on. I'll come back here afterwards.'

'OK. We've had the girl in,' Webb said. 'Sally Barnes. The body that rented the Vectra was white, about thirty, tall and lean, with cropped hair and tattoos.'

'What sort of tattoos?'

'You're going to love this. Got a black swastika on the underside of his right wrist.'

'She's observant.'

'Right-handed. She saw it as he signed the form.'

'How did he pay?'

'Cash.'

'No credit card?'

'Not this hire company. Small outfit, isn't it.'

Swann put the phone down and drove up to Muswell Hill.

☆

Webb waited at the Portakabin until the manager was ready to take him up to the valeting company in Uxbridge. It was on a back street off the main drag, a couple of lock-up garages knocked together. He found four people working; Asians, all of them brothers. A

73

young lad called Mustaq had cleaned the car the day before.

'What overalls were you wearing, Mustaq?' Webb asked him.

Mustaq looked at him out of black, suspicious eyes. Two of his brothers, with long hair and bracelets, stood with their arms across their chests.

'I need to know.' Webb looked at him closely.

Mustaq plucked at his chest. 'These ones.'

'How many cars have you cleaned since?'

'Two.'

'OK. Have you washed them – the overalls?'

'Yes.'

Webb frowned. The overalls looked pretty grimy. 'You sure, Mustaq. I'm not from Environmental Health.'

Mustaq looked at his brothers. 'Listen,' Webb said. 'This is very important. I don't care either way about your overalls, Mustaq. But I do need to know the truth. It isn't going to matter to you – except if you lie to me. I really don't like people who lie to me.'

'They haven't been washed.' One of his brothers spoke: the tallest one, thin, pockmarked face and hair falling across his eyes.

Webb went up to him. 'What's your name?'

'Ronnie.'

'And how would you know, Ronnie?'

Ronnie's face broke open in a smile. 'Because I do the washing.'

Webb laughed out loud then. 'Good lad,' he said. 'Get him another pair. I'm going to need these ones.'

By the time they got back to the Portakabin at Heathrow, the team from the exhibits office had arrived. The manager gave them the keys to the Vectra.

'You've not touched it, Webby?' Tania Briggs asked him. Webb shook his head.

The manager of the hire company watched as the car was wrapped in sterile tarpaulins and then hoisted on to the back of a truck. Webb stood with him on the steps, breathing in his cigar smoke.

'Will I get it back in one piece?'

Webb paused and peered closely at him, pushing the smile from the corners of his mouth. 'Only if we don't blow it up.'

☆

Swann's ex-wife and children lived in a terraced house close to Muswell Hill Broadway. It was rented, which he did not like particularly, but she hadn't bought because there was the possibility that her boyfriend would actually get his business off the ground and take them all off to Australia, a thought he liked even less. Rachael answered the door. She still looked attractive, and he stood for a moment a little awkwardly. This was never easy.

'Cup of tea?' she said.

He followed her through to the kitchen and squatted on a stool as she plugged the kettle in.

'You're earlier than I thought.'

'I know. I'm sorry. The Soho bomb.'

'Will you be able to stay for a bit when the children get in?'

'I've got to go over to Hammersmith.'

She folded her arms and leaned against the work surface. 'I hear the IRA didn't do it. Have you any idea who did?'

'We're looking at a couple of things.'

She looked wryly at him. 'Nothing changes then.'

Swann took the mug of coffee and sipped at it. 'So tell me what's going on,' he said. 'You talked on the phone about your job and everything. Peter?'

Her face clouded then and she sighed. She sat opposite

75

him and pushed a hand through her hair. 'I never get to see him,' she said.

'Doesn't he come here?'

'It's too far when he's busy in the week, and these days he spends most of the weekend working as well.'

Swann tried not to smile. Those were the very reasons she had left him, because the job demanded so much. 'Why don't you just move in together?'

She shook her head. 'He doesn't want to do that until he can earn enough to support all of us.'

'*I* pay for the kids.'

'Well, support *me*, then.' She got up. 'If I lived with him, I could help him get things moving. Help him with the selling side of the business.'

'What does he do exactly?'

'Makes furniture.' She pointed to a mock Queen Anne chair in the corner. 'He made that.'

Swann was impressed. He did not want to be, but he was. 'So you want to live with him?'

'Yes.'

'And the children?'

'He's not ready for that yet.'

Swann nodded slowly.

'It's not like that, Jack. I'm trying to get this dance teaching off the ground. Have you any idea how difficult that is when you have to be there for the children? All my classes seem to start just as they're about to come home.'

He put his mug on the table. 'What d'you want me to do about it, Rachael?'

She looked at him then. 'I want to know if you'll have the children.'

'Permanently?'

'No. Just until I can get this sorted out.'

He thought about it. 'I'd love to have them,' he said.

'But I'm not sure it'd be that good for them. I work almost all of the time.'

'Then change your habits.'

'SO13, Rachael. You know it goes with the territory.'

'Tell me about it. "Short on sleep but long on memory."' She rolled her eyes to the ceiling.

He stood up then and put his hands in his pockets. 'I won't be able to do anything immediately,' he said. 'It'll take a couple of months at least to sort something out.'

'I know that. All I'm asking is that you think about it. See if you can help out at all. You've *got* your career, Jack. I need to get mine.'

He left her then and went back to the car. From his mobile he phoned George Webb.

'What's happening?'

'Hire car's gone to DRA. How you doing?'

'Rachael wants me to have the kids full time.'

Webb was silent for a moment. 'What do you want?'

'I want them. I just don't see how I can.'

'What're you doing now?'

'Going back to Hammersmith. I'll see you back at the Yard after.'

'OK. Listen. Caroline's coming in tonight. We're going to get some solids somewhere. Join us if you want.'

'Thanks, Webby. I will.'

Swann drove to Hammersmith and parked outside a small three-storey hotel at the far end of the road from number 4, then made his way along the street. A mechanic was working on a taxi outside the blue garage doors of his workshop. He eyed Swann cautiously. Swann ignored him, climbed the steps to number 4 and rang the bell. He heard footsteps in the hall and then the door was opened.

He was faced by a smallish good-looking man, mixed race, hair curling, like a West Indian, cut tightly against his scalp, fine bronze skin and high cheekbones. He looked up out of very black eyes.

'Yes?'

'Mr Davies?'

The man looked puzzled. 'Er, no,' he said. 'My name's Morton.'

Swann held up his warrant card. 'Police, Mr Morton. Can I have a few words?'

'Of course.' Morton ushered him inside.

The front door opened on to a high-ceilinged hallway with stripped and polished wood on the floor. Two large rooms led off it and, at the back, three steps descended to a very spacious kitchen. A wide-banistered staircase, the wood again stripped and polished, climbed the wall to the right of the door. Morton led Swann into the lounge at the front of the house and motioned to leather armchairs. 'What can I help you with, Mr . . . ?'

'Swann. Detective Sergeant.'

'Sergeant then.' Morton sat across from him, one socked foot tucked under his backside. He wore a designer T-shirt and running pants. Swann squatted on the edge of the chair and loosened the buttons on his jacket.

'Is this your house, Mr Morton?'

Morton shook his head. 'I rent it. Well, the company I work for pays.'

'And what company is that?'

'You won't have heard of it.'

'All the same.'

They looked at one another for a moment, then Morton smiled. 'It's an American company, Mr Swann. Medicourt Communications.'

Swann nodded. 'What do you do for them?'

'Consultant. Electrical engineer. I look after most of

Europe, so London's an ideal base, although I'm having a bit of time off at the moment.'

Swann sat further back in the chair. Morton spoke very well, not plummy but almost. 'You been here long?' He motioned round the room.

'Only a few weeks.' Morton nodded to the furnishings. 'Not really my taste.'

'Nice all the same.'

Morton sat forward then and looked keenly at him. His expression was clear and he exuded confidence. 'What can I do for you, Sergeant?'

Swann took the copy of the driving licence out of his pocket. 'I was looking for an Edward Davies,' he said. 'We believe he hired a car at Heathrow on Tuesday afternoon. The licence gives this address.'

Morton leaned across to look at it, but didn't take it. 'It is this address,' he said. 'But he doesn't live here.'

'No?'

'Afraid not. Must be some mistake.' Morton shifted himself on the seat. 'What's it all about?'

Swann pursed his lips. 'You heard about the car bomb in Soho?'

'Of course. Terrible. No coded warning and PIRA didn't claim it.'

Swann stared at him for a moment. 'You know much about them – PIRA?' he said.

Morton laughed then. 'Should I?'

'I don't know.'

Again Morton laughed. 'I heard it on the TV, Sergeant. It's been all over the news.'

'It has, hasn't it.'

'So tell me. What's this got to do with it?' He nodded again at the driving licence.

'We believe that a car possibly used in the incident was hired by somebody using this licence. Skinheaded man,

79

tattoos.' Swann upturned his right forearm and tapped it. 'Black swastika here.'

Morton shrugged his shoulders. 'It's possible he lived here,' he said. 'I don't know who the tenant was before we took it on. You could check with the rental agency. Pearson's – they're just the other side of the Broadway on Fulham Palace Road.'

'Thank you. I will.' Swann looked at him again. 'There were two people involved in the bombing, Mr Morton.'

'So I heard. One parking the car – one driving away.'

Swann nodded. 'This is just routine, but I'd like to see some ID. You see we don't have a description of the other driver.'

'I understand perfectly.' Morton got up and took his wallet out of his pocket. 'What would you like – driving licence? Hang on, I'm not sure where I've put it. I can get my passport if you want.'

Swann waited while he went upstairs and fetched it. He noticed the book Morton was reading, lying open on the coffee table. *Geronimo the Apache*, some kind of biography. Morton returned and handed him a red European Community British passport. 'There you are,' he said.

Swann took the passport. 'Where are you from, Mr Morton?'

'Originally? Portsmouth. My father was in the Navy. He met my mother in Africa.'

'They still live down there – Portsmouth, I mean?'

'No.' Morton looked at the floor. 'They're both long dead, I'm afraid.'

'I'm sorry.' Swann looked at the passport again and noticed it had only been issued six months previously. 'Recent,' he said and held it out to him.

Morton nodded. 'The last one expired.'

'Have you got something with a previous address?'

Morton looked at him closely. 'Is that really necessary, Sergeant?'

'In this instance, yes.' Swann smiled at him. 'The hirer of the car said he lived here. I need to check everything, Mr Morton. I'm sure you understand.'

Morton went back upstairs and this time returned with his driving licence. 'You've done me a favour actually,' he said, 'forced me to find it. Knowing my luck, I'd get stopped and not have it with me. Not only that – I need to change the address.'

Swann looked at the licence. 'Fleet,' he said. 'That where you lived before?'

'For a while.'

'D'you mind if I ask where you were about four o'clock on Wednesday morning?'

'Not at all. I was here asleep.' Morton smiled at him.

'Can anybody verify that?'

'No. I live alone.'

'OK.' Swann stood up. 'Thank you for your time. I'm sorry to disturb you.'

'Not at all.' Morton showed him to the door. 'Good hunting,' he said as Swann walked down the steps.

# 4

After the interview with Morton, Swann went round to the letting agents in Fulham Palace Road. The manager told him the house fetched seven hundred pounds a week in rent, and gave him a photocopy of the lease agreement. Swann questioned him about Edward Davies, but was told that nobody by that name had ever lived there. He related all this to Colson, Clements and the others at the afternoon briefing upstairs.

'Coincidence then,' Clements said.

'It happens, Guv, doesn't it. Addresses are picked at random.'

'You don't sound convinced.'

Clements was watching him. Superintendent Colson was watching him. Swann brushed a palm across the thigh of his trousers and sighed. 'I don't know,' he said. 'There's something about Morton that bugs me. He's a little bit too sure of himself.'

Clements stood up. 'OK,' he said. 'We know the driving licence is fake. Given that, we've probably found the car. George?'

'Waiting for DRA's evaluation,' Webb told him.

'In the morning?'

'Probably, yes.'

'Right.' Clements glanced at Colson. 'In the meantime, we start looking for a skinhead with a swastika tattooed on his wrist.'

☆

They had dinner in the West End; Swann, Webb and Caroline. Swann had much on his mind.

'How can you have the children?' Caroline asked him. 'You're never there.'

He looked at her, laying down his fork and picking up his wine glass. 'I don't know. But you imagine how they must be feeling right now. Jo's not even ten yet and Charley's only six. They think that their mummy wants to be with her boyfriend, but she can't because of them.'

Caroline leaned across the table and covered the fist he had made with a palm. 'Oh, Jack. It's not as simple as that.'

'I know it's not. But that's what they're going to think.' He sat back. 'I'll have to figure it out, somehow.'

'You'll have to get a nanny.'

'I can't afford a nanny, Caroline.'

Caroline cocked an eyebrow at him. 'Jack, that's an Armani suit you're wearing.'

'Well, you know what I mean.' He drummed his fingers on the table top. 'I suppose I won't be paying child support.'

Webb was silent, toying with his food and watching them both. He was hardly listening, other things on his mind. The veroboard from the Soho car bomb disturbed him, its origin: even from the small fragment he had recovered, he could tell that the dual circuitry had been put together by a professional. The TPU that it came from was undoubtedly more sophisticated than the Provisionals' Mk 15.

Caroline was speaking. 'Listen, Jack,' she said. 'Why don't you try and find out about those student au pairs who come over?'

Swann frowned at her. 'Pia's going to love that.'

'If it bothers her that much, tell *her* to look after them.'

Swann grinned at Webb. 'Pia, the surrogate mother. Can't quite see it, can you?'

Caroline shrugged. 'Her problem then, isn't it.' Again she laid her hand over Swann's. 'Listen,' she said. 'They're advertised in *The Lady* magazine. They come over to study English. You don't pay them, only board and lodging. They look after your children in return. If you contact the agencies and explain your situation, I'm sure someone'll help you.'

Coffee came and the conversation inevitably turned to work. Morton bothered Swann. He could not say why: his story had checked out and in no way did he fit the description of the man who had hired the second car. They didn't have a description of the first man, however. All at once he looked up and stared at Webb. 'PIRA,' he said.

'What about them?'

'No. *He said, PIRA.*'

'Who?'

'James Morton, the body at Queen's House Mews.' Swann crushed out his cigarette and gestured with a palm. 'Who says PIRA?'

'I'm not with you.'

'Listen to me. You talk to the public, anyone not in the know – and they call it the IRA. Even on news bulletins, it's the *IRA* claimed responsibility or whatever. Morton referred to them as *PIRA*.'

☆

The following morning, the results came in from Jane Mason at the Defence Research Agency. They had swabbed the hire car and come up with indisputable explosive traces. She spoke to George Webb on the phone as he sat in the exhibits office. Webb put the phone down and walked the length of the corridor, past the morale-boosting stuff on the wall that the Branch had gathered over twenty years of fighting terrorism: photographs, bomb scenes, SO19 taking out armed suspects. Swann was at his desk, talking on the phone. DI Clements was looking through the initial reports on the blown-up car from Soho.

'Guv'nor.' Webb walked across the floor towards him and Clements looked up. 'Jane Mason just on the phone.'

'And?'

'RDX in the hire car.'

'From Semtex?'

'Jane thinks so, yeah.' Webb touched the edges of his moustache. 'There's something else I wanted to show you.'

Clements followed him back to the exhibits office where he took a sheaf of papers from his drawer. Earlier that morning, he had printed them off from the computer records stored in the Bomb Data Centre, which took information from terrorist incidents all round the world. Under the terms of the Trevi Committee Protocol, international police forces and counter-terrorist officers shared information. Webb took a diagram he had discovered in the files and laid it on the desk. He pointed to the circuit board and the wiring. 'Red and green,' he said. 'This is a dual integrated circuit used in a timing and power unit from an abortive ETA incident in 1987. Barcelona Airport.' He laid the piece of circuit board from the car bomb alongside it. 'Not the same, but the pattern of the wires is similar.'

Clements chewed his thumbnail. 'ETA?'

'Possibly. Who knows. ETA and PIRA share information.' Webb shrugged his shoulders. 'Maybe they're trying to fool us. Maybe it is PIRA and they're adopting a new tack. They know how many they've lost to us in recent years. Maybe they're going to share operatives for a while. Irishmen in the Basque country and Basques over here.'

Clements leafed through the papers. 'It's possible, I suppose.'

☆

The day after he was visited by Jack Swann, James Morton, the dark-skinned man in number 4 Queen's House Mews, bought a car. He got the train to Peterborough and went to an auction of ex-company cars. There he inspected a number of vehicles all being sold off cheaply and bought a Ford Mondeo. He paid for it in cash, drove back to London and parked outside his house. Then he scoured the *Yellow Pages* for long-term underground storage.

☆

Swann went back to the letting agents on Fulham Palace Road and spoke at length with the manager, a Greek called Monoyos. The house in Queen's House Mews was owned by an Arab, who spent most of his time out of the country. It was one of many such houses, dotted here and there around London. Most of the larger premises in the non-exclusive areas had been converted into flats, but this particular businessman had discovered a market for the large Victorian property. He also owned the one along the same street which was for sale. Swann had noted it and his next port of call was the estate agents who were selling it.

He rechecked the rental history of number 4 and found nothing that aroused his suspicions. Then he got the bank details of Medicourt Communications, the US-based company that Morton claimed he worked for, and found they had an account at Lloyds on Hammersmith Broadway. He copied all the documents and then asked Monoyos about prior tenants. He discovered that as Morton had said, he had only been in the house for two months. Prior to that it was empty for a month, with a twelve-month let before that. He questioned Monoyos further about the Medicourt letting. 'Who actually rented the house?' he said. 'It's just got the company name on the documents.'

Monoyos nodded. 'A woman viewed it first.'

'Woman?' Swann looked sharply at him. 'Who was she?'

Monoyos scratched his head. 'What was her name? I've got it here somewhere.' He rummaged in a drawer and came up with a pad of paper, the used pages folded over rather than torn off. He flicked back over them and then tapped a page with his fingernail.

'Joanne Taylor,' he said. 'That's the woman. Joanne Taylor.'

'Any address?'

Monoyos shook his head. 'She did everything through the bank.'

'What d'you mean?'

'Well, she told me that the company had no office base in the UK, so *she* would call me. She rang from a cellphone, I think.' He paused then. 'It's not unusual.'

Swann nodded. 'What about signing the lease?'

'It was delivered to Lloyds Bank round the corner. It came back to me signed, with the deposit electronically transferred and confirmation of funds for the remainder of the lease.'

Swann thanked him then and left. On the pavement he remembered something and went back inside. 'One more thing, Mr Monoyos,' he said. 'Prior to Medicourt taking the tenancy, did you show anyone else around?'

Monoyos looked back at his diary. 'One man,' he said. 'O'Brien, I think his name was.'

Swann leant forward. 'What did he look like?'

'Blond hair, I think, quite well dressed. Nice man. He spoke with an Irish accent.'

Swann crossed the road and went into Remmington & Son, the agents selling the other property. He spoke to a negotiator called Julie Baker who had shown most of the prospective buyers around. She got out her diary and flicked back over the past three months, the length of time the house had been on the market.

'It needs quite a lot of refurbishing,' she said. 'The owner has a number of such places and I think he's getting bored. He's not prepared to drop the price, though, and considering what needs doing, he'll have a job to sell.'

'More money than sense, then,' Swann said.

'Very probably, yes.'

She looked through the viewings and wrote a list of them all for him. When she was finished, he took it from her and scanned the names. No Joanne Taylor among them and no O'Brien. There was another name that interested him, however. 'This Mr McIlroy,' he said. 'Irish?'

'Irish name maybe, but his accent was English. South London, I'd say.'

'What did he look like?'

'Quite tall. Blond hair, longish. Blue eyes, I think.'

'Thank you,' Swann said. 'Thank you very much.'

He went to the bank on the Broadway, showed his ID and waited for the business manager who looked after Medicourt Communications. He had to wait a few minutes, flicking through the *Financial Times* on the small table between the twin settees in the waiting area. A man in his mid-twenties, slightly overweight, with a mass of slicked-back hair and a goatee beard, came out from the small office behind the business banker's desk.

'Andy Roberts,' he said.

'DS Swann.' They shook hands. 'Can we talk somewhere privately?'

Roberts led him back into the office and they sat down. 'Medicourt Communications,' Swann said. 'What can you tell me about them?'

'Not a lot. They only use this account to pay the rent on the house they lease round the corner.'

'That's it?'

'Yes.'

'Where does the money come from?'

'From another account. It's electronically transferred every couple of months.'

'From where?'

'Ireland.'

Swann looked at him. 'Your bank?'

'No. Allied Irish in Belfast. Apparently the company has connections over there.'

Swann chewed his lip for a moment. 'When the lease was signed, the letting agents told me they sent it here.'

Roberts nodded. 'Yes, they did. It was collected, I think.'

'Who by?'

'That I can't tell you. It would've been left with the messenger.'

'Does the name Joanne Taylor mean anything to you?'

Roberts shook his head.

'Who opened the account?'

'Let me see.' The manager flicked through his records. 'It was done by proxy via the Allied Irish account in Belfast. They gave us their reference. There's no borrowing facility, so it wasn't a problem.'

'So you've never actually met anyone from the company, then.'

Roberts shook his head.

'And the lease?'

'Returned to us here, I think.' Again Roberts looked at his notes. 'Yes,' he said. 'It was. We forwarded it to the agents, with a letter declaring enough funds in the account to pay the rent for six months.'

'Which is eighteen thousand two hundred pounds.'

Roberts' eyebrows shot up. 'Is it?'

'Yes,' Swann said. 'It is.'

He drove back to the Yard, parked underground and pressed the lift call button. He bumped into Webb as he came out on the fifteenth floor. He was standing in the open doorway of the Special Branch cell talking to Christine Harris. Swann went down to the squad room where a couple of his colleagues were gathered. There was a note on his desk to phone Pia at work. A smile spread across his face and he realized then just how much he missed her. Stripping off his jacket, he dialled her direct line.

'Pia, it's me.'

'Jack. How are you?'

Her voice melted him, the hint of European in her accent, when she spoke his name it was almost 'Jacques', but not quite. He bent his face to the desk, free hand over his ear. 'I'm fine. You got back early, then.'

She sighed. 'Yes. The meeting wasn't exactly productive. Are you still very busy?'

'Working on the Soho bomb, yes.'

'Are you getting anywhere?'

Swann sat up straighter. 'We're making a few inroads.'

'I missed you, Jack. When can I see you?'

Swann drew circles on a pad of paper. God, he loved this woman. Webb told him he loved them all, but he really loved this one. 'Just as soon as you want. What about tonight?'

'What time?'

'Seven, eight, maybe.'

'Shall I cook?'

'I could pick something up.'

'Thai.'

'OK. I'll bring it over to your place.'

Swann put the phone down and went to get himself some coffee. He stood with it in the corner of the squad room overlooking Big Ben. He had been seeing Pia for about six months now. He and Webb and a few of the other guys had been raucous at a leaving do one night in Waxy O'Conors. One of the lads had taken promotion back to uniform to look after the security section at Heathrow. He was due on a refresher course with SO19 at 7 o'clock the following morning. At midnight, they were planning which nightclub they could drag him to.

Pia had been there with a group of her friends from the bank. They were celebrating somebody's birthday party and all ended up going to the club together. There had been something about the way she looked at him. Big oval eyes, so elegant and small-boned; short black hair and leggings that hugged her flesh like a second skin.

'Jack.'

He started and looked over his shoulder. Webb stood at his desk, pushing a pencil end through his notes. Swann tossed the empty coffee cup into the bin and went over to him.

'Clements has called the meeting.'

'Now?'

'Yeah. Couple of things have shown up and we need to see who's doing what.'

They went upstairs to the sixteenth floor and the conference room. Most of the team were gathered already. Swann looked at the chart on the wall: he had some additions to make to it. Colson went over what they had established so far and Webb imparted the information regarding the circuit board and the Barcelona incident.

After he had finished, Swann related the events of the morning, the banking facilities of Medicourt Communications and the blond-haired men, O'Brien and McIlroy.

When he had finished, nobody spoke for a few minutes, then Colson moved off the edge of the desk where he squatted. 'It's getting interesting,' he said. 'Lots of Irish bits and pieces, but no PIRA.'

Swann placed his hands on the top of his head. 'I think we ought to get somebody to check the bank account over the water, sir.'

Christine stood up. 'I'll give someone a call for you, Jack.'

'Thanks.' Swann looked at Clements then. 'I haven't checked the passport yet, but I will. Something's not right about Morton.'

# 5

Swann left the Yard early that evening. He drove first to Muswell Hill to see his children, not wanting to miss them again, having done so the day before. He rang the bell, saw Joanna's small face at the upstairs window transform into an expression of glee, then, even from outside, he could hear her feet thumping down the stairs. The next thing he knew she was in his arms. 'Hey, darling. How you doing?' He carried her inside and kicked the door closed with his heel. Rachael was upstairs and he could hear the sound of Charlotte, his youngest, moaning about Joanna getting all the cuddles. He climbed the stairs, still with Jo in his arms, telling him all about what she had been doing at school. She loved school, the only person alive, he thought, who couldn't wait for Sunday to become Monday.

He took her into the bathroom and set her down. Charlotte stood up and hugged him, plastering his jacket with soapy water. Rachael had a wry smile on her face as he extricated himself from his daughter and dabbed at his suit with a towel. Swann ignored her.

'And how're you, little short person?' he said, crouching on to one knee as Charlotte sat down in the water again.

'Fine,' she said. 'Fine.'

Jo was hanging round his neck, her face under his chin, pushing his head right back. 'Mummy says we might come and stay with you for a bit, Dad,' she said.

'Because she's got to go to work,' Charley added.

'Will I have to change my school?' Joanna looked up at Swann. 'I don't want to, Daddy. I'll miss all my friends.'

'I don't mind. I don't like my school.' Charlotte splashed a pink arm up and down in the water. Swann got to his feet and stepped back to avoid the waves.

'You live in Waterloo, don't you, Daddy,' Jo said. 'It's not as nice as here.'

'I like Daddy's house.' Charlotte grinned at him. 'I like Mummy's too, though. I like them both the same.'

Swann looked at them and smiled. So different. Jo, the elder, very prim and proper, long blonde hair tied at the neck in a ponytail. Dark eyes like his and a thoughtful expression on her face most of the time. Charley, on the other hand, had the same blue eyes as her mother, and shorter, darker, more curling hair than her sister, though most of the curls had dropped out now. He stepped out of the bathroom. 'You guys coming to stay with me this weekend?' He looked at Rachael then. 'That's what we planned, isn't it?'

'Yes.'

'Good. What about it then, girls? We'll go over and see Caroline's horses.' Caroline had two horses, one for Webb to ride, though he never did. Swann kissed both his daughters and left them to their baths.

He went downstairs, Rachael following him. 'I've been thinking about what you said,' he told her. 'It'll take some sorting. What about Jo's school?'

'I know. The last thing I want to do is disturb her.'

'Why don't you just get the Aussie to move in here then?'

She placed one hand on her hip and shook her head at him. 'I've told you, Jack. It's too far from his workshop. And he has got a name.'

'Whatever.' He sighed and flapped a hand at her. 'We'll sort something out. Don't worry.'

It was eight-thirty by the time he got to Pia's in Shepherd's Bush. She lived in a one-bedroomed ground-floor flat in Lime Grove. Swann pressed the doorbell and she answered it dressed in a bathrobe. He kissed her, laid the food on the work surface in the tiny kitchen at the back, then turned to her again. He pulled her very close; lips on her lips, then neck and down between her breasts. 'Missed you, darling.'

She held him, fingernails in his shoulder blades. 'I missed you too.'

He kissed her again, then they broke and she rested the flat of her palms against his chest.

'I was just getting into a bath.'

'This'll keep. We can nuke it,' he said, nodding towards the food parcels. He followed her through to the bath-room with the sunken bath and the huge mirror on the back of the door. He watched as she slipped off the robe and lowered herself into the foaming water. Her hair was cut short up the back of her neck, almost shaved it was so close, heavier on top but still cropped, spiky at the front accentuating the jet black of her eyes.

'God, you're beautiful,' he muttered.

She smiled at him, the water reaching up her thighs to the dark mound of pubic hair. Her skin, though pale at this time of year, still had the rich depth of her Mediter-ranean birth. She lay back and gently smoothed the soap over her breasts, then down her belly and eased it between her legs. She touched the tip of her nose with her tongue and Swann tugged loose his tie.

They ate dinner on the floor of the lounge, with candles dripping wax over the Victorian fireplace which housed the mock coal fire. It was lit, but low, and apart from the candles it threw out the only light. They ate and talked and drank wine. 'I've got the kids tomorrow,' Swann said. 'They're coming for the weekend.'

'How are they?'

'Great. Rachael wants them to come and live with me, though.'

Pia looked up, a little startled. 'Permanently?'

'For a while at least.' He explained the week's conversations.

She sipped her wine and shrugged. 'It's fair enough, I suppose. She should be allowed to work.'

Swann nodded. 'I'll have to get a nanny or something.'

'Can you afford it?'

'No.'

'What, then?'

'Caroline thought I could get one of those student au pairs, the ones who want board and lodging only.'

Pia looked up then and her brow furrowed darkly. 'And how will you manage that? You've only got two bedrooms.'

'The sofa upstairs is a bed, remember? I can kip down on that.'

'What – give her your room?'

'Don't see as I've got any choice.'

She waggled her wine glass at him. 'Just as long as there's no tiptoeing in the night, Jack Swann. I know what they call you, remember.'

He laughed then and tweaked her chin with his fingers. 'That's because of the suits, darling. Not the dirty raincoat.' He sat back and lit a cigarette. 'I thought we'd go over to Amersham on Saturday, if you fancied it. The kids love Caroline's horses. We could stay over till Sunday?'

'Why not. I might persuade the fat detective to cook.'

Pia stared into the gas flames, eyes hooded and thoughtful. For a moment Swann studied her face, then rested a hand on her thigh. 'What's up?' he said. 'You look preoccupied.'

Pia stretched, her robe falling open, revealing the curve of her breasts. She hunched forward, rubbing the stem of the wine glass between her palms. 'Oh, I'm all right,' she said. 'Paris was a pain.' She glanced up at him then. 'I'm getting a bit sick of all the bullshit, that's all.'

'Bullshit?'

'You know, Jack. Rich people's bullshit.' She was silent again for a moment. 'Ignore me. I think I'm just tired, that's all.'

They made love again, on the floor of the lounge, with the fire hissing quietly and the candles twisting into darkness. He roamed her body with his, stiff and hard and desperate. Later, in bed, with the curtains thrown back and cold air blowing into the room through the open window, they lay side by side while the sex dried on their skin. At six in the morning he got up, showered, and went back to the Yard.

He got coffee and went to his desk. He had the details from James Morton's driving licence, which listed Fleet in Hampshire as his previous address. He had checked the electoral register with the council and found that Morton was listed. He clearly had lived in Fleet and paid his council tax. It added up. On the face of it genuine, but there was that nagging doubt at the back of his mind. At nine o'clock, he rang the Passport Office and gave them the number he had taken from Morton's passport. After a short delay, the operator came back on the line.

'You say the passport was renewed?' she said.

'That's right.'

'Not according to our records.'

'What d'you mean?'

'When we issued it last year – it was for the first time.'

Swann sat very still. 'You're sure?'

'Positive.'

'Can you send me a copy of the application form?'

'Only on microfiche, the original would've been shredded ages ago.'

'Soon as you can then, please.' Swann gave her the fax number.

When he put the phone down he went to the exhibits office and found George Webb.

'James Morton lied to me,' he said.

'How?'

'Told me his passport was a renewal. It's not. First application.'

'Is it indeed?'

Swann nodded. 'I'm waiting for the microfiche copy of the form.'

Webb looked at him with a puzzled expression on his face. 'Stupid mistake to make,' he said.

'That's what I thought.'

They took the application details to the Family Records Centre in Islington. 'Why lie to me, Webby?' Swann said, as they parked. 'He must know we'd check.'

'I don't know, mate. It doesn't make any sense.'

Inside, the building was not as yet heaving with people researching family trees. Every time they went into the place these days, the world and his wife seemed to be there. Morbid fascination with the past, Swann called it. They went to the births section and pulled out the relevant indexes. Then it was a matter of going through them one by one. According to his passport Morton was born in 1961, so they got the four books for that year, which listed all the births in England and Wales in alphabetical order. It took them a while, but they located James Morton. Swann took the reference to the clerk at the desk and showed him his warrant card. 'I need to know if anyone made a copy of his birth certificate – about six months ago,' he said.

The clerk took the reference from him and checked the records. 'Yes,' he said. 'Somebody did. Almost exactly six months ago.'

Swann traced the line of his lips with his tongue and looked sideways at Webb.

'More and more interesting,' Webb said as they left the desk again.

'But now the hard part.'

Webb pushed air from his cheeks. 'You're telling me.' He looked at the rows and rows of books. 'Every single death since 1961.'

Swann pulled a face. 'It'll take a while, Webby, but we've got a lot of bodies back at the Yard. He lied to me, didn't he. I want to know why.'

☆

Over the next two weeks Swann and several colleagues devoted two hours a day to going through the death registers at the Islington records centre. A general election was beckoning and PIRA were determined to create as much havoc as possible. A number of railway stations had to be closed down when a whole raft of coded warnings came into the central command complex on the same day. The London Underground system came to a stop as more warnings were received by radio stations and newspapers. The capital ground to a halt. Traffic backed up and George Webb discovered he could drive on the pavement.

The RUC Special Branch inquiry into Medicourt Communications discovered that the Allied Irish Bank account was one of a number with reasonably substantial credit balances. Medicourt was a non-trading company, owned by another which was owned by yet another. The main banking activities appeared to take place in Germany and northern Spain. Banking references were given by West Deutsche Landesbank in Frankfurt, and from there the trail ran cold, money being transferred in and out electronically from companies all over the world.

Other priorities took over. Security on the mainland was at its zenith with the possibility of a change of government. As usual, it was a question of budgets, manpower and the relative merits of risk management. The domestic threat from PIRA would grow with every day that passed before 1 May. John Major had called the election in mid-March, a full six weeks before voting day.

Swann found himself alone, spending more and more time poring over old tomes in Islington, as others were tasked elsewhere. In the middle of the third week, he was about to pack it in for the day when he felt a sudden burst of excitement. The death of James Morton was right there on the page before him. He checked and rechecked the details, then he sat back and rubbed his hands through his hair.

Back at the Yard he looked for DI Clements, but he was out on a confidential inquiry. He looked for George Webb, but Webb was at the Old Bailey giving evidence. The witness box in Number 1 court, the loneliest square metre in the whole world when the Queen's Counsel was picking holes in everything you said and did. Swann headed back to the squad room and saw the commander's door was open. Colson was sitting across the desk from him. Swann hovered in the doorway and Colson motioned for him to come in. 'Just give us a minute, would you, Jack,' he said.

Swann sat down and waited for them to finish their conversation. The commander had pictures of native American Indians hanging on his walls, high-quality oils from renowned Western artists. It had been something of a joke amongst the ranks and Garrod had been dubbed 'Cochise' behind his back. He pointed out to them that the modern-day terrorist learnt most of his trade from the likes of Crazy Horse and Ten Bears. Hit-and-run, the original guerrilla fighters. Geronimo, the Chiricahua Apache, was perhaps the best at evading capture. He would lie wrapped round the bole of a tree and sleep as patrols all but rode over him. On one occasion, he placed a handful of stolen blue coats on cacti and held a cavalry patrol at bay for four hours because they could not tell how many horsemen they faced.

'Yes, Jack.' Superintendent Colson was speaking to him.

Swann started and looked up. 'Queen's House Mews, sir. James Morton, the man I interviewed.'

'What about him?'

'He died of leukaemia when he was five.'

Colson stared at him and then at the commander. Swann handed him the copy of the entry from the Family Records Centre. 'Two things bother me, sir,' he said. 'First, he gave me the passport, and yet still managed to come up with a driving licence when I pressed him.' He hunched his shoulders. 'That's odd. Ninety-nine people out of a hundred could lay their hands on their driving licence before they could their passport.'

Colson nodded.

'Secondly, he lied to me. Stupid mistake to make. Too stupid in my opinion. He told me the passport was a renewal, when he knew I'd find out it wasn't.'

Colson looked at him and frowned. 'I agree,' he said. 'I'll muster the troops. We need to consider our options.'

Swann got up and went to the door.

'Jack,' Garrod checked him and Swann turned in the doorway. 'Well done.'

'Thanks, Guv,' he said.

They gathered upstairs at 2 p.m. Clements was still out, so Colson took the briefing. He spoke for a few minutes, then turned to Swann. 'Jack, perhaps you'd like to tell everybody what you've discovered.'

Swann moved to the front of the room and told them about James Morton's death.

'Result, Flash,' Webb said. 'Bloody excellent result.'

The others echoed his comment and Colson caught Swann's eye. 'Hard work,' he said. 'It always seems to pay off in the end.'

Webb looked back at Swann. 'How're we going to play it?'

'Surveillance. Joint SB and Box.' He glanced at Christine and Julian Moore. 'That's if you guys can work together.'

Julian looked witheringly at him.

'We need to recce for a static observation point,' Swann went on, 'and we'll need plenty of bodies on the street. You got any teams free right now?'

'We're pretty tight,' Christine said. 'There's a bit going on, isn't there. We could drag a few in from SO11.'

'Not necessary,' Julian said. 'We've got all the manpower you need.'

'I still want an SB presence,' Swann said. 'Make it easier to liaise.'

'Fair enough.' Julian looked at Christine.

'I'll sort something out,' she said.

'We'll give him a week or so, then do a covert on the bins,' Swann went on. 'I want to see what he's throwing away.' He glanced at Webb. 'You and me?'

'Dead of night.' Webb rubbed his hands together. 'Digital interference, just the way Caroline likes it.'

'In the dark, George,' Christine said, 'why am I not surprised?'

MI5 and Special Branch set up a joint surveillance

operation. Despite the jokes, it was a fact that since Special Branch had got used to the idea of civil servants aiding them with police work, they had won far more than they lost. The end of the cold war had spelled redundancy for informant handlers and surveillance-trained operatives. More manpower. No budget implications. Better results.

Covertly, they set up an observation point in the building across the road from number 4. An attic flat with a good view over the street and the houses opposite. Television men arrived with a delivery of cardboard boxes and were greeted by the owner of the flat, a middle-aged lady who thought this police presence was wonderful.

The surveillance was round the clock, twenty-four-hour video tapes linked to the camera, which appeared as a disc-like ornament behind the net curtains. Special Branch and MI5, two officers occupying the room at any given time. Morton was followed every time he stepped out of doors. His newly purchased Mondeo was watched by a full team, its every movement monitored by an array of different vehicles and motorcycles. When he went anywhere on foot, he was shadowed and not once did he show any sign of antisurveillance techniques. He bought his food from the supermarket in Hammersmith. He never went into a pub or off-licence. When he ran short of milk, he would jog round the corner to the shop run by the little Asian man and buy some more. He did not appear to go to work and spent long periods in the house, visible to the spotters across the road, seated at a desk in the bay window of the lounge. GCHQ monitored his telephone calls. Two weeks into the surveillance, Swann and Webb stole his plastic rubbish bags.

They did not know what if any value could be gained from them, but you could learn a lot about a person's activities by what he throws away. They took the substituted dustbin liners back to the exhibits office at the Yard. Tania Briggs was there with DI Clements who was duty officer and they crowded round as Webb laid sterile paper on the desktop and tipped out the contents.

It was all the usual sort of stuff – empty cans, milk cartons, bread wrappers, old food, apple cores and orange peel, cereal cartons and other bits of rubbish. Swann was beginning to feel a little deflated when Webb scraped something else on to the table. A PP3 battery wrapper. He paused, turned it over in his gloved hand and then set it to one side. Nobody spoke. He tipped out the rest of the contents and worked his way through them.

'Look,' Swann said, aware of the hairs on the back of his neck. He picked up another piece of cardboard with a torn strip of clingfilm still attached to it. 'The wrapper from a hot-glue gun.' Clements picked up the Branch copy of the surveillance log and flicked through the pages.

'Guv'nor?'

He looked up at Webb, who was holding something between his forefinger and thumb. Not very much and obviously stripped from the copper core, a tiny piece of green electrical wire.

Now they stood in silence. Clements looked again at the log. 'Since we've been looking at him, he hasn't bought batteries or glue gun or wire,' he said. 'We've had eyeball every minute of the time he's been out, no cracked ice at all.'

Swann gazed at the items, separated now from the others on the desktop in front of them. 'So when did he buy this little lot?'

'And why throw them away today?' Webb added.

☆

The following morning James Morton walked out of his house and got into his maroon Ford Mondeo. Immediately the spotters were on the radio to the motorcyclist on Glenthorne Road. 'Four/two from Control. X3, Dave. Target on the move. Repeat, target is on the move.'

They watched as Morton turned the car round and drove the length of the street. As he turned right, the motorcyclist fell in behind him.

Morton drove round the Broadway and then back on himself and crossed beneath the A4 flyover and on to Hammersmith Bridge. The motorcyclist was a dozen cars back now and a white van had taken over. On the far side of the bridge, a Peugeot 406 slipped in behind him at the lights, then stalled and called the following surveillance cars up while he held up the traffic. A second motorcyclist had eyeball contact further down the road. Morton drove on until he came to the South Circular Road and then turned east and headed for Putney. He crossed at the junction with Putney High Street and again the lead car put the block in to allow the other cars to catch up. It was important to try to keep together, especially on the scale of this operation. Blocking a set of traffic lights, although irritating the hell out of a number of drivers, allowed the trailing cars to catch up, overtake the lead car and go on together in convoy. Always up ahead there was at least one vehicle with eyeball.

Morton drove sensibly and quite clearly there was no third eye. They had not expected one: a second car specifically designed to watch for signs of surveillance, acting as guard for the main vehicle. Morton had had no visitors and had visited no one either overtly or covertly in all the time they'd had him under surveillance. GCHQ had monitored which phone numbers he called and which had called him. On three occasions he had called a telephone box in Highgate. They had set up separate surveillance on that particular box, but the new Home Secretary denied them permission to bug it.

Morton went through Putney and into Wandsworth and then turned north towards the river and the solid waste transfer station. He drove the Mondeo into the long-stay underground car park beyond the Delta business park, overlooked by Wandsworth Bridge. The lead car waited a few minutes before following him down the slope, beyond the attendant and into the darkened concrete hole. He drove slowly, apparently looking for space. Morton was not difficult to locate. He had parked on the lowest level, close to the stairs exit, and was locking the boot when the surveillance vehicle swept past him and parked in a space further away from the stairs. In his rear-view mirror the driver saw Morton leave the car and disappear into the stairwell. The information was relayed to the following vehicles and he was picked up as he left the car park on foot. He walked to Wandsworth High Street and took a taxi back to the premises in Queen's House Mews. The information was relayed back to the Yard and Swann contacted the car park. He was told that a vehicle could be parked there for as long as was required. The keys were left with the attendant, who would ensure the car would start properly when the driver phoned to say he'd collect it.

The surveillance continued and Morton was in and out of the house. He bought various items on his trips into the West End, including a large black travel bag. He had left no specific time to return for the car in Wandsworth, and for three days a surveillance team watched it. On the fourth night, George Webb made a covert entry into the boot by unscrewing the number plate and flipping the lock mechanism. Inside, he found a small black holdall which contained an empty plastic sandwich box and a large padded envelope. In the envelope he found a pack of PP3 batteries, the same type as the package they had recovered from the bins, together with a full box of Havana cigars and a Memopark timer.

Bill Colson took the briefing the morning after Webb made his covert entry. It was the beginning of June and getting warmer. Every member of the team was present including Christine Harris from the Special Branch cell and the representatives from MI5. Swann sat at the back of the room and drank coffee. Webb told them what he had found in the boot of the Mondeo and Colson stood up again when he had finished. 'We've got the bits and pieces recovered when Webb and Swann did the sneaky beaky on the bins,' he said, 'and Webby's just told us what's in the boot.' He paused then, rubbing the palm of one hand across the knuckles of the other. 'I think we have two choices. Number one, keep watching the Mondeo and the target to see what happens. Number two, we scoop him up now.'

Swann cleared his throat. 'I think we should take him out, Guv. Last Box log mentioned him buying a big bag for his holidays.'

'If he takes a trip, we can pull him before he gets on the plane,' Christine said.

'Why not wait to see who comes for the car?' McCulloch the ginger-headed Scotsman suggested.

Swann glanced at him. 'We could wait for ever, Macca. I think we should scoop him up now. We know he's using the identity of a dead person. We don't need any more.' He looked at the superintendent. 'Guv, we don't know who this guy is or what his motives are. He knows how to build a Mk 15 TPU, but he only uses it as a dummy. The other TPU is potentially much more sophisticated. Right, Webby?'

Webb looked across at him, fingered his moustache and nodded.

'You just want to interview him, Flash.' Christine was grinning at him. 'Teeth sharp, are they?'

Swann returned the smile. 'You're only jealous because you don't get to do it any more.' He licked his lips like a wolf. 'Nothing like the look on their faces when the gates at Paddington close.'

Colson sat down and pondered. 'I think Jack's right,' he said. 'If we bring him in now, we've got the potential for good forensics in the house. Not only that, but it might prompt any second player to go and get the car.' He stood up. 'I'm going to give SO19 a ring and make sure we have a team on standby. They can do their reconnaissance over the weekend and hit him either Monday or Tuesday.'

☆

While Swann was falling off Pink Void at Baggy Point, with memories of the past flaring up in his mind, Sergeant Nicholas Graves, of specialist firearms officer blue team, was watching the video taken from the helicopter they had used to fly over the area around Queen's House Mews. He was down in the basement at Old Street with his men, the inner sanctum of the SFO teams, where they held their own preliminary briefings. Graves was fifty-one years old, still fitter than most men half his age, six foot two, with a broken nose and eagle-blue eyes. What little hair he had was shaved so close that from any sort of distance he might as well have been bald. He had joined the department in 1991, when the first armed response vehicles were being commissioned. He had been a skipper then and was a skipper now, had moved from the ARVs to the SFO teams, with a period of two years instructing between. He had held his pink firearms ticket for fifteen years, serving three of those in the Diplomatic Protection Group, guarding Downing Street.

The members of blue team lolled about him in easy chairs, drinking coffee, a couple of them smoking. Joe Pollock – or Mumbles as he was affectionately called – the gigantic, method of entry man, with biceps like tree-trunks, sat with Twelve Hits Phil Gibson, who, at ten and a half stone, was the smallest member of the team. The two of them worked together, Mumbles taking out doors and Twelve Hits (so named because it took him twelve attempts to batter open a door on one abortive mission) being the MP5 cover man while stun grenades were thrown in. Between them they formed the front of the 'stick'.

They were studying the street plan that had been taken off the computer and enlarged so they could fully detail the route to the rendezvous, form-up and final assault points, in order to determine the best method of attack. Over and above the Squirrel fly-by, they had undertaken a detailed reconnaissance from the ground. Four men had arrived in a British Telecom van and had begun inspection work on the telephone connections around the target premises. They had gone into the car workshop next door and discovered that the premises went back a long way and had a yard off to the right. The yard was basically used for dumping old taxi cabs before stripping them for parts that could be used on others. It ran a good way behind the target premises, with a breeze-block garden wall in between. The wall was six feet high and they could tell from the aerial photography that there was no way out of it except over and into the yard. This meant that the rear would need only two men and they might complete the whole operation with just the one team.

Graves was discussing the method of attack, working out who would do what in the line of the stick. Mumbles, of course, would be the MOE man as ever, although this operation would require more stealth than strength. A hydraulic ramp for the door and then let it swing gently open, rather than just battering the lock. Gibson would back him up with another behind him to secure the door, probably Rob MacGregor with the bang box. MacGregor was twenty-five and from Glasgow, the newest recruit to blue team. The rest of the team would follow after that. Two ladder men for the front windows. One across the road with a sniping rifle in the observation point and two more on the roofs further down.

☆

Caroline drove home as she always did when the three of them were out together. Swann and Webb had finished the last of the wine on completing Kinky Boots. Again Swann had led the climb and this time he moved well, no hint of the mishap on Pink Void being repeated. His handholds were considered and well measured, following the line of the crack, pivoting on the balls of his feet, which were closely encased in the rubber-soled friction boots. He got to the top of the final pitch and eased himself up until his arms were locked with his fingertips all but touching, then he swung his foot up in one smoothly executed movement. He felt great as he belayed Webb up after him. The wind was coming off the sea in gusts now, a lull and then a sudden rush of salt-baked air to tug at the roots of his hair.

Webb snoozed in the back seat while Swann sat up front with Caroline. When he had first joined the Branch, he could not understand how his colleagues seemed to be able to sleep anywhere at any time. After a few months of eighteen- to twenty-hour days, however, he learned the trick himself. Caroline drove quickly, music low on the stereo. Swann was still feeling pleased with the final climb of the day, so much better than the laboured stuff of yesterday and then again this morning. He was quiet, thinking: Pia was back from the Middle East today and he wanted to see her. Caroline glanced at him.

'You look like the cat that got the cream,' she said.

Swann grinned. 'Last climb, sweetness.'

'You enjoyed it?'

'Yes. I did.'

She overtook a red Ford Escort and gunned the car forward in the outside lane, eating up the miles back to London.

'When're they coming?' she asked. 'The children, I mean.'

'Next weekend.' Swann chewed his knuckle and looked at her. 'I've got one of those student nanny placements you told me about. It's only fair. If Rachael doesn't get this teaching certificate for the RAD, she's never going to get a career off the ground.'

Caroline looked sideways at him. 'I admire you, you know.'

Swann cocked one eyebrow. 'Why?'

'The way you treat her. You know, one of my greatest regrets is that my ex doesn't even speak to me.' She shook her head a little bitterly. 'We were together for eighteen years, Jack, since we were kids really. We met when I was fourteen.'

'He doesn't talk?'

'Never. Not once. I don't think he ever really believed I'd leave him. He'd dished out so much punishment over the years, I suppose he thought he could just keep on doing it.'

Swann looked ahead again. 'I can't understand men who hit women. Never have been able to. Never will.'

Caroline glanced sideways at him. 'He really did love me, you know.'

'Yeah – so why did he hit you so much?'

111

She had no answer for that, pushing out her lips a fraction and slowly shaking her head.

They were almost back to Amersham when Webb's pager vibrated on his belt. He unclipped it and showed the message to Swann.

*Operation Ding Dong. Dig-out confirmed. Parade call 7 a.m., Monday.*

Swann lifted the mobile phone from where it lay on the dashboard. He dialled the Yard, spoke briefly with the ops room and hung up again. He twisted round to Webb, one arm across the back of his seat. 'The Ninjas did their recce this morning. It's definitely on for Tuesday. They'll call the attack at four a.m.'

'Best get some sleep tonight, then,' Webb said, and winked at him.

☆

Swann got out at Amersham station and took the Metropolitan line to Baker Street and then the Jubilee to Charing Cross, before finally heading to Waterloo and home. The sun was getting low as he walked down Waterloo Road, past the park where a group of kids were kicking a ball about. His flat was baking, the heat striking at him as he opened the door, as if desperate for some form of escape. He went round opening every window in the place and wondered why he had bothered to close them in the first place. The flat was on the top floor and the chances of being burgled were pretty much next to nothing.

He shuffled through the pile of bills that he had collected from downstairs, then picked up the phone and dialled his ex-wife's number.

'Hello,' he said. 'It's me.'

'Hi.'

'Everything settled?'

'I think so, yes. The girls are really pleased they don't have to change schools.'

'Worked out well. The nanny, or whatever I'll call her, will bring them as far as Highgate. Her classes don't start till nine-thirty. You'll meet them at Highgate and run them to school from there?'

'Either me or Peter.'

'Right.'

'I'll drive them over on Saturday morning.'

'Fine.' Swann laughed then. 'I'm looking forward to it.'

They said goodbye and then he dialled Pia's number and got her answerphone. He swore under his breath and then it occurred to him that she might already be on her way, so he went through to the bathroom and showered.

The water was hot and sharp against his skin. He lathered his head with shampoo, and it dripped over his eyes and ran down his chin. He could feel the ache gathering in his muscles. That was the trouble with climbing irregularly: it made different demands on the body and he knew he'd be stiff in the morning.

He dressed in a T-shirt and shorts and set about cleaning the flat. Friday had been a long day and then they were off straight from Webb's. Nothing had been done in his place for over a week. The dust settled in layers, accentuated by the strength of the evening sunlight as it streamed through the kitchen windows. Flies from the open door to the roof garden buzzed about his head and he swatted at them with a dishcloth. The phone rang and he picked it up. Pia's voice. 'Jack. It's me.'

For a moment his heart fell. He looked at his watch. Nearly eight o'clock. 'What's happening?'

'I'm late is what's happening. I didn't get in till this morning and everything's got behind.'

Swann smiled to himself, her tone of voice so plaintive. 'How long will you be?'

'An hour.'

'No worries. I'll see you when you get here.'

It gave him more time to clean up and he relaxed. Down on the lower of the two floors he occupied, he stripped the bed and stuffed the dirty linen into the wicker basket in the bathroom. He then set about cleaning the basin and toilet, and had just sat down with the top off a bottle of beer when Pia arrived. She brought a bag for the morning and Swann took it from her and kissed her. She followed him upstairs and he poured her a glass of wine.

'So how was Israel?' he asked.

She stood with the wine glass in one hand, the other cupping her elbow, dressed in white shorts and a pink, skintight top. 'OK. Not as good as I hoped. I thought I'd get the client for sure.'

Swann spooned chicken bhuna on to rice. 'You didn't?'

'Not yet.' She threw out a hand. 'It's how it goes. You get all the introductions. It was a dinner party as well, so I suppose I could only expect so much.'

'But you will get him?'

She made a face. 'I hope so. There's a lot of competition though, Jack.'

'Other banks?'

'He's a player, very much in demand.'

It had taken Swann a little bit of time to establish exactly what it was that Pia did. She worked as an international private banker in Upper Grosvenor Street. The bank was Luxembourg-based, but she worked with a UK team in the international office. London was a better base than the Continent, and they enjoyed the same access to places such as Bermuda and the Cayman Islands as did the British banks. Pia had come to England from Italy in the late eighties. She got a degree in economics from the LSE and then studied for a Master's at Berkeley,

California, after first completing a management training course with NatWest. From there, she had moved to Luxembourg Directe and worked as a trainee under the eye of her present boss Paul Ellis.

Ellis had guided her at first. Her Israeli contacts, derived she had said through her late father's business, had been attractive. Ellis had thought he could bolt her on to his department without actually treading on the toes of his Arab clientele. She was officially part of the African/Asian arm and worked out of the adjoining building, so protocol was not tested by Arabs and Israelis arriving for meetings at the same time.

They ate dinner and afterwards went up to the roof garden to enjoy the relative cool of the evening. Swann lit two cigarettes and passed one to her. The stars were out, sky hazy and pink from the light thrown up by the city. Cars rumbled over Waterloo Bridge and voices lifted in laughter from the street below. Swann sat on the bench facing the old MI5 building and smoked. 'Your job's getting you down, isn't it,' he said gently.

Pia looked at him, standing with one arm hooked round her waist, flicking the ash from her cigarette.

'I suppose.'

'Paris,' he said. 'Now Israel. A lot of pressure.'

She sighed. 'Too much. Sometimes I think I'd like to do something else.'

Swann gently drifted an arm round her shoulders. 'Like what?'

'I don't know, Jack. Something a bit more worthwhile.'

He stared across at the buildings over the street. 'Worthwhile wouldn't pay so much.'

'Money isn't everything, is it.' She tasted her lips with her tongue. 'I'm sick of the travelling as well. Always away. I've got to go to the States again next month.' She looked through the darkness at him, then tossed her

115

cigarette over the parapet and for a moment they sat in silence. 'Take me to bed,' she said.

He undressed her, sitting on the edge of the bed while she stood before him, peeling her top over her head. She was naked underneath, breasts rising, nipples bunching into curling points of flesh under a smattering of goose bumps. Swann felt his breath tighten and he drew her towards him, arms gentle about her narrow waist, until one nipple was between his teeth, and he tugged, softening it and then licking it stiff again. She rested her forearms on his shoulders, fingers entwined in his hair, and kissed the top of his head. Swann sucked her breast into his mouth, burying his face deeper and deeper into flesh. She let go a little moan and he eased her shorts down over her thighs. Her knickers came with them and pubic hair brushed against him. He eased himself lower, moving her round so she lay back, naked in the moonlight against the white of the sheet. He traced little circles on her skin with the tip of his tongue, then moving between her legs he tasted her.

Pia arched her back, Swann watching the contortions of her features as she pressed the points of her fingers deeper into his scalp, holding him between her legs. He felt her shiver and her legs lifted, knees clutching his ears. She pushed him back and rolled him on to the bed before dragging his shorts away. She took his penis in the palm of her hand, smoothing the skin with her fingers; and then she took him in her mouth, softly at first and then deeper. Swann groaned, twisting the sheet into knots with his fists. She moved up his body, breasts over his groin, then belly and chest, until she lowered herself on to him with the tiniest of gasps in her throat. Swann watched her face as she rotated her hips, eyes closed and broken up at the edges as if she were silently crying.

He lay with her later, just the sheet over them, the

room close and airless even with the windows wide open. She half rested her head on his shoulder and he could feel the moisture gathering deep in her hair. 'I love you,' she whispered.

He felt the squall of emotion in his breast and held her very close to him. Lightly he stroked her hair. 'I want to take care of you.' She didn't answer. He stroked the down of her cheeks, so soft under his fingers.

They lay in silence for a while, then Pia said, 'Will you stay with me tomorrow night?'

'I can't. I'm working.'

She eased back on the pillow, the sheet falling away from her breasts. 'What're you doing?'

'Scooping somebody up.'

'IRA?'

'No. Somebody else.'

'OK. Wednesday, then.'

'Wednesday and Thursday and Friday.'

# 6

The following afternoon, James Morton took the plastic
bin liner from the flip-top bin in the kitchen and walked
to the front door. He opened it wide, stepped out into the
sunshine and placed the bag carefully on the step. He
yawned and stretched and for a second glanced up at the
third-floor window in the house across from his. He
glimpsed the tiny silver disc that had been there for four
weeks now.

In the observation point, Christine Harris watched
Morton place the bin bag outside. Next to her Julian
Moore, the surveillance operative from MI5, chewed on
a sandwich. He swallowed and picked up his cup of
coffee.

'Doesn't look like he's going out today,' Christine
muttered.

'Oh well, that'll make the last day that much easier.'

She sat back in her chair. 'We won't be up here when
they hit.'

'No.' Julian looked at the remainder of the sandwich
and decided against it. 'Pity,' he said. 'I've never seen
them put the stick in before.'

Twenty minutes later, a car drew up at the far end of
the road and a young man in a suit got out. Christine
glanced briefly at him and then looked away again. The
car was a red Escort cabriolet with the roof folded away.
She looked across at the target premises, then back up

the road. The man was still there, standing on the corner and looking at his watch. He carried what looked like a clipboard under one arm. A second man came round the corner. He wore a grey suit with the jacket over his shoulder. The two men shook hands and then the first one led the way up the steps.

'A buyer for number thirteen,' Christine said.

'What?'

She pointed along the road. 'The agent's showing someone around.'

She lit a cigarette and sat back. Julian moved into the forward chair and scanned the street through the zoom lens of the camera. Five minutes later, the front door to number 4 opened and Morton appeared for the second time that day. This time he came out, wearing a running top with the hood pulled up. Julian clicked the shutter on the camera. Christine lifted the radio. 'All units from Control. X3. Target moving, walking, Glenthorne Road, turning left towards the Broadway.'

Morton walked as far as the Broadway station and then went inside. He was followed as far as the newsstand, where he bought a copy of the *Evening Standard*. Five minutes later, he was back inside the house again. They watched from the observation point, but he did not come out again. Further down the road, the estate agent came out with his client. They meandered down the steps, the client looking back up at the building and pointing. On the pavement they held a discussion for a few minutes, then they shook hands and the estate agent got back in his car. The two spotters in the observation point took bets on how long it would be before the 'SOLD' board went up.

☆

One a.m., and the SO13 investigation squad were gathered at Shepherd's Bush police station for the SO19 briefing. Swann arrived with Webb a little later than the others. They had done a final drive-by along the Glenthorne Road end of Queen's House Mews. The operational commander was there, as was Clements and the rest of 4 Squad. The arrest team were present, standing apart from the SFOs in order that no firearms contamination could be passed on. Out in the car park they had a sterile car prepared – swabbed, papered and the seats covered with plastic.

Swann nodded to Mumbles and Twelve Hits. Most of blue team had worked with the Branch at some point. They liked the work: it was exacting and also highly lucrative in terms of overtime. At 1.15, the briefing began in earnest. The scene had been photographed and videoed from above, as well as covertly from street level by the bogus telephone engineers who had been working on Sunday and Monday mornings. The area was mapped in pen on Sasco whiteboards which were placed round the tables at the front of the room.

Graves spoke at length with Colson and DI Clements, a black Glock 17 nuzzling against his hip. Clements was giving him the updated information from Box and SB. Morton was safely put to bed and the house was in darkness. They had seen the lights go off in the front room on the first floor, which they knew to be his bedroom. When he was satisfied, Graves moved to the front of the room and cleared his throat. 'Ladies and gentlemen,' he began, his voice soft yet very firm. 'If we can begin.'

The hubbub hushed and those who hadn't already done so took their seats; plain-clothed officers from the Branch and the men with many pockets: SO19, dressed like Ninjas apart from their black respirators. The briefing followed the normal pattern: information; intention; method; administration and communications. Graves introduced himself and DSU Colson formally. 'We're here to assist SO13 in detaining a suspect who's currently residing at number four, Queen's House Mews in Hammersmith,' he said. 'Mr Colson will fill you in on the details and update us on the surveillance log.'

When Colson sat down again, Graves indicated the maps blown up on the boards behind him. 'The property is a three-storeyed Victorian terrace with a basement,' he said. 'No basement access from the street. This building has not been converted. We are *not* – repeat *not*, looking at a flat within it. It's one building with one occupier. The bedrooms are located on the first and second floors.' He stopped talking again and checked his notes. 'There's a garden at the back with no way out except over a six-foot-high breeze-block wall.' He indicated the position on the map. 'Beyond that is a yard where taxis are repaired. We can gain access from the first wall at the junction of Queen's House Mews and Adie Road. It's a possible escape route, so I want two guys covering.' He nodded to two officers seated directly in front of him. 'Phil D and Eddie. You've been tasked on the black.'

He picked up a plastic coffee cup and sipped from it. 'The intention is to detain James Morton,' he said. 'We'll safely secure and surround the premises – or rather on the white and black in this case – breach the door quietly and move upstairs. We'll have assault ladders ready for the windows. The stick will go upstairs and attack from the landing. Stealth, gentlemen, stealth. Mumbles is MOE man. We'll use the ramp and open the door quietly. Rob's shield man. Long shield, Rob?'

MacGregor nodded and adjusted the MP5 carbine in the sling across his chest. Graves continued. 'Phil Gibson, MP5 cover on the white.' He went on to confirm the other tasks finalized in the basement at Old Street earlier in the day. 'When this briefing's over, we'll load up the vehicles and assemble in convoy order. The rendezvous point is the junction between Adie Road and Queen's House Mews. The cordons will be in at either end of Glenthorne Road and at the Adie Road junction. The arrest car will wait at the form-up point at the top of Queen's House Mews itself. The team will move forward on foot to the final assault positions. Phil and Eddie on the black – you two will have to get over the wall and take up positions in the taxi yard.' He looked then at the duty officer from Shepherd's Bush who would put in the cordons. 'Assuming a successful outcome, the cordons will remain in place till the team withdraws. Control will be the Special Branch observation point across the road.

'Right,' he went on. 'Contingencies. If there is a shooting, SO19 will control the situation. There will be no other intervention unless specifically invited by me. In that event, the armed officers involved will go to Ealing police station and I'll ask Mr Colson to nominate a liaison officer for CIB. If the target is non-compliant, we'll drop into siege mode and negotiate. If he gets out, jumps, gets down the stairs, whatever – SO19 will deal with it. If he runs, the dogs will deal. The debrief is back here. Comms will be back to back – and secure cougars only.' He looked again at Colson. 'Any tension indicators we need to know about – late-night drinkers, street activity, etc.?'

Colson looked at his team and slowly shook his head.

'Good,' Graves went on. 'Now, is everything clear?'

'One thing, Nick.' It was George Webb who spoke. 'Forensics.' He stood up and looked at the gathering. 'You've all been to the fat detective's lectures,' he said. 'Clearly, safety and securing the situation is paramount, but, remember, only touch what you have to.'

Graves nodded. 'Good point,' he said. 'No point in

nicking him if we fuck up the forensics. The armed operation number is 13-B/24. We assemble in forty-five minutes.'

☆

In the small hotel overlooking Queen's House Mews, a man with a black beard and horn-rimmed glasses sat at his window, reading a book. He yawned, glanced at the flickering but silent TV screen and then at the illuminated hands of the clock beside his bed. Three-thirty in the morning. He leaned closer to the window and looked out. No movement, a meagre light falling across dirty pavement from streetlamps. Across the way, a light burned in the upstairs flat next door to the house for sale. Further down the road, number 4 was in darkness.

☆

The convoy rolled. The lead vehicle driven by Graves with Colson next to him and Swann and Webb in the back. After that, the dark green Leyland DAF SFO kit vans. Two benches inside, men cramped together with MP5s and Kevlar shields, blankets and respirators. On the floor were two black plastic suitcases. On the front of one was written the word *Distraction* and on the other *Bang*. The convoy moved as one, overtaking what little traffic was on the road. They moved along the agreed route at speed. No sirens, no blue lights. When they reached the rendezvous point, the vehicles formed up, then rolled slowly to the top of Queen's House Mews.

At the window of the hotel room, the bearded man stirred where he had dozed in his seat. He sat up, rubbed his eyes under his fine-lensed spectacles and hunched himself further forward. He heard the faint hum of idling engines and then silence. Seconds later, car doors opened and he moved still closer to the window. The curtains were drawn, but did not fully cover the glass. The man stiffened, watched closely, and as he did so he saw darkened figures begin to make their way along the opposite side of the street. One of them, the lead man, seemed to be carrying something very heavy. He counted six of them and then saw two more moving along Adie Road and out of sight. If he craned his neck far enough, he could see number 4 quite clearly.

Graves, carrying a sniper's rifle, left Colson, Webb and Swann in the lead vehicle, then made his way ahead of the team to the house where the joint surveillance operation had been taken over by an observation team from the Antiterrorist Branch. He climbed the fence at the back and walked up to the door, which opened as his foot reached the top step. Upstairs at the window, he moved between the observers, holding twin radios in his hands. He set a mobile phone on the windowsill in front of him, then he spoke quietly into the radio. 'Mumbles from Graves, confirm you're in position.'

He was answered by three clicks on the radio.

'Phil G. Twelve Hits, confirm.'

Three more clicks. 'Rob?' And so it went on until every member of the team had called in. They were ready – two on the black, four on the white, with two on the roof above.

Graves watched as Mumbles bent his weight to the hydraulic ramp and moved towards the steps at the front of the house. The darkness was good but not total; the lamp outside number 4 appeared to be overbright.

'*Go*,' Graves said very quietly.

The massive figure of Mumbles moved forward and placed the hydraulic ramp in position. Two slabs of metal at either end of an extendable boom, fed by compressed air. He placed the ends carefully against the doorposts, just below the height of the Chubb lock, and began to feed the air. Slowly, the ramps tightened against the wood. Mumbles fed more air and still more. Now the ramps bit and the wood began to hiss. A groaning sound as it fractured and he grimaced under his respirator. Behind him, MacGregor bent and flexed his arm in the slings of the long-faced Kevlar shield. He had his MP5 strapped over his other shoulder, Glock loosened in its holster. Mumbles fed more air. The wood moaned again, cracked and splintered, then it gave and the door moved in its housing. He released the pressure, hauled back the ramp and moved up to the door. He bent low, Glock in his right hand now. MacGregor was with him. Gibson, at the bottom of the steps, snapped his MP5 the length of its sling.

Mumbles pressed the fingers of his gloved hand against the front door. As he did so he crouched ready to enter. The door swung open and the first thing he saw was a gaping hole in the floorboards. They'd been ripped up three feet back in the hall. He half rose, then felt a sudden rush of air, and his eyes balled in their sockets. What looked like a lawn mower swung down the stairs and almost crashed into him. Someone started firing. Three shots. Three more. Rapid fire. Mumbles leapt back. Gibson returned fire, rattling off half a dozen rounds in quick succession. Graves watched from the window. 'Pull back,' he commanded. 'Covering positions. Now.'

The three men at the front of the stick dropped back quickly and took up positions across the road, beyond the pedestrian bollards. Graves watched the front door swing shut again. 'Siege mode,' he said into the radio.

In the lead car, the three officers from SO13 heard the shooting and sat very still, listening to the radio. Colson, in the driver's seat, rubbed the line of his lip with the heel of his thumb. Behind him, Webb's face was grave. Swann shifted restlessly. 'George, you'd better organize some technical back-up,' Colson said. 'I think we're going to need it.'

Webb got on the radio and spoke directly to the operations room on the sixteenth floor, requesting a full Technical Support Unit from SO11. He set the phone down then and joined Swann on the pavement, where he was watching the scene at the far end of the road. At the window of the hotel room above them, the bearded man watched, a light in the dark of his eyes.

Further along the road, lights were coming on and windows were being opened in houses on both sides. Graves was on the phone to base in Old Street requesting a second team. He glanced behind him to the wall where he had set the sniping rifle, then summoned every available Trojan in the area. Mumbles, MacGregor and Gibson were still containing the front entrance. At the rear, the black was secure with Phil Davies and Eddie Butler in the yard. Graves watched the front of number 4 for movement, then he heard Davies's voice in his ear.

'Control from Davies. Light on the black. Window three/two.'

Graves was silent for a moment. Outside, the rest of the team were preparing to evacuate the house immediately next to number 4. Graves spoke to Colson in the lead car. 'Can somebody bring down a kit van? Quickest way to get these people out.'

Swann heard the transmission and was behind the wheel immediately. He drove the length of the road at speed, spun the van in a three-point turn and backed it up. The occupants of the flats next door to number 4 were loaded hurriedly into it, with cover from the entry team protecting them. Swann drove them back up the road and they were moved away by local uniformed officers.

In the observation point, Graves had a telephone held

to his ear and was listening to the endless ringing from the unanswered line at number 4. 'Come on, you fucker,' he muttered. 'Answer the bloody thing.' But nobody did and he put the phone down. He lifted the radio again.

'Colson from Control. How long till we have technical?' he asked. 'I want to know what's going on in that house.'

Webb answered him. 'Graves from Webb. On its way now. I'll let you know as soon as they get here.'

Graves picked up the telephone and dialled again. Again it rang and rang, but still nobody answered.

The Trojan units, marked armed-response vehicles, were backing up the SFO team. At the rendezvous point, at the junction with Adie Road, the Technical Support Unit had arrived and Webb radioed through to Graves.

'OK,' Graves said. 'I still can't get him to pick the phone up, but we've got an upstairs light on the black.' He glanced through the window again, five o'clock now and the sun was lifting over the grey streets of the city. 'Bring the support team up, Webb. Park on the target side of the road and stand by.'

Webb and Swann got into the van with the TSU and moved up Queen's House Mews, stopping halfway along on the right-hand side of the road. The SFO team had secured the front entrance to the house next door to number 4 and backed them up as the technical men moved in, walking swiftly, heads low. They were joined by Webb, Swann and two firearms officers.

They worked first in the ground-floor flat where the adjoining wall backed on to the hallway of number 4. Gauging the height as best they could, they tried to figure out where the stairs would be and work slightly above. They chipped away wallpaper and plaster until the brick-work was exposed. Using a very small, very powerful, diamond-headed drill, one man started to cut a tiny hole in the brick, little flurries of red dust flying into the air.

The drill made barely a sound, the head rotating slowly with a light buzzing noise. The officer worked until he was through the brick, plastic goggles covering his eyes. As soon as there was no more pressure on the head it died and rested against the inner side of the wallpaper. The officer removed the drill and fed a fibre optic listening probe, the size of the inside of a ball-point pen, into the hole. It came up against the wallpaper next door. The free end was fixed to a speaker and the device activated. They all listened in silence.

Upstairs, in the first-floor flat which abutted the landing of number 4, a second technical support officer was working away at that wall. He finished with the drill, inserted the probe and activated the speaker. Swann moved up to him with an SFO, respirator hanging loose about his neck. They, too, listened in absolute silence.

Downstairs, Webb was monitoring the first device. All at once they heard movement, footsteps creaking on the staircase. It was unmistakable. Webb winked at his colleague. 'Got himself a loose one.'

The footsteps reached the bottom and then they heard the sharp click of a weapon being made ready. Webb spoke into his radio. 'Control from Webb. Movement. He's downstairs, right now. Just cocked a gun.'

'Received.'

Again Graves picked up the telephone. Across the road, Webb and Swann could hear the phone ringing through the wall. Nobody answered it. Then Swann heard somebody muttering to himself upstairs.

'Control from Swann. Upstairs. He's talking to himself.'

Downstairs, Webb frowned. He had not heard him go back up. He moved out into the hall and beckoned for the technical support officer to follow him. They went up to the first floor and joined Swann and the other officers. Webb ushered them out of the flat, back on to the landing. He pointed to the top flat. 'Let's look in the loft,' he said, looking at the TSU men. 'If it's shared, we can drop a probe through the ceiling rather than go through the wall up here.' As he was talking, they heard more movement coming from the next-door landing. A door was closed and then footsteps along the landing and then another door closing. Swann rubbed the stubble that had built up on his jaw. 'Busy boy, isn't he.'

The SO19 officers brought a small assault ladder into the house and then moved up to the loft. Very carefully, they eased the trapdoor up and peered inside. It was fully light outside now, five-thirty. Graves was monitoring the situation, again trying to get the man to answer the phone. People were watching from the windows all along the far side of the street and the armed officers from the ARVs ordered them to keep inside through loud hailers. Two Trojans were now parked in the street, blue lights flashing, doors open with ballistic blankets thrown over them to protect the officers from fire. Graves used the same loud-hailing system to speak directly to Morton.

'James Morton, this is Sergeant Graves of the Metropolitan Police Firearms Unit. You are completely surrounded by armed officers. Throw your weapon out of a window and come out the front door with your hands over your head.' He received no answer.

Upstairs in the attic, Webb stared. Not only was the loft not partitioned with number 4, it stretched the full length of the building. He glanced at the SFO who squatted next to him.

'You didn't know?'

'Never showed up on the plans.'

The lead SFO placed wooden treadboards over the beams on the floor, then Kevlar ballistic blankets were laid over the boards and Webb eased his way across them until he came to what he'd hoped he was going to find: an ancient, rose-type light fitting, holding a substantial chain-linked connection for a heavy chandelier. He slipped a final listening probe down and they waited. Somebody coughed directly below them. Everyone fell silent. Webb was on his hands and knees on the Kevlar blanket, praying it was as good as they claimed. He had never had cause to find out. If whoever was in the room below heard so much as a whisper, he would probably do so now. Again the cough, then a door creaked and closed. Webb let go a sigh. He and Swann moved out of the loft and went downstairs. They slipped out of the house and Swann glanced up to see a sniper on the roof of the building opposite: he was training telescopic sights on the upstairs windows of number 4.

Graves watched the scene from the observation point. The listening devices were in place. There was no means of escape. He lifted the radio to his lips. 'All units from Graves. Stand off,' he said. 'Maintain positions. Let him soak for a while.'

He left the OP then and went out the back, climbed the wall of the yard and dropped down the other side. He walked the length of the next street and came out in Adie Road. The second SFO team had arrived and Graves sent one of them back the way he had come with an assault ladder for the garden wall. Swann, Webb and Colson moved back up the road to the form-up point.

'Worst nightmare stuff,' Graves said as they got to him. 'Someone who actually knows what he's doing.'

☆

From his window in the hotel, the slightly built man with the beard watched them. He saw Swann, he saw Webb and he saw Colson. From the travel bag at his side, he took a camera, focused the lens and snapped all three of them.

☆

'We'll let him sweat it out for a few hours and then I'll send the teams in,' Graves said. 'I'll do the windows with shotguns and then the gas. We'll storm them on ladders. At the same time I'll drop a couple of lads through the loft space.'

'Stun grenades?' Webb made a face. 'Could be lots of dets in there, Nick. Concussion waves could set them off.'

'I know.'

'You're going to do it anyway.'

'Well, Webby. The way I look at it is this – if they do go off, he'll be the only one in there apart from the team and they take that risk every time we use them.'

'I hate the fucking things,' Swann said. 'Guy in 22 lost a hand to one.'

'Jim Robertson. He was training with us at the time.'

As they were talking a bearded man with glasses and a stick came out of the hotel, carrying a travel bag. He turned the wrong way down Queen's House Mews and started walking towards the siege. Jack Swann spotted him.

'Sir. Sir. Excuse me, sir.'

The man stopped and looked round.

'I'm afraid you can't go that way, sir.'

The man smiled at him, heavy-browed, the beard straggling almost to his chest. He wore a fez-style cap on his head. 'So sorry,' he said. 'I always walk that way.'

'Not today though eh, sir,' Swann said. 'The road's blocked off.'

The man nodded, crossed the street, then disappeared round the corner. Swann shook his head as he went.

Graves stood off for four hours. He would've liked to

have waited until it was dark, but there wasn't the time. Already, the whole thing was being filmed by a crew on rooftops at either end of the street. Pressmen gathered at the outer cordons and a helicopter was flying overhead. Graves looked up at the sky and pushed the sleeves of his coveralls higher against his elbows. 'Somebody shoot it down,' he muttered.

The street was evacuated long before the stand-off period ended. Graves moved back to the control point and reassessed. He had men in front of the house giving cover fire with MP5s. Butler and Davies were still at the back and he had three men inside the house next door. That was enough to go in through the attic. There was still movement being monitored by the sound probes through the walls of number 4. All had been quiet for an hour and then the target was heard once more on the landing of the first floor. Graves knew the sound probes were his marker for the attack. He had to get men in there as quickly as possible, when they were the least likely to get shot at.

At 2 p.m., he called the attack. Gibson, MacGregor and Mumbles were in the loft of the next-door flat, crouched in readiness on Kevlar ballistic blankets. Downstairs, one of the technical support officers was monitoring the second probe they had inserted. He heard something at one minute to two.

'Control from TSU-1. I've got movement.'

'Where?' Graves held the handset very close to his mouth.

'Second landing. He's . . .' The officer suddenly broke off as he heard the distinct sound of a toilet flushing. 'Toilet. Second floor.'

'GO. GO. GO,' Graves shouted into the microphone.

In the loft, Gibson and MacGregor hauled up the trap door and dropped a stun grenade. Gibson held it, pulling out the pin and keeping the safety arm pressed tightly against the canister. Nine separate explosions, indentations in the metal casing. He hurled it into the room below and it bounced off the floor and the walls; explosions and smoke and fire. The two men dropped as the ninth charge went off. They secured the door and then Mumbles dropped down behind them and moved on to the landing.

At the same time, shotgun fire took out the windows on the first floor, then CS gas canisters were lobbed inside. Assault ladders were up in seconds and the attack team swarmed up them and smashed in the remaining glass. Quickly, they moved through the house. Gibson, Mumbles and MacGregor on the second floor. The toilet door was closed. They took up positions; Gibson one side, carbine high, the butt pressing into his shoulder.

'Armed police,' Mumbles shouted. 'You in the toilet. Come out with your hands over your head.'

Nobody answered him. Smoke drifted and as it cleared, Gibson spotted a tape recorder on the stairs leading down to the second floor. It was wired to some sort of electronic timer. Downstairs, the other team had secured the rooms. That only left the ground floor and the basement. Mumbles ripped open the door to the toilet and two MP5s were levelled at the empty seat.

'Control, from Gibson,' Gibson spoke into his radio. 'Second floor clear. No bodies. But we've found a cassette recorder and timer.'

Graves frowned heavily, the creases cutting the skin of his forehead.

They had deliberately not attacked the front door. It was covered in case Morton tried to run, but, with the lawn mower in the hall and the floorboards taken up, rapid entry was impossible. Inside the house, the team moved through the smoke. Gibson put out the fire which had been started by the stun grenade in the bedroom. They searched everywhere, tossing the beds over and opening wardrobes. They went through it room by room, but found nothing except two more tape recorders. The lawn mower that now nestled among the broken floor-boards in the hall had been attached by two cables on a trip switch. Gibson spotted two passive infrared move-ment sensors above the front door. A hole had been cut in the ceiling a little way back and a gun barrel poked through. Gibson got one of the smaller assault ladders and climbed up to investigate. The gun was an Ingram SMG. He looked at it closely, wedged as it was in the hole. There was something fixed in the trigger housing, a small cam-style motor which turned electronically. He left the weapon where it was. The jagged edges of the hole had fibre in them. He could see it clearly in the cuts in the plaster. Graves came in. He stood with his hands on his hips and looked at the lawn mower.

'Movement sensors, Sarge,' Gibson told him. 'One for the mower, one for the SMG.' He rubbed a hand through sweat-soaked hair. 'He was gone long before we got here. The light on the black was on a timer, the noises we heard were from tapes. He knew we'd use listening probes.'

Graves looked up at the gun in the ceiling, then again at the lawn mower. 'What's more important,' he said quietly, 'is how he knew we were coming.'

☆

Graves confirmed the house to be clear and handed it over to the antiterrorist officers. Webb and his colleagues from exhibits now dressed in paper suits, boots and gloves, took over. The area was cordoned still, but the homes that had been evacuated were returned to normal and the SO19 perimeter taken down. The firearms officers returned to Shepherd's Bush for a debrief with the unused arrest team. Jack Swann went with them. He drove with Colson and Clements. All three of them were subdued. Swann sat in the back staring out of the window. At Shepherd's Bush, they found a free briefing room and crammed inside. Swann and the senior officers from SO13 faced Graves and his firearms team across the table. Graves rubbed a palm over the bald dome of his skull. The energy exerted over the past seven hours had all but drained him and his head ached with stopped-up adrenalin. Opposite him, Colson and Clements were still. Swann broke the silence.

'He knew we were coming,' he said. 'It's why he wasn't there.'

Graves looked at him. 'I thought your team had put him to bed.'

Colson picked up the surveillance log. He tapped an entry with his index finger and offered the page to Graves. 'He went out at 14.05. They had X3 contact every second and he was back in the house by 14.15. He didn't go out again.'

At the far end of the table Phil Gibson shifted his position in the chair. It was hot and his Ninja suit was sticking to him. 'He got out through the attic,' he said. 'We searched. He must've got down through the house at the far end. The one that's for sale.'

Everyone looked at him. 'There's a footprint up there,' Gibson went on. 'Me and Mumbles checked it out.' He looked at Mumbles, who nodded his acknowledgement. 'We should've known about the attic.'

Colson spoke to Swann. 'Jack, give SO12 a ring, would you. See if you can get hold of Christine Harris. I'll want to talk to Julian Moore as well.' He looked back at Graves. 'What do you make of it?'

'Well, he certainly knew we were coming, which begs the question – how?'

Swann put away his mobile phone. 'Someone must've told him.'

☆

Webb co-ordinated the search at Queen's House Mews. They photographed everything initially, every room from varying angles, so they could refer back once evidence had been recovered, bagged and tagged. The house was expensively furnished and well kept. A rumble of unease moved in the pit of Webb's stomach – somebody had paid an awful lot of money to house James Morton.

Upstairs they found a mini darkroom. All the materials for developing pictures were still there, but no pictures themselves. There were no clothes in the bedrooms, the place had been cleared out: dishes were done, no mess in the kitchen, nothing even vaguely hurried about anything. Webb had been in many such search situations over the past seven years. He knew what to look for – haste; the mistakes left by somebody making a swift exit. He saw none of those things here.

They took the place apart, dismantling chairs, lifting carpets, checking the chimney. Cupboards were pulled out and beds turned inside out. The toilets were taken apart as was the bath. In the kitchen, Webb checked the usual places for hides: behind the kickboards of the fixed units, the back of the fridge for Semtex rolled flat. He found nothing.

The basement could only be accessed from inside the house and appeared to have been used as an office. Webb and Tania Briggs went down after the kitchen had been taken apart. There they found a twin set of wall-mounted units, set at ground and eye level. Webb opened the doors of the middle cupboard and scanned. Books and papers piled high. He shifted them out and started flicking through them. Then he laid them aside. The back of the cupboard was unplastered. He stared at the brickwork, something odd about it, but he could not say what. Then three bricks caught his eye; the mortar around them was yellow and cracked. He traced the line of the cracks and measured them, running the length of two bricks and the height of three more. He called Tania over. She was standing over the desk with a set of thick fibre-tip pens in her hand. Setting them down on the desktop, she moved over to Webb.

'See what I see?' Webb asked her.

Tania stared, then smiled and very carefully she reached inside and slid out the first loose brick. Webb was right, in total there were six, the mortar intact but not actually sticking to anything. In the space behind they found two boxes of Iraco detonators and two timing and power units. Webb lifted them out and laid them on the work surface.

Plastic boxes, grey and black in colour. He measured them: $15 \times 7 \times 5$cm. At one end of each box were two black plastic screw terminals with a red light-emitting diode set between them. On the left side there was a decade switch, ten positions, and next to it a small digital clock with a liquid-crystal display and separate alarm indicator. On the top edge four black microswitches were mounted. Webb looked closer. Sealed to the casing inside was a piece of brown perforated circuit board. It matched the section he had recovered from Soho. There were two integrated circuits on the board, two transistors and a miniature 6-volt relay. At the top end was a press stud-type battery connector which would take a PP3. The wiring was red and green.

'Webby?'

Webb heard Tania but was staring at the TPU. He had

seen this before, not in a picture, but had had it described to him. He looked at the clock. Spanish – Plastia, the manufacturer.

'Webby.'

He now looked at Tania, who was holding a passport in her hands. It had been wrapped in clear plastic and placed in the alcove behind the detonators. She opened the pages and showed the photograph to Webb. 'Not very good,' she said. 'But definitely Target One.'

Webb took the passport from her. Syrian, in the name of Ibrahim Huella. He handed it back and looked again at the TPU. Then he glanced over the rest of the room and his gaze fell on the pack of pens that Tania had been holding. He lifted one eyebrow. 'Where'd you find these?' he asked as he picked them up.

'Desk drawer.'

He took one out and turned it over in his hand, then carefully he unscrewed the non-writing end. 'Jesus Christ,' he whispered.

'What is it?'

Webb held the pen like a piece of priceless crystal. 'Tania, get everyone out of here now.'

'What is it?'

'Evacuate. Not just the house, the street. Get upstairs and do it now.' He let go a breath. 'Call the Yard and get an Expo here right away.' Still she stood there. For a second Webb ignored her, as very, very carefully he laid the pen down on the desk.

'What is it?' she demanded.

'TATP,' he said, picking up the passport and TPU. 'Triacetone triperoxide, about as deadly a base explosive as you can get. If you want a home-made grenade – throw a jam jar full of this.'

Upstairs, he ordered everyone out and relayed the evacuation order to the local uniforms. Tania contacted the explosives officers and Webb got on the phone to the Defence Research Agency. They would have to deal with it, an oil drum full of acetone to separate the particles and render it safe. He was still sweating when he put down the phone. One of his colleagues had trodden on three tiny crystals of TATP after the Israeli Embassy was attacked. He was thrown halfway across the road.

Beyond the cordon he wiped the moisture from his brow and looked again at the timing and power unit. Tania was at his elbow. 'Arab,' she said. 'We had a batch like this before.'

Webb shook his head. 'These aren't Arab. And they're not Spanish either.' His face clouded again. 'Tania, if this is what I think it is, we have a very big problem.'

# 7

Harrison tied his hair in a ponytail and inspected the lines in his face. He grimaced, stepped out of his trailer and flipped away the Merit. Rodriguez was seated on the steps to his trailer. Harrison wiped the back of his neck under the black, sweat-stained baseball hat and walked to his '66 Chevy pick-up. He carried his canvas bag of tools and tossed them into the back.

'You go for a beer, *amigo*?' Rodriguez tipped back his hat.

Harrison shook his head. 'Gonna see if Chief's home.'

'Ah. OK. See you later then.'

'See ya, Rodriguez.' Harrison climbed into the truck and twisted the key. The old V8 rumbled into life and shook a little around him. He put it in first, rolled the steering wheel under the palm of his hand and drove out of the park. At the top of the hill he headed south on 75. He knew Chief wasn't at home.

About a mile down the highway, he saw Jesse Tate pulling out of the entrance to Jake Salvesen's ranch. Tate recognized the black Chevy and they nodded briefly to one another. Harrison watched Tate's truck disappear in his rear-view mirror. He lit a Marlboro, unconscious movement, one hand snaking into the right breast pocket of his shirt and plucking the cigarette from the pack. He rolled it between forefinger and thumb before snapping open his Zippo.

Tate had been coming from the compound or at least the ranch buildings that skirted the edge of the property. He'd be going into town, maybe to get a beer at Joe's club or the Dollar. Harrison scratched his chin and hooked his ponytail back over his shoulder. He thought for a moment: he hadn't banked on seeing Tate. The reservoir, if anybody asked. East Magic, to see if Chief was fishing.

He drove the seven or so miles to the junction with Highway 20. It was seven-thirty now and he did not pass any other vehicles he knew. He pulled off into the rest area and went in to take a piss. There was no one else in the men's room. Harrison spat, unzipped, urinated and washed up. Outside, the evening sunshine bounced in a glare off the roof of his truck. He glanced at the highway, then walked round the side of the men's room and lifted the drainage-inspection cover. From inside his shirt he took a small plastic bag, sealed at the top and wrapped over. He dropped it down by the pipe and replaced the cover, then he dusted his hands on his jeans and got back in his truck. As he pulled on to the highway, he could see the back of Chief's green Continental disappearing into the distance.

Back in Passover, he followed Chief on to Lower Canford and across the Big Wood River, still high with snow-melt from the mountains. A few minutes later and they hit the dirt road and then the entrance to Lower Canford Ranch and the cabin that somehow Chief had rented for only four hundred dollars a month. Chief parked the Lincoln, reached in the back and pulled out the paintings, four of them about two foot square apiece. Harrison climbed out of his truck and took a cigarette from his pocket. Chief was six foot six and weighed 260 pounds. He looked down at Harrison, flicking long black hair from his eyes. 'Hey, what's up?' he said.

'I'm good, buddy.' Harrison slapped him on the back and they walked into the yard.

Inside, the house was cool, shaded for most of the day by the trees that grew in the yard. It was basically two rooms and actually not much bigger than Harrison's trailer. High-ceilinged and wood-panelled, it comprised a front room with two couches, then a kitchen and sort of bedroom combined. Indian rugs, skins and paintings hung on the walls, and some of the bone and bead chokers that Chief made lay on the table along with his Southwestern art books.

'So how was Boise?' Harrison asked him. Chief handed him a beer from the refrigerator.

'Busy.'

'They gonna display the pictures?'

'Fucking A, man.'

'Right on.' They touched knuckles and Harrison raised his bottle in a toast.

Chief sat down on the couch. 'You seen Belinda?'

'Think she might be up in Westlake. She didn't leave you a note?'

'Nope.'

'Women for ya.'

'Yep.' Chief squinted at him. 'You wanna smoke a bowl?'

Harrison made a face. 'Maybe later. Let's go get a drink.'

Jesse Tate's truck was parked in front of the Silver Dollar. The bar was not overly full. Wednesday night, basketball on the TV. Charlie Love was at one end nursing a Bud draught. Harrison nodded to him. Chief touched him on the shoulder and they both sat down on bar stools. Jesse had his hat tipped back on his head and rested long, tanned arms on the bar, a bottle of Miller before him. Two Mexicans hogged the pool table.

They drank a couple of beers. Jesse sat slightly away from them, chatting to Vicki, the bartender, and watching the TV. Every now and then he would ease a palm over the hairs on his forearm. A truck pulled up outside and Slusher came in, shook hands with Jesse and sat down. They talked for a while, then Jesse went out and climbed into his truck. He headed north in the direction of Westlake.

Harrison and Chief talked about hunting. Chief was going to shoot elk in the season and he wanted Harrison's company. 'Bows or rifles?' Harrison asked him.

'Bow, Harrison. You don't get a second shot with a rifle.'

'I can shoot a bow.' Harrison lit another cigarette and blew smoke from the side of his mouth. They sat for a moment in silence and then he swivelled off his stool and moved across to the open door of the bar. He carried his bottle in one hand and rested against the doorpost. The sun was low now, burning a last fiery path across the snow-block trails on the mountains. He felt movement beside him and Chief leaned a loose arm on his shoulder.

'What you looking at, man?'

Harrison thinned out his eyes against the direct glare of the sun. 'Just watching the day close down.'

'Thought there was some piece of ass out here you weren't telling me about.'

Harrison shook his head. 'You're so pussy-whipped, you couldn't do nothing about it, anyways.'

He looked north up the street again. Tate was a vet, Green Beret vet, and Harrison knew if he ever came up against the sonofabitch it had to be on his terms. At five foot ten he was not tall, lean and mean enough maybe, but Tate was a big mother, muscular and rangy. At forty-three he was in shape. Chief sat down on the step and bummed a cigarette. Harrison flipped his Zippo. Both he

143

and Chief had been in Vietnam, though neither of them talked about it much. Thirty years since Harrison got back for the second time, almost that for Chief. He had done two tours as well: 101st Airborne Rangers, two-man teams flown in on Hueys to secure a hill or a clearing before the grunts hauled in. Dangerous work, only fit for Indians and blacks. Harrison let smoke drift from between his lips. He knew from both Chief himself and photographs at headquarters that when Chief left the service in '72, he went home to Pine Ridge in South Dakota. There he stood with Banks and Means, when the American Indian Movement had their showdown with the FBI.

'You wanna come up to my place and play some guitar?' Chief said.

Harrison did not answer him. Jesse's truck was coming down again from Westlake. He had a passenger with him this time. Harrison sipped at his beer and watched. Jesse drove by and Harrison glimpsed the suited man sitting next to him.

They drove back to the cabin. The sun was gone now and the light began to fade. The clutch of buildings that was Passover spread out in the valley, with mountains on either side. In winter, the snow piled up to the blacktop, then, with the thaw beginning in April, the river rushed full and brown, foaming with melted ice from the hills. Now the hills were bald, those closest to the highway grassy and smooth, with only the odd scattering of aspen across their flanks. Harrison was thoughtful: Jesse Tate's Suburban on his mind, and the suited passenger, another unknown face in the county.

Harrison poured peppermint schnapps while Chief took his boots off. From the heel of the left one, he lifted a little plastic package, then pulling the pipe from his shirt pocket he pressed a bowl of pot. They sat in silence, listening to the crickets in the grass outside. The darkness was falling fast now and Harrison was restless. He wasn't in the mood to smoke, too much on his mind. Chief seemed to sense it. Harrison could tell by the way he slanted his eyes when he watched him. 'Guffy working tonight?' he said.

'Up in Westlake, yeah.'

'What time does she finish?'

'I ain't seeing her tonight.'

'Wondered what was up with you.'

The pot was good though and it smoothed a path through Harrison's twisted veins as he eased back in the chair. Chief sat with his fingers spread across his stomach and watched the room out of half-closed eyes. They had been friends for a while now, good friends; and Harrison often wondered what would happen when, as he eventually must, Chief found out the truth. He sank the last of his schnapps, stretched and got up. 'Gotta go,' he said.

Chief nodded. 'Work again tomorrow.'

'Yeah, work.' Harrison twisted his lip, prized a Merit out of one pocket and stuck it in his mouth. He fumbled for his lighter, then realized Chief still had it and he bent to pick it up.

'You look beat yourself,' he said.

Chief nodded. 'One more hit and then bed.'

Harrison pushed open the screen door and stepped into the yard. The sky was lit up with stars, crystal in velvet black. No cloud, the moon all but full, and he squinted as he climbed into his truck. He rolled down the track and out on to Canford Road, leaning into the window and driving with his hand on the gear stick because it liked to jump out of third. He went back to his trailer where he closed the door and pushed a path through the pile of junk on his bed just in case Guffy was here when he got back. He'd tell her he'd been fishing or something if she asked. It was risky going at this time of night, a lot of people about and he had to get down the road to the old mine and the edge of Salvesen's property.

Rodriguez was still out on his stoop with a bottle of Cuervo beside him and his hat tipped over his eyes. He wasn't about to see anything. Harrison took his mountain bike from its housing on the back of the trailer and pushed his way down through the undergrowth to the road. Here he paused. Laying the bike on its side, he sat down in the bushes and waited. He needed to let his night sight get in some sort of shape before he could move. He sat and watched the road that wound between the houses, crossing the river twice before finally meeting up with the highway again by the airport in Westlake.

When his eyes were accustomed fully he got back on the bike and began to cycle hard along the road running parallel with the dull height of the mountains. He crossed the river, could hear it tearing along, the water tumbling in choked waves over rocks and weed, carrying with it the weight of the snow from the mountains. He cycled in silence with no lights showing, past the affluent properties that bordered the Big Wood River. He saw the broken-down mine with the slag heap of rocks up ahead to his left, the far edge of Salvesen's ranch on this side. Two thousand acres of prime Idaho grazing. Scattered about the outer fringes were the cabins he had built for those followers closest to him. Jesse Tate and his family had one just a little way off the mile-long track that led up to the compound itself.

Harrison rode beyond the old mine workings and jumped off the bike a hundred yards further on, where a grove of cottonwoods swayed alongside the stream that fed off the river. He walked his bike into the brush and then hid it. Now he had to hike a mile up into the mountains to his permanent equipment hide in Dugger's

Canyon. That meant up Little Mammoth Gulch, across the saddles of both Mammoth and Star and down to the old Magdalena mine that had been operated for forty years by Danny Dugger's father. He waited for a few moments before he set off. He always did, enough time to let the ground settle, a few moments to watch and listen. All was quiet about him, no cloud, no wind; nothing save the crickets at his feet and the rustle of a crow's wing overhead.

He moved through the cottonwoods and quietly stepped over the fence on to the Forest Service land that bordered Jake Salvesen's property. The old mine shack was directly above him now, with the heap of loose shale to his left and the 'No Trespassing' signs beyond that. Half a mile in was Bill Slusher's cabin, the furthest outpost on this quarter of the property. Slusher lived there with his wife and four children, one of the inner circle. Harrison now scanned the same trail he had walked for eighteen months. Up past the cabin, keeping close to the hillside, and then higher still, climbing the gulch to the first break in the hills. Slusher's cabin was set just beyond it.

Tom Kovalski had contacted him personally. Harrison was undercover trained and working out of the Minneapolis field office. Kovalski was GS15, unit chief of the Domestic Terrorism Operations Unit at FBI headquarters in Washington D.C. They had known each other for years; Harrison a rookie, when Kovalski was the assistant special agent in charge at Indianapolis. He'd been an ASAC there for two years and he knew of Harrison's history as a border agent in Arizona and New Mexico, and his upbringing in Marquette on Lake Superior. Kovalski had called him into headquarters with a proposition.

'How'd you like to go undercover again, Johnny?' He had sat at his desk with a hopeful expression on his face.

Harrison bunched up his eyes. The last time he'd been a UCA was in the Florida Keys, trying to infiltrate a drugs gang. 'It's been a while, Tom.'

Kovalski looked at the file in front of him. 'Small town Idaho,' he said. 'I'm looking to put in a long-haired drifter like you.'

Harrison raised one eyebrow. 'What's the deal?'

'Jakob Salvesen.' Kovalski sat more upright. 'You heard of him?'

'Oh yeah. Lots of money.'

'About five billion, we reckon.' Kovalski showed him a picture. 'Taken at Estes Park in Colorado,' he said. 'October 1992, just after the Randy Weaver fiasco.'

Harrison looked at the picture – heavy, round-faced man with a mass of reddy brown hair and walrus-like moustache.

'That was the big Christian Identity meeting,' Kovalski said. 'Every right-wing fundamentalist there you can imagine, anti-abortionist to Aryan Nations.'

Harrison nodded. 'The Leaderless Resistance call.'

'That's right.'

'Why Salvesen?'

'Because we've been monitoring his activities on the Internet, John, and I think he might be trying to bind these groups together.'

'You mean some sort of central command structure?'

'Exactly.' Kovalski pushed a hand through his hair. 'Leaderless Resistance causes us a whole set of problems, little pockets of violence here, there and everywhere. A central command gives us something to go at, but it also makes them much more of a force. We don't know what Salvesen's trying to do, but he is doing something. If he's uniting the militia – I want him.'

Harrison blew out his cheeks. 'So, what're we looking at, Tom? These groups are small. You'll never infiltrate the cell.'

'Not asking you to, Johnny. We want covert recon', that's all.'

'Wires?'

'Not enough probable cause. I need someone in there to ascertain the risk. If we can prove probable cause, we can take it further.'

'Small town Idaho.' Harrison made a face. 'You're talking about a long haul.'

Kovalski nodded. 'We've done our homework. Pocatello's assimilated a lot of information. Salvesen's got a compound outside Passover, the bottom of Sun Valley. Lot of transients there. It's mountain country, hunting and fishing. You've been up there on the big lake. Your Vietnam history is good and you look the part.' Kovalski tapped the pages in front of him. 'Also you're old enough. People are less suspicious of older guys. We're talking about arriving and stopping, getting a job and living. Stage Hands'll set you up with the background. The Salvesen compound is set in two thousand acres, surrounded by government land so you can lay up and watch without breaking the law. We think he might be arming and training these groups, John, and we don't want another Oklahoma.'

He had arrived in Passover in April. The snow was still edging the highway and he slept under the camper top in the back of his pick-up. The problem with any small town is who are you, what are you doing there, and why are you on your own? Harrison was forty-six when he got there, long hair tied at the back in a ponytail, scruffy, oil-greased baseball hat on his head. He got drunk in the Silver Dollar and slept the whole of the following day in his camper. Then he got drunk again. A drunk is a threat to nobody and he's unlikely to be a cop. One night in Joe's club when he was on his eighth whisky coke, somebody asked him what he was doing in the town. Harrison leaned on his dirty palm and looked at him out of rapidly closing eyes. 'Undercover Fed,' he said, and promptly fell off his stool.

When he went back the next night the story was round the bar and people were backslapping him as a joker. Slowly, he sobered up and then he got a job landscaping with the Mexicans. He went to work, came home, drank and shot a little pool. At first they took him for a hustler, but when his eight-ball game did not improve, they realized he was just no good. He would sit at the end of the bar and take the cuts about living with beaners. After a while, though, he started to slip into place and the suspicions grew less and less. He was just a good old boy from Marquette who liked nothing better than ice-fishing the big lake in wintertime.

Most evenings after work he would get out his bike and cycle up and down the river road pretending to get fit, but in reality probing gently; logging every property; who owned them, where they went and when. He would check the perimeter line of Salvesen's land for the best points of observation. After eight months he started to figure out his close lay-up points. He moved very very slowly; dressed in cam' gear and gilly suit he crossed the river and cut up the draws at a snail's pace. Somebody moving fast is visible at night and very noisy. Gently, he probed the ranch boundaries and came upon Slusher's cabin. The smoke gave it away long before the light did. He could smell it. The world smells different at night, a fact he had noted, making sure he smelled of nothing whenever he made an entry.

He saw elk and heard owls calling and the screech or two of a crow not quite settled for the night. He logged the exact location of the cabin and on his next venture he skirted the best trail round it. The next time out, he found a different trail and made sure he alternated movement. There were a full two miles of mountain from the cottonwood grove by the mine to the compound and the Southern-style mansion that dominated it.

A mile north of Slusher's place, across the twin saddles, was his keep hide, hidden in the thickest grove of cottonwoods deep in Dugger's Canyon. Further inland from Slusher's cabin was Drake's, the last one on this side of the compound. Over time he had probed further and further, making ground every time he went out. He had two good lay-up points before Drake's cabin where people could walk over him all day long and not see him. The initial problem with the keep hide had not been digging the hole, that only took him three visits. It was walking in with a big green Coleman cooler to store the equipment in. Dugger's old place was on Bureau of Land Management ground, the only concession being the hogan Chief had built before the government took it back. The three of them used it – Harrison, Danny and Chief. That enabled Harrison to drive his truck up there and sink the cooler into the earth.

He did not visit the hide often; he had a temporary one located just inside the cottonwoods at the bottom of Little Mammoth, where he kept his full cam' and gilly suit. Now, he pulled on the two-piece camouflage suit complete with hood and fold-over flaps for his hands. He wore tight-fitting leather gloves in the real cold, with the snowsuit flaps over that, but in this weather or any other time except deep snow, he preferred the dexterity of open fingers.

Suited, he moved out, silently, slowly up through the trees on to the open ground of the trail. Once above the old mine, he knew the trail and could risk moving more quickly. Even so, a two-mile hike would take him the best part of an hour through this country and he rarely did it in the week. Most of the activity happened at the weekend. He wasn't sure what he would find tonight, but that new face bothered him. He had seen the man before but did not know where, and something about Jesse Tate's mood disturbed him. They moved around a lot at night. The training compound was a mile further back in the hills and most new visitors got the full tour in darkness. Nothing quite like a display of night-sight shooting to get your blood running high. If there was such a show tonight he would be up most of the night. This guy had arrived late as it was, nine or more before Jesse picked him up. They might wait until morning, but Salvesen had nothing if not a sense of drama and he liked to show off to guests.

The last time Harrison had been in, about three weeks before, he witnessed Jesse drilling twenty new faces. The training compound reminded him of the Alamo, an adobe and wooden construction built on three levels, where Jesse put in the 'recruits', then attacked them with men of his own. He seemed to school them more in survival than guerrilla tactics, which somehow didn't make sense. Tonight Harrison needed his night-vision SearchCam, so a trip to the hide was necessary. He never got there.

Two hundred yards this side of Drake's house, he was on the downward slope of a small grassy hill which shouldered its way between two peaks, both of which carried snow right into June. Moving more slowly now, he was aware of the proximity of Drake and his penchant for shooting elk in the night. Salvesen had a big herd roaming his property and the government land that bordered it, and sometimes his men shot meat for their families, taking no notice of the season. A lot of the non-believers from Passover knew about the elk and Harrison had had to lie low more than once to avoid an over-eager poacher. If Salvesen caught you shooting on his land, that would be the last shot you ever made. The sign at the entrance off the highway said it all: 'Trespassers will be shot. Survivors will be shot again. Federal trespassers will be tried and hanged for treason.'

Harrison had made it as far as the last line of fir when he felt the motion sensor vibrate against his hip. He stopped stone cold and allowed the weight of the gilly suit to fall over him. The hood was low, covering his face, and he stood as still as the grave. He had two passive infrareds set up on wire hidden in the branches of these trees. The wire followed the line of the bark to the grass where the transmitters were located. He had put them there because the third time he was out he was almost compromised by a poacher. The sensor jaggled against his hip again and then, very softly, he heard voices. Whispers, two men away to his right, just inside the line of trees. Harrison cut his breath to nothing, felt in his pocket for his knuckle knife and squatted on his haunches. Now he was just one of the rocks on the hillside. The voices drew nearer, low, but no longer a whisper. 'I tell you I heard something.' Drake's eldest boy, Tommy, sixteen and already built like a wrestler.

'Course you did. What d'you think we're out here for?'

'No, Dad. Not deer. It weren't moving like no deer. I know how a deer moves. Goddamn, you've been showing me since I was but five years old.'

'Don't cuss, boy.'

Silence. They were now no more than fifteen feet away. If Harrison lifted his head he would see them. All was stillness. The night above purple, the moon casting a haze of watery light through the prickles of uppermost branches. Harrison did not breathe. They moved closer to him still. Slowly he lifted his head, inch by inch, not jerky but smooth, just far enough so he could see out

153

from under the hood of the gilly. Drake and his boy were not ten feet away, lower on the hill than he was, peering through the darkness. Harrison's face was coated with cam' cream. Tommy Drake looked right at him.

'If it was deer, why didn't we hear it run?'

For a moment his father did not answer. He hefted his rifle to his shoulder and looked where his son looked. Harrison looked right back. He saw them. They did not see him. He did not move so much as a fingertip.

'It was a deer,' Drake said finally. 'God, you're spooking me, boy.'

His son crouched down for a moment as if he was looking at the ground. He straightened again and their heads jerked this way and that like roosters in a farmyard. Then they moved off, back down the hill towards the lights of their cabin a hundred yards below. Harrison remained where he was. He watched them, saw them moving until the darkness completely enveloped them, then he stood up, looked at the clarity of the sky and cursed. The wind and the rain, a covert man's best friend.

He went home. He had lost too much time and there was every possibility that Drake would call someone up just to be certain. He could not risk that. There would be other times. The face bothered him, though. He had seen it somewhere before. He was in the yard tomorrow, however, and if Jesse or one of the others drove by with him, Harrison would make some excuse to call by the airport. One way or another he would get a second look at him.

☆

It rained in London the day after Queen's House Mews was raided. The previous evening, James Morton, alias Ibrahim Huella, had checked himself into St Ermin's Hotel opposite Scotland Yard. It appealed to him, being right on their doorstep. He got a room on the fifth floor which overlooked the Yard itself and he made a point of watching them all return. He saw Jack Swann get out of a car, which someone else was driving, and go in through the main entrance. He saw two more cars arrive and disappear into the underground car park. He left the window then, and taking the roll of film from his camera he went downstairs to the payphones. He dialled and waited, lightly tapping his fingernails on the desk, and then she answered.

'Yes?'

'I have a package for you.'

'What is it?'

'Film to be developed.'

'OK. When and where?'

'The Lady Chapel. Now.'

'How d'you want the pictures transported?'

'I don't. These are for my own use.' He hung up and went outside.

The streets were wet, the rain had ceased and the sun was endeavouring to break up cloud, although so far with little success; it was muggy and the pavement steamed under his feet. He walked along Broadway to join Victoria Street. Parliament Square was already busy with taxis bunched up one behind the other. The police officer on the corner of Victoria and Broadway stood with his arms folded over his chest and ignored him.

Huella turned right on Victoria Street and continued as far as the Esso Building. Here he stopped and crossed the road into the square. Westminster Cathedral lifted against the sky at the far end: a square building with a tall round spire on the left as he faced it, almost Moorish to look at. Huella walked across the square, ignored the young man selling copies of the *Big Issue* and climbed the steps. The notice on the door always intrigued him. 'Closed Circuit Television in operation.'

Inside, it was cool and darkened. Three huge domes in the ceiling ran the length of the main aisle to the altar at the far end. Just before the altar, the Christ hung on a cross twenty-five feet in height. Huella paused and they looked at one another. The walls were pillared in marble, pink and green and blue. He scanned for the cameras, hidden carefully from view so as not to disturb the ambience.

To the right was the Lady Chapel with the huge octagonal font which the priest would have to climb upon to perform any baptism. Huella sat down in the third row of chairs, four seats from the right. Bending his head, he stared at the ground. He would stay in St Ermin's until the others arrived. He thought a little about the future, weighed up what it meant to him, but dismissed it. There was much to be done before then. He looked at his watch and considered who should make the delivery. There were security cameras everywhere. He could use the foot soldiers maybe, but he wanted them for other things later on.

He heard the sound of a woman's footsteps behind him and he stiffened a fraction, then slowly raised his head but did not look round. The woman moved between the chairs and sat down in the seat directly behind him. Huella stared ahead and waited. She sighed and said, 'The candles are lit.'

'No, my dear,' he replied. 'The candles are alight.' He placed the roll of film to be developed under his seat. The woman reached forward and picked it up. He heard the clack of heels as she walked away.

☆

George Webb sat in the exhibits office at the Yard. Swann was with him and McCulloch from the investigation squad, together with DI Clements. Webb had sketched out the finds thus far: TATP in the pens, which had been rendered safe by the explosives officers and DRA; two complete timing and power units. Searching under the floorboards they had found the component parts for at least two PIRA Mk 15s. They had also discovered nearly a kilo of Semtex, rolled flat and stored in plastic office envelopes in a separate compartment under the top of the desk. The passport they had seen before, or rather they knew it was one of a batch of fifty counterfeits, Syrian in origin. The paper quality was good but not perfect, first seen by the Israelis.

There had been a number of other papers in the desk, scribblings, the odd word. A date, a time. Stuffed at the back of the drawer they had also found an *A–Z* of London. Webb had flicked through the pages and stopped at page sixty-one. Moor Street was circled in pencil. They also found a receipt from a glass supplier in Bermondsey for four eight-foot sheets of armour-quality glass.

Clements looked at the glass receipt encased in a nylon evidence bag. 'How're we doing for prints, Webby?' he asked.

'Got to get this lot over to Lambeth.'

Clements nodded. 'What about the general dusting?'

'Not finished yet, but we have *some* prints. They're fuzzy and we've no way of knowing whose they are yet. There was a clear set on the outside door handle, mind you. They're most likely to be his. The spotters definitely confirmed no gloves when he went out walking.'

'The car?'

'The OP's still set up. If you want me to do a covert swabbing, I will.'

Clements shook his head. 'Let's leave it a few more

days – see if anyone comes back for it.' He looked at his watch. 'The meeting's set for eleven. Will you be ready by then?'

Webb made a face. 'I want to do some work on the TPUs. Give me Jack for an hour and I will.'

Clements left them then and went back to the inspector's office. Swann sat down opposite Webb and rested his elbows on the table, chin in the palms of his hands. 'So talk to me,' he said.

Webb scratched his moustache. 'TPUs bother me, Jack. They remind me of something. I want to go through what we've got in bomb data.'

Swann cocked an eyebrow at him. 'You want to tell me what we're looking for?'

'Something using a Plastia clock.'

They went through to the Bomb Data Centre and sat down with Brian Johns, the DS who ran the office. Webb told him what they were after and he gave them access to the computer. Webb tapped in his password and started flicking through the files. He recalled that two years previously information had come in from Spain over a possible ETA attack in Madrid. Whenever information came in, Webb always had sight of it and any coded warnings were sent under separate cover. He trawled through the information, with Swann sitting next to him, until he came to what he was looking for. He printed two copies, handed one to Swann and they both sat and read.

New Year's Day 1995 – Madrid car bombing
Suspect: Ramon Jimenez

(Translated from the Spanish)

On New Year's Day in 1995, a violent explosion involving a Seat Ibiza car occurred outside the Madrid regional office of the Banco Bilbao. The car was gutted and the badly charred bodies of two men were discovered within. The vehicle was identified by the engine number as having been rented by one Ramon Jimenez in Barcelona the day before.

The two victims (identified by Spanish counter-terrorist officers from their dental records) were Hans Dieter Maier – nephew of Carl Gustav Maier – active during the Baader-Meinhof years in the late 1970s and Emilio Luca – known to be active with the Basque separatist movement ETA.

An examination of the scene showed that the car had not been in motion at the time of the explosion. The roof was located later on top of a nearby building some 25 metres up and 150 metres from the point of detonation. The positions of the bodies indicated that they had occupied the front seats. Parts of a hand were also found on the roof of a nearby building, indicating their close proximity to the centre of detonation.

Examination of the vehicle revealed that the central symmetry of the hole in the floor, coupled with the intimate damage to the propelling shaft beneath it, clearly showed that detonation had occurred centrally between the two seats, a theory reinforced by the symmetrical pressure damage to the inner uprights of the seats.

The timing spring from a mass-produced Plastia Spanish watch, copper detonator, and plastic fragments of the Arab equivalent of the timing and power unit were recovered, together with the wrist-watches of the two victims and a fragment of black/grey plastic, presumably from the housing. The Arab-originated 11-hour 15-minute timer is quite commonly used by the Basque separatist group ETA.

Two parts of a pair of scissors were recovered from the chest and liver of Maier, and it was clear that these had been in close proximity to the explosion, due to the bent configuration of the blades. Marks on the metal showed that the explosive used was high performance and traces of Eastern Bloc Semtex were later recovered.

Exactly at the time of detonation a coded warning was telephoned to the headquarters of the Madrid Guardia Civíl. The target was not given in specifics, only a reference to the further eradication of Spanish identity. Clearly, the device exploded prematurely. ETA have never been known to issue coded warnings at any time in their history. The warning words were *Tormenta Corneja* – Storm Crow.

Swann laid the sheet of paper very carefully back on the desk and felt the flesh pucker on his cheeks. For a long moment he stared at Webb.

'The watch was made by Plastia, Jack. Same as the clock in the TPUs.'

'ETA.'

'Maybe.' Webb tapped the sheet of paper. 'But ETA don't give warnings. They never have done.'

For a few moments the silence settled like a sudden weight in the room, then Swann sighed. 'Have we got a picture of Jimenez?'

Webb went back into the programme. 'E-fit,' he said. 'I'll print it.'

They were both standing by the printer as Clements came in with Superintendent Colson. 'Have you found anything, chaps?' Colson asked them. 'I want to get the briefing started.' The printer finished rolling and Swann picked up the coloured E-fit image. For a moment he stared at it and then passed it across to Colson. 'James Morton,' he said.

☆

Tommy Cairns read the morning papers and scanned the pictures of Queen's House Mews. 'The Antiterrorist Branch raided the premises after a tip-off concerning the recent car-bomb attack in Soho.' Folding the paper under his arm, he went out to his car and drove over to the builder's yard where he and the others worked. Charlie Oxley was reading the same thing in the *Sun*, a cigarette burning between his fingers. He looked up when Cairns came in and held up the paper. 'That was the address on the driving licence, Tommy.'

'So what? He got away, didn't he. And nobody's looking for you.'

Oxley looked at him then. 'Well, they haven't found me anyway.'

'And they won't. If they had a really good description they'd have been round here by now. You've got no form, Charlie. How the hell can they find you?'

Oxley dropped the newspaper on the floor and placed both hands on his crew-cut head. 'We've still got the glass,' he said. 'That means they'll want us again.'

☆

Colson took the first full briefing since the debacle at Queen's House Mews, and the feeling that somebody was laughing at them was tangible. Immediately after it became clear that Morton had escaped, Swann spoke to Christine Harris and Julian Moore, who had been operational as watchers on Monday. When he told them what had happened, and that SO19 believed Morton had escaped through the attic, they recollected the estate agent's visit.

Swann went to see the agency and they confirmed that they had *not* shown anyone round that day. He rechecked the list of people they *had* shown round since the property was put up for sale. Some of them had addresses, some of them had telephone numbers, but quite a few had only left their names. He looked for single men and found three. Single women, he found five. The name McIlroy stood out.

It would not be difficult for someone who knew what they were doing to get a key. A flat piece of clay in your hand, asking to go back inside for another look on your own just as the estate agent was getting in his car; him waiting there while you go in, key in the clay and bingo – you could enter any time you pleased.

'He had no visitors in all the time we had him under surveillance?' Colson asked, sitting at the front with his arms folded.

'Nobody, sir,' Swann said.

'Yet somebody picked him up from Moor Street in a rented Vauxhall Vectra. And now somebody has got keys to the empty property in Queen's House Mews.'

'One and the same person,' Christine Harris suggested.

'Possibly, but who?'

Swann could sense the additional air of unease. Morton/Ibrahim Huella had known that SO19 were going to attack him. That meant he knew he was under surveillance, and the fact that on no occasion did he endeavour to use any third eye or other obvious antisurveillance techniques told them he didn't need to. He was confident he would know exactly when they planned to scoop him up. Swann looked round the room: SO13, the best domestic antiterrorist force in the world, save perhaps the Israelis; the source agencies, Special Branch and MI5. Somewhere there was a leak. The only other possibility was the SFO team involved, but Huella's activities, or lack of them as regards antisurveillance manoeuvres, discounted SO19. He was sure of his ground long before they got involved.

Colson got to his feet again. 'Storm Crow,' he said, face suddenly grim. 'George dug up a file that came in from Spain a few years back, an incident where a Plastia Spanish watch was used as the timing device. It was originally thought to be ETA, but the authorities received a coded warning. He looked at Webb then. 'The codeword was Storm Crow.'

Webb folded his arms. 'We've heard the name before. We've never seen him here and we never wanted to.' He sucked at his teeth. 'I've only pulled that one incident so far, but the name has been whispered since 1989. We don't know much about him or them, no one can even confirm whether it's an individual or a group. It could be an individual. It could be an amalgam of lots of things. I know that some of his work resembles ETA, as we've seen today. We also know Phil Cregan pig-sticked a dummy Mk 15 at Soho, so there's been contact with PIRA. Bombings, assassinations, nothing that can be connected with any one group or cause in particular. Bomb data lists an FBI agent called Louis Byrne as the man in the know. Apparently, he was in the Middle East in 1989 when the first incident took place. I'll pull all the files later and brief you on everything.'

'We don't know that this was anything to do with Storm Crow,' Christine Harris broke in on him.

Webb glanced at her. 'No, we don't know anything for sure. I'm just working on hunches.'

'Storm Crow incidents generally get claimed, don't they?'

Webb nodded. 'Either that or a codeword. Madrid, for example. Spanish police weren't well up on him then, that's why they thought PIRA may have been involved. No one gives coded warnings but PIRA.'

'Cross-fertilization?' Colson said. 'Storm Crow some kind of joint statement maybe. We know ETA and PIRA have links.'

Webb twisted his mouth down at the corners. 'The only problem with that theory is most Storm Crow incidents have little to do with the specific cause of any one group. That suggests money and power are the motives. Some of the incidents have been assassinations. There's lots of reasons to kill people and top hit men get top money. If you want my opinion, Storm Crow's another Carlos but without the PFLP, and we all know what a nasty bastard he was.'

'Innocuous little man when you meet him, apart from being carried in on a pole.' Dave Collins from 2 Squad had been to Paris to interview the Jackal earlier in the year. For twenty-four years the Branch had wanted to speak to him over the shooting of Edward Sieff, the brother of the then chairman of Marks & Spencer. Carlos had shot Sieff in the face, after forcing his way into his home back in 1973.

Colson paced round the table. 'What about TATP? The last time that was used was against the Israeli Embassy.'

'Triacetone triperoxide,' Webb stated. 'Crystal form, a base explosive about as volatile as it gets. Friction sets it off. Makes pure PETN and lead azide look stable. Normally used in the Middle East. Hamas have been making home-made grenades out of it for years, not to mention car and suicide bombs.' He shook his head. 'In felt-tip pens – takes some bottle just to put it in there.'

The briefing broke up. Swann and Webb wandered back to the fifteenth floor and bought coffee from the machine. Swann sipped his, leaning against the window in the exhibits office looking out over Buckingham Palace.

Webb stood next to him. Both of them were silent. Then Swann said, 'Nobody mentioned it, did they.'

'No.'

'It's there all the same, though.'

'Maybe. No doubt Colson and the old man are talking about it.'

Swann looked sideways at him then. 'It's either Box or SB or us, Webby.'

Webb nodded grimly. 'It could be other things, Jack. If this is Storm Crow, then we know from the files just how clever he is. Surveillance is surveillance, isn't it. All he had to do was clock one of the footpads, do a bit of covert antisurveillance and he'd know. Then he could locate the OP. That's not difficult if you know what you're looking for.'

'What about the hit, though?'

Webb chewed his lip. 'That's the hard bit, I grant you.'

'Timing and everything.'

Webb nodded. 'He could've clocked their recce. Phones, wasn't it? If he's that clever he would have contacted BT and asked the question.'

Swann made a face. 'He could, I suppose. He was so fucking cool when I spoke to him. GCHQ have no record, though.'

'Out and about, Jack. He could've used a call box. Mobile, loads of ways he could check.' He picked at his teeth with a matchstick. 'Should've bugged the car.'

'Tell you something else,' Swann said. 'The way he's set this thing up – the car bomb, the hire car, address and everything. Passport and not driving licence. It's as if he wanted us to find him.'

'But then he got away.'

'Right.'

'That could take care of your conspiracy theory, Jack.

If he wanted us to find him he'd know the drill, in which case he could figure out when we were going to hit him.'

'But why should he want us to find him?'

'I wish I knew, Jack. I really wish I knew.'

Together they went back to the Bomb Data Centre and printed a selection of documented Storm Crow incidents going back to 1989.

4 July 1989, US Ambassador – Tel Aviv
Said Rabi
Brigitte Hammani

On Friday 4 July 1989, the US Ambassador to Israel, Theodore Welford-Jennings, was travelling back from a function given in honour of US Independence Day by several members of the Israeli Cabinet. The ambassador was returning to his residence, guarded by a joint Mossad and Diplomatic Security Service convoy, when a grenade was thrown from a Citroën Dyane car, idling at the intersection with a side road. The grenade exploded and there was fragmentation damage to windows and several of the cars. The ambassador's car received only minor damage to its rear section. Two people fled from the scene on foot (a man and a woman), leaving the Citroën, which was later found to be booby-trapped with a small device containing half a pound of the Russian-manufactured explosive Ammonal.

Israeli Secret Service officers pursued on foot and the man was cornered and shot six times, being fatally wounded after entering a courtyard in a residential area and firing on his pursuers. The woman was never captured.

The device in the Citroën was rendered safe by

means of a controlled explosion. No trace of any other device or weapon was recovered, but the car was registered to one Brigitte Hammani – unknown to the security forces before the incident. The deceased man was Said Rabi, a member of Yasser Arafat's Fatah, who had recently fallen foul of the leadership. The grenade was home-made, using tri-acetone triperoxide. Two hours after the ambassador returned safely to his residence, a phone call was taken from a French-speaking male and the attack was claimed in the name of *Tempête Corbeau* – Storm Crow.

Webb looked up at Swann. 'First recorded incident.' He passed it over and Swann read through it. Webb flicked through the screen and something else caught his eye. 'One more,' he said, 'then I'm going to phone the FBI and talk to this Louis Byrne.'

28 June 1995, Alessandro Peroni – Paris
Pier-Luigi Ramas
Tal-Salem

---

On 28 June 1995, Alessandro Peroni was in Paris for a conference on the convergence criteria for European monetary union. He was there in a dual capacity as adviser to the Italian government and chief economist of Banca Di Roma.

At 8.30 a.m. he left his hotel and walked the short distance to a waiting taxi. As he opened the door, another man, also apparently waiting, pushed him into it and the taxi sped off. The taxi was later found abandoned with Peroni still inside, fatally wounded, having been shot five times with 40-calibre shells, possibly from a Beretta.

The concierge of the hotel was able to give good

descriptions of both the taxi driver and the assailant. An E-fit image was created and the information circulated internationally. The men were identified as Pier-Luigi Ramas and Tal-Salem, a tandem hit-man team wanted in Germany by the BKA.

At 6 p.m. that evening, the offices of *Le Figaro* were telephoned from a call box outside Paris. The caller was Spanish or South American and the assassination was claimed in the name of *Corneja Tempestad* – Storm Crow.

# 8

Tal-Salem sat on the balcony of a rented apartment in Javea, southern Spain, a glass of beer at his elbow. He was watching topless girls on the beach, out of slightly glazed eyes. Between forefinger and thumb he held a long fat joint, the effects of which were working their way steadily through him. Those who had gone before him, long long ago now, had eaten theirs in cakes. Behind him the telephone rang and he looked at it for a moment before answering.

'*Hola.*'

'Hello, old friend.'

Salem smiled. 'A long time since I hear from you,' he said. '*Qué pasa?*'

'*Nada.*'

'*Nada* is not what I hear.'

The voice on the other end of the phone laughed then. 'Your Spanish doesn't get any better.'

'Neither does my English.' He sat on the arm of a chair. 'So, how is London in the summertime?'

'Better than in the wintertime.'

'Is what I'm hearing correct?'

'It is. Once again we share an employer.'

'The way of the world, my friend. When the work you do is good, the right people remember.'

For a moment neither of them spoke, then the caller said: 'And our other old friend. How is he?'

'Well.'

'He's with you?'

'No,' Salem said. 'He is only ever with me when we're working. Right now he is in Rome. His favourite city in summertime.'

'I thought that was Paris.'

'Paris is OK, but he prefers the girls in Rome.'

'Can you contact him?'

'Of course.'

'Then do so. August will be a good time to be in London.'

'August then.'

'We'll speak again.'

'You are aware that the price has gone up.'

'Inflation, a terrible thing.'

'So I read in the papers.'

Tal-Salem went back out to the balcony. Late afternoon, the sun was moving steadily closer to the sea. Some of the girls on the beach had already put their clothes back on, yet the heat of the day still burned his face. He picked up the beer, slightly warm now, and swallowed. Then he went back inside and made a phone call to Rome.

☆

The airplane was only half full. At midday the man in the dark suit left business class and went through to the toilet. He moved up the economy cabin, smiling at the flight attendant, and settled in an empty seat. He unclipped the phone from its housing, ran his AT&T card through, waited and dialled. It was late afternoon in London. She picked up the phone after three rings.

'Hello?'

'Good afternoon.'

'I wasn't expecting to hear from you.'

'Of course not. It wouldn't be good business if you knew when I was going to call.'

She did not reply.

'Everything going as planned?'

'Yes. I have the pictures back.'

'Pictures? Oh, the pictures. Good. Good.'

She paused. 'Can I ask you a question?'

'Just one.'

'Is it you that I meet?'

For a moment he was silent and then he said: 'In the cathedral? Westminster Cathedral, such a beautiful, awe-inspiring place. Did you know they have closed-circuit television there? Make sure you don't get caught on it.'

'It is you, isn't it.'

'Is it?' He could hear the lightness of her breath.

'What if I were to sit down in front of you instead of behind?' she said. 'What if I were to turn round and look you right in the face?'

'Then you would die.' He laughed then, a cruel sound, low and loose in his throat. 'Or be sent back where you came from.' The flight attendant was on her way up the aisle. 'Enough,' he said. 'Games are for other people. Stage two is at hand.'

☆

Louis Byrne took the call from Scotland Yard. He was seated at his desk, working on some papers for a lecture he was about to give in conjunction with the Bomb Data Center. In the wake of the Timothy McVeigh trial, the Bureau was polishing up its public image and Byrne was its best advert. Thirty-eight years old and already GS14. Supervisory special agent in the International Terrorism Operations Unit, National Security Division, and argu-ably the most able agent they had. 'Byrne,' he said as he answered.

'This is Detective Sergeant George Webb, Scotland Yard Antiterrorist Branch.'

Byrne sat back. 'Good morning. How's it going over there?'

'Busy.'

'You guys are always busy.'

'Tell me about it.'

'What can I do for you, George?'

'I think we have a problem over here and I'm told you're the man to help us.'

'I am?'

'Apparently so.'

'All righty. Shoot.'

Webb paused. 'We're not sure,' he said. 'But we think the Storm Crow's in London.'

Byrne was silent, his hand a fist on the desk, eyes fixed on the black feather pinned on the office wall. 'Go on,' he said quietly.

'We had a car bomb in Soho back in April.'

'I heard about that.'

'Well, what you won't have heard is how we raided a house and found nothing except timed tape recordings and a gun operated by movement sensors.'

'Really?' Byrne sat up straighter.

'Unfortunately, yes. Reception committee, Louis. We've seen nothing like it in years.'

Byrne moistened his lips with his tongue. 'So tell me, George – why Storm Crow?'

'*Modus operandi*. We've got details over here of one or two events in Europe. The assassination of an Italian banker, Paris in 1995, and a car bomb in Madrid.'

'*Tormenta Corneja*,' Byrne said.

'Right. A watch made by a company called Plastia was used in the timing and power unit. We found dual circuitry in Soho and complete TPUs with the same integrated circuits in Queen's House Mews. The timing unit was a Plastia LCD clock. At first we thought maybe the IRA and ETA were trading operatives, but now I don't think so.'

Byrne glanced at the photograph of his own face framed on the cabinet by the desk. Above his right eye, a mock bullet hole had been punched through the paper. 'Have you received anything from him?'

'Received? You mean as in a coded warning?'

'No. I mean *received* received. Anything in the mail?'

'Such as.'

'Well, I don't know if you guys are aware, but we bumped into him in Texas, right after Oklahoma.'

'Don't remember it, no.'

'Fort Bliss got mortared. A few days later, our field office in El Paso got something in the mail. A black crow's feather and a picture of me with a bullet hole in my head.'

Webb blew out his cheeks. 'We've had nothing like that.'

'Then maybe it's not what it seems. This guy's specific, George. Got a big ego. Makes Carlos look modest. If it is him, he'll let you know.'

'What about the TPU?'

'Could be, sounds kinda familiar, but he likes to confuse people. He's used stuff from just about every known group there is. He can make it look like Hamas or Hizbollah or the IRA if he wants to.'

'That makes sense,' Webb said. 'We had two TPUs in the car bomb. One was a decoy, PIRA Mk15.'

Byrne was silent again for a moment. 'Now that *does* sound like him. Tell me something, George. You got any idea what he's doing?'

'Not so far. There doesn't seem to be any obvious motive.'

'That sounds like him too.'

'Our bomb data files tell us you've had more to do with trying to catch him than anyone else around.'

'I have been kinda interested, I guess.'

'What makes you so sure it's a him?' Webb asked.

Byrne exhaled audibly. 'Hunch, I guess. I went to Tel Aviv in 1989. At the time I was working out of the legal attaché's office in Athens. My old marine lieutenant was the regional security officer in Israel.'

'Right,' Webb said.

'So what I'm saying is – when they hit Welford-Jennings' motorcade, I was all but on the spot. That was the first recorded incident.'

'I've got it on file over here. Brigitte Hammani and Said Rabi.'

'Right. The thing is, Rabi was a disaffected Fatah member. He fucked up or something and I think Arafat's guard were out to slit his throat. I had a theory that the attack on Jennings was him and Hammani working alone. His way of trying to appease the Fatah. Because he got killed, I think somebody else may've claimed it.'

'Storm Crow.'

'Exactly.'

'One man?'

'I'd say so. Kinda like putting himself on the market right there and then.'

'So you're saying he wasn't actually responsible for it, but claimed it because nobody else did.'

'Well the Fatah didn't. Neither did the PLF or anybody else.'

'What about the girl – she was never caught. Right?'

'Right.'

'Working with him?'

'Could be.'

'We've got a woman here in London right now. We

174

don't know who she is, but she's rented a property on behalf of a company. The name being used is Joanne Taylor, blonde hair and blue eyes.'

'Brigitte Hammani was a Palestinian, George. She looks like one – dark skin, very long, very black hair. Real pretty.'

'D'you have any pictures of her?'

'There was one, seized from an apartment in Bethlehem. It got destroyed by mistake.'

'That was fucking handy.' Webb was quiet for a moment. 'If it is Storm Crow, what's he likely to be up to?'

'Who knows, George. He's basically for sale. Whoever's prepared to pay his price. The Fort Bliss thing was drugs. He's done the same in Colombia.'

'Any idea who he is, where he's from or anything?'

'That's why he's so good. Nobody has a clue. Look, I gotta go now – I'm late for a lecture. PR thing, trying to remind the public that the FBI's not the enemy. I'm coming to England in August for the Shrivenham conference, though. I'll bring over what I have if you want.'

'That'd be good.'

'If you need me in the meantime, just call.' Byrne put down the phone and stared long and hard at the black feather on the wall.

☆

Ibrahim Huella checked out of St Ermin's Hotel and called a taxi. He had been there a week and had learned all that he could. He left the taxi idling in the Broadway, strolled past the guards at Scotland Yard and went into the foyer. The eternal flame burned on his right and the desk sergeant looked up at him.

'Can I help you, sir?'

'Just dropping something off for a friend of mine in

SO13. Jack Swann, DS. Room 1521.' He handed him the large envelope he was carrying. 'D'you think you could see he gets it?'

'The floor's not sealed if you want to go up. You got your warrant card?'

'No time. I'm due at a briefing.'

'Who shall I say left it?'

'Just tell him Jim. SO12. A Squad.'

'Right you are then.'

Huella thanked him, walked outside and climbed into the waiting cab.

Swann, Webb and the rest of the team were discussing the information that Webb had gleaned from the FBI. Garrod had gone public with a photograph of Huella/ Morton again, but as yet they had had no response other than the normal crank callers. Trying to trace the ringed Cortina had proved all but impossible, and they still had no lead on the man who had hired the Vectra. Various Nazi groups had been considered, but no individual identified. The assistant at the hire company had been shown book after book of mugshots and had not recognized anyone. They had a reasonable E-fit, but nothing you could hang your hat on. Swann was on his way out to revisit the glass supplier in Bermondsey when the call came into the squad room. 'Jack, it's Campbell. There's a package for you downstairs. They're screening it now.'

'OK. Thanks, mate.' He put the phone down and looked at Webb. 'Package for me.'

Webb looked at his watch. 'Bit early for Christmas.'

The envelope came up and Swann sat down at his desk. He slit open one end and eased out three large photographs. For a long time he stared. Webb was sitting opposite him.

'What is it, Jack?'

Swann didn't reply, just kept staring at the pictures.

Webb walked round the desk and looked over his shoulder. Goose flesh broke out on his cheeks. Three photographs, close-up shots – Colson, himself and Swann. They all had a hole in their heads, as if someone had shot a round through the paper. 'I think we better talk to the guv'nor.'

They walked the length of the corridor to the superintendent's office. Colson was just handing over to DSU Robertson, his counterpart. Swann tapped on the door and he looked up.

'What is it, Jack?'

'Can we have a word, Guv?'

Colson beckoned them in and Swann laid the pictures down on the desk. 'These were hand-delivered downstairs.'

Colson stared at the photographs, a hole right between his eyes. Webb's was on his right temple and Swann's on his left. He recognized the scene from behind the cordon tapes on Adie Road.

Swann picked up the telephone and dialled the front desk. 'This is Jack Swann, SO13 Reserve. You've just had a delivery for me.'

'Yes. We sent it up.'

'The person who delivered it, what did he look like?'

'IC3. Black beard, glasses. Said you knew him. Certainly knew you. Your name, your floor, even the room number. Said his name was Jim. Prot' from Special Branch.'

Swann felt the shiver run the length of his spine. 'Thanks.' He put the phone down and looked at the others. 'Afro-Caribbean male, black beard and glasses. Said his name was Jim – Prot' from SB.'

'Storm Crow,' Webb said quietly.

'What?' Colson looked over the desk at him.

'Has to be, sir.' Webb motioned to the pictures. 'Louis

Byrne, the Fed I talked to, had one like this sent to him two years ago. That was from the Storm Crow.'

Colson looked again at the photos. 'Special Branch A Squad,' he said.

'Close protection.' Swann drew in his lips. 'He's telling us we need it.'

Colson looked up at Webb. 'George, he could only have taken these from Queen's House Mews. Get a team down there now and check the angles.'

'Hotel,' Swann said. 'The one on the corner. First, second floor maybe. Last place to be evacuated.' And then he remembered, the little brown-faced man with the horn-rimmed glasses and beard, the one he had checked when he set off the wrong way up the road. 'Jesus Christ, I spoke to him. Guy with the hat and a stick. Little fucking bastard.'

'Get that team, George,' Colson said again. 'But don't go yourself. You and Jack stay here. We need to talk to the old man about this.'

Garrod had a senior MI5 operative in his office. Colson interrupted them. 'Sorry, John,' he said. 'I'm afraid we need to talk to you.'

Swann and Webb followed him inside. Swann glanced at the Indian pictures. He always did; they had a way of drawing your eye. It was then he remembered the book that Morton had been reading when he interviewed him. It had been lying on the side table, a biography of Geronimo, the master of illusion. Colson told Garrod what had happened and showed him the pictures. Garrod pressed his glasses higher up his nose, then looked at Webb and Swann. 'Right,' he said. 'This floor is sealed until I say otherwise. For Christ's sake, we've just issued a picture of the man.' He looked at Colson then. 'D'you want personal protection weapons?'

Colson pursed his lip. 'Maybe for a week or so.'

Garrod looked at Webb who nodded. 'Swann?'

'Jesus,' Swann said. 'A gun. I've got two kids and an au pair in the house. I suppose I'd better, yes.'

'Pick them up when you're ready. I'll write the authorization now.'

Swann suddenly needed to go home. The girls were there with Annika, the new au pair. He took the tube to Waterloo and walked home. Charley was leaning out of the lounge window and waved frantically when she saw him. Swann realized then just how much he had missed coming home to them. 'Get back inside, Charley. You'll fall,' he called.

Upstairs, they jumped on him, knocking him on to the sofa. 'Girls, girls,' Annika clucked at them. 'Be careful of Daddy's suit.'

Swann smiled at her. 'They're all right.'

'I'm cooking,' she said. 'Would you like some?'

'What is it?'

'Spaghetti.'

'She makes great spaghetti, Daddy. Better than yours.' Charley tugged round his jaw so he faced her.

'*She* has got a name, young lady,' Swann said. '*She's* the cat's mother.'

They both started laughing then and Swann tickled them. 'Not Annika,' he said. 'You know I don't mean Annika.'

Joanna sat up straight, pushing her hair out of her eyes. She patted his chest, then pulled his jacket open. 'You've got a lump . . .' She saw the butt of the gun sticking out of the shoulder holster. Swann pulled his jacket closed. Annika stared at him. He put his finger to his lips. 'That's enough now. You're too noisy. Bath time.' He clapped his hands together.

They shuffled downstairs to the bathroom and he heard Joanna whisper, 'Daddy's got a gun, Charley.'

He stood with his hands on his hips for a moment, then turned back to Annika. 'You OK?'

'Fine.'

He patted his jacket. 'Don't worry. I don't usually carry one. We've got a bit of a threat on at the moment, that's all.'

Annika shrugged her shoulders. 'All our policemen have guns.'

The phone rang then and he picked it up. 'Swann.'

'Jack, it's me, Pia.'

'Hey, you.' He sat down on the couch crossing one leg over the other, entwining the cord round his fingers. 'How're you?'

'I'm OK.' Her voice sounded a little awkward.

'What's up?'

'Nothing. I just needed to speak to you.'

'Another bad day?'

'No more than usual. Can I see you tonight?'

Swann looked at Annika. 'I'm home with the kids tonight, love.'

'Oh.'

'Come round. Stay. You've not tried out the couch yet.'

She hesitated. 'I don't like it with another woman in the house.'

Swann put his hand over the receiver and spoke to Annika. 'Fancy a night out?'

Her eyes lit up. 'I could see my boyfriend.'

'Great.' He spoke to Pia again. 'Annika's going out. Come round whenever you want.'

He read Charley the story of *The Elves and the Shoemaker*, the original Ladybird hardback that he had read as a child. She loved the pictures, he loved the pictures, the texture in the leather of the shoes after they were sewn together. Joanna read her own book. When the story was finished he kissed them both and then Charley pulled his head close to hers. 'Daddy,' she whispered. 'Why have you got a gun?'

'It's complicated, darling. But don't worry, it'll only be for a few days.'

Upstairs, he took a bottle of beer from the fridge and put some music on. Pia arrived just after seven-thirty, let herself in and appeared beside him in the kitchen. She flung her arms round his neck and kissed him hard on the mouth. Swann looked deep into her oval eyes.

'Missed me, did you?'

She hugged him again. 'I don't like this other woman in your house.'

He held her at arm's length. 'She's eighteen, Pia. I really don't think we've anything to worry about.'

'She's pretty.'

Swann cocked an eyebrow at her, letting his gaze drift over her face, neck, breasts. 'There's pretty,' he said, 'and then again there's pretty.'

She kissed him again, mouth working into his. Swann broke to breathe and then he poured some wine.

Pia spotted the shoulder holster lying with his jacket on the couch. 'Jack.'

'What?'

'Why've you got a gun in the house?'

'Take no notice of it. It's just a precaution.'

Pia looked at him with her head to one side, arms tight across her chest. 'Precaution against what?'

He sighed, took her hand and sat down with her on the couch. He stroked her cheek with the backs of his fingers. 'There's been a bit of bother over the Soho bomb.'

'What sort of bother?'

He slipped the Glock from its holster and weighed it in his hand. 'We're dealing with a bad one, love.'

Pia stared at the gun. 'Put it away, Jack. Somewhere out of sight. I can't stand guns.'

Swann placed the gun and holster above the kitchen cupboards. 'Sorry,' he said, 'there was no need for you to see it.'

She stared at him, eyes broken up at the edges. 'Jack, if you're carrying a gun, I want to know about it.'

He sighed. 'It'll only be for a while. A couple of us have got them. Personal protection weapons. For a week or so, no longer. Just till the threat dies down.'

'What threat? Tell me, Jack.'

'It's probably nothing. Happens now and again. Webby carried one once before, when we found his name on a PIRA list.'

'But why now? What's happened, Jack?'

Swann tipped the neck of his beer bottle to his lips and swallowed. He wiped his mouth with the back of his hand. 'This is for your ears only. Understand?'

She nodded. 'Of course.'

'Today we received three photographs at the Yard. Hand-delivered by the target from Queen's House Mews.'

'Oh my God.'

'Pictures of me, Webb and Colson, you know, the operational commander. Three holes in the faces, as if someone had shot them.'

Pia sat down and then got up again and went to the window. 'Jesus Christ, Jack.' She hugged herself, staring over the street. Swann touched her lightly on the shoulder. 'Nothing'll come of it, love. This guy likes to play games, that's all.'

'Does Caroline know?'

He looked at his watch. 'She will by now.'

They made love on the floor, naked; with the children asleep in their beds downstairs and the prospect of Annika bursting in on them at any moment. Pia gripped him with long fingernails, his back, arms, shoulders, raking herself against him as if she couldn't quite get close enough. She straddled him, working him deeper and deeper inside her. Sweat broke out on Swann's body and cries stopped in his throat. Afterwards they lay together in the bath and still she held him tightly, while he kissed wet hair where it was cropped close at her neck.

☆

Harrison bought a case of Budweiser from the Valley Market at the far end of Passover. He was just off work and there was nothing in the fridge. He also bought a pack of Marlboro reds and a pack of Merit menthols and paid for them and the beer. The Mexican kid, Rico, served him and grinned at the twin packs. 'How come you smoke two types, Harrison? You never did tell me.'

'Well, the thing of it is, Rico,' Harrison said, 'when I was in 'Nam, before I went down the holes, I was caught up in a firefight with Charlie that lasted two whole weeks. The landing zone was so hot it was smoking and there was no way in even for the dust-off. We had but the one medic and his arm got shot off. Anyways, those chopper pilots buzzed in and out, but they just couldn't land. Old Charlie had us buttoned flatter than a squashed rattler in a wagon rut. They dropped us C-rations and cigarettes, but they only had these.' He picked up the soft pack of Merits and flipped them over in his hand. 'After two weeks I was hooked on the menthol and just couldn't give 'em up.' He chuckled then as he picked up the Marlboro reds. 'Trouble was, I couldn't give these up neither.'

He drove back to the trailer park and took his beer inside. He flipped the top off a bottle and stacked the rest in the refrigerator. The trailer was hot, the tiny windows hardly opened at all and there was no air conditioning. He squatted on the couch and flipped through the latest bunch of pictures he had taken. The man Jesse had picked up the other night was still about. On Saturday, Harrison had spent the entire day in his observation point on the hillside at the back of the compound. Salvesen had built it well, on a mini plateau above the canyon with mountains rising behind, the tallest one with snow still clutching its flanks. Harrison had placed his lowest lay-up point just outside the grove of aspen that scattered the belly of the hill at the edge of Salvesen's land.

The security was weakest at the rear of the compound, which housed the Southern-style mansion complete with pillars and a small place of worship where Salvesen sought inspiration. Not only was he founder of the Omega Foundation, dedicated to the pursuit of divine inspiration and biblical prophecy, he was the self-styled pastor of the Church of God's Prophecy. He preached regularly on his own AM radio station, called Network of the Lord, and he took services in the churches he had built along the Salmon River. Five in all, stretching from Passover north over Galena Summit, up to Stanley and Challis. He rotated every fifth Sunday. Harrison wondered what he would do when he fulfilled his dream and had them clear to Coeur D'Alene.

He sipped beer and looked through the pictures. The man he had seen riding into town was BobCat Reece, leader of the West Montana Minutemen. Reece was the third known 'patriot' leader that Harrison had seen in the last four months. Kovalski had told him that Salvesen was not officially linked to any unorganized militia, but he had dabbled with the 'Posse' in the eighties and they had written about hanging government officials for committing unconstitutional acts. Reece, for one, would go along with that. He stowed the photographs in the padded envelope and wrapped it in rolls of sandwich wrap. Then he placed it under the flooring until he could get it to Max Scheller, his contact agent.

He took a shower and drove up to Westlake to see Lisa. She had her back to him when he walked into Grumpy's diner, and he slid on to a swivel stool at the counter.

'Hey, Miss Lady Mam,' he whispered.

Lisa turned, looked at him and smiled. She pushed her hair back from her face, one hand on her hip. 'Hey, honey. What's up?' At thirty-eight, she was ten years his junior; slim-faced with high cheekbones and hazel eyes. In her younger days she had modelled swimwear and adorned the pages of the Harley Davidson calendar. She leaned over the counter and kissed him. 'What can I get you?'

'Corned beef on rye, half and half onion rings and French fries.' Harrison patted his stomach. 'Got to watch my waistline.' On the TV above the counter, the NBA final was being played out between the Bulls and the Utah Jazz. Most people favoured the Jazz as Utah was a neighbouring state.

It was a warm evening and Harrison wore only his jeans and a tank top. Lisa poured coffee and he scratched the image of a grinning rat holding a whisky bottle and a pistol, tattooed on his upper arm.

'Been busy today, hon'?' he asked her.

'So so. I guess.'

The door opened and Jesse Tate walked in with Wingo and BobCat Reece from Montana. Harrison stirred sugar into his coffee. They sat at a table by the window and Jesse snapped his fingers at Lisa. Harrison felt the hackles begin to rise. He said nothing though, but squinted at Reece from one eye. He remembered the face now, thin black hair and quick darting eyes. Reece had been arrested for shooting a forest ranger way up by the Canadian border. Harrison had seen those eyes on FBI pictures back in D.C. There were no witnesses, however, and Reece had claimed self-defence. The ranger's gun had been fired and they could not prove whether it was after he was killed or not, so Reece walked away.

Lisa served his dinner, but he had suddenly lost his appetite. He picked at the food with his fork.

'Not hungry, honey?'

He looked up into her eyes and smiled. 'I was. Not so sure any more.'

'That the food or the company?' She looked over his shoulder.

'Hey, what about a little service round here?' Jesse snapped his fingers again.

Harrison bristled and swivelled round on his seat. 'Mind your manners, Jesse. The lady was serving me.'

Jesse stared coldly at him. 'I don't see no lady.'

Harrison felt Lisa's hand on his arm. 'Leave it, honey. White trash is all.'

She served Jesse and his friends. Harrison pushed his plate away and got up off the stool.

'I'm going to the hotel for a drink,' he said. 'They give you any trouble, you call me.'

She smiled at him and cupped his face with a palm. 'I can handle those motherfuckers, honey.'

At the door Harrison paused and looked back. Jesse was still watching him. 'Hey, Harrison,' he said.

'What?'

Jesse nodded to his arm. 'Real tunnel rats wouldn't broadcast it.'

Harrison held his eye, one hand on the door. 'Is that a fact,' he said.

☆

Swann was looking for Ibrahim Huella, alias James Morton, alias Ramon Jimenez. He, Webb and Colson carried side arms for two weeks before reviewing the situation.

186

The forensic team had located which room Huella had rented in the hotel in Queen's House Mews and gone through it with a fine toothcomb. Webb gave them an update at the afternoon briefing. 'We're making some progress,' he said. 'At least forensically. SO3 have identified only one clear set of prints, although we've got a reasonable flange mark which the UV light sensor picked up. We're assuming he wore gloves when he was inside the house. Hell of a thing to keep up for that length of time. The fingerprints came from the door handle. Remember, Box and SB confirmed that when he went out he wasn't wearing gloves. He closed and opened the front door and he could hardly wipe it in broad daylight, especially given that we now believe he knew we were watching him. We've also picked up some prints from inside the house.

'We've done ESLA lifts all over the house and the hotel room. We've got fibres from both and at the moment Lambeth are looking for a match. One thing we do know is that the rug used to cover the second TPU in the Cortina was in contact with the carpet in the basement study at number four. Fibre persistence is pretty good with the two types of synthetic involved, and we can say for definite that at some point the rug was in that house.'

Colson nodded his appreciation.

'Footprints,' Webb went on. 'We've got them from the kitchen floor. He may have worn gloves inside, but he still put the kettle on in his bare feet first thing in the morning. We've got a clear set from both the kitchen and the bathroom.'

'What about the RDX trace?' McCulloch asked him.

Webb made a face. 'Not so clear. It's in the car all right. We've also got some firearms residue. Since the initial search at Queen's House Mews we've come up with a bulb and wire, so we can pretty much prove he was circuit testing.' He paused and looked at Colson. 'I'm going to swab the inside of the Mondeo tonight, sir, and then we'll put a tracker on it and leave it. I don't see anyone coming back for it in the short term.'

'He'll forget about it,' Swann put in. 'If he knows we were watching him, he'll know we know about the car. He won't go anywhere near it and neither will anyone else.'

'Tow it in?' Tania suggested.

'No.' Webb looked again at Colson. 'I think we should leave it, sir. If it's got a tracker we don't have to worry.'

'I agree.' Colson got up. 'Jack, what about the glass?'

Swann got up. 'CapScan Glass Supply in Bermondsey Wall,' he said. 'On the twenty-fourth of March they sold four sheets, eight by four. Also base plates and hinges to fit.'

'A room,' Webb said. 'What would he want with a glass room?'

Colson half closed his eyes. 'Let's not even think about that.'

'They do remember the purchaser,' Swann continued. 'Most of their customers are builders with accounts, trade sales, that sort of thing. They do have a retail counter though, and this guy bought it from there.'

'Description?' Clements asked him.

'Cropped hair and earrings, that's all they can tell us. The glass was loaded on to an unmarked flatbed lorry. The warehouseman couldn't remember the colour.'

'So, we're looking for another skinhead, driving a lorry this time,' Webb said. 'What – a couple of thousand in London.'

'Have we found out any more about the company that rented the house in the first place?' Colson asked Swann.

'Medicourt.' Swann sat down and flicked through the notes he had. 'Not really. We know about the London end and Belfast. That was for show I reckon. There's nothing Irish about this. We've been trying to unravel what's further up the ladder, but it's a nightmare. Companies here, there and everywhere, investments, share dealings. The trail splits a hundred different ways.'

That night Webb went back to the car park where Huella had left the Mondeo. He was backed up by plainclothes men from SO19, and Jack Swann accompanied him. They got to the location in Wandsworth and the surveillance team confirmed that the area was quartered and secure. One of the Gunships moved into the car park first and settled its position. The other remained outside. Swann drove down the ramp to the lower levels and parked in a space opposite the Mondeo. They could see the Gunship from here and Swann scanned the area before he and Webb got out.

Webb moved round to the left-hand side. He peered at the nearside window and decided that best access was gained from there. Once inside, the swabbing would take about an hour. Meanwhile, Swann would fit the tracker. Webb slid his wire down the window to get to the lock, and then he heard something tinkle, a metallic sound at the back of the car. He looked at Swann. Swann looked at him, then they moved to the back of the car. It was pitch-black now, and Swann bent to his haunches and briefly shone his pencil light. Lying under the nearside rear wheel was a small tube of metal no more than a quarter of an inch across and three inches in length. He looked up at Webb. 'Canny bastard, isn't he.' A fine layer of dust coated the bumper, and Swann probed with his pencil light until he saw a tiny circle imprinted at the nearside end. He grimaced at Webb, upended the metal tube and replaced it in exactly the same spot.

'Wasn't there when I did the boot,' Webb hissed at him.

Swann nodded and placed the tube back on the ground. 'I'll put it back when we're done.'

They opened the passenger door and Webb set about swabbing the car. All at once his headset crackled in his ear. 'Underground from Pater. Possible X-ray. Repeat, possible X-ray. Stand by.'

He froze and looked at Swann. Somebody moving above ground. Swann forced the tightness from his chest and looked across the car park where one of the firearms officers had opened the car door.

'Stand by.' Again the call in their ears. 'Two males, walking towards the entrance. Still moving, still moving. Stand by.' Swann stared at the sloping entrance to the lower levels where thin light drifted.

The radio crackled again. 'Negative, Underground. Repeat. X-ray negative.'

Webb let breath slip audibly from his lips. 'Let's do the tracker and go,' he said. 'This geezer's got a picture of me with a hole punched in my head.'

# 9

August 4 dawned hot and sticky in central London. The sun lifted at 5 a.m. with no hint of cloud in the sky. By 9.30 the temperature was in the eighties and tempers frayed on the congested streets in and around Victoria. Cab drivers sat in their steaming black diesels, with their frustrated fares sweating it out in the back. Three men moved from separate directions towards the Roman Catholic cathedral in Westminster.

Tal-Salem flew in to Gatwick and took the Express straight to Victoria. He had been to London many times before, although the authorities, for all their vigilance at airports, never knew he was there. Pier-Luigi Ramas took a flight from Rome to Heathrow, and looked on in mockery as armed uniforms patrolled with Heckler & Koch carbines, sweating under the weight of their Kevlar body armour. Ibrahim Huella, dressed in the flowing black of a Greek Orthodox priest, took a taxi. He carried a brown leather briefcase and toyed with the crucifix that hung to his breastbone.

He arrived first, walking along the concourse that led to the steps of the cathedral, Scotland Yard only minutes away. He had glimpsed the armed officers of the Diplomatic Protection Group as he made his way up from Parliament Square. An armed police car funnelled a route slowly through the traffic, two white-shirted officers in the front and one in the rear. Huella had seen these cars before, as they blocked the entrance to Queen's House Mews when he made his quiet escape. Twin aerials and a yellow spot on the roof so they could be identified by helicopters. Each car carried two MP5 carbines in addition to the handguns of the officers inside, but he knew that at any one time there were only six of them on the street.

He walked into the cool of the cathedral and smiled at the elderly woman behind the desk. 'Good morning,' he said. 'Such a beautiful day.'

'Lovely, isn't it. Are you here for a holiday, Father?'

'Conference. I've just come to pay my respects.'

'I suppose you must be used to the heat.'

Again he smiled. 'Oh yes. I'm from a little town called Olympus on the island of Karpathos. Do you know it?'

'I've only been to Greece once,' she replied. 'Corfu.'

'To the north. Very beautiful. Very green.'

'Where is Karpathos exactly?'

'To the south, between Rhodes and Crete.'

'Ah. I've not been there.'

'You must visit. It is equally beautiful.' He smiled again and left her, wandering down the aisle. At the altar he paused, whispered a blessing then made his way to the Lady Chapel.

Ramas arrived next, wiping the moisture from his brow, in a collarless white shirt and faded Levis, a pair of dark brown Sebago Docksides on his feet. He paused to pick up a visitor's guide from the woman. 'The organ is tuned every Monday afternoon,' she told him.

'I shall avoid that time then.'

'Best,' she said, wrinkling her nose. 'Awfully noisy.'

Ramas moved down the aisle and took in the magnificence of the altar. He crossed himself and then wandered back, before moving to the Lady Chapel. In front of him an Orthodox priest sat in prayer. Ramas leaned forward. 'The candles are lit,' he said.

'No, my son, the candles are alight.' Huella sat upright again.

Within minutes they were joined by Tal-Salem, who took the chair in the row behind Ramas, two seats to the side. Salem carried a briefcase similar to the one that now rested against Huella's chair leg. Salem passed his case to Ramas, who laid it on the floor beside Huella's. They sat there the three of them for two minutes or more and then Huella bowed his head a final time, reached back for the second case and walked out of the chapel. Tal-Salem picked up the other case. It was heavier than the one he had been carrying.

☆

Tommy Cairns sat in the pub with his brother and watched the television screen above the bar. The lunchtime news was on. Earlier in the day he had received another phone call.

'We need a black taxi and a driver,' the woman had told him.

'Do you?' Cairns had been in bed at the time, his girlfriend lying next to him.

The caller was silent for a moment. 'Do I detect a note of hesitancy?'

'Did I say that?'

'Did you need to?'

'I want to meet with you.'

'Impossible.'

'Why?'

'It's not safe – either for me or for you.'

'What're you trying to achieve?'

'Why should that matter? You and I are on the same

side, Mr Cairns. You have concerns about the future as do we.'

'You're not English, are you.'

'Does that matter?'

'It might.'

'Action 2000,' she said, a hint of mockery in her tone. 'What exactly is your manifesto?'

'We're an army, not a political party. The politics is for others.'

'Clearly. Although they appear to have disowned you. I can no longer speak to Mr Ingram.'

'Ingram.' The word tasted sour on his tongue. 'Ingram has no stomach for a fight. All I'm asking you is what you're doing. This is my country. How do I know you're not just one of those Irish bastards.'

'Did the Irish claim the Soho incident?'

'No.'

'Then I'm not one of those Irish bastards, as you put it, am I.' She paused then. 'Listen, we find you useful but we *can* manage without you. The money appeared to satisfy you before. But perhaps I should just move on to somebody else. I dare say the Irish would help me.'

'I'm not saying we're out. I just want to know what you were trying to achieve with Soho?'

'If you stick around, you'll see.'

Cairns sighed. 'A cab then,' he muttered. 'Where and when?'

He looked at his brother now. Frank was older than him by four years but not as bright. He was bigger, sallow-faced with pockmarks beneath his eyes. His hair, like Tommy's, was not cropped, as was the norm with the more overt Nazis among them. Cairns had always thought the skinhead look was too easy for the police. They were brought up in the East End, Frank the hitter, Tommy the thinker. Their dad had been a fan of Oswald Mosley and had been active with Colin Jordan's National Socialist Movement in the 1960s.

While they were in prison for robbing a sub-post office in Kent, they met some activists from Combat 18, but Tommy didn't like the way they operated with other European groups. Another inmate talked to him about James Ingram's British Freedom Party, and its street-level offshoot Action 2000. When he and Frank got out, they went to an Action 2000 meeting and subsequently joined the BFP. Ingram gave them a job in one of his many building firms. That had been seven years ago. Neither of them had been nicked since and Tommy had risen to foreman in the yard, which comprised Action 2000 soldiers. He had also assumed the leadership.

Frank sat down again, spilling a little of the thin lager as he set the glasses before them. He ran a forefinger through the spillage and sucked it. His brother took two cigarettes from his packet of Embassy Regal and passed one to him. 'Charlie's late. Is he bringing Kenny?'

Tommy nodded.

'A cab.'

'Wait till they get here. We're the inner sanctum, Frank. We discuss this between the four of us.'

'What about the rest of the lads?'

'The rest are just soldiers. Any army has its officer corps. You've watched Sharpe, haven't you?'

His elder brother grinned and dragged knuckles across his mouth. 'So I'm an officer now, am I?'

'Non-commissioned, Frank. Non-commissioned.'

Oxley and Bacon arrived a few minutes later, bought beer and sat down at the table.

'So what's happening?' Oxley said, sipping the froth from his pint. He was tall and lean, three earrings in his left ear and a swastika tattooed under his right wrist.

Bacon lit a cigarette, spider's webs stretching in blue across the backs of his hands.

'They want us to work again,' Cairns told them.

'Great.' Oxley rubbed his hands together and Cairns squinted at him. 'Well, it's better than working, isn't it.'

'We don't know what they're doing,' Cairns said. 'This is our country. This is fucking England and she's a spic bitch or something.'

Oxley pulled a face. 'The guy I drove was a nigger, but the pay was fucking good. Who gives a shit, Tom?'

'We're a racist organization, Charlie. Action 2000 starts where all the other pricks leave off – Combat 18 and the National Front and all those other wankers who couldn't organize a piss-up in a brewery. If we're seen to be taking money from blacks or spics or Jews . . .'

'Arabs use Jews all the fucking time.' Oxley looked right back at him. 'We got a bucket load of money for hiring a car and picking up a nigger. He was only actually half a nigger anyway. We got another bucket load for buying four sheets of glass and storing it in a lock-up. Somebody's got money to chuck around, I say we take it.'

Cairns thought for a moment, lit an Embassy Regal and blew smoke rings. 'Ingram don't want to play no more,' he said.

'Good.' Bacon twisted his mouth at the corners. 'Guy's a sap, anyway.'

'Just us, then.'

'Why not?' Oxley swallowed half his pint in one mouthful. 'Like you told me, Tom, no sign of the Old Bill, is there.'

'OK. We're agreed.' Cairns sat back. 'They want us to nick a black cab and make a pick-up.'

'That's it?' Frank said.

'Yep. Kenny, you can steal it. Who wants to drive?'

'I will,' Frank said.

'Right. Just make sure you wear some fucking gloves.'

☆

Harrison eased himself inside Lisa and she moaned in the back of her throat. 'How's that, Miss Lady Mam?'

'Good.' She smoothed her hands over the skin of his back.

He stroked once, twice, three times. 'And that?'

'Better.' She dug her nails in hard.

He rolled off her a while later and she curled herself foetally into his body. The sweat poured off him, the dry heat of an Idaho August sapping the air from the room.

'You're a great fuck, Harrison.'

'Well thank you, Miss Lady Mam.'

'You're not as old as you thought you were.'

They lay in silence for a moment, then she said, 'You've never told me you love me.'

'Well, now why would I want to go spoil a thing with all that shit?'

She sat up and slapped his chest. 'What shit? What shit, Harrison?'

'There ya go, gal, getting all shitty on me.' He sat up and reached for his beer. He sucked at it and froth bubbled up the neck. 'I'm an old man, Guffy. What'd you want with love from an old loser like me.'

Lisa looked at him for a moment, her face bunched up, then she lay down and her fingers wandered between his thighs.

'I ain't that young,' he said.

They laughed and he lay back and stared at the rotating fan on the ceiling.

'That thing don't work real well, does it?'

'Never did.' She wiped perspiration from her hair. 'Will you ever take me home, honey?'

'Home?'

'Michigan.'

'You mean Marquette? Marquette isn't really home, just where I was for a while.'

'I'd love to go fishing on the lake.'

'Lake's best in the wintertime. When it's all froze over. I'll take you in the wintertime.'

He looked at her, breasts flattened against her chest, nipples hot and red and easy.

'You ever dream about 'Nam, Harrison?'

'Nope.'

'Not ever? I thought all you vets had dreams.'

'Not this one.' He looked at her through the darkness. 'I ain't been in a tunnel for thirty years and change. I ain't going in one again, so why the fuck should I dream about it.'

'You're lucky,' she said. 'I know other people who dream.'

He looked at the ceiling once more and eased her further under the crook of his arm.

'God, you're so skinny.' She poked him in the ribs with a finger.

'Always was, honey.'

'You don't eat properly is your problem.'

'No, but I sure as hell drink properly.' As if to emphasize the point he sucked again at the beer. 'How come you stuck to Guffy?' he asked her. 'After your divorce and everything?'

'My kid's name.' She shrugged. 'I didn't want a different name to my kid.'

'That's good.' He kissed her lightly on the forehead. 'I like that in a woman.'

They were quiet for a moment, then she said, 'Where d'you go at night?'

The question stung him. 'What?'

'Where d'you go at night? You don't poach. Sometimes I call you up after work and you aren't there.'

Harrison lay back and stared at the ceiling.

'You got another woman – that why you don't say you love me?'

Harrison shook his head. 'One's enough for me, Miss Lady Mam.' He sat up again. 'I walk, Guffy. Ask the doughnut man. He's seen me when he's been baking. Sometimes I stop by for coffee with him. When I can't sleep, I walk.' He looked her in the eye then. 'That way I don't dream.'

☆

Tal-Salem had the contents of the soft leather briefcase laid out on the bed of his hotel in Hyde Park. The map, the schedule and the guns. Two Beretta 40-calibre pistols complete with silencers. He took the twin magazines and the spare and laid them on the pillow. Lifting one, he flipped out the cartridges, counted them and pressed them back into place. He did the same with the other two clips, then he placed one into the butt of each gun and made sure the safety catches were on. In the ashtray beside the bed a joint sent spirals of smoke to the ceiling.

Ramas came through from the bathroom. 'The shower is free if you want it.' He picked up a Beretta and flipped out the magazine. 'Mine?'

'If you want. They're both the same.'

'They're never both the same.'

'I tell you what,' Salem said. 'You choose.' He took one last toke on the joint, inhaled and closed his eyes, letting smoke dribble from his nostrils. He swung his legs off the bed and went into the bathroom. Ramas ejected the cartridges from the magazine and counted them. Then he pressed each one back into place. He aimed the gun at himself in the mirror, flipped off the safety catch and aimed again. He twirled the gun on his forefinger and reset the catch. He put on a pair of jeans, stuffed the Beretta into the waistband and adjusted it. He took it out again, removed the magazine, replaced it, then tried the gun in the other side of the waistband. When he was satisfied he put it under the pillow of the bed where he was sleeping.

He sat in the chair and studied the map. The taxi would wait outside Victoria Station. Tal-Salem would be just inside the entrance. The cab would idle with its *For Hire* sign turned off. He would be on Victoria Street at three minutes to eleven. The meeting was due to break up at eleven. As soon as he saw them he would call Tal-Salem on the mobile, then he would wait for the cab. He looked at the photograph of the target. Jean-Marie Mace, French economist with Banque Nationale de Paris: forty-three years old, married with fifteen-year-old twin sons. Then he rolled on his back, stared at the ceiling for a few brief moments and went to sleep.

☆

Kenny Bacon and Charlie Oxley sat in Oxley's Ford Escort on the corner of Lea Conservancy Road. Bacon had just been into the newsagent's to buy cigarettes, one of which he now rolled as he sat squashed against the window in the passenger seat. Oxley was watching the black taxi cab parked across the road from the recreation ground. The cab was parked outside some newish maisonettes that backed on to the canal, at the bottom end of Hackney Marsh. Bacon shifted in his seat, lit the cigarette and blew smoke. 'He won't go out now,' he said. 'Let's go get a pint and come back later on.'

Oxley started the engine. 'Where we going to get a decent pint round here?' he moaned. 'Place is full of spades.'

'You ever shagged a spade, Charlie?'

'Once when I was drunk.'

They looked for a suitable pub. 'What's it like, then?' Bacon asked him.

'What?'

'Black woman.'

'Same as white, only you don't need to turn the lights off.' Oxley slapped his thigh.

They found a relatively black-free pub on Victoria Park Road and ordered a couple of pints. Still only half past ten. They drank three before wandering back to the car.

'You can get into this cab, then,' Oxley said.

Bacon looked sourly at him. 'You know me, Charlie. What can't I get into?'

'You ever been nicked?'

Bacon grinned like a wolf. 'No. Have you?'

'Not so far.'

Bacon stole the taxi just after midnight. He left Oxley in the Escort, moved quietly down the road and got in through the driver's window using a wire coat hanger. The cab was old: he had deliberately chosen an old one, watched the guy for a couple of days, silly fat bastard with his building-site bum hanging out of his trousers. He knew it would not be alarmed. Lying briefly under the car he disconnected the steering lock, then knocked out the ignition with a slide hammer. Seconds later the ancient diesel engine rumbled into life.

☆

At nine-fifteen, the delegates attending the DTI conference on the business implications of a single currency gathered in Victoria Street. Pier-Luigi Ramas watched as he made his way towards the Army & Navy store, where he browsed for half an hour.

Tal-Salem waited at the hotel until ten o'clock and then

made his way across Hyde Park, where already sun-worshippers were gathering on the banks of the Serpentine. He walked to Kensington Gore where he stood on the corner, briefcase in hand, and waited. Two cabs passed him and then an older one with a sallow-faced driver in his late thirties. He pulled over and wound the window down.

'Going to Victoria, sir?'

Tal-Salem climbed into the back.

He sat with his legs slightly apart, catching the glances cast in his direction via the rear-view mirror, as he took a pre-rolled joint from his pocket. He straightened out the ends before cupping his hand to the match. 'You know what to do?' he asked.

The driver nodded. 'Drop you at Sloane Square and then go to Victoria.'

Tal-Salem opened the briefcase, glanced inside and closed it again. The cab took him along Kensington Gore and then all the way down Sloane Street. Cairns stopped outside the station.

'Victoria,' Tal-Salem said. 'Wait for me there.'

'What're we going to do exactly?'

'Pick up another fare.'

Jean-Marie Mace sat with a glass of water at his elbow, his jacket draped across the chair behind him. 'It is important that we reassure businessmen throughout the whole of the Union that the introduction of the euro will be smooth and the transition to a single currency easy,' he said.

His counterpart from Barclays Bank cleared his throat. 'We've tried to be proactive here,' he said. 'But with the previous government's wait-and-see policy it wasn't easy. We have published business guidelines on the subject, however.' He glanced at some of his competitors from the other major clearers. 'We were the first, I believe, to do so.'

'Excuse me,' the man from the Department of Trade and Industry interrupted. 'We know what we hear on the television and from other parts of Whitehall over here,' he said. 'But how do you think having Monsieur Jospin as Prime Minister will affect things as regards the timing. I mean we're now in the target-testing period. It's this year that the convergence criteria will be assessed.'

Mace shrugged his shoulders. 'France is committed to the idea of a single currency. Chirac made some mistakes with his austerity measures, but before him the conservatives had to deal with Mitterrand. Now Jospin and his socialists will have to deal with Chirac. I don't foresee a problem.'

Pier-Luigi Ramas walked down Victoria Street and stopped at Pret A Manger. He bought a sandwich and cappuccino, and sat in the window looking up and down the road. Fifteen minutes before eleven. The meeting was a preliminary one and scheduled to last just the ninety minutes. He would wait until 10.57. It would take them a while to say their goodbyes and leave. Thirty delegates in all, quite a mêlée on the pavement. No doubt some of them would have ordered cabs, perhaps a few would have drivers. He took the photograph of the Frenchman from his pocket and studied it.

At five minutes to eleven he left Pret A Manger and started walking along Victoria Street. Now the thrill began to rise in his veins. Their target would come out of the DTI building diagonally across from the corner of Dacre Street, and on that corner an armed police officer stood guard. Diplomatic Protection Group. He knew them from his previous visits to London, the red police cars with the blue lights on top. Still, the danger was why he did this. If they were careful, nobody would even notice. He called Tal-Salem on the mobile.

Tal-Salem was waiting just inside the main entrance to Victoria Station. He could see Cairns in the cab, window down, smoking a cigarette, waving the other cabbies ahead of him. The phone rang. He pressed SND and lifted it to his ear. Pier-Luigi's voice.

'Five minutes. They will break up any time. Wait two minutes, then come.'

Tal-Salem looked outside at the congestion. 'We'll come now,' he said. 'Traffic.'

'OK, but do not arrive too early. Remember we have police on every corner.'

'All the more fun.' Tal-Salem weighed the briefcase in his hand. 'Remember the Israeli Embassy? They didn't fire a shot.'

'All the same.'

'I hear you.'

He walked out of the station, hailed Cairns, and got in the back of the cab. 'Victoria Street,' he said. 'Pull over where I tell you.'

Cairns swung round the traffic loop and stopped at the red light. Behind him Tal-Salem had opened the brief-case. He transferred the Beretta to his jacket pocket.

Ramas walked purposefully down the road, past the junction with Dacre Street and the DPG officer. He paused across the road from the DTI Conference Centre – smoked glass, black metallic pillars – and saw the gathering of suits, male and female, in the foyer. Any moment now the doors would open and they would start to file on to the pavement. He looked again across the road; the main doors were open now and the first few people were coming out. Some of them started walking up towards Victoria Station, others crossed the road for St James's Park tube. Mace stepped on to the pavement:

he would hail a taxi; he always travelled by taxi and his next appointment was in the City. Tal-Salem's cab came along Victoria Street and pulled over to the wrong side of the road. Mace smiled, having not even lifted his arm. From an upstairs window in the DTI building on the other side of the street, a secretary sipped coffee and watched the comings and goings below her.

Tal-Salem climbed out of the cab and handed five pounds through the window. Mace got in, then Tal-Salem got in behind him and slammed the door.

'Excuse . . .' Mace started. Then the other passenger door banged as Ramas got in from the road side. He glanced briefly at the policeman on the corner. He hadn't moved. Tal-Salem had a gun in Mace's ribs. Ramas drew the other one. For a moment Mace was paralysed, head twisted, staring for a second out of the rear window. Cairns pulled on to the street and slowed for Parliament Square.

At her window the secretary stared after the taxi. That man had got out, paid the driver and then suddenly got back in again. Then the man on the road. The last thing she saw was the face of the man in the middle. She shook her head and went back to her typing. Then she noticed a couple of people standing on the pavement outside the conference centre looking equally puzzled. One of them crossed the road. Getting up from her desk, she walked the length of the corridor to see her section supervisor.

Cairns drove the cab at speed. 'Where are you taking me?' Mace tried to control his voice.

Tal-Salem jabbed him with the gun, gloved hand, though the day was steaming. Cairns glanced in his rear-view mirror. 'Drive,' Ramas hissed at him. 'Take us off the main road.'

'What're you going to do?' Mace squealed.

Nobody answered him.

Cairns swung round Parliament Square, the traffic lights with him, and crossed Westminster Bridge. At the far end he headed a short way along Lambeth Palace Road, across the roundabout and on to the Albert Embankment. Then he turned left and right into Vauxhall Walk and harsh left into Jonathan Street. He crossed Vauxhall Street, then right and a sharp left, before another left into Wyndham. The next right was Aveline Street and a dead end. Cairns hit the brakes.

'Out.' Ramas waved the gun at him. 'Go. Now.' Cairns jumped from the driver's door, heart pumping in his chest. One look back at Mace's stricken face. For half a second he paused. Then he was running hard, back the way he had come.

Mace looked into the faces of his assassins. He knew now that's what they were. 'I have money,' he whispered, the words sticking to the back of his throat. 'I'm wealthy.'

Ramas just looked at him, worked the action on the silenced Beretta and backed out of the cab. Tal-Salem opened the other door.

'Please. I have a family. Please . . .' Mace lost control of his bladder and they all heard the faint trickling sound. He squirmed in the seat, lowering his back, raising both hands to his face. Ramas wrinkled his nose and shot him six times in the face and chest. Mace's body jerked, his hands wavering, fingers stretched and tight. Blood spurted from his clothing. He twisted, then arched his back, one hand to the holes in his face. Then he slumped to one side and slid down the back of the seat.

# 10

The direct line from the central command complex rang on the sixteenth floor. Campbell McCulloch was manning the base. 'SO13,' he said.

'Chief Inspector here. We have a reported kidnapping.'

Downstairs, McCulloch found Swann and Webb in the corridor. 'Kidnapping,' he said. 'DTI Conference Centre on Victoria Street.'

Swann stared at him. 'You're winding us up.'

McCulloch handed him the CAD.

They met Clements in the foyer and walked to Victoria Street. The Diplomatic Protection Group officer had a throng of people around him and had already called for back-up.

Clements spoke to him. 'SO13. What's up?'

'A man was kidnapped.' A short, dark-haired woman of about thirty, in a navy blue suit, stood with her hands on her hips.

'You saw this?'

'Yes.' A whole group of other people started speaking and Clements raised his palms in a gesture of calm. Swann took the woman by the elbow and gently eased her to one side.

'Detective Sergeant Swann,' he said. 'What did you see exactly?'

'I was in the foyer,' she said. 'The meeting had just broken up.'

'What's your name?'

'Mary Pearce. I work for Luxembourg Directe.'

Swann lifted one eyebrow. 'Can you tell me what happened?'

'The meeting had just broken up and a few people had already gone out to get cabs.'

'What meeting?'

'Banking/business initiative meeting. The euro, implications of a single currency on manufacturing business. Jean-Marie Mace,' she said. 'That's the man's name. He was bundled into a cab.'

☆

Jonathan Bell was dropping rubble down bin shutes from scaffolding on the corner of Loughborough Street and Wyndham. He saw the cab take the corner at speed and knew it was a dead end. Then first he saw one man sprinting back the way he had come, followed a minute or so later by two more. The second two separated, one of them moving quickly towards Kennington Lane, the other disappearing round the corner.

'Hey, Ben,' Bell called to the lad who was working with him. 'You see that?'

'What?'

'Those two blokes.'

'What two blokes?'

Bell looked back along the street, then he began to climb down the ladder.

'Oi,' Ben called after him. 'Where you going?'

'I'll be back in a minute.'

Bell walked round the corner and saw the cab at the dead end with both its rear doors open. He stopped. Then, almost careful where he placed his feet, he stepped closer. Ten feet away he could hear the faint pat pat pat as if a tap was dripping. He took another few paces, then he stopped and stared. Half slumped on the back seat, a man lay with one eye fixed on him. The eye was dull; there were holes in his face, and blood pushing out from his chest had smeared the seat and coagulated in a lumpy puddle. The dripping sound he could hear was the overflow that spattered on to the road. The man was breathing, just. Bell could see bubbles of blood against his lips.

☆

Swann wrote down what Mary Pearce had told him and felt Webb's hand on his shoulder. He took him to one side. 'The cab's just been found south of the river. White male, shot six times. Kennington are attending.'

Swann sprinted back to the Yard and flashing his warrant card at the guard he raced underground to the SO13 car-parking spaces and jumped in the Mondeo Estate. The engine whined as he revved hard and tore out of the car park. He stuck the blue light on the magnetic pod on the dashboard and flicked on the siren. Webb jumped into the passenger seat. 'Guv'nor's going to follow,' he said.

Swann hauled the steering wheel over and the car sped down towards Parliament Square. 'Fucking tank.' He cursed the weight of the thing. It was armour-plated underneath and fitted with a Talos alarm.

'This all there was?'

'Why else would I choose it?'

They drove along Lambeth Palace Road and on to the Albert Embankment. A minute later they were at the crime scene. Swann flipped off the siren but left the light whirling on the dashboard. Paramedics were lifting a bloodied figure on to a stretcher. Two uniforms from Kennington were there and two more were cordoning off the roads. Swann motioned to the paramedic nearest him as they covered the man with a blanket. He looked up and shook his head. Webb moved over to the cab and placed his warrant card in the top pocket of his shirt. One of the uniforms approached him.

'SO13,' Webb said.

'Shot six times,' the constable told him. 'My guv'nor's alerted AMIP.'

'No need,' Webb shook his head. 'This is one of ours.'

'You sure?'

'Oh, yes. I'm sure.'

Webb went to the back of the Mondeo and took out his gear. 'Everyone back behind the cordon, Jack,' he said. 'And get some help from the office, will you.'

Inside the back of the cab Webb found a blood-spattered, leather briefcase. He lifted it with two gloved fingers and laid it on the bonnet of the car. It was not locked and inside he found the French European Community passport of Jean-Marie Mace. Unrolling a large nylon bag, he stowed the case inside.

He walked over to Swann. 'That's a positive, Flash,' he said.

'Mace?'

'Yes.'

'Right.' Swann called the Reserve, then he stepped back beyond the cordon and went up to the lad who was standing with the uniform from Kennington.

'Jack Swann,' he said, shaking hands. 'Scotland Yard.'

'This is Jonathan Bell,' the uniform told him. 'He found the body.'

'He's dead, then?' Bell looked into Swann's face.

'Can't confirm that.' Swann looked beyond him to the constable, who coloured and moved away.

'He was still alive when I found him. I could see bubbles of blood on his lips. That means he was alive, doesn't it.'

Swann nodded slowly. 'Listen, Jonathan. I know this

has been one hell of a shock for you, but I need to know exactly what you saw. We'll sit in the car there and you can take as much time as you need.'

Bell told him what he had witnessed: the taxi coming round the corner at speed and turning into the dead-end street.

'Did you hear any shots?'

'No. But this bloke came running round the corner as if a pit bull was after him.'

'Bloke?'

Bell sighed. 'I was above him. Jeans, yeah, blue jeans and T-shirt. White T-shirt.'

'No jacket?'

'No.'

'Did you get a look at his face?'

'Not really. He had brown hair, I think, quite long.'

'Tall?'

'Ish.'

'Anything else?'

'God, he was really shifting. I only saw him for a moment.'

'Which way did he go?'

'Back up Loughborough Street.'

Swann flicked the remains of his cigarette out of the window. 'What happened after that?'

'Two others. I was watching this time and they were walking not running.'

'Go on.'

'Foreign. Well, not what you'd call British white anyway.'

'Can you describe them?'

Bell scrunched up his eyes, tasting his lip with his tongue. 'One had a beard,' he said. 'Both had black hair.'

'Clothes?'

'One without the beard had a white shirt and jeans, black jacket over his arm.'

'The other?'

'I don't know. Jeans, coat, yes, short jacket, I think.' Bell looked sideways at him then. 'He was carrying a briefcase, I think.'

'Thank you.' Swann radioed through the descriptions to the operations room. Within minutes every police officer in London would be looking for them. He took the rest of the statement and then went back to the tapes, where he watched Webb bending over a puddle on the pavement, the driver's side of the taxi. Water gushed from a broken overflow pipe above.

Webb had already called in the Serious Crimes Unit from Lambeth and DI Clements arrived. Swann joined the search team that scoured the immediate vicinity; Antiterrorist Branch officers together with as many as could be spared from Kennington and Southwark. Half an hour later, they found a 40-calibre Beretta in a dustbin on the corner of Kennington Lane.

☆

After he had got rid of his gun, Pier-Luigi Ramas got on the Victoria line at Pimlico and followed it north all the way to Finsbury Park. There, he changed to the Piccadilly line and continued to Cockfosters. Outside the station he watched for police activity, then crossed the road and went into a café.

Tal-Salem took a taxi to Waterloo Station. He walked into the main entrance, crossed the wide concourse and stepped into W.H. Smith's. A dark-skinned man in a brown suede jacket stood browsing through the motoring section of the magazines. At his feet was a Harrods shopping bag. Tal-Salem moved alongside him and, bending for a newspaper, placed the briefcase on the floor next to the shopping bag. He flicked through the paper, then replaced it on the shelf and picked up the Harrods bag.

He went down to the toilets at the far end of the station, paid his twenty pence and went into a cubicle. Inside the bag he found the traditional clothes of a Muslim. Quickly he changed, then, folding his own clothes carefully, he placed them inside the Harrods bag. Once he was ready he left the cubicle, washed his hands and went back upstairs. He bought a ticket for the Underground and went down to the Northern line. On the platform, he took a train north and changed at Warren Street for the Victoria line to Walthamstow. At Walthamstow station he climbed the stairs, then walked the length of the car park until he found the blue Omega Estate with a roll-back flap over the boot. His wife was waiting for him, dressed in black with a veil across her face. Tal-Salem greeted her, then climbed behind the wheel. She got into the passenger side, and from the glove compartment took out his driving licence with the home address in Birmingham.

He drove through traffic to the North Circular Road and was stopped by a police officer on a motorcycle.

'Good afternoon, sir,' the officer said as Tal-Salem wound down the window.

'Good afternoon.' Tal-Salem smiled at him, showing white teeth between the strips of his beard. 'Is anything the matter? The car is new. There shouldn't be anything wrong with it.'

The officer looked at him. 'Just routine, sir. Is this your car?'

'Yes. I've only just bought it.'

'Can I see the documents?'

'But of course. My dear?' Tal-Salem spoke to his wife, who went again to the glove compartment. She produced a registration document and insurance certificate and handed them to her husband. Tal-Salem took his driving licence from his wallet and passed everything through the window. The policeman went round to the back and checked the number plate.

'From Birmingham?' he said.

'Yes.' Salem nodded to the Harrods bag behind him. 'We have friends here in Walthamstow and my wife did a little shopping in town.'

The officer glanced at the bag on the back seat. 'What've you got in the boot?'

'Nothing.'

'Would you open it for me, sir?'

'But of course.' Tal-Salem got out of the car and walked round to the back. 'There,' he said, spreading his fingers at the empty boot.

'Thank you, sir,' the officer said. 'Sorry to have bothered you. Have a pleasant journey.'

Tal-Salem smiled. 'Perhaps you could help me there,' he said. 'I understand you're privy to the traffic problems.'

The officer shook his head. 'Only in London, sir.'

'Ah. Of course.' Tal-Salem thanked him, took back the documents and got behind the wheel.

He drove round the North Circular to Southgate and from there up through Oakwood to Cockfosters. Pier-Luigi Ramas drank coffee and saw him pull up outside the station. Dabbing his mouth with a napkin, he left the café and crossed the road. Tal-Salem reached over and opened the back door. The seats were already down and Ramas slid straight into the boot. Tal-Salem lifted the seats behind him. In Birmingham, his wife dumped her veil and robes, then caught a train for London.

☆

Harrison lay on the couch, one arm crooked behind his head, and contemplated the loneliness in his gut. Two years this time, four years before that. He should've grown used to it by now. Ninety-seven per cent of the undercover agent's story is true, but the final three per cent – that lie was all that really counted. Many UCAs were married and so had a balancing factor in their lives. Tom Kovalski had voiced the lack of anything in Harrison's life as a concern, but Harrison had never gone native and he didn't intend to now. But it was true, there was no life other than the lie he wound about himself for the benefit of people who trusted him. Not for the first time he vowed this would be the last undercover job he did. He was forty-eight years old and had found some kind of something with Lisa Guffy. In his weaker, more fanciful moments, he entertained thoughts of leaving Passover, leaving the Bureau even, going back to the lake and taking Guffy with him.

He looked at his watch and switched on the radio. He tuned it to the AM frequency and set the tape rolling. Salvesen was preaching up in Salmon tonight, in the newly built church he had established there. He always broadcast his sermons and Harrison had made a habit of taping them. He had the sound low while the actual service part was broadcast, the singing and handclapping. He couldn't stand the 'leaping and wailing' brigade, as he called them. But it was not long before the music died away and he twisted the volume control up higher. He took a menthol Merit from his shirt pocket and lay on his back with his eyes closed. Outside he could hear the scrape and rattle of Little T on his skateboard.

There was always a certain amount of trepidation as he awaited Salvesen's voice. It was deep and warm and he could imagine thousands of disaffected Americans tuning in to him right across the country. He could imagine the scene. He had been to the church in Salmon, just for a poke around one day, white clapboard outside and deep mahogany inside. Salvesen had built a traditional pulpit in the style of the fire and brimstone churches of the Old West, and Harrison visualized him now in his white suit, standing with ham fists massed over the edge of the lectern.

'We shall continue this evening with our studies of the prophet Daniel,' Salvesen began. 'This book of the Bible, as you may recall, was written in the sixth century before the birth of our Lord and Saviour. But there are some so-called scholars around the world who would have us believe that Daniel was actually written only one hundred and sixty-five years BC. That, I might say, is a most convenient way of negating his early prophetic statements and thus rendering those which apply to latter years null and void.' He broke off and cleared his throat. 'I might also add that there are significantly more Bible scholars who believe, as I do, that the book *was* laid down in the sixth century BC, about twenty-six hundred years ago, if my math serves me correctly.'

Harrison stubbed out his cigarette, then got a beer from the refrigerator. He sucked on it, leaning against the door to the trailer.

'Chapter two,' Salvesen went on, 'is when Daniel first saw visions of the future kingdoms of the world. We will discuss this in much greater detail when we come to what I, and many others, consider to be *the* most important passage in the Old Testament – Daniel, chapter seven. But, suffice to say, tonight will be a good introduction to what must surely come to pass.' Again, he hesitated for a moment. 'I know I have many listeners all across the nation. Oh, a lot of people will be out drinking and suchlike on a fine summer's evening such as this. But there are, I may tell you, enough good and true Americans who still believe in virtue and the moral texts of the Bible.

'While the rest of the country sleeps the dull slumber of secularity, we must remember it is us who keep the vigil. Think of that, my friends; the vigil, the watch, the future of this great country, the future of the free world in the hands of God-fearing Americans like you and me. Those of us who remain true to our founding fathers and the God-given constitution.'

'God bless America,' Harrison muttered into his bottle.

'Daniel. I digress. In chapter two, Daniel comes forth as the only true adviser to Nebuchadnezzar, King of Babylon. We read how the king had a dream which troubled him greatly. He summoned his so-called advisers and asked them to tell him what he had dreamed. If they did that, then they would truly be able to tell him what it meant. He was sick and tired of them telling him lies, so he figured anyone who could give him what he asked for must be a true prophet, and thus adviser to the kingdom. You have to remember that the Israelites were under the dominion of Babylon then, and Daniel, of course, was an Israelite.

'The advisers told the king that what he asked was impossible. Verse twelve tells us that the king flew into a rage and ordered the execution of all of them, including Daniel. Daniel prayed to the Lord for mercy and the Lord, in his infinite wisdom, showed Daniel what the king had dreamed. Thus, in verse twenty-four, we learn that Daniel was able to go to Arioch, the king's commander, and tell him to advise the king not to execute anyone, for he, Daniel, would not only tell him what he dreamed but also what it meant.

'In verse thirty-one, we read:

Thou, O king, sawest, and behold a great image. This great image, whose brightness was excellent, stood before thee; and the form thereof was terrible.

This image's head was of fine gold, his breast and his arms of silver, his belly and his thighs of brass.

His legs of iron, his feet part of iron and part of clay.

Thou sawest till that a stone was cut out without hands, which smote the image upon his feet that were of iron and clay, and brake them to pieces.

Then was the iron, the clay, the brass, the silver, and the gold, broken to pieces together, and became like the chaff of the summer threshing floors; and the wind carried them away, that no place was found for them: and the stone that smote the image became a great mountain, and filled the whole earth.

This is the dream; and we will tell the interpretation thereof before the king.

Thou, O king, art a king of kings: for the God of heaven hath given thee a kingdom, power, and strength, and glory.

And wheresoever the children of man dwell, the beasts of the field and the fowls of heaven hath he given into thine hand, and hath made thee ruler over them all. Thou art this head of gold.

And after thee shall arise another kingdom inferior to thee, and another third kingdom of brass, which shall bear rule over all the earth.

And the fourth kingdom shall be strong as iron: forasmuch as iron breaketh in pieces and subdueth all things: and as iron that breaketh all these, shall it break in pieces and bruise.

And whereas thou sawest the feet and toes, part of potters' clay, and part of iron, the kingdom shall be divided; but there shall be in it of the strength of iron, forasmuch as thou sawest the iron mixed with miry clay.

And as the toes of the feet were part of iron, and part of clay, so the kingdom shall be partly strong, and partly broken.

And whereas thou sawest iron mixed with miry clay, they shall mingle themselves with the seed of men: but they shall not cleave one to another, even as iron is not mixed with clay.

And in the days of these kings shall the God of heaven set up a kingdom, which shall never be destroyed.'

Harrison was interrupted by a knock on the door. Hurriedly, he switched off the tape and found Danny Dugger waiting on the stoop, Dodge Dakota baseball hat set back on his head.

'Hey, Harrison. You coming down to the hotel to shoot some pool?'

Harrison looked at him. Danny's Shoshone girlfriend had left him the previous week. She worked up at Atkinson's Food Hall in Westlake and had gotten involved with some other guy. Danny had figured something was going on because she started not coming home. He had followed her one night and caught them in bed together. Rough on any man, that. He stood there with his hands in his pockets, looking up. Harrison switched out the light in his trailer and climbed into his truck.

☆

It was almost midnight when Swann fitted the key in the lock and wearily climbed the stairs. The children were both sound asleep. He tiptoed into their room and lifted the sheet over Charley, who had got herself all tangled up. The pig she called Teddy was lying on the floor. He kissed Jo on the forehead and she wrinkled her nose but did not wake. Then he went upstairs. There was one message on the answerphone. Pia. He called her back and a sleepy voice answered.

'Hi, darling. It's me.'

'God, Jack. It's late.'

'Yeah. Sorry. Busy day.'

'I heard. Mary Pearce from our bank. She was on the news.'

'I spoke to her.'

'I know. As soon as I heard about it, I phoned her.'

'You told her it was me who spoke to her?'

'Yes. Is that a problem?'

'Not at all. Does she work with you?'

'Different sector.'

He yawned. 'What've you been up to, anyway? Whose money have you been spending?'

'I don't spend it, Jack. I invest it.'

'Yeah, right. Sorry.'

'You sound tired. Get some sleep.'

'I will. Listen, all this means I'm going to be pretty busy.'

'Don't worry. I've got to go away again myself. The States, remember I told you.'

'Yeah. How long for?'

'Week or so. I love you, Jack.'

'Yeah. I love you too.'

That night he dreamed. Why, he did not know. Since he had been climbing again he had not dreamed so often. But that night – perhaps it was the shooting, the harsh brutality of sudden and violent death; perhaps it was because he knew that out there a spectre was slowly beginning to haunt them and no one had any idea why. That morning, the picture of him with a bullet hole in his head was brought home with a stone-cold clarity, when he saw Jean-Marie Mace lying on the stretcher with his face ripped open. Whatever the reason, he dreamed.

☆

Bivouaced high on the Diamir face of Nanga Parbat in the Himalayan mountains, Swann coaxed gas out of the stove for soup. Next to him in the tiny Gore-tex tent, Steve Brady lay back in his sleeping bag. Swann nursed the soup till it steamed and then they shared it, each dipping a spoon from either side of the billycan. Outside, the wind blew in a hoarse rasp and drifting snow pressed at the flimsy sides of the tent. Neither of them spoke. Today had been difficult, the weather closing about them as they climbed hard from the Mummery Rib, where Ellis and Bowen had pitched the second camp. They had been first choice to attack the summit at the south shoulder, but this morning Ellis's knee was worse and, without him, Bowen was not keen to climb.

The party had been split like that right from the off. It was their expedition – Ellis and Bowen, two seasoned climbers from Derbyshire. There had been four of them originally, attempting the Diamir face alpine-style, having gained permission the previous year and booked the time for late July. Ellis and Bowen were also police officers; Bowen, a uniformed inspector from Derby itself, and Ellis, a traffic officer from Matlock. They had been climbing partners for years. Four weeks before the expedition was due to set out, the other two dropped out. Frantically, Bowen had advertised for replacements in the police magazine. Steve Brady, from 3 Area Major Incident Pool, had seen the advert and phoned Jack Swann. Swann had ice-climbed in Scotland and in the French Alps, but had no experience of anything vaguely like an 8000-metre peak in the Himalayas. It was the chance of a lifetime, however, and he jumped at it.

They had met Ellis and Bowen for the first time at Heathrow Airport, just as they were about to fly out. It had been a good meeting, but pretty quickly the divisions between the four of them were obvious. Bowen was forty-three years old, Ellis forty-one, both veterans of many an expedition to the Himalayas. Bowen had climbed Hidden Peak three years before and had made a solo attempt on Everest by the Northwest Ridge. He had only been beaten by the weather. Ellis had climbed with him on K2 in Pakistan and had also attempted Lhotse. He was well known for his solo ascent on the north face of the Eiger and his exploits in Patagonia. In comparison, Swann and Brady were rank amateurs, but they were younger and full of enthusiasm.

Late July had been full of storms and for a week the four of them were marooned in their tents at base camp, watching thousands of tons of snow billow in crashing waves over the Mummery Rib, which was the planned route of ascent. But on the first day of August the weather broke, the sun rose above the summit and the mountain was encased in a blaze of heat which could be felt on the valley floor. Swann got up at first light, crawled out of the tent and pulled on his boots. Sun reflected on the Rupal face, firing the rock in crystal pink across the Merkl Gully. Further down, it blackened ominously where it was cast again in shadow. Swann stood with his hands on his hips as Brady joined him, taking a piss right there through the zip in his salopettes. From the other tent, Bowen and Ellis appeared, and Bowen's chapped, brown face stretched into a smile. 'Get set, you two, we're climbing.'

They had made good progress and walked steadily up the glacier from base camp. On the first night, they camped on the freshly packed snow that only a day earlier had sprayed over the Rib above them. The night was still and calm, very cold, but as silent as any Swann could remember. The following morning, they were climbing as the first threads of dawn streaked the Diamir face. Awesome, was the word Swann thought of, this silent, lonely place, where all was rock and snow and great walls of packed ice as high as 4500 metres in places. Two parties, alpine-style. Swann belayed Brady and seconded up after him, walking roped together on the easier stretches. Bowen and Ellis were ahead of them and as the day wore on the distance between them increased.

It had been bitterly cold when they started, but as the day grew, the sun beat on them from a perfectly cloudless sky. Swann found himself sweating under the weight of his gear, feet swimming in moisture inside his double plastic boots. By late afternoon on the second day, they caught up with Bowen and Ellis at the bivouac they had set just above the Mummery Rib. It was there that they discovered Ellis's crampon problem. The bail bar on the toe had gone and he had fallen fifty metres from just above the Rib. Bowen had broken his fall and Ellis came to a halt before the Rib wall itself, but his knee was badly twisted and his chances of making the summit were small to non-existent.

Swann had sensed something was wrong as soon as he and Brady got there. Given the distance the two older men had gained on them during the day, their second camp could've been an awful lot higher. The sun bounced off the mountain side, half blinding him even behind the lenses of his snowglasses. He coiled in the rope and watched Bowen apply some strapping to Ellis's knee.

Nobody spoke, there was nothing anyone could say. Ellis cursed his crampons and his own stupidity for falling, but there it was, his attempt on the mountain was over. That night, they all crouched in the bigger tent and discussed the forced change in plans.

'What d'you want to do?' Bowen looked at Brady first,

the more seasoned of the two of them. Swann sat on his haunches and sipped coffee.

'Go for it,' Brady said. He glanced at Swann. 'What we came for, wasn't it.'

Bowen tasted cracked lips and looked at Ellis. 'I'm going to get him down.' He looked at them again. 'Unless you need me to stay up here for back-up.'

Swann looked at Ellis's knee. 'That's going to swell and swell,' he said quietly. 'If you don't get him down tomorrow, you'll be struggling. Besides, this weather isn't going to hold for ever.'

Bowen placed his hands behind his head. 'You sure you're up to it, Swann?'

Swann gazed evenly back at him. 'What do you think?'

Bowen relaxed then and patted him on the arm. 'Sorry,' he said. 'Disappointment. We've planned this trip for years.'

Swann let his hackles drop and he looked over at Ellis. 'If you want, I'll take you down,' he said. 'Let Pete go up with Steve.'

'No.' Bowen shook his head. 'You go for it, Jack. We're partners, so are you two. It wouldn't be right.'

Swann nodded and then he and Brady went back to their own tent.

They lay in the darkness, not able to sleep. The wind had risen a fraction and the temperature was falling steadily. Swann wriggled the neck of his sleeping bag higher, working his head deeper into the hood.

'Tomorrow night, Jack, we'll be just below the Merkl Gully,' Brady said. 'I tell you now, that's as steep as you'll have climbed at any kind of altitude.'

Swann gazed blankly at the gently flapping walls of the tent. 'I'm up for it,' he said.

That was the previous night, and now they shared soup, with the weather gone bad on them once more. By now,

Ellis and Bowen would be off the mountain. Going down the slopes around the Rib was a lot easier than going up. It was the descent from the summit itself that was the difficult bit. The wind howled right outside the tent. Swann looked at his partner. 'I've never known weather to change so quickly.'

'That's how it goes up here.' Brady finished his soup and rubbed a gloved hand across his face. 'We'll have to see how it is in the morning.'

'The storm could last a week.'

'It could.' Brady grinned then and patted him on the arm. 'It won't, though. I'm going to climb this fucking hill, if it kills me.'

Swann remembered sleeping only fitfully that night. This was the same route that the Messner brothers had taken in 1970. Only Reinhold came back.

The first thing he noticed when he woke was the quiet. Through the walls in the tent the day looked grey, but the wind had gone. He sat up and saw Brady at the door on his hands and knees.

'What's the weather like?' Swann asked him.

Brady looked back over his shoulder. 'I don't know yet.' He pulled on his outer boots and stepped outside. Swann, albeit reluctant to leave the relative warmth of his sleeping bag, followed him.

Cloud was everywhere, grey and black in places, and pressing low against the peaks and spires all about them. Swann stood on hard-packed snow, frozen solid by the overnight drop in temperature. Brady was looking directly upwards. Swann followed his gaze and saw the summit a thousand or so metres above them. Brady turned to him.

'We can make it and back today,' he said. 'No wind, Jack.'

'Shitloads of cloud, though, Steve. It could start snowing any time.'

'It's either that, or we go down.'

Swann scanned the summit ridge again and felt a sudden rush of adrenalin. 'Go on, then,' he said.

They got rope and ice axes and strapped on crampons. Swann packed a little food, but no stove. They had water from the snow they had melted last night, and left the tent behind. Attack the Merkl Gully now, reach the summit, and then down again before nightfall. Tomorrow they could check the weather and take all the time they needed on the descent.

'Jack,' Brady said as they were about to rope up. 'Don't forget the camera.'

Swann patted the pack strapped between his shoulder blades and then they started walking up the slope to the bottom of the Merkl Gully. It was almost vertical. Axes and points all the way, 150-foot pitches with ice screws for protection.

They climbed well, the sun did not come out and the day remained a frostbitten chill. But they were invigorated by the summit shoulder that drew steadily closer with each kick on the wall. Brady led and Swann watched the smooth ease of his movement. He followed at some speed for his relative lack of experience, and he could not get over the sensation of awe: it was not just the height, but the utter desolation of this place. Below them, somewhere on the glacier, Ellis and Bowen were back at base camp, but up here they could have been the only two people in the world.

Late morning, however, the weather closed in on them. Brady was almost at the top of the gully when the clouds just lowered on top of him. Damp and colder than the day, Swann felt the moisture testing the scant protection offered by his Gore-tex suit. It was as if the mountain all of a sudden grew weary of the irritation on its flanks, and sought to be rid of them. Swann had seen nothing like it: it grew noticeably darker and a knot of anxiety twisted round his intestine. Brady had tied off and was beckoning him up. Swann let go the rope and swivelled the axe heads round, gripping the shafts in heavily mittened hands. He kicked into the ice and a piece splintered, as if serving him with a warning. He paused, checked his footing and kicked in again. Good holds this time; he dug at the ice with the curved picks of his axes and started into the cloud. Halfway up, he lost sight of Brady and climbed by the tightening length of the rope. He crested a ramp and there was Brady, looking down from above him. He was perched on a ledge, screwed into the wall, carefully paying the rope through his hands. Swann could see he was shivering. He pulled up on to the ledge and rested.

'We can't make it,' he uttered as soon as the breath returned to him.

Brady looked up. The summit was shrouded in cloud now. 'We can, Jack. The summit's just above us.'

Swann looked up, then down between his feet. He could no longer see anything, the gully hung with tendrils of smoke-coloured cloud.

'It's going to snow,' he said.

'Maybe not.' Brady's eyes were shining, his breath coming in bursts of steam. 'We can do it, Jack. Nanga Parbat. You and me.'

Swann looked to his left and saw the cloud lowering steadily. They were close to 8000 metres and the air was very thin. He could hear the slow roar of breath trying to escape his lungs. 'Steve, we need to go back.'

☆

He woke up and saw Brady beaten and bloodied, standing at the end of the bed. He screamed, high pitched like a woman. Somebody started to cry. And then he realized it was Joanna, his daughter. He recovered himself and sat up, reaching out both his arms for her. She pushed against him, sobbing. 'I'm sorry, darling. I was dreaming,' he said. 'I'm sorry, I didn't know it was you. I didn't hear you come in.'

He held her close to him then, near to tears himself while her own sobbing subsided.

'I couldn't sleep,' she said. 'I woke up and I was frightened.'

He took her into bed with him and held her till she was asleep, then he carried her back to her own bed.

Back on the couch in the living room he lay down and closed his eyes, trying to ignore the cramps round his gut. He saw the mountain, felt again the sudden, terrible weight as Brady lost his grip. He threw off the bedclothes and stood naked in the middle of the floor. The same point, the same point every time he dreamed. The clarity of it, as if a film were replaying again and again in his head. Everything was still all right, then. But the breath choked in his throat and the air in the room seemed suddenly rancid and still. Pulling on a pair of shorts, he climbed the steps to the roof. The windows of the old MI5 building were cold and dark and empty, like so many sightless eyes.

Guffy was working all weekend in the diner and Harrison had told everyone he was going fishing at his favourite spot a few miles along the East Fork of the Salmon, south of Willow Creek. Friday night he had a beer with Junior and Big John, the Italian, in the Silver Dollar. They sat at the far end of the bar, bullshitting while the band set up in the corner. 'You want company this weekend?' Junior asked him.

'Nope.' Harrison glanced at him. 'No offence, Junior, but I always fish on my own. I'm around folks all week long and I like to get off on my own.'

The doors flapped and Jesse walked in with Slusher and Wingo. He eyed Harrison darkly, but did not speak. Outside, the harsh crackle of engines split the air, and Harrison slid off his stool. Dark now, past ten and the evening cool, with a breeze blowing in from the mountains. From the stoop, he could see Fathead and Randy Miller parking their Harleys.

'Hey, Harrison. What's up?' Fathead slapped him on the shoulder, almost spilling his beer, as he walked into the bar.

Harrison left at eleven and watched Tyler Oldfield, one of the Passover marshals, cruise the length of Main Street. Rodriguez and a couple of his friends were sharing an illicit bottle of Cuervo on the steps of the Mexican Import Shop.

'Hey, Harrison. You wanna drink?'

Harrison held up his hand. 'Not tonight, Rodriguez.' He glanced at the others and spotted Pedro looking sorry for himself. He had just been stopped by the sheriff for driving without privileges, the sixth time it had happened and he was looking at three years in the pen. 'Don't let the cops see you drinking on the street, Pedro,' he said, 'or your three will be five to ten.'

At midnight he packed his fishing gear into the truck and left the trailer park. He rolled north through Westlake, the streets quiet. He knew the police patrolled every half-hour along Main Street, not that it mattered much at the weekend. He'd told enough people in town where he would be till Sunday. Next to him on the seat, he had a small canvas bag containing rations and water for the weekend, together with a selection of polythene bags and toilet tissue.

He smoked one cigarette after the other, Merit, then Marlboro, never pulling out the packs, just feeling for one in his shirt pockets, sticking it against his lip and lighting it with his ancient brass Zippo. He needed his fill of nicotine for two reasons: number one, an undercover agent never got over his fear – every time he went covert, he was nervous; number two, these would be the last smokes until Sunday. In downtown Westlake he turned left off Main Street, out of town and then on past the scattered ranches until he came to the dirt road that led to Dugger's Canyon.

The track took him a mile or so into the hills before sweeping round in a circle and down into the canyon itself. Colorado Gulch was its real name, but everyone in town knew it as Dugger's Canyon, being as how the Dugger family had mined it for years. The trail dipped down to the river and the bridge that Danny and his father had built. He pulled off before then and drove the truck into the clearing where Chief had built his hogan. There was good fishing just north of here and, if anybody asked, Harrison would tell them he changed his mind at Galena Summit. This weekend Chief was working on his pictures for the buyer in Boise, and Harrison knew that Danny would not come up here. The old Magdalena mine was closed down, although the entrance still gaped where the roof had partially collapsed. One night when he was drunk in the Westlake Hotel, Danny had mapped the tunnels for Harrison. The hogan was Navajo or Hopi, Harrison could never remember which. Chief had spent a year down in Arizona on the reservation during his wanderlust days and had a spell living in one. Wood-pole construction with a mud roof, cool in summer and well insulated in winter. It was better than hauling a tent for hunting.

He left the truck, hid his fishing gear in the brush and shouldered the canvas bag. In the depth of the cotton-woods, he stripped the top sod of earth from his keep hide and dug down through the loose dirt to the sealed cooler inside. He took out his spare cam' suit and gilly and dressed quickly; first, the two-piece summer cam' suit, not quite desert-style but close. The gilly he put on last and it fell to the ground at his feet, the hood down over his face and flaps over his hands. If he stood still, he was part of the hillside.

From the hide he also took his Glock 17 automatic pistol, garrotte and his two knuckle knives. These he stashed under the gilly and then lifted out his camera with the macrozoom lens. He had a cover sheet made and ready at each of his lay-up points, so that wherever he watched from the hillside the sun would not catch the lens. Down in the bottom of the box, he had an MP5 with retractable stock, ten clips of ammunition along with three rolls of fishing line, and head-fixed, night-vision glasses which he avoided wearing whenever he could. He also kept an NVG telescope, extra rations and his distraction box, just in case things got really nasty. At the very bottom of the cooler was an infrared suppressive suit. Everything was wrapped in plastic to keep the moisture out, though the cooler had a pretty good seal. When he was ready he stowed what he needed in the canvas bag, slipping in two extra rolls of film and finally a motion sensor, which he would set in place while he was watching and remove when he was gone. The last thing he did was smear his face and hands with cam' cream.

Once his eyes were as accustomed to the darkness as they were going to get, he set off. The country was rugged, the trails pitted and full of loose rock and shale. His eyes were good. Six months of crawling tunnels in Vietnam had set him up for life. Yes, you could use a flashlight down there and most of the time you did; but there were those occasions when Charlie was so close you could almost hear the breath break from his body, then you crawled in darkness.

Compared to the blackness underground, open country under a flat and full sky was daylight. The world was grey/brown rather than black and Harrison had hiked this trail many times before. The going was steep at first. He pressed a path between the hills, cutting through groves of aspen and Douglas fir trees. He almost stepped on a chukar, and in the trees, crows called as he passed. He startled a group of elk and had to watch for the bull as he skittered away from the trail. Birds lifted from the branches of trees, with the sudden flurry of movement. That was bad, moving too fast. Birds flying like that could alert somebody looking. He recalled the night back in June when Drake's kid had been so vigilant.

A mile into the canyon, he came to the outcrop of reddy brown rock that lifted in a small bluff to the north-east of the trail. He could spot it from some distance as the sky greyed above his head, a slim fissure of a cave edging fifteen feet into the rock. Sometimes he would use this as a sleeping hole if Jesse had troops on the hill. In the roof, bats hung in clusters. Harrison hated bats. They were OK scuttling about in the open, but when you disturbed their sleep they were frantic, screeching and crying and fluttering into your face with wings of moist leather. He moved more slowly now, too visible on open ground: he could never be completely sure that they did not patrol at night. In the daytime, they used three-man teams on the perimeter of the compound itself. Whatever Salvesen was planning, he was paranoid about people close to his land. Harrison checked his watch, almost three o'clock. He was careful, eyes peeled, ears pricked for sounds which shouldn't be there. He wished it would rain or the wind would blow instead of this dead calm.

He had lay-up points at height and distance intervals mainly on the hillside to the back of the compound. He moved from one to the other at a snail's pace, spending a good few hours in each. In summer, Salvesen entertained guests on a specially seeded lawn with trees growing up against the inner fence. The compound was accessed by the dirt track that ran for a mile between the foothills all the way from the highway. You had to cross a small wooden bridge over the river, and there Harrison had hidden passive infrared sensors to count vehicles crossing. When he couldn't use his eyes to see what kind of traffic was moving up and down the highway, he checked his car counter. Mucho activity meant mucho surveillance, which, given the size of the town and the general interest in other people's business, was not that easy. There are only so many weekends in which a man can be invisible.

It was three-thirty when he moved to the top of the gulch and settled in his first observation point. High on the hilltop, which overlooked the grassy canyon where Salvesen had his compound, the gulch saddled between two outcrops of rock. Underneath the one on the right flank, an overhang jutted about three feet and Harrison used it to lie under. A dried-up gopher hole pitted into the rock, and it was here he stowed the first of his camera hides.

He took the camera and binoculars from his bag and pulled the chicken-wire shade from the hole. He unravelled it, pulling the wire out on to the prongs, which he set deep in the earth. The covering was the same colour strips of cloth that he used on the gilly suit. When it was set up, not only did it protect his lens from reflection but it kept the sun from his face. The cam' cream had dried now and when it got light the sun would mush it into a sticky coating on his skin. He lay on his side, under the lip of rock, and set his camera on to the mini tripod. The lens was extendable, but had been adapted by FBI scientists for ease of transportation. When everything was ready, he rolled himself in the gilly suit and slept the rest of the night.

He woke with the sun warming his face. Three men with dogs were walking the outer perimeter fence, five hundred yards below him. The fence was twelve feet high with razor wire on the top. He recognized Jesse's mottled green baseball hat. He adjusted his position; below him, in the foothills, cattle grazed. A couple of men on horseback were rounding them up, hats turned to the sun. If he listened hard, he could hear their whistles. He watched as they gathered the stray steers, then drove them ahead, down the slopes towards the outer rim of the compound. Harrison lay there until the foot patrol was gone and the horsemen had driven the stock far beyond the front of the compound. Then he moved, crabbing his way down the hill a few feet at a time. Far in the distance, clouds gathered and he knew he would get wet tonight.

It took him over an hour to make his second lay-up point, about a hundred yards further down the hill. There, he had the benefit of a rising bank of grass with some scrub sage tightly curled in clumps. Wrapped around one was his second chicken-wire shade. Again he unwound it, no sudden movements, everything slow and easy. Now and then he would peer back up the hillside to make sure he was not observed from above. He could see a gathering of tiny figures in the backyard of the compound. The house stood tall and white against the sun. The huge marquee, where Salvesen held church services by special invitation only, took up half the spare ground at the back. Beyond it, to the right as Harrison looked, was the stretch of seed grass where the barbecue area was. He could see a tendril of smoke rising towards the sky. Now he set up his camera for the second time, adjusted the zoom lens and watched. It wasn't as close as he would like and he knew that he would have to make the final observation point if he was to get any decent shots. The compound was busy, people thronging here and there. Harrison imagined pitchers of lemonade, and the chicken and racks of ribs hissing in their own fat.

It was almost ten and he knew that a half-hour from now another patrol would check the outer perimeter. From his forwardmost lay-up point, they would still be fifty yards in front of him. There was no wind, so the chances of one of the dogs sniffing him out was remote. It remained a chance, however, and he had to decide whether to move now or wait till they had passed. He decided that time was on his side, so he settled down to wait. At exactly ten-thirty the second patrol came by, different men this time and the pit bull was running free. It gambolled away from them, running back and forth, up and down the hill, no more than twenty-five feet from where he would have been lying. His mouth dried at the thought.

At the forwardmost lay-up point he settled in for a long stint, propped up on his elbow under the protective cover of the gilly. His camera was set up, the chicken-wire cover over it as part of the hillside. He could see clearly and he snapped away at the faces eating chicken and ribs and platters of green salad. He recognized a couple of people; businessmen from upstate with whom Salvesen was acquainted. Then he saw Congressman Redruth from Boise. Twice now he had photographed him in this compound. He looked for other out-of-towners, but could not spot anyone he recognized. One man stood apart, looking a little awkward. Harrison focused his camera, closing in on the man's face. The subject was young, younger than most of the other guests, his face tanned dark by the sun, with long blond hair. There was something vaguely familiar about him, but Harrison could not say what. One man he did recognize was Gil Davidson out of Missouri. He had been here at least three times before, a preacher in the mould of Salvesen, only not as bright. He was part of the leadership of the Missouri Breakmen, one of the best-attended militia groups in the country. He had brought forty men and women out for a weekend's training with Jesse Tate.

Harrison lay back and slept for a while and when he woke it was afternoon. The gathering was less busy now, the smoke from the barbecue had gone and the trestles were being cleared. He saw Salvesen walking beyond the marquee with the blond-haired man who had stood on his own. Harrison got behind the camera and followed them. God, he wished he could hear what they were saying. Salvesen was a big man, taller and much broader than the blond guy. They walked close, strolling almost, heads together as though deep in conversation. The younger man was showing Salvesen something, but Harrison could not tell what it was. He trained the camera on Salvesen's reddened features, bull-nosed, with that great walrus-like moustache spreading across his lips. He was fifty-five years old, but you'd have to look hard to find a grey hair on his head.

That night Harrison did get wet. Early evening and a stillness descended on the country, holding the air against the ground. Then all at once the wind started to blow, slow at first, then harder and harder until the trees were bent all but double. Clouds gathered darker and darker and then lightning lit up the sky in pink and orange, before it forked at the ground like the devil spearing for fish. The rain fell in vertical lines, iron rods hammering the dust into mush. Harrison used its cover to move as close to the outer perimeter fence as he dared. He had no NVGs with him, but they would have been useless anyway with lightning strikes all around him. The thunder rolled, the rain hissed against rock and dirt and he was able to move much more swiftly than he normally would. He had been this close before, again using the cover of a summer storm to shield his path and allow him up to the fence. He had noted that when the weather was this bad the perimeter patrols were non-existent. He knew where the light and motion sensors were, and they were fewer than at the front. Everybody bars and chains their front door. Human nature, he called it. Salvesen was no different, his back gate was locked but it wasn't bolted. He had goon towers twenty feet high on each corner of the compound, but they were not manned twenty-four hours a day. They were manned tonight, however; a show of strength for his guests, no doubt. One man in each, armed with an M16 automatic rifle. Salvesen allowed no Chinese or Russian guns in his compound. Harrison knew the movement of the guards, and right now they would be tucked up under cover having a quiet chew or a smoke.

He was able to get right up to the fence and check it from one end to the other. The trip wires were visible to the naked eye, if you knew where to look. Fifty yards to the back of the fence was a rising hillock with a grove of aspen behind it. Harrison moved there and lay up against the edge, the best cover near to the compound. It was too close for any feeding animal to crop at the grass and the regular movement of men kept most of them away. Harrison lay flat now, with the rain beating off his gilly and soaking right into his bones. He was cold, wet through, but this was his best chance in years. If ever he was to find a weak spot in the wire, it was now. So he picked his way at a crawl, the entire length of the fence and found what he was looking for. The wire had been dug down into the ground, rather than just being tied off, but underneath the northern goon tower it was solid rock. They had had no option but to fasten it down and leave it. As Harrison tested it with his fingers, he knew he could cut effectively and tie back again afterwards. If Kovalski could get him a warrant – he had his point of covert entry.

Exhilarated, he watched the inner wall. Lights were mounted, facing out at twenty-foot intervals. They were activated by motion and cast a beam over the outer pasture that ran up to the fence. Twin security cameras were set up at each corner, facing across one another so they could pick up any movement. He had filmed them recently with the SearchCam Recon IR, a tactical surveillance camera that the Bureau had furnished him with. It was made of anodized aluminium and allowed him to survey activity covertly and behind the line of fire. The information ended up in the Domestic Terrorism Unit in D.C. After Oklahoma, 'potential terrorists' was how the

FBI viewed some of the active militia groups. Salvesen had as yet committed no crime against any person or person's property in the United States, but he frequented the company of known militia leaders and was undoubtedly training their members, perhaps even arming them. Harrison saw his role as terror prevention. According to the Bureau, terrorism prevention was: 'A documented instance in which a violent act by a known or suspected terrorist group or individual with the means and a proven propensity for violence is successfully interdicted through investigative activity.' Investigative activity, that was what this was, sitting out here with rain falling like lead pellets from an ashen sky and lightning bolts tearing up great chunks of the hillside. Salvesen could not be deemed to have a proven propensity for violence, but some of the men he spoke to did – BobCat Reece of Montana for one.

Harrison checked above him to make sure the guard had not had a sudden urge towards vigilance and then he moved back up the hill. He had as much as he needed; the day had been more than a success and the thought of getting some sleep in Chief's hogan was far more appealing than spending the rest of the night out here. Collecting his gear, he made his way much more quickly up the hill and headed for Dugger's Canyon. He made good time, the wind got up and the rain slanted at his back, pushing him along trails which now ran with water. He was not as vigilant as he had been earlier, but he reckoned he could walk right by someone in this weather and they would never know it.

He didn't see the figure that crouched above the entrance to the cave where the bats lived, water dripping off his uncovered head. He squatted against black rock, hunting bow over his knees, as if keeping a silent vigil on the valley below. He heard Harrison long before Harrison

239

got to him and then he saw him shadowy against the sky, moving quickly through the rain with his coat tails dragging in mud.

In the cottonwood grove in Dugger's Canyon, Harrison stripped off the gilly and quietly shook it out. The cam' suit was soaked and he kept it on. He could dry it out in the hogan. He scrubbed at his face and the backs of his hands with Cam-off wipes and then replaced the lid on the cooler. He had his roll of film, and the information logged in the back of his mind. He put the film in his pocket inside its sealed plastic container and moved out of the trees. Not ten feet from him the figure crouched again, head to one side, dark eyes watching him. When Harrison had gone, the figure slowly uncoiled and moved into the cottonwoods. Here he stood for a long moment, studying the ground as it was lit up by lightning: a faint undulation in the earth. The figure bent, pressed the soil, worked his fingers around and then lifted. He looked down at the top of the cooler.

# 12

Swann's dream soured his mood. Webb noticed the sudden quietness that had come over him, though it was perhaps reminiscent of the general atmosphere on the fifteenth floor. Security was tight; MI5 intelligence officers had to wear their ID tags, anyone else had to have a warrant card and nobody from outside the department or Special Branch came up unaccompanied.

Webb sat in the exhibits office with Tania Briggs and DI Clements. 'There you go,' he said, handing the information he had sourced from bomb data to Clements. 'Descriptions given by the lad on the scaffolding, the secretary upstairs at the DTI and the other witnesses match the E-fits from the assassination of Alessandro Peroni in Paris in 1995. Not only that but the MO is the same.' He paused, licked his moustache and looked up. 'Tal-Salem and Pier-Luigi Ramas. Hit men,' he said. 'Both are in their mid-thirties, originally trained by the Syrians in the Bekaa Valley. They've worked in Europe, Israel, Egypt and the Lebanon, amongst other places. They're professional killers, but they have done other work. Sheikh Omar Abdel Rahman of Gamaa Islamiya has had contact with them.'

'The Blind Egyptian,' Briggs said. 'World Trade Center. They were involved in that?'

'Could've been. Not in the actual attack, but the planning, maybe.'

Webb looked back at the print-out on Tal-Salem and Pier-Luigi Ramas, information fed to them from various antiterrorist organizations worldwide: the FBI, BKA in Germany, the French, and an awful lot from the Jonathan Institute in Israel, where every year there was an international conference on terrorism. The institute had been set up after Entebbe and named in honour of Jonathan Netanyahu – the brother of the Prime Minister, Benjamin – who had been killed leading the attack on the plane. 'They've done stuff for Abu Nidal in Israel.' Webb pointed out three instances where their assassination handiwork was apparent to the Israeli Secret Service. 'They also carried out bombings for the PLF and Hizbollah in France in the 1980s.

'The Israelis and the FBI suspect them of being active during the Gulf War,' he went on. 'There were a hundred and seventy-odd terrorist attacks during the war, only thirty of them actually carried out against Western targets, though. The rest were in Third World or Arab countries. These two are consummate professionals. They're probably better than anyone we've come up against.' He took a long breath. 'I reckon what we've seen so far is just for openers.'

Clements looked sourly at him.

'You know what I mean, Guv. Queen's House Mews – why give the right address on the wrong driving licence? Shit, they could've done the old Flat 36G when it only goes up to F routine. OK, Jack Swann worked bloody hard to find out James Morton was dead, but we know how it works – find someone who's dead and get their birth certificate. If they died before sixteen you can get their national insurance number as well. Anyone with Huella's credentials would do it a different way. He did it with Ramon Jimenez. I've checked with the Spanish authorities. The real Jimenez was a barman in Cadiz who'd never applied for a passport. Huella got a passport in his name and his only mistake was that Jimenez had a record. When the Spanish did their checks on the Jimenez who hired the car, they found the guy in Cadiz. They showed him pictures and he recognized Huella immediately. He had hung out in Cadiz for six months, just to get an ID.'

'I think we need to get on to that Fed again, Webby,' Clements said.

'I'll phone him this afternoon.'

☆

Swann and McCulloch were co-ordinating the house to house in Hackney. Every occupant was spoken to, every business, every pub and shop. Swann went into the newsagent's under the Eastway. The little Indian man looked thoughtful. 'The night before,' he said. 'A man came in to buy cigarettes.'

'What man?'

The Indian smiled. 'You will understand why I remember him when I tell you.'

'Go on,' Swann said.

'White, quite small, with a skinhead haircut and tattoos.'

Swann felt his pulse quicken a fraction.

The Indian man touched his left ear lobe. 'Lots of earrings too. Four, I think. Two studs and two round ones, you know, the loops.'

'Sleepers,' Swann said.

The man nodded. 'That's right, sleepers.'

'The tattoos,' Swann asked him, 'anything particular that you remember?'

'Spider's webs on his hands.'

Swann narrowed his eyes. 'Anything else – no Nazi insignia – swastikas, stuff like that?'

'No, I only remember the webs.'

Swann thanked him and left.

He and McCulloch went into the King's Head pub on Victoria Park Road and spoke to the landlord. 'Skinhead,' Swann said to him. 'Lots of tattoos. Four earrings.'

The landlord nodded. 'I remember. There were two of them.'

'Two?'

'One small. He was the one with the earrings. The other was quite a bit taller.'

'Can you describe him?'

The landlord sighed. 'Skinhead,' he said, making an open-handed gesture. 'Green bomber jacket, I think. He had tattoos, too.'

'Any that you remember specifically?'

'No.'

'Swastika, maybe?' McCulloch put in.

The landlord looked at him for a moment and shook his head. 'Not that I noticed,' he said.

☆

Webb phoned Louis Byrne for the second time in as many months. He could not get hold of him right away as he was attending a memorial function in the quadrangle. Byrne called him back an hour or so later.

'George Webb,' Webb said as he picked up the phone.

'George, this is Louis Byrne. FBI. You called me.'

'Louis, how're you doing?'

'Pretty good. You?'

'So so.' Webb leaned an elbow on the desk. 'Couple of developments over here. I never got round to letting you know but we received a delivery, not long after I spoke to you.'

'Delivery?'

'Photographs. Three of us with bullet holes in our heads.'

Byrne was quiet for a moment. 'It's him, George. No question.'

'I was afraid you were going to say that. Can you send us a file, Louis – the work that you've done on him so far?'

'I'll be in London myself next week. Shrivenham. Bringing my wife. I've got a spare day or two before the conference, I'll bring in what I've got. You can show me what you guys got and maybe we can cross-reference.'

'OK,' Webb said. 'Listen, let me know the flight you're on and we'll send a car.'

'Thanks, George. But the leg-att'll organize a cab for us. I've got to check in at the embassy anyway and we'll be staying at the Marriott.'

'You been to London before?'

'Oh yeah. Several times. My wife's first trip, though. I guess she can do plenty of shopping while I'm in Oxford-shire.' He paused. 'The other thing I'd suggest you do is talk to the Jonathan Institute. They've got a file over there as well.'

'Anyone in particular?'

'Ben Dubin. Good guy. Criminal data section.'

☆

Tommy Cairns sat at his kitchen table with his brother, a cigarette burning between his fingers. He was reading the newspaper and Jean-Marie Mace's face looked up at him. He laid the paper down, twisted his mouth at the corners and sucked on the cigarette. Frank was very still beside him. 'Makes me an accessory to murder,' he said.

His younger brother said nothing.

'Doesn't it.' Frank passed a hand over his scalp. 'Tom?'

'Shut up, Frank. I'm thinking.'

Frank was silent then. Getting up, he looked out at the overgrown grass in the garden. The day was hot and sticky. He opened the door and let the dogs in. Two Staffordshire bull terriers, they sniffed about at his feet. 'I didn't know what they were going to do,' he said as if to reassure himself. 'I didn't want to be no terrorist, Tommy.'

'What d'you think Action 2000 is – fucking teddy bears' picnic?'

Frank looked round at him and Tommy held his gaze. 'Frankie, every time you smack a Paki or put burning paper through a Jewboy's letterbox, you're terrorizing. That's what we do.'

'Yeah, but they've killed people, Tommy. You do a lot of time for that.'

Tommy slapped the open newspaper with the back of his hand. 'Tell me where in here it mentions a description of the cab driver?'

'I haven't read it.'

'Well read it.' He threw the paper at him and it fluttered against his chest, pages falling everywhere. 'Everything's fine, Frank. We're making a lot of money.'

☆

Bob Jackson, Harrison's supervisor, sat in the air-conditioned comfort of his office in Salt Lake City. He had been feeling a bit easier of late. After McVeigh was convicted in June and subsequently sentenced to death, security had been the tightest he had known it in thirty years with the FBI. They had been expecting, almost anticipating, some form of 'patriot movement' backlash, but it had not materialized. Jackson was married with four grown-up kids and three grandchildren. His wife worried about him much more than she used to. But that feeling of security, the little bit of breathing space he seemed to have been allowed these last couple of weeks, dissipated like evaporating water as he stared at the latest product from Idaho. Opposite him, Harrison's case agent, Tom Brindley, and contact agent, Max Scheller, watched him. Jackson got up and moved over to the window. The traffic was backing up downtown. It was late afternoon and pitifully hot on the street.

'So, what d'you reckon, Bob?' Brindley said after a few moments. Jackson went back to his desk, sat down in the swivel chair and looked once more at the pictures. 'I don't know, but it could be.'

'I think it's him,' Scheller said. 'Maybe we ought to speak to headquarters.'

Jackson looked at him thoughtfully, then back at the pictures of the blond-haired man with Jakob Salvesen. He looked up at his computer screen and decided against E-mail. This was too sensitive to send electronically. Most of the militias used the Internet and they had picked up FBI information before. Jackson himself had come across the names of field agents and their families in Montana and northern Idaho, the one time they had broken the 'pretty good protection' software surrounding the militias' web sites.

He picked up the phone and dialled the direct line. He could not get hold of Kovalski, so he tried him through the Strategic Intelligence Operations Center. 'I'm trying to locate Tom Kovalski in Domestic Terrorism,' he said.

'One moment, please.' Jackson rapped his fingertips against the wood of his desk, then the operator came back on the line. 'He's at the Arizona field office.'

Jackson rang Phoenix.

'Kovalski.'

'Tom, this is Bob Jackson over in Salt Lake.'

'Bob, how's it going?'

'It was going good, Tom. Now I'm not so sure.'

Kovalski's voice dropped an octave. 'What's up?'

'Just got a fresh batch of product from our man out west. It'll be coming over to you tomorrow.' He paused and looked across the desk at Brindley and Scheller. 'You're not going to like this, Tom. We've got a guy deep in conversation with the main man. They're taking a stroll in the garden.'

'Who is he?' Kovalski said quietly.

'We think it's Bruno Kuhlmann, the John Doe from Atlanta.'

☆

Louis and Angie Byrne flew into Heathrow. Angie sat at the window and gazed over the city as the plane drifted under the clouds. She had her face all but pressed to the glass, trying to take everything in at once.

'You'll see it all, hon',' Byrne said, patting her arm. 'Don't worry.'

Angie looked back at him out of piercing blue eyes, the sort of eyes that cut you down in a courtroom. 'Don't patronize me, Louis. I want to remember it from the air.'

Byrne shook his head and smiled.

They landed, collected their bags and took a taxi into the West End. The cabbie loaded their bags and looked Angie up and down. She was tall, slim and statuesque, in a two-piece red suit. She wore a white chemise with a low neckline and her breasts lifted together. Gold hung from her neck and from her ears and flashed in the sun on her wrist.

'First time in London?' the cabbie asked them.

'For my wife, yes. Not for me.' Byrne looked out of the window.

'Holiday, is it?'

'Business.'

'Where'd you want to go, then, sir?'

'Hotel Marriott in Duke Street.'

'American,' the driver said. 'Visiting the embassy, are you?'

'Possibly.' Byrne glanced at his wife.

The driver dropped them at the Marriott just off Grosvenor Square and the doorman took their luggage. Their room was on the fourth floor, overlooking the street. Byrne tipped the porter and looked at his wife. 'Hope you like it, honey.'

'It's a hotel room, Louis. I've seen one or two before.'

'You gonna be OK with me gone all week?'

She fisted a hand on her hip. 'Think I'll manage. Don't you?'

'I guess.' He kissed her then, her scent thick in his nostrils. 'I just gotta go over and see the leg-att. I'll be right back.'

'Now?'

'Yeah. I want to pick up my bag.'

He crossed Grosvenor Square and went into the embassy through the side door. A British armed police officer from the Diplomatic Protection Group patrolled the corner, in white shirt and body armour. Byrne nodded to him, showed his badge at the door and went inside. The FBI office was on the third floor. Byrne knew Matheson, the legal attaché, from D.C. Government service grade 15, fifteen years older than he was and looking towards his pension. Still, London was as decent a place as any to do that. Matheson had a good file, almost as good as his own, but then he *was* that much older. Byrne went straight into his office and Matheson looked up from behind his desk.

'Lucky Louis Byrne. You've arrived, then.'

'Looks that way, Bill.'

Matheson stood up and they shook hands. 'Over for

the Shrivenham conference. I expected you to go straight to Oxfordshire.'

'Yeah, me too. But I brought my wife with me.'

'Angie – over here?'

'That's right. She's taking a week's vacation to see the sights. Her first time in London.'

'Well, I shall have the pleasure of looking after her while you're at the conference.'

'I'd appreciate that. She thinks she's a tough attorney, but she doesn't know London.'

He sat down and rested an ankle on his knee. 'Bill, is my bag here? It got packaged in D.C. and sent across in the pouch.'

'RSO'll have it. Why'd you do that, anyway?'

'Because I've got papers for the cops over here that I didn't want broadcast if they searched me at the airport.'

Matheson squinted at him. 'You didn't bring anything else with you, did you?'

Byrne looked puzzled for a moment and then he laughed. 'Oh, I get it. No, I didn't, Bill. If I want a gun, they got them at the naval building.'

The conference was due to begin at Shrivenham in Oxfordshire the following Monday. Byrne phoned Scotland Yard from his hotel room and arranged to go straight over. He took a taxi across London and was met by George Webb in the foyer. It was another hot day and Webb was dressed casually in jeans and a polo shirt. Byrne was tall and lean, hair cut high on his head – a throwback to his days in the Marines. After so long in the service, he had got used to not having to comb it.

Webb pressed his card through the swipe and they went to the lifts. 'Fifteenth floor,' Webb told him, as they began to rise.

Byrne nodded. 'I guess you get pretty good views from up there.'

'Not bad.'

They looked at one another. 'IRA been busy?'

Webb made a face. 'Last month was marching season.'

Swann came out of the squad room. He wore his four-button, dogtooth-check suit and a yellow tie. He offered his hand to Byrne. 'Jack Swann,' he said.

'Louis Byrne. FBI.'

Swann nodded. 'We've heard a bit about you?'

'Yeah. What's that?'

'*Lucky* Louis.'

Byrne pulled a face. 'Who you been talking to, Jack?'

'Leg-att. Drinks with us now and again over at the Foxhole.'

'USAF Intel in Ruislip,' Webb explained. 'The Marines that guard your naval building have barracks there.'

Swann looked at Byrne. 'Bill Matheson told us you were blown up in Beirut in '83.'

Byrne nodded. 'I was guarding the roof when the truck hit us. Went sixty metres up in the air and came down with the rubble.'

'And you walked away?'

Again Byrne nodded. 'Just cuts and bruises.'

'Lucky Louis indeed.'

They went to the exhibits office and Colson came in with DI Clements and a handful of the other detectives. Byrne took off his jacket and sat behind Webb's desk. 'Can I see what you got?' he asked.

Webb went to the Holmes computer and printed off what they had on the investigation so far. Byrne narrowed his eyes as he read. 'Who're the guys with the tattoos?' he asked.

'We don't know yet.'

He read on. 'Tal-Salem and Pier-Luigi Ramas.' He looked at the E-fits from Paris and then at the descriptions given by the witnesses to the shooting of Jean-Marie Mace. When he was finished he sat back. 'Motive?'

Colson made a face. 'We don't know. There doesn't seem to be one.'

Byrne nodded his head slowly. 'If this is Storm Crow – the motive will become apparent as time goes on. He'll have more planned than just this.'

Swann flicked his eyebrows. 'Well, that's wonderful news.'

Colson glanced at him, then back at Byrne. 'You think it's one man?'

'My theory, yes. I stress that, guys. It is only my theory. Nobody really knows for sure. The name Storm Crow first came about in Israel in '89. I guess you all know that already. US Ambassador's car.'

'TATP grenade,' Webb said.

'Right.' Byrne looked up at him. 'Did you check with Dubin?'

'He's not there right now. But they said he'll get back to me.'

'OK. Ben's a good man. I've worked with him on these incidents. I was assistant legal attaché in Athens in '89. That's the office that covers the Middle East. Went over to Israel that first time and I've had an interest ever since. We had one attack in the States, which I believe was down to him. Special kind of TPU was used.'

'Hang on a minute.' Webb went through to the evidence cages and brought back one of the timing and power units they had recovered from the basement of Queen's House Mews. He laid it on the desk. 'Like this?' he said.

Byrne cocked his head to one side and then carefully lifted the grey-black box encased in the nylon bag. The swing lid was open and he studied the interior, the liquid-crystal clock, LED for circuit testing, dual green and red wiring on the circuit board. He set it down again. 'I've never seen a complete one, but the components, the clock for example . . .'

'Spanish,' Webb told him. 'Mass-produced.'

Byrne looked from one face to the next. 'We found parts of one of these on the Texas/Mexico border. We've had troops down there helping the border patrol with the Mexican drug problem since 1989 – peace dividend from the cold war. Marines are used to do recon' work along the Rio Grande. A law was passed in the United States in 1878, the Posse Comitatus Act. Basically it forbids soldiers from doing police work, but they're allowed to carry out non-combative surveillance. In 1981, Congress passed legislation that allowed them to share equipment with law-enforcement officers, which is useful because they have stuff like NVGs which the border agents don't. The US/Mexico border is nineteen hundred and fifty-two miles long and we've only got sixty-two hundred border agents. Since the Marines have been down there, we've had a pretty good detection rate.

'Anyway, the point I'm making is that the Mexican drug barons have been losing a lot to us in recent years. Don't get me wrong, they still get the stuff through – heroin, cocaine, marijuana – but we've stopped a lot. In May 1995, a bunch of mortars hit the joint task force barracks at Fort Bliss. It was only a couple of weeks after Oklahoma. They were set up in the sage brush, back of a small hill, half a mile away. It was a good place to set the launch vehicle, not overly patrolled by Marines. This fourteen-year-old kid used to let his family's goats graze there. The mortars were timed to go off right about the point he arrived. Trouble was, only five of the six made their target, the other one blew up inside the pipe barrel. Kid got torn to pieces by shrapnel.

'Anyway, the fort suddenly found themselves in a war

zone. A platoon working the river came under fire from what were perceived to be bandits the other side. Another explosion happened a hundred and fifty miles away at Fort Davis. That's where we found the parts to this.' He held up the TPU again. 'Initially, we thought it was militia activity. Back in March of '95, there was all manner of lunacy going back and forth on their Internet bulletin boards. They thought that we and the ATF were training for a nationwide assault on their weapons. They're paranoid that the government's going to take them away. I wasn't working the investigation at first, but it wasn't very long before it came to light that this was nothing to do with the militia. Somebody was using their paranoia as a front. The DEA Intel Center in El Paso discovered that in that one day twenty million dollars worth of cocaine entered the United States from Mexico.'

Colson rubbed his lip with a thumbnail. 'So these explosions were just a decoy, then.'

Byrne nodded slowly. 'Three Marines were killed and two civilians. The bandits held the river platoon down for three hours until back-up got there, then they just melted away.' He lifted the TPU and turned it over in his hands. 'As I said, the component parts we recovered from Fort Davis were like these. Plastia watches and clocks can be bought in any general store in Mexico. This type of wiring is standard in the United States.'

'What was the explosive at Fort Davis?' Webb asked him.

'High grade. Government C-4, two and a half pounds. The IED was in the trunk of a car.'

'Parked outside the fort?'

Byrne shook his head. 'Inside, I'm afraid.'

Swann smiled grimly. 'Listen, it happens.' He looked at his colleagues. 'Lisburn. Remember?'

Nobody spoke for a moment, all eyes seemed to be on

the timing and power unit lying between Byrne's hands on the table. 'And you believe that was Storm Crow?' Swann said.

'Yes.'

'Codeword?'

'No. Interestingly enough, my only knowledge of him using codewords has been in Europe. I understand that groups like ETA or Action Directe have never used them.'

'Only PIRA,' Colson said.

Byrne bent to the briefcase on the floor by his feet. 'A few days after the explosions we received this. It was sent to our field office in El Paso. I kept it as a souvenir.' He took out a clear plastic envelope: inside was a black feather. 'Crow,' he said. 'A day or so later, they received a photograph of me with a bullet hole in my head.'

Colson glanced at Swann. 'That sounds familiar,' he said.

Byrne gestured with an open palm. 'That's his style, always the one for drama. But that's why I talk about motive in the manner I do. Gentlemen, it's my belief, and again I can't prove it, although street-level intel' in Mexico City kinda bears me out, that Storm Crow looked at the problems the Mexican barons were having and offered up his services. He had a pedigree, didn't he. Israel, 1989.' He took out a file from his briefcase. 'You've probably got all this stuff, but you may not've been able to relate it to Storm Crow. Israel again – 1991 and '92. In 1993 – the headquarters of the Guardia Civíl in San Sebastian. A covert DEA helicopter in Colombia. That chopper was undercover as a short-distance freight carrier, but somehow their surveillance got compromised. They were hit by anti-aircraft weapons.' He paused. 'May '95, it was us. Suppose the Mexicans paid him a million dollars for hitting Fort Bliss. Wouldn't it be worth it?'

Outside, a cloud had momentarily shrouded the sun and the room dulled about them.

Webb cocked an eyebrow. 'And you believe it's one man?'

Byrne nodded.

'Why?'

Byrne drew breath audibly through his nose. 'Because it's for profit. Groups surround causes – Hizbollah, Hamas, PIRA. They have political or religious ends. That deal in Texas was for profit. It was drug money, nothing more. The shooting down of the DEA chopper, the same.'

'What about the others – Madrid, the shooting of Alessandro Peroni in Paris?'

'Markers, maybe? He'll be watching for other clients. Maybe he knows something about them that we don't.'

Swann frowned at him.

'Keeping his hand in, Jack. Keeping his profile high. Name in the papers. That way he's marketable, isn't he. Basic economics.'

Colson stared at him. 'So, you're telling us we're dealing with a businessman?'

'Pure and simple. He plies a trade and gets paid for it. No different to a hit man, only the stakes are a lot higher, and so – I imagine – is the pay-off.'

Swann showed him a surveillance photograph of Ibrahim Huella. 'The man we're looking at,' he said. 'So far he's had three aliases – Huella, which is on a Syrian passport, James Morton, one he picked up over here, and—'

'Ramon Jimenez,' Byrne finished for him. 'The Spanish connection. He's also used Raoul Mendez.'

Swann nodded. 'Could this be him – the Storm Crow?'

Byrne looked at the photograph and scratched his head at the temple. 'It could be, I guess. Nobody ever ID'd him.'

'We've got a clean set of prints from the house we raided,' Webb told him.

'That might be useful. I could run them through CJIS in Clarksburg.'

'CJIS?'

'Criminal Justice Information Services. Fingerprint boys. They might be able to come up with something, but don't hold your breath.' Byrne stood up. 'Gentlemen, I have to go. I'll be at Shrivenham from Monday, and my wife wants me to show her the Tower of London. Any of you guys going, by the way?'

'To the Tower?' Swann winked at him. 'We'd never get out again.'

# 13

The man in the 4 × 4 drove from Blanchland towards
Hexham. Passing through Slaley, he headed over the
moorland towards Healey. The farm was signposted a
mile and a half to the east of Healey itself, which was no
more than a clutch of stone cottages. The road in was a
dirt track beyond a five-bar gate which stood open. The
driver cut his headlights, dead slow now, pitch darkness,
with no moon piercing the weight of the cloud that
pressed against the moor. The track broadened into a
farmyard with a sprawl of L-shaped buildings to one side.
Across the concreted yard, more buildings lifted against
the gloom in a flat, narrow line. The driver cut the engine
and reached over the seat for his bag. Outside, he paused
to listen, lifting his head like a hunting wolf. The wind
coursed through the eaves of the buildings, rustling at
loose tiles. He could smell the rain in the air.

He made his way across the courtyard until he got to
the last building, rubber-soled shoes making no sound on
the concrete. The door was solid oak and fixed in place
with a heavy padlock. He took a pencil-light torch from
his pocket and twisted it on; then he played the light
around the bottom of the bag until he found the set of
picks he carried. Standing again, he checked his position,
listening; then shone the light on to the flat face of the
padlock. It was old and had one of those little shutters
that ran across the keyhole. He looked carefully, gauged

the little spike which the key fitted over and selected a pick from the metal ring. He worked one pick round at a time, making sure that none slipped against another. The lock was old and stiff and it did not want to give. The man cursed under his breath, checked behind him and worked at the lock once more. Two more minutes, three, then the pin clicked and turned and the lock broke free in his grip.

The barn smelled of damp and he heard the scuttle of rats on flagstones. He shivered; the one thing he hated more than anything else was rats. Again he shone the torch, not for long, just enough to take in where the workbench was and the shelving beneath it. He gauged the distance in paces, flicked off the torch and crossed. A grimy window, directly in front of his face, allowed a trickle of grey light to filter in from outside. Again he allowed the use of the torch, but again just for a moment. He crouched, set the bag on the floor beside him and looked at the shelving. There were a number of rusty paint tins, some boxes of nails and a half-size metal bucket. He shone his torch; the bucket was both empty and dry. Now he opened his bag and reached for a length of copper tube. Holding it very carefully, he slid it out of the bag and laid it on the floor. Then he took the strip of oil cloth he had brought and wound it round the copper. Two hands again, he placed the oil-cloth package inside the metal bucket and slid it under the bench.

He paused to listen once more and then went back out to the yard. The first spots of rain had begun to slap the concrete. He closed the oak door and reset the padlock. Back in the 4 × 4, he sat a moment with the window half-down to listen. Nothing save the wind rising and the faint splash of the raindrops. He started the engine, turned round and crawled back up the track in darkness. At the junction with the road he paused and looked for traffic; seeing none he pulled out, then drove for fifty yards before switching on the headlights.

☆

Harrison was working in the Passover Lumber Yard, shifting tree trunks with the big crane, when Jesse Tate drove past in his pick-up truck. Below him, Chief was standing on the partially assembled wall of the house they were building, while Harrison swung the boom. Chief had finished his paintings and was doing a bit of spot work. The log dangled above him and he eased it into place with gloved hands. Harrison set it down. Chief unbuckled the nylon strap and he swung the boom away again. He looked at the sky, saw nothing, but then a few minutes later he heard the familiar roar of the Lear engine and Omega 2 swung in across the valley. That would be Willy Johnson piloting, he always flew Omega 2. Harrison did not know where he had been, but he flew out three days ago. Below him, Margarito and Ezequiel fetched another hunk of timber for the house. The jet banked east over the town, mottled against the rise of the mountains, and then descended into Westlake Airport. Ten minutes later Jesse drove by, heading back towards the ranch with a man in a cowboy hat and sunglasses sitting next to him. Harrison did not recognize him.

'Hey, Harrison.' He didn't hear Margarito calling up to him. 'Home, boy!' He looked down then. 'We're all set.'

Harrison lifted the boom.

☆

Colson chaired the meeting in the wake of the visit from Louis Byrne. He went through all the information they had gathered so far and added Byrne's file notes for the benefit of those who had not seen him. 'From what we've seen already and from what we've learned from the FBI, we are almost certainly dealing with Storm Crow,' he finished. He lifted his hands, palm upwards. 'Unfortunately, it makes sense, particularly when you consider the tactics employed at Queen's House Mews.'

Swann stared across the room at him. 'Talking of Queen's House Mews, how did he know we were coming?'

Colson rubbed the flat of his palms together. 'You think somebody told him, Jack?'

'Yes, Guv. I do. We've never had a leak in this department. I think it's a serious question and nobody's even mentioned it.'

Colson glanced at DI Clements. 'We agree with you, Jack. But short of a witch-hunt – what d'you suggest we do?'

Swann had no answer. He looked between his feet, compressing his lips into a line.

'It isn't actually that simple,' Julian Moore spoke quietly. 'He *knew* we were watching him, because he wanted us to watch him. He made sure we did. Nobody had to tell him anything. I remember at an earlier briefing, Jack, you raised the point yourself, about giving the real address on a false driving licence? Why use the term PIRA? Why the passport as proof of ID?'

'That doesn't change the precision, Julian. The exact time of the SO19 attack.'

There was silence for a moment, then Webb said: 'What's more disturbing than any question of a possible leak is how he knows what we do. He knew at some point we would do those bins, Jack. He knew that a fast SO19 entry is through the front door, so he took up the floorboards and rigged up all those movement sensors.'

'The Storm Crow is good, Webby. According to Byrne, the best.' Swann moved his shoulders. 'SO19 use basic military strategies; they're not difficult to work out. But the exact day and time of the attack? He was out before the Ninjas even got plotted up.'

'If he wanted us to know he was there,' Colson said, 'he would've been watching everything we did. He would've spotted the SFOs coming along as BT men and then he would've checked. He's a professional. Maybe he's been in the job somewhere, the military, perhaps. As soon as he knew they weren't authorized, he would have been alerted. He left right away. But he came back to watch, didn't he, to see if he was right. The hotel, remember. Why do that if he knew the exact time of our attack?'

It was a fair point and Swann had to concede it. 'OK,' he said. 'No leak. No conspiracy. Sorry I interrupted you, Guv.'

Colson smiled at him. 'Forget it, Jack. If it wasn't for your vigilance and overtly suspicious mind, we wouldn't even be sitting here.'

Swann looked at the floor.

'OK,' Colson went on. 'Where was I? Oh yes. George, have we got anything definitive yet from Lambeth on the cab?'

Webb cleared his throat. 'The initial forensic reports indicate clothing fibres, in particular, a piece of yellow thread on the driver's seat. There's hundreds of fingerprints, but none we can identify. We now know who the killers were, but we've no ID for the driver. I did get a footprint, mind you, which we photographed. The sole indicates a training shoe. The heel and instep wear can give us a match and subsequently the wearer – that's if we find the shoe.'

Swann sat forward, hands clasped together. 'We know the cab was stolen from Lea Conservancy Road,' he said, 'and two skinheads were seen the night before. I've run a CRO check on known villains with swastika or spider's web tattoos, but couldn't find anyone who isn't already banged up.' He looked at Christine Harris.

Christine leafed through her notes. 'The swastika could be for bravado or it could point to some Nazi affiliation. There's still a few groups operating, but nothing compared to what we have seen. We know about Combat 18 – the letter bombs we had earlier in the year, for example.

'The main political party now is the BFP. British Freedom Party. They got going around the time Ray Hill did so much damage to the BNP and British Movement. The BFP is run by James Ingram, a silver-spoon solicitor who was once a Young Conservative. He always denies it publicly, but there's a link between his party and a street outfit called Action 2000. We've looked at them in the past and they number a few hundred at best. They're not as organized as Combat 18 and they don't seem to have any affiliation with German, Dutch or Belgian Nazis. They're racist all right, but wholly British in it. Most of them work for Ingram in some capacity. He's got various building firms dotted about the country. A lot of them are skinheads and they've been known to have swastika tattoos. Again, there's nobody with form that we can positively identify.'

Colson sat down at the desk once more. 'There's something else we need to remember,' he said. 'At Queen's House Mews we found a receipt for four sheets of armoured glass.' He stopped and turned his mouth down at the corners. 'They paid in cash, yet still got a receipt. Not odd in itself, I suppose, but in these circumstances . . .'

'Somebody wanted us to know they have it,' Swann said quietly. 'Just like they wanted us to know they were in Queen's House Mews and that they planted a bomb in Soho, and now they've killed a French banker.'

'Europe?' Webb put in. 'Something to do with Europe?'

Colson looked at him with his head to one side. 'Go on.'

'Alessandro Peroni was a single-currency adviser. Mace did something similar for Banque Nationale de Paris. That DTI conference was about single-currency issues. The Storm Crow planted a car bomb in Madrid near the Banco Bilbao, didn't he.' He made a face. 'Spain will join any single currency.'

DI Clements looked doubtful. 'Who in this country gives a toss about what goes on in Europe? Nobody cares whether we have a single currency or not.'

'Except half the Tory Party,' Swann said. 'And maybe a bunch of anti-European skinheads.'

'Not enough,' Webb put in. 'If Action 2000 are involved, it's as foot soldiers, gophers. Skinhead may have nicked a cab, skinhead hired a car. But Huella, Tal-Salem and Ramas are the doers here. Huella seems to be the brains. Mind you, he likes being on the ground too. Got more front than Carlos, walking into the Yard like he did.'

Swann looked back at Colson. 'He wanted us to know he has the glass,' he said again. 'And now we do. What we don't know is *why*.'

☆

Bruno Kuhlmann knew he was being watched: after three years in the service, he'd picked up a working knowledge of counter-surveillance. The United States was a big country, however, and he knew that there were only ten thousand FBI agents in the whole place. He knew their field office was in Salt Lake and they had resident agency offices in Pocatello, Coeur D'Alene and Boise, but they couldn't follow him everywhere. They had tried to tail

264

him when he left D.C. the last time, but it had not been difficult to lose them.

He sat at the bar in the White Lion. Billy was serving beer to some girls, and this older guy was upstairs on his own reading the paper. That meant there would be a car out front. Sure enough, there was a blue Dodge truck parked across the street with one guy sitting in it, eating a sandwich. He wore a red T-shirt and working man's gloves lay under the windshield. Billy was leaning on the far end of the bar now, talking to the three girls. A dopehead sat at the table by the window, sucking noodle soup off a spoon. Kuhlmann could see the trouser leg of his observer against the railing of the balcony upstairs. He slid off his seat and wandered towards the stairs as if he were going up to the men's room. One glance to make sure Billy's back was turned and he stepped through the curtain into the little hallway between the bar and the kitchen. He could smell cooking fat and mayonnaise. From here it was easy, the back door open, down the steps and away. Billy's jacket hung on the peg by the door and Kuhlmann snatched it as he went past.

The Irishman sat in the August sunshine waiting for the Washington Flyer at East Falls Church. This place had always struck him as odd, no church that you could see, nothing like the Falls Road, just a futuristic entrance to a Metro station and lots of car-parking spaces. He sat on the wall behind the bus shelter with his face to the sun and hummed 'Whiskey in the Jar'. He heard a train arriving and watched out of squinted eyes as the passengers got off. Not very many of them, just the few that would be getting in their cars or taking the Flyer for Dulles Airport.

He saw Kuhlmann come out of the station, guardedly check in either direction, then meander towards the empty bus stop. The Irishman remained where he was.

The Flyer pulled off the freeway and swung round the loop to park just in front of where he was sitting. Two women were walking slowly ahead of Kuhlmann, pushing their children in three-wheeled strollers. They passed the bus stop and climbed into a Jeep parked in one of the bays. The driver of the bus jumped down, black man, head shiny with perspiration.

'How long?' the Irishman asked him.

'You got five minutes, buddy.' The driver started towards the station.

The Irishman got up, smoothed palms down his jeans and climbed aboard the bus. He sat on the left-hand side about halfway back. Kuhlmann got on, walked up the aisle and sat in the seat directly across from him. The Irishman looked ahead and rubbed his tattooed knuckles. 'So,' he said. 'Are ye set?'

'Yeah, I'm set. Now things get a little bit warmer.'

The Irishman pursed his lips. 'Aye,' he said quietly. 'It'll get warm, right enough.' He took an envelope from his back pocket, passed it across the aisle and stood up. The bus driver was ambling down from the station, a cigarette in his mouth. 'Everything ye need is in there.' The Irishman looked at Kuhlmann, then stepped back into the sunshine.

The driver looked up at him. 'What's happening, man?'

'Changed me mind, so I did.' He walked back to the station.

The driver dropped his cigarette and ground it under his heel, then climbed on to the bus. Bruno Kuhlmann sat there on his own.

'You want one way or round trip?'

'What?'

'I said, do you want one way or round trip?'

'One way,' Kuhlmann replied.

# 14

Harrison went to the post office as he did every day: there was no mail delivery service in Passover. He opened his box and found a postcard from Lake Superior. He turned it over and read: 'Hey, buddy. How's it going? Things are fine here, but I saw your grandma the other day and she seemed a bit lonesome. I guess she'd appreciate a phone call. Take care. Jeff.'

He stuffed the postcard into his pocket and went back to the lumber yard. After work he went for a drink in the Westlake Hotel, with Chief and Danny and Lisa. Belinda was in the bar, shooting pool for a buck a stick. Chief had broken up with her, but was itching to get back. Belinda was Lisa's age, with smooth skin and long legs, which she displayed to everyone as she played pool in her shorts. Harrison sat with Lisa and watched Chief watching Belinda's legs, firebird tattoo on her calf. 'Get after her, man.' Harrison nudged him in the ribs. 'You should never've let her go. Great piece of ass.'

Chief looked on impassively; the problem with Belinda was that every mother's son sniffed about her in the bar and she was in the bar most nights. Harrison took a Marlboro from his shirt pocket, lit it, then turned to Lisa. 'Honey, I gotta call my grandma.' He fished the postcard out of his pocket. 'My conscience up in Marquette. I'll be right back, OK.' He slipped off the stool and walked round the bar, being careful to avoid a staggering Charlie Love who lurched through the door.

He picked up the telephone which was set against the wall opposite the men's room door.

'Harrison.' Max Scheller's voice. 'You in a payphone?'

'Yeah. Hi, Grandma. How you doing?'

'The blond man with our subject in the compound is the John Doe from Atlanta.'

'No kidding? Did you get that TV Direct I wired you the money for?'

Lisa stood next to him, her arm about his waist and started kissing him. He could smell the Mudslide on her breath.

'Has he been back?' Scheller said in his ear.

'Nope. I don't reckon so.'

'They lost him back in D.C.'

'Is that right, Grandma? No, the weather's still pretty good out here. Fixing to snow up there, huh.'

'If he surfaces again, let us know.'

'I'll do that. I promise you, I'll write real soon.'

'We got the green light for a covert search warrant, if you can find a way into the compound. ATF can prove one of his companies is supplying weapons to the militia. With that and the John Doe, we've got enough probable cause. Brindley's writing the affidavit, but the US Attorney's Office isn't exactly breakdancing. Your man's got influential friends.'

'OK, Grandma. You take care now. Goodbye.'

Harrison hung up and Lisa draped her arms round his neck. From the corner of his eye he could see Chief had started to hit on Belinda again. The other Lisa, the bartender, was pouring her a Kamikaze Slammer and Chief was fishing in his pockets for dollars. Smitty left the bar where he'd been bullshitting with Junior and winked at Harrison as he made his way to the men's room.

'Let's go home, Harrison,' Guffy whispered in his ear. 'It's too noisy in here and I'm feeling all kinda sexual.'

Harrison kissed the end of her nose. 'OK, Miss Lady Mam. Go get your jacket.'

☆

Swann worked with Christine Harris on the Nazi connection. Together they ran a number of checks on nominals and potential nominals from the Special Branch cell on the fifteenth floor. They had criminal record information on Tommy Cairns, the leader of Action 2000. Together with his elder brother Frank, he ran a gang of builders from a yard in Mitcham, owned by James Ingram the leader of the British Freedom Party. It was decided that MI5, under Julian Moore, would operate a short-term surveillance to see what they could find out.

After two weeks, they came up with a group of four individuals that were worth looking at a little more closely. Tommy and Frank Cairns, Kenny Bacon and Charlie Oxley. The Cairns brothers were not skinheads and sported no tattoos. Bacon and Oxley, on the other hand, were 'definite maybes'. Bacon had a spider's web tattooed in blue on his right hand and Oxley sported a black swastika on the underside of his wrist. They concentrated initially on Oxley.

He lived in Croydon and was picked up for work every morning by a man named Denis Smith. They lived close. Smith drove a white Escort van. From Monday to Friday, and occasionally on Saturdays, they would drive the half-hour or so it took them to get to the yard in Mitcham. Once there, it would be a cup of tea and then out on the lorries to whatever site they were working at.

At the end of the second week, Julian reported back to the team. Friday afternoon with the summer waning now; leaden, oppressive skies threatened thunder.

'Not much to report,' he was saying. 'They've been working on a house in Penge. Oxley's been there all week. They eat their lunch at a café round the corner from the plot, sausage, egg and chips every day. He smokes forty cigarettes and drinks at least four pints of Holsten Pils a night.'

'And that's it?' Colson asked him.

'One thing. They use flatbed lorries a lot.'

'The glass purchase,' Swann said.

Julian looked round at him and nodded. 'It's a possibility.'

He looked at Colson again. 'Nothing out of the ordinary has gone on,' he continued. 'No third eye anywhere, no attempt at any form of antisurveillance.'

'He didn't meet anyone we might want to look at?'

'No one. He goes to work, comes home, goes to the pub and then home to bed.'

'Women?' Swann asked.

'None that we saw.'

'Any losses?'

'No.'

Colson pursed his lips. 'We've shown pictures of Oxley to Sally Barnes,' he said, 'the girl who hired out the Vectra, but she can't give us a positive ID. Give it another week or so and then we'll reassess.'

☆

The blonde-haired woman stood in the telephone box with the receiver to her ear and her fingers depressing the black buttons. It was almost five o'clock. The phone rang once and she released them.

'Good afternoon.' His voice was cold and clear.

'The police are watching the Nazis.'

For a moment he was quiet. 'You checked?'

'I'm a professional. Of course I checked.'

'They're distinctive, aren't they, the Nazis. And they'll be known. Special Branch will have monitored their activities. They always do.' Again he was silent. 'Do they know they're being surveilled?'

'I don't think so. *I've* seen the cars though, different ones, sometimes a motorbike. They follow them all day.'

'Have you been spotted?'

'No.'

'Third eye?'

'If they're looking for one, they haven't found it. Don't worry, I've been selective. It's me I'm protecting.'

'Brigitte, you're getting clever in your old age.'

'Don't call me that. Not even over the phone. Certain people monitor phone boxes that're called on a regular basis.'

He laughed then. 'This is a clear line. D'you think I'd do anything to jeopardize your safety, unless I deliberately chose to?'

Her breath was suddenly tight in her chest. 'Don't play games with me.' She licked her lips, watching the street about her. 'Do you want me to use them again?'

'They have the glass?'

'Yes.'

'Then use them. Before you do – suggest the situation to them. See what they can do about it. If they can't cope – dispense with them.'

'How will I transport the glass?'

'Think of something.'

'The others?'

'You can't use them. Not in London.'

'How then?'

'And just now you were being so clever.'

Her knuckles tightened round the receiver. 'What about the property?'

'The American will do it. He'll contact you when he arrives.'

☆

Ricky Gravitz flew into Manchester Airport, made a telephone call, then rented a car. He was to drive to Newcastle upon Tyne, a city in the north-east of England. He would stop before he got there, though, those were the instructions, a place called Consett, where apparently they made potato chips. He would be met at a roadside diner, the last before he hit town, coming in on the A68. Leaving Manchester, he had a little bit of trouble negotiating the weird way the English drove. Not only did they travel on the wrong side of the road, they all seemed to drive at a hundred miles an hour. He kept at a steady sixty-five, and looked for traffic cops.

Cars whizzed past him as he slowed to check the map, people hooting their horns and making obscene gestures. He had always thought England to be a sedate, polite place. Already, he was missing home. It took him a long time but he made it to the rendezvous point, just before the prearranged time of five o'clock. The parking lot was solid with cars and he had to wait a few minutes while a family sorted themselves out and then he took their space. As he parked, he saw a woman with long blonde hair get out of a car in the other aisle. She wore jeans and a short jacket. It was September now and northern England was getting colder. Gravitz parked his rented car and got out. She was waiting for him at the entrance.

'Joanne, right?' he said.

She nodded but did not smile, merely took his arm and together they went inside. They had to wait to be seated and then got a table in the smoking section. Gravitz watched her take cigarettes from her purse and shake one out. She lit it and inhaled deeply.

'What d'you want to eat?' Her accent was British as far as he could tell.

He glanced at the menu. 'Hamburger.'

'Fine.'

The waitress came over and stood there in her red uniform. They ordered two hamburgers and two cokes and Joanne finished her cigarette. Before the food arrived, she lit another one. 'Your instructions,' she said, and passed the envelope to him. 'It's all in there. You just go and rent the property. Pay for six months with the money order. You have that with you, don't you?'

'Of course.'

'Dollars or sterling?'

'Do I look stupid?'

'Don't ask questions I can't answer.' Her mouth was tight, lips thin, eyes blue and stone cold in her face.

Gravitz sat back and rested a fisted hand on the table top. The hamburgers came and she put out her second cigarette. They ate in silence and afterwards he leaned towards her.

'One question?'

'What?'

'How close are you to him?'

'Close.'

'I want to know how close.'

'Fool. You know as much now as you really ever want to.'

He shook his head. 'I want to know more.'

She stared at him then, a new darkness in her eyes. 'Believe me, you don't.'

He nodded, mouth twisted, and sat back. She started to get up. 'I'm leaving now. I have to tell you, I didn't want it done this way.'

'What way?'

'Meeting face to face.'

'I'm new in town, honey. I needed to see a face.'

'Did you?'

He nodded.

She leaned close to him then, fists resting on the table. 'So now you've seen one. If anyone ever describes it – I'll cut yours to pieces.' She kissed him hard on the mouth and left.

Gravitz booked into a forty pounds a night travel lodge and watched English television. The soccer season was under way and he could not quite understand the passion of the Newcastle United fans. In the morning he got up and drove into Consett in the rental car. He parked in the town centre car park and walked the short distance to the real estate agents, Caspar & Gibbs. The receptionist was blonde and tanned and very pretty. Gravitz smiled at her and set his briefcase down on the floor.

'My name's Gravitz,' he said. 'I wrote you from the United States. I've come to lease Healey Hall Farm.'

☆

Ibrahim Huella had a new driving licence. Colin Leaming was a thirty-two-year-old black man who worked at McDonald's in Coventry. For two months Huella had worked with him, making Big Macs with not enough mayonnaise. One afternoon during his break, Huella had stolen Leaming's driving licence from his jacket pocket, photocopied it in the office, returned it, and then written to the DVLA in Swansea claiming two things: firstly, that he had lost the licence and secondly, he had a change of address. Within seven days he had a new licence sent to the room he was renting just outside the city. Three weeks after that, he had left the room and rented a car in Colin Leaming's name, using a Bank of Scotland credit card.

He drove the car to Northumberland where he delivered it in good order to the Avis depot. Then he caught the bus to Consett and phoned Healey Hall Farm. Gravitz drove out to pick him up in a car he had bought at an auction in Sunderland.

'Ricky Gravitz,' he said, as Huella got in the car.

'Colin Leaming.'

'We're going to be working together.'

Huella glanced sideways at him. 'You sound excited.'

'I am.'

Huella nodded and looked out of the window.

Gravitz had settled into the farm and had continued with the pretence he had used as his reason for renting it in the first place. He was in the north of England for a sixth-month sabbatical to finish his research on northern European mineral deposits for his Ph.D. from Harvard. Just another American trust-funder spending his family's money. At least he was putting it to good use.

Huella only had a small case which he carried up to his room. He checked the lie of the stairs first, whether there were any windows halfway up and whether he could be seen from the landing. Satisfied, he moved to the second bedroom, noting the mess already made by the master.

'Go in and close the curtains,' he said.

'Why? There's nobody for miles around.'

'Just do it, please.'

Gravitz went in, looked out of the window, which faced over fields and then moorland at the back, then he pulled the curtains across and only when they were fast did Huella enter the room. He scanned it quickly and nodded. Then he placed his bag on the bed.

'Now,' he said, turning back to Gravitz. 'Show me the passageway.'

Gravitz frowned. 'Passageway. What passageway?'

'You mean you haven't found it?'

'Hey.' Gravitz lifted a finger. 'No need for that, man. We're in this together.'

Huella's eyes narrowed for a fraction of a second and then widened again. 'This farmhouse is nearly six hundred years old,' he said. 'Six hundred years ago the English and the Scots were tearing one another's throats out every other week. The man who built this house was called Elliott. Mr Elliott had a large family and he wanted to protect them. So he built a passage from the cellar to the outbuildings, which in those days were stables. The passage is still there. It's why we chose this house.' He took a step closer to him then. 'With what we're doing, we don't want to be opening too many doors, now do we.'

The cellar door had a lock on it and Gravitz had no key. 'I guess we weren't meant to go in there,' he said. Huella picked the lock in three minutes. The cellar was racked with wine, every bottle marked and labelled, some of them over thirty years old. The passage had been built to almost walking height and stretched about fifteen feet. At the far end were wooden steps which led up to a tight-fitting trap door in the floor of what would have been the stables. Some years previously they had been converted into three separate workshops, but all had adjoining doors. Huella went through to the last one and bent to the small metal bucket under the workbench. He lifted out a piece of oil cloth, slowly unwrapped it and held up a length of copper tube sealed at both ends.

Back inside the house, they ate some food and then Gravitz cleared away the dishes. Huella sat at the table and drank orange juice. He watched Gravitz for a moment, then snapped his fingers. 'Let me see the letter.'

Gravitz went up to his room and came down again with a piece of paper. He unfolded it and handed it to Huella, who read it and smiled. It was a piece of Harvard

276

University-headed paper, the Geological Sciences Department under Dr Irving P. Wright. It was 'To whom it may concern', and it explained that Richard Gravitz III was a Princeton honours graduate, writing his thesis for what promised to be an excellent Ph.D. on the geology of northern Europe. He was in England to do the final research and analysis on the strength of mineral deposits in the rocks of northern England and southern Scotland. In order to do this, he would need access to certain scientific equipment and also hydrochloric and nitric acids. As Mr Gravitz would not have access to any English laboratory conditions, he would be funding the provision of his own. The university would be most grateful for whatever assistance he could get in the UK.

Huella handed back the letter. 'Perfect,' he said. 'Now, tomorrow you will go shopping.'

☆

Tommy Cairns took the call on his cloned mobile telephone. As soon as he answered and heard the short silence, he knew who it was.

'Did you know that certain interested parties have been looking at one of your number?' she asked him.

For a moment Cairns was stunned. 'No.'

'Oxley.'

'Police?'

'Who else?'

'You're sure? I mean, how do you know?'

'I just know. What're you going to do about it?'

Cairns thought quickly. He was sitting at traffic lights in Peckham on his way home from work. He scanned the rear-view and door mirrors. 'Just Charlie?'

'So far. But he works with you and the others, doesn't he.'

Again, Cairns was quiet.

'Do you want out?'

He bit his lip. 'How much more work is there?'

'Two jobs. Both involve the hire or theft of a vehicle.'

Cairns thought about it. Oxley had stolen the cab, but Frank had been driving it. 'What about Frank?' he asked her.

'What about him?'

'Is anyone looking at him?'

'Not that we know of. But you've been careless.'

'Oxley,' he said. 'Oxley's been careless.'

'Do you want out?' she asked him again.

'No.' He said it very quickly, then bit his lip again.

'All right. But you need to consider exactly what you're going to do when you receive the instructions. They'll be in the usual place.'

'OK. Don't worry about it. I'll straighten things out.'

'Make sure you do.'

Three days later, he waited for the postman in Crouch End. He saw him driving up the road in his van and he waited. At number 43, the postman jumped out of the van and walked up the steps. Cairns walked along the pavement behind him. 'Anything for F, mate?' he asked.

The postman shuffled the stack of mail in his hands. 'Just this.' He walked down the steps and handed Cairns a padded A4-size envelope. Cairns thanked him and went back to his car. Inside the envelope, there was another £3500 in cash and a typed sheet of paper. He read it carefully, then folded it into his pocket.

He had thought about phoning Oxley at home as soon as the woman had phoned him, but decided against it. Old Bill listened to phones, didn't they. Aware of it all now, he had watched as Oxley arrived at the yard the morning after the phone call. Sitting in the Portakabin, he had a good view of the gates and the road beyond. Charlie arrived at eight o'clock. Cairns watched him get out of the van, then watched the road. A motorcycle courier drove slowly past.

Three other lads were drinking tea in the Portakabin when Oxley came in. Cairns spoke quietly to them. 'Go get the van ready, lads.'

They looked at him. 'All of us?'

'Yes, fucking all of you.'

Oxley turned to go with them, but Cairns stopped him. 'Not you, Charlie.'

When they were alone, Cairns leaned on the desk and folded his arms. 'Old Bill's clocked you,' he said.

Oxley stared at him. 'What you on about?'

'They're watching you.'

'Who are?'

'The police, you fucking wanker.'

Oxley jumped up to look out of the window.

'Don't be a prick. Take my word for it. I know.'

Oxley sat down again and stuck a cigarette between his lips.

'I've had another phone call,' Cairns told him. 'They want us to do two more jobs, but the trouble is Old Bill's looking at you.'

'Why me?'

'Can only be the cab.'

'Kenny did the cab and Frank drove it.'

'Yeah, but you drove Kenny.' Cairns stroked his jaw. 'Where'd you go that night?'

'What night?'

'When you nicked the cab, stupid.'

Oxley scratched the shaven hair on his scalp. 'Hackney, wasn't it.'

'I know that – what did you do – pub, shops – what?'

'Pub. We had a couple of pints on Victoria Park Road.'

'Landlord clock you, did he?'

'I don't know.'

'Fucking skinheads in Hackney. You pair of twats. You're gonna stand out a mile.' He tugged at his hair. 'Why d'you think I grow it like this?'

Oxley said nothing. He bit his already bitten-down nails and spat what he could on the floor. 'What d'you want me to do?'

'Nothing. Let me think about it for a while. But don't start looking over your shoulder. Don't do anything any different than you are now. I reckon, if they think you've clocked them, they'll pull you.'

'What can they nick me for?'

'I don't know, do I. Just don't let them know you see 'em. If nothing happens, they'll get bored and fuck off.'

That was a few days ago now and Cairns sat in his car with the cash and the typed sheet of paper. He drummed his fingers on the steering wheel and then he made a phone call.

'Hello?'

'Hello, Mr Ingram. Tommy Cairns.'

'What do you want?'

'Nothing really. Just that we're a bit slack right now, so I thought a bunch of the lads might make a start on the flat in Brighton.'

'I wanted that done before the summer. I could've let it.'

'We were busy then, weren't we. We might as well get on with it now, though, make sure it don't get no worse over the winter. You might get a long-term let.'

'OK.'

'It'll mean the lads staying down there.'

'Why? It's hardly a long drive.'

'In the flat, Mr Ingram.'

'Oh, I see.' Ingram sniffed. 'All right, then.'

'I'll come and collect the keys.' Cairns switched the phone off and then dialled another number.

'It's me – Tom. Listen, I need a driving licence. Don't care whose, so long as he's away and his old lady don't know me.'

'OK,' the voice said in his ear. 'How soon?'

'Yesterday'd be good.'

☆

Swann still could not shake the mood, as if a cloud of depression had settled on him. 'What's the matter, Daddy?' Joanna asked him as he sat on the settee on Saturday morning. 'You don't seem to be very happy at the moment. Is it because me and Charley are naughty?'

Swann took her by the shoulders and held her in front of him, looking into her eyes.

'Darling,' he said. 'You and Charley are the best-behaved children in the world, and even if you weren't – Daddy's moods wouldn't be because of you.'

'So what's the matter, then?' She put her hand on her hip and cocked her head to one side.

Swann looked at her and smiled. 'Oh, I don't know really.'

'Is it Pia? I thought you loved Pia.'

'I do.'

'Is she coming over today?'

'We're going over to get her, then go and see Caroline and George and the horses.'

Joanna went to get ready and Swann went up to the roof and smoked a cigarette. He rested his foot against the parapet and leaned on his thigh. Rachael had left him partially because of this. Every now and then, just when he thought he was doing OK, something would happen, trigger a dream and then he would slip down the slope some more. He fought against it continually, brave face, snappy clothes, boosting the way he felt about himself. It was strange though this time – that photograph had started it, Ibrahim Huella, or whoever he really was, sending him the picture with a mock bullet hole in his head. Webb had laughed it off, as Webb was apt to do. But he couldn't. It was not the threat that bothered him, but the deliberateness of the act; as if the sender knew his weakness, sought it out, then picked at it over again.

*You should talk to someone*, Rachael had told him time and time again. *All you do is bury it. Then it resurfaces and everyone else suffers.*

*I'm not talking to some stranger.*

*Then get some fucking pills.*

Which is what he had done for a while, but that only helped in the short term, so he stopped taking them. The climbing helped definitely. Maybe he needed to go again, this winter perhaps; Scotland, maybe tackle some snow and ice on his own.

'Daddy, we're ready.' The girls' voices lifted up to him in unison from downstairs. He threw the remains of the cigarette into the street below and went back inside. They were standing in the lounge side by side, with their overnight bags packed and ready before them.

Swann scooped them up in his arms and hugged them. 'Come on, then,' he said. 'Let's go and get Pia.'

☆

Tommy Cairns stole the van and drove it to the yard in darkness. It was five days since he had sent Oxley, Bacon and the other boys down to Brighton to work on the seafront flat. At the yard, he unscrewed the licence plates and fixed the fresh set that Willis had given him. It was less risky than hiring a van, even with a new driving licence. If for some reason Frankie got pulled, the plates would check out with the type of van. He had been ultra careful, not knowing whether anyone was watching him or not. He had a beer or two, watched the faces in the pub and looked for people he didn't recognize. When he left, he took a long route to where he knew the van was parked and kept looking behind him. He had no real idea about any tried and tested antisurveillance techniques, but he did make sure he stopped regularly, doubled back before finally getting to the van and stealing it. It was easy: he hated doing it himself, but there was nobody else. He was actually better at having them away than Bacon, but he let Bacon think he was better so he could use him more often.

The glass was in the lock-up at the yard. They had moved it from Bacon's garage weeks ago. Frank came down and together they loaded it into the van and secured it.

'You know where you're going?' Tommy asked him.

'Yeah. Supermarket in Crook.'

'We got one more job after this, Frankie, and then we're out. So listen, when you're up there, stay out of the way.'

The following morning, Frank Cairns drove the van north, with the four sheets of toughened glass in the back. A mile before he got to Crook, he stopped at a newsagent's to ask how many supermarkets there were and was directed to one close to the centre of town. He parked the van, slipped the keys up the exhaust pipe and went to find a pub. His instructions were to come back for it at two-thirty, when the keys would be back in the exhaust pipe.

Ricky Gravitz sat in his car and watched as Cairns walked away. He waited five more minutes and then got out, locked the door and wandered over to the van. The supermarket was busy but not heaving. He quickly checked round and bent for the keys in the muffler.

Huella was in the furthest workshop from the house when he heard the van arrive. He had the wooden trap door up and was just finishing with the foam he had taped round the rim, so that it would seal fully when closed. He tried it and it fitted, stiff to lift, but the foam remained intact. He stood up and rolled the last of the foam tape into a loop and placed it under the workbench. Set up on top was a microscope, some Tanita weighing scales and two gas burners linked to twin bottles on the floor. He had a metal clamp with a bulbous, heat-resistant bottle hooked over one burner and a second, slimmer tube set next to it.

Gravitz turned the van in the farmyard and backed up to the workshop. When he got close, Huella opened the door and Gravitz stopped. Together they unbound the tapes that held the four sheets of glass in place and then lifted them into the workshop. From the cab, Gravitz collected the box of hinges and fastenings and placed them next to the glass. When he was finished, he went back out to the van. Huella closed the workshop door and watched him drive away. Now he stood in the silence, thinking of Jack Swann and George Webb and all of those other policemen he would soon have scurrying for their lives. He looked again at the glass, then sat down on a stool at the bench. There was nothing he could do until Gravitz got back. It would take both of them to build it.

# 15

When they had built the glass-panelled room, Huella relaxed for nearly a month. He did nothing but sit in the house and read books: Tolstoy and Chekhov – the short stories rather than the plays. He did not watch TV, did not go out, but he exercised in his bedroom, countless numbers of press-ups and stomach crunches. Gravitz got bored. He hated English TV. There was no satellite dish, so he couldn't get any American sport and he could not stand soccer. He could not understand why they did not just get on with it. When he asked, Huella looked at him sadly.

'Timing, Richard.'

'What d'you mean – timing? We're paying for this.'

'You are. And you're getting your money's worth. There is planning here, an immense amount of planning. There's a certain way of doing things.'

'Why don't we just go boom bang and get on with it?'

'Like you did in Oklahoma?' Huella sneered at him. 'McVeigh was caught within eighty minutes, wasn't he.'

Two weeks into October, Huella made a phone call. He spoke for only a few minutes and then hung up. The following night, a car drove up from the main road with no lights. Gravitz was watching television and did not hear it. Huella heard it from the kitchen and stiffened. He waited, the front door open a fraction, and listened as it drove along the main road at the top of the track. The driver stopped and sat idling for almost a minute before turning into the farm itself. Huella went through to the living room, where Gravitz sat with one leg draped across the arm of a chair.

'We have a visitor,' he said. 'He'll be hungry.'

Gravitz looked up at him.

'Go and make him some food.'

The car pulled up outside and a man got out. From the boot, he took two dark-coloured bundles and carried them under his arms. Huella opened the door quickly and he stepped inside. Tal-Salem, no beard and cropped hair like a skinhead. He looked through the kitchen doorway at Gravitz.

'That the one?'

'Yes.'

Tal-Salem's lips parted in a thin smile and he handed Huella the bundles.

Huella took them, plastic sealed suits in green, with rubber overboots and inner and outer gloves. Two waist bags with straps and, inside, two respirators.

'That one is yours,' Tal-Salem told him and patted one of the bags. Huella nodded and lifted the other one. He took out the black mask with the twin eye goggles in rubber and unscrewed the metal casing on the respirator. One glance told him all he needed to know and he rescrewed it again.

'Have you got everything else?' Tal-Salem asked him.

'The crystals came in copper.'

'Is it as good as we're told?'

'We don't know yet. But we will.'

Tal-Salem nodded. 'You will need this,' he said, and from his pocket he fished a tiny bottle of pentyl acetate. Huella took it quickly and slipped it into his own pocket. 'And this.' Tal-Salem handed him another bottle and Huella put that into a separate pocket. Tal-Salem went through to the kitchen then and sat down. He did not speak to Gravitz, just ate his food, smoked a cigarette and left.

In the morning Huella was up at six. He knocked on Gravitz's door and told him this was the day he had been waiting for. By seven o'clock they were in the cellar. Huella had laid out the suits. 'You've done this before?'

Gravitz looked at him. 'I was in the service.'

'Then I'll dress you first. You're more used to being in the suit than I am.' Huella smiled at him and broke the seal on the nuclear, biological and chemical warfare suit. It came in two pieces, the trousers with tie-up braces and a jacket with plenty of pockets and a hood. Army olive green and lined with charcoal. He had to prise the legs of the trousers apart and then Gravitz leaned against him while he pressed his feet through. Huella wrapped the ties over Gravitz's shoulders, then fastened them at the waist. Next, he pulled the smock-style jacket over his head and tied the strap at the bottom. There was Velcro on the bottoms of the trousers and on the sleeves. Huella helped him into his overboots and fastened the laces for him. Then he sealed the trouser legs with the Velcro fasteners. Gravitz pulled on the white cotton inner gloves and Huella fastened the Velcro on the sleeves. The rubber gloves were awkward. Huella made Gravitz stand side-on with one foot facing forwards and held open the gloves while Gravitz worked his hands into them. Huella flattened the joints between the fingers for maximum dexterity. He wrapped the tops above the wrists in reams of black DPM tape to ensure that nothing could get inside. Then he picked up Gravitz's respirator bag and took out the rubber mask. Gravitz pulled it on and pressed it into his face.

'Can you breathe?' Huella asked him.

Gravitz nodded. Huella made him bend forwards and

he pulled the hood up, pressing the elasticated edges round the rim of the mask.

'OK?'

Gravitz gave him the thumbs up and Huella handed him a plastic bottle of Fuller's Earth. 'If you touch or spill anything, use this straight away.'

Gravitz nodded.

Finally, Huella took the second bottle that Tal-Salem had given him and unscrewed the lid.

'Acetate?' Gravitz asked him.

Huella nodded and waved it under his nose. 'Can you smell anything?'

Gravitz shook his head.

'Good. Now do me.'

When Huella was suited, he took the other bottle of pentyl acetate and checked his respirator. He could smell nothing. They were ready. He led the way into the passage from the cellar, the door of which he had also fitted with the sealing foam. The outside door to the final workshop was locked and sealed with mastic. The same had been done to the small window at the back.

They closed the doors behind them as they went, passage door to the cellar, trap door to the first workshop and the two adjoining doors after that. The glass room was ready, the door they had fashioned standing open. Inside was the bench with the heating apparatus and the bottles of nitric and hydrochloric acid. The sealed copper tube was still wrapped in oil cloth on the other bench. Huella picked it up with gloved hands and they both stepped into the eight by four 'dirty room'. On the shelf under the bench lay a short length of scaffolding pipe.

The workbench was three feet wide and two feet deep. The heating apparatus and the glass bottles were set at the far end. Huella placed the copper tube into the fixed vice and tightened it. Gravitz picked up a small hacksaw they had laid out in readiness and started to saw off the top of the tube. It took him a few minutes and when it fell off, he stepped back. Huella had laid a sheet of white paper on the bench next to the vice. He held the tube in one hand while slowly loosening the pressure of the vice. He lifted the tube clear and poured the contents very carefully on to the paper. Gravitz bent low, aware of the rasp of his breathing through the respirator, and studied the crystals scattered now on the paper. Blue-white metal, already they were beginning to oxidize, turning a browny black at the edges. Huella lifted the paper from each side and the crystals slid into the furrow. He poured half of them into the bulbous glass jar, set at an angle of forty-five degrees over the burner.

Gravitz unscrewed the lid on the bottle of nitric acid. He poured it over the top of the crystals, which immediately fizzed and began to dissolve. As soon as he had finished, Huella fixed the vaporizing tube fitted with a thermometer over the top of the jar. It was now a sealed unit, the pouring spout blocked by a rubber bung. He turned on the gas, lit the burner and moved away from the bench.

He held the copper tube while Gravitz poured the remaining crystals back. Then Huella took a separate rubber bung from the bench and secured the sawn end. They both moved out of the dirty room and Huella laid the tube on the other workbench. He leaned his head close to Gravitz. 'Get the charge.'

'Now?'

'Yes, now. I want to shape it. Don't worry, without a detonator it's harmless.'

Huella watched the rising temperature carefully through the secure glass panel. It had to heat to 120 degrees and remain at that temperature for exactly four minutes. Any longer and it could explode. He could feel the tendrils of sweat on his brow, the mask pinching his face. He was suddenly aware of his breathing, consciously taking in each gasp of restricted air. Gravitz came back with the Semtex and laid it out on the other bench.

'Watch the temperature gauge and the clock,' Huella told him.

Gravitz took over from him, face close to the wall of glass, and Huella set about making a conical-shaped charge from the Semtex, less than two ounces, but more than enough for his requirements. When it was ready, he left it on the bench. Gravitz looked over at him and nodded. They both went back into the dirty room and Huella cut the gas supply to the burner. The blue flame died and the vapour in the jar began to settle. They watched as it cooled and began to re-form as a yellow-coloured liquid, like bad mescal or urine.

'What's the crystal derivative?' Gravitz said. 'I thought we'd have to do a lot more than this.'

Huella shook his head. 'That part was done months ago. All it needed was heat and acid.'

'What is it?'

'Do you really want to know? If you knew, you could tell someone.' Huella felt the sweat in his eyes now. When the solution was cool, they had to pour it. He looked at Gravitz.

'You OK?' His voice was muffled and Gravitz cocked his head to hear him. 'Are you OK?' Huella repeated.

'Fine.'

'Good. Get the water.'

Gravitz picked up the larger jar, which contained half a gallon of water, and set it down by the burner. Huella uncoupled the sealed jar from the bracket. He looked sideways at Gravitz. 'You pour it. I've got to put the charge in the pipe.' They swapped places and Huella lifted the scaffolding pipe from underneath the bench. Gravitz picked up the jar.

'Take the bung out and wait for thirty seconds before you pour.' Huella indicated the clock on the wall. 'It has to oxidize for exactly thirty seconds before dilution.'

Gravitz nodded and Huella stepped outside the door and eased it to with his heel.

He carried the pipe to the bench where he had prepared the shaped Semtex charge and then looked round. Gravitz had the bung out of the neck of the spout, his eyes fixed on the second hand of the clock. All at once he jolted, almost dropping the bottle. Huella moved to the glass. Gravitz looked at him and Huella could see his eyes were balling inside the mask. He put the jar on the bench and coughed, body buckling over. He stumbled, got to the door and pushed it open. Huella stepped aside and let him past, then quickly he replaced the bung in the jar.

Gravitz was choking. Huella could hear him and he stepped out of the dirty room. Gravitz looked at him again and then retched. He vomited into his mask and hauled it over his head. His lips were blue and the blood vessels had burst in his eyes. He felt his bowels go and excrement slip down the backs of his legs. He tried to get to Huella, but he moved aside. Gravitz fell against the bench, his fingers gripped the scaffolding pipe and locked. He spasmed, then crashed to the floor and rolled on to his back, still holding the pipe. His body went rigid and his eyes rolled. He started to blabber incoherently and then the muscles in his face locked up.

Huella had seen enough. He left Gravitz lying on the floor with his eyes beginning to push against their sockets and went through into the second workshop. From there, he made his way to the cellar and climbed the steps to the hall. The door directly across was a shower room. He moved quickly over to it, knowing he was taking a chance, and then stepped into the shower, still dressed in the suit. The water was freezing and he stood under it for nearly twenty minutes. When he was finished, he patted the suit down with paper towels and then stripped it off and dumped it in the plastic bin liner lying on the floor. He had not touched Gravitz and he had only touched the bung and jar with his gloves. These he washed and rewashed before he took them off.

When he was naked, he climbed the stairs to the other bathroom. Here, he showered and soaped himself for a further fifteen minutes, then he dried and dressed. Hurriedly now he packed his things, being careful to leave nothing behind. Outside was the car that Gravitz had bought and registered. Huella fastened his bag and then went through to Gravitz's room. He took all evidence of his ID and most of the money from his wallet. Then he went outside, leaving the farmhouse door open. He resisted the temptation to walk across the yard and peek through the window to see if Gravitz was dead yet. He should be. Huella must have watched him for about two minutes. He would lie in a state of paraesthesia for three minutes more and then his heart would stop.

He drove south and on through Stanhope, where he passed the police station housed in the old building on the corner. He carried on south until he got to Eggleston, then he pulled over at a phone box and dialled 999.

'Which service, please?' the operator asked him.

'Police. I want to report a burglary.'

'What's your name, sir?'

'Leaming. Colin Leaming.'

'And your address?'

'Never mind that. I think the burglars are still there.'

'Where?'

'Healey Hall Farm.' He put the phone down and got

back in the car. It was low on fuel and he stopped at a Texaco station on the A68. From there, he drove back to the A1 and then south. When he got to the first Leeds exit he stopped at the service station, got out of the car and walked to the red Lancia that was waiting. Tal-Salem, sitting behind the wheel, leaned across to open the passenger door. 'Just the one of you, then.'

Huella looked through the windscreen and smiled.

☆

Harrison went to church. Jakob Salvesen was preaching in Passover that night and Harrison told Lisa he was going. October, Sunday, and still quite warm. Five of them were nigger-fishing out at Magic Reservoir: Harrison and Lisa, Chief now more than ensconced with Belinda again, and Danny Dugger still on his own, but with hope; three poles between them, lying back on the beach, with a cooler full of beer.

'Church, Harrison,' Lisa said when he told her. 'When did you ever go to church?'

'Never,' Harrison said. 'But my grandma's sick and she's the only family I got.'

'So, you're going to go to church?'

'Yep.'

'Jake Salvesen's church.'

'What other church is there?'

'Goddamn, Harrison. I never figured you for religion.'

'Neither did I, Guffy. But I'm forty-eight years old and I haven't tried church yet. I don't mean to make a habit of it, but I'll give it a shot one time.'

'Fine,' she said. 'I'll be in the bar when you come out.'

Jesse Tate was there and so were Bill Slusher, Drake and his wife and kids, Wingo and a whole bunch of townspeople from Passover. They were singing the first hymn when Harrison slipped inside and quietly took a seat at the back. He scraped the faded baseball hat from his head, but he didn't sing. He hadn't come here for the singing, he'd come to listen to what Salvesen was going to say to his flock. As usual the address would be broadcast nationwide and Harrison imagined the likes of BobCat Reece and his friends glued to their radio sets.

He had to sit through two more hymns and the people got a little louder, hands started being raised and people were swaying in the aisles. Harrison felt more than a little uncomfortable. The things I do for this job, he thought to himself. At last, though, the congregation settled down and Salvesen got up in the pulpit, resting his hands on the lectern. If he spotted Harrison hunched in his seat at the back, he did not show it.

'Daniel, chapter seven,' he was saying, 'has been considered – right from the earliest Hebrew scholars to modern-day evangelicals like myself – the most important chapter in the whole of the Bible. I'll read you some and then maybe discuss it a little bit.' He cleared his throat.

'In the first year of Belshazzar king of Babylon Daniel had a dream and visions of his head upon his bed: then he wrote the dream, and told the sum of the matters.

Daniel spake and said, I saw in my vision by night, and, behold, the four winds of the heaven strove upon the great sea.

And four great beasts came up from the sea, diverse one from another.

The first was like a lion, and had eagle's wings: I beheld it till the wings thereof were plucked, and it was lifted up from the earth, and made to stand upon the feet as a man, and a man's heart was given to it.

And behold another beast, a second, like to a

bear, and it raised up itself on one side, and it had three ribs in the mouth of it between the teeth of it: and they said thus unto it, Arise, and devour much flesh.

After this I beheld, and lo another, like a leopard, which had upon the back of it four wings of a fowl; the beast had also four heads; and dominion was given to it.

After this I saw in the night visions, and behold a fourth beast, dreadful and terrible, and strong exceedingly; and it had great iron teeth: it devoured and brake in pieces, and stamped the residue with the feet of it: and it was diverse from all the beasts that were before it; and it had ten horns.'

Salvesen stopped talking for a moment and looked at the written word in front of him. Then he looked up at his audience and his eyes were tight, pitted almost in the reddened flesh of his face. 'Those four beasts, my friends, were four empires, kingdoms if you like, that would "bear rule", so the Bible tells us, which literally means have authority over all the known world at the time.' He paused and scratched the side of his nose with a fleshy finger. 'Now, when we look at chapter two, you'll recall the dream of King Nebuchadnezzar. He saw a beast divided in gold, silver and bronze; feet and toes of clay and iron.' He inhaled audibly. 'The interpretation that the angel of the Lord gave to Daniel in both cases is the same – four kingdoms which would hold dominion over the earth.

'The first of those four kingdoms or empires was Babylon itself, which came to power in 606 BC after it had conquered Egypt. It became a world kingdom when Nebuchadnezzar took over from his father after he died. In 530 BC, the Babylonians were conquered by what was then the Median-Persian Empire. This was the second beast in Daniel's dream. The third was the ancient Greek Empire, installed by Alexander the Great in 331 BC. See how the prophetic line becomes a reality?' Again, he swept the congregation with penetrating eyes and they seemed to alight on Harrison. 'It was also predicted that the third kingdom would be split into four – the four wings on its back? Well, after Alexander, four of his generals divided the empire and it lasted in that way until it was finally conquered by the Romans in 68 BC.' Salvesen paused to dampen his lips with his tongue. 'The fourth kingdom was Rome. If you read on in chapter seven, my friends, you'll see how that fourth kingdom ruled the whole world until the time of the Lord's return. "Behold, he cometh with the clouds; and every eye shall see him, and they also which pierced him: and all kindreds of the earth shall wail because of him."'

His voice was low and controlled, but the power in it seemed to reverberate round the whole church. Harrison could feel the hairs lifting on the nape of his neck. He squinted at those around him. Every eye was rooted on Jakob Salvesen. Right now, Harrison thought, you could make them do anything you wanted.

'But how, I hear you ask, can this be?' Salvesen went on. 'The Roman Empire fell apart. It took a long time, but by AD 400, hordes of barbarians sacked the city. That was sixteen hundred years ago, near as makes no difference. And yet – here it is in God's living word that the Roman Empire, the fourth kingdom as prophesied by Daniel, will be in power just before the Lord's return.' He leaned on the pulpit then and looked at them. 'Well, let me tell you, my friends, that fourth kingdom is alive and well as we speak. It's already been resurrected and right now it's taking its final form. And I shall tell you something else – in the last days of this world, America will have no place. She will cease to be the pre-eminent power in world affairs. Like the first Rome, she will have fallen apart from within. She will have suffered from every conceivable degradation and depravity known to man. We see it every day of our lives. We see it in the government. We see it in the one-world religion seekers, the one-world government seekers. We see it in rights for homosexuals, for lesbians, and those who dish out abortion like Hershey bars. We see it in federal laws which strip the common man of what he, by virtue of the God-given constitution, was born to. Brother will turn against brother. Children will rise up against their parents. Drugs, gangs, gang rapes, drive-by shootings. The removal of prayer from school. Did you know there's an organization in this country working to take Gideon Bibles from hotel rooms?

'Heed my words, my friends, the United States of America is going the way of Rome. And in its place – a new Rome, the Rome that Charlemagne tried to put back together, the Rome that Napoleon Bonaparte tried to put back together, the Rome that Adolf Hitler tried to put back together. This isn't my opinion, friends. This isn't just old Jake Salvesen shooting off at the lip.' He stabbed the Bible with a forefinger. 'It's here. It's here in black and white. It's what I've been warning against for years.' He stopped then and looked at them. 'That is my word to you tonight. That is my word across this country to the good people of America, to my friends in Montana and Kansas, Texas and Missouri and Nebraska; South Dakota and back east there in Delaware. It's my word to you in Washington D.C., if you hear me, to you on Capitol Hill; and you, sir, in the White House. Yes, sir. This is my word to you. I tell you, our day is all but over and the coming times . . .' His voice softened then. 'Well, the coming times are upon us.'

After the service Harrison got up to leave. He stood for a moment with his hat in his hands and then walked outside. The sun was sinking and he was thirsty.

'Harrison, isn't it?'

He stopped, squared his hat on his head and looked back. Jakob Salvesen was standing in the doorway of the church, his white suit gleaming like gold in the evening sunshine.

'That's my name.'

Salvesen walked down the path to him, a big man, bearlike, towering over Harrison. They looked at one another, not so different in age, but from completely different worlds.

'Not seen you in my church before,' Salvesen said.

'I listen on the radio sometimes.'

'Why tonight?'

Harrison scratched his head. 'Well, that I can't answer for you, sir.' He looked Salvesen in the eye.

'God works in mysterious ways.'

'So they tell me.' Harrison took a Marlboro from his shirt pocket and scraped his thumb over a match. The smoke drifted in Salvesen's face. Jesse had come to the door and Bill Slusher with him. They eyed Harrison suspiciously.

'So, you're just waiting for it all to go bang, are ya,' Harrison said. 'That why you live up on the hill in that old fort of yours?'

Salvesen's eyes darkened. He had his hands in his trouser pockets, belly thrust forward, moustache twitching. 'Just minding my property, Mr Harrison, like any other American.'

'I guess.' Harrison had the urge to spit, but he fought it.

'Will we see you next Sunday?'

'Well.' Harrison looked into the sun and scratched the

tattoo on his arm. 'You never know, Mr Salvesen. You just never know.' He fixed his hat then and walked off down the road. He could feel Salvesen's eyes on him, Jesse's and Slusher's, too. Halfway to the bar he stopped and looked back. Townsfolk were still milling about in front of the church, but Salvesen was looking at him. Harrison took a tin of chew from his jeans pocket and pressed a fingerful under his lip. He sucked and spat and walked into the Silver Dollar.

☆

Police Constables Walker and Jennings were patrolling the A68 just south of Broomhaugh, when the call went out to any car in the area. Disturbance at Healey Hall Farm. Jennings lifted his radio to his lips.

'Control from five/six, we're at Broomhaugh now. What've you got?'

'Possible break-in. Can you attend?'

'On our way.'

They hit the blue light, sped along the moorland road, with the land rising on one side and falling away on the other. 'Where is it?' Walker asked.

'Next right.'

They came to the entrance and turned off. The farm-yard was deserted, but the front door of the house stood open. Walker and Jennings got out of the car and looked at one another.

They went up to the door and Walker pushed it back on its hinges. A light wind was blowing from the north and the door creaked as it swung back. The house was in silence, no sound, no movement from anywhere. They looked at one another.

'Hello?' Jennings called. 'Anyone at home?'

Silence. He called again. 'This is the police. Is anyone here?'

Walker laid a hand on the radiator in the hallway; it was warm. He made a face and wandered into the kitchen. The remains of a meal was still stuck to dishes piled in the sink. He felt the kettle, but it was cold. They went through to the lounge, the dining room and the large study at the back. Nobody. Jennings stood at the bottom of the stairs, a hand on the banister, and called out once more. Again he received no answer. They started up the stairs. Clothes were strewn across the unmade bed in the master bedroom, a stereo system standing on the dressing table. The wardrobe doors were open and clothes hung from the rails. They moved on to the second bedroom and it looked as though it had been inhabited, sheets on the bed, a little rumpled. The wardrobe doors stood wide, but it was empty. The chest of drawers looked as though somebody had cleared it recently, empty drawers only half pushed in.

Downstairs again, they checked the other rooms and came to the closed door to the shower room. Walker swung it back and saw the plastic bin liner in the corner. He bent and checked the contents – a rubber respirator. He narrowed his eyes, looked again and recognized the bundle of green cloth and rubber boots. 'Jesus Christ,' he said. He stood up then and sniffed. Nothing. The shower-head still dripped water.

Out in the hall, Jennings had the cellar door open and was shining his torch downstairs. Walker touched him on the shoulder. 'There's a chemical warfare suit back there.'

'What?'

'An NBC suit.'

'You sure?'

'Course I'm sure. I've worn the fucking things.'

Jennings looked at him and then started down the steps to the cellar. Rows and rows of wine bottles. He whistled. 'Christ, Len. There must be a fortune down here.' They moved between the bottles and then came to the inner passage door.

'Who owns this place?' Walker asked him.

'I don't know, man. Some big noise in London.'

Walker tried the passage door. It was stiff, but it opened. He noticed the foam lining on the outer skin. Jennings shone his torch. 'Secret bloody passage.'

They moved on and came to the steps which led up to the trap door. Walker could feel his heart beating. Jennings lifted the door and it sucked air through the foam. They climbed into the first workshop. Benches, tools. They looked at the second door. It opened again with a stiffness and Walker frowned. Something was wrong. He could feel it. Something was very wrong. They saw more benches, only this time they were littered with an array of electrical items.

Walker moved to the bench and saw two PP3 batteries, electrical wiring and liquid-crystal clocks. Two black and grey plastic boxes and, individually wrapped in polythene, four Iraco detonators.

'That's it,' he said. 'We're out of here.'

'What about the other door?' Jennings indicated the final one.

Walker looked at the insulation foam round the edge. 'Don't open it.'

He led the way back to the house and then out into the yard, where they crossed the concrete to the outside door of the third workshop. Walker could see that it was sealed with mastic. There was no window at the front, so they made their way round the back and came to a small, grimy-glassed aperture. Walker moved up close and cupped his hand against the window. He could see a man lying on the floor in a green NBC suit, one hand clutching what looked like a length of pipe. Beside him was a discarded respirator. His face was pink and bloated, blood covering his lips and tongue. His eyes looked as though they had burst.

'Oh my God,' he breathed.

'What is it?' Jennings pushed to see. Walker was already on his way back to the car.

'Whatever you do, don't try to get in,' he said.

'What is it, man? What is it?' Jennings was following him across the farmyard.

Walker called over his shoulder. 'You remember that trouble with PIRA?'

'Aye. Course I do.'

'This is ten times worse.'

At the car, Walker picked up the radio. 'Control from five/six.'

'Go ahead five/six.'

'Healey Farm. We've got some kind of terrorist incident. There's batteries and detonators and stuff like that in a workshop.'

'OK. We'll—'

'Hang on a minute. It gets worse. We've got a fatality and it looks like some kind of chemical.'

The control room called Superintendent Gooding, the senior duty officer, and told him what they had.

'Right,' Gooding said. 'Implement major incident procedure and get the cordons in quickly.' He put the phone down and dialled Scotland Yard. 'I want to talk to your Antiterrorist Branch.'

☆

Jack Swann was talking to Julian Moore in the Special Branch ops room. Moore was just back from Brighton, the surveillance on Oxley and Bacon cancelled. The line to the communications room rang. 'SO13 Reserve. DS Swann.'

'Swann, this is PSU Gooding, senior duty officer at Ponteland, Northumberland. We've got a problem here.'

302

He told him what they had and Swann felt a chill brush his spine.

'Right. We'll be there. You got cordons in?'

'Of course.'

'Any explosives?'

'We've found detonators and batteries.'

'OK. I'll come back to you.' Swann put the phone down, then dialled Colson's office.

'Northumberland, sir,' he told him. 'Chemical incident at Healey Hall Farm.'

Colson glanced at the map on his wall. 'OK, Jack. Get the CAD and we'll move.'

Colson hung up, then dialled the Meteorological Office. 'This is the Antiterrorist Branch, Scotland Yard. Which way is the wind blowing and at what speed?'

'Right now?' the voice came back. 'From the north-east, at about fifteen miles an hour.'

Upstairs, the computer-aided dispatch was pumping through the printer in front of Jack Swann, when the phone rang again.

'Colson, Jack. The wind speed is fifteen mph, blowing from the north-east.'

'Right, sir.' Swann hung up and dialled the Chemical and Biological Research Establishment at Porton Down in Wiltshire.

'Duty officer, please.'

'Speaking.'

'Jack Swann. SO13. We've got a chemical incident in Northumberland.'

'Substance?'

'Not known.'

'Wind speed?'

'Fifteen mph from the north-east.'

'OK. Without knowing exactly what you've got, persistency etc., I can't confirm a downwind hazard. Initial evacuation, one mile upwind and four miles down, funnelling two to four. But that might change.'

'I understand.'

'Can you give me the exact location, please?'

'It's Healey Hall Farm. We'll give you a grid reference in the air.'

When Swann hung up he called Gooding back. 'Right, sir,' he said. 'Everything's rolling here. Evacuation radius, one mile upwind, four downwind, and two rising to four either side of the farm. That may change when we've had a chance to assess. Where's the nearest army base?'

'Catterick.'

'You'll need them. Perimeter guard. What about 11 EOD?'

'What?'

'Bomb-disposal team. If there's explosives there, you're going to need an ATO.'

Gooding paused.

'Bomb man, sir. Ammunitions technical officer.'

'Of course. We're on it, Swann.'

'We'll see you when we get there, then. Porton Down scientists are on their way. They're flying direct from Wiltshire. They'll need a map reference. I've told them, you'll give it to them in the air. Call sign Foxtrot Unicorn two/five/zero. Repeat, Foxtrot Unicorn two/five/zero.'

# 16

_____

It was four-thirty in the afternoon by the time they arrived at the rendezvous point, established on the northern side of the outer cordon, upwind of the farm. Soldiers were everywhere, armed and spread out at intervals around the perimeter line. The scientists had been there for well over an hour and were already down at the farm. Webb rendezvoused with PSU Gooding.

'Explosives?' he asked.

Gooding shook his head. 'We've had an EOD officer check. There are explosives there but only a small quantity of Semtex. No improvised explosive device.'

'OK.' Webb looked at the soldiers. Already a tent city was appearing above the perimeter line on the flat of the moors.

'Evacuation?'

'Done. So far, we've not been told to increase it.'

The breeze blew from the north, tugging the grass into knots. It ruffled Webb's hair and he looked back at Tania.

'DRA coming or not – d'you know, Tania?' he asked.

'Jane's flying up, I think.'

An army truck was sitting with its engine running, waiting to take those required into the inner cordon and the changing station. Webb showed his ID to the driver and they climbed into the back.

The truck dropped them at the forward control point to the north of the inner cordon and 'dirty line'. Beyond that point, everyone was dressed in full NBC gear, complete with mask and respirator. Three clear-plastic inflatable tents had been erected for the three stages of decontamination, hosepipe showers hanging in lines from hooks attached to the ceiling. No cubicles, just duckboard to walk on. The water would drain from the troughs and run through a single pipe to a pit that was already being dug by twin JCB excavators.

Separate from the decontamination tents, on the other side of the control point, two more were set up for people to change into NBC suits. Webb set down his boxes and looked for the scene commander. He could see a number of people at the farmhouse and he assumed they would be from Porton Down. Their helicopter had been squatting on a flat piece of moorland, just above the rendezvous point. The scene commander was a major from Catterick. He introduced himself as Peter Carter.

'Antiterrorist Branch?' he said.

'Briggs and Webb. Any idea what we've got yet?'

Carter shook his head. 'The scientists are in there now.'

Webb glanced about them. Land-Rovers were patrolling the dirty line south of the farm and well into the downwind hazard. The sky overhead was cloudy, grey and black in patches as the daylight gradually faded. A Lynx helicopter buzzed above their heads. He looked back at Carter. 'The wind's lifted.'

'I know.'

'Have they said anything about increasing the downwind hazard?'

Carter shook his head.

'What about the press?'

'No one's tried to break the line just yet.'

'Now, there's a first.'

'There's five hundred soldiers here, Webb. They've all got guns.'

They stood outside the first of the plastic tents, both holding their warrant cards. 'Exhibits officers,' Webb told the corporal in charge. 'Antiterrorist Branch.'

'Right.' The corporal pointed to some benches set out on the far side of the tent. 'Change there and put your clothes in a bin. There's tape on them. Make sure you mark your name.'

Webb carried his kit over and unfastened his bag. From inside he took a freshly sealed NBC suit and his respirator. Soldiers milled about them, some of them preparing to patrol the dirty line. Webb could smell food cooking as he stripped off his clothes. 'Hope the army feeds us,' he said to Tania. 'They're renowned for what they can produce in the field.' He whistled as he changed, but underneath he was aware of the growing sense of unease. Bombs he could handle, but you just never knew with chemicals. He and Tania buddied up to get themselves fully suited. When they were ready, DPM tape round their wrists and masks squashed against the skin of their faces, they each produced their own bottle of pentyl acetate and checked to make sure they could not smell pear drops.

When they were ready, they moved out of the tent and up to the cordon tape that marked the dirty line, five hundred metres upwind of the farm. Webb looked across at the farm, as a group of suited figures started to walk up the cordoned approach path towards them. 'Aye, aye,' he said. 'Something's going on.'

The group got closer and went into the first decontamination shower. Webb could hear the water rushing off charcoal-lined suits. The word came from the tents that the crime-scene team could now enter. They would be briefed on the far side of the inner cordon. Webb and Tania picked up their tongs, nylon evidence bags and the other tools they might need. Webb stuffed the bags into the respirator case strapped about his waist and the tools in the breast pockets of his NBC smock. He glanced at Tania. Again they checked their respirators, then crossed under the tape.

They were met by the duty officer from Porton Down. He nodded to them and looked at the name tag under the plastic cover on Webb's sleeve.

'Webb?'

Webb nodded. The man showed his own name tag. Billings.

'What've we got?' Webb asked him. He spoke loudly, voice muffled through the respirator.

'We don't know. The contamination looks like it's confined to the end shed over there.' Billings pointed to the row of workshops standing in a line at right angles to the farmhouse. 'There are marginal traces in the house itself, though. So far we've swabbed outside and done some atmospheric testing. We've got some positive readings, but they're minimal.'

'Nerve agent?'

'We don't know. The chaps you saw getting cleaned up have got what we think is the base crystal. There was a bottle of solution in there, nitric and hydrochloric acid, together with heating apparatus.'

'What, just open in the workshop?' Webb said.

Billings shook his head. 'They've built a dirty room out of glass.'

Webb went very still. 'How big is it?'

'About eight by four.'

Webb looked at Tania and she stared back through the separated eyes of her mask.

Billings pointed out the approach path, between the two lines of orange tape. 'That'll take you to the front door of the house,' he said. 'There's another one of *us* in there with the pathologist.'

They walked between the tapes and Tania leaned her head close so she could be heard through the respirator. 'Glass, Webby. Eight-foot dirty room.'

'I know, Tania.'

'What d'you reckon?'

'I don't reckon anything till I've seen it.'

At the farmhouse door they were shown down into the wine cellar and Webb caught a glimpse of some of the labels on the bottles. Someone's going to be very upset about this lot, he thought. Lights had been set up on cabling, running through the cellar and into the passage to the workshops. The trap door was closed and they opened it. The Porton Down man with them made sure it was closed again before he opened the first workshop door. Webb examined the foam sealer that had been stapled over the rim. 'Someone knew what they were doing,' he muttered.

In the second workshop they found the detonators, still packaged. Tania photographed everything while Webb took a closer look around. On the workbench he saw the PP3 batteries and the circuit tester, and then his gaze fell on an LCD Spanish clock with separate alarm display, squatting in a grey and black plastic box. Tania lowered her camera. 'Oh, fuck,' she said.

Webb laid out white paper sheets while they were dusting and placed the items for recovery on those, before wrapping each piece in three nylon bags and then labelling them. In the last room, they found the pathologist bending over the dead man.

His body was lying prostrate on the floor, naked now, having been carefully cut out of the NBC suit, which was piled in a black plastic bag. Webb moved closer. The flesh was pale, rigid almost over the bones. The man's face was bloated, burned about his mouth and nose. Blood was smeared dark and congealed round his eyes. His mouth was open a fraction with the thickness of his tongue protruding. He knew it was pointless asking the pathologist anything. The body would be wrapped in three nylon body-bags and then carried to the perimeter line where it would be decontaminated. Then it would be placed in a sealed casket and shipped by helicopter to Porton Down. Only after they had carried out X-rays and a full autopsy under contamination conditions, would they pass any information back.

He left the dead man and turned to the glass room, then he paused and crouched again by the doctor. 'I want to photograph his fingerprints while you've got him like that,' he said. 'We've got a digital camera.' The doctor nodded and Webb motioned to Tania, who knelt down beside the dead man and set about assembling the equipment.

Webb watched her for a moment, then looked at the eight-foot glass room with the workbench and the heating equipment. Bottles of nitric acid, bottles of hydrochloric acid; he left them for the scientists. Everything he touched, he did so with tongs, working hard not to brush against anything. He turned to the other workbench and examined the shaped charge: Semtex, not very much, looked about two ounces or so to him. On the floor the dead man was still clutching the piece of scaffolding pipe. Webb bent to the pathologist once more. 'Can you get that pipe out of his hand?' he asked.

He nodded and curled back the fingers with a cracking sound. The pipe fell loose and rolled on to the floor. Webb bent gingerly over it. He could not use the tongs, it was too big and heavy. Tania looked at him. Webb felt sweat on his brow for the first time. His paper suit started to stick to him under the charcoal-lined outer. He pressed his lips together, and carefully, just holding the ends, lifted the scaffolding pipe.

It was a mortar or bomb casing of some kind. He stood it on its end and checked the conical Semtex charge. Designed to fit the pipe and force maximum blast pressure at the trajectory. Mortar. He shone his torch inside the piping and saw what they had planned to do. Halfway down was a barrier, what looked like a bung made of plastic or nylon and heat-sealed into place. They were planning to pour the solution into the pipe and seal the top. The shaped Semtex charge would be pressed into the other side of the bung and a detonator into that. A chemical dispersal-mortar bomb that would make the subways of Tokyo look tame. He looked at the glass again and checked its gauge and thickness. It measured exactly the sizes he had in his mind, imprinted there from a receipt found in Queen's House Mews.

'George.'

He didn't hear her.

'George.' Tania came alongside him. She was holding the discarded respirator. 'Look.' She had unscrewed it and showed Webb the inside. He bent his head, not seeing anything at first, and then he realized the fine mesh filter had been hacked to pieces. Deliberately. The mask would have been totally useless. 'Jesus Christ,' he said.

He looked back at the stiffened corpse and took a moment to recover himself. This was as evil a thing as he'd witnessed. He'd seen the shattered and burned remains of innocents in bomb scenes, women, children with their clothes and flesh burned off by the searing heat of the blast wave. That was cynical, cowardly. But this was systematic evil, doctoring a respirator to see if the poison you've perfected works.

He knelt down once more by the body and spoke to the pathologist. 'Any ID on him,' he asked, 'when you cut him out of the suit?'

The pathologist shook his head.

Webb straightened up again. 'We're going to check the house. We've got what we can from here.'

'You'll never be able to do a fingertip search,' the pathologist told him. 'When we've finished, they'll burn it down.'

'I know. Don't worry. We've got most of what we need.' Webb looked at the body one last time and noticed a signet ring of some kind on the third finger of the right hand. He had seen the like before, many times, in the Foxhole bar at Eastcote barracks in Ruislip. It was a US varsity clasp ring. He leaned close to the doctor again. 'I want that ring,' he said.

'Be my guest. Try not to damage the finger.'

Webb took a set of slim wire cutters from his pocket and fed them under the back of the ring. He snipped it off and used the tongs to pick it up and place it in one of the smaller nylon bags. He then placed that bag in another and then that in yet one more. Three layers of nylon between him and the contaminated ring. He turned to find Tania looking at the dirty room.

'Storm Crow, isn't it,' she said.

☆

Swann and McCulloch drove to Consett to speak with Caspar & Gibbs, the estate agents in charge of Healey Hall Farm. The press were now milling about the outer cordons in their droves. Swann saw every conceivable newsman: BBC, Tyne-Tees, Grampian, Granada, Sky. The radio reporters were all there and so were the newspapers.

He wondered how long it would be before somebody tried to break the cordon. The evacuation had been swift and few people were affected. This was a remote corner of the country and the population within the downwind hazard was minimal. The news coverage had been limited, a chemical spillage had been noted, but then John Garrod had been recognized and had to give a statement. However, the evacuation had been managed sensibly and quickly with very little panic, soldiers from Catterick and Kielder with trucks to load people into. They had been moved beyond the hazard line and set up in an array of small hotels and community centres, a few thousand at most.

They drove into Consett and Swann wondered how Webb was getting on at the scene. It was nearly six now and the streetlights were on. Grey skies, not dark yet, but a fresher wind than there had been and the definite threat of rain. The doors to the offices of Caspar & Gibbs were closed and locked. A whole gaggle of newsmen were camped on the pavement. Swann could see lights inside and he rapped on the glass. Nobody came. He rapped again and held his warrant card up to the window. He saw a man looking nervously from the rear office. Swann knocked yet again and the man finally came forward. He was waving Swann away, when he saw the warrant card and opened the door. The newsmen heaved and Swann and McCulloch blocked them and eased inside. The man locked the door again. Swann flapped his warrant card against the glass and waved the press away. They ignored him. He shook his shoulders and turned to the man who had let them in – portly, in his fifties, balding head gleaming under a film of sweat.

'Detective Sergeant Swann,' he said. 'Scotland Yard.'

The man led them into his office, where he offered them seats in leather chairs and poured out coffee. Swann glanced about him – spacious, leather desk, more like a solicitor's office than an estate agent's. The man was the Caspar of Caspar & Gibbs and he sat down heavily in his chair.

'Feel like I'm under siege,' he said. 'What with that lot

out there, and you're the second lot of policemen I've had here today.'

'Locals?' Swann said.

'Ponteland.' He fished in his pocket for a card and passed it across. 'DC Newham.'

Swann noted the number.

'Scotland Yard,' Caspar said. 'Antiterrorist Squad?'

Swann nodded briefly.

'I saw your commander on the TV just now.'

'The farm,' Swann said. 'Who rented it?'

Caspar opened the top drawer of his desk and fished out a copy of the lease. He pushed it towards Swann.

'American student. Richard Gravitz III.'

Swann picked up the document. 'What was he doing over here?'

'Ph.D. Minerals, I think. Something to do with rocks, anyway.'

'How did he pay?'

'International money order. Full six months in advance. Sterling.' He shook his head. 'Best tenant we've ever had. That farm is not cheap, Sergeant. It's over two thousand pounds a month.'

Swann looked up at him. 'Who owns it – the farm?'

'Ah, now that's delicate. We have one very upset individual.'

'I'm not surprised. He's about to see his country pile razed to the ground.'

Caspar leaned forward. 'He's got a wine collection that's worth a fortune. I don't know how the insurance company will view it. Not only that, but the farm's been in his family for years.'

'Who is he?'

'Down your way, actually. Solicitor, which is bound to make matters worse. He'll probably try and sue us for letting to undesirables.'

'His name?'

'James Ingram.'

☆

By eight o'clock that night Webb was finished. With no IED to disrupt things, the farm lights had been used and the approach path from the inner cordon was lit with spotlights. He and Tania had been completely through the house and it was clear from the downstairs shower that someone had washed off there. The water had drained into the mains and the information had been passed on to Northeast Water, but nobody else. Now they were busy sampling the sewerage for signs of contamination.

The men from Porton Down, however, were satisfied that there had been no actual spillage inside the far workshop. Their swabbing had revealed no signs of liquid and they were rapidly coming to the conclusion that the leakage had been in the form of a gas. They still had a number of tests to do on the area and the cordons and army presence would stay in place for at least forty-eight hours. Webb and Tania left the outbuildings and walked back through the fields to the decontamination tents. They had been working in the suits for over three hours; the recommended limit in any one spell was about half an hour. It was fully dark now, though the sky was lit up and the landscape upwind of the farm had a strangely lunar quality, dominated by the luminous bubble tents where the decontamination process was going on.

They arrived together and were met by two soldiers in full NBC gear. They passed over their evidence bags which were put through the three-tent process first, and then each of them went into the shower. Freezing cold water all over them, still completely suited, standing on

315

duckboard in the metal trays with the run-off to a single pipe.

When the first shower was over, they patted themselves down with paper towels which they dumped into bins for incineration, then each of them was assisted by one of the suited orderlies. The orderly unwrapped the DPM tape from around Webb's ankles and wrists and then pulled the rubber overgloves back to halfway. He loosened off the collar tapes and the smock at the waist, and, for the first time in three hours, Webb felt air flow over his skin. Then it was the second shower, colder it felt than the last one. Again, Webb patted himself dry and walked along the duckboard to the next tent. He could see the pale moon through the roof, distorted by plastic and the glare of lights from the ground.

The next orderly cut his smock up the front with shears and told Webb to stand with his arms out in a crucifix position. The man loosened the sleeves, then told him to turn round. He did so and placed his arms behind him like a bad swallow dive. The orderly pulled the jacket down his arms in two pieces and the rubber gloves came with them. They were all placed in a bin beside him. The jacket came away inside out, so that any contamination on the material stayed there. Next, Webb had the trousers loosened and pulled halfway down. The white paper suit was black with charcoal and stuck to his flesh like glue. He sat on the chair provided and the orderly cut the laces on the rubber overboots. They, too, were discarded and then the trousers came off the rest of the way, once again inside out. The only thing that Webb wore now was the paper suit and his respirator. The orderly unzipped the suit and peeled it off him inside out. His body, naked and shivering now, was black with running charcoal.

He moved along the duckboard and into the final shower. This time soap was provided and he washed every inch of his body in freezing cold water. He washed his hair three times and shivered all the way through it. He washed the outside of his mask thoroughly, then took it off and washed the inside. This was the only piece of the suit he would take with him when he left the tents.

At last it was over and he was dried and back in his own clothes. Exhausted and hungry, he and Tania took the truck to the outer cordon and could smell cooking from the army field canteen. Soldiers were everywhere, the press camped not far away. Webb looked for familiar faces and saw Swann standing with another man, smoking a cigarette. Swann spotted him, dropped the cigarette and ground it under his heel.

'What've we got?' he asked.

Webb looked gravely at him. 'The glass from Queen's House Mews.'

He took Swann's arm, walking him slightly apart from the mass of soldiers and police officers around them. 'Chemical mortar bomb, Jack. Scaffolding pipe and conical-shaped charge. About two ounces of Semtex. Packs of Iraco dets and LCD Spanish clocks.'

'Definitely *the* glass?'

'Almost certainly.' Webb looked at him then. Swann's face was pinched. 'What?' he said.

'I figured as much.'

'Why?'

'Guess who owns the farm?'

'I haven't got a clue.'

Swann looked in his eyes. 'James Ingram. Leader of the British Freedom Party.'

☆

Swann drove them back to London. The commander had ordered a parade call at 7.30 a.m. He dropped Webb at home and then Tania. By the time he crawled into his own flat, it was two in the morning. He grabbed three hours' sleep, showered and dressed and was at his desk by 6.30. He had not seen the kids; they and Annika had still been asleep, so he might as well have been away for the night. Webb came in at 6.45, looking red-faced and refreshed. Colson had been at his desk since six o'clock apparently. He was on the telephone when Swann had walked past his office to get coffee. Gradually the rest of the squad filtered in and Colson came down to the squad room.

Swann was suddenly tired. Colson sat on a desk and hitched his trouser legs up at the thigh. He let the team settle and then spoke. 'All right everyone, it's early, I know, especially for the team who went north yesterday, but think of all the overtime.' He looked at Webb. 'George, maybe you or Tania would like to give us a run-down on what you found.'

Webb told them about the Semtex, detonators and timing and power units, all of which, together with the pipe bomb, had gone to Porton Down. 'The bad news is we've finally found the glass,' he finished.

'What about the fatality?' Colson asked him. 'Do we know who he is?'

'Name's Richard Gravitz, sir,' Swann put in. 'American. He rented the farm supposedly to do his Ph.D.'

'I took a varsity clasp ring from him,' Webb said. 'GWU on the back.'

'What does that mean?' McCulloch asked him.

Webb glanced over at him. 'Graduation ring, Macca. He obviously went to GWU.'

'Which is what?'

'How the fuck should I know?'

'It's George Washington University,' Colson cut in on them. 'It's in Washington D.C.' He paused. 'Someone better give Louis Byrne a ring.'

Webb moved in his seat. 'I've got film of the body and his fingerprints via the digital camera,' he said. 'I'll call Byrne myself, soon as they wake up over there, and get it downloaded to him.' He stopped then. 'Just so everyone knows – Gravitz was murdered by whoever was working with him. They doctored his respirator, mashing up the filter with a knitting needle or something. I assume they wanted to see if what they were making worked.'

'In which case, why leave when they did? Why Semtex? And why a half-made bomb?' McCulloch said it to no one in particular. 'If you only want to see if it works, you don't need to bail out when it does.'

'The locals got a 999 call,' Tania added, 'somebody claiming the farm was being burgled. He gave his name as Colin Leaming.'

Colson chewed the ends of his fingers. 'Campbell's got a point,' he said.

Swann looked at the floor. 'He's doing it again, isn't he.' He shook his head. 'He's telling us he can make a chemical bomb and he can kill people with it.'

☆

Louis Byrne looked at the set of digitized fingerprints that George Webb had sent over. He studied the image in detail, photocopied it, then packaged it for CJIS in Clarksburg. Leaving his desk, he went up to see his unit chief, Randall Werner. He was looking at an after-hours communication that had come into the SIOC overnight, and waved Byrne to a chair. After a moment he looked up. 'What d'you want, Lucky?'

Byrne loved it when men such as Werner called him that. He knew he was the favoured son, but it still helped to hear it once in a while. You could be out of favour just as fast as you were in with the upper echelons of the Bureau. He placed the copy of the prints on Werner's desk. 'Fatality in northern England. US national, Randy. These just came in from Scotland Yard.'

Werner placed half-moon spectacles on his nose and studied the copy of the prints. He lifted his brows, wrinkling the tanned flesh of his forehead, and took the glasses off again. 'We know him?'

'They've got a name. Richard Gravitz III, supposedly a student from Harvard, but they have a clasp ring from GWU.'

'Yeah?'

'The Harvard bit is supposed to be a Ph.D., so it might've worked, but this guy died mixing a chemical bomb.' Byrne looked straight at him. 'It's the Storm Crow, Randy.'

'As in Bliss and Davis?' Werner lifted his eyebrows. 'Your favourite topic of conversation.'

He pushed his chair away from the desk and clasped fingers across his belly. 'You gonna organize the FEST?'

'If that's OK with you.'

Werner nodded. 'Who're you gonna take?'

Byrne shrugged. 'Won't need many. All we'll get to do is tag along. UK counter-terrorism's good. They'll let us shadow, at best.'

'OK. Who?'

'I need to talk to the State Department and the CIA. I want Larry Thomas from Weapons of Mass Destruction and I thought I'd take Cheyenne Logan if Tom Kovalski can spare her. She was working with me at Bliss.'

Werner nodded. 'You want me to talk to Tom?'

'I can do it.'

'OK. I'll contact the leg-att over there and set you up.'

Byrne went back to his office and picked up the phone. He called the Criminal Justice Information Services in West Virginia. 'This is Louis Byrne from International Terrorism. I'm sending you down some digital prints of a deceased US citizen, which just came over from London. If you can't get a criminal fix, check the military. Maybe the guy did some service.'

'You got it.'

Byrne hung up, then he rang Angie's office across the Federal Triangle. 'Hi, honey. It's me. I've got to go back to London. And I might be gone for a while.'

# 17

James Ingram sat in his office staring at the wall. Two hours earlier he had got off the plane at London City Airport. He had been to Northumberland to try to see what was going on at his farm, but he could not get within a mile of the place. It was like arriving on the set of some disaster film and he was still a little shell-shocked even now. A mobile army camp with tents everywhere, vehicle checkpoints and armed police officers. A great gaggle of pressmen had descended as soon as he was recognized, but he refused to comment. They had strung a mobile perimeter line as far south as Derwent Reservoir and most of the local talk was about whether it had been contaminated.

He was not allowed anywhere near the farm and had been told in no uncertain terms by a Major Carter that, once they were satisfied that any contamination had been contained, the farmhouse, outbuildings and all the contents would be incinerated. The farm had been in his family since 1852 and it contained one of the best wine collections in the north of England.

The telephone rang on his desk. Ingram did not seem to hear it; still sitting with his cheek cupped in a palm, staring out of the window. It rang again and this time he stirred and picked it up. 'Yes?'

'The police are here to see you, Mr Ingram.'

Ingram jumped. He knew they would come. Caspar

had told him that people from Scotland Yard had been in the office, yet still he was disturbed. He hated the police, always had done, hated any form of dealings with them, even down to a traffic offence. 'Send them in,' he said quietly.

He got up, went to the mirror over the fireplace and adjusted his tie at the collar. Then he turned and stood there waiting for them with his hands behind his back. His secretary showed in two men, both in suits and ties. One was tall and slim, with dark hair and the sort of eyes that would hunt you across a room; the other was huge, with long, reddish blond hair and green eyes.

'Mr Ingram?' The dark-haired one spoke.

'That's me.' Ingram was stern-faced now, the injured party here. He held out his hand.

'Detective Sergeant Swann. This is Detective Constable McCulloch.' Ingram shook hands, then offered them the seats across the desk from his. He clasped his knuckles together and looked from one to the other.

'What've you come to tell me, gentlemen?'

For a moment Swann did not say anything. He crossed one knee over the other and looked at the solicitor. He had never seen him in the flesh before and he was smaller than Swann had imagined. Once or twice, BFP events, marches and so forth had been given a tiny airing on television and he had seen Ingram interviewed on the odd occasion.

'We want to talk to you about the situation in Healey, Mr Ingram. Your farm.'

'Ex-farm.' Ingram looked keenly at him. 'They're about to burn it down.'

Swann nodded. 'Nothing else they can do.'

'It's six hundred years old, Sergeant. Been in my family since 1852.'

'What d'you know about the people who rented it?' McCulloch spoke for the first time.

Ingram stared at him. 'Nothing, Constable. Why should I?'

'It's your property.'

Ingram looked at Swann again. 'I understand, Sergeant, that you've been to see Caspar & Gibbs, the letting agents?'

Swann nodded and Ingram glanced at McCulloch. 'Then you'll know I have absolutely nothing to do with who they let to. It's why one employs an agent.'

Swann nodded. 'So you had no knowledge whatsoever?'

'None.'

'You do know Charlie Oxley, though?' McCulloch said.

'Who?' Ingram stared at him.

'Charlie Oxley. You should know him, he's a skinhead, active with Action 2000.'

'Action 2000 has nothing to do with me.'

Swann lifted his eyebrows. 'You're leader of the British Freedom Party, Mr Ingram. Come on.'

'I've said it many times,' Ingram pinched his lips together, 'there is no association between my political party and Action 2000.'

'Then how come they're always at your rallies? How come ninety per cent of the ones we arrest for violent racist crimes have knowledge of your party, or even literature about it on their persons?'

Ingram ran his tongue over his lips. 'It's a free country, Sergeant. People can buy and read what they please.' He sighed then. 'You know, it's a sad indictment of our society when I realize that I expected this. Here am I, innocently awaiting some word on how the people who ruined my farm might be caught. But, no. *I* get interrogated once again over a perfectly legitimate political party and another organization over which I have no control whatsoever.'

'Charlie Oxley works for you, Mr Ingram.' Swann's voice was low and calm.

'Does he? A lot of people work for me. I have many business interests.'

'A lot of people who're members of Action 2000 work for you,' McCulloch said. 'That's a nasty coincidence.'

Ingram looked at him again. 'Nasty, Constable. What are you trying to imply?' He didn't give McCulloch the chance to answer. 'Gentlemen,' he said, 'being police officers you should know that one way of stopping young, potentially violent men from reoffending is to offer them gainful employment.'

'It's also a good way to build up a private army,' Swann replied.

The tip of Ingram's nose lost its colour. He stared at Swann for a moment. 'Are you suggesting that I might have use for a private army, Sergeant?'

Swann looked evenly back at him. 'I was merely making an observation, Mr Ingram. Reflecting on British society – much as you were a moment ago.'

They stared across the desk at one another, then Ingram said: 'Was there anything else?'

'Not right now.' Swann stood up. 'We'll want to see you again though, as this investigation widens.'

Outside on the pavement, McCulloch lit two cigarettes and gave one to Swann. 'He's lying through his teeth, Jack.'

'Tell me about it.'

☆

Swann went home and found Rachael in the flat. Annika looked a little awkward and disappeared down to her room.

'I'm finished work for a few days,' Rachael told him. 'I'll have the girls, if you like.'

Swann scratched his head. And then he realized that as soon as Rachael had her life together again, she would take the children back. He had had them for over three months now and he was getting very used to it.

'You don't mind, Daddy, do you?' Jo tugged at his hand. 'We've hardly seen Mummy since the holidays.' Charlotte looked up at him with equally expectant eyes. Swan sighed and shook his head.

'No, I don't mind.' He looked at Rachael. 'What day is it today?'

'Wednesday. You that tired, Jack? The girls tell me you never got home last night.'

'I did. From about two till five-thirty. I was back at the Yard by half past six.'

'Were you up north?'

He nodded.

'That was terrible. Chemicals, wasn't it. You weren't anywhere near anything, were you? I don't want anything to happen to the children.'

Swann rolled his eyes. 'Nothing's going to happen to the children. I investigate, Rachael. George Webb does the sharp-end bits.'

'The what?'

'Oh, never mind.' He sat down. 'Today's Wednesday. When will you bring them back?'

'Monday. Peter and I are going to take them away this weekend.'

Swann nodded. 'OK. Go and pack a bag, girls.'

Charlotte lifted hers from where she held it behind her. 'Already done it, Daddy. We knew you wouldn't mind.'

When they were gone, Annika came through and looked at him. Swann did not notice her. He sat there feeling strangely lost. She coughed and he stirred. 'Sorry, Annika. I was miles away.'

'They've gone away till Monday?'

'Yes.'

'Ah.'

'Did you want something?'

'Do you need me?'

Swann looked about the living room. 'I don't think so.' Then he realized what she meant. 'Oh, sure, right. Go to your boyfriend's, if you like. They're coming back on Monday afternoon.'

When she was gone, he felt even more lost and he sat for a minute and then went and took a shower. He stood for a long time with the curtain pulled across and the water falling over his head. He imagined George Webb under the freezing hosepipes in Northumberland. He wondered why it had not occurred to him until just now that Rachael would take the children back. God, he thought. How empty the place will be without them.

He met Pia in the West End and they had Chinese food in Lisle Street. He preferred the restaurants in Lisle – real Chinatown, he called it. Gerrard Street was for tourists. Pia watched him picking at his food and halfway through the meal she laid a hand over his.

'What's up, Jack?'

He blew the air from his cheeks and looked across the table at her. 'God, you've got the most beautiful eyes,' he said. He could see himself reflected there in the onyx.

'What's the matter?'

'I don't know, Pia. I wish I did.'

'Have you been dreaming again?'

'Not since the last time. But it sort of clings to you.'

She sighed and rested her hands in her lap. 'You're not going to want to hear this, but Rachael was right, you know. You need to talk to someone.'

'Oh, God. Don't.' Swann rubbed the heel of his palm in his eye.

'Jack, what happened to you was incredible. I don't know anyone who wouldn't need to talk it through with somebody.'

He stared at her then and took a long pull from his wine glass. 'It was years ago.'

'So what? You've never got over it. You've never even talked about it.'

'I'm going to Scotland, if there's any snow in November. Talk to Alec, maybe.'

'Alec?'

'You haven't met him. Old climbing friend from years back. Talk it through with him. I'll take Webby with me. Maybe the two of them can straighten me out.'

'You're going to climb snow and ice again?'

'Yes.'

'You sure that's the right thing to do?'

Swann sighed. 'No,' he said. 'I'm not. But it's better than a psycho's chair.'

They went back to Swann's flat and he was so preoccupied with his own inner turmoil that he didn't notice how quiet Pia was herself. He opened a bottle of red wine and turned to find her staring out of the window with one arm cupped round her waist. Swann stopped and stared at her, the set of her back, her forehead against the glass.

'Pia?'

She didn't turn.

'Pia.' He laid the glasses down and moved alongside her. She was staring blankly into the glass, with tears in her eyes.

'Jesus, love. What's up?' Swann slipped an arm about her shoulders.

She sucked breath and flicked at her eyes with her fingers. 'I'm sorry.' She held up her hands, palm outwards, then fumbled in her bag for a cigarette. Swann lit it for her and guided her over to the couch. 'I'm sorry,' she said. 'I just . . .'

'No, *I'm* sorry.' Swann kissed her lightly on the forehead. 'I'm so bloody selfish. We only ever talk about me: my problems, my job, my past.' He lifted her chin with gentle fingers. 'Talk to me,' he said. 'What's the matter?'

Pia drew on her cigarette and exhaled heavily. 'Oh, I don't know,' she said. 'Everything's just getting on top of me.' She looked at him then, the tears glasslike in her eyes.

'Work?'

She nodded. 'It's getting to me – the greed, the lies. I can't seem to do it like I used to.'

'Then give it up.'

She looked beyond him then, mouth half-open. 'How can I give it up?'

'Easy. Just go in and tell Paul Ellis you're quitting.'

She laughed. 'If only it was that simple.'

'It is that simple, love. Just quit.'

She shook her head, crushed out the cigarette and lit another. 'I can't just quit. I've got too many commitments.'

'There are other jobs, Pia.'

'Not with the money I'm on.' She got up then and picked up the wine from the kitchen work surface. 'Ignore me, Jack. I'm just going through a bad patch. I'll get over it. I always do.'

☆

Louis Byrne studied the report CJIS had sent over from Clarksburg. There was no Richard Gravitz III and the prints he had received from England did not fit anyone on their criminal files. They belonged to a man who had served three years in the army, Bruno Kuhlmann, suspected of being involved in the Atlanta pipe bombing.

He went across to the Domestic Terrorism Operations Unit and found Cheyenne Logan talking with Tom Kovalski. Byrne laid the prints on Kovalski's desk. 'Bruno Kuhlmann,' he said. 'Your John Doe from Atlanta.'

Kovalski squinted at him. 'What about him?'

'He's been found dead in England.'

Kovalski stared at him, then picked up the sheet of paper. 'He'd been under surveillance,' he said. 'We lost him downtown.' He passed the prints to Logan and looked up at Byrne. 'The UCA in Idaho photographed him in Jakob Salvesen's compound.'

Byrne bunched his eyes at the corners. 'That doesn't make any sense.'

'It certainly doesn't now.'

Byrne leant against the radiator. 'I'm going over to London with the Foreign Emergency Search Team, Tom. I want to take Chey with me, if you can spare her. She worked with me on Fort Bliss, and if she's looking at this product from Idaho she might be just as useful to *you* over in London.' He tapped the picture of the blond-haired Kuhlmann with a forefinger. 'If they've got a Storm Crow problem in England – maybe we do too.'

☆

Harrison replayed the message on the answerphone in his trailer at lunchtime. Outside it was raining. Fall was upon them. He walked to his truck where Chief was waiting for him. 'What is it?' Chief asked him.

'Nothing.' Harrison looked sideways at him. 'Phone rang is all. Buddy of mine from Marquette. I gotta call him back.'

Harrison twisted the key in the ignition and turned the truck round. They rolled up the hill and then the few blocks to the lumber yard. Chief went back to the house kit they were setting up and Harrison stopped at the payphone. 'Just got your message,' he said when Scheller answered.

'We need a meet.'

'When.'

'Tonight. Usual place. Usual time.'

Harrison put down the phone.

At five o'clock he got off work and went back to the trailer park. A large gathering of Mexicans were clustered outside Rodriguez's trailer. He parked up and wandered over. The women were all chattering away in Spanish and the men were gesticulating. Harrison peeked through the crowd and saw Little T – Tony Vasquez Junior – sitting on the stoop in tears.

'*Qué pasa?*' Harrison said to Margarito who was standing next to him.

'Look.' Margarito grabbed Harrison's arm and dragged him over to the boy. Margarito turned him round and lifted his shirt. Harrison cocked an eyebrow: red weals lined the boy's back, running below the waistband of his pants to his butt.

'How'd that happen?'

'Tate.' Margarito spat in the dirt and the women started yammering again. 'He say Poquito T was on Salvesen land. He say he was trespassing. Tate say that he catch any beaners trespassing on Señor Salvesen's land, he shoot them. He cannot shoot this boy, so he whip him instead.'

Harrison pushed his hat higher on his head. The boy had taken a hell of a beating. His father stood slightly apart, in his black Wranglers and pointed Mexican boots. He was smoking his way through a pack of Basic 100s. Harrison touched his shoulder.

'Ah,' Tony said with a twist of his lip. 'Gringo.'

'Whoa, buddy. Time out.' Harrison looked him in the eye. 'You came to his country, *amigo*. You can't stand the heat, then get outta the kitchen.' Tony jutted his jaw and Harrison stared right back. 'There's good Americans and there's bad, just like there is Mexicans.'

Tony looked at him a while longer, then laid a hand on his shoulder. 'Forgive me, *amigo*. I have much anger in my heart today.'

'I understand that.' Harrison placed a pinch of chew under his lip. 'What you figure on doing about it?'

'Maybe I teach Tate a lesson. A lesson in Spanish.' Tony's dark eyes flashed cold.

Harrison nodded slowly. 'Well, I guess you'll decide when you're ready, but watch yourself, Tony. You gotta remember that nobody's looking for a war round here and if one gets started, you'll lose. You can't fight the whole of Blaine County, which is what it'll amount to. There's a lot of good people in this valley, though Tate ain't one of 'em. Not many white people like him. But you go to war with him and you go to war with them. That's just the way it is.'

'*Si*, I know it.'

'Your boy's hurt, but he ain't hurt so bad.' He looked across at him. 'Pretty soon he'll be bragging to his buddies about how he got on Salvesen's land.'

Tony said nothing. 'He is my son. You don't have children, so you could not understand how a man feels about his son.'

'No, I reckon not. But before you go into battle, you gotta make sure you're in the right war. And I know about wars, Tony.'

He drove south on Highway 75, past the rest area and his dead drop and on down to Shoshone. He had to wait for a full ten minutes while a freight train crossed the lines in front of him and then he headed on, through

Jerome and down to the intersection with 84. Once on the freeway, he drove more quickly. He had not had a meeting with his contact agent for a couple of months. They spoke on the phone a lot and there were the postcards. It was a five-hour drive from Salt Lake City to Passover, so they always met halfway at the Valley Hotel in Logan, Utah. It was big and inconspicuous and the chances of Harrison meeting anyone he knew were next to nothing.

He got to the hotel first and ordered an MGD. He'd stick to two or three; the last thing he needed was an over-zealous cop and a DUI to deal with on the way home. He sat at the bar and watched the slim black girl serving. She was pretty and young and probably very firm. Her arms were bare and the skin full and rich. He noticed the set of her collarbones and the way her neck arched when she laughed. He thought of Guffy then and how much of a woman she was. Youth was nice for a night or so, but not the kind of thing to take home.

Scheller came in at eight-thirty. Harrison slid off his stool and shook hands. He had expected maybe Jackson and Brindley as well, but Scheller was on his own. Buying a fresh round of drinks, they went through to eat dinner.

'Bruno Kuhlmann,' Scheller told him. 'The guy you photographed in the compound.'

'He ain't been back.'

'I know.' Scheller looked left and right and leaned across the table. 'He's dead, JB.'

Harrison stopped chewing.

'Somebody killed him. In England.' Scheller went on to explain what had happened and when he had finished, Harrison sat back in the chair. He had left half a prime rib on his platter.

'England?'

'Yeah.'

'I don't get it, Max. What was he doing in England?'

Scheller clasped his hands together on the table. 'Who knows, Johnny, but right now we got Louis Byrne on his way to London with a FEST. Kuhlmann was making some sort of chemical device, very worrying to the Brits. The latest in a series of events, apparently. They think they're dealing with Storm Crow.'

Harrison narrowed his eyes. 'Storm Crow. That is one motherfucking sonofabitch. So that's why they're sending Byrne, huh?' A thought struck him then. 'Max, that deal in Texas in '95. Drugs, right?'

'Twenty million bucks worth of nose candy.'

'We sure about that?'

'What d'you mean?'

Harrison leaned across the table. 'That was right about the time the militia were panicking over Joint Task Force Six. Right?'

Scheller nodded.

'Kuhlmann shows up in Salvesen's compound two years later, then dies in a Storm Crow incident in England.' He opened his hands. 'Maybe there *was* a connection.'

'With the militia?' Scheller shook his head. 'DEA Intel confirmed the coke hitting the street.'

Harrison sat back again. 'Then it don't make fucking sense.'

'I know.'

'Are the Brits sure about Storm Crow?'

'They know their terrorists, Johnny. They're positive.'

Harrison stared beyond him then. 'Salvesen's getting ready for something, Max. But it's got nothing to do with England.'

Scheller made a face. 'He still got militia men in the compound?'

'They come and go all the time. Tom Foley of the New Texas Rangers was the last one.'

Scheller ordered coffee. 'What I haven't told you yet, and what the British haven't told anybody except us, is that Kuhlmann was murdered. He was wearing a mask, you know, a breathing respirator. Whoever he was working with punched holes through the filters. He breathed in fumes and croaked.'

Harrison stared at him. 'That makes even less sense.'

'Tell me about it,' Scheller said.

He sat back and sighed. 'There may not be any connection with Salvesen. Hell, probably isn't. We haven't seen Kuhlmann in the compound before.'

'Coincidence though, eh.' Harrison sat forward and scraped the end of his cigarette round the lip of the ashtray. 'I went to his church,' he said.

Scheller lifted an eyebrow.

'You hear him that night, Max, just the other Sunday?'

'I listened to your tape.'

'You figure what all that shit was about?'

'Nope.'

'Me neither. The fourth kingdom, Roman Empire and all that stuff.' Harrison thinned his eyes, then looked back at Scheller. 'He ain't like the rest of them, Max. He's not going on about the conspiracy or concentration camps or black fucking helicopters. But he sent out a warning that night.'

For a few moments neither of them spoke. Around them the restaurant was busy. Harrison sipped at the last of his beer. 'What d'you want me to do right now?'

'We need to know what's going on,' Scheller stated. 'He's had a lot of activity so far, let's see what happens after this. If there is a connection, we might get some kind of reaction. If somebody's killed one of his men over there, then maybe he'll want to do something about it.' He looked again at Harrison. 'What about a full week's covert?'

Harrison twisted his mouth down at the corners. 'Grandma ill?'

'Gotta get back to Marquette.'

'You want me to try and get inside?'

'*Can* you get inside?'

'I think I could, yeah. Compound at least, anyway. Fence is weak at one point, Max. If I can get by the dogs, then who knows. Might be able to site a transmitter.'

'I'll get you some T-17s.'

Harrison took a Merit from his shirt. 'I'm running short of rations.'

'We'll drop some off.'

'OK. I'll talk to the lumber yard tomorrow.'

Guffy was in his bed when he got home. Harrison walked down the hallway and leaned against the doorway. She was propped against the pillows reading a book, breasts exposed, large and heavy with full red nipples.

'Where you been?'

'Running some errands.' He sat on the edge of the bed and pulled off his boots. 'I got to go away for a while, Guffy.'

'Where?' She put the book down and sat forward.

'Home. Jeff called me up this morning. My grandma's real bad.' He sighed then. 'Well, she ain't really my grandma, but as good as. She brought me up when my mom and daddy got killed.'

'Oh, baby doll.' She reached over and laid a hand on his arm. 'You want me to come with you?'

'You can't get the time, hon'. I gotta go see Eddie in the morning and ship out right away.'

'You gonna fly?'

He nodded.

'Want me to take you to Boise?'

'That's real sweet of you, honey, but I'll take the truck. It needs a few things done and I can only get the parts in

Boise.' He stood up and peeled off his shirt. Lisa looked at the tattoo on his arm, the grinning rat with the whisky bottle, the gun and the motto in Latin underneath: *Not worth a rat's ass.*

'Will you tell me about that one day?'

He squinted at his upper arm. 'I did tell you. When I finished with the Rats, I got shitfaced in Saigon and had it done. Regretted it ever since.'

'Not the tattoo – the army, Vietnam, the whole thing.'

Harrison pinched up his eyes. 'You don't wanna hear about that. Shit, Guffy. It was thirty years ago. I've forgotten most of it.'

He went through to the refrigerator and got two beers, flipped off the tops and took them back to the bedroom. He handed one to her. 'How's Chief and Belinda?'

'Just fine.'

'What about Danny – you seen him tonight?'

She shook her head. 'I've been down here. Danny'll be in the hotel tonight.'

Harrison nodded. 'Needed to see him before I go. Never mind.'

'You think Eddie'll give you the time?'

'If he don't, I'll quit.' Harrison finished the beer and got another.

'Udal got a DUI.'

He poked his head round the door. 'Again?'

'Yep. He's got to go to meetings now three times a week.'

'He taking the cure?'

'I doubt it. He'll do the meetings, but that'll be it.'

'Udal, huh.' Harrison shook his head. 'He's too old to be driving, anyways.'

In the morning he went to work early, parked the truck and went through to the back office. Fast Eddie, the boss, so called because he could never make first base on the softball field without being thrown out, was in his office on the telephone. Harrison hung about outside till he had finished, then he went in and told him the situation.

'No problem, Harrison. You wanna take some vacation time?'

'Yeah. I ain't took but a week this year.'

'Is another week gonna be long enough?'

'That'll work, yeah.'

'When you flying?'

'This afternoon.'

'OK. You got it. Call me if you need longer.'

'Thanks, Eddie. I appreciate it.'

He drove south on 75 and then turned off on the mountain road. He stopped at the rest area and lifted the drainage cover on his dead drop. There were fresh food supplies and some T-17 transmitters left by the courier at some godforsaken hour this morning, no doubt. Harrison stuffed them in his bag and then got back in his truck. Two hours later he was in Boise. He parked at the airport and went inside to the luggage lockers, where he stowed his suitcase for one week. Then he took the truck to Matt Briggs who owned the classic Chevy shop on Orchard Drive. He knew Matt well, having watched him this summer in the Mud Bog Challenge, at the forty-eighth annual outlaw weekend in Richfield. Matt was a Chevy man through and through and drove a modified 454, cherry red with twin exhausts sticking straight up through the hood.

'Third gear keeps jumping out, Matt,' he told him.

Matt rubbed his oiled hands on a rag. 'Right on. Been that way ever since you bought her. You finally gonna get it fixed.'

'I am, Matt. I am. Sick and tired of grabbing the gear all the time.'

Matt nodded. 'How long you got? I'm pretty busy about now.'

'A week?'

'Oh right, no problem. You wanna borrow a truck?'

'Thanks, man.' Harrison shook his head. 'I'm flying back to Michigan. My grandma's not very well.'

Matt made a face. 'Sorry about that, man. You give her the best from Idaho, y'hear.'

Harrison walked the short distance to the Alamo rental lot and hopped a ride on their bus to the airport. He had only his bag now and he went back into the terminal. He made his way past Delta and United and the Northwest desk and watched the Sun Valley Stages counter in the far corner of arrivals. The bus went at two-thirty. Harrison could see the driver, in his Texas-collared shirt and with his slicked-back hair, writing on a clipboard. He stood in the shop, reading while he watched who went up to the counter. Between one-thirty and two-fifteen he saw only three people, none of whom he recognized. At two-twenty he crossed the concourse and stepped up to the counter. The driver still had his head bent. 'Be right with you, buddy.'

Harrison waited, watching. The man looked up and smiled. 'You wanna take the bus?'

'Which way you going?'

'Mountain Road. Came through Shoshone this morning.'

'Got many riding?'

'Just three, so far.'

Harrison took forty dollars from his billfold. 'You got four now,' he said.

☆

The Foreign Emergency Search Team arrived in London on Sunday 12 October. The following morning, they went to Scotland Yard. Webb and Swann came down to meet them. They shook hands with Byrne and he introduced the team. 'Larry Thomas,' Byrne said. 'Supervisory agent, Weapons of Mass Destruction Unit, FBI. Graham Ketner, CIA, and Bob Hicks, DSS.' Swann was looking at the slim, elegant, black woman as yet unintroduced. 'And this is Cheyenne Ortez Logan, special agent in our Domestic Terrorism Ops Unit.'

'Cheyenne,' Swann said. 'Very nice to meet you.'

Webb looked at the ceiling.

They went upstairs and joined the briefing. The farm in Northumberland was going to be incinerated that morning. Two officers from Porton Down were there. John Garrod had left his meeting with the Home Secretary early, to hear at first hand what the scientists said. The duty officer was Dr William Firman and it was he who outlined exactly what they were facing. Colson quietened everyone down and then Firman stood up. He had a few slides to show them, the various stages of their testing, in order that should they come across it again, they would be fully aware of what they were dealing with.

'Before I go into what we think we've discovered,' he said, 'I take it you all know about the all-clear round the contaminated area. Basically, we're positive now that the leak was in that dirty room and there alone. There was a possibility of some contamination passing from the NBC suit found in the downstairs shower room, but the sewerage system has been fully tested and shows nothing positive. Over and above that, although it was never officially made public, the Derwent Reservoir was considered a potential problem: if that became infected, then so would the rest of the water supply. Mercifully, given the initial containment and wind direction, the reservoir water has again tested negative.'

'Good news,' Garrod said.

Firman looked at him then. 'That's where it ends, I'm afraid.'

Swann glanced at Webb who half lifted his eyebrows. Firman checked the notes in front of him and then flashed up the first slide, a piece of blue metalline crystal enlarged by a microscope. 'Stage one, in terms of our recovery from the point of contamination,' he said. 'Unfortunately, we think stage ten from inception.' He stopped. 'That's not strictly fair. They began with a crystalline form and ended with this one. But between then and now, they have altered it at least ten times. They broke down the original crystal and then adapted its molecular dynamics with various chemical additives. It eventually came out in the form you see on the slide. Blue-white metal. If exposed to the atmosphere, it forms a browny black oxide. We believe it started life as pirillium E-7, a rodenticide first manufactured in the United States, similar in make-up, I suppose, to something like thallium.'

Thallium, Swann thought. They had not seen thallium since the late eighties, when a number of Iraqi dissidents in London and Baghdad found themselves drinking orange juice laced with it.

'E-7 was a lot more virulent than thallium,' Larry Thomas, the FBI man, said. 'It crippled the nervous system.'

Firman looked up at him. 'You're part of the liaison?'

'Weapons of Mass Destruction Unit.'

'Ah, this should be particularly interesting to you, then. When I'm done, you're welcome at Porton Down.' He looked back at the slide. 'As I said, crystalline form. I won't bore you with the technical jargon regarding evolution procedures, but, suffice to say, what we found in Northumberland is about as dangerous as it gets. Think of sarin or tabun – then think much worse – and you'll be getting close.' He paused and looked at them all, particularly the commander. 'We haven't faced this threat openly before and I have to tell you, we're still a long way from finding an answer in terms of serum or antidote.'

'What does it do?' Webb asked.

Firman flicked through the slides. 'I'll tell you. These crystals, when diluted in either nitric or hydrochloric acid and then heated to a temperature of 120 degrees, and kept at that level for four minutes, become this yellow liquid.'

'Looks like piss,' McCulloch said as the slide came into focus.

'Tastes considerably worse and unlike your own urine it has no life-enhancing qualities.'

Firman flicked to the next slide. 'On exposure to the atmosphere, or pure oxygen, the liquid vaporizes. It does it whether it's neat or diluted in water. We're still testing the persistency of that vapour in the atmosphere. It's been three days so far.'

A chill went through the room. Larry Thomas scratched his head. 'You've got airborne persistency for three days? No decomposition?'

'Oh, it's decomposing,' Firman said. 'But it's still lethal.'

'What about in the ground or the water system?' Swann asked him.

'We don't know yet, but we're talking a lot of years.'

He flicked to the final slide: Bruno Kuhlmann's corpse. 'The subject was contaminated by respiratory ingestion of the gas,' he said. 'The solution we found had not been diluted at all, but, as I've just said, its dilution ratio is high. You don't need very much of it to cause a massive problem.

'Symptoms,' he went on. 'Initially, coughing, respiratory restriction and pains behind the eyes. Once absorbed – be it by the respiratory system, orally or through the

342

skin – it swells your blood vessels, and increases your heart rate. Nausea, diarrhoea, muscular pain, paraesthesia and delirium. The gas burns – note the marks around the subject's nose and mouth. The expansion of the blood vessels comes round the heart and lungs, the spinal cord at the neck and the main arteries to the brain. There is a massive build-up of blood, causing pressure behind the eyes. In his case,' he tapped the screen, 'he's bled from vessels actually in the eyes. Ultimately, the brain comes under massive pressure and the heart rate intensifies to a point where it just arrests.'

'How long does that take?' Colson asked him.

'About five minutes.'

When Firman had finished speaking, there was absolute silence in the room. 'Have they made this themselves?' Tania asked him.

Firman shook his head. 'I doubt it. Pirillium E-7 has been around for thirty years. Lots of people know about it. This derivative could have its origins in the States, or it could be anywhere, the Middle East, here even. It takes some manufacturing, mind you, so somewhere, somebody knows what they're doing.' He made an open-handed gesture. 'Aum Shinrikyo got sarin, didn't they.' He looked at Garrod again. 'I'm told you think this is Storm Crow-related. As far as I understand it, they can get anything they want.'

When the men from Porton Down had gone, the tension in the conference room was tangible. Garrod stood talking to Colson. Swann sat back, rested an ankle on his knee and looked at the ceiling. Again he saw the photograph that Huella had sent in, his forehead with a hole in it. The Feds were talking together and then Colson called them all to attention.

'OK everyone,' he said. 'Bad tidings, I know. But that's what the crow brings.' He looked at them. 'Remember, we've been fighting a domestic terrorist threat in this country since 1973. We've got bloody good at it. With respect to our American guests, I think we're as good as it gets. So far the Storm Crow has given us the runaround. He thinks he's led us up the garden path and back again. But he hasn't. We're still ahead of the game.'

'You think so, sir?' McCulloch looked unconvinced.

'Campbell, if you want off this investigation, that's fine with me.'

McCulloch flushed bright red and looked between his knees.

'We're going to get him,' Colson went on. 'We've got enough forensic evidence to put him away for thirty years. Think how you're going to feel when he gets driven up that ramp at Paddington and the gates close behind him.' He paused and looked at each one of them in turn. 'You know what you're working on and you also know what we might be up against. I think we all agree that the death of Bruno Kuhlmann was premeditated. The pipe bomb, dets, etc. were deliberately left for our benefit. He wanted us to know that he has what he has and exactly what it can do. We've had *that* confirmed now from Porton Down.'

'Question is, Guv,' Swann broke in, 'what's he going to do?'

'Do? He's not going to do anything, Jack, because we are going to nick the bastard.' He looked directly at Swann then. 'In many ways this is your deal. I'm looking forward to watching you interview him.'

☆

Harrison sat on the Sun Valley Stages bus as it turned off Highway 20 and on to 75. As it trundled on towards Passover, he sank lower in the seat. Fortunately, the windows were tinted and he knew nobody could see in. It had been a long trip, almost three hours so far. At the front, the driver yawned. 'I think we're finally gaining on it,' he said.

Harrison stared out of the window: Little Mammoth Gulch, to his left, where the old mine workings guarded Salvesen's land; the long grove of cottonwoods, where he hid his mountain bike before trekking to the top of the ridge and crisscrossing the saddles to Dugger's Canyon.

He was going there now, but not by the normal route. He would take the winter trail where he snowmobiled as far as the canyon and the deep hide in the cottonwoods. He could not risk the bus driver setting him down in Westlake, so he went north about a mile and then asked him to stop. It was five-thirty now and there was a lot of traffic. He jumped off the bus, ducked across the cycle path and down to the banks of the Big Wood, where he waited till it got dark.

From here, he had to cross the road and pick an unseen path between the properties before climbing into the hills and eventually accessing Dugger's Canyon from the East Road. It was a mile or so walk up the winding track that was favoured by mountain bikers. He thought about Danny Dugger's father and Danny himself, having worked that canyon for years and years and years only to have the lease sold from under them. When Danny came to renew it with the BLM after his father moved to Carey, the bureau said he didn't have enough money. They let it to Jake Salvesen two years before Harrison drifted into town.

He crossed the highway and recognized a solitary figure in jeans and a black hat trying to hitch a ride to the valley: Charlie Love, still flush with his winnings from the NBA finals back in June. Harrison avoided him, cut a path into the foothills and disappeared into a clump of Douglas fir. Then he began to pick his way up the hillside, being mindful to walk just below the ridge. The sky was greyer than the mountain and he knew how conspicuous movement on a hilltop could be, even at this time of night. He thought about Charlie Love as he walked and the friends he had made, not just in Chief and Danny, but Guffy, Chris Shea, Mike Burrell and little Billy Ellinger. He thought about Tracey Farrow and Cody, Monty with his Jack Russell called Missy. Everyone called her Miss-er because Monty'd be lost without her. Then there was Randy Miller, Sandy and Smitty, Junior, and Brian, the tattoo artist from Denver he'd met up at the Sun Run.

When he'd been this deep before, it had been at infiltration level in Chicago, and before that, Key West. Infiltration so deep that his buddies were the enemy. That, he had always been able to justify in his mind. This time, however, it was different – this time he was on the outside. People like Salvesen operated among a close-knit group to stop such infiltration. This time, his friends were on the outside. He wondered how betrayed they'd feel, when he finally came out in public. He wondered how Guffy would feel having slept with a man called Harrison who did not really exist. How the rest would feel, having being lied to for two solid years, the worst of which would be Chief, his best friend, who'd faced down the FBI with a gun in his hand at the second Wounded Knee.

It took him an hour and a half to get to Dugger's Canyon and the keep hide in the cottonwoods. It was much colder now and pretty soon the first snows of the season would hit the valley. He'd thought about using the mine to bury his Coleman cooler, but Danny sometimes used it even now, on the quiet. He knew the Magdalena tunnels like the back of his hand and any disturbance would be noticed. Sometimes Danny would drive up and just sit in the dirt when he got fucked up on booze, and start thinking about the old days. At least he didn't do that any more, with a DUI hanging over him.

Harrison opened his hide and listened to the rustle of the wind through the cottonwoods. There was bear up here and bobcat, as well as mountain lion. He had never actually bumped into a bear, but had seen a nine-foot lion one day when he was hiding in the lay-up point under the rock overlooking Salvesen's compound. He'd figured it was in the area when he was hiking in at first light, and came across scratch marks in the dirt which were fresh. The lion was ahead and travelling away from him. Mountain lions generally scratched facing the way they were headed and you could tell that from how the marks lay in the ground. Fresh scat was another indicator; sometimes it was a little, sometimes a lot, depending on how long it had been since the lion killed. Up here, a problem with one was rare, but he had heard of a few joggers being taken down in Nevada, when game was scarce in the drought years at the turn of the decade.

The only bear round here was black, though they were cinnamon-coloured to look at. Harrison had seen a few of them on his sojourns, but they had never bothered him – they spent most of their time hunting through garbage. There were no grizzlies, although a bunch had been transported to northern Idaho from Yellowstone one time, when there was a problem with hikers up there. They had all migrated though, back through Montana, and were shot when they got to Yellowstone.

☆

When the briefing was over, the US team separated. Byrne and Logan attached themselves to the investigation squads, Thomas went to Porton Down, and the CIA and State Department men were introduced to Special Branch and MI5. Swann stood in the conference room with his hands on his hips, scanning the Annacappa chart on the wall. He scrutinized the early events: driver of the Vauxhall Vectra unidentified, origin of the ringed Ford Cortina, as yet unknown; the emergence of James Morton, the first alias used by Target One; Joanne Taylor, the phantom woman who rented property; McIlroy, the blond-haired man with the South London accent. He felt somebody at his shoulder and looked round to find Byrne studying the chart. 'Everything you got so far?'

Swann nodded.

'Tal-Salem.' Byrne pointed to the shooting of Jean-Marie Mace. 'Throwback to the eleventh century.'

Swann glanced sideways at him.

'You ever hear of the Hashishin?'

'I can't say I have, no.'

'Shiite assassination sect. Used to get stoned on hashish before they carried out attacks on their Seljuk oppressors.' He paused. 'Tal-Salem always smokes before he kills someone.'

Swann sat on the desk and folded his arms. 'You know a lot about all this, don't you, Louis.'

Byrne moved his shoulders. 'The job, Jack. Everyone's got their area of expertise. Not many people handle domestic terrorism like you guys. Up until recently we've not had too much of a problem in the States, though I figure that's all changing.'

'Was McVeigh working on his own?'

Byrne puckered his lips. 'Apart from Nicholls, you mean? We don't know for sure.'

'Militia? The "patriots", or whatever they call themselves?'

'The use of that word's a moot point, I can tell you.'

'I bet it is.'

Byrne sat down. 'Cheyenne's the one to talk to about the militia problem, Jack. Me, I move around the world.

348

I already told you about the Mexican situation we had. I tracked him for a while in Colombia, too. There's not been anyone like this guy since Carlos the Jackal.'

'You're convinced it's one man.'

'Ego, Jack. The feather, the photos, use of the Spanish, the French for Storm Crow when he claims stuff. Theatre, isn't it. One man's ego.'

'Any idea who it is?'

Byrne lifted his foot to the desk. 'That's the difficult bit. Unlike the Jackal, we don't have a starting point. We knew he was recruited by the KGB in Venezuela, before going to school in Cuba and Patrice Lumumba.'

'Moscow.'

Byrne nodded. 'He had a history. *El Gordo* – we knew about him right from the beginning – Ramirez Sanchez, rich boy revolutionary.'

'We interviewed him recently,' Swann said. 'Shooting he did over here, twenty-five years ago.'

'Edward Sieff.'

Swann's eyebrows shot up. 'Shit, you do know your stuff.'

'You gotta remember,' Byrne said. 'I got blown up in '83. Victim of terrorism, myself. I was lucky – I got out with a few cuts and bruises. Two hundred and forty-one of my friends didn't. I've pursued these bastards ever since. Call it my life's work.'

'We call it job pissed.'

'Job what?'

'Pissed. Drunk. Drunk on the job, nothing else mattering.'

Logan looked up from where she was reading the notes that Dr Firman had left. 'That's Louis Byrne,' she said.

'What about this Idaho militia, then, Cheyenne?' Swann asked her.

'It's not really a militia.' She laid down the notes and

came over. 'Sam Sherwood's the Idaho militia man. This guy Salvesen's in the south, the rest are almost in Canada.'

'So what *is* he, then?'

'We think he might be the man to bring the militias together.'

'It's what we don't want to happen,' Byrne explained. 'We think there may be upwards of a hundred thousand of them around the country. They have at least one presence in every state, something like eight hundred militias in total, four hundred and forty of them armed. They communicate via web sites on the Internet, and now and again they might conduct some mini-battle manoeuvres up in the Dakotas, but apart from that there's not much physical contact between them. So far, they've practised what they call "Leaderless Resistance", small cells of about seven or so people. That way, if a cell gets knocked out, the whole is not affected.'

'Like PIRA,' Swann observed.

'Sort of, but PIRA have a war council, an established chain of command. So far, the militias don't have any such council, or a groundswell of public support, and we hope it's gonna stay that way.'

'You don't need many of them, though, do you,' Swann said. 'With your gun laws, any fucker can own a grenade launcher.'

'They're waiting for some kind of revolution,' Logan told him. 'They stockpile food, weapons, that kind of stuff. Women as well as men. Some of the toughest ones are women, particularly the Christian Identity people, they believe they carry on the seed. They all think that the government's been infiltrated by communists, that we have concentration camps all ready to put them in when we take their guns off them. They avoid paying taxes, drive without licence plates and try to claim they're no longer citizens of the United States, therefore they don't have to abide by its laws. They think the Federal Reserve is a Jewish conspiracy, with the IRS its collection agency.'

Byrne ran a hand across his scalp. 'They see black helicopters in the sky and believe they're covert government agents. They think the Russians are massing along the Canadian border, and that we're secretly training the Crips and the Bloods in LA to take their guns off them.'

'And you think this bloke Salvesen is uniting them?'

'We think he might be trying to. The ATF know he's supplying weapons. That isn't illegal though. He owns a munitions company or two. If he wants to give M16s away, he can. He's got a lot of money, Jack. Runs two private airplanes and flies their leaders in from all over the States.'

'What's his connection with the fatality in Northumberland?'

'There may not be one. All we know is that Kuhlmann was spotted in his compound.' Logan took Harrison's product file from her case and sifted through the photographs. 'There you go,' she said, 'that's what he looked like before his face got burned.'

Swann studied Kuhlmann's face. Then he looked at Salvesen. 'This the man you're talking about?'

Logan nodded. 'Jakob Salvesen, heir to Salvesen Connaught, or at least his father's shares. I think he's sold them all now. He's holed up in southern Idaho with a bunch of churches and about five billion dollars.'

'Going back to the original point about ID'ing the Storm Crow,' Byrne said. 'I talked in detail to Ben Dubin before I got on the plane. The only clue we have is a John Doe with Carlos when he bombed the French police train in 1982. Dubin believes that one of the players there, a man of about twenty-one, might be the guy who became the Storm Crow. He was mixed race, which might suggest your man Huella. Also, Huella would be about the right age now. Anyways, Dubin has intelligence sources that got into GRU, Soviet Military Intelligence, which suggested that Carlos may have had a protégé who had some training in Russia and also in Cuba. Since the Wall came down, we've got some information out of the DGI in Cuba, which was effectively Soviet Intel, anyway. They confirmed the same. But nobody knows who he was or what his *raison d'être* was. My own feeling is that he did have a connection with Carlos for a time, but he was smart enough to see what would happen if he had a particular cause. Carlos worked for causes, and finally he lost his usefulness. First the Russians, then the Syrians. They sent him to Sudan, where the French extradited him in their own particular fashion.'

Swann pushed out a cheek with his tongue. 'So you think this boy took some training and went solo?'

Again Byrne spread his palms. 'Jack, at this stage, it's conjecture.'

'What about the prints Webb gave you – did you get anywhere with them?'

'Not so far. Trouble with the States is not every county sheriff or police department uses the national crime info center properly. We've got too many different law-enforcement agencies, I guess.'

Swann chewed the end of his thumb. 'He's a *doer* this guy, which makes me wonder.'

'What d'you mean?'

'What we've seen so far has taken two things above all else, a hell of a lot of planning and a hell of a lot of money. He's blown up a car in Soho, letting us think it was PIRA, which means he's had access to a Mk 15 TPU. The driver he used to collect him from that scene gave an address where Huella was actually living. We think he wanted us to find him. We had him under surveillance for a month and somehow he knew it, though we saw no sign of antisurveillance. We hit him on the ninth of June and somehow he knows we're coming.'

Byrne stared at him then. 'You got a leak here, Jack?'

The hubbub around them suddenly ceased, everyone looking at Byrne. Swann shrugged his shoulders. 'He knew we were watching, maybe he saw us substitute his dustbins. Anyway, he had an escape route already planned and he used it. Somehow his intel' is very, very good, which makes me wonder if *he* could have planned this, or whether there's someone else in the background. He knew how SO19 attack, and he had the whole house rigged up to keep us there all day.' He broke off, conscious of his colleagues looking at him. 'I don't know how he knew, Louis. Maybe he's just the best antisurveillance man on the planet.'

# 18

Swann and Webb went up to Northumberland for a few days with Louis Byrne, while Logan remained in London to brief the Operational Command Unit on the possible militia connection.

They were allocated an office in Ponteland, where the local officers had already conducted a house-to-house inquiry. People remembered Ricky Gravitz: a talkative, open young man, typically American but pleasant enough. They traced his movements back to his arrival in the UK, where he hired a car at Manchester Airport after flying in from Denver, Colorado. Nobody had seen any second occupant. There had to have been two, at least, if only to build the dirty room, and sabotage the respirator.

Swann sat at a desk and studied the map, picking out the most direct route from Manchester. Kuhlmann could have gone two ways, he decided, either up the M6 to Carlisle and then across the A69, which to the man in the know would have been the least busy route, but more likely he would have tried the more obvious route – M62 to the A1 and up. Swann had confirmed that the rental car was full of petrol, which he had paid for when he left Manchester. That gave him enough to get across to Consett, so there was no point in dispatching officers to check the filling stations along the way. He had arrived in Manchester just after lunch. Lunch would've been on the plane, which might mean a stop before Consett for food, given the size of aircraft portions. Swann looked over at Webb, who was reading some of the witness statements regarding Kuhlmann's movements.

'If you were going to get some grub on your way from Manchester, where would you stop, Webby?'

Webb bunched his eyes. 'Little Chef, probably. Easiest, isn't it.'

Swann nodded. 'But where, round here?'

Webb came over and looked at the map Swann had in front of him. 'I reckon he came M62, then A1,' Swann said.

'Jesus. Hundreds of places.'

'Maybe he met someone.' Swann scratched his chin. 'Just in from the States?'

'Unless it was set up by phone. Nothing we've got so far shows us anyone meeting anyone else.'

'Except the estate agent at Queen's House Mews.'

'True,' Webb agreed. 'It's possible.'

'I want to check all the cafés. See if he was seen and if so whether he was with anyone. There can't be that many Americans in the north-east at any one time.'

Webb tapped the map. 'If he did stop, it wouldn't be until he got more this way. You've got the A1 or the A167, then you've got the A691. I'd go the A68 – but that doesn't mean he would.'

Swann made some phone calls and located the restaurants on the roads in question. He took Byrne with him to check them. Five minutes after he left, Webb took a phone call from Nick Patterson at the forensic science laboratory in Lambeth.

'The fibres you scraped from the second bedroom at Healey,' Patterson said.

'What about them?'

'I've got a match with Queen's House Mews.'

Swann decided to start with Consett and move out on

one road. If that proved unfruitful, they would come back in on another and then out again on another. He had close-ups of one of the surveillance photographs that the undercover FBI agent had taken.

'You ever been up this way before, Louis?' he asked.

Byrne looked out of the passenger window and shook his head. 'Furthest north I ever got was Shrivenham, the last time I was over.'

'Good conference?'

'Not bad. You ever been to the ones they hold in Israel?'

'At the Jonathan Institute?'

Byrne nodded.

'Can't say I have. The commander's been over once, I think.'

They stopped south of Consett at the first restaurant on the A691, but nobody remembered Bruno Kuhlmann. Not everyone working the day in question was on duty, however, so Swann left them a picture and the phone number of DC Newham's office in Ponteland.

'So what about our man, Louis?' Swann asked as they drove on to the next one. 'Who is he?'

'Storm Crow?' Byrne made a face. 'If I knew that, Jack, I'd take him for what he did to us in Texas.'

Swann glanced at him. 'How close have you got to him?'

'Well, I've got close to somebody, whether it's him or not I don't know. He knew I was gunning for him in Texas. I'm damn sure he was holed up in Mexico at the time. Covertly, myself and a few other guys tried to trace him using our embassy in Mexico City. But he got wise to us and disappeared. He's the master of disguise: one of his favourites is a Greek Orthodox priest, but he's been everything from a Sikh to a Rastafarian. It's hard to track a man like that.'

356

They drove on in silence and then pulled into the car park of the second restaurant. 'What about Huella?' Swann said. 'From what your man in Israel said, he must be a definite maybe.'

Byrne wrinkled his brow. 'Could be. We've never had a positive sighting of him in the States, so I can't tell you. We had a John Doe at Fort Bliss, but he was a Mexican driving sheep on a horse. The Chicanos couldn't tell us anything.'

'Chicanos?'

'American-born Mexicans.'

'Huella could pass for a Mexican,' Swann said. 'His hair's IC3, but he keeps it short. Easy to wear a wig.'

'IC3?'

'Afro-Caribbean.'

'Right.' Byrne nodded. 'Longer hair, Fu Manchu moustache and a hat. I guess it could've been him.' He shifted sideways in the seat. 'There's something else familiar about him, but I can't get a handle on what it is.'

It was not until the sixth restaurant that they got anywhere. Swann went straight in and asked the girl standing at the till if she recognized Bruno Kuhlmann. She looked at the picture, screwed up her face and looked again. Then her eyes brightened. 'Yes,' she said. 'I do.'

Swann felt the first surge of excitement since this Northumberland thing blew up. 'American,' he said.

'That's right. He came in with a woman.'

'Can you remember what she looked like?'

The waitress thought for a moment. 'Blonde hair, quite long I think, and blue eyes. Yes, I remember, because she kissed him just as I picked up their coffee cups.'

Swann's heart was beating that little bit faster now. 'Would you recognize her again?'

'Probably.' She shrugged her shoulders. 'I suppose so.'

'Thank you,' Swann said. 'Thank you very much.' He

took her details and then he and Byrne went back to the car. 'Joanne Taylor,' Swann told him. 'We've had the description before.'

'Brigitte Hammani,' Byrne said. 'I've been thinking about it, and I reckon they're one and the same.'

They went back to the headquarters at Ponteland and Webb greeted them. 'How'd you get on?'

'Eyeballed,' Swann told him. 'Little Chef on the A68. Woman with him, long blonde hair.'

'Joanne Taylor?'

'I'd say so.' Swann looked at Byrne. 'Louis thinks she's Brigitte Hammani.'

Webb looked at Byrne then. 'The body from the first recorded incident?'

'In 1989.'

'Long time ago, Louis.'

'Yes, and she's never been seen since.' He lifted his shoulders. 'Just a theory, George. It doesn't mean I'm right.'

Webb sat down on the edge of a desk and told them about the results from Lambeth. Swann lit a cigarette and dropped the match in a metal bin. 'Huella,' he said. 'Why am I not surprised?'

'There's something else,' Webb said. 'The glass. We've got a bloke with a London accent asking directions to the supermarket in Crook.'

'When?'

'Five weeks ago.'

'Driving a van?'

'Yes.'

'Hire companies?'

'Already done. I've been on to the lads back at the Yard.'

Swann looked at him then. 'If he came up from London, he would've bought petrol,' he said.

358

Webb nodded. 'How many possible routes are there?'

'A1, M1 maybe, or even the M6.'

'Carrying four eight-foot sheets of glass. How big a van, d'you reckon?'

'Luton?'

'Or a high-sider, maybe. What's that going to do – two hundred and fifty, three hundred miles to a tankful?'

Swann nodded. 'Full when it's picked up. You could get to Newcastle on that.'

'Yeah. But you'd have to fill up pretty quickly afterwards. Say, forty miles south. Let's check the red priorities.'

They went through to see John Newham. 'How many bodies can you give us, John?' Swann asked him. 'We need to hit every petrol station going forty miles south of here, for videos.'

Newham looked doubtful. 'Lads, you'll be lucky if they've kept them this long.'

'We know,' Webb said. 'But we need to do it anyway.'

Newham arranged it, a bomb-burst of personnel covering every possible filling station forty miles south of the farm. Swann, in the meantime, went to the supermarket to try to find out if anyone had seen the van. While he was out, a call came in from Carter's Car Auctions in Sunderland. The investigation team had been aware that Kuhlmann had been seen driving a white Ford Escort with a G prefix letter on the number plate, and they had requested anyone who had sold a G-registered Escort to an American to come forward.

That first night they stayed at the Holiday Inn near Newcastle Airport. None of them had checked in yet, having driven straight to the headquarters at Ponteland. Louis Byrne dumped his case by the reception desk and made for the toilets. Swann showered, phoned Pia and got her answerphone, then went down to the bar for a drink. Byrne and Webb came in a few minutes later and they went into the restaurant. The waiter handed a wine list to Byrne. He laid it on the table and ordered two bottles of Barolo. 'Bureau's paying,' he said.

Back at the Yard, Bill Colson was poring over the undercover product brought across by the Foreign Emergency Search Team. 'If this Kuhlmann got killed by Huella, then Huella must be working against Salvesen, if there is a Salvesen connection at all,' he commented.

Logan rubbed a hand through her hair. 'I guess. It's possible there is no connection, but it's very coincidental. Kuhlmann was a fringe lunatic, did some service time and he was on the far right of society. He had dealings with militia in other parts of the States, but he wasn't a compound dweller like some of them.'

Julian Moore sat with them, together with David Campbell from MI6. Campbell picked up a photograph and studied it. Two men sitting at a wooden table in front of a huge log building, drinking steaming coffee from tall glasses with handles. 'Where is this?' he asked.

Logan took the picture and squinted at it, then she looked at the marker on the back. *SVL* and dated *12 Feb 1996*.

'Looks like the lodge. Sun Valley Ski Lodge in Idaho. That guy's Jake Salvesen. I don't know who the other one is.'

'Can I make a copy of this?'

Colson looked quizzically at him. 'What is it, David?'

Campbell laid the picture down and tapped the second man with his fingernail. 'Him, I recognize. Can't tell you his name right now. But I do recognize him.'

Moore looked at it and furrowed his brow. 'It's Sebastian May,' he said.

'Yes.' Campbell nodded. 'You're right. Sebastian May.'

Colson looked from one to the other of them.

'Sebastian May,' Moore explained. 'A Hertfordshire MP until 1992. He lost his seat to the Lib-Dems. He's always been ultra right-wing, hugely Eurosceptic.'

Campbell nodded. 'Then he surprised everyone by not only running, but winning a seat in the European Parliament two years later.' He stood up. 'I'll make that copy.'

Colson touched him on the forearm. 'I want to be kept informed, David. No Box 850 silences, please.'

Campbell smiled at him. 'Of course, Bill. If there's something you need to know, we'll tell you.'

'I bet you will,' Colson muttered after he had gone.

☆

The following morning, Swann and Webb were back in Ponteland early. Newham had video tapes from seven garages so far. 'You're lucky, lads,' he said. 'They've kept quite a few of them. On the other hand, you're not so lucky. Now you've got to watch them.'

They could do nothing, however, until they knew what they were looking for. Hundreds of vans stopped at filling stations for petrol. They had to wait until they got something from DI Clements in London. At ten-thirty, however, they got another phone call: the Ford Escort purchased by Ricky Gravitz had been found in a service station car park near Leeds. Webb told them to cordon it off and leave it. He got his gear together and drove down the motorway.

Swann was talking to McCulloch and Newham when DI Clements finally phoned him.

'We've got something on the van, Flash,' he said. 'Nothing's been hired that gives us anything. But we have got a stolen one. Blue Transit nicked about five weeks ago.'

'Recovered?'

'Wallington in Surrey. Plates had been changed, Jack.

The ones on it now belong to a different van, which was scrapped two years ago. The owner recognized some bodywork marks and the engine number checks out. He says it's done five hundred more miles than it should have.'

Swann was smiling. 'Sounds like our van, Guv.'

'The index number you're looking for is E112 EEV.'

'OK. We've got some videos up here to look at.'

'Good lad.' Clements paused then. 'How's it going with Byrne?'

'Good. He really knows his onions.'

'Heard a bit about him since he arrived.'

'Yeah?'

'Serious player, apparently. He's the FBI's top agent in international terrorism. I'm told the Arabs want him dead because he knows so much about who's playing for them these days. It was him who got the intelligence on the bombers for the World Trade Center.'

☆

Harrison was settled in his mid-level lay-up point at the back of Salvesen's compound. He lay on his side, the gilly suit covering him completely. Ten minutes previously, he had seen Tate and Slusher make their sweep of the area. They passed below him, disappearing into the grove of fir trees which drifted up the gulch above the groundswell, some fifty feet from the outer perimeter fence. Above him clouds were massing, pressing the sky ever flatter towards the mountains. The tops of the highest ones were already lost in curling grey cumulus like thick ribbons of smoke.

One of his motion sensors was suddenly activated, jaggling the pager on his belt. He lay very still and from above him he could hear something moving. Had he missed a patrol? He lay as still as the grave, only his fingers inching over the ground until they fitted the hilt of his knife. The wind was blowing straight off the mountain from behind him. The sound moved closer, slowly – footsteps. And then Harrison relaxed. He ought to know the difference between a man and an animal by now. Those were hooves he could hear. Moments later, the head of a bighorn sheep jutted into view. It sniffed the air as if it knew something was wrong, but its eyes could not equate with its snout. Heavy, curling horns and thick neck, it moved right past him and stopped again, then it cropped at the grass for a moment, eyes ever watchful. He could see it all now, not ten feet from him, deep tan body with a white patch on its rump and down the backs of its legs. Another movement caught his eye, down in the compound this time, and he put one eye to the lens of his camera. In the yard at the back of the house, Salvesen was walking with another man. Harrison looked harder and snapped off a couple of shots. Stocky little guy with cropped grey hair. Harrison felt as though he should know him.

He watched for three full days and saw no further activity. The older, squat man stayed for two days and then he saw someone load his luggage into Jesse's truck and drive him out of the compound. On the evening of the fourth day, he knew he could make better use of his time. He watched as the final patrol of the day wound its way round the perimeter fence, then he moved.

Already it was dark and a stiff, wintry rain had begun to fall. The goon tower lights were on and he could see a figure moving under the roof. It was at the foot of that same tower that he knew the wire was weakest. Crouching by the lay-up point, he checked his gear: Glock 17 automatic with two spare clips, his garrotte and two stun grenades, together with knuckle knives, a set of wire cutters and doped meat for the dogs. That was going to be his biggest hurdle, two Dobermans running loose on the other side of the wire. There was fifty yards of open space to negotiate before he got to the inner wall. Many times over the past two years he had got right up to the outer fence and lain there unnoticed, while he picked out the lights and passive infrared mountings using the SearchCam Recon IR. The security was tight and he knew he would be lucky to site the T-17 transmitters without anyone finding them.

He watched until the patrol was out of sight and then he stowed the gear he had checked back into the pockets of his cam' suit. The rain slapped off the ground now, spattering the hood of his gilly suit. Taking fresh cam' cream from his pockets, he smeared his face and the backs of his hands, and then took off the gilly. He stowed it with the camera and camera hide deep in the hole at the observation point, and then began to make his way forward. He moved close to the ground, with stealth and not speed. He would rely on the rain and the ever-increasing wind to camouflage the sound. The figure in the goon tower continued to move about, restless no doubt with the rain and anxious for his relief at ten.

The ground was still firm, though the scrub grass was greasy under-foot. Harrison, eyes peeled, moved forward at a zigzag, covering the ground at a snail's pace. He had to time it just right, aware of the wash of the lights, which were set to sweep the fence automatically every three minutes. So he moved and lay flat, moved and lay flat, allowing himself two minutes forty-five seconds to make the distance he could, before flattening himself against the ground.

He made it to the exterior perimeter and sat there, halfway between the towers on the south-east side of the compound. He could see the dogs from here, gambolling together midway between where he was and the inner wall. The wind was blowing from him to them, which was what he wanted. Already he had the packed meat in his hands and was pressing it through the wire mesh of the fence. Three handfuls to ensure they could not miss it. Then he waited. Maybe it was the force of the wind, or perhaps the sudden harshness of the rain, but it took them a minute or so to pick up his scent. Then they barked and Harrison moved back up the hill into the grove of Douglas fir. He dropped behind the groundswell, slithering down to the drainage culvert, where now water was rushing.

The dogs barked again, but then stopped. Harrison waited. They were trained to pick up any scent and pursue it to its source. They had smelt him and he had retreated, but he had been long enough in one place to settle a spoor. They could only get as far as the fence, and there they would find the meat he had drugged earlier in the day. Crushed tranquillizers in each rolled handful. Hopefully, they would get most of it down them. It wouldn't put them totally out, but they would be unsteady on their feet and lie low. It would also dry out their mouths, which ought to keep them from barking.

He waited: ten minutes, fifteen, twenty. On twenty-five minutes, he crawled to the top of the rise, damp earth soaking into his cam' suit, and looked out over the compound. The light swung and he pressed his nose to the dirt, forced away a cough and looked again. One of the dogs tripped a wall light. Harrison watched the animal stagger a little, then sit awkwardly, rump swinging out behind it. He looked for the other, could not see it, then spied it on the far side of the tower, lying on the ground.

Now, Harrison moved back to the fence, avoiding the play of the searchlight, and crabbed his way to the base of the tower. Above him no one stirred, and he allowed himself a wry smile as he took the wire cutters from his breast pocket and his fingers brushed the packet of cigarettes habit had made him place there. The thought of going into the hotel or the Silver Dollar for a beer suddenly ran high in his veins. He shook the desire away as rain rolled off him, and quietly closed his fist round the wire cutters. He cut, then curled the wire with his fingers until it was raised about ten inches off the ground. Flat on his belly now, like a snake he eased his way underneath, working with fists to his jawbone and his elbows levering him through. From the other side of the compound, one of the Dobermans gave a halfhearted bark.

Harrison squatted right under the tower. The rest of the compound was in darkness. He checked the face of his watch. It was 9.38. Twenty-two minutes before they switched the guard. He needed to be inside the inner compound long before then. He moved off, watching the motion sensors on the walls. He knew that Salvesen did not have any closed circuit TV cameras on the inner wall. They were mounted on the side of the house and kept watch on the inner compound grounds. He wondered if they carried sound as well as movement. He made it to the inner wall unhindered, passing right by one of the dogs. It looked at him out of confused eyes, tongue hanging out and panting very heavily.

'Hangover tomorrow, buddy,' Harrison whispered.

Salvesen had planted fir trees along the inner line of the wall, to protect the house from the throw of light when one of the dogs tripped a sensor. Now they provided the cover he needed to pull himself up. There was no wire on top and thankfully nothing like broken glass. Salvesen obviously figured the exterior wire and dogs were enough. Harrison straddled the wall and peered through the evergreen branches. He could see the back of the marquee and the small building behind that. The house, huge, like some ancient Southern mansion, was to the front, with another slightly smaller building backing off it at an angle. He dropped inside and squatted.

The rain fell more sharply now and the wind shook water from the trees to spray him still further. He waited, not moving, eyes peeled, ears pinned back, listening like a timber wolf on the scent. He heard nothing, saw nothing. Nobody walking about on the inner side of the wall. He moved forward slowly at first, then scuttled to the edge of the marquee. He worked his way down the side which would bring him to the lawned area off the back of the house. Halfway along the tent wall was an opening and Harrison slipped inside. Chairs in aisles, a lectern and a piano. Church. Harrison noted it in his mind, to be transferred to tape later. There was nowhere obvious to place a transmitter. He moved through the marquee which had a kind of straw matting as a floor, but kept to the grass at the side, so muddy footmarks would not betray him. At the far end he paused, crouched and looked out. The lawn was bathed in light from the back of the house.

From outside, he heard voices and realized the guard was changing over. He stayed exactly where he was until all was quiet again. From somewhere, he heard a door slamming, and then just the rain and the rustle of wind through the trees. Cautiously, he moved forward until he was against the wall of the house. A shadow fell across the lighted lawn and Harrison became part of the wall. For what seemed an eternity, he waited for the cameras to move. There were only two pivot points: depending on how wide-angle the lenses were, they would see so much and no more. He worked out his movement. There had been no cameras in the marquee and he figured he was all right. He would soon know if he wasn't.

And then a sliding door opened at the back of the house and Jakob Salvesen stood under the lee of the balcony, just out of the rain. Harrison was about seven feet from him, pressed against the wall. If Salvesen turned right, he would see him. Harrison did not breathe. Salvesen looked at the sky and lifted something to his lips. 'Seven crowned heads.' He muttered the words into a Dictaphone. Then he stepped back inside. Harrison could still hear him. 'Omega Foundation. Statement 321. Israel 1948. Rebirth. Jeremiah, chapter twenty-three: "Therefore, behold, the days come, saith the Lord, that they shall no more say, The Lord liveth, which brought up the children of Israel out of the land of Egypt; But, the Lord liveth, which brought up and which led the seed of the house of Israel out of the north country, and from all countries whither I had driven them; and they shall dwell in their own land."'

His voice grew louder again and Harrison saw his shadow fall once more across the lawn. He could see the points of his boots fractionally overlapping the deck. 'Nineteen sixty-seven,' Salvesen went on. 'Fifth of June 1967. The Six-Day War. That was when it began. Lindsey was right about that. Jerusalem. They retook Jerusalem for the first time since AD 70. Luke chapter twenty-one: "And they shall fall by the edge of the sword, and shall be led away captive into all nations: and Jerusalem shall be trodden down of the Gentiles, until the times of the Gentiles be fulfilled."' Salvesen paused for a moment. 'Their time was fulfilled in 1967. That's it,' he muttered. 'That's when it began.'

The sliding door closed then and the shadow retreated. Harrison remained where he was, aware of the sound of his own heart in his ears. Then he retreated, back through the marquee to the wall and over. The dogs were on their feet, but wobbly. He made it to the fence, wriggled under, then painstakingly rolled down the wire, straightening it as best he could without sending a vibration to the top, which would alert whoever was on guard. He pressed the cut ends back into the earth and packed it a little higher.

All the way up the hill his mind was working: *the fourth kingdom, Rome,* and now this – *1948, Israel, the Six-Day War. Luke twenty-one.* Luke twenty-one and Jeremiah what? *Jeremiah twenty-three.*' He got to the lay-up point and whispered what he remembered into the Dictaphone. *Seven crowned heads,* and *the times of the Gentiles be fulfilled.* He shook his head, looked at his watch and decided he had had enough. He knew now that snippets here and snippets there would not give him what he needed. The key to what Salvesen was doing lay on the other side of that sliding glass door.

# 19

They checked the videos taken from the red priority routes, and Swann spotted the van filling up with fuel at a garage just south of Durham on the A1. The driver was caught on film as he paid. That night the three of them ate dinner again at the hotel, due to leave the north-east early the following morning. Swann watched Louis Byrne looking at the wine menu. Something was odd about it and he didn't realize what until the meal was over. Byrne had gone upstairs to phone his wife, and Swann and Webb were alone in the bar, having a nightcap.

'What's that matter, Jack?' Webb asked him. 'Something's been bugging you all night.'

Swann sipped at his whisky. 'Ignore me, Webby. I've just been in the job too long.'

'We've all been in the job too long. What's bugging you?'

Swann flicked ash from his cigarette.

'Come on. What?'

'OK,' Swann said. 'The other night we had dinner. Right?'

'Yes,' Webb said, drawing out the word.

'And tonight we had dinner.'

'So?'

'Louis chose the wine both times.'

'Did he? I don't know. He paid, which to me is all that counts.'

Swann laid a hand on his arm. 'Tonight he looked at the wine list, but last time he didn't. He just ordered Barolo, like he knew it would be there.'

Webb looked at him then. 'He must have looked at the list. He's never been here before.'

'Exactly.'

Webb wagged his head then. 'You're right, Jack. You've been in the job too long.'

☆

Byrne flicked through a file. Special Branch and MI5 were watching James Ingram. GCHQ monitored his telephone calls for a while, noting who he called and who called him. One number, which he had rung three times in the two days after Swann and McCulloch interviewed him, had been Tommy Cairns's, the self-styled leader of Action 2000. MI6 had informed them that Sebastian May and Jakob Salvesen had been at Cambridge University together in the early 1960s. They were confident there was nothing more to their relationship than that, but would keep on looking.

Logan was sitting at the desk in the squad room that the Foreign Emergency Search Team had been allocated, studying a copy of Harrison's report, which had come over in the diplomatic pouch to the regional security officer at the embassy.

'Louis,' she said quietly.

Byrne looked up. 'What is it?'

'Take a look at this.' She handed him a photograph of a squat, iron-haired man with Jakob Salvesen.

'That's Abel Manley,' Byrne said.

Swann came in then, glanced at Byrne and called them to the briefing. Byrne told Logan to go on ahead. He had to go to the embassy to pick something up and would be back as soon as he could.

Upstairs, Swann flicked through the papers on his knee. 'We clocked the van filling up with petrol on the A1, and we've got the driver paying at the counter, though I don't know how good it is.' He switched on the TV and video. 'The van,' he said freezing the frame, so they all could get a good look. He wound it on again and stopped. 'And the driver paying.' They could see the man – albeit not very distinctly – short-cut hair but not a skinhead, tall, and paying with cash. 'It's not very clear,' Swann said, 'but I reckon that's Frank Cairns of Action 2000.

'Another garage and another video,' he went on and replaced the tape with a different one. He froze the frame on a dark-skinned man with long black dreadlocks. 'Another disguise. Raghead this time, but that is Ibrahim Huella. The car is the one that Kuhlmann bought from Sunderland.'

Webb cleared his throat. 'DRA have confirmed explosive traces in that car,' he said. 'They've identified mercury, barium nitrate and tetrazine, so whoever was driving had been handling detonators. We've also got fibres which match the second bedroom in the farmhouse and those found in Queen's House Mews.'

'For such a pro he's a bit of an amateur, isn't he,' McCulloch stated.

Swann looked at him sourly. 'Except for the fact that he hasn't been nicked yet, Macca.'

Colson looked round the room. 'Where's Byrne?'

'He had to go back to the embassy to collect something,' Logan said. 'He'll be here any time.'

Colson nodded. 'As you know, we put the word out on Huella, Ramas and Tal-Salem. I'm positive Huella is still in this country, because he hasn't finished with us yet. I don't know about the others. But we did have a call from a Colin Leaming. He told us that somebody answering Huella's description worked with him at McDonald's in

Coventry. We're going to interview him later today.' He paused then. 'In the meantime we concentrate on the Nazi angle here. I can't believe they're anything more than runners, but I think it's time we leaned on them.'

Louis Byrne came in then, carrying a file under his arm. 'One other thing,' Colson continued. 'Part of the stuff we've seen from the FBI undercover agent in Idaho has thrown up something that Box 850 are looking into. A picture of this chap Salvesen with Sebastian May, a Conservative Euro MP. It was taken at a ski resort over there. Box are doing a little bit of digging of their own and if it's pertinent, we'll hear from them.' He looked at Byrne then. 'Cheyenne said you went to get something?'

Byrne scraped a hand over his crew cut and held up the paper file. 'We had something sent over from the States today.' He passed the picture Logan had shown him earlier to Colson. 'That guy is Salvesen, as you know,' he said, pointing. 'The other one is Abel Manley who used to be a Minuteman.'

He stood up then and laid the file on the table. 'The Minutemen were an insurgent group back home in the sixties. A forerunner to the Posse Comitatus, a seventies and eighties group which led to today's militia or "patriot movement", who are preparing for some kind of bloody showdown with what they describe as the "Satanic Federal Government", i.e. the United States. Jakob Salvesen had links with the Posse. To give you some idea what they were like then, they used to advocate hanging federal officials from main street. The Minutemen believed that the United States was being taken over by communists, with the government complicit in the act. That's a belief first put forward by the John Birch Society. They produced a guerrilla warfare guide with plans of how to raid, ambush, sabotage, etc. Again, government officials were the enemy, traitors to the constitution.' He paused and selected a document from the file. 'Back in D.C., we put together a few facts, comments, etc. on these kinds of groups, going back as far as the Klan. Let me read you something: "Minutemen also developed chemical and biological weapons. 'They're portable, inexpensive to manufacture and easy to conceal,' said chemist and Minutemen leader Robert DePugh. 'One man with a test tube in his pocket could wipe out a whole army base.'" '

Byrne handed the document to Colson. 'Robert DePugh was arrested in 1970 and the group pretty much disbanded. We haven't seen Abel Manley since. But like DePugh, he was a chemist.'

☆

Swann drove to Coventry and Louis Byrne accompanied him. 'You sure you don't want to stay back at the Yard?' Swann asked him. 'It's a two-hour drive for a two-minute interview. All we're going to do is confirm that Huella was there.'

'I'll stick around, Jack. I want to be close to things.'

They drove up the motorway and Swann looked round at him. 'How long're you going to be over here?'

'We'll be back and forth till the job's done.'

'You don't mind just watching.'

Byrne shrugged. 'Sometimes watching's the best thing you can do. You learn a lot when you watch.' He looked out of the window. 'Now and again we get involved if the country in question has no real counter-terrorist capacity. But here,' he patted Swann on the back. 'You taught us everything we know.'

Swann left the motorway. 'Word on the street is that you're one of the most wanted police officers in the world.'

'Am I? Where'd you hear that – Logan? You shouldn't believe everything she tells you.'

'Seems like a bright girl to me.'

'Yeah, and pretty. She got a degree in psychology from Columbia.'

'Who's after you, then – Hizbollah?'

Byrne shook his head. 'No. Gamaa Islamiya aren't too happy with me, though. They think I kidnapped one of their own.' He shook his head. 'I know who the players are, Jack. I try to track their movements. I guess they know I'm doing it.'

'And Storm Crow?'

'Him in particular.'

☆

Harrison sat across the counter from Lisa Guffy in the diner, where she had just served him a platter of fried chicken, baked potatoes and onion salad. He looked at the food, resting his crossed forearms on the counter, and then he looked in her eyes. 'Well, thank you, Miss Lady Mam.'

'Eat,' she said and pulled his baseball hat over his eyes. He did eat and he watched her serving the last tourists of fall, with her short skirt and hair piled on her head, breasts thrusting at the material of her shirt. She felt his gaze trailing around after her and she flicked at him with a towel.

'Eat,' she said.

'I'm eating.'

When he was finished he wanted to smoke, but couldn't in the diner, so he paid the check, left two dollars' tip and slid off the chair. 'I'm going to shoot a little pool in the hotel,' he told Guffy. 'You wanna come by after work and drive me home.'

'Only if you're sober.'

'Deal.'

Harrison hitched up his jeans and crossed the road to

the Westlake Hotel. Then he remembered he had promised to pick Danny up from the Silver Dollar in Passover, because he had backed his truck into a post and knocked the muffler off.

He drove south out of town and saw Tate's pick-up coming the other way. Jake Salvesen was in the passenger seat. Harrison slowed and they passed without seeing him. They pulled into the airport and Tate drove him straight out to the runway, where Willie was waiting by the steps to Omega 2. Harrison pulled over and flipped the hood on his truck. He leaned under it and watched Salvesen climb the steps to the plane, and then Willie helped Tate with the luggage. Three big cases; it looked like he was going away for a while.

He parked the truck at the back of the bank by Danny's little condo – more of a cabin really, built in the twenties and a little lopsided now – and handed Danny the keys. 'You can keep it till tomorrow, Dan. Guffy's driving me home tonight.'

'How's that third gear?' Danny asked him.

Harrison looked sideways at him. 'You see me grab it?'

'Nope.'

'That'll work, then.'

Danny got two Bud draughts and some quarters for the pool table. Long-haired Mike was in the bar and shooting on the far table with Jimmy, the English ex-pat, who'd worked all over the country before moving to Idaho with half a million dollars in the bank. He had a tattoo of a swallow between the forefinger and thumb of his right hand, and an ageing Elvis Presley haircut. Harrison nodded to Cecil and Junior, then saw Belinda talking to Tracy, Lisa Guffy's home girl.

'You seen Chief, Belinda?' he asked her.

She shook her head. 'I think he's home painting or

something. I was gonna go over later, if I can get me a ride.'

Harrison nodded. 'Guffy's coming for me. We'll give you a ride.'

He took off his jacket, just a white singlet underneath, and he picked up a pool cue. He rubbed the rat tattoo on his shoulder and yawned, then spied Tony Vasquez sitting on his own in the corner. Harrison tweaked a Marlboro from his jacket and lit it, watching as Danny racked. He was leaning over the table to break, when Jesse came in with Drake and Wingo. They bought beer, then moved to a table close to the pool tables. He caught snatches of their conversation.

'No, I ain't seen the little beaner since,' Jesse was saying, 'whipped his ass for him good. Can't he read no signs.' He laughed then. 'No, I guess he can't at that. Don't speak nothing but Spanish.'

'Should ship 'em all back,' Wingo, a tall rangy man with blond hair and muscles, added. 'Little mothers, alls they do is drive around in low riders all day, with boom boxes banging at you every fucking minute.'

In the corner Tony Vasquez knocked back his shot and slid his chair away from the table.

Harrison bent to the table. 'Five ball, corner pocket.' He missed and swore. Then he took a pinch of chew from his tin and placed it under his lip. When he looked round, both Jesse and Wingo were staring at him.

'Dude's got a rat crawling up his arm,' Wingo said.

'Yeah, well, he ain't worth a rat's ass, anyways.' Jesse laughed, a cruel guttural sound.

Harrison's first instinct was to whip his cue over Jesse's head so hard he'd never get up, but he ignored him and bent to his shot.

Tony Vasquez leaned a palm on the table and stared beyond Harrison to Jesse. His eyes were glazed from

Cuervo. 'Hey, motherfucker.' He slurred the words and Jesse pushed back his chair. 'What did you say?'

The bar had quietened considerably. Harrison potted the one ball and then reached for the chalk. Jesse was on his feet now, Wingo with him. Tony reeled a little as he pushed his weight away from the table. Out of the corner of his eye, Harrison saw Chief walk through the main door.

Jesse and Wingo moved towards Tony Vasquez. Harrison laid the pool stick down on the table.

'What did you call me, beaner?' Jesse's lips curled in a snarl.

'Motherfucker. I call you motherfucker. It's what you are – you beat my boy, motherfucker. Maybe you like to pick on someone your own size.' Tony staggered, losing his footing, one boot sliding across the dust on the floor. He regained himself and leaned against the wall. Jesse picked up a pool stick and Harrison stepped in front of him.

'He's drunk, Jesse. Let him be.'

For a moment Jesse stopped, looking down into Harrison's eyes. 'Get out of the way.' Wingo stood at his shoulder. Chief moved away from the bar.

'You assholes wanna fight – do it in the street.' Sula-Mae, the bartender, screeched across at them. 'Tell you what . . .' She had the phone in her hand. 'I'll call 911 now, so the cops can be ready for when you're done with it.'

Jesse looked at Harrison. Harrison looked back at him. Tony could hardly stand.

'I got your marker, Harrison,' Jesse said quietly.

Harrison felt the sudden desire to kill. He had killed before: underground in Vietnam, one on one. You, your flashlight and your six-shot revolver. Him, his AK47 and the M-26 grenade he stole from you.

'Then you better get the drop on me,' he replied, 'because if you don't, I'll kill you.'

Chief moved between them, six foot six and 260 pounds. 'Didn't you hear the lady?' he said.

Wingo took a step backwards. Jesse glanced at Chief's black eyes and nodded slowly. 'I got a long memory, Harrison.'

'So do I.'

Jesse looked once more at Tony. 'You watch your mouth, beaner. Or it won't be a beating you take.' He picked up his hat. 'Come on, boys. We got work to do.'

☆

Byrne and Logan ate with Swann and Webb at the Wonkei on Wardour Street. No cheques, no credit cards, just cash – a three-course meal at five pounds a head. Cheyenne told them a bit about herself, her background, her three years in Naval Investigation before joining the FBI.

'You married, Chey?' Swann asked her.

'No.'

'Boyfriend?'

'Oh, Jack. Give it a rest.' Webb hit him lightly on the arm. 'Just because Pia's out of town.'

'I'm just asking. Polite conversation, it's called.'

'In other people's language, maybe.'

Byrne's pager went off. He frowned and glanced at Logan. 'Leg-att wants me to call him.' He went outside to use his mobile phone.

'Do *you* think there's a connection between your militia investigation and here, Chey?' Webb asked her.

She sat back and adjusted the napkin on her lap. 'On the face of it, it makes no sense,' she said. 'The militia's beef is with the US government. They think we own their lives just because they've got a social security card. Oh, it's more complicated than that – conspiracy theories – New World Order – international Jewish banking cartels. They even believe we're training the Hong Kong police and the Gurkhas to take their weapons away. I can't see how any of that fits with what you've seen over here. But Kuhlmann in Salvesen's compound is a helluva coincidence. And now Abel Manley?'

Byrne came back then, his face serious. 'Remember the fingerprints you gave me, George, the first time I was here?'

'Yeah. Huella's from Queen's House Mews.'

'I just got an ID. The leg-att received a definite confirmation from CJIS. Huella's a US citizen. His real name is Ismael Boese.'

Logan frowned, eyes intent upon Byrne's. 'James and Morag Maguire,' she said slowly.

'And the SLA before them.'

'You chaps want to explain this to us?' Swann asked quietly. 'Who's Ismael Boese?'

Logan glanced at him. 'Sorry, Jack. It's a long story.'

'Tell them,' Byrne said.

'Back in 1974,' she began. 'Two members of the Symbionese Liberation Army were convicted of terrorist activities. You remember the SLA – they kidnapped Patty Hearst.'

Webb nodded. 'Who could forget Patty?'

Logan pushed her plate away. 'The SLA wasn't around for very long. After that episode with her, we hit them hard and it all ended with a Los Angeles SWAT team. Anyway, in an unrelated incident, two other SLA members were tried for terrorist activities in 1974. Pieter and Leona Boese. They got ninety years apiece. He was German-American, she Afro-American. They had a son called Ismael. He was thirteen years old when they went

380

to jail, and they gave him to two of their friends to bring up. James and Morag Maguire.'

Byrne leaned forward. 'IRA fund-raisers.'

'Ismael was mixed race, a good-looking boy,' Logan said. 'They put him through high school, then college. I think he majored in electronics.'

'James Maguire was arrested in Belgium in 1984,' Webb interrupted, 'trying to blow up an off-duty British major.'

'Sandford-Adams,' Swann added. 'What happened to the kid?'

'In 1984 he was twenty-three,' Logan said. 'He'd left home long before then.'

'Born to two terrorists, then brought up by two more.' Webb stroked his moustache. 'Where is he now?'

She made an open-handed gesture. 'We lost touch with him years ago. Morag Maguire's doing time for conspiracy. That's back in the States.'

'And the kid got a degree in electronics?'

'I think so. I can check.'

They were silent for a moment and then Webb pushed air from his cheeks. 'If ever there was a blueprint for an habitual terrorist, that's it.'

'Ideologue,' Byrne said.

Swann felt a shiver prickle his scalp. 'That fits with something else. What you told me, Louis, about the French police train in 1982. Carlos and the mixed-race unknown. Your man in Israel, Ben . . .'

'Dubin.'

'Yes, him. Your theory about the Storm Crow being in this for money. First the Russians and then the Syrians stitched up Carlos when they didn't want him any more. Imagine, you're brought up by two people with a cause and they end up doing life. Then you go to two more with a similar cause and they end up in prison as well. The connection is the cause. Think about it – your parents, your adopted parents, and eventually Carlos the Jackal himself.'

Webb looked at Byrne. 'How did you get the prints?'

'We didn't. It was the ATF in California, years ago. This kid tried to buy some blasting caps. The ATF had an undercover man working Venice beach. They checked him out and found he was Ismael Boese. With his past, they tailed him for a while, but he seemed to be pretty clean. One night in a bar, however, the UCA lifted the glass Boese'd been drinking from. Always useful to have a set of prints on file. Only they never made it to the national crime computer. That's why it took us this long.' He sat back, shaking his head. 'I would never have thought of him, but it's true, his profile's got to be the most pathological terrorist ever.' He gestured with an open palm. 'I think we just identified the Storm Crow.'

# 20

The following morning, Swann briefed Clements and Colson on what had transpired. Colson sat in his office swivelling back and forth in his chair.

'Louis Byrne came up with this?'

Swann nodded. 'The leg-att paged him while we were in the Wonkei, Guv. They'd had word from Washington – Bureau of Alcohol, Tobacco and Firearms.'

'Ismael Boese, the Storm Crow. That's a hell of a result, Jack.'

Swann pushed out his lips. 'Only one thing bothers me, sir. What we've seen so far has taken a tremendous amount of planning, not to mention the money . . .'

'Meaning Boese's too much of an action man to be Storm Crow,' Clements cut in.

'Carlos was an action man, Jack. He also planned his operations in the minutest of detail. How d'you think he evaded capture for twenty-odd years?'

'I'm not arguing, Guv. Byrne's probably right.'

Colson came down to the squad room after imparting the news to the commander. Byrne and Logan were checking files. Swann had got agreement to bring in Frank Cairns, even though the video evidence was far from clear, and was about to go and get him.

'Ismael Boese, Louis,' Colson said, sitting down across from him. 'Now we know who he is – what about a motive?'

Byrne laid down the file he was reading. 'Money.'

'Is Jakob Salvesen paying him? Is that why Bruno Kuhlmann was in the compound?'

'I don't know.' Byrne sat forward. 'Everything we know about the militia indicates their fight is with the US government. Yet Salvesen is arming them. Kuhlmann could be a coincidence, so could Abel Manley. It's possible, probable even that the two things are entirely unrelated.' He stood up and pointed to the information pasted round the walls. 'There's never been a specific pattern with Storm Crow,' he said. 'He goes where the money is. But since Fort Bliss, in 1995, he's only been active in Europe.' He looked back at Colson. 'Five separate incidents, and three of them to do with banking.'

Swann watched him, one foot resting against the edge of his desk. 'I can't believe that Kuhlmann is just a coincidence,' he said.

Byrne looked sharply at him. 'Why not, Jack? What possible reason could Salvesen have for being behind what Storm Crow is doing in Europe? The people who frequent his compound are US militia leaders.'

'Apart from Sebastian May. The right-wing Euro MP.'

'MI6 have cleared him.'

Swann held his gaze. 'I don't believe in coincidences, Louis.'

'There is one thing,' Logan interrupted them. 'We told you that Salvesen runs this religious foundation called Omega. He claims it's funded to research Biblical prophecy. Some of his sermons are transcribed for people who didn't catch his radio broadcasts and are published on the Internet. Recently, he's been talking about the "fourth kingdom", something to do with the ancient Roman Empire.'

Swann raised one eyebrow. 'That helps a lot, Chey.'

He stood up and looked at Colson. 'I'm going to nick Frank Cairns,' he said.

☆

The Catholic priest walked into Westminster Cathedral and smiled at the woman behind the desk. Around him, the organ pipes groaned as if someone who could not play was trying to. 'They're being tuned,' she said.

He smiled at her and wandered to the font at the back of the Lady Chapel, where he sat down to pray. He sat a long time and then he heard footsteps on the flagstones, slow deliberate steps and the creak of the chair behind him.

'Such a fine autumn day, so it is.'

The priest straightened and half smiled. 'A good day to be in Dublin.'

'Aye.'

The Irishman leaned forward in his seat. 'Are you prepared?'

'Of course.'

'I don't think you're hearing me, Father. I mean, are *you* prepared?'

The priest paused then and stared at the lighted candles on the altar. 'Yes,' he said. 'I am.'

'Talk to our mutual friend,' the Irishman told him. 'She'll have the last of everything ready.' He scraped back the chair and stood up. The priest felt the heat of his breath on his neck. 'In the meantime, try to enjoy your vacation.'

☆

'And I stood upon the sand of the sea, and saw a beast rise up out of the sea, having seven heads and ten horns, and upon his horns ten crowns, and upon his heads the name of blasphemy.

And the beast which I saw was like unto a leopard, and his feet were as the feet of a bear, and his mouth as the mouth of a lion: and the dragon gave him his power, and his seat, and great authority.

And I saw one of his heads as it were wounded to death: and his deadly wound was healed: and all the world wondered after the beast.'

Jakob Salvesen addressed his audience in Ely. He was a guest of the Nevada Unorganized Militia, whose leader – Evan Robinson – sat at the front of the hall with him. There were three hundred people crammed inside, some of them having to stand. Salvesen leaned on the lectern. 'Sound familiar, friends?' He stood up again, pushing out his belly under the white suit, and stroked the length of his chin. 'The situation that arises before the final struggle. We all recognize it. We know of the conspiracy, the New World Order, the global government which will mean an end to US sovereignty. The likes of Mikhail Gorbachev in this country right now, an office in the San Francisco Presidio.' He threw out a big hand to his left. 'The liberals who want to see an end to the family as we know it – not American citizens, but citizens of the world. Homosexual freedoms, AIDS and abortion. The World Bank pouring billions into abortion and other forms of contraception to stop what *they* call the population explosion and what *we* call family life. You've got the United Nations giving orders to American forces. We pay and they play. That's treason, friends.' He stood back and hooked his thumbs in his belt. 'It began with Ruby Ridge, and then the Brady Bill and finally, Waco. No wonder that gal in Indiana called on the people to arm themselves and go arrest Congress. No wonder people see black helicopters in the skies, and concentration camps from Alaska to Jerome, Idaho. No wonder people don't want to pay federal taxes, when the money they pay gets pumped into liberal, demonic causes like the New Agers, whose very origins are based in Satanism.'

He stepped back from the lectern and put one hand in his trouser pocket. 'In 1971, I read a book that started me thinking. I was quite a young man then, before I became a pastor. Some say I'm from a privileged background and in many ways I am. I was born into a whole bunch of money and sometimes I wondered why. It gave me an edge though, an advantage. I was able to study with the best students and learn from the best teachers and I took it upon myself to do just that. I was in a position to see things that most ordinary hard-working, patriotic Americans were not in a position to see, because they were too busy just trying to feed their families. I tell you, my friends, I saw and I acted. What you are doing is right, organizing yourselves into groups such as this one. That is your Second Amendment right as God-fearing American people. Heck, we've been subjugated before. That's what the fourth of July is all about. But the demon is not here, my friends; the stain of the beast is not yet with us. It is coming, however, mark my words. But it won't grow here; that diabolical foetus is weaning in malice elsewhere.'

He paused then and touched his moustache with his tongue. 'The Omega Foundation is just that. Omega, the last, the end. I've been watching and preparing my ground for thirty years and you must do the same. The fight may yet come to this country's soil. The UN is just the beginning. The time of desolation that was foretold seven hundred years before the birth of our Lord and Saviour Jesus Christ is at hand. I charge you, my friends, to read the second and seventh chapters of Daniel. You'll read about four kingdoms – only the fourth one, the beast of iron that smashes and tramples all before it, is a broken kingdom. It comes in two parts and right now the second stage of that kingdom is all but complete. We're told by the Lord himself in the gospels of Matthew, Mark and Luke that: "The abomination that causes desolation, the nameless one, will stand in the temple of the Lord and claim to be the Lord."'

He looked straight at Robinson. 'Evan,' he said. 'Lead these folk in the name of the Lord. The foundations are laid and time grows short. Keep your guns loaded and your powder dry.'

☆

Swann and McCulloch sat across the table from Frank Cairns at Paddington Green police station.

'Who stole the van, Frank?' Swann asked him.

Cairns sat with his arms folded, next to the duty solicitor. 'What van?'

'The van you drove to Consett.'

'Never heard of fucking Consett.'

'Frankie,' McCulloch wagged his head, 'we've got you on videotape buying petrol.'

'No, you haven't.' Cairns leered at him across the desk. 'I wasn't there. I was with friends in Croydon. I can give you half a dozen witnesses.' He looked at his lawyer. 'This is a fucking stitch-up. When I get out of here, I want you to sue these bastards.'

Swann shook his head at him. 'Real hard case, aren't you, Frankie. Little Nazi boy running around whacking blacks and Pakistanis.'

'I object to that, Sergeant,' the solicitor stepped in. 'You cannot make accusations which have no basis in fact.'

'He's a member of Action 2000. They, in case you didn't know, are Nazis.'

The solicitor shook his head. 'You have not established that my client is a member of any political group.'

For a moment Swann was silent, then he changed tack. 'Who did the talking, Frank? Was it Joanne Taylor that spoke to you? Was it you, even? No. More likely to be Tommy. Yeah?'

Cairns shook his head. 'I don't know what you're talking about.'

'I suppose it was James Ingram to start with. Maybe he put them on to your firm. Got somebody else to do his dirty work.'

'There you go again,' Cairns said. 'Rambling. You want to watch that, you know. First sign of madness.'

They took him back to the cell. Swann called Webb at the Yard to find out the results of the Section 18.

'Find anything, Webby?' he asked. 'We're getting nowhere here.'

'Nothing,' Webb told him. 'No shoes we can match to the puddle tread and nothing for the thread in the cab.' He paused. 'He's either dumped them or stashed them somewhere else.'

'Or it wasn't him.' Swann scratched his head. 'He reckons he's got half a dozen witnesses for the time we think he was driving the van. I thought the Paddington Green treatment might shake him up, but it hasn't.'

They held him for forty-eight hours, but he stuck to his story. The solicitor knew they had nothing more concrete than the video evidence, which was not good enough on its own. They had no choice but to release him. He waved to Swann as he was driven away.

☆

Autumn in London was wet and cold. In January it snowed hard. Swann and Webb went to Scotland and climbed ice-crusted waterfalls. They stayed in a small hotel on the banks of Loch Tay with Pia and Caroline.

He lay upstairs with Pia. They had the curtains drawn back, so they could see the wafer of light from the moon over the darkness of the loch. Long after they had made love and Pia slept against him, her body soft and warm, Swann lay on his back with the pillow raised, one arm behind his head, and looked out at that moon.

He fell asleep and dreamed. Steve Brady, standing at the bottom of the bed with his head caved in and blood dripping over the ice axes, which dangled from smashed wrists. He woke up screaming.

'Jesus, Jack. What the hell's the matter?' Pia sat bolt upright, her fingernails digging into his shoulder blades.

She switched on the light and stared at Swann's ashen face, his eyes sunk back in their sockets. 'You were dreaming again, weren't you. The climb. You and Steve Brady.' She sat down and sighed. 'You should never have gone on to the ice, Jack. That's not the way to deal with it. You need to talk about it. Don't you see, you have to. You've bottled it up for years.' She got out of bed and stood there, naked, goose pimples rising on her skin. 'I can't go on like this. I really can't, Jack.'

He reached out and took her wrist, pulling her back towards him. 'I'll be all right,' he said.

'No, you won't, Jack. You won't. You'll go on and on and on.' She flared her nostrils at him. 'I love you, you know. I really love you. You can trust me. Talk to me. Talk to me now. How can I help you, if you won't even talk to me?'

Swann poured a shot of whisky from the bottle on the bedside table. He held the glass with white knuckles, fingers gripping the wet sides like ice, sweat still sticky on his brow.

'The Diamir face,' he began. 'Steve wanted to go on.' He looked at Pia. 'I'll tell you, Pia. I'll tell you now. Just don't leave me.'

Ice crusting the vertical walls of the Merkl Gully, where Hermann Buhl had stepped before him and the Messner brothers, Gunther never making it off the mountain. Swann looked across at Brady, as the clouds rolled in around them, massing against the summit and yet still allowing a glimpse at 8000 metres.

'London's a long way from here, Jack,' Brady said. 'When're we going to be here again?'

Swann looked up at those steep, grey curves where buttresses of ice had dripped in the sun that had blinded them earlier, replaced now by thick dark cloud that promised snow and perhaps the threat of avalanche.

He gazed below to where Ellis and Bowen had been; but surely now Bowen had got him down, thousands of feet below, upon the grey-black centipede of the glacier and the safety of walking on flat ground where you were sure of your axe and boots. He looked back at Brady and caught the fever of light in his eyes.

'We should go back, Steve. We won't make it before the weather breaks.'

'We can make it, Jack. I'll lead. Come on. You and me, alpine-style. This is Nanga Parbat. The Himalayas. We can make it. Look, you can see the bloody summit.'

Swann did look and Brady was right, you could still see the summit cast in pink with the final glow of the sun.

'OK, go for it, you bastard. But we better fucking make it.' Swann kicked in with the points of his crampons, legs slightly bent at the knee. He checked his weight against the slim metal screw twisted into the fissure of grey ice at his chest. He peered at the screw, not seeing it and seeing it, then he rested his weight, took the slack through the sticht plate and looked up. Brady was already climbing and the cloud seemed to murmur with voices of caution as Swann watched him, ice axes inverted, the shaft loops loose about his wrists as he plunged in the picks and hauled himself up the face.

'The bastard's not putting in enough protection,' Swann murmured. He wanted to shout, but the cloud swirled about him now and the first flakes of snow were settling on his jacket.

He knew then that they would not make it. The cloud was too low; already the sun, which had glided across the summit in false caress only moments earlier, had betrayed them. Above him, Brady faltered, stopping on the ice as if, with the descent of the cloud, his confidence had drained away. For a moment he looked back, down the funnel of the gully, with ice and rock and mountain, steep and unforgiving, all about him. 'Come back,' Swann said to himself, Brady being too high to summon from here. He felt the rope go slack, the weight of it damp now against his arms. He paid out a little more as Brady seemed intent on one more effort. Thoughts of bivouac entered Swann's head, but where could you bivouac in the Merkl Gully?

Brady moved up again; Swann saw the arc of the axe and then the left foot rising and kicking in. He saw the ice splinter, an image imprinted on his mind from sixty feet below. And then the rope sang and Brady was in space, adrift all at once from the face. Even then, Swann thought of descent; only Brady's descent was loose and fast and lost from the wall. The rope fizzed under his hands and Brady was sliding, slithering off the face, desperately trying to twist one ice axe round for a brake. And then he was past, floundering. For an instant, Swann saw his face, lips drawn back, the red of his gums – and then gone. The rope bucked and kicked and then hauled at the muscles in Swann's forearms as he rammed it over the sticht plate. It buzzed and hummed with the vibration. Never would he forget that sound. In the deepest sleep, in the quiet of the morning, he would feel the snap of his muscles and the sudden weight that racked his body, forcing his feet down in the ice till it crumbled and cracked, and then *he* was loose, hanging horizontally in his harness, the rope between him and the belay point harsh and taut and tearing into his body.

For what seemed an eternity, Swann hung there, holding the stricken rope, eyes fixed on the sliver of metal that plugged them both to the wall. And the snow fell harder, flakes of ice it seemed, in his eyes, his nose, coating his body in a fine mist of white so he could no longer see the ice screw. He calculated the distance in his mind. No protection between them. Sixty feet up, one hundred and twenty of falling. He had felt the shudder through his arms as Brady bounced off the packed ice of the gully wall, and now the weight was such that he knew, though he could not see, Brady was hanging as he was, adrift from the mountain. No movement: either Brady was unconscious or he could not get a grip on the wall.

Swann took the loose end of the rope, twisted it round his right leg and tied off. Now, at least, he had his hands free. But he was still lying on his back in mid-air; his harness seemed to have worked itself down and he could not get straight. But more than that, it was the weight of his partner which pulled him. Swann found breathing hard, tight and constricted in his lungs, no room for his diaphragm to work. He knew he had to get upright, too long like that and he would pass out, not much longer and he would die of asphyxiation. He still had both axes on his wrists, and he let the loop of one slide down his forearm until he could grip the shaft. He swung it upwards with all the strength he could muster, and the pick bit into the ice and held. Swann hauled on it and the rope tore at him. For a moment he gasped; he could feel the restricted flow of blood to his lower body, a fizzing sensation as the veins were squeezed shut. After a few moments of manoeuvring he managed to get himself semi-upright, and he sat there, hanging on to the shaft of the axe.

He could breathe now and he peered below, dangling like a spider from a single thread, as the snow fell in flurries about him, hiding the world beyond the wall at his nose. Looking up he could see nothing, right in the thick of the clouds now; he should never have agreed. They should have gone down when they still had the chance. He thought about the ice, and the atmospheric change from the heat of the day when your clothes fairly wring with sweat to the sudden shift as the clouds roll in and the temperature drops like a stone. For a time the ice is weakened, still partially melted by the sun and not yet given over to the hardening of the night. That's why starting at first light was so important: the ice is packed hard, having frozen solid during the night. It is bitterly cold to begin with, but your feet and axes are more certain then than at any other part of the day.

He looked below, but could not see Brady anywhere. He knew he was in space over the gully. He had an abseil rope over his shoulder. Leaning against his axe head, he pulled the rope round and taking another ice screw, wound it into the wall with the head of his second axe. He buried it as deep as it would go and pulled down on it hard. You never knew with ice: with rock you can almost be certain of your belay, but ice moves, it contracts and expands and what is sure to begin with does not necessarily stay that way. Once the screw was in the wall, Swann took a sling and two karabiners and hooked himself on to it. He tied off the climbing rope, then unclipped himself. The rope jerked and Brady slipped that bit further, and now he was hanging on his own, only the single ice screw to hold him. But there was only half the weight and Swann had faith in that screw. The relief was incredible, but he was aware of a dull pain, between his belly and his bowels, and he wondered if he had ruptured something. No time to think about it now, he had to find his partner and somehow get down to their tent before the weather blocked their retreat.

He abseiled, kicking out from the wall and sliding down on a figure of 8. He came to where the wall pushed out in a ledge to the drop below and saw Brady dangling twenty feet further on. Fifteen feet more and he would be back on the slope. It was steep but not vertical. Swann got to the ledge and stopped. 'Steve,' he called. 'Can you hear me, Steve?'

No answer. Swann looked at the way his body was hanging. His left foot was at an awkward angle and he was bleeding from somewhere. Swann dug home another piece of protection and tied off. He pulled the rope down, clipped in to the new ice screw and abseiled down to the wall above which Steve Brady was hanging. It was getting darker now and the snow fell harder. If he could just get him down to the camp. But then he wondered, where was the camp? Were they following the same route? Then he felt panic overtake him. No they weren't, the lower slopes of the gully had been too steep and they had traversed some distance before going up it again. So where did that leave the tent? The fall, Brady hanging in mid-air; everything was a blur all at once. He forgot about the tent. What he had to do was to get Brady.

Once on the wall below Brady, he tied off again. What he would give right now for a bolt gun. He climbed back up. Brady was unconscious, but his eyes were flickering.

His head was badly gashed, mouth split and his left foot definitely broken somewhere. There was no way he could climb. Swann looked down and the mountain slopes seemed treacherous beyond belief. He had no choice: if they did not get off this face both of them would die.

Moving above Brady, he fixed another belay point and tied off the abseil rope. Then he fixed a rope sling between himself and Brady, about ten feet apart. Brady still twirled in space. Swann unclasped his pocket knife and cut through the rope that held Brady to the ice wall above them. He took in the slack on his own rope, but there was still a terrific jerk as Brady fell a few feet more. Swann felt the wrench at his middle again and Brady groaned below him. 'You OK, Steve? Can you hear me?' he called. Brady looked up at him for a moment and his eyes seemed to expand and contract in his head.

'Jack?'

'You fell, Steve. Don't talk. I'm lowering you down, abseiling along with you.'

'Cold, Jack. Cold.'

'I know. Don't talk.'

So they began the long descent with snow falling all about them. Every now and then mini-avalanches would overtake them and Swann would press himself tighter to the wall and pray that the ice screw would hold. He got them three hundred feet, six hundred, nine hundred, and then the darkness was closing in so hard he had no idea where they were on the wall. The tent and the final camp were but distant memories; every sensation, every bearing had been turned upside down. Below him, Brady kept talking as if the very words would keep him alive. He told Swann he could feel nothing below his waist. 'Am I paralysed, Jack? D'you think I'm paralysed?'

'You're fine. It's just shock.'

'Yeah. Shock. That's it, Jack, just shock.'

At twelve hundred feet it got steeper and Swann cursed himself for not being able to find somewhere to bivouac. Below him, as the gloom grew, he could see a snow ledge, about ten feet across. Beyond that he saw nothing, but it might be good enough for them to huddle together. They had no tent, no food, no sleeping bags. Their intention had been to reach the summit and get back to the tent in eight hours. That was history now, consigned to the dustbin of foolishness. Swann was angry. Brady would not be hanging there if they had retreated when they should have done. The one thing a climber never messes with is Himalayan weather.

He looked again at the ledge, sixty feet below. It looked full and snow-covered and maybe there would be enough depth to dig some sort of snow hole before it got too dark.

Above him he felt something give. A jerk in the rope, which at first he thought was a chunk of falling ice or heavy snow, but it jerked again and he could see the rope loosening in his hands. He looked below and started to move again, only sixty feet, fifty, forty. Then he felt a terrific snapping of the rope and for a second he thought he was going to fall. The ice screw holding them to the wall was working itself loose, the combined weight of both of them too much for the fragile housing. Swann looked again at the ledge below and then at Brady's upturned face.

'The ice screw's coming out, Steve,' he said, voice stumbling over the words. 'It can't hold both of us.'

Brady looked up at him, opened his mouth and closed it again. Swann had one hand in his pocket, looking at the ledge below them. The screw jerked again and he felt a shiver run from the top of his spine and disappear between his buttocks. The cold chipped at his face, ice on his partial beard and sticking his eyelids together. The rope jerked again and Swann took out his knife.

'Jack. No.' Brady lifted a hand as if to ward off a blow.

'It can't hold us.' Swann had the knife open, his heart so high in his chest it all but stopped up his throat. 'Look, Steve. Look below you.' Brady was whimpering like a child.

'FUCKING LOOK, STEVE.' Swann bellowed it at him and Brady looked below. 'Snow ledge, Steve. It's only about fifteen feet.' Again the screw moved. Swann did not dare slide any further in case it pulled out altogether.

'Don't cut the rope, Jack. Please don't cut the rope.'

Swann blocked his ears. The weight was too much. He remembered Simpson and Yates in the Andes years before. Yates cut Simpson. The first law of mountaineering: you have to save yourself. Simpson fell 150 feet and survived. All Brady would do was drop about fifteen and land in the soft, freshly fallen snow on that ledge.

'Don't cut the rope, Jack. You'll kill me. Don't kill me, Jack.'

Swann held the rope that bound them together and began to saw. Again the ice screw shuddered – it must've been all but out of the wall now. Swann sawed and sawed and all the time he did so, Brady pleaded in his ear. 'Don't cut the rope, Jack. Please don't kill me.'

Swann sawed, snow in his eyes, and the rope was fraying and fraying and then finally it broke. Brady fell. He did not cry out, just looked up, eyes falling away as he lost height, and then he landed with a thump on the ledge. Swann watched him roll and stop, and relief flooded through him. And then the ledge collapsed, and Brady fell with a cry in his throat that Swann would remember for the rest of his life.

And silence. Not even the wind, just a perfect stillness,

with night falling and the snow dropping soundlessly on to him. Swann clung to the wall like some exhausted insect, with the frayed end of the rope dangling between his legs. He stared at the ledge: it had been a good ledge, full of packed snow, and now it was no longer there.

He clung there all night and the voices of dead climbers whispered to him through the moan of the wind. He must have slept, because he woke up in the morning still hanging on to that wall, with the clouds all about him and no sign of the sun. He was stiff and freezing cold, and wondered what he was doing there.

He shook his head and remembered. And then he began to cry, still tied off on the abseil rope, somehow having survived the night, with his body temperature so low he was but degrees from hypothermia. He sobbed and sobbed until he could not cry any more. And all around him the mountain seemed to ring with voices, whispers, cries, guttural voices of men, the clink of axes in ice, the stamp of frozen feet on rock, as if every climber who ever set foot on the Diamir face was raging at what he had done.

Somehow he got moving, abseiled the rest of the way, and then one more rope length and he could walk, climb backwards and scramble the rest of the way down the mountain. Every inch of the way he prayed he would find Brady – lying in the snow, hurt yes, but still alive – but there was no trace of him anywhere. The last few thousand feet he stumbled in a state of delirium, the cold, the lack of food and the sheer emotional trauma taking his senses from him. He saw other climbers, far distant, in woollen breeches and carrying hawser ropes. A woman's voice urging him on. Once he saw Brady, heard him calling and he started to lurch across the pack ice before he realized there was nobody there.

Sometime that evening he stumbled down the final

stretch of the glacier and into base camp on his own. Bowen was on his feet, grabbing Swann as he fell forward, pitching into the tent. He took him and lowered him carefully, wiping the flecked snow from his face.

'Where's Brady?' he said.

☆

Pia was silent after Swann had finished speaking. He sipped whisky and flicked at the build-up of tears in his eyes. 'I killed him, Pia. I killed Stephen Brady.'

She touched his cheek with a soft palm. She was naked, her beauty framed in silhouette against the moonlight. 'He killed himself, Jack. You tried to save him.'

'I cut the rope.'

'Yes, you cut the rope. But *he* made the mistake.'

'He pleaded with me.' Swann's eyes buckled into knots of grizzled flesh. 'He pleaded with me not to kill him.'

Pia kissed his eyes. 'If it'd been the other way round, he'd have done the same thing.'

'No.' Swann shook his head.

'You know he would, Jack. You've told me yourself. Every climber who ever steps on to a hill knows the risks. He should not have gone on. The weather closing in like that, temperature dropping. Even *I* know it was madness.' She stroked his hair and eased herself back into the bed beside him. 'Ssshh,' she whispered. 'It's all right. It's all right. You've got it out, talked it out, Jack. Everything will be all right.' She kissed his face and chest and neck, gently, like the wings of a butterfly fluttering over his skin.

Swann closed his eyes as she moved lower down his body, her hand on his thighs, his belly, lips brushing against him. He reached for her then, the breath stuck in his throat; warm skin, the softness of her breasts, he kneaded them with stiff fingers. He worked himself against her and she caressed his buttocks, then took his penis in her hand, stroking him as he stiffened.

On her back now, a light in her eyes and her legs wrapped about his waist, ankles locked, squeezing the love out of him as he moved inside her. He could not get close enough, could not get deep enough; frantic now, his skin on fire, the muscles of his face twisted in a mask of pain. Her fingers raked his hair, pulling his head down, pushing it back again, her tongue in his mouth. Then he came with a roaring in his throat like the guttural cry of an animal; and all the fear, the pain and the weakness flowed out from inside him.

☆

Tommy Cairns believed he had heard the last of them. Nothing on the phone, nothing in the mail. When he first found out it was Ingram's farm that had been incinerated, he thought it was hysterical. But on reflection he had sobered. Why choose Ingram's farm? How did they know about it? The reports in the papers said that the workshop was accessed by a passage from the wine cellar, something to do with the original owner's being terrified of marauding Scots. Maybe that's why it was chosen. But he knew that whatever Ingram said, the police would think he knew about it. That gave *them* a hold over him. Not that they needed one; no one knew who they were. Not only that, but Frank had been arrested. He did well and they had to let him go, but it had been close. The press reports about the death of the American at the farm hinted that it might not have been an accident. That disturbed him. Maybe they killed those whom they used, like the female praying mantis.

He was working at the back of a flatbed lorry in early March, loading some sheets of plywood, when the mobile

401

sounded on his belt. Almost before she said anything he knew that it was her.

'Hello, Tommy,' she said.

He stood still, then rested against the back of the truck. 'What d'you want?'

'The last job I told you about.'

'No. Frank got nicked. We're not doing any more.'

'It's a very simple job, purchase and delivery. Fifteen thousand pounds.'

Cairns stopped. He was pretty sure that if the police had been watching Charlie, they were not doing so now.

'Frank got arrested.'

'And he got released, didn't he. This is the last job, Tommy. After that, we'll leave you alone.'

'I don't want nothing to do with chemicals.'

For a moment she paused. 'You *will* help us, Tommy.'

A chill went through him then and he could feel his mouth drying. 'What do we have to do?' he said carefully.

'Just buy some more glass.'

'Fucking glass. Jesus Christ. I'm not hiring any more vehicles. And it's too risky stealing them.'

'Then use one of your own lorries. You're a building firm, aren't you?'

'Oh yeah. I'm really fucking stupid.'

'So, you're out.' The way she said it sent a shiver scuttling down his back. 'Because if you are, I want you to remember that we know who you are.'

'Frankie knows who you are – two of you at least.'

'Yes,' she said. 'That's a mistake that needs rectifying.'

Cairns did not scare easily. He'd been in Belmarsh and other nicks and held his own with the worst of them. Growing up, he and Frank had been in fights galore and had often taken people on when the odds were more than two to one. But he recalled seeing Frank's ashen face after he dumped the taxi. *He knew what was going to happen. The bearded one's eyes*, he kept saying, *you should've seen his eyes.*

'OK,' he said. 'Last time. After that, you leave us alone. You fuck off back where you came from and never call me again.'

She laughed in his ear. 'That's more like it, Tommy. Action 2000, remember. A little before 2000 – but action all the same.'

☆

Apart from the cold, Harrison preferred surveillance in winter. The difficulty was getting on to the land unnoticed. But, once there, a winter gilly suit would hide you from anything. During the winter Salvesen was less active. Harrison knew that he had been on a preaching and speaking tour throughout most of the fall. He was not only invited by leaders of the militia, but by some of the mainstream churches: Baptists in Arizona, Seventh Day Adventists in Colorado, Assembly of God in California. Much of the tour was broadcast on his radio station, and Harrison had listened to his sermon in Nevada. Afterwards, he had looked up some of the passages in the Bible.

Harrison had also written down what he had heard him dictating when he made his one covert entry into the compound. The Gentiles' day and all that. 1967. The Six-Day War when the Israelis recaptured Jerusalem from King Hussein of Jordan. He had sat in his trailer when he wasn't seeing Guffy and flicked through an old copy of the Bible. He looked up Revelation, chapter thirteen and found the beast with seven heads, one of which had been wounded, and the ten horns with ten crowns upon them. He read more, trying to get a handle on where exactly Salvesen was coming from, and he found another beast in chapter twelve, a red dragon with seven heads and ten horns, only this time the heads had crowns and none of them had been wounded.

In early March the snow was still banked up to the highway and Harrison went to Nevada for three days to visit a friend. He drove out of Passover with his bag packed, having already requested his handlers to procure some item of interest from the casinos in Reno and leave it in the dead drop for his return. He hid his truck off the highway near Shoshone and waited for Scheller and Brindley. They gave him a new truck, loaded with a snowmobile, and he drove back to the valley looking like any other tourist. He headed through Passover and West-lake unnoticed, and parked off the road to Dugger's Canyon.

He snowmobiled to the hogan and made it to the high lay-up point, using snowshoes and two long ice axes. In the wintertime the rocky outcrop formed the basis of a natural snow hole and he could sleep there in some semblance of comfort.

Salvesen did not ease up on his patrols just because it snowed. Rather than have his men trudge around on snowshoes, they used snowmobiles and sped around the outer perimeter fence. They also conducted the odd military manoeuvre inside the compound itself. Sometimes they would be conducted at night and the odd poacher had mentioned the coming and going, quietly in the bar. Normally, though, they would go north of the compound, deep into the hills and draws, to the training centre. Harrison had joked about it with the guys back in Salt Lake. Some kind of Bekaa Valley in Idaho.

He settled down in his snow hole and watched for a while, then fell asleep and was awoken in the morning by a six-point royal bull calling to his herd from the rocks above his head. It was like a foghorn going off and Harrison nearly cracked his head as he woke up. He heard it again, thought the world was falling in on him, then he smelled the rancid scent of its breath. He could see the points on the rack as the huge elk shook its head and bellowed across the mountain. Its front hooves were right on top of the snow hole, supported by the outcrop of rock. Danny Dugger had got an eight-point bull the year before last. He was hunting with Chief, Chief using his bow. He had loosed one off and missed. Danny brought it down with a rifle they had taken as back-up. They never kept the rack, but it was eight points and the elk weighed over a thousand pounds, bigger than some of the horses on the ranch where Chief lived. Danny's pride and joy were the two ivory teeth he had kept as souvenirs.

Harrison ignored the bull. He watched the cows in the valley below, looking up at their lord and master and pretty much ignoring him. He put his binoculars to his eyes and scanned the compound. Jesse Tate came out of the bunkhouse with three other men and walked across to the main house. Quite a few of them stayed there in the winter. Salvesen was not home, Harrison knew that much. He had reputedly gone to Michigan to speak to a group up there. Governor Platt was supposed to be going to listen to him. Harrison had never really watched when he was away before, but the word was that Jesse was sergeant-at-arms.

Since that one time, Harrison had not been able to gain entry. What he needed was to place a listening device somewhere, but it had to be in the house itself, and it was wired and alarmed like a bank vault. He decided to move. There was definitely nobody in the tower on this side and he had the cover of the snow, then the grove of Douglas fir. He made it in just under an hour, which was good going in this weather. As he got to the top of the line of trees, he saw Jesse, Wingo and another man go into the building that jutted from the house on the side. Harrison had named it the armoury because he had seen them come out with M16s, when they were preparing for an exercise in the hills.

He got to the forward lay-up point and settled. Jesse came out again and yelled across the compound to one of the others, who came running towards him. Together they disappeared back inside and the silence of the day descended. Harrison yawned, wondering why he put himself through this, wondering what else he could do with his life, wondering why the Bureau spent such a lot of money on a seemingly fruitless exercise. He thought of Guffy and the fact that he was lucky to have such a good and loving woman to whom he lied every day of his life. He ought to make the most of her while he had the chance, instead of lying in a hole in the middle of winter playing at being James Bond. Not many men of his age and battered appearance got the chance at an old lady like that. He was lying there, thinking about the warmth of her body still tucked up in bed, when he heard Jesse's voice in the trees behind him.

'Wingo, your snowshoe's loose, buddy.'

Harrison physically jumped, then stilled his breathing to nothing. He had seen them go into the armoury not fifteen minutes before. He heard the tramp tramp of crushed snow under shoes moving directly towards where he lay. With one silent hand he eased the hood down on his gilly and lay flat. If they turned up the hill from the trees, they would see his tracks in the snow.

They did not though, they walked past him in winter combat gear and set off round the perimeter fence, M16s packed over their shoulders. A pace to the left and they would have stepped on him. Three of them: Jesse and Wingo, and the other one looked like Slusher from the back. Harrison breathed again and watched until they were round the far side, then he rolled on his back and looked up at the sky. Blue today, with wispy cloud reminiscent of summertime. He closed his eyes and he pondered. Jesse had gone into that building and Harrison knew that the door on the side was the only way out. Maybe there was another that led to the house, but that still didn't explain how not fifteen minutes later, they had walked out of the draw and nearly stepped on top of him.

He rolled back on to one elbow and peered through his binoculars. They were now almost back to the main gate, level with the road they cleared every day in order to get out. He could see two shiny black snowmobiles, like dolphins stranded on a beach. The men got on board, two on one and one on the other, and set off across the flat, white-topped pasture, weaving trails in the snow. He watched until they were no more than dots on the horizon and then he turned his glasses to the goon towers. If there had been anybody there, he would have seen them. It's very difficult for a person to remain absolutely still unless they have been properly trained.

Harrison got up and moved quietly back into the semi-darkness of the trees. He deliberately moved round the groundswell and then he squatted and looked at the tracks. He could hear the trickle of water from the culvert, running out and freezing in the snow. The compound was built on a slight plateau, with the ground running away from it on all sides except this one to the east, where the mountains rose. It gave Salvesen excellent visibility and kept his rear more than guarded. Any opposing force trying to reach the relative cover of the trees would be spotted before they'd got fifty feet down the hill. Harrison crouched and listened to the caress of the wind in the trees. Above his head a black crow cawed at him, then lifted on a wing span of almost four feet. For a while it circled like an eagle, then dropped back to the tree line.

He listened to the trickle of water. The footprints led directly to the culvert, about forty feet to the back of the groundswell, just before the hill started climbing. Harrison sat there and stared. And then he understood.

Lai Khe base, or Rocket City because of how the VC used to lob mortars in every night. Just a little north of Ben Cat in Cu-Chi District, Vietnam. Nineteen years old and a volunteer for the 1st Engineer Battalion, intelligence and reconnaissance section, Tunnel Rats. He had been in Vietnam for over a year. He could have got back in the world after twelve months, that was the most they expected of you. But Harrison had volunteered for more. Looking back now, he was a punk kid with a hair stuck up his ass. He had seen the Rats, and heard about Robert 'Batman' Battens, and he volunteered for the underground work on two occasions. Batman was the number one man underground and the only NCO in Vietnam to be on the ten most wanted list of the Vietcong. Although there was always a Rat Six, the term given to the officer commanding the section, everyone knew that Batman led the Rats. Harrison had been told he was in his third full year in 'Nam. What he didn't know, however, was that Batman got his date of estimated return from overseas before Harrison put in his second request to join them.

Harrison was the perfect size for a Rat, not too tall, wiry and showed them no fear. A lot of them were Cuban or Mexican, because of their size. There were no blacks – Batman wouldn't allow it. The fact that Harrison was no longer a draftee impressed them and within two hours of arriving he was backing up the point man in a tunnel system deep in the Iron Triangle. Fifteen-minute standby from Lai Khe, they would be flown in by chopper and rappel down ropes to the ground. From there they would go into the tunnels and do what had to be done, one man on his own sometimes. Harrison had done that more than once, just your fatigues, your flashlight and gun.

During his first tour Harrison's best friend, Eli Footer from Chicago, had been killed by a VC who popped out of a tunnel entrance and threw a US M-26 grenade that had blown him to pieces. Harrison remembered finding his hand. It had all happened so fast that he did not know it was Eli they got, but Eli had a diver's watch and that's what he found on the hand. He remembered their unit pulling out and the Tunnel Rats taking over. There and then he volunteered, but was refused because his own unit was down on men and they were about to make a big push to the north. They packed what they could find of Footer into a bag and carried him out in the dust-off. Harrison had seen the VC that did it; his face, his NVA helmet and the arc of his arm as he lobbed the grenade from the trap door to a tunnel. He never got another chance to transfer, so he volunteered for a second tour.

He approached the water culvert cautiously; booby traps, punji stakes and spears. He shook his head at himself. Salvesen had dug escape tunnels under that compound, somehow they were linked to the culvert. The entrance was snow-packed, but still Harrison checked for booby traps: in his mind's eye the snow and packed ice around the lip was replaced by dust and sweating vegetation and the perpetual hum of mosquitoes. He looked for snakes and spiders in grass that wasn't there, then squatted back on his haunches. For a moment he gathered himself, so many sudden images in his head, memories he didn't remember having; the rest of the team, him the youngest by some four years. The way they talked about Batman and what had happened to the last Rat Six. Conversations he thought he had forgotten; people he had not seen since and would not see again.

He let it all sink through him, let his head clear, as the

sun died in the sky and a new chill settled over the country. Then, taking his Mag-lite from his pocket, he crawled into the culvert. He crawled in water, just a dribble, but wet enough to soak through his clothing in seconds. He shone the light and the darkness of the pipework opened out in front of him. He stopped. The last time he had shone a light like that – the very last time – he had fucked up and that had been that. But he couldn't think about it now. He clenched his jaws together, this was Idaho in '98 and not Cu-Chi in '69. He was almost forty-eight years old and this was FBI work. He could only see the drain and that somehow didn't make sense: the piping was too narrow to do anything but crawl forward on your belly.

He backed out again and sat there thinking, ignoring the chill of the water on his knees. He checked the area immediately around the culvert for some other kind of entrance. He remembered hearing how the first of the tunnels in 'Nam were found. The army couldn't understand how the NVA were getting inside the heavily guarded Cu-Chi base and shooting GIs in the night. Then one day, some guy out on the point sat on a scorpion and leapt ten feet in the air, only it wasn't a scorpion, it was a nail in a wooden trap door bevelled into the earth.

Quietly he scraped around, not wanting to disturb anything, and then he was forced back to the lay-up point as Jesse's patrol came riding round the fence on their snowmobiles. He knew then that he had been too eager, too lax in his approach, so he settled himself down and went to sleep until dusk. He woke to cloud cover and the threat of a storm, with the wind licking through the trees like it does in summer: nothing to begin with, that still, weighted air, and then all of a sudden the first rush of the storm. The trees were bending like that now, as if the sky threatened to break up in thunder. He checked the goon tower and knew that Jesse was now being that bit more vigilant, as a shadow moved across the white line of the sky. Harrison got his gun and his flashlight, his wire garrotte and knife, then he rose and moved back to the culvert. Again he crawled inside. He had missed it the first time, maybe subconsciously he did not want to find it. But now he spotted it, a flap of corrugated iron set on a rivet hinge in the ceiling.

# 21

Harrison crouched in the culvert and checked his gear.
When he was ready, he eased himself up on his haunches
and unfastened the metal clip on the culvert ceiling. The
circular trap door dropped a fraction and he paused
before revolving it back. His light was still switched off
and he squatted there in pitch darkness, listening. He
could hear the trickling of the water, but no sound from
above. For a long moment he remained there with his
mouth dry and his senses heightened in a way that they
had not been for thirty years. He realized in that moment
just how much he had forgotten. But he had not forgotten
everything and gently he reached up and probed the rim
of the hole with his knife. Only when he was satisfied
there were no booby traps did he ease himself through.
That had been the most dangerous time underground,
moving up from one level to another. It was then you
were at your most vulnerable. Normally, the point man
would lift the door and fire off three rounds before you
went on. But you never knew where the VC was: he
could be sat right on top of you and drop a grenade in
your lap, or just as easy – lean over and slit your throat.

Harrison eased the trap door back in place. No sound,
he could see nothing ahead or behind, but he could feel
the floor of the tunnel; not earth crawling with spiders
but concrete. He switched on the flashlight for the first
time and shone the length of it. Four-foot-diameter con-

crete piping. Salvesen had been clever. When they built this place and put the drains in, he made sure that a second layer of piping was laid over the first. One for sewerage and one for men to escape. Harrison looked after the beam of light, throwing out some thirty feet, and then he began to move.

He crawled on all fours, holding the flashlight ahead of him in his left hand. The Glock was stuck in the belt of his winter cam' suit, the gilly he had left in the lay-up point. He knew from the entrance angle at the culvert and the dead straight run of the tunnel that he was travelling south-west. The hardness of the concrete pushed at his knees, making them ache before he had gone a hundred feet. The roof was close to his head, closer than he remembered. Those tunnels had been hard-baked earth and they twisted and turned, and every so often you would be probing with your knife for tiny little wires or tree roots that should not have been there. If you didn't, you'd find yourself tripping a booby trap and that would be the last thing you did.

It all flooded back now, the silence of when he was working alone, or moving point. Two trap doors and the point man changed, that was always the rule. When somebody fired, or worse if a grenade went off, the sound was deafening. Two of the Rats, when he first joined them, had their eardrums burst and came out with blood spilling down the sides of their faces. He remembered seeing it for the first time and wondering what it felt like. He only had to wait three weeks and then he was in hospital having grenade shrapnel dug out of his knees and with padding on both of his ears.

He moved forward quite quickly now, as silently as he remembered, with the flashlight beam bobbing ahead of him. The slightest sound and he switched it off, lay flat and listened. Only when the silence returned did he switch the beam back on and continue under the compound. He tried to gauge the distance in his mind as he moved, measuring out what would have been paces. If he did meet anyone along the way, they wouldn't be expecting him, so surprise would be on his side. That'd be nice for a change. Most of the time in Cu-Chi, Charlie was up ahead there somewhere, with his AK47 cocked and waiting for you.

He crawled for about ten minutes and then he saw the first trap door above him, and a little way beyond it, the first junction with another tunnel. The door was right above his head and made of wood, bevelled to fit in the slot, just like they had been before. Now he paused and rose to his knees with his head bent over, listening. He listened and listened and the only thing he could hear was the rasp of his own breathing and he cursed himself for all the years he'd filled his lungs with smoke. His flashlight was off now, but he could make out the underside of the trap door through the gloom. Quietly, he pressed both hands to the base, twisted it slightly and lifted; so very slowly, no noise, holding the breath back in his chest. Nothing, no sound, but light, not bright but dim, as if it entered a room from outside.

Harrison lifted the door completely and moved it to one side. He dropped back into the tunnel and waited. If anyone was up there he would hear them. He heard nothing, but slipped his Glock from his belt. The action was already worked, a round in the breech with the trigger safety on; all he had to do was squeeze and he was firing. He squatted, listened and then rose up through the hole where the trap door had rested. He moved around on the balls of his feet and looked about him. He was in the middle of a room, maybe thirty by thirty, a row of chairs, two rows, ten in all. In front of them was a table with another, bigger chair behind it. Harrison climbed out of the hole and carefully replaced the trap door. He looked at the table and at the single chair which stood to one side. It looked like a meeting chamber of some sort, or an interview room, except there were the twin rows of chairs like an audience. He saw video cameras mounted on the walls. Two doors, one at either end of the room. He moved to his right and pressed his ear to the panel. He could hear nothing, so he opened the door very slowly. A passageway with another door leading off it. He knew he was facing away from the house now. This was the smaller of the two buildings, the one that backed on to the marquee before the armoury. The marquee was no longer standing, Salvesen having taken it down as he always did in the winter.

Beyond the door was an anteroom and then another small one with a glass wall in it. Beyond the wall was a desk and some headphones and all manner of radio equipment. It was obviously from here that Salvesen made his broadcasts. Harrison closed the door again and went back to the first room. The door in the far wall was locked and he assumed it joined the back of the marquee in summertime.

Back in the tunnel, he moved up to the intersection, shone his torch and went on. Now he was moving across the compound. He considered direction for a moment and decided that this tunnel would take him straight under the house. About thirty feet in, he came to a second trap door and again he paused and listened. He lifted it, a tighter fit than the first one, but he got it loose. Freezing cold air hissed at him and he knew it was outside, would've been under the marquee. He let it settle again and moved on. Sixty maybe eighty feet further, he stopped and looked up. The third trap door, this one would be right under the house, and from the angle he had approached he had a pretty good idea where it would bring him. His heart beat faster now; all thoughts of Cu-Chi and the past were banished. This was the here and now and a different task was appointed. He waited and waited, and when he was sure he lifted the wooden portal above his head. Darkness save a fragment of light, which came from under a door. He could see it as he got to eye level. He could smell leather and wood and he knew he was in Jakob Salvesen's office.

He eased himself up and this time he left the trap door lying where it was. From outside in the hall, he heard voices, two of them, men speaking in soft tones. He crouched by the entrance to the hole with his gun in his hand and waited. He was behind Salvesen's desk and still covered from view from the door. He looked about him in the gloom. Great iron helmets were hung on the walls along with huge pictures of ancient Nordic warriors. Harrison gently rose to his feet and cursed silently as his knees creaked. He could see shadows moving over the crack of light that came from under the door and he hovered before crouching again. Then the voices faded and the shadows drifted away and he stood once more in silence. He looked at Salvesen's desk and saw books, the Bible, and two others whose titles he could not see. He did not dare risk the flashlight. One wall was a full glass door where Salvesen had stood speaking into his Dicta-phone. He looked closer and saw papers and maps and a book with *Hungary* written in bold black letters, which he could see plainly enough. On the wall was a map of the world. He moved closer to it and saw plastic-topped pins stuck into various countries round Europe.

Then he heard footsteps in the hall outside and he ducked back down the hole. He had only just got the trap door settled when somebody came into the room. Harri-son squatted cross-legged on the concrete floor of the tunnel, with both hands on his Glock, pointing directly upwards. Nobody came, nobody opened the door but he could feel the sweat dripping off his forehead. He looked ahead and then back the way he had come. He moved on; fifty feet further the tunnel branched right and he came to another trap door. Lifting this, he smelled food and refixed it. People were still moving about; he would not risk going into the house again. He followed this tunnel, due north now as far as it would go, and came to a trap door at the end of it. Beyond that, just earth like the dummies Charlie built in Cu-Chi. He tried to lift the wooden door, but it would not shift. It felt colder here and he was aware of a thin slice of air coming at him from around the crack. He moved back to the fork under the house, then, turning to his right, he crawled its length until he came to another trap door. He was deathly quiet, suddenly aware of just how cold he was. He could hear footsteps above his head. The bunkhouse, he told himself. He had mapped that from the air.

Now he retreated, the layout fixed in his mind. Back at the first turning, where he would go left to get back to the culvert, he stopped and looked right. The final bit, which hopefully would take him under the large building he called the armoury. He moved right, getting used to the concrete now and crawling with more freedom. Unless he was very very unlucky, he was not going to meet anyone. He came to the trap door and stopped. He listened again for a long time, the breath heightened in his chest. He raised himself to his knees and listened again. Then he lifted the door. He could smell it: gun oil, metal, weaponry.

He climbed out and stood in darkness. There were no windows in this building. He risked the flashlight and let go a low whistle. On specially manufactured wall racks he saw rows of M16 automatic rifles. He counted thirty in all. Next to them were grenade launchers, pump-action twelve-gauge shotguns, Beretta 40-calibre pistols, Colt 45s and Ruger 9mms. In a smaller closet with the doors standing open, he counted a further ten Ingram SMGs, like an Uzi but smaller. He looked at the boxes against the wall and lifted the lid of one of them. They were filled with dynamite and he counted ten four by four cartons. Metal closets were screwed to the walls and inside one, he found boxes of blasting caps, six to a box and over fifty boxes. In a separate closet on the other side of the room, he found thousands and thousands of rounds. Salvesen was preparing for war.

He moved to the far wall and tried the door, but it would not open. This building was on two levels, he remembered that. He moved to the other door and it did open. Now he was in a passage and he paused, listening like a hunting dog. He saw a flight of stairs and another door above them. Immediately in front of him was a door which presumably joined with the house. He could see no light under it. He went up the stairs. The door was locked and heavy, made of armoured steel. Harrison frowned. The key was in the lock though and it turned easily enough. He opened it and it creaked very slightly at the hinges. Inside it was pitch-black. Again, no windows. He stood a moment, allowing his eyes to grow accustomed, but they did not. He switched on the flashlight and stared. The room was long and thin and split in half by a glass panel and a door on one side. Beyond the glass panel, a wooden platform and hangman's noose.

He stood there and stared for a long time at the gallows. Six chairs were set out on this side of the panel. He let go a breath and felt a sickness deep in his gut. Slowly, he moved to the door and stepped on to the wooden platform. The trap door was open and below he could see the floor. The door downstairs was where one went to collect the bodies. He stood for a long moment and then turned. A new chill stopped the blood in his veins. Positioned above the door where he came in, a video camera was focused on the gallows.

Harrison left the tunnels, shaken and disgusted by what he had seen – so-called 'patriots' ready to mete out their own brand of 'justice' for those government agents they deemed to be unconstitutional. He crawled to the culvert, much on his mind, and as he made it to the portal he found himself whistling 'Dixie' – softly, but there all the same. He stopped, cocked an eyebrow and shook his head at himself. Thirty years and he was still whistling 'Dixie'. Every Tunnel Rat did that, to let the guys on the surface know exactly who you were when you reappeared from the earth with half a ton of mud on your head.

☆

At the end of February, Joanne Taylor had looked over the apartment while the estate agent hovered in the background. It was OK, she thought; two bedrooms, quite spacious, a good-sized living room with a small open-plan kitchen.

'Very popular here,' the agent told her. 'None of these properties stay very long on the market. I've only got three on the books right now.'

She looked at him and nodded. Dark glasses, long blonde hair and red painted fingernails. She walked to the window and looked out. From this height the view was spectacular. She could see the lakes and St Giles Church and the height of the buildings beyond it.

'Who's the property for, exactly?' the agent asked her. He was a young man, with oiled hair and a heavy pin-stripe in his suit.

'Some Spanish bankers,' she said. 'Well, one, anyway. Raoul Mendez, but the lease will be taken in the company name. Señor Mendez is advising the government on

British and Spanish business interests apropos the single currency.'

The agent nodded. 'That's supposed to come in next year,' he said.

'Supposed to. The currency in your pocket won't change until 2002. We need to be ready,' she said, 'whether the first phase goes ahead or not.' She looked at him then. 'The rent?'

'Three hundred and fifty pounds per week, plus the service charges. There's an underground car park with a lift straight up. The car park is secure and we have video-taped CCTV.'

She nodded slowly. 'We'll take it. Prepare a lease and send it to our bankers.' She handed him a card and then left.

☆

Ismael Boese flew into London from the United States and checked into the Stakis Hotel overlooking Hyde Park. He settled into a room on the fourth floor, with views all across the park and Kensington Gardens. He checked in as Raoul Mendez, an American citizen from Albuquerque, New Mexico. He was only going to stay a few nights, he told them, as he was here on business and would need to find something more permanent. He had a lengthy moustache and the thick, black hair of the Spanish. From his room he made two telephone calls, one to Birmingham and one to Manchester. When he was finished, he lay back on his bed and slept.

In Birmingham, Tal-Salem sat on his bed in the small hotel where he rented a room on a weekly basis, and which was close enough to commute to the Indian restaurant where he had been working. He had just rolled a long slim cigarette, sprinkled with Moroccan black hashish. Now he smoked and as he did so his eyes glazed and he felt the ease of his diaphragm, moving up and down in his chest. He stared at the tear in the wallpaper on the wall facing his bed. He had been working at the restaurant for six months now and he missed the beach and the girls in Spain. Pretty soon, he would have all the time he needed just to kick back and relax.

In Manchester, Pier-Luigi Ramas packed his case for the morning. He would take the train to London and check into the Stakis Hotel in Regent's Park. He stared at his reflection in the mirror, not him at all to look at: bearded, long hair, tied behind his head in a ponytail. And the glasses – little John Lennon's. It was amazing how just a small change in your appearance was all you needed to deceive the casual, even not so casual, observer. When he saw himself on television, *he* didn't recognize the pictures.

In the morning, Boese got up and ate a leisurely breakfast before making his way to the tube station. He took the Piccadilly line as far as South Kensington and then changed for Victoria. From there he walked to Westminster Cathedral, just another Spanish tourist paying his respects. He smiled at the woman as he always did, only she didn't recognize him as the Greek Orthodox priest, and then he wandered amid the magnificence, crossed himself under the great crucifix and made his way to the Lady Chapel, where he found a young woman with blonde hair already seated in front of him.

'The candles are lit,' he said quietly, as he sat down behind her.

'No,' she replied. 'The candles are alight.'

He leaned forward as if in prayer and she passed a package underneath her chair. 'The agent's name is Franklin Rees & Co, you'll find them in Long Lane on the right-hand side, as you go down towards the meat market from the Barbican station. The details are all in there and everything has been settled. Make yourself known to the concierge. He will have the key.'

'Are they aware of the others?'

'Your two colleagues from the bank? Of course. They know that time is short and you will be working from home as well as the office.'

'And the papers – the money?'

'Everything you need is in the package. You even have membership of the health club.'

He smiled then and, bending forward, he pressed his face into her hair. She stiffened and he delighted in her sudden revulsion. When she looked round, he was gone.

☆

The Foreign Emergency Search Team came back to London for the third time in March. After they had positively identified Ibrahim Huella as Ismael Boese, Louis Byrne and his colleagues, now knowing that Storm Crow was a US citizen, had gone back and forth to Washington, to follow their own inquiries. Within two days of their return, the Antiterrorist Branch was contacted by a glass supplier. After the incident in Northumberland, they had been in touch with every supplier of toughened glass in London and insisted they be contacted confidentially if anyone bought a similar quantity to what they had found before. Anyone who was not known, any non-account holder, and anyone paying in cash. Rayburn's of Sutton called them.

Swann and Webb went down to see them right away. Cheyenne Logan went with them.

'You find anything out in the States, Chey?' Webb asked her, leaning his arm over the back of the seat. Swann was driving, quickly, pushing his way through the traffic.

Logan shrugged. 'Not a lot. Louis thought we had a

sighting of Boese in Las Vegas, but it turned out to be nothing. I don't think he was in the States at all.'

'Why not?'

'I don't know. Instinct, I guess.'

Webb nodded. 'He was probably here all the time.'

They pulled into the glass-supply depot. A young lad of about sixteen was serving.

'We're police officers,' Swann said to him. 'Is your Mr Matthews in?'

'I'll get him.' The boy ducked away and Webb had a look outside. There was a loading bay backing on to the trade counter and a number of vans were parked against the burnt red of the wall.

'Good afternoon.'

They turned and the manager, Mr Matthews, the man who had phoned them, opened the hatch in the counter. He was small and slightly lopsided, a beer belly hanging over the waistband of his trousers. 'Come through. Won't you?' he said.

They followed him to a small office at the back and he sat down. 'Glass purchase,' he began. 'You sent us a circular asking us to report any strange purchases of armoured glass.'

'That's right,' Webb said. 'We did.'

'Here we are.' Matthews took the letter from his desk drawer. 'All purchases that are not known trade customers or are made with cash.'

Swann rolled his eyes to the ceiling. 'You had one today,' he said, 'why you called us.'

Matthews looked up at him. 'No, not today. That's somebody's error. It was yesterday, I'm afraid.'

Swann bit his teeth together. 'Yesterday?'

'That's right.' Matthews flicked through the ledger on his desk. 'Afternoon, four sheets four by six, Pro-Max glass. Not armoured but very tough.'

Swann went back to the counter and looked up at the ceiling. He came back through again. 'Your CCTV, do you tape it?'

'Oh, yes. We're very careful like that.'

'We'll need yesterday's tape.'

'Yes, of course. I'll get it for you.'

Webb looked at Matthews as he scrabbled in the box under his desk and came up with an assortment of video cassette cases. 'Who served the buyer?'

'Let's see.' Matthews checked the receipt book. 'Mark did, that young lad out there.'

'I'd like a word with him,' Swann said.

'Be my guest. Sorry we didn't tell you sooner. If I'd been here, I would've done it. You can't trust the staff to remember anything.'

Swann went back to the counter again and took Mark to one side. 'I'm Jack Swann, Mark,' he said. 'Scotland Yard. Yesterday you sold some glass.'

'I sell a lot of glass.'

Swann nodded. 'I know you do. This was four sheets of four by six toughened glass. Max-plus or something. It was a cash purchase. Yesterday afternoon.'

Mark still looked doubtful, then he nodded. 'I remember, bloke on his own. Paid cash, told me he was building an aquarium somewhere. Worcester, I think he said.'

'Can you remember what he looked like?'

'Just normal.' He pointed to the video cameras above the counter. 'We'll have him on tape, though.'

'Thanks, Mark. What did he load it into – the glass I mean?'

'Van, I think. Somebody else collected it.'

Swann narrowed his eyes. 'You mean he didn't take it there and then?'

'No. I think someone else picked it up later on.'

'What did he look like?'

'I don't know. He would've gone straight to the yard.'

'D'you remember the colour of the van?'

Mark shook his head. 'Ask the lads outside. They do the loading.'

Swann did ask them. They couldn't agree. It could've been white. It could've been blue. One thing they did remember, however, was that the driver wore a woollen hat with no bobble and an old Harrington jacket.

Matthews had a video recorder set up in his office and Swann, Webb and Logan sat down to watch with Mark.

'Your boss said it was in the afternoon.' Logan looked at the timer on the screen.

Mark squinted at her. 'You a copper as well?' he said.

'Sort of.'

'How come you're American, then?'

'I work for the FBI.'

His eyes widened. 'What, like Mulder and Scully?'

'Not quite. No.'

They wound the tape through to the afternoon and then played it more slowly. They watched for a few minutes, then Swann wound it on again. 'That's him.' Mark pointed and Swann froze the image, rewound and played it again. A man in a bomber jacket, maybe blue or black, the image was not good enough to tell. He was bare-headed and dark-skinned. As they watched, he slowly lifted his head and stared into the lens of the camera.

Ismael Boese, the Storm Crow.

Swann stared at the screen and Boese stared at him: face cold, eyes the black of a shark. Nobody spoke. Swann looked at Webb and then at Logan. Still none of them said anything, but they could all feel it, the sudden ice in the air.

'Thanks, Mark,' Swann said. He left them then and Swann wound the frame back and froze it once again.

'Son-of-a-bitch,' Logan said softly.

'Taking the piss, Chey,' Swann muttered. 'Bastard's taking the piss.'

On the way back to the Yard, Webb phoned in and spoke to Campbell McCulloch. 'We need a van, Macca,' he said. 'Nicked or hired in the last few days. The bastard's here again.'

When they got back, they showed the tape to the whole team. Nobody said anything at first and then Colson shook his head. 'Who the hell does he think he is?'

Byrne stared at the screen. 'The baddest man on the planet.'

Colson shot him a glance. 'You think so? Well, I'm going to put him away. I'll have him in Paddington Green so fast, his feet won't touch the ground.' He stood up and looked at the troops. 'We need a van,' he said. 'And you know what – we need it now. So get out there and find it.'

☆

Harrison went back to the tunnels the night following their discovery. He hiked back over the saddle in snow-shoes to Dugger's Canyon and spent the day sleeping in the hogan that Chief had built. He locked the door from the inside and curled up in one of the sleeping bags they stowed there. He woke up just before dark and went out to his keep hide. The Magdalena portal seemed to yawn at him, hung with broken timbers like the jaws of some silent beast on the hillside. From his hide, he took his infrared video camera with the macrozoom lens he needed for close-up work.

He was still disturbed by what he had seen, rattled by both the huge amount of arms, but mostly by the execution chamber. What was that – a throwback to his Posse days? Then he recalled the sign on Salvesen's gate about federal trespassers being tried and hanged. The other room, the first one he had gone into. He knew now it was a mock courtroom. He desperately wanted to get in touch with his contact agent in Salt Lake City, but he also wanted to get into Salvesen's den before he got back from his speaking tour.

He hiked back to the culvert through light flurries of snow, which enabled him to move that bit more quickly. It didn't matter that the tracks were deeper, they would be covered almost as soon as he passed and there was no way in the world that anyone would be abroad tonight. He moved swiftly, aware of a tightness in his chest as he got closer to the culvert. Today his sleep had been fitful as it always was in the daytime, but the dreams were dark, dreams he had not had in a long time and he woke up in a sweat. He was shaky. For the first time since coming here almost two years ago, he was genuinely concerned. So many memories now: the irony of it, the only way to gain entry was from tunnels underground.

He lay up under the rock on the hill until midnight and then he made his way down. It was still snowing and the goon tower lights were on around the compound. He could see movement as he drew closer and slowed his pace accordingly. At his final lay-up point he halted and sat in his gilly suit against a mound of snow for half an hour, then he made his way back to the tunnel entrance again. Somehow it seemed colder tonight. The hike from the canyon should have warmed his blood, but it hadn't. He was shivering as he entered the darkness for the second time in two days. The iron trap door seemed stiffer than it had done and Harrison's fingers were chill against the metal.

He slid back the portal and prised himself up on to concrete. Again he squatted, Glock in his right hand, flashlight as yet unused in his left. He listened, head high, slightly to one side, and waited. He could hear the water dripping, but he could not hear anything else. On his way through the mini-labyrinth yesterday night, he had noticed that at certain points along the way the tunnels had passing areas. Salvesen had obviously anticipated activity underground. Harrison crawled and thought about the weapons. He thought about the men and women that were flown in and then shipped out to the compound's mock town for training. Defensive, that had been what he noted, the training was defensive rather than offensive. Hell, he thought, they all believed that federal agents were coming to take their guns.

He moved cautiously, not using the flashlight. He had mapped the tunnels well in his head the previous night and could roughly gauge the distance to the first trap door. Tonight there was no need to go anywhere except straight for Salvesen's office. No need for the light except to count the trap doors he passed. He got to the first junction, turned right and pressed on. Halfway along the tunnel, he heard something moving towards him. Harrison froze. Somebody breathing and then the bob of a flashlight. He lay flat and tried to recall where the passing place was. The light moved nearer. Carefully, soundlessly, he began to move backwards, facing the oncoming light with his gun in his hand. The urge to fire was intense; a light ahead was Vietcong.

Why would anyone be in the tunnels tonight unless they had spotted him entering? Impossible, he had been too careful. He moved backwards, never turning away, moving quickly enough to keep out of the fall of the light. Whoever it was was also moving quickly; he could hear the laboured rush of their breathing. The irregularity of the light told him that they were using both hands on the floor. The beam bounced off the walls and the ceiling instead of illuminating the expanse of the tunnel ahead.

He felt the pressure of the concrete, the ice in his knees and the palms of his hands. At the junction he paused. Which way? Where were they going? Instinct told him that they must be heading outside; why else use the tunnels? Maybe Jesse had some kind of exercise going. Harrison thought about the culvert and knew that his lay-up point would be secure. He moved round the corner to his left, backing all the way, and then pressed himself against the wall with his gun across his chest.

The man grunted as he got nearer. Harrison could hear him cursing under his breath. The light played all across the junction wall and Harrison pressed himself even closer into the darkness. He had the Glock in his belt now and his hunting knife in his hand.

'Fucking Jesse Tate.'

Wingo. Harrison twisted his mouth down at the edges; all his senses tingled, the desire to kill in his chest. That's what you did underground. Whoever you met you killed, because if you didn't – he killed you. He was back there now in the heat and the dirt, in singlet and jungle fatigues, with moisture in his eyes and dirt spilling on to his head from the runs in the tunnel roof. The flashlight was the enemy with an AK47 and grenades and a wire for your throat, as you moved from one level up to the next.

'Fucking Jesse. Thinks he's fucking Rambo. Middle of the fucking night.' Wingo got to the junction and Harrison tensed. *Look this way, motherfucker* ... the thought dulled into the thud of blood that lifted against his temple. Wingo did not look, he turned left and headed off into the darkness.

Harrison's head ached, the sudden heart-stopping tension. He sat a moment to gather himself, sweating through the cold in his cam' suit. Clearly, Jesse did have some kind of exercise running, the kind of night-time thing that would appeal to his sense of power with

Salvesen being away. Harrison knew he had to be doubly careful. He considered getting out there and then, but could not for fear of meeting Wingo coming back. He steeled himself, rubbed the sweat from his palms and gathered up his pistol and knife. He was here, he had to get into that office and he had to do it now.

He met no one else. Maybe Wingo had pissed Jesse off and was on some kind of punishment mission of his own. Harrison paused under the next trap door and listened, but all was quiet above. And then he was under the house and above him was the bevelled wooden door that led to Jakob Salvesen's den.

He sat where he was, tasting the salt on his lips from the sweat that rolled off his brow. He had been cold, but now the blood ran high and his skin was moist under the cam' suit. He sat for a few minutes with his ear close to the trap door. Only when he was satisfied his senses were in control did he pivot on one foot and twist the wooden circle above him. It moved and lifted and this time there was no light whatever. That meant the hallway was in darkness, which suited his purpose exactly. Sliding the trap door to one side, he straightened and stood up in the hole. He could smell leather and wood and opulence. Quickly now, he hoisted himself up and crouched on the carpet, listening.

From his jacket, he pulled out the infrared video with built-in torch to enhance the light source, then he moved to the desk. Now he could see what he had not been able to see last night. Two books: *The Late Great Planet Earth* and *Planet Earth 2000 AD,* both by Hal Lindsey. He photographed the covers and scanned the rest of the desk: Bible open at the book of Revelation and the book on Hungary; various scribblings and notes that did not mean very much. In the top drawer he found a chart entitled 'Planned timetable for the introduction of the euro 1994–2002', with various dates and events signified in black boxes. It was a poor photocopy of probably a coloured original. Harrison also found a large envelope, slipped out the contents and filmed them. Photographs. He frowned. It looked like a bomb scene; he thought it might be Oklahoma. No time to analyse, he needed to film and get out.

A noise in the hallway disturbed him, the creak of a floorboard. He stiffened, watching the bottom of the door for sudden light. He stayed exactly where he was, aware that if Wingo had gone out via the tunnels he may very well come back by them, and Harrison had no way of knowing which portal he would enter. He heard nothing more, put it down to the way a house likes to creak and shift its weight in the night, and went back to work. In the next drawer he moved the papers and filmed them, a receipt with something stuck underneath it, a bunch of other notes.

Leaving the desk, he moved to the maps on the wall and worked his way over them with the camera, seeing nothing, merely ensuring that he had captured it all on film. His nerves were calmer now, the pistol in his belt, the knife against his thigh, and the re-entry to the tunnels reminding him that once upon a time he had been a killer, worthy of the badge he had worn with such pride until that last abortive entry. He paused in his filming and looked about the room. He rechecked the desk and carefully went through the last of the drawers. When he was confident he had as much as he could get, he slipped back underground. He would've liked to have planted a T-17, but Wingo in the tunnels put him off. That would take over an hour and he could not afford the time. He crawled back to the culvert in darkness, eyes skinned, waiting for the sudden bob of a flashlight that would tell him Wingo was on his way back. He never saw him and he made it to the portal, sliding down with outstretched hands and coiling up like a ball. Outside he stood straight, looked up at the sky and breathed.

☆

SO13 were looking for a van. No theft had been reported that would coincide with the purchase of glass from Sutton, so they concentrated on the hire companies. Swann, McCulloch, Tania Briggs and George Webb went through the *Yellow Pages* and checked every hire company within a thirty-mile radius. Logan and Byrne gave them a hand. They came up with four possibles, vans that had been rented for short periods and returned. They separated and went out to pay each of the companies a visit. Webb drew a blank, as did McCulloch and Briggs. They confirmed the names and addresses of the hirers together with the drivers' licences, and they all checked out. Louis Byrne went with Swann and they visited a Rent A Wreck outfit not far from the glass supplier itself.

The company operated in an industrial yard and had hired out a white Renault van the day the glass was bought. It was returned the following morning. Swann looked through the name and address on the licence and asked for a description of the hirer. Smallish man with a black woollen cap on his head. Swann got on the phone to the Yard.

'DI Clements.'

'Guv'nor, it's Jack Swann. I might have a result here.' He gave Clements the details and then went to look at the van. It had not been cleaned since it was returned. The manager opened it up for them and he and Byrne took a good look inside.

'Jack,' Byrne called, as Swann was inspecting the driver's seat and doorwell.

Swann came round to the back and Byrne lifted his hand, palm upturned. A fragment of glass rested against the tip of his index finger. Swann went back inside and spoke to the manager once more.

'How many miles did they do?'

'I'll check.' He flicked through the agreements. 'Forty-one,' he said.

The phone rang on Swann's belt and he unclipped it. 'Jack Swann.'

'Clements. Result on the licence. William Montgomery is doing fifteen years in Parkhurst for attempted murder. Went down in '94.'

Swann nodded to himself. 'Mislaid his licence, did he?'

'Convenient, wasn't it.'

'We've found traces of glass in the van, Guv. Can you send down a team?'

'On its way.'

'Guv'nor.' Swann looked Byrne in the eye as he spoke into the telephone. 'The van's only done forty-one miles. I reckon it's about ten from here to the supplier and ten back again. That only leaves twenty-one. The glass is somewhere in London.'

An exhibits team arrived, searched the van and then took it to the Serious Crimes Unit at Lambeth. Swann and Byrne went back to the Yard where Colson had called a mini-briefing. They all sat in the squad room, atmosphere tense between them.

'The glass is somewhere in London.' Colson's words fell like stones. Swann glanced out of the window across the park towards Buckingham Palace. He thought about Pia and his children and then Boese's eyes.

'We have to find it,' Colson was saying. 'We have to trace its movements. I'll get the commander to draft in as much uniform as we can get and check every CCTV camera in London if we have to.'

☆

From his window on the twenty-third floor, Ismael Boese could see part of the ruins of the old city wall. Tower blocks dominated the skyline, and he recognized the Commercial Union Building and the recently reopened and renamed NatWest Tower. Below him was the lake and the City of London Girls' School, and, to his left, the Guildhall School of Music and Drama. He had wandered through Smithfield at 4 a.m. while the meat vendors set up for the day's trading. He walked past Bart's Hospital and sat watching the early Guinness drinkers in the Bishop's Finger, the cabbies and the market traders finishing and preparing the day. The smell of early morning beer, coffee and cigarettes, and the resinous hint of animal fats.

At eight o'clock Tal-Salem arrived with his sports bag and the first of the scaffolding pipes. Boese had already erected the metal rack to house them, and he began to put them together. Behind him on the kitchen table, four car batteries stood in their packaging next to the coiled roll of detonator cord and a pot of black paint for the window.

# 22

Harrison sat hunched on the worn couch in his trailer, watching the video with the door locked, a lighted cigarette between his fingers and an open bottle of Coors on the table. He noted the titles of the two books and would request copies from his contact agent when they met later tonight. The camera moved over the desktop, then focused on the open drawers. He had zoomed in on the contents of the top one, and now he froze the image – a receipt for a meal in Paris, France. There was something protruding from underneath the receipt, what looked like a handwritten slip of paper. He tried to make out what was scribbled on it, 'Ten, ction, aces', bits of words running vertically down the edge of the page.

He pulled hard on his cigarette, letting the smoke eddy in little curls from his nostrils, and watched as the video moved across the desk. He stopped and froze the picture once again, cocked his head to one side and stared at a piece of newspaper, *USA Today*, 11 June 1997. A huge advert for UMB bank and next to it the world round-up section. He read the various headings: CONGRESS WARNS ARAFAT THAT AID MAY BE CUT OFF, CONGO EVACUATION, FRENCH IMMIGRANTS, SRI LANKA FIGHTING, CZECH SAVED – and then at the very bottom of the page – PROTESTERS: DEVIL'S IN EU PACT'S DETAILS. There was a picture of a nun beneath it. Harrison screwed up his eyes and read, 'In Athens Greece: a Greek Orthodox nun joins a thousand clergy and others in a protest on Tuesday outside Parliament, which votes today on joining a European Union pact to remove border controls. Religious groups say that EU identity cards will carry the number 666, a sign of Satan, in their bar codes.'

Next to it was another clipping, this time from a paper he didn't recognize. It was dated 25 March 1997 – ROME SALUTES 40 YEARS OF EVER CLOSER UNION.

Harrison crushed his cigarette, immediately plucking another from his shirt pocket, and moved the film on again. He saw the wall map now, Europe marked out with a dotted line round its borders, and next to the map on a separate sheet of paper somebody had listed:

Rome

West Germany
Holland*
Belgium*
Luxembourg*
Italy
France
_____

Spain*
Greece
UK*
Denmark*
Sweden*
Portugal
Finland
Austria
Ireland

Harrison looked at the map itself again and saw Hungary marked and underlined twice, the Czech Republic and Poland underlined once. He rewound the video to the stuff he had photographed in the drawers and stopped at the chart relating to European monetary union.

Switching off the tape, he placed it in the bag to give to Scheller, who would be driving up from Salt Lake at this very minute. Harrison had arranged the meeting in Twin Falls and he needed to leave now if he was going to make it. He drove without concentrating on the road, his mind wandering every which way. Why was Salvesen so interested in Europe when he was spending so much time with the militia over here?

Scheller was waiting for him in the bar. He was seated at a table in a dimly lit corner, with two bottles of Bud before him. Harrison quartered the room and slipped into the seat opposite him. He took out a cigarette, did not light it immediately, but held it end-on between his index fingers.

'Tom Kovalski's on his way,' Scheller said.

'From D.C.?'

'No. He was over in Pocatello.'

Harrison took a long draught from his beer.

'What gives?'

'I got into Salvesen's office.'

Scheller's eyebrows shot up.

'He's built tunnels under that compound, Max. Concrete piping over the drains.'

'How'd you find out?'

'Patrol. Saw a bunch of guys disappear into the armoury, and next thing I know, they show up right behind where I'm at. It was snowing. I followed their tracks to a drainage culvert.' Harrison looked him in the eye. 'Took me right back, Max.'

'I'll bet it did. Jesus, Johnny.'

'He's got over thirty M16s in there, SMGs, grenade launchers and shotguns, not to mention dynamite and fucking blasting caps coming out of his ears.' He narrowed his eyes. 'Something else too. Remember the Posse in the old days, talking about trying government representatives and hanging them?'

'Yeah.'

'He's got a courtroom and gallows built right inside that house.'

Harrison lit his cigarette. 'I got a videotape for you, Max. He's got maps of Europe and shit all over the place. A whole bunch of countries listed.' He passed the paper sack he had in his jacket across the table. 'You know something else, more and more people up there are starting to listen to him. The more the movie stars take over the valley, the more disaffected the regular people get. One actually told me the other day that he'd seen an old Japanese internment camp being refurbished in Jerome. Reckons it's a concentration camp for after the UN takes over.'

Scheller sipped his beer. 'Did you get a wire set up?'

'Didn't have the time. But I'm going back. One in his office, the other in one of the cameras he's got in the courtroom.'

Scheller nodded slowly.

Harrison leaned forward then. 'I want two books, Max, both by a guy named Hal Lindsey. *The Late Great Planet Earth* and *Planet Earth 2000 AD*.'

Tom Kovalski walked into the bar. Like Scheller he was dressed casually. He bought himself an MGD, sat down and shook hands with Harrison.

'How's it going?'

'Pretty good.' Harrison told Kovalski what he had told Scheller and Kovalski's face was grave.

'Kuhlmann was no coincidence,' he said. 'Salvesen *has* to be linked to what the FEST are looking at in London.' He scratched his head. 'So why the fucking militia?'

'I don't know, Tom. But I think we should take him out.'

Kovalski shook his head. 'We can't prove he's done anything.'

'Kuhlmann was in the compound.'

'First amendment, John. Man can have anyone he likes over to dinner.'

'But he got killed in England.'

Kovalski pushed out his lips. 'Not enough. We can't prove a link other than by association. You know the deal. The public scrutiny we're under right now. Salvesen has some very influential friends. We screw this up and they'll hang us by our balls. You don't know half the shit I went through to get you that search warrant.' He shook his head. 'I want to get Salvesen good. We've had this operation running too long to jeopardize it now. Until we have a cast-iron evidential case, we have to sit tight.'

☆

The fingerprint team gleaned a partial set of prints from the rear-view mirror on the hired van and Swann ran them through the PNC, but could not locate a match. They spent literally hundreds of man hours, collecting video tapes and watching them. Every filling station where the angle of the forecourt cameras picked up part of the road, the London traffic cameras, local businesses and shops. Everybody, even the Foreign Emergency Search Team, took it in turns to sit for hours and watch them; looking for a clue, a glimpse of the number plate on the van, some idea of where it might have gone.

Swann met Pia after having a drink with the explosives officers and the Americans, and they went back to his flat. The children were still up, undressed and bathed, but jumping around on the bed settee in the lounge. They hadn't seen Pia for over two weeks and they leapt on her as soon as she came upstairs.

'When are you and Daddy going to get married?' Charlotte asked her.

Pia's cheeks burned with colour. 'Daddy's never asked me.'

Swann was stunned. He had never thought about it. Marriage was not something he was very sure he wanted to do again and he had always thought that Pia was not the marrying type. 'Bed, you guys,' he said and patted Joanna on the bottom. She yelped and then both she and Charlotte descended into the giggles. In the end, Pia had to agree to read them a story to get them to go to bed.

While she was downstairs, Webb phoned up.

Swann could hear the hubbub of conversation in the background and knew immediately that Webb was either still in The Annexe or some other licensed premises.

'Jack, it's me.'

'What you doing?'

'Drinking.'

'Still?'

'Yeah. Old man showed up with the DSU.'

'You still in The Annexe?'

'Yes.'

'Feds with you?'

'Yeah. Byrne can drink, but I'm not sure about Larry Thomas. Don't think his wife lets him out too often back in the States.'

'Anything happening?' Swann sat back, lifted the sole of his foot to the coffee table and lit a cigarette.

'Julian Moore showed up from Box. They've got a possible from the Cairns mob.'

Swann sat more upright. 'Who?'

'Denis Smith. Skinhead with no form. He fits the description of the bloke who hired the van. Louis suggested Box do a number on him, like the ATF did to Boese. He drinks with Charlie Oxley and the other one, with the spider's web tattoos.'

'Beer glass?'

'Either that or a covert on his car.'

Swann blew smoke rings. 'Try and match the prints.'

'Yeah. At least we'll know we've got the right bloke.'

Swann felt brighter. 'Is Garrod going for it?'

'Oh, yeah. Got nothing to lose, have we.'

☆

Oxley and Bacon stood at the bar with Denis Smith and drank pints of lager. From the back they looked the same – green nylon bomber jackets, tight-legged jeans and Doc Martens. Bacon had a set of red braces that trailed over the backs of his thighs. Behind them at a table, two women sat talking, casually dressed, one in leggings the other in figure-hugging Levis. Oxley kept looking over at them.

'What about the one with the short hair?' he said, nudging Smith who leaned at his elbow. Smith swigged his beer and looked round.

'Bit of a babe,' he muttered. The girl smiled at him and looked away again. At the table behind them, a man in his thirties read the newspaper.

'Go and chat her up,' Smith said.

Oxley shook his head.

'Go on.'

'You fucking do it.'

Smith shrugged his shoulders, then sauntered over to their table. He was skinny and tall, lean face with sunken cheeks and slightly overlarge eyes.

'Hi,' he said.

The dark-haired one looked up at him. 'Hi,' she said and smiled. 'What're you guys doing tonight?'

441

Smith waggled the beer glass in his hand and sat down on an empty stool. 'Just having a drink.'

'Bit crappy, isn't it,' she said, wrinkling her nose. 'There must be a better pub than this round here.'

He looked her in the eyes then. 'I could show you a better pub.'

She looked beyond him to the bar where his mates were watching. 'Yeah?' she said. 'I bet you could too.'

For a few moments he looked as though he thought she was making fun of him. The other girl smiled at him and got up. 'Come on then, show us,' she said.

When they were gone, the man with the newspaper folded it over his arm and stood up. He moved past the empty table and slipped the spread of his fingers inside Denis Smith's beer glass.

☆

Boese worked into the night. He had secured the metal rack to the floor, just in front of the French doors that opened on to the balcony. He had had to adjust the shelving panels in order to create a better angle, but that had only been a matter of twisting a few screws. Tal-Salem and Pier-Luigi Ramas worked alongside him. Two large plastic sports bags were discarded on the couch and Ramas was comparing the lengths of pipe. So far they had fifteen sections. The glass they had brought up in the lift at two in the morning, after hiding it in the garage downstairs. Six by four; it had only just fitted. Now it rested, four sheets together with hinges and fastening brackets, against the far wall. A sealed length of copper tubing lay on the kitchen work surface.

Ramas was placing seals one-third of the way down the scaffold piping. Tal-Salem had a block of Czech-manufactured Semtex in front of him, which he was cutting and preparing into conical-shaped charges. On the far side of the room, thirty-five Iraco detonators were still individually wrapped. Boese moved to the window and looked out. The net curtains were pulled together, but he could still see the grey outline of the city beyond them. He turned once more to the rack and fixed another length of pipe at an angle of forty-five degrees.

'When do we black out the window?' Ramas asked him.

'Just before we leave.'

☆

Webb sifted through the evidence they had accumulated on Ismael Boese. His exhibits cage was open and Logan was messing about with the 7.62 Tokarev that Webb had confiscated a year ago, but as yet had not sent away for destruction.

'Neat little gun,' she was saying. 'I never handled one before.'

Webb heard his extension ringing through in the exhibits office. 'George Webb,' he said when he got to it.

'Mike Richards, Webby.' Richards was one of the fingerprint team from SO3.

'What you got?'

'Your suspect was in that van.'

☆

Denis Smith opened his front door, yawned and looked at the sky. He shivered, yawned again and zipped his jacket to the neck. He walked down the hill to where he had parked his van and fumbled in his pocket for the keys. Three men got out of a car across the road. Smith was still fishing for his keys when he felt a heavy hand on his shoulder. He jumped and instantly balled his fist. Campbell McCulloch's fleshy face stared down into his, long red hair and green eyes glinting like a cat.

'Hello, Denis,' McCulloch said. 'I'm arresting you under the Prevention of Terrorism Act.' Smith looked at Swann, who was standing next to McCulloch. He could see the butt of a gun bulging at his armpit. McCulloch read him his rights while Swann slipped plastic handcuffs over his wrists. They marched him to the car where DI Clements was waiting.

Swann drove very quickly, siren blaring, and McCulloch phoned ahead to the reception committee at Paddington Green police station. In the back, Clements ignored the prisoner, who sat stony-faced, having not said a single word. At Paddington Green, Swann pulled up the ramp beyond the security gates and stamped hard on the brakes. Smith lurched forward in his seat. The door to the custody suite was opened and DSU Colson stood there. He looked at Smith, face pressed right up against his, and then stepped to one side. Swann and McCulloch frogmarched him down the hall to the custody sergeant.

At the desk, Swann spoke softly to him. 'Nice to have you here, Denis,' he said. 'Bet you didn't expect it when you woke up this morning. Had your normal breakfast, did you? Weetabix and toast. You like Rose's lime marmalade, don't you, and it's coffee and not tea.' He shook his head at him. 'You look a bit pale, Denis. Bet you wished you'd got home earlier last night now, don't you. Playing cards in the week's not good for you. And all that beer, six pints of lager on a Wednesday night, not to mention the whisky and coke.'

Smith stared at him, mouth slightly open and his eyes orbs in his skull. Swann patted him on the shoulder. 'I need to tell you what's going to happen to you. First of all, we're going to take your clothes and shoes. Don't worry, we'll give you one of those paper suits I expect you've seen on the telly. Then we're going to put you in a cell by yourself and somebody'll want to have a look at you. They'll want to tape your face and look at your hair for bits and pieces. OK?'

Smith looked at him but did not speak.

They strip searched him, then gave him the paper suit to wear. Samples were taken from his face with strips of sticky tape, and from his hair and the palms of his hands. They knew they weren't going to find anything, but Swann wanted information when they interviewed him and needed him to be as malleable and frightened as possible. Four hours after they arrested him, they sat him down in the interview room, Swann across from him and McCulloch alongside. Smith had not requested a solicitor. He hadn't said anything, not even asked to use the phone. He had been photographed and fingerprinted and they were preparing an identity parade for the manager of the van hire company.

'Denis,' McCulloch said in a genial tone. 'You hired a van from Rent A Wreck in Mitcham using a false driving licence.'

Smith narrowed his eyes.

'Yes?'

'No.'

'Ah, you do speak.' Swann nodded. 'There's me thinking you were actually as dumb as you look.'

'Hey.' McCulloch touched him on the shoulder. 'I'm talking.' He looked again at Smith. 'We know you did, Denis. Then you collected four sheets of heavy-duty glass from a place called Rayburn's in Sutton. What I want to know – is what happened to it afterwards?'

Smith shook his head, looking from one to the other of them. 'I don't know what you're talking about.'

Swann was suddenly in his face. 'Maybe you should get the brief now, Denis. You're definitely going to need him.'

Smith flinched, half lifting a hand to his face.

'You see, we can prove you hired that van and that you

picked up the glass. You used a licence in the name of William Montgomery, who just happens to be doing fifteen years in Parkhurst. Tommy get the licence for you, did he?'

Smith did not reply.

'Makes no odds whether you talk or not, Denis,' Swann went on. 'Not to us, anyway.'

He looked at McCulloch who leaned forward and said, 'Might make a bit to you, though. You see, at the moment we can prove that doing what you did links you to a really nasty man called the Storm Crow. You ever heard of him? Like Carlos the Jackal, only worse.' He smiled then. 'He's a terrorist, you see, which makes you an accessory to the murders he's been committing. You'll do at least fifteen years.'

Swann looked Smith in the eye then. 'They like skinheads inside, Denis. Especially the big black guys called Suzie.' He paused for a moment. 'Terrorists do their time. Did you know that? There's no parole and no remission. So when you walk down those steps in the Old Bailey, you won't come out again till you're forty.' He stood up. 'Get that lawyer, eh. Who shall we call – Mr Ingram, is it?'

Outside, Swann looked at McCulloch. 'He'll talk,' he said, 'when I've wound old Ingram up.' He made the call himself and was put through straight away.

'Mr Ingram. This is Detective Sergeant Swann of the Antiterrorist Branch. Remember me?'

At the other end of the phone, Ingram sat white-knuckled. 'Of course I do, Sergeant. What can I do for you?'

'I'm phoning from Paddington Green police station. We've got one of your Action 2000 lads down here, a Denis Smith.'

'Sergeant, please. They are not *my* Action 2000 lads as you put it – and I don't know any Denis Smith.'

'Well, he knows you. We've arrested him under the Prevention of Terrorism Act and he wants you to come down and represent him.'

Ingram swallowed, air backing up in his throat. 'Sergeant, as I'm sure you know, I'm not a criminal lawyer.'

'Aren't you? He seemed to think you were.'

'I'm afraid he's wrong. Now if there's nothing else . . .'

'When there is, I'll come and get you.' Swann put down the phone.

Back in the interview room, Swann sat down again with Smith. McCulloch had gone to get coffee for them and Swann folded his arms. 'Ingram's not coming, Denis. Says he doesn't practise criminal law. Typical that, isn't it. Serve the bloke on the street all these years and when you need him, he's history. Had to get you the duty brief instead. Probably only be a solicitor's clerk, but better than nothing, eh.'

Smith's eyes had lost their arrogance. Swann squinted at him. 'You want to talk to me, Denis?'

McCulloch pressed open the door with his foot and placed three coffee cups on the table. Swann took out his cigarettes and slid them across to Smith. 'What d'you want to tell me?'

Smith blew smoke and rubbed one tattooed arm with his palm. 'What d'you want to know?'

'What you did with the glass.'

'I just drove the van to a back street.'

'Where?'

'Whitechapel.'

'What did you do then?'

'Just left it. Went and had a cup of tea. Put a bet on.'

'Where *exactly* did you leave it?'

'Winthrop Street, behind Whitechapel tube. Left the keys up the exhaust pipe.'

'For how long?'

'Hour and a half, maybe.'

Swann thinned his eyes. 'Then you went back?'

'Yeah.'

'And?'

Smith shrugged his shoulders. 'And nothing. Van was where I left it. I got the keys from the exhaust and took it back.'

'The glass?'

'Glass was gone.'

☆

Byrne and Logan were sitting in the leg-att's office in Grosvenor Square. They had just received copies of the latest submission from Harrison. Still photos from the infrared video he had taken in Jakob Salvesen's office. Logan leafed through them, brow furrowed, and handed each one to Byrne. She saw the chart on currency union, the books by Hal Lindsey and the stuff from the top drawer, the meal receipt with the scribbled paper beneath it. Byrne looked through each one in turn. He came to the bomb scene and frowned. The images weren't very clear, but he recognized them. 'Think we better show these to the guys at the Yard,' he said.

Swann briefed the team on the interview with Denis Smith. 'Coughed,' he said. 'Gave up Tommy Cairns. Told me it was Cairns who set up the van hire, gave him the driving licence and everything. We've got enough to pull him now. We can get a Section 18 on his address and the builder's yard. You never know – we might find Frank Cairns's shoes.'

'What about the glass?' Colson asked him.

'I think it's somewhere in the City.'

At that moment Byrne and Logan came in and made their apologies. Byrne looked at the bomb-scene photographs pasted up on the wall and he nudged Logan.

'Bring in the Cairns brothers,' Colson was saying, 'and Oxley and Bacon. Oh, and bring in Ingram too. Ask him why every time we speak to him, he speaks to Tommy Cairns. And I want Legion patrols, all over the City.'

'Sorry to interrupt, Bill,' Byrne said, 'but we've just picked up a fresh report from our UCA in Idaho.' He took the photos from the envelope and passed them across to Colson.

'This is the Soho bomb scene,' Colson said.

Byrne sighed heavily. 'I think we've established our link.'

Swann stood with Webb. 'How the fuck did he get them?'

'Press syndication library. About a tenner apiece.'

Swann looked sharply at Byrne then. 'Salvesen's employing the Storm Crow,' he said.

'Looks that way, doesn't it.'

'So nick him.'

'We can't. He hasn't committed any felony. All we've got is Bruno Kuhlmann in his compound and these photographs.' He looked at Webb. 'You said just now, George, anyone can pay for them.'

Colson stared coldly at him. 'And in the meantime we're hunting down a chemical bomb.'

Byrne looked helpless. 'Even if we did bust Salvesen now,' he said, 'it won't make any difference. Boese'll carry on, Bill. Once he starts something, he always likes to finish it.'

☆

John Henry Mackey sat in his trailer in Hagerman, Idaho, and watched the sport on HBO. At his feet lay his huskies and on the wall two high-tension bows were hanging. He had been checking through some of his legal papers, because the cops had stopped him again for speeding. He found what he was looking for and smiled. Those mother-fuckers didn't even know their own law. He'd stand up in front of the judge and stick them with it. Title 18 of the United States Code: 'If no person or their property has been injured, no crime has been committed.' He had hit nobody, he had trespassed on nobody's land and he had damaged nothing. He'd have his day in court.

The telephone rang and he jumped. His mind had been elsewhere and he was wary of the phone at the best of times. He had been one of those ready to march on Congress in September '94, and had stood with Jesse Tate at the eighty-one-day Freeman stand-off. He was absol-utely certain the Feds had tapped his phone.

'Yeah?' he said when he finally picked it up.

'John Henry?'

He frowned, a softly drawling voice he didn't recognize. 'Who's this?'

'Friend.'

'How'd I know that?'

'You don't, but you gotta trust me. I can't talk for long because I know they listen. I seen Russian tanks being freighted through Buffalo, Wyoming, just last Tuesday.'

'What's your name, friend?'

'That don't matter, John. But you gotta know some-thing – the Feds are watching Jake Salvesen. They got an undercover agent in Passover, Idaho, and they're about ready to jump his ass. You's a friend of Jesse Tate, John. I know you got respect for him. Get a hold of Jesse and tell him before it's too late. The people of this country ain't gonna take no more Waco or Ruby Ridge.'

The phone died then and Mackey held the receiver loosely in his hand for a moment. He crossed to the window and peeked through the drape. The exterior lights were on as they always were and if anybody was out there, the dogs would let him know. The voice rang in his ear, fear in it, desperation. Unknown caller in the night – maybe it was some kind of trick. He dismissed it, sat down again and went back to his beer. But it wouldn't leave him, the voice breaking in on his thoughts. Then the phone rang again.

'You're sitting there thinking on what I said, John Henry. I know it. The thing of it is, we don't have a whole lotta time. But I know you're nervous. When you talk to Jesse, you tell him this: when the crow flies, he sees everything beneath him.' Again the line went dead. Mackey got out of his chair.

He drove the seventy-five miles from Hagerman up through Shoshone to Passover. It took him an hour and a half and he kept his eyes skinned for cops. On the seat next to him lay a .357 Magnum, just in case. He had been to the Salvesen ranch just one time, when Jesse invited him to join in an open training day the year before. Salvesen had impressed him and the facilities were excellent. He turned off the highway and bumped his truck across the cattle trap. 'No Trespassing' signs were everywhere. The track was over a mile long and then he saw the lights of Salvesen's compound. God Almighty, the man was well set for when the shit hit the fan. Two armed men stopped his truck. He knew them, Drake and Wingo. 'What's up, John Henry?' Wingo said. 'What you doin' out here in the middle of the night?'

'I gotta see Jesse and Mr Salvesen and I gotta see them now.'

Salvesen wore his white suit and sat behind his desk with his arms loose and his hands in his lap. Jesse sat across from him, his face set and cold.

'That's exactly how it went, Mr Salvesen,' Mackey was saying, 'and then he called back.'

'What did he say the second time?'

'Oh, like how he knew I'd be suspicious, but he said to tell you something about a crow.'

'A crow?' Salvesen sat bolt upright, both fists on the desktop. 'What did he say about a crow?'

'Something about it flying. I can't recall exactly. When the crow's flying, it can see most everything.'

Salvesen's eyes were pinched now, lips a white line in his face. He snapped his fingers at Jesse. 'Check. Check now. Now, I tell you. Do it now.'

Jesse was out of the chair in a flash. Salvesen sat back and rested one balled fist against his teeth. He no longer seemed to see Mackey.

'So I did right to come out here, Mr Salvesen,' Mackey said.

Salvesen looked at him then with a cold light in his eyes. 'What do you think, John?'

Mackey stared at him: his face had changed, darker, the thoughts furrowing great lines in his brow. Again Salvesen looked up. 'You need to get home, John. Be ready. Don't you know the hour is late.'

When Mackey had gone, Salvesen still sat there, and then his gaze fixed on the papers on his desk. Opening his drawers, he took every note, every scrap of paper and piled them into the metal dustbin. He took the map from the wall and the charts and the writings and threw them in after. When he was done, he opened the sliding door and placed the bin outside. Then he threw in a match and watched it burn.

# 23

On the twenty-third floor of Liddesdale Tower, Boese watched while Ramas and Tal-Salem painted the window black. When the paint was dry, Boese himself took the roll of detonator cord and set about wiring up the glass. Movement sensors were mounted on the walls. Each of the thirty-five metal pipes had been sealed inside, one-third of the way down, and then sealed again at the top. They were fixed on the metal rack like pipes from an organ and pointed at an angle of forty-five degrees to the window. Inside the four-inch pipes, pressed against the nylon bung was a two-ounce conical-shaped charge. An Iraco detonator had been inserted in each one, with the wires extending down into a four by two wooden box. Boese set the last of the micro-switches on the lock clasp and then they packed their bags.

Outside in the hallway, Ramas kept watch while Tal-Salem sealed the door and keyhole with black waterproof sealant. When that was done, they descended one by one in the lift and went their separate ways. Boese, grey-haired, with a straggly beard and dark suit, limped into the Barbican tube station, leaning heavily on a cane. He passed an armed, watchful police officer and took the Circle line to Paddington.

☆

John Garrod, the commander of the Antiterrorist Branch, spoke on the phone to Major Ronald Hewitt of 11 Explosives Ordnance Disposal. 'Storm Crow, Ron,' Garrod was saying, 'responsible for the incident in Northumberland.'

'And you say there's a dirty room somewhere in the City?'

'We don't know for sure, but all the evidence points to it.'

'Why?'

'God only knows. But we need you on standby. I'm going to speak to the Home Secretary shortly, because if this *is* what we think it is – we'll be facing the worst threat this country's known in peacetime. Operation Stormcloud, Ron. It'll be a category A incident, no soak time, a disposal operation will have to be activated immediately.'

For a moment Hewitt was silent, then he said, 'D'you know how many category As we've dealt with, John?'

'I can't remember one.'

'No, neither can I.'

Garrod put down the phone, glanced briefly at the pictures of his daughter and granddaughter on the desk, then he dialled the Home Office.

'I'm sorry, sir, but you need to be aware,' Garrod told him. 'The threat is very real. You saw what happened at Healey Hall Farm. My instincts told me then that we were being put on notice and this fresh purchase of glass confirms it. Right now, we think the target could be the City because this is something to do with the European Union, maybe currency convergence, I don't know.'

'Why would an American be that concerned about currency convergence?' the Home Secretary asked him.

'I don't know, sir. I can't believe that's all there is to it.'

'We can't have the City closing down, Mr Garrod. We need to find this dirty room and find it very quickly.'

Garrod looked briefly at the ceiling. 'I know that, sir. We've got every available officer on it now. We're checking anything that's happened in the City over the last six months – business rentals, fresh employment, residential rentals and purchases. We're working round the clock.'

☆

Swann stared across the table at Tommy Cairns, who sat dressed in a white paper suit with his arms folded. Cairns stared back impassively.

Swann said it again: 'Tell me about Joanne Taylor.'

Cairns shrugged. 'I've told you. I don't know what the hell you're on about.'

'OK.' Swann sat back. 'For starters, we've got you for passing a false driving licence to Denis Smith, so he could hire a van.'

'Not me.'

'That's not what he told us.'

'His word against mine.'

'Is it?' Swann leaned towards him then. 'Frank drove the cab that Tal-Salem and Pier-Luigi Ramas used when they shot Jean-Marie Mace. That makes Frank an accessory to murder. When I tell him that, and tell him that we can prove it, he's going to have a lot to think about. I don't suppose it'll take him very long before he decides to tell us the rest.'

'Frankie was with me the day that Frog got shot,' Cairns said. 'We were playing cards with Charlie Oxley. Ask Charlie's mum, she was there.'

'Yeah?' Swann shook his head at him. 'Then explain to me how we found a thread from Frank's Levis on the driver's seat?'

Cairns stared at him and for a moment his eyes wavered. 'If you did, you planted it.'

Swann began to laugh then. Behind the two-way mirror, Byrne and Logan watched them. Swann snarled at Cairns. 'It won't wash, Tommy. When we get old Frank into the Bailey, he won't have a leg to stand on. That's him and Denis, accessories to murder. They'll be gone for ever. We've also got Frank's training shoe splashing through a puddle and leaving a nice fat print. We found them in the locker at the builder's yard.'

'He lent them.'

'Oh, do me a favour.' Swann rolled his eyes to the ceiling. 'You know, I credited you with more intelligence than that. We've got a witness who can identify him.'

'I want my lawyer.'

'Ingram's in custody.'

'Not fucking Ingram.'

'Why don't you tell us about Ingram, Tom?' Swann said. 'Do yourself a favour.'

☆

Webb and Christine Harris were in the City, traffic fumes choking them, taxis and motorcycle couriers rushing by. They were checking the serviced offices off London Wall for any hint of Joanne Taylor. Elsewhere, hundreds of other officers were doing the same thing. The Legion patrols had been running for three days now and police officers were everywhere. SO19 armed response vehicles, helicopters from Lippetts Hill, the City police and even some specialist firearms officers had been seconded.

'What about residential, Webby?' Christine said, as they came out of their eighth property management company with yet more reams of paper.

'Couple of the others are doing it. Let's get this lot back to the Yard. My feet ache from all this walking.'

They found Swann and McCulloch talking to Byrne and Logan. 'We can make it stick with Frank Cairns and Smith'll testify against Tommy,' Swann was saying.

Byrne scratched the hair that bristled on his scalp like fur. 'Doesn't get us any closer to the main man, though. Does it, Jack.'

Swann shook his head. 'Joanne Taylor's the key. She's the lynchpin, body on the ground, co-ordinating.' He looked at Webb, who had just dumped a great pile of papers on the desk.

'What's happening?'

'Shit is happening, Flash. Haven't you noticed?'

DI Clements came in then with Colson. They had just completed an interview with James Ingram.

'What've you got, Guv?' Swann asked Clements.

'Not much. Ingram's pleading ignorance and harassment. Did Cairns give him up?'

Swann shook his head. 'Cairns isn't saying anything. He'll happily let his brother take the fall along with the rest of them.'

'If he does – they'll hang him for us.'

'Yeah.' Swann sighed. 'We've got the foot soldiers all right, but then they're easy to get. What we need is Ramas and Tal-Salem and, above all, Boese.'

Christine Harris looked over at them then. 'Why haven't we been contacted?'

'He won't necessarily call,' Byrne said to her. 'Not until afterwards, anyway.'

The door opened then and the commander walked in. 'What's happening?' he said to nobody in particular. They told him what they had and the lines deepened above his eyes.

'I've just been on the phone to the Prime Minister. He isn't very happy.'

'Yeah well, shit happens to all of us.' Webb yawned as

he said it. 'What's he think we're doing – lying around scratching our arses?'

☆

Police Constable Ray Stewart drank a pint of Guinness in the Bishop's Finger in Smithfield. He had just finished a twelve-hour shift of Legion patrols and was enjoying one quiet pint before he went home to his family. The days had been long of late, the tension tangible, SO13 officers charging around all over the place. It made the activities of PIRA look small fry. He sipped the froth off the top of his pint, and licked his lips.

Two stools down from him, a bunch of window cleaners were enjoying a joke. He knew them vaguely, part of the team that looked after the tallest office blocks and some of the residential ones. One man in particular was having a good laugh, tall and thin with lank, mouse-coloured hair and a thin drooping moustache. 'Unbelievable. Wasn't like it last time I cleaned. Painted completely black,' he said.

'The window?' his mate next to him asked.

'Yeah. I reckon there's some kind of shagging party going on there. Some old slapper servicing all those rich geezers or something.'

Stewart looked at him then and frowned. The man caught his eye, held it and looked away.

'What did you say?' Stewart asked him.

The window cleaner stared at him.

'*What* did you say?' Stewart asked again. 'A window painted black?'

'What's it to you, mate? This is a private conversation.'

Stewart swivelled round on his chair and took his warrant card from his pocket. 'City police,' he said. 'Now tell me about this window.'

☆

458

Swann phoned Pia at his house. She was not working and Annika was away for a few days. Swann had asked her if she would look after the girls till he got home.

'How you doing?' he said.

'Fine. I'm quite enjoying myself actually. Are you coming home soon?'

'Can't, love. All hell's breaking loose.'

'What's going on?'

'We're looking for something and we really need to find it.'

'You can't tell me any more?'

Swann sighed. Before him on the desk was the series of photographs that the FBI agent had taken in Idaho, the Parisian receipt uppermost in the pile.

'It's the Northumbrian thing,' he said. 'We think he's doing something similar in London. Can you stay with the kids till I get there?'

'Jack, darling. I'll stay all night if you want me to.'

'You're wonderful. I'll get home as soon as I can.'

He put the phone down and looked again at the pictures. Louis Byrne was standing the other side of the desk. 'I'm going to go to Paris, Louis,' Swann said. 'Check this receipt out.' He lifted the picture. 'Salvesen must've met somebody there.'

Byrne nodded. 'I'll tag along, Jack. If we can pin something on him here, the Hostage Rescue Team can take him back home.'

Swann looked at the receipt again and squinted. 'What d'you reckon that is?' He pointed to the scrap of paper that was poking out from underneath the receipt, bits of words written on it. 'Ten, ction, aces'.

Byrne lifted his shoulders. 'Probably nothing,' he said. 'Our UCA couldn't have thought it that important or he'd have snapped it separately.'

Swann looked at it again. 'Somebody's handwriting,' he

said. 'Looks to me like some kind of Winthrop directions. "Aces" could be paces, "ction" could be action or junction maybe.' He laid it down again. 'I'd need to see the rest.'

The phone rang then and Swann picked it up.

'Jack, it's Campbell. Upstairs. We've just had a uniform on the phone from the City. There's a flat on the twenty-third floor of Liddesdale Tower with the window painted black.'

☆

Jesse Tate checked the outer perimeter fence with the rest of the men from the compound. They walked slowly, feeling their way along the wire to see if it had been breached. Ever since Mackey had showed up, Salvesen was a different man – angry, smarting with indignation. A federal agent watching him. They were trying to figure out who it was, somebody from the town, somebody on the move maybe. Jesse stopped at the back fence and scanned the hillside climbing up to the saddle. The snow was gone from the lowest slopes, but still drifted up in the draw. If anyone was going to watch, it would be from up there. He would have seen them, twenty years in the service taught him that much. He had been trained in covert observation and he knew its limitations. Yet Mackey and his phone call. Salvesen took it very seriously, the bit about the crow had convinced him. Jesse didn't know why he needed foreign terrorists anyway. They could've done it themselves.

'Hey, Jesse!' Wingo was calling to him.

'Whatcha got, buddy?'

Wingo pointed to the bottom of the fence wire, directly beneath the goon tower. 'It's been cut,' he said.

Jesse dropped to one knee and inspected the wire at the base. Wingo was right, the wire had been cut and curled back, then rolled again and pressed into the earth. 'Sonofabitch,' he said.

'Who?' Salvesen thumped the desktop. 'Who, Jesse? By God, when I find him, I'll hang him myself.' He stared at Tate then. 'It's beginning. You know it's beginning. We must act before they do. Treason. That's what it is. I want everyone in that town checked out. Everyone. I don't care how long they've been there. Start with the ones who're newest. Check out their lives, Jesse. Call whoever you need to call. I don't care what it costs. I'll find the sonofabitch whoever he is and when I do, I'll hang him.'

☆

Harrison smoked one cigarette after the other as he sat in his trailer and pored over the papers spread out on the coffee table. He had both books by Hal Lindsey and a copy of the Bible, plus his own selection of the pictures from Salvesen's office.

He remembered Salvesen's words on the Dictaphone and he checked it against the books. In 1970, Hal Lindsey, an evangelical preacher from Texas, had written *The Late Great Planet Earth* and traced certain prophecies of the Bible, linking them with the modern day. That had been almost thirty years ago. In 1995, Lindsey had updated events with *Planet Earth 2000 AD*. Harrison found comments in both books referring to the restoration of Israel as a nation in 1948. According to Lindsey's interpretation of events, the end times would come about in the generation that witnessed the rebirth of Israel. On page 149 of his second book, he referred to Matthew twenty-four. 'When its branch has already become tender, and puts forth its leaves, you know that summer is near: even so you too, when you see all these things, recognize that He is near, right at the door. Truly I say to you, this generation will not pass away until all these things take place.'

According to scholars, a Biblical generation was regarded as about forty years. 'Well, that makes it way past time,' Harrison muttered to himself. Over the page, though, Lindsey went further: 'Did it perhaps begin in 1967 not 1948?' Harrison recalled Salvesen's words about the Gentile times being over. The Gentiles had ruled Jerusalem until the Israelis took it back in the Six-Day War.

He sat back, sucked the froth of a Coors and lit another cigarette. Salvesen was always going on about the fourth kingdom as dreamed by Daniel and King Nebuchadnezzar of Babylon. He turned back to *The Late Great Planet Earth*, chapter eight: 'Rome on the Revival Road'.

Lindsey believed that the fourth kingdom was the resurrected Roman Empire. A ten-nation confederacy as foretold in the books of Daniel and Revelation. Harrison knew that in 1957 the European Community was born. Six countries – France, West Germany, Holland, Belgium, Italy and Luxembourg – signed the original Treaty of Rome. He glanced back at the pictures he had taken in Salvesen's study. Those six countries had topped the list with Rome marked in red above them. Three of the countries, Holland, Belgium and Luxembourg, had asterisks next to them. Why? He looked at the next nine countries on the list. Four of those had asterisks too – Spain, the UK, Denmark and Sweden. Seven in total marked out as separate from the others. What did they have in common?

He heard a car pull up outside and Chief wandered in. Harrison had no time to shift the stuff from his coffee table, but he managed to cover the product from the office itself. Chief looked down at him, saw the Bible open and squinted. 'You really do got religion, don't you, Harrison.'

Harrison looked up at him and shrugged.

'What's Guffy gonna say about that?' Chief sat down next to him and Harrison shuffled the covert papers and stacked them on the floor. 'Guffy's got my religion,' Chief went on. 'Man, she burns more sage than I ever did.'

'Wards off evil spirits. Why not – hell, there's enough of them around.'

Chief picked up *The Late Great Planet Earth*. 'You reading this?' He laughed then and flicked through the pages. 'Man, I used to study this stuff when I was a Pentecostal.'

'You were a Pentecostal?' Harrison looked sideways at him. 'What about all those war songs?'

'Back on the Res' when I got back from 'Nam,' Chief told him. 'Right about the time we were fighting the FBI. They threw me out because I couldn't get a handle on it.'

'The Pentecostals threw you out?'

Chief nodded. 'Said I was disruptive. Told me I couldn't be in their church and a member of the American Indian Movement.'

'Figures, I guess.'

'Hell, it was the Christians that fucked us over in the first place.' Chief picked up Harrison's beer and took a swig.

Harrison gave him a cigarette. 'You know much about it?' he said, nodding to the books on the table.

'I guess.' Chief looked at the second book. 'Never saw this one. How does he explain the fact that Europe has fifteen countries and not the ten he kept harping on about?'

'He doesn't,' Harrison said. 'He just reiterated what he said. Ten, not fifteen. He thinks they're the ten horns of the beast in Revelation.'

'Right on, and the little horn being the Antichrist. God, I remember all that.'

'He says five countries will drop out or amalgamate.'

'How're they gonna do that? European countries are splitting all over the place. Bosnia and Serbia, the Czechs. No one's gonna amalgamate.'

'That's what I figured.'

Chief took a pipe out of his pocket and pressed in a little pot. 'How come you're so interested, anyways?'

'Just am I guess. Comes of going to Jake Salvesen's church.'

Chief regarded him thoughtfully. 'Talking of which, that guy's one agitated man.'

'How come?'

'I don't know. But Jesse and his boys are in town right now, drinking in the Dollar and looking meaner than fuck.'

Harrison took the lighted pipe from him and sucked on it, pulling the aromatic smoke deep into his lungs. He passed it back again. 'What've England, Denmark, Spain, Holland, Belgium, Sweden and Luxembourg got in common?' he asked him.

Chief closed his eyes and blew a steady stream of smoke at the ceiling. 'Kings and queens.'

Harrison frowned. 'Yeah?'

'Well, all except Luxembourg, that's what they call a dukedom.'

Harrison stared at him. Revelation, chapter twelve. *Seven crowned heads.* In chapter thirteen the horns were all crowned, but in chapter twelve it was the heads. 'How come you know all this stuff?' he said.

'Went to school, didn't I. Shit, you think I'm just some dumb Indian?' He stood up then. 'Anyways, you coming for a drink? That's what I came over for.'

Harrison closed the Bible and stood up. 'You drive,' he said.

They sat at the bar in the Silver Dollar. Cecil and Margarito were shooting pool for five bucks a stick. Jesse and Wingo were seated a few stools along from them and Jesse had a mean look on his face. He kept staring at Harrison.

'Am I wearing something of yours?' Harrison said after a while.

'I don't know, hick. Are ya?'

The bar fell quiet. Chief shifted in his seat, a slow smile on his face. 'Hey, cool down. It ain't the fucking weekend.'

'Fuck you, Indian.'

Chief looked at the floor. Harrison could feel a tingling sensation all across his skin. Wingo touched Tate on the arm, but Tate pulled away. Harrison looked in his eyes. 'You need to learn to be a little more polite,' he said quietly.

'And you're gonna teach me. Right?'

Vicki, the bartender, slapped her palm on the counter. 'That's enough,' she said.

Red Mayer, one of the Passover marshals, walked into the bar and twirled his hat in his hands. 'That your Lincoln out there, Chief?' he asked. 'You got a busted tail light.'

☆

Swann and Byrne sat up front with the pilot. The Squirrel had been scrambled from Lippetts Hill and picked them up from the roof of the Yard. They flew low over the City and Swann checked the grid reference on the map. They could see Liddesdale Tower as they approached, at the eastern end of the Barbican complex, abutting Aldersgate and Beech Street, across the road from the tube station.

They ran a fly-past, the pilot winging slowly across the tower, rotor blades whirring with a whump whump above their heads. Swann saw the blacked-out window straight away, though the sun glinted off it. He indicated to the pilot to ease them in closer and he set the Squirrel almost motionless in a hover alongside the window. Swann peered at the dark panels of glass. He made a circular motion with his index finger and the pilot lifted away again.

'Set me down where you can,' Swann told him, and picked up the radio. 'Control from Squirrel four/nine,' he said.

'This is Colson, Jack. Go ahead.'

'Fly-by complete, Guv. I'm not happy. Pilot's going to set us down and I'll speak to the concierge. It would pay to get an Expo down here.'

The pilot swung round and set them down on the HAC ground, just off City Road. Swann and Byrne climbed out of the helicopter and made their way through Chiswell Street to the underpass on Beech Street. At the far end was Liddesdale Tower. The concierge, a young man in a blue shirt with sweat marks at the armpits, was dipping a roll into a mug of soup and sucking off the moisture.

Swann laid his warrant card on the desk. 'Flat thirteen on the twenty-third floor,' he said. 'Have you got a tenant in it?'

'I don't know. I'll check.'

'Quickly, if you would.'

The concierge took a clipboard from his desk and ran his finger down the list of names. 'The flat's owned by Mr and Mrs Bridgewater,' he said. 'They're in Saudi right now and yes – you're right, they have let the apartment.'

'Who to?'

'A Spanish gentleman. Mr Raoul Mendez.'

Byrne tapped Swann's arm. 'He's used Mendez before,' he muttered. 'Colombia.'

Swann felt a spider walk over his back. 'Has he had any visitors?'

'Only his assistants that I'm aware of.'

'Male or female?'

'Male. Two of them. Foreign gentlemen like Mr Mendez.'

Swann thought for a moment. 'Did they use the car park?'

'Oh, yes. Frequently.'

'Can you get the lift straight up from there?'

'Yes.'

'Are they still in residence?'

'As far as I know, although I haven't seen anyone for a day or two. They rented the apartment from Franklin Rees on Long Lane.'

Swann could hear the wail of a siren as they stepped out of the lift. He glanced at the wall sign which denoted the spread of the numbers and followed the corridor left. They came to number 13, moving quietly now. Swann looked at the door. The edges and keyhole had been sealed with black mastic.

As they came out of the lift again on the ground floor, Webb and Phil Cregan, the explosives officer, were coming in through the revolving doors.

'That's a positive,' Swann said. 'We've found them all right. Raoul Mendez is renting, a name Louis says he used in Colombia. Had two visitors and I'll give you three guesses who they are.'

'Fits with the glass,' Webb said. 'Right mileage.'

'I want to take a look,' Cregan told them.

'Door's sealed with mastic, Phil.'

'I still want a look.'

467

'I'm going to walk down to the estate agent's on Long Lane,' Swann told them.

They left Webb and Cregan to do a second walk-by upstairs, and crossed between the cars. Franklin Rees were halfway down Long Lane, on the right-hand side of the road. Swann showed his warrant card and spoke to the manager.

'Yes, we rented it, about three months ago,' he said. 'Spanish-American, good references.'

'I'll bet,' Byrne muttered.

The manager squinted at him and Swann said, 'Who came to view it – Mendez?'

'No, I don't think so. Hang on a second.' He went over to one of the desks and spoke to a young man in a striped blue shirt and gold cufflinks. The two of them came back. Swann looked at the younger man.

'A woman viewed it,' he said.

'What was her name?'

'Jane Taverner.'

'You remember her?'

'God yeah, she was drop-dead gorgeous. Long blonde hair.'

☆

Cregan stared at the door, then scratched his jaw and looked at Webb. 'No,' he said. 'Don't like it. Don't like it at all.'

They made their way back downstairs. 'You staying here?' Webb asked him.

'Till EOD arrive. After that, it's their problem.'

'I'll get back to the Yard.'

'Ring Cannon Row. Will you? Let them know what's happening.'

Outside, Webb climbed into the Expos' Range Rover

where Nicholson was still sitting in the driver's seat. 'Does Phil need me?' he said.

'Not this time, Tom. Going to be a military job.'

'Definitely chemicals, then.'

'Looks that way.' Webb leaned over the dashboard and picked up the phone. He dialled Colson's direct line.

'George Webb, sir.'

'What you got, Webby?'

'Wheel's come off. Big time. Cregan's staying here. The front door is sealed with mastic.'

'Hang on a second, George.' Webb heard the phone being laid on the desk and then voices. After a moment, Colson picked it up again. 'George, get back here as fast as you can.'

'What's happened?'

'We've just received a phone call. The one we didn't want.'

Colson had got straight on to the duty officer at Snow Hill, and the City police put in cordons and started evacuating. When Webb and Swann got back to the fifteenth floor, everything was in 'go' mode. The floor was sealed and all non-essential personnel were gone. Clements was on the phone to Porton Down and the Meteorological Office. Webb looked at the computer-aided dispatch that had been issued by the central command complex.

*Operation Stormcloud is live. Chemical bomb. Flat 13, twenty-third floor, Liddesdale Tower, Barbican. Suspect confirmed – Ismael Boese, alias Storm Crow.*

Colson called Swann and Webb into the commander's office. Sir Paul Condon, the Metropolitan Police Commissioner, and force duty officer for the day, was there.

'Close the door, Jack,' Garrod said. Swann did so and leaned on it.

'We've just had a phone call from your girlfriend.'

'Pia?' Swann stared at him. 'Is something wrong with my kids?'

Garrod held up a palm. 'They're fine. She's at your house with them and they're fine.' He looked at Condon and then at Webb and finally back at Swann. 'A little while ago somebody rang your doorbell. Pia answered it, but nobody was there. She found an envelope on the doorstep. It had a crow's feather in it.'

Swann took a moment to digest it. 'I need to speak to her, sir.'

'Of course. Go ahead.'

When he had gone, Webb looked from Colson to the commander. 'The door's sealed with mastic, sir. Jack's . . .'

'Tell me as we go, Webb. Tell me as we go.'

'Go where?'

'Ever met the Prime Minister? You're about to.' Garrod picked up the phone and dialled the Ministry of Defence. He spoke to the duty officer. 'This is Deputy Assistant Commissioner John Garrod, Antiterrorist Branch Commander. Operation Stormcloud code E-7/D10 is live. This is not an exercise. Repeat. This is not an exercise.'

Louis Byrne sat across the desk from Swann and watched his face. 'Don't take it personally, Jack. It's the way he likes to do things.'

Swann glared at him. 'You know what, Louis. I do take it personally. I take it very fucking personally.' He had just come off the phone to Pia who sounded very shaken. He wanted to go to her, go to the children, but it was impossible right now. He had told Pia to take them over to Caroline Webb's house in Amersham. He sat where he was and stared at the pictures that were pasted up on the wall. Ismael Boese stared back.

☆

470

On the fifth floor of Old Scotland Yard on Cannon Row, Nick Knight stood at the window of the spacious office he shared with another explosives officer. He heard the siren long before the BMW pulled up outside the gates to Downing Street. The DPG officers opened them and the car swept up to Number 10. He watched as John Garrod, Paul Condon and then George Webb got out. 'Good God,' he said. 'The fat detective – going up in the world.' He watched as the door to Number 10 was opened and they all trooped inside. 'Hope you haven't had your tea, Mr Blair,' Knight muttered. 'You're going to get indigestion.'

☆

Jakob Salvesen glowered across the desk at Jesse Tate. 'Who?' he said. 'Who breached my walls, Jesse? Which federal agent dared to trespass on my land?'

Jesse had never seen him like this, a changed man: gone was the genial giant with the soft Louisiana voice and the 'for the people' ministry. In his place was a cold, calculating man, under threat.

'I don't know.'

'Somebody in the town.'

Jesse narrowed his eyes. 'Somebody who knows what they're doing,' he said softly. 'Someone with experience, maybe.' Then his eyes darkened. 'Harrison,' he said.

'Who's Harrison?'

'The Tunnel Rat.'

'Tunnel Rat? Ah yes, I remember.' Salvesen sat back in the chair. 'He was in church one Sunday. Never saw him before. Never saw him again.'

'He lives in the trailer park with the beaners,' Jesse said. 'Works at the lumber yard on Main Street.'

'Find out, Jesse. Do it now. I want to know everything

about him. Find out where he comes from and contact our nearest friends. If it is him, I'll hang him.'

☆

Lisa was asleep and Harrison was reading Revelation, chapter thirteen. 'Then I saw a beast coming up out of the sea. It had ten horns and seven heads; on each of its horns there was a crown ...' He scribbled a note 'ten crowned horns'. '. . . and on each of its heads there was a name that was insulting to God.' He wrote the number seven and put a circle round it. 'The beast looked like a leopard, with feet like a bear's feet and a mouth like a lion's mouth. The dragon gave the beast his own power, his throne and his vast authority. One of the heads of the beast seemed to have been fatally wounded, but the wound had healed.'

He lit another cigarette, took up his pen once more and began to look at his notes. He had scribbled down what he had seen of Salvesen's etchings from the video he had taken. The number 17 and the number 16. The number 6 was ringed and then 1. 6+1=7. He stared at it, then back at the passage – seven heads and ten horns. Ten crowns on the horns. The telephone rang and he picked it up.

'Yes?'

'It's Tom.'

'What's up?'

'Two things. Leg-att's been on the phone from London. Storm Crow's planted a chemical bomb right in the middle of the city.'

Harrison whistled softly.

'They've got your product and Byrne's planning to go to Paris to check out the receipt. We might be able to put Salvesen with someone and hit him.' Kovalski paused.

'The other thing is – somebody just rang one of your "hello" lines in Marquette.'

Harrison sat very still. 'They did?'

'Yes. Someone's checking you out.'

Harrison flicked ash from the end of his cigarette. 'So they're checking me out, so what? The lines are good.'

'We can pull you out.'

'No.'

'You sure?'

'Yep.' He paused. 'Any of you figured out the Biblical stuff yet?'

'Some.'

'What you got?'

'Number seventeen.'

'Me too. Salvesen disagrees with Lindsey on this ten-nation confederacy stuff.'

'Right.'

'There's fifteen countries in the European Union right now.'

'That's right,' Kovalski said. 'And if they go ahead with the single currency, that's gonna effectively make them a federal state.'

'Does it look as though it's gonna happen?'

'Depends on who you read.'

'Salvesen thinks the Antichrist is going to rise out of the European Union. Six Six Six and all that.' Harrison scraped the blunt end of his pen over his notes. 'What I wanna know is what all this has got to do with the militia.'

'You sure you don't need some back-up?'

'Back-up'll blow everything, Tom. We still got nothing to book Salvesen with.'

He hung up. Salt Lake must've been spooked for Kovalski himself to call. He looked back at his notes again. Ten crowned horns, ten nations. Six heads, one of which had been mortally wounded. He flicked back to the

Old Testament and the dreams of Daniel. Chapter seven and verses twenty-three and twenty-four: 'Thus he said, The fourth beast shall be the fourth kingdom upon earth, which shall be diverse from all kingdoms, and shall devour the whole earth, and shall tread it down and break it in pieces. And the ten horns out of this kingdom are ten kings that shall arise: and another shall rise after them; and he shall be diverse from the first, and he shall subdue three kings.'

The resurrected Roman Empire. The ten kings where Lindsey got his ten-nation confederacy and the EU began in Rome. But it was not ten, it was fifteen. Harrison looked again at the second of Lindsey's books and thought it was a bit of a cop-out to just stick to what you'd said twenty-five years earlier without any real explanation. Clearly Jake Salvesen didn't agree with him and Salvesen was the dangerous one of the two. He looked again at Revelation thirteen, stubbing out his cigarette and lighting another. Through in his bedroom, Guffy sighed and he heard her roll over. Seven heads, one of which had been mortally wounded but had been miraculously healed. Lindsey believed that wound to be a physical one to the man who was the Antichrist, indicating that one of the seven heads, i.e. the one that was wounded, signified him; and yet in the same breath he seemed to be saying that the little horn rising from the ten horns was the Antichrist. How could it be both?

Harrison looked again at his notes: six nations signed the original Treaty of Rome – six heads? But there were seven in chapter thirteen. And then it dawned on him, the seventh head, mortally wounded yet healed. Could the wounded head be the symbolic rising of Rome?

# 24

George Webb looked across the Cabinet table at the Home Secretary, the Foreign Secretary and the Prime Minister and had to remind himself where he was. The Prime Minister was speaking to him. 'You're definitely sure it's chemicals?'

'Not sure, sir. No. We can't be sure until we get a look at it. But the door's sealed with mastic, so is the keyhole. It bears all the hallmarks of what we saw in Northumberland.'

The Prime Minister looked at Dr Firman who had been helicoptered in from Porton Down.

'Only this time it's in London.'

'Operation Stormcloud, sir,' Garrod said. 'We've been preparing for it ever since the incident at Healey Hall Farm. I've got an explosives officer down in the City right now and 11 EOD are on their way in from Didcot.' He leaned forward. 'We need to evacuate, sir. And we need to do it immediately.'

The Prime Minister looked at Dr Firman. 'How many people do you think we need to evacuate?'

'That depends on what we've got. If the device has been planted on the twenty-third floor of a tower block, he's going for maximum atmospheric dispersal, which would indicate a large quantity of the derivative. The airborne persistency is potentially as long as seventy-two hours. The wind can blow it a long way in that period.'

'How many people?'

'Wind speed is twenty miles an hour, a northeasterly,' Firman said. 'Downwind hazard of say, twenty miles initially. I would suggest the funnel to be four miles at the top and spreading to perhaps fifteen. That's as far north as Stratford, spreading from Stoke Newington to West Ham.' He thought for a moment. 'Southern borders – Greenwich, Penge, Croydon. Draw a line to Shepherd's Bush, Isleworth, Hounslow, as far south-west as Shepperton.' He passed a hand through his hair. 'You know, it'll make sense to use the natural boundaries for cordons, North and South Circular Roads perhaps, and the M25 at the bottom of the funnel.'

'That's the whole of London,' the Home Secretary said. 'You can't evacuate the whole of London.'

'We can, sir,' Garrod told him. 'We have to.'

'OK. OK.' Blair held up his hands, his face pinched and serious. 'For how long?'

'Till whatever we've got is completely rendered safe,' Firman told him. 'As I said, the last time we tested its atmospheric persistency it lasted three days. Just how many years it remains in the water system or in the ground, I cannot tell you.'

'Have you got an antidote, serum, whatever?'

'We've been working on it since October.'

'That's not what I asked you.'

'No,' he said. 'Not yet.'

☆

When the meeting was over, Garrod, Condon and Webb drove back to the Yard. The phone rang on the dashboard and the commander picked it up. 'Garrod.'

'Major Hewitt. 11 EOD.'

'Where are you, Ron?'

'Approaching target area now. Will be at the EOD control point in fifteen minutes.'

'OK. Control command is the Antiterrorist Branch. We're pulling back to the BBC building in White City. Designated entry and exit road is the A40, limited to security forces only. MOD are calling out every available army unit in London, who have NBC capability. The Prime Minister will be on TV any time, the broadcast will be nationwide. He'll declare a state of emergency.'

☆

Major Hewitt and his EOD operators arrived at the Barbican under armed police escort. The streets were already clear. Phil Cregan and his driver were waiting for them. Cregan knew three of the initial six warrant officers, who parked their vehicles in convoy on the Beech Street underpass control point. Tiny Tim Porter and Pete Mitchell, who made up the entry team, and also one of the diagnostics men, a warrant officer called Colin Salmons. Hewitt, he knew from various exercises they had been involved with. Cregan knew the drill and had prepared as much as he could for the questions that Hewitt would pose in order to make his evaluation. Standard procedure: PIT–STOP–PLAN–FELIX. The P in STOP was *priority, only take risk if category A*.

A few minutes earlier, he had listened to the Prime Minister broadcast a message over every radio and television station in the country. He had declared a state of emergency and hundreds of square miles of London were about to be evacuated. Already, Liddesdale Tower and the surrounding area had been cleared. Cregan had used his authority to get cordons in at four hundred metres and had the area fully searched by the City police. He remained on-site himself. If the device went off, he knew that he'd be dead anyway. Outside the four-hundred-metre mark there was pandemonium. The police and armed forces were trying to encourage a coherent set of evacuation procedures, but people were already panicking.

Cregan spoke to Hewitt. 'We've got a possible chemical IED,' he said. 'Twenty-third floor, flat thirteen. The door and keyhole are sealed. There's a balcony with a large window and French door. The whole thing's been blacked out with paint.'

'Access?'

'Got to be the stairs – unless you want to risk the lift.'

Hewitt shook his head. 'Are the engineers on their way?'

'Should be here any minute.'

'What're the possibilities for remote RSP?' Hewitt asked him.

'Not good.' Cregan looked up at the tower. 'Whatever happens, somebody'll have to get into the flat. I've checked the door and my guess is, it's booby-trapped. Knowing what we do about Storm Crow methods, the booby trap will be delicate and almost definitely linked to the main IED.'

'Cordtex the door?' Hewitt asked him.

Cregan made a face. 'Could do. Best possible outcome, the booby trap is neutralized. Worst possible outcome . . .' He let the sentence hang.

'In your opinion, Phil. What's most likely to happen?'

Cregan remembered Swann showing him the photograph with a bullet hole in his head. 'I think he's a total bastard, sir.'

The mobile phone rang in the Range Rover and Tom Nicholson called out to him. 'John Garrod,' he said.

Cregan picked up the phone. 'Sir?'

'Are the ATOs there yet, Phil?'

478

'Just arrived. Major Hewitt's making his evaluation now.'

'Engineers?'

'They're on their way.'

'OK. When you've finished briefing Hewitt, I want you in White City.'

Cregan put the phone down and walked to the first EOD lorry where Tim Porter and Peter Mitchell were being helped into NBC suits. He lit a cigarette and watched them. After they were dressed, their aides helped them into the wraparound bomb suits – Kevlar-layered, with a cuff rising round the neck to the chin and an acrylic blunt trauma shield built into the chest area. He was glad it was them and not him. In any normal IED incident, i.e. categories B to D, the EOD team would allow for a soak time or waiting period, in order to ensure that the risk to military personnel was minimal. It was also the time for evaluation and planning. Category A demanded immediate action and Hewitt would have to plan the render safe procedure as the various EOD operators discovered exactly what they were up against.

Hewitt watched the two members of his entry team start towards the tower block and considered his options. Disposal operations had to be started now, regardless of personal risk. The entry team had no choice but to physically assess the best method of gaining entry, while minimizing the risks to themselves and the Engineers, who would undoubtedly be working with them. They were carrying all their entry equipment together with scientific testing gear, including the portable isotopic neutron spectroscopy system, which could identify high explosives, as well as nerve and blister agents within a sealed container. The evaluation took anywhere from one hundred to one thousand seconds, but assuming the entry team were successful, the PINS system would be on hand for the diagnostic team to make their analysis. Over and above that, there was the weight of Buck-eye – the smaller remote-controlled robot. They could not risk the lifts. If the bomb went off and they got stuck, there would be no way out.

Halfway up the stairs, Porter was contacted by his second.

'Engineers are here, Tim.'

'Good. Get them to come up and meet us. A couple, Barry. No point in risking any more lives than we have to.'

Hewitt monitored the conversations from the EOD control point in the trucks parked in the underpass on Beech Street, from where he would endeavour to plan the render safe procedure, as and when the pertinent information was relayed to him. He hoped, although without much conviction, that once they had gained entry to the apartment itself, they might be able to move whatever device they encountered using hook and line, in order that a remote RSP could be implemented.

He sat in the back of the lead truck and switched on his equipment, computers, radios and the VDU for Buck-eye, which linked to the portable screen that the entry team would use. The truck was in direct communication with the operations room at Scotland Yard.

Webb was already there, kitted out for chemical war. Larry Thomas of the FBI and Christine Harris from SO12 had volunteered to assist him. Webb was operating the main communications computer linking the EOD control point to the commander in White City. Half a dozen officers had volunteered to remain in the central command complex to co-ordinate radio and telephone contact for the evacuation. Apart from them, the rest of the Yard was empty.

Porter and Mitchell climbed the stairs and outside the

City was silent. Late afternoon, the day muggy and heavy with cloud. Porter doubted the wind was travelling at twenty miles per hour. Most City occupants were daytime dwellers fortunately, leaving their offices for other parts of London at night. From the staircase windows, he could see the NatWest Tower dominating the now impotent financial centre of Europe; and the pyramid-like summit of Canary Wharf further down the river. He was sweating. It was early April now and warm, and the heat of the charcoal-lined NBC suit and the weight of the Kevlar bomb gear pressed the sweat back against his flesh. Already, the respirator pinched the skin of his face, squeezing his eyes in their sockets. His breathing was a rasp and hearing was greatly restricted unless he and Mitchell put their heads close together. Finally, they made it to the twenty-third floor and sealed front door of Flat 13.

☆

At White City, Swann watched the Prime Minister on television again to repeat his emergency statement. He told the public the truth: there was a deadly terrorist threat in the City of London, and the nation faced the worst potential disaster ever encountered in peacetime. Each London borough would issue emergency notices through local radio stations and via the police using loud hailers. People were instructed to take only the bare essentials and leave in an orderly fashion. Hospitals, old people's homes and hospices would be evacuated by ambulance and the army. They were to wait for contact by designated army and police personnel to arrange the transportation of patients. All roads out of London were to be used, bar the A40. This was for security forces and emergency services only. Any vehicle found on the A40 would be stopped. The Prime Minister again specified the affected areas and pleaded for those who were outside the downwind hazard to remain in their homes, to alleviate the weight of congestion.

Byrne joined Swann and watched as the cameras shifted back to the BBC studio housed below them, and the gravity of the newscaster's face. 'That was the Prime Minister,' he said. 'We can now go to our correspondent, Tim Gutteridge, close to the scene in the City.'

Swann stared at Byrne. 'What the fuck is he still doing there?'

'John,' the reporter said, 'I'm standing at the site of the initial cordon put in by the police. As we now know, this is not nearly sufficient, with most of London being evacuated. Any minute now, we will have to move out of the affected area by helicopter. I can just briefly tell you that the army is here en masse. We have bomb-disposal teams from the Royal Logistical Corps and the Royal Engineers, and they are currently trying to evaluate just what they are dealing with.' A siren cut into him and the image was lost.

'There's no bomb-disposal team from the Engineers,' Swann muttered. 'They don't have IED capability.'

The newscaster came back on screen. 'I'm afraid we've lost those pictures from the City,' he said. 'The police have requested that people do not panic.' He stopped then, touched the radio in his ear and said: 'We're just getting reports of a serious car crash on the A406, north of Muswell Hill.' The picture shifted and Swann saw two cars coupled together and burning out of control. People were standing around in a daze; he could hear a woman sobbing bitterly and somewhere a baby was crying.

The newscaster came back on screen, and went on to tell them that the councils of Essex and Kent, Surrey, Berkshire and Buckinghamshire were implementing their emergency planning procedures in conjunction with the police and fire services. Schools, hotels, community centres, church halls and every other available building were being commandeered to accommodate the expected flood of refugees. The residents of those areas not affected were expressly requested to remain at home.

The camera then cut to Euston Station where the platforms were inundated with passengers. The reporter was jostled and shoved. 'As you can see,' he said, 'the trains are already overloaded. Normal travel is non-existent. There are no fares; people are just crowding on to trains in the hope of getting away from the carnage. Outside, cars are jammed on the roads and we're told fleets of ambulances have begun arriving from as far afield as Hertfordshire and Cambridge, to begin the delicate job of evacuating the hospitals that are within the inner cordon, or "dirty line" as the security forces refer to it.'

The picture returned to the studio and the newscaster continued. 'The army have been scrambled: the Duke of York Regiment, the Guards, the Territorial Parachute Regiment from the King's Road. Soldiers, fully armed and wearing nuclear and biological warfare suits, have hit the streets in a convoy of lorries that move like an endless green centipede along the A40.' His voice was interrupted by overhead video footage.

'The stock market ceased trading some time ago,' he went on. 'Contingency plans take them only as far as South Quay, but South Quay is being evacuated. We're told by City analysts that computer systems will take over, but many economists fear the effects will still be disastrous. When the Dow Jones opens in New York, the value of sterling is widely expected to plummet. In Brussels, an emergency meeting of the European Parliament has been called, and the Foreign Secretary will be flying in to make a statement. The spectre of Storm Crow has closed like great black wings over the lives of millions of people.'

Swann switched channels and saw two men fighting in front of their cars. An old lady on the pavement was bundled to the ground. Helicopters flew overhead. He thought of his children and thanked God he had told Pia to take them to Amersham as soon as she received the feather. Byrne shook his head at the screen. 'Look at it,' he said, gesticulating. 'How can one man wreak so much havoc?'

☆

Jesse Tate knocked on Salvesen's office door. 'Come in,' Salvesen called. He was watching CNN on the television. Every news programme worldwide had been interrupted to broadcast what was happening in London. Jesse stopped to watch for a moment and saw the crowds of people panicking on the streets. The reporter was in a helicopter flying over the city and cars and buses and trains were shunting nose to tail. The pavements moved in a single mass of humanity, like millions and millions of bees crawling over one another. Salvesen was staring at the screen. 'They don't realize what I'm doing for them,' he said. 'They'll never unite now. I'll never let them unite. Storm Crow. He's not bringing bad news but good. Don't they know this is their salvation?' His eyes were cold as stone. 'Somewhere in the fires of Hell, Jesse, the Devil is gnashing his teeth.'

Jesse nodded slowly. 'Harrison,' he said. 'His phone numbers check out in Marquette.'

'They do?' Salvesen frowned.

'I got our friends in the police department up there to check him out.'

'But?' Salvesen caught the glint in Jesse's eye.

'I checked something else out. Harrison claims he was

a Tunnel Rat in Vietnam. He's got their badge tattooed on his shoulder.'

'Go on.'

'I checked the war records through one of our military contacts on *The Register*. There weren't that many Tunnel Rats and only one called Harrison. He was from Michigan, but Detroit not Marquette. He got his DEROS, but the plane bringing him home crashed in the Pacific. There was another Rat from Chicago, but his name was Johnny "Buck" Dollar. His mother's maiden name was Harrison.'

'What happened to him?'

'That was the difficult bit, Jake,' Jesse said. 'We're lucky you got so many friends in so many places. John Dollar worked as a border agent for three years in New Mexico. After that he joined the FBI.'

☆

Swann took a call on his mobile from Rachael, his former wife. She had gone to Scotland on a course the week before. 'Jack, what's happening? I can't believe the news.'

'You better believe it, Rach. It's real.'

'Where're the children?'

'Safe. I got them out of London long before anyone else.'

'Where are they?'

'Caroline Webb's house. Pia's with them.'

'Thank God.'

'You still in Edinburgh?'

'Yes.'

'I'd stay there if I were you. If this bomb goes off, we'll have a contamination problem for years and years and years.'

'Storm Crow,' she said. 'Who is he, Jack? Why's he doing it?'

'We don't know, Rachael. Why do any of them do

485

anything?' He looked up and nodded as Byrne gesticulated to him. 'I've got to go now. Don't worry, the kids are fine.'

He put the phone down and Byrne came over. 'Colson's called a meeting,' he said.

☆

Tim Porter and Pete Mitchell were joined by Captain Robert Ryman and four soldiers from the Royal Engineers, and they moved up to the twenty-fourth floor of the tower block. They had been fully briefed by the Antiterrorist Branch and had worked out a plan of containment. As yet the IED was unknown, but the blacked-out window indicated that some kind of dispersal device was set up on the other side of it. In Northumberland, Webb had found a four-foot length of scaffolding pipe, blocked and sealed two-thirds of the way along. A sealed projectile for a liquid, with a small shaped charge to set it off. The minimal explosion but maximum dispersal, twenty-three floors up, exploding the gaseous E-7/D10 into the atmosphere above London. It was all they had to go on. They had no definite idea what kind of timing and power unit had been installed, but it was likely to be the same kind as had been recovered from Queen's House Mews. That was fitted with an LCD clock, with separate alarm display and a ten-day decade switch. They had no idea what point the safety-arming switch had been set to. The bomb could go off at any time.

Ryman and his men had to try to find a way of containing the derivative if it was exploded into the atmosphere. During exercises certain options had been considered, for a given situation, but none of them had proved overly successful. This one was doubly difficult in that the target area was so high above the ground. Any form of wall construction had huge logistical problems.

They had to try and keep the toxin out of water supplies, so any form of dilution containment was out of the question, unless they could seal the spillage in tankers. That in itself caused other problems. As it was, every vehicle that was inside the dirty line was potentially contaminated, and, if so, could never be brought out again. JCB diggers were on standby outside the inner cordon on Shepherd's Bush common, and alongside them the decontamination tents had been erected.

The Engineers had racked their brains for alternatives and then one of their number had come up with a potentially good idea. They contacted an ocean salvage company in Tilbury and commandeered an underwater balloon. This was a massive lightweight tarpaulin bag that was inflated with helium underwater and used to assist the raising of wrecked ships from the seabed. It measured one hundred feet in length when deflated, and they believed it would be strong enough to hold the exploding chemical if the device went off. If they could secure it efficiently, they might be able to catch as much as seventy per cent of the material before it vaporized in the atmosphere.

The bag had been picked up in a Chinook helicopter and winched down on to the roof of Liddesdale Tower. The Engineers made their way up and transported the twenty-foot package down to the twenty-fourth floor. The plan was to break into the flat directly above the target and then abseil down the balcony and secure it in place with explosive bolts and sealant. The five of them, together with the two operators from 11 EOD, were now standing right over the bomb. The explosive bolt guns were risky: concussion waves could set off the detonators, overt vibration might trip a mercury tilt switch. But there was no viable alternative. To try to quietly drill holes in the concrete surround of the balcony would be time-consuming and awkward while hanging from abseil ropes.

The Antiterrorist Branch had secured plans of the building and they knew that the layout of the target flat was the same as that on the floor above. A large living room with a kitchen off it and two bedrooms. The front door opened straight on to the living room and the EOD operators had already made the assumption that it was booby-trapped. The best point of entry was through the wall of the flat next door. The Engineers were busy scraping away plaster in the flat above, in order to assess exactly what the wall construction was. This confirmed, the two men from the entry team could access Flat 14 and work on the adjoining wall.

They could hear the other Engineers setting up their abseil ropes, as the two who were assisting them opened the door to Flat 14 with a hydraulic ramp. Here they needed stealth rather than force: the wrong sort of shock wave through the walls might trip whatever device had been set. The heat was intense; the sun had broken through the clouds and was magnified by the size of the windows. Porter and Mitchell worked side by side with the two Engineers, listening to the thud outside as the abseilers fired home their bolts. At each mini-explosion, Porter held his breath. His eye holes had misted in the respirator, making him twist his head sideways to see. He had checked it again on the way up, even though it had been checked and rechecked with pentyl acetate outside.

Using diamond-headed drills, they broke a hole through the mortar between the grey breeze blocks that had been exposed in a patch two feet square in the wall. Porter had an infrared endoscopic probe ready for insertion and the camera set up to replay what it saw. The drill cleared the brickwork and automatically cut out. Porter knew they had struck the plaster beyond. Resetting the drill, he broke the plaster and came up against wallpaper, pushed on through and then withdrew the drill bit. They worked low down on the wall. It was unlikely to be booby-trapped, but they did not know what sort of light or movement sensors might have been set up on the other side. Phil Cregan had briefed them on the elaborate hoax that had been pulled at Queen's House Mews and they were taking no chances.

Once they were through, Mitchell selected the fibre-optic probe and passed it to his colleague. Porter took it in hands encased in black rubber and cursed the fact that the gloves were so cumbersome. He worked with the probe and, taking his time, began to feed it through the tiny hole in the bottom of the wall. Outside, he heard another shuddering thud, as an explosive bolt was set into the concrete balcony. The sooner they had that bag set up, the better they all would feel. Once it was done and secure, the Engineers would fall back and only he and Mitchell would be left. From somewhere above, he could hear the whirr of rotorblades and he imagined other soldiers, hooded and masked, patrolling the perimeter line with guns.

☆

George Webb manned the operations room. Once again he was caged inside his charcoal suit, listening to the hoarse wind of his breath through a respirator. Christine was NBC-trained and she was watching the traffic cameras while Webb manned the radio. From here, he could talk to any officer or soldier out there; he could talk to the two 11 EOD entry men or Major Hewitt, and he could patch them all through to Garrod in White City. He looked out of the window and saw the hubbub of Westminster. It would be a good few hours yet before the evacuation was complete and he imagined the turmoil in the counties, as the respective councils battled with emergency-planning procedures that would be more than overloaded. How many boroughs? How many people? Hackney, Stepney, Poplar, the City, Tower Hamlets, Camberwell, Brixton, Clapham, Battersea, and all those stretching south-west in the path of the downwind hazard. Parliament had gone already, MPs scuttling for their constituencies like pack rats. The government had removed to Chequers and Whitehall was rapidly deserting. The Foreign Secretary was going as far as Europe.

☆

Porter had the probe in place and was now able to scan the contents of the darkened room through the infrared lens: the images were relayed back to the mini-monitor he held in his hand. Mitchell pressed his head close, so their bomb helmets were touching and they could speak to each other. The radio line was open, and, downstairs, Hewitt wanted to know what they saw. The camera probed the far side of the wall and, as it did, the layout of the room was exposed to them piece by piece. There was no furniture, or rather there was, but it was all pressed against the opposing wall, directly across from where they squatted next door. That left the exposed space of the floor and the window to their right. The probe twisted right and Porter saw what looked like a large wooden box, like the chests people have at the bottom of their beds. He moved closer and higher and he saw a metal wall rack fixed to the floor right in front of the window. On the rack he counted a substantial number of short scaffolding pipes, set like mortars at an angle of forty-five degrees. He could see the twists of wire extending from the base of the tubes.

'Jesus Christ,' he muttered.

'What've we got, Tiny?' Hewitt's voice in his ear.

'The biggest fucking mortar I've ever seen.' He described the IED and then said, 'They've layered the window with det cord. Glass'll go a nanosecond before the bomb, which is bolted to the floor. There's no chance of moving it, sir. We might get Buck-eye active, once we see what we're doing. But if the box is booby-trapped, we'll have to do a manual RSP, and fuck that won't be easy.'

Sitting in the truck in the underpass, Hewitt could feel the perspiration gathering on his palms beneath the taut rubber of his gloves. Already he was considering options and the possible consequences of choice. *What's the best that can happen? What's most likely to happen? What's the worst that can happen?* The latter didn't bear thinking about.

Porter studied the camera images and paused to consider the movement sensors. They were wired to one another along the walls; four he counted, all linked, possibly by collapsing circuits, to the main device. He could not tell for sure, but it looked like the sensors were crossing each other at about chest height.

'Four-sensor booby trap,' he said. The scope twisted the other way and now he could make out the door. 'Booby trap on the door, separate device linked to the handle and wired to the IED. The door is twenty-millimetre boxwood. We could get through it with one strand of Cordtex 22, but it might trip the main device.' He sighed heavily through his mask. 'Now we've decided on this hole, I'd rather use Buck-eye to pig-stick it. At least we can see what we're doing.'

Webb listened to the conversation between Hewitt in the underpass at Beech Street and his entry team twenty-three storeys above his head. The Engineers had the balloon in place and Hewitt's men on the ground described it as one hundred feet of condom dangling down the side of the building. If it wasn't so serious, they'd laugh. Two Engineers were now back on the twenty-third floor to cut a hole in the wall large enough for the entry team to get through. They had drilling equipment which would take out the mortar on two breeze blocks and then they could haul out the stone. Four men in immediate danger.

Swann, impotent all at once, watched the evacuation as it was played out on television, in a surreal, almost movie-like fashion. He wished now he had volunteered to man the ops room with Webb. The news broadcast told him that, as yet, no one who was outside the cordon had tried to break back in. One enormous problem was rounding up the homeless and loading them into open-back army lorries that had flooded the city from every available barracks. Helicopter cameras zoomed in on the masked and suited soldiers, shifting cardboard city at gunpoint. Swann wondered how many of them would slip the net, and return to the no-go area as looters. They could have a field day. So far, the Prime Minister had said nothing about looters. The army or police would arrest them, but one or two might slip the net. Once inside the dirty line, they could never come out again. He shrugged his shoulders. If they were exposed to D10, they'd die. They'd burn the bodies there. The TV pictures jumped to another massive pile-up on the M25 at the M3 intersection. Swann watched, as tempers flared and two men started a fist fight on the hard shoulder.

Larry Thomas, the FBI weapons of mass destruction agent, was listening to the pandemonium over police radios north of the city. Police forces nationwide had been alerted, and around London the county forces were assisting with the refugees fleeing the potential carnage in the city. TV crews had descended in number and press-men were massing at the outer cordon. Those living outside the specified areas were equally panicking, refusing to ignore the government advice to stay in their homes. Some older people inside the dirty line had refused to go at all.

Back in White City, Swann watched the pictures as some drivers tried to avoid the congestion by getting on to the A40. They were promptly stopped by police and forced back on to the other roads. Another fight broke out and he watched three uniforms bundle one of the antagonists to the ground. Ten minutes later, Tony Blair went back on TV from Chequers and appealed for calm. He cited the British quality of combined fortitude when facing a massive threat. 'Work together,' he urged them, 'not against each other'.

Outside London, the county councils were desperately trying to cope with the deluge of incomers from the capital. There were not enough hospital beds and makeshift wards were springing up in army camps, community halls and hotels to cope with the infirm from the London hospitals. All doctors' leave was cancelled and naval medical personnel were flown in to assist from Haslar. Empty hospitals inside the inner cordon were under armed guard as were the banks, against the threat from looters. Swann watched as the images flicked from London to the counties: Oxford and Reading; the concrete mass of Basingstoke where people fled in their droves.

☆

Harrison spoke on the phone to his contact agent. 'What's happening?' Scheller asked him.

'Don't know. Something's up. Tate tried to pick a fight with me the other night. The atmosphere's changed. I can smell it.'

'You need back-up?'

'I can handle it.'

'The main man?'

'Not been seen. Plenty of movement from the others, mind you. I've got the T-17s set up. I'll check them out tonight.'

'Johnny, we're thinking about coming in anyway. This thing in London.'

'And lose, Max? No way. I already told Kovalski, we have no evidence against Salvesen. Busting in on him now isn't gonna stop what's happening in London.'

'They're worried about you in D.C. Your "hello" lines were called.'

'I know that, Max. I can handle it. I've got to check those T-17s. If I don't, we'll never have anything on Salvesen. I'll call in every twelve hours. If you don't hear from me in twenty-four, send in the cavalry.'

He rang off and walked back from the Valley Market to the lumber yard where Danny was operating the crane. Mark Eddington watched him. Eddington was a casual crony of Wingo and worked in the yard scraping logs into shape by hand. He claimed to be very knowledgeable about the US constitution and subscribed to the underground military magazine *The Register*. Rather than refuse a driver's licence, he had signed for one 'without prejudice' and 'under duress'. He argued that under the constitution he had a right to travel granted him by God. By imposing the licence on him, the state had taken away that right and forced him to accept a privilege of the state instead. According to the authors of the Bill of Rights, no right should ever be abrogated by a privilege. Harrison thought it was bullshit paranoia. Eddington was the one who'd sworn he'd seen Gurkhas training in The Pioneers. He could feel the man's eyes on his back all the way to the crane.

They quit work at lunchtime that day and Harrison went for a drink in Joe's club. It was dark inside and a couple of Mexicans were shooting a game of pool. There was drizzle in the air and Harrison had his jacket zipped to the neck, his grubby baseball hat pulled low to his ears. Five minutes before one, Wingo drove by in Jesse's truck.

Back in his trailer, Harrison picked up the second book by Hal Lindsey that Max Scheller had got for him and he flicked through the first few pages. He was so absorbed he did not hear the truck move slowly through the trailer park. The door swung suddenly open and Jesse Tate levelled a Casull 454 handgun at him, complete with telescopic sights. It could take down a bull elk at two hundred yards. Harrison looked at the gun, then at the others; Drake and Wingo. They both held sidearms. He felt sweat creep between his legs.

Jesse stared at him with a light in his eyes that reminded him of darkness. Drake looked at the notes on the table and grinned. 'The evidence,' he said, nudging Jesse. Jesse looked down and his face lost its colour. Harrison watched his finger over the trigger of the Casull. He'd always boasted about the 300-grain hollow points it sported. For a second, Harrison thought he was going to shoot him there and then. He did not. He spoke in a low menacing voice.

'You're a federal agent, Harrison. And the way you've been conducting yourself goes against the highest law of this United States. You're unconstitutional and that means you've committed treason.' He paused then and smiled. 'You know the penalty for treason.'

He moved towards him then and handed him a piece of paper. Harrison looked at it and shallowed his breath; a warrant for his arrest issued by the 'Common Law County Court'. Jesse motioned for him to get up, then he glanced down at the pile of papers on the table. 'Bring the evidence, Drake.' He looked again at Harrison, the barrel of the Casull no more than twelve inches from his chest. 'Your real name's John Dollar,' he said. 'We're arresting you under county common law. You'll be taken before the court, tried, and hanged by the neck till you're dead.'

# 25

Swann went to see DI Clements. 'Guv, what about having another go at Cairns and co?'

'Right now?' Clements looked at him. 'We've got enough hassle trying to shift prisoners out of the contamination area, let alone interview them.'

Swann coloured. It was true, all the prisoners in London had had to be evacuated along with everyone else. The nightmare was where to put them. If ever there was an ideal time to try to escape it was now.

He went back down the corridor and bumped into Logan. 'Cheyenne, have you got that last batch of surveillance product?' he asked her. 'I want to take another look.'

'Sure.' They went back into the makeshift squad room where Logan opened her briefcase and laid out the pictures from Jakob Salvesen's office.

Swann skimmed the pictures and stopped at the one which he thought might be Winthrop instructions underneath the receipt for the meal in Paris. 'Be nice to get hold of the original to this,' he said, tapping the picture. 'Somebody's handwriting. I'd bet my flat this is Winthrop.'

'Directions to get to a dead drop or something?' Logan said.

Swann nodded. 'PIRA use it all the time. Concealment and accessibility, the key to a decent weapons hide.' He studied the receipt then. He had been about to go to Paris when the blacked-out window was discovered. Taking the photograph with him, he went in search of Clements once more and found him in conference with Colson. Swann hovered in the doorway and Clements rolled his eyes at him. 'Yes, Jack.'

'I want to go to Paris, Guv.'

'Paris?'

'Yes. I was due to go before all this blew up. Remember?'

'The receipt,' Colson said.

Swann nodded. 'Might as well go now. It might give us a body the FBI can use to hit Salvesen.'

Clements looked at Colson, who nodded. 'Fine with me. Get yourself on a chopper to Southampton, Jack. You can get a plane from there.'

Back in the outer office, Swann phoned Caroline Webb's house and spoke to Pia. 'I'm going away for a day or so, Pia. Will you be all right with the kids?'

'I can't go to work, can I. To tell you the truth I like having them.'

Swann paused, thought for a moment, then bit the bullet. 'Listen, this is hardly the time, but will you marry me?'

Silence, save the softness of her breathing.

'Sorry,' he said. 'Ridiculous thing to ask you.'

'No, it's not,' she said. 'Jack, I'd love to marry you. But I can't.'

'Why not?'

'I just can't get married.'

'But why?'

'Oh, I can't explain on the phone.'

'Right.'

'Don't be like that. You said yourself it was a ridiculous time to ask.'

'Yeah. Right. Sorry.' He looked at the receipt in his hand. 'Anyway, I've got to go. I'll call you from Paris.'

'You're going to Paris?'

'Yes.'

'There are no planes.'

'There are plenty of planes, Pia. They're just oversubscribed. I'm Old Bill, aren't I. I think I can get a seat.'

'What're you going to Paris for?'

'Just checking on something. I'll phone you, all right?'

'OK.' Again she was quiet. 'Listen, we'll talk when you get back.'

'Sure. Kiss the kids for me, will you?'

He was on the common waiting for a ride to Northolt and the helicopter, when Louis Byrne came down. Across the green, the army were setting up a field canteen, the other side from the decontamination tents. Byrne stood upwind of his cigarette smoke.

'You going to Paris?'

'Yes. I want to find out who Jake Salvesen had dinner with.'

'I'd still like to come along.'

'Be my guest, Louis.'

They hitched a ride on a lorry going back along the A40 to Northolt, and witnessed first-hand the plight of the people still fleeing the capital. The TV had reported two overloaded trains almost running into one another because of a signal failure in Kent. Near misses and not so near misses everywhere you looked. At Northolt, they got a helicopter ride with two scientists who were returning to Porton Down. Until the entry team had got an idea on what was inside the flat, there was little they could do at the crime scene. At Porton Down, Swann got hold of a car and he and Byrne drove to Southampton. They had to wait for a couple of hours, but squeezed on the last flight to Orly.

'Have you been wondering what Boese's doing while all this is going on, Jack?' Byrne asked him as the plane took off.

'I have, yeah.'

'What d'you reckon?'

'Well, the best time to escape is during the pandemonium. Who's going to get stopped?'

Byrne nodded. 'He stuck around to watch once before.'

Swann shook his head. 'He stuck around to check out SO19's tactics. That was a bit of research. He doesn't need to research any more. He'll be long gone, Louis. Back to wherever it is he came from.'

'Yeah, I guess you're right.' Byrne looked away from him.

Swann tightened his seat belt. 'He has to have a safe haven somewhere. Every terrorist needs friendly faces.'

'He's different though, isn't he,' Byrne said. 'Thinks of himself more as a businessman than a terrorist. That's why he's guarded his identity so carefully.'

'He's been clever, all right. I've never come across a more cunning bastard than this one.' Swann frowned. 'We were very lucky with your ATF connection. That was a serious result.'

Byrne looked at him. 'You still think somebody snitched, don't you.'

Swann made a face. 'Not snitched. Made a mistake. Loose talk in a pub, maybe. It happens.' He looked sideways at him. 'He knew far too much to get it just from antisurveillance.'

☆

From the deck of his father's trailer Little T saw them walk to the truck, Harrison between two men, and the one who beat him behind them. Harrison sat between Drake and Wingo in the back seat, handcuffed behind his back. Jesse drove through town to the highway. Harrison saw Danny Dugger's truck with the white camper top parked out in front of the Silver Dollar. The cloud was low still and a fine drizzle washed over the windshield.

'Looks like it might storm up,' Harrison said.

Drake looked sideways at him. 'Shut up.'

'You'll have every Fed in the state camped on your stoop by the morning.'

'I don't think so.'

Jesse watched in the rear-view mirror. 'I don't think so either.'

They drove him into the compound with the rain falling harder. The dogs were out and they barked as Tate stopped the truck. It was cold when they set him on the ground, the wind coming in off the mountains to bend the trees against the inner compound wall. Wingo got out first and, grabbing a handful of Harrison's shoulder, hauled him out afterwards. The house stood huge and white and silent. Harrison looked at an upstairs window and saw Jemima Salvesen watching him, a look of disgust on her face.

They marched him inside the walls of the inner compound and closed the gates. Then Jesse went up the steps to the house. Wingo and Drake escorted Harrison across the yard to the armoury. Harrison thought of all the M16s down there and wished he'd had the opportunity to substitute the firing pins. It was too late now. Wingo unlocked the side door, threw him inside and locked it again after him.

Harrison knelt in the darkness; no windows, no interior light switch that he could find. He stood up and allowed his eyes to grow accustomed and, as they did, he gradually made out the gallows above his head. The trap door was open and he glimpsed the thick loop of the noose. He thought about Guffy then and all the people he knew in

501

town. He flexed the fingers on both hands. The cuffs were the plastic type used by the state police, and they bit into the skin round his wrists. He leaned against the wall and caught his breath. He knew from his reconnaissance in the tunnels that there was a second door. Turning his back to it, he tried the handle. Locked. Ironic really: beyond that door was more firepower than a man could ever need and here he was helpless. He could feel the knot in his stomach. Fear. He was locked in, hands tied fast. Again he looked at the gallows and he knew they *would* hang him.

☆

Porter and Mitchell, the two entry operators, waited while the Engineers worked on the hole in the wall. All four of them had stick-on chemical indicator paper attached to their arms and legs. If there was contamination immediately, the paper would turn blue. Porter watched his as the first breeze block came clear, one more and Mitchell would be able to get through at least. Porter wasn't so sure that he would. The sweat was in his eyes again, running down his face, mask sucking at flesh beneath the rubber housing. He would have given anything just to ease that pressure for a moment and wipe the moisture from his eyes. Twenty minutes was the optimum time that anyone should spend working in one of these suits, and over it he had the modular bomb gear with the heavy Kevlar lining. He wished he had opted for the lighter one and allowed his arms to remain free at least. If the device went off while he was gaining entry, he would be history anyway. But caution was always the watchword and you never think of those things while you're preparing yourself. If you thought you were going to die, you wouldn't do this job in the first place. Cregan had the right idea, getting a job with the Met when his time was up. The Met handled more IEDs than they did, but none stuffed full of chemicals.

The Engineers were through and they looked back at Porter and Mitchell. 'All yours, boys,' one of them said. 'You want us to stick around?'

Porter shook his head. 'Fuck off out of it,' he said. 'You've been here too long as it is.'

The Engineer laid a gloved hand on his shoulder. 'Good luck,' he said.

When they were alone, Mitchell and Porter looked at one another. The time was ticking away, both of them knew it. Whatever time had been allowed on the safety-arming switch, there was less of it now than when they started.

'Control from entry team,' Porter spoke into the radio clipped to his bomb helmet.

'Go ahead, entry team.' Hewitt's voice. He could hear the tension in it. You want to be tense, he thought. You ought to be up here.

'Porter here, sir. We're through the wall. Engineers are on their way down.' He glanced down at the indicator paper. 'So far, negative contamination. Indicator paper remains clear. We're going to send Buck-eye in to take a look around. Retreating to distance of one hundred metres.'

'Received, Porter. Standing by.'

Mitchell set up Buck-eye, the portable version of the weapons-mounted Alvis Wheelbarrow. He could climb stairs and look over walls if you wanted him to. They had carried him up here between them and now he was activated, armed with three disrupters, drive and attack cameras. They moved away, feeding out the fibre-optic cable and the portable monitor. Porter had rigged up the radio control for the drive and attack cameras as well, but he doubted whether Hewitt and the others in the control vehicle would get any pictures, too much concrete around them. One hundred metres took them two floors down and they checked their position before using the remote handset to drive Buck-eye towards the hole. The little robot would get through easily enough, infrared sight on the cameras. They could risk no additional light and had worked the last few minutes in darkness. There was no way of knowing whether the movement sensors were also activated by light. There was also no immediate way of knowing whether Buck-eye himself would set them off; it all depended on the angle of the infrared beam. The moment he was at the wall was a tough one. Both Mitchell and Porter watched the monitor with the drive camera picking up the full expanse of the hole. Once through, the whole thing could go bang.

They eased Buck-eye through the aperture and gently into the flat. Porter operated the lower hamper at a snail's pace, using the attack boom to give them gradual all-round vision. He kept the weapons mount boom low, almost to the lower hamper itself, and carefully swept the area.

'Control from Porter. Buck-eye is in the target area. You getting anything, sir?'

'Negative. Too much interference.'

'I'll talk you through it.'

Through the twin cameras on the robot, Porter could see the room in a pale wash. Keeping the boom fully flat, he zoomed the macrolens in on the booby-trapped door: a separate IED, but linked to the main device, about half a kilo of Semtex attached to a PIRA-style timing and power unit, with a mercury tilt switch on one side.

'Booby trap on the door,' he said. 'But linked to the main device. I think we can do a con-ex on that and get the door open.'

'How far is it from the main IED?' Hewitt spoke in his ear.

'Right across the room, probably thirty feet.'

'Concussion waves?'

'Possible, sir. We can leave it if you want, but it's held on a mercury tilt switch.'

'What about the rest? You said there were passive infrareds?'

'Stand by.'

Porter guided Buck-eye 360 degrees and then slowly across the carpet. He stopped and scanned the rest of the room. A glass cubicle had been built against the wall of the kitchen. They had not been able to see it with the fibre-optic camera.

'Control from entry team.'

'Go ahead.'

'Located dirty room. Four-sided glass in the kitchen.' He moved the robot closer. 'Plastic drum on the floor. Empty,' he said. 'About twenty to twenty-five litres. The cap is missing.' It lay on the floor alongside the empty drum. He raised the boom now, gently, so he could see the rest of the room. On the surface inside the dirty room lay a number of glass bottles and a small gas burner. Discarded by the sink was a piece of copper tubing, with one end hacksawed off. Porter reported it back.

He and Mitchell had a discussion. They left Buck-eye where he was and sat on the steps of the tower block. Outside, the City was silent, dark now as the day faded. They had scanned and filmed the rest of the room and counted thirty-five tubes in total. The information had been relayed back to the control point and in turn to the scientists from Porton Down, who were still beyond the inner cordon at the command control point in White City. The tubes all had twin lines of detonator wire in them, which meant each one was charged separately. On the

505

floor was the four by two wooden box with a hinged lid. They had filmed it up close and Mitchell had picked up a microswitch booby trap set under the hasp on the front. A tiny hole had been drilled at the back of the hasp and the wires threaded through to whatever was in the box. Seventy pieces of detonator wire in total, negative and positive leading down from the tubes. They were intertwined after that and fed into four other holes at the back of the box. They had risked lifting Buck-eye's boom sufficiently to see over the top.

'Take out the booby trap on the door,' Mitchell was saying. 'The wall-mounted stuff we can't do with the robot.'

It was true. They had counted movement sensors in all four corners of the room, separately and mutually wired, as if somebody had been setting up a stereo system. The wires ran down into the box. That presented them with another dilemma. They had no way of knowing what would happen if they disconnected the wiring. It would probably have been armed with a collapsing circuit, so that if the wires were cut, it set off the main charge. Porter got back on the radio. 'We're going to pig-stick the door,' he said. 'There's no way to render safe the booby traps other than manually and I want to see what's in the box before we do that. Diagnostics will have to X-ray. We'll breach the door and enter for a manual look.'

Hewitt did not answer for a moment.

'Copy, Control.'

'Affirmative. Go ahead, Tim, and good luck.'

In the operations room at Scotland Yard, Webb, Thomas and Christine Harris listened to all that was being said. 'Eerie,' Thomas commented, 'listening in like this. That apartment must be the loneliest place in the world.'

☆

Harrison was scraping the plastic handcuffs on the hinges of the door and knew he was not getting very far. Normally, you needed wire cutters to get them off. His hands throbbed now, and with the stopped-up blood so his anger mounted. He thought of Jesse Tate and the look of cold fury on his face as he levelled that 454 at him. Another thought was beginning to bother him: Scheller and Kovalski had told him that his 'hello' lines in Michigan had been called. 'Hello' lines were secure confirmation for any over-zealous questioner, and had been more than enough in the past, even when people like Joe Pistone were layers deep in the Mob. So why not now? Why had Salvesen looked further? There could only be one reason and that was that Salvesen was sure beyond any doubt he was a Fed. The only way he could be that sure was if somebody told him.

Who had burned him and why? It meant death. Here he was, sitting under a home-made gallows, with the self-styled Judge of Idaho about to pass sentence. How did he get compromised? It could only be from someone who knew. And then a thought struck him: Chief had come into the trailer and seen him working on the Biblical stuff. Chief's tone, his comments; standing with Banks and Means against the FBI in 1972. But how could Chief know? And would he really tell Salvesen? Harrison was positive he had entered the tunnels unnoticed, and more than covered his tracks on the way out. But had some-body seen him?

He sat and considered the timing. The last thing he had done was send in the report and pictures, after entering Salvesen's office. That was the first clear evidence that linked Salvesen to anything. But what had he photo-graphed – a bunch of notes, the titles of some books, maps on the wall. Nothing that could be conceived to be incriminating in a court of law. Suddenly he heard voices outside, then the key turned in the lock. Jesse stood there with two other hands from the bunkhouse.

'Get up,' he said.

Harrison worked his way to his feet. Jesse handed his pistol to one of the other men and then spun Harrison round. He cut through the flexi-cuffs and Harrison winced as the blood started to flow again.

'Hurt, did it?' Taking a set of metal cuffs from his belt, Jesse slapped one on Harrison's wrist and the other on his own, then he led him outside. As he closed the door, he looked Harrison right in the eye. 'Next time I come in here – it'll be to drag your body out.'

They crossed the yard, Harrison with Jesse fastened to him and the other two slightly behind, both of them holding rifles. Harrison looked left and right. The afternoon was waning now and lights burned in Salvesen's office. Outside the wall, the dogs, smelling an unknown scent, suddenly barked. Jesse opened the door to the radio building and they walked into the courtroom. Every chair was taken bar the one that stood on its own. Jakob Salvesen sat in the judge's chair with his hands across his belly.

Harrison felt the rage begin to grow inside him. They were going to try him in their kangaroo court. These assholes actually believed they had the right. He looked Salvesen in the eye. 'If you're gonna try me, mother-fucker, take this fucking thing off.' He hauled his hand up and brought Jesse's with it. Salvesen's eyes flickered a fraction and then he lifted a finger and pointed. Jesse unfastened the cuffs and took his gun back from the other man who moved to the door. Jesse directed Harrison backwards to the witness chair and then went to stand behind Salvesen. Harrison's chair was positioned to the left of the table. The trap door was five feet from him, looking like part of the floor. He knew then that they did not know he had been underground. Somebody had tipped them off, but that somebody did not know about the tunnels, or if they did, they hadn't seen him enter them. Thank God, that counted out Scheller and Brindley at least. Bob Jackson, he would trust with his life.

'This will be a very short trial, Mr Johnny "Buck" Dollar, who claims the alias of Harrison, resident of the town of Passover, Idaho.' Salvesen's voice had lost its charm, harsh now and purposeful, in a clipped almost metallic way. His eyes were cold and dark. 'Federal Agent Dollar. An appropriate name. A unit of measurement. We have yet to weigh you for the gallows. You wouldn't want us to get it wrong and pull your head off, now would you.' He sat up straighter. 'How did you get into this compound?'

'Never been here before now,' Harrison said.

'Liar. You better tell the truth, Mr John Dollar, or I'll just go ahead and sentence you anyway.'

'Fuck you, asshole.'

Jesse was out from behind his chair, but Salvesen had a hand on his arm. 'Let him cuss all he wants, Jesse. He's gonna have to face his maker sooner than you or I.' He looked again at Harrison. 'I shall ask you one more time,' he said. 'How did you get in here?'

Harrison had one hope and that was the T-17 transmitter. It was in this room, wired to the video, and if it would only work, then all of this would be captured on tape. Even if they killed him, Scheller would locate his forward lay-up point from the maps he had provided them with and find the tape. Salvesen would not only be hanging him, he would also be hanging himself. A slight whirring sound caught his ear and he glanced up to see the head of the video camera moving. He felt suddenly sick. Salvesen was filming it all for posterity.

'You broke my fence,' Salvesen said. 'Trespassed on

private land.' His voice was rising. 'I have a right to shoot you for that.'

'Only if you catch me, Jake. And you didn't.' Harrison was eyeing the trap door. He might just be able to make it without Jesse shooting him. He could feel the adrenalin beginning to build. 'I don't recognize this court and I don't recognize you as a judge,' he said. 'I don't recognize Jesse Tate there or any of these others. What we got here, Slusher and Drake and Wingo. That you over there, Mark? And, oh look, the Passover marshal himself. Tyler Oldfield. You're a cop, Oldfield. What're you doing here?'

'Harrison, you're charged under common law for conduct unbecoming a government official,' Salvesen said. 'You have infringed my rights and trespassed on my land, gained employment under false pretences and carried out treasonous acts.'

'Treason? I don't know what you mean, Jake.'

'Ignorance is no defence even for police officers, Harrison. If you had bothered to read any of the judgements given out by the Supreme Court of the United States, you would know that.' Salvesen rapped his fist against the table. 'Your work for the FBI, a corrupt and murderous instrument of the New World Order, is by definition unconstitutional. Any act or work carried out by a government official on behalf of the same New World Order is by definition treason. Treason is punishable by death.'

'You just gonna convict me, Jake? Or do I get a say?' Harrison could feel his heart thumping. He needed more on tape.

Salvesen looked cautiously at him, then at his watch, and he nodded. 'You can have your say.'

'I just wanted to ask you a question.' Harrison moved

to the edge of his chair. 'Something I can't figure – aren't you a little ahead of yourself?'

'In what way?'

'Well, all this New World Order stuff. Who is it you read – Hal Lindsey?'

'Among others.'

'What, like Robertson and that other guy with the videos – what's his name – Jack Van Impe?'

Salvesen looked at him with a slant in his eyes. 'They're all good men, men bold enough to speak the truth.'

'But you're ahead of them. Seems to me that they're interested in the souls they save and the money they get donated to them. They're making a buck, Jake. Nothing wrong with that. Shit, it's the American way.' He paused then and cocked his head to one side. 'What's the hurry, Jake? How come you went and planted a bomb in the middle of London?'

Salvesen looked at him carefully then. 'The time is upon us,' he said, leaning forward and clasping his hands together like Harrison had seen him in church, bent over the pulpit like some spiritual benefactor. 'The problem is, Harrison, that those other men only see half the picture. The militia, people I'm close to, who try to protect the constitutional rights given this nation by God himself, only see half the picture. I'm doing this country a favour. People see black helicopters and concentration camps and the United Nations, but that's just a ploy.'

'Ploy?'

'Oh, it's probably real enough, but it's still so much rumour. The whole situation is a product of the Devil. The Bible tells us that in the last days of the world there is little or no mention of the United States. People like Lindsey and the others recognize it, but they don't seem to have too much to say about it. Now me,' he poked himself in the chest. 'I've had a better education than most and I've had a little more money than most and maybe because of that I can see things a little more clearly than most. What better way for the Antichrist of the revived Roman Empire to undermine the only truly independent power left in the world?'

'I'm not with you, Jake.'

'I wouldn't expect you to be. You work for them.'

'Enlighten me. Call it a last request.'

'I'll put it to you this way,' Salvesen said. 'What better way for the Devil to create his own world than to undermine the US with revolution. There's people here in Idaho, people in Michigan, in Texas and Arizona; people in Florida, Nevada, Louisiana and Baltimore ready to go to war right now. Only a couple of years ago, there was a call to arrest Congress. All of that undermines the stability of America.'

'So why the fuck are you arming them?'

'Not just arming them, Harrison, educating them.' Salvesen shook his head. 'Me, I'm your saving grace. They want to go to war now. I'm telling them the war'll come here soon enough. All I'm doing is showing them how to defend themselves when it does.'

'War from Europe?'

'The New World Order under the sign of the Beast.'

'So that's different to the war on the Internet, then?'

Salvesen's gaze shallowed. 'It's one and the same, only the timing is different. The Antichrist wants civil war on US soil, so the rise to power in Europe is that much easier. Me, I'm just trying to prevent it.'

'By planting a bomb in London.'

'Sometimes that's what it takes.'

'Storm Crow.'

Salvesen threw back his head and laughed. 'This time he's bringing good news. He might just be bringing salvation, only they don't know it.'

'An international terrorist worse than Carlos the Jackal.'

'In times of war, Harrison, a man uses everything at his disposal. What were the British in Palestine after the war, if not occupying terrorists. They themselves presided over the second generation of concentration camps, when they stopped the Jews going back to Israel.'

'That why you got something against them?'

'They were foremost in trying to prevent the reformation of Israel. Ernest Bevin, the greatest exponent of it all. Maybe he knew what would happen when Israel was reborn.'

'"And Jerusalem shall be trodden down of the Gentiles, until the times of the Gentiles be fulfilled." In 1967, Jake. When they kicked Hussein back into Jordan.'

Salvesen lifted his eyebrows. 'You've done some homework. In other circumstances, I might even congratulate you.'

Harrison cocked his head to one side. 'Don't you think you might just be a little off the mark, though. I mean, Lindsey and those other boys who talk about the revived Roman Empire, the fourth kingdom that you preach about – they reckon it's the ten horns in Revelation. Ten nations, Jake. I don't know if anybody noticed, but there's fifteen in Europe right now.'

Salvesen smiled then, the light cold in his eyes. 'Exactly. And that's where I part company with them. It seems to me they're just making money out of it, after all. Now me, I got all the money I ever needed, so my desire is righteous. I looked a little further than they did, Harrison. I took account of chapter twelve in Revelation.'

'The dragon with seven heads and ten horns.'

'Seven whole heads. Seven crowned heads, Harrison. Seven crowned heads at the time that this begins. You know how many kingdoms or royal families there are in Europe right now?'

'Tell me.'

'There's seven, Harrison. If you include Luxembourg.'

'Which you obviously do. But what about the ten nations? You got me there.'

'Not ten. Sixteen.'

'Now, you have lost me.'

'Listen to me, fool. In 1957, six countries of Europe signed the Treaty of Rome. *Rome*, Harrison. *Rome*. West Germany, France, Belgium, Holland, Luxembourg and Italy. Six nations. The six good heads in Revelation thirteen.'

'I read that. And the bad head?'

Salvesen licked his lips. 'The wounded head that was miraculously healed. The others think that's the mortal wound of a man, something he'll recover from and the world will be amazed. But people come back from the dead all the time. Thirty minutes with no heartbeat is the longest I heard of so far. That isn't gonna fool anyone.' Salvesen shook his head. 'The seventh head in Revelation thirteen is Rome. Symbolic, not literal. The second phase of the kingdom, mortally wounded in AD 400 and resurrected in 1957. Now that *is* amazing.'

'And the ten horns?'

'The other ten nations who joined after 1957.'

'That makes sixteen, Jake. There's only fifteen right now.'

'Fool,' he said. 'Hungary is waiting to join.'

Now Harrison saw it: Jakob Salvesen's urgency. For a split second, his logic and his voice, Harrison wondered if he might not be right. He sat very still and remembered what Kovalski had said to him on the phone. With a single currency Europe would become a federal state. And then he knew exactly why so many militia leaders had been in this compound. Their avowed goal was a violent showdown with the Satanic Federal Government, the United States of America. But for Salvesen, it wasn't America at all. It was the United States of Europe.

Jesse Tate was restless behind Salvesen's chair. Across from him, the others shifted in their seats. 'We're off the point,' Salvesen said. 'You've said your piece. Now we get on. You've been charged with treason and I find you guilty.' He stood up then. 'John Dollar, at six o'clock tomorrow morning you will be taken to a place of execution and hanged by the neck till you're dead.'

Harrison stared at Salvesen, then at Jesse Tate. 'Not worth a rat's ass, eh, Jesse.' He leapt up and threw his chair across the table. Then he was on his haunches scrabbling for the trap door and hauling it open. Jesse recovered himself. A shot rang out, but Harrison was already dropping into the darkness.

# 26

Porter armed the central disrupter on Buck-eye's modular weapons system, and sighted the attack camera. If it failed, the whole place would go up.

'Preparing to con-ex,' he said into his microphone, voice hoarse and distant. They looked briefly at one another, sweat speckling Mitchell's face through his mask. Porter fired the pig-stick. They heard the dull thud from above and the image on the camera wavered. Porter watched as the camera focused again, aware of the pulse at his eye. 'Con-ex successful,' he said.

They climbed back to the twenty-third floor, overheated and weary under the weight of their suits. Nearly six hours had passed since they received the call telling them that the operation was live. Taking a manual lever, they opened the front door to Flat 13, where the remnants of the ruined booby trap still dangled from the handle.

Five minutes later, they were joined by Salmons and Richards from the diagnostics team, carrying the X-ray machine and their cases.

'We can't tell where the wires from the booby traps end,' Porter told them, 'but the det cord on the window finishes up in the box. Once you two have X-rayed everything, we'll come back up.'

Salmons was strapping night-vision glasses over his bomb helmet. 'Don't worry about it, Tim. Major says you boys have had enough.'

Porter looked at him gratefully. 'See you back at the ranch, then.'

He and Mitchell made their way back down the twenty-three flights of stairs to the incident control point. They debriefed Hewitt and the render safe team, then climbed aboard a lorry to be ferried back to the inner cordon and decontamination. It was late now, and the streets were absolutely deserted. Everyone had gone and London seemed crippled by an eerie silence, accentuated by the sound of the diesel engine. Porter sat in the back of the tarpaulin-covered truck, letting the air flow over his charcoal suit. The weight of the Kevlar and the bomb helmet was gone and he felt strangely light and free. They passed nobody on their journey from the Barbican to Shepherd's Bush; no sound, no movement, only the fragile glow of street lights and the expanse of the sky above them.

☆

Colson sat with Dr Firman and the commander, who was on the phone to the Prime Minister at Chequers.

'We're working on it now, sir,' the commander said.

'Is it safe yet?'

'Not yet, I'm afraid.'

'We need the City open, Mr Garrod. The country cannot afford this.'

'I know that, sir. But it's delicate. They've discovered a very large and very intricate improvised explosive device. It's booby-trapped and they had to enter the flat through the next-door wall. The Royal Engineers have erected a balloon on the outside of the window to try and catch most of the chemical if it goes.'

'What about contamination?'

'Well, they're only just entering the room, but it's been negative all the time they've had a hole in the wall.'

'That's good news at least. We must work fast, though

– international confidence is falling. The economy will suffer, Mr Garrod, and people need to be back in their homes.'

Garrod rubbed at his eyes with a palm. 'I appreciate that, sir. But if we get this wrong, there won't be any homes to go back to.'

'I understand, Mr Garrod. Believe me. You have my direct line; please keep me posted of any developments.'

'PM wants his capital city back,' Garrod said as he put down the phone.

Colson rubbed at the stubble on his jaw. 'Don't we all.' He got up and looked out of the window, across towards the luminous blue glow of the decontamination tents.

☆

In the operations room at the Yard, Christine Harris dozed, her head resting against a rubber-gloved palm. Larry Thomas sat by the window, looking out over the deserted city and thinking about his wife and children back in Virginia. Webb monitored the communications. It occurred to him that all they needed now was PIRA to break their ceasefire and then they'd be really stuffed.

☆

Salmons and the less experienced Richards checked one another's respirators and Richards made sure his indicator paper was properly attached, and that he had a bottle of Fuller's Earth in his pocket. They had the door open and entered Flat 13 in pitch darkness, using their NVGs. The movement sensors were still live and they knew from Buck-eye's boom what was a safe height to work at. So they crawled on their hands and knees and between them brought in the X-ray machine and PINS analysis system. Richards gawped as Salmons removed the weight of his helmet.

518

'If it goes off with me right over it, the helmet'll keep my head in one piece,' Salmons said. 'It'll still be four miles from my body.'

He could see more easily without it. He had done it many times, taken the helmet off up close. It really did not matter: from five to ten yards it might make something of a difference, depending on how lucky you were, but on top of the box itself, luck had nothing to do with it. He worked quickly, making the most of his energy before the heat of the suit began to sap it. Richards was alongside him, preparing the plates and deciding which way to approach the box. They had to X-ray from all angles, so they could get a clear idea of exactly what was inside. If they were very lucky, they might be able to find out how much time they had left. They would X-ray some of the tubes as well, see their make-up, what kind of detonator and charge had been applied and what the liquid content was.

Cautiously, Richards approached the empty plastic drum which stood alongside the glass wall of the dirty room. He watched his indicator paper through the fuzzy light of the NVGs that protruded from his forehead like a Dalek's eye. When he got near the container, the paper started to fade and he felt his heart rise in his chest.

'Col?'

Salmons was busy with the X-ray machine, setting it carefully along the front of the box. He could see the microswitch booby trap just under the hasp.

'Colin?'

'What?' He turned and Richards pointed to the colour of his indicator patch.

'Shit.'

'It's that container.'

Salmons looked across the room and bit his lip. 'Is there anything in it?'

'No.'

'Run the PINS,' Salmons said.

Richards set up the isotopic neutron spectroscope, checking the time on his wristwatch, strapped over his black rubber glove. It could take up to twenty minutes to get an accurate reading and he was painfully aware that they might not *have* twenty minutes.

'Control from diagnostics,' Salmons spoke into the radio.

'Go ahead, Colin.'

'Preparing to X-ray. There's an open plastic container on the floor, and we've got the first traces of positive contamination.'

He X-rayed, moving round the wooden box to take pictures from all sides, inching his way, being careful not to disturb or move it. He counted a second microswitch under the lid on the right-hand side, close to the hinge. As the lid was lifted, so the switch would push out and complete the circuit. There was no way of opening the box with det cord without disturbing them, so they would have to be dealt with manually. For a moment, he thought of the mind that had rigged this thing up. Perspiration ran off his nose and he licked at it.

While he was working, Richards started the spectroscopy analysis. He tested the general atmosphere, then the plastic drum and then the piece of copper tube in the dirty room. Inadvertently, he touched the fallen container, and patted down with Fuller's Earth. The signs in the room were positive but minimal. He moved back to Salmons who was now X-raying the pipes. 'Positive in the dirty room, although marginal, Colin. Positive on the plastic container, and the copper tube.'

Salmons nodded.

'I'll start on the pipes.'

'Just do a couple, Mike. We need to get the pictures developed quickly.'

☆

Swann and Byrne walked alongside the Seine, a world away from London. Paris, as always, was heaving. Swann checked the directions he had got from Yves Mercier of the DCPJ, his counterpart in the French police. An old friend, Mercier had been on the fifteenth floor more than once recently to discuss four Algerian activists they had arrested up in Manchester. He had given them directions to the floating barge restaurant close to Notre Dame Cathedral. Byrne had hailed a cab and they were walking the rest of the way. Swann pointed out a flight of steps which led down to the quayside.

'You speak French, Louis?'

'Don't you?'

'Pidgin.'

'I'll figure it out, Jack. Don't worry.'

Byrne took the receipt from him and they made their way into the barge, which turned out to be an extremely exclusive place with only a handful of tables. All of them were full, with well-dressed patrons who could afford the luxury of Notre Dame as a backdrop and the horrific nature of the prices. Byrne took the *maître d'* to one side, showed him his FBI shield and then began to speak to him in perfect French. Swann caught the words 'Scotland Yard' and he showed the man his warrant card. Then Byrne handed him the photograph of the receipt. The man wandered over to the payment counter, where he began checking through a book.

Swann touched Byrne on the arm. 'You've been here before?'

'Not Paris, but France a couple of times.'

'How come you're so fluent?'

'Studied it at school.'

'What else d'you speak?'

'Bit of Spanish. German. Russian. Little bit of Arabic. It helps with the Middle Eastern guys I have to interview.'

The *maître d'* came back with a copy of the reservations book. He checked the date on the receipt and then opened the pertinent page. Swann saw the name before his finger ever got to it. 'Monsieur Salvesen'.

'Who was he with?' Swann asked. 'Louis, ask him who he was with?'

'It is all right, my friend. I speak English.'

'Good,' Swann said. 'Who was he with – do you remember?'

'Of course.' The waiter smiled then. 'Beautiful girl. Very beautiful girl.'

'Could you describe her?'

'Oh, yes. He comes here quite a lot, always with the same girl. Dark hair, short.'

Swann peered at him for a moment. He had expected it to be long and blonde. 'If I got an artist down here, could you describe her to him in detail?'

The man looked puzzled and Byrne translated for him. He nodded his head vigorously. 'I've seen her many times. I know what she looks like. Monsieur Salvesen – he always eat here with her when he is in Paris.'

Swann called Mercier, who said he would arrange for someone to come down right away. Byrne explained it to the *maître d'*, who looked at his watch, shrugged his shoulders and nodded. They left him then and took a cab to the hotel from where Salvesen had made the booking. On the way, Swann phoned Webb at the Yard.

'What's going on back there?' he asked him.

'Diagnostics are in. Entry team couldn't do anything about the booby traps. They're crawling about in NVGs.'

'Have you spoken to Caroline?'

'Not recently. They'll be all right, Flash. There's a two women to two kids ratio.'

'Yeah, right.'

'Have you come up with anything?'

'Possibly. Salvesen had dinner with a woman. The waiter at the restaurant says he's seen her before. Yves's getting an E-fit done for me. Tell the old man I'll be back as soon as I can.'

'Shouldn't worry about it, mate. Not much for you to do over here. Not much for any of us to do till EOD get this sorted.'

'How bad's the contamination?'

'So far? Not too bad. Dirty room mostly.'

Swann rang off and he and Byrne went into the hotel. It was elegant and privately owned, boasting the historic patronage of Hemingway and Gertrude Stein. They spoke with the manager in his office behind reception.

'I know Monsieur Salvesen well,' the manager told them. 'He always stays here when he visits Paris.'

'On his own?'

'*Oui.*'

'The last time,' Swann asked him. 'On his own then?'

'*Oui.*'

'He went out to dinner. Did he come back on his own?'

The manager looked at him then out of partially down-cast eyes.

'You need to tell us,' Swann said. 'We're police officers, remember. This is an international investigation, and we have the backing of the French police.'

The manager twisted his mouth at the corners. 'I have to be careful. You understand?'

'We do understand. But it's important. Was he here on his own?'

The manager shook his head. 'He came back to the hotel with a girl the last time he was here. They went up to his room together. He tried to be discreet, but she was there in the morning when the cleaners went in.'

Swann looked closely at him. 'Would you know her if you saw her again?'

The manager shook his head. '*Moi? Non.* The cleaner. Perhaps, yes.'

'I'm getting a picture made,' Swann said, 'a drawing. When is this cleaner working?'

'Tomorrow morning.'

'I'll need to see her as soon as I have the picture. Can she make herself available?'

'I will see to it, monsieur.'

☆

Jakob Salvesen stared at the hole in the floor of his courtroom and his face began to boil.

'Get after him,' he bellowed. 'Get after him now. Kill him. Do you hear me? Kill him.'

Harrison could not hear him. He was scampering along the concrete pipe in darkness, unarmed, and men with guns were breathing down his neck. Soon he would hear shots, the sound would be deafening, the first man into the hole would loose off shots. He had to make the bend in the pipe before then or lie flat on his belly and pray. He heard the shot ring out, and lay down against the concrete, hands over his ears. He could see the bob of the flashlight behind him. Bullets zinged off the walls. And then the years rolled back, thirty long years, enough time to forget. He had forgotten, banished that time to the far reaches of memory.

Halfway through his second tour, still barely nineteen years old, the youngest Rat in the division. They were called out from Rocket City. A unit of grunts had been pinned down by tunnel fire deep in the Iron Triangle.

He went into the tunnel as point man, with Ray Marti-

524

nez behind him, and was lowered down the shaft in a Swiss saddle, with a flashlight and gun in his hands. He wasn't scared and looking back, maybe that's what should have worried him the most. Being lowered into a shaft was the most dangerous thing the point man could do, save come up through the trap door to change levels. Harrison wasn't bothered, he had his gun ready and he dropped, crouched and held his fire. He signalled above and set off at a crawl. The tunnel had been hit by shellfire and the earth was loose, damp and muddy. Behind him, Martinez was twenty feet back. Harrison would do the first two levels and then give up the point. He crawled low, holding the flashlight way above his head on a piece of bent wire.

He moved forward and stopped. Sixth sense. He hadn't even seen it: a punji stake mantrap, sharpened bamboo spikes pointing up at you from a pit in the tunnel floor. So far he had managed to avoid them; others had not been so lucky and ended up impaled on a dozen razor-sharp poles. He shone his light and recoiled. There were two black snakes intertwined in the spikes below him. He looked back to Martinez. 'Mantrap, Ray,' he hissed. 'Motherfucking snakes in it.'

Martinez hated snakes more than any of them. Harrison hated them, but it was how the spiders crawled on his back that really got to him.

'Johnny.' A voice soft and singsong, coming out of the darkness. 'Wanna fuck with me, Johnny.'

Harrison froze, the breath dying in his throat. Instantly, he shut off his flashlight. The voice, calling his name so close. It was not his name, they called them all Johnny. The underage hookers called them Johnny. But it *was* his name, his mom called him Johnny and his little sister. For a second, he was back on the big lake fishing the ice with his grandpa.

Martinez heard it too. Harrison looked back, trying to pick out his face in the darkness.

'Keep coming, Johnny.' Thin voice through the darkness. 'Keep coming, Johnny. I got something for you.'

It sounded almost American, but it was not. He knew it was not – it was VC: he had an AK47 and he knew these tunnels like the back of his hand. A fear gripped him then like he had never experienced; the darkness and the voice. He could not see. Shutting off the flashlight darkened the eyes, so sight for a while was impossible, globs of black and grey dancing before your pupils. He tightened the grip on his gun.

'I'm going to kill you, Johnny.'

He fired; one-two-three, a pause; four-five-six. He was empty. You never ever emptied your gun underground. Fire three, swap guns behind you and fire three more. The second man reloads. Harrison was out. The VC knew he was out. He threw himself flat against the earth and felt something damp crawl across his face. Behind him, Martinez opened the flashlight and fired three.

'Back up, JB. Back up now. We'll blow the fucking hole.'

Harrison crawled back beyond Martinez, dragging his useless pistol with him.

On the surface nobody said anything, but it did not matter. He knew and they knew. He sat on his own, smoking a Marlboro and staring blankly into the steaming vegetation. Another team went down the hole, crossed the punji stake mantrap and killed the VC. Then they blew the hole. That was his last mission. He was shipped out and went to Saigon and got drunk. It was there he got the tattoo, no longer a Tunnel Rat.

And now he was underground again, crawling for his life, fleeing the flashlights and the guns, tearing up that hole just as fast as he could. He was beyond the bend, the voice thin and cruel like a chill wind in his head. Memories from thirty years ago. They were coming for him; Jesse Tate's voice yelling out at him through the darkness. He just crawled and hoped, round the bend with only fifty yards to the culvert. Outside the culvert was daylight. Fear, tangible; he could smell it in his own sweat. He crawled on. Another deafening shot, the boom of Jesse's 454. The shell ricocheted off the concrete walls and he felt the rush of air by his head.

He made it to the culvert and fiddled frantically with the catch, the beam from the flashlight behind him. Head first, he dropped down into the drainage pipe and water splashed over his arms and his face. On hands and knees again, crawling through three inches of water, he could see the weakening day through the portal and felt the crisp air on his face. Outside, he straightened up, and sprinted a few yards away from the trees. He could already hear somebody at the exit. Behind him, the compound was in turmoil, every hand on the ranch scrambling into vehicles. Already two trucks were racing round the perimeter fence. A shot rang out, pinging off rock just to the left of him, and he knew the guard in the goon tower could see him.

He needed to move, get out of here, disappear into the boonies where they could not see him. But he had no cam' gear, no gilly suit. He was unarmed and they would pick him off like a duck sitting on water. The culvert. He got to it and hefted a large hunk of rock from the pile just at the edge. Here he was camouflaged from the goon tower by the trees, but the engines of the trucks drew closer. He stood above the culvert and waited. A hand extended from under the corrugated iron, a right hand, black gun gripped in it. Harrison felt blood rushing as he lifted the rock. Then he saw the back of Wingo's head.

'Motherfucker.' Harrison crashed the stone on to the

back of that skull and was instantly spattered with blood. Wingo died there and then. Harrison flared his nostrils and spat, then he grabbed the pistol and took off up the hill. The body would hold them for a little while at least.

☆

Salmons and Richards took the results of their swabbing and the PINS analysis, together with the X-rays, down to the incident control point. Major Hewitt had summoned the assistance of Webb and Cregan, given their knowledge of Storm Crow handiwork. Webb was already suited and an army truck drove into the Broadway and picked him up from Scotland Yard. He had seen the city quiet before, deserted even, but never like this. The night was around him and the clouds were low and steaming. Everything was as it should be: the height of the buildings, the road signs and the matt black of the tarmac. There was no bomb damage, no debris. Previously, when he had seen it so quiet, it was in the wake of St Mary Axe or Canary Wharf. But this quiet was different – ghostlike, a terrible, terrible emptiness.

The gathering in the underpass had grown larger. Cregan was on his way in from Shepherd's Bush where he and the other Expos had remained on standby. Hewitt, Salmons and Richards were already looking over the freshly developed X-ray pictures. Webb glanced at the scientists from Porton Down. They had the swab samples and the first results of the spectroscopy analysis that Richards had taken, and were working on persistency qualities there and then.

Hewitt had the pictures set out on the table, and the render safe team of Wilson and Johnson were looking at the passive infrared layout and wiring. Cregan sat down next to them. 'Like a wild woman's knitting,' he muttered. 'TPUs are the same, Webby.'

Webb nodded, and, feeling in his respirator bag, he produced one of the grey and black boxes they had recovered from Queen's House Mews a year ago. He pointed out the twin black plastic screw terminals and the light-emitting diode sitting between them. On the side was the ten-position decade switch and the Plastia LCD clock with the mini-alarm setting on the face.

'Two integrated circuits,' he said. 'Two transistors, miniature six-volt relay and PP3 battery connectors. Time delay – three minutes to ten days.' He looked through his mask at Wilson and rotated the thumbwheel on the digital decade switch through zero to nine. 'Pick how many days you want,' he said, 'then set the alarm. Simple. Trouble is, we don't know what it's set to.'

Wilson studied the circuitry in detail, trying to figure out where and how to disarm it safely when the time came. The X-ray images were not definitive, but they gave them sufficient data to formulate a plan. Time was against them already, and every second they spent here was precious. He could see the power supply was from four car batteries: the PP3 relay nowhere near sufficient for thirty-five mortars. Between the source and the TPUs was a secondary circuit linked to a mercury tilt switch. Wilson rasped breath through his mask. 'Bastard knows how to make things difficult, doesn't he.' If they got their render safe procedure just the slightest bit wrong and knocked that switch out of line, the mercury bubble would shift and complete the circuit. He shook his head and tried to follow the X-ray negatives with a rubber-gloved finger. The TPUs fed the detonators via the cluster of wiring that entered the wooden box through holes at the back.

'Booby traps we can do from the outside,' Johnson said. 'Look, Tug. See what I mean? There's no collapsing circuit.'

Wilson nodded. 'Needs to be at box level, though. We can't stand up.'

Next to him, Salmons was making drawings for them to take back upstairs. Wilson had to figure out which wire was which once they were inside the box.

'You might want to drill a little hole first, Tug,' Salmons suggested. 'Here, maybe.' He pointed to the front of the box about halfway down, low enough not to disturb the microswitches, but high enough to avoid the wiring and TPUs. 'Put a fibre-optic torch in, so you can see what you're doing.'

Wilson nodded, exhaling a short breath. 'We'll do the booby traps first,' he said. 'At least that way we can move around in there without having to crawl.'

'Buck-eye's still up there,' Salmons told him. 'Don't go any higher than the boom.'

Wilson looked once more at the X-rays. 'The pipes are half filled with liquid. What about PINS?'

Richards shook his head. 'I only had time to test four of them. We're still waiting for the results.'

'It's the same as Northumberland,' Webb said. 'You'll have two ounces of conical-shaped Semtex and an Iraco detonator in each piece of pipe.' He looked again at the pictures. 'You've also got secondary wiring in the bottom, just to be going on with.'

'Fuck it,' Wilson said and stood up. 'We could sit here all night. We'll get on with the booby traps.'

'We'll study the pictures for you, Tug,' Hewitt told him. 'See if we can work out an answer. When we do, we'll radio up.'

'We'll have to get the box open anyway,' Wilson said. 'I can't figure the wiring from these. I'll end up cutting the wrong ones. And I plan to live a bit longer.'

☆

Swann and Byrne had a late snack in the hotel. Mercier had called and told them that the E-fit man was finished at the restaurant, and the *maître d'* had been moaning at the lateness of the hour.

'You from Washington originally, Louis?' Swann asked Byrne as he pushed away his plate.

'Texas.'

'Never been there. Disneyland in LA once, with the kids, but that's my lot.'

'It's hot and dry and big,' Byrne said. 'I started in Dallas as a street agent, then did some tours overseas as assistant leg-att before going to headquarters.'

'You still got family down there – Texas, I mean?'

'Mom and Dad. My sister teaches politics at Berkeley.'

'Anyone else?'

Byrne looked away. 'Older brother. He's a helicopter pilot in the Navy. Apple of my daddy's eye. Always was, I guess.'

'Your sister younger than you?'

'Eleven months.' Byrne sipped more wine. 'She never let me forget that it wasn't even a year. Used to really piss me off. She always learned quicker than me, got dressed quicker, that kinda stuff. Funny the things that bother you as a kid.'

'You've done pretty well.'

'My old man hates the Feds. Blamed us for Waco.'

'Religious, is he?'

'Seventh Day Adventist.'

'Like the Branch Davidians?'

Byrne nodded.

'That must've been strange.'

'Oh, he didn't believe the stuff that Koresh was into. Was kinda funny, though. Him and me, I mean.' He toyed with a fork. 'What about you?'

531

'My dad was a copper like me. Retired now. Old school.'

'The Met?'

'Flying Squad. Sergeant under Slipper in the sixties.'

'Jack Slipper?'

'Yeah. He never stops talking about it. The Great Train Robbery was the best thing that ever happened to him.'

'At least you've got something in common.'

They moved through to the bar. Neither of them had any intention of sleeping and there was a plane back to Southampton at 6 a.m. 'A couple of the guys on the floor told me you and Webb like to climb,' Byrne said to him. Swann swirled the ice in his whisky.

'We do a bit, now and again.'

'Just rock, or snow and ice?'

'Both,' he said, holding his eye. 'I don't do so much snow and ice any more.'

☆

Jesse Tate came loping through the trees and Harrison ducked behind a rock, breathing hard. Drake followed Jesse and behind him Slusher and Tyler Oldfield. They all had rifles except Jesse, who carried his Casull in his right hand. He stopped and squinted into the fading sunlight. Harrison looked for more cover, higher up. Somehow he had to work his way back up to the saddle and cut a path to Dugger's Canyon. That was two draws back of here, with maybe fifty to a hundred yards between himself and his pursuers. He checked the clip in Wingo's gun, and tried to remember how many shots had been fired in the tunnel. Wingo, as the first man after him, would've fired them. But then he *had* heard the Casull. If he could just divert them long enough to get to his keep hide, he would have all the firepower he needed.

Jesse was some distance below him, but the hillside was

naked, scarred here and there at the top with late snow. Harrison needed cover. His heart beat faster and he could see Jesse and the others strung out in a line now, cutting their way across the lowest flanks of the hill. Looking back up, he followed the line of fir and aspen that crept up through the draw to the right of the saddle, some five hundred yards above.

He started to move again, crabbing his way up the hillside, then stopped. Another truck was rolling across the grass outside the compound. Jesse had stopped and was shouting something to Slusher. Harrison took the opportunity to get higher, climbing over boulders and rocks and pressing himself between the trees until they thinned. He was getting ahead of them and he looked back and saw Salvesen get out of the truck, carrying a rifle. There was no mistaking his bulk in outsize cam' gear. He handed something to Jesse. Then they went to the back of the truck and Harrison heard the barking of pit bulls.

☆

Wilson and Johnson climbed to the twenty-third floor. The early hours now. Outside, the moon pressed a sickle-shaped hole in the cloud. Johnson carried the drawings and the NVGs. The flat was still in darkness, and they could not risk switching on a light until at least the booby traps were taken out. There were four movement sensors in total, one in each corner of the room, all wired to one another and then down into the box. They laid the drawings on the floor and Wilson put an infrared torch to the paper. He traced the line of the sensors with his finger, muttering to himself through his respirator. There was so much wiring he could not be sure, so he stopped, checked himself and analysed it all over again. Johnson did the same and they compared. 'The four here,' Wilson said, 'and the other four there. Yes?' They spoke with their heads close together. Johnson thought it over again and then nodded.

'You sure?'

Johnson twisted his face round so their eyes met through the masks. 'I'm sure,' he said. 'Let's do it.'

Wilson traced the first set and worked his way very gently round to the back of the box. They had to snip the wires low down, for fear of setting off the sensor. 'Red?' he said.

'Yes.' They did not know the colours from the X-rays but the diagnostic team had told them red and green. Webb and Cregan confirmed it. Storm Crow configuration: every TPU man liked his own way of doing things, and the booby-trap wiring would be the same. 'They better be fucking right,' Wilson muttered, and felt in his jacket pocket for wire cutters. He had to prise the red wire so gently away from the green, in order to get the jaws round it. With mercury tilt switches in the box, he dare not jog against it. He cut the first wire, just a little snipping sound, barely audible through the weight of the masks. Sweat ran into the corners of his mouth, the pressure of the rubber making his forehead ache just above the bridge of his nose. His eyes seemed to be pulled down in their sockets. Between them, they disarmed the rest and finally were able to stand up.

Wilson could feel the moisture working over his body and he knew that when he finally got to shower, his skin would be black with charcoal. His palms were soaked and all he wanted to do was wipe them down on his thighs. He looked across at his colleague. 'You OK?'

'Yeah.'

'Call it in.'

Johnson squatted down on his haunches. 'Control from Johnson.'

'Go ahead.'

'The booby traps are neutralized. We're just left with the box.'

☆

Harrison got to the outcrop of rock and his highest observation point before the saddle. It was getting darker now, but he counted ten men coming up the hill after him, maybe a hundred yards away. Shots rang out and a slug zipped off the rocks by his feet. Jesse's pistol was good for two hundred yards, let alone the rifles. He needed to get to his cooler and his own guns. The pit bulls were tearing up the hillside after him. Harrison took Wingo's gun from his belt and worked a round into the chamber. The dogs were almost to him. Taking cover behind the rock, he gripped the pistol in both hands and aimed. He shot the first one in the chest. It yelped and spun and came down on its back. The second paused, looked at its mate and sniffed. Harrison shot it through the head. It gave him a certain amount of pleasure. They were Jesse Tate's dogs.

He scrambled to the saddle, ducked over the rise and then he was racing, stumbling down the other side and the adrenalin rush buzzed through his veins. Anger; taut, hard anger flaring inside him. No more fear. The odds were ten to one, so let them come. He knew exactly where he'd take them. He was still a mile from Dugger's Canyon and he needed the cover of the trees in the draw to keep their fire off him. He jumped over some rocks and lost his footing, tumbling head over heels, crashing through the sage and the bunch grass that crusted out of the loose snow, which was still clinging to the upper slopes of the hillside. Two minutes, maybe three and they would be on the rise and could take all the time they needed to sight and pick him off.

He would not lose now. He had lost before and he would not do so again. He thought of the gallows and the crazy light in Jakob Salvesen's eyes, and he fell into the trees as Jesse's tall frame appeared over the rise above him. Harrison was on his feet again, pushing himself up from the dirt. A startled black-tailed doe skittered away from him and crashed out into the open. He heard the crack of rifle fire, glanced left and saw the deer cartwheel in the snow.

The gulch dipped away from him now, down to the valley floor, then the next rise cloaked with thick douglas fir that would bring him to the lip of the canyon. He started running again, the breath sticking in his lungs, a firelike acid in his side. Shouting from above him. He looked back, but could not see them through the trees. He hit the gully floor and started to climb again, on a crude track that once upon a time had been a partial logging road. The saplings had become new trees, and he picked his way through the weight of them, then vaulted ancient stumps of fir, which the English had used to mast their ships.

He heard more shouting behind him – Salvesen's voice booming out across the expanse of the hillside. Then rifle fire and a branch split thirty feet in front of him. They had spread out: Salvesen in the middle, Slusher and Drake to his right, the others to the left of him, with Jesse way out on the flank. Harrison saw him feeding fresh 300-grain shells into his 454.

He climbed on, crested the rise and looked down through thick vegetation to the mud roof of Chief's hogan below him. From here, he could see the slim fissure of darkness backing into the clay that was the half caved in portal of the Magdalena mine. He smiled then. He had been in that mine before. Danny was proud of his past and delighted in taking him down. They should've had a gun that day, should've looked for tracks around the entrance, but they didn't. The cougar heard them long before they heard her. Fortunately, she gave them warning and they backed out slowly, then stood stock-still as she slunk into the cottonwoods. Harrison looked at the mine now and something stirred in his heart. Out here, he was chicken feed. Ten on one, the odds were stacked against him. But in there, the darkness of tunnels stretching over a mile into the hillside. The past grew up in his mind and he heard that VC's voice and a shiver ran through him again. But it remained his turf: he had crawled tunnels alone and killed with just a pistol.

He pushed his way down the slope, keeping off the track and hacking a path with his arms through the thickest layers of undergrowth. It was much darker now. Within five minutes, he was deep in the cottonwood trees and heard the sound of his pursuers above him. He scrabbled at the earth and ripped away the top layers of dirt, revealing the green lid of his cooler. His MP5, with its retractable stock and three clips of ammunition, was wrapped in black plastic. He slung it over his shoulder and reached for the flashlight, his Glock and his knife. His cheesewire garrotte he stuffed into the pocket of his shirt, and then he pulled on his cam' suit. The blood fizzed in his veins. He was back in Vietnam, contemplating the enemy, and the rush was building inside him. At the bottom of the box, he had four stun grenades, nine explosives in each. He slipped these into his breast pockets and spread cam' cream over his face. Then he crouched and waited. Somebody was moving close to him, a matter of yards away. He heard the crunching of twigs underfoot.

The sound moved closer and for a second Harrison thought he could be seen, but the vegetation was thickest here, which is why he had chosen the place for his hide.

Footsteps and breathing, laboured, somebody not used to such exertion. Tyler Oldfield, one of the Passover marshals, and he was holding an automatic rifle against his chest. Harrison heard the crackle of static and realized they had radio contact. Oldfield was ahead of him now and Harrison slowly rose. He could see the butt and barrel of the rifle poking out on either side. Three feet away. Harrison lifted one foot and pivoted, hunting knife in his hand.

'Can't see a damn thing,' Oldfield muttered. 'Everything's fucking green.'

Harrison slipped a hand over his mouth and rammed the knife to the hilt, up under his ribs. He twisted the blade sideways before pulling it out. The warmth of Oldfield's blood spilled over his fingers. His body went rigid, then slack and a little bubbled gasp escaped his lips. Harrison lowered him gently into the undergrowth. He bent over him before he died, looked into his eyes and lightly patted his cheek. Oldfield stared and stared, the terrible fear of sudden and violent death.

'You lose,' Harrison whispered.

For a moment he crouched like a lion on her kill, and tasted death on his lips. He felt nothing, no sensation, no emotion. Oldfield's headset crackled, and Harrison placed it over his own ears and listened.

'Tyler, you copy? Where is the sonofabitch?' Jesse Tate's voice.

Harrison looked through the clearing to Magdalena's portal. 'He's gone into the mine.'

He moved swiftly and ducked into the blackness. He could smell the water, probably still eighteen inches deep in some places with the last of the ice-melt. He could see Jesse now, moving towards the entrance from the trees. It was sand and clay around the edges, and the roof had dropped in some more. Jesse stepped towards it like someone walking on eggshells, gun extended in front of him. Harrison backed up and listened. He could hear Jesse talking to Salvesen. 'Tyler said he went into the mine.'

'Then go in after him. Slusher. Where you at?'

'Back of you.'

'Get down there with the others. Tyler, get down there. Tyler, you copy?'

Harrison straightened up. 'Copy,' he whispered.

Drake and Jesse hesitated at the portal and Harrison moved further into the drift, the darkness complete within a few feet of the entrance. He saw Salvesen step into the clearing by Chief's hogan, then Slusher behind him. He could shoot one of them here, but one was all he would get. He needed them deep in the mine.

Drake and Slusher looked at one another and Harrison dared them to come inside. The vein ran the length of the Bloodline drift, at an angle of thirty degrees, with adits coming off it in three separate places. The Duggers had opened new tunnels, packed them with wooden supports and cut fresh stopes for the ore. The drift ran for two hundred yards, with the Star Raise climbing to the top of the mountain, some fifty yards in from the portal. There the drift sloped down and gradually steepened, with the Widow-maker tunnel dropping from the shaft and heading back underneath it. The roof had never been good and three men that Danny knew of had died there.

'Tyler, you copy? Where the hell are you, Tyler?' Salvesen was talking into the radio.

Harrison moved back a further ten yards to where the drift bent to the left, and spoke very softly. 'Tyler's dead, Jake.'

Static and silence, and then Jesse's voice. 'He's got Tyler's radio.'

'Fucking A, asshole.'

Shots split the air, the savage boom of Jesse's 454 Casull. Harrison laughed at him. 'I'm still alive, motherfucker.'

He heard Salvesen's voice. 'I'm going back to the house, Jesse. Find him and kill him. Leave his body in the mine, but bring me the tattoo off his shoulder.'

Harrison felt a little cold then. Jakob Salvesen, good Christian boy that he was. He saw the bob of the first flashlight bounce off the rib walls and he thought very quickly. He wanted Salvesen alive, but he needed to change the odds first.

☆

Lisa Guffy had been phoning Harrison all day and kept getting his answerphone. She tried again halfway through the evening and got no reply, so she got her battered Subaru and drove over to the trailer park. His lights were on, the door was open and his '66 Chevy Rig parked where it normally was. She drove into town and checked Joe's club and the Silver Dollar, but nobody had seen him. She asked Tracey Farrow and Cody and Fathead, but none of them knew where he was. She drove back to Westlake and called into the hotel. Smitty and Junior were shooting a game of pool with Wayne O and Big Kevin. Patty was cocktail waitressing and Danny Dugger sat with Cecil from Galveston Bay, but none of them had seen him at all. She phoned Chief, who was at home with Belinda.

'I haven't seen him,' Chief told her. 'You checked the water holes?'

'All of them. I'm in the hotel right now.'

'Well, don't worry, honey. He's a big boy.'

'Don't patronize me, Chief. I am worried.'

'OK. OK. Drive by his trailer. I'll meet you there.'

Chief was there when she got back, looking at the open

540

Bible on the table, with a frown creasing his face. It was dark now and she could hear TexMex music coming from Tony's trailer next door. 'What's with this?' Chief asked her.

'I don't know. He's been looking at it ever since he went to Jake Salvesen's church.' She frowned then. 'He told me you got him into it. Something about being a Pentecostal.'

They knocked on Tony's door and he answered, a half-empty bottle of Cuervo in his hand.

'Hey, Chief. You wanna drink?'

'No thanks, Tony. We're looking for Harrison. You seen him?'

'*Amigo*, look at me.' Tony lurched against the door frame. 'I'm all fucked up, man. I don't see nothing.'

They left him and wandered over to Harrison's truck. 'I'm worried, Chief,' Lisa said. 'It's not like him to take off without his truck.'

'Pssst.' The sound came from behind them. 'Hey.' They looked through the gloom towards Tony's trailer and saw Little T's head poking out of the bedroom window.

'You should be asleep.' Chief walked over to him. 'What's up?'

'You looking for the Rat man?'

'Yeah. You seen him?'

Little T nodded. 'Three guys come and drive him away.'

'Which three guys?'

'The big one with the dogs. The one that whopped me.'

Chief stared at him. 'You sure about this?'

'I seen them. This afternoon.'

'OK. Go to sleep, and thanks.' Chief cuffed him about the head and turned to Lisa. 'Go home, honey. I'll handle this.'

'What d'you mean, go home?'

'What I say, girl. Stay home and lock your door. I'll come over when I can. Harrison's in trouble, and I gotta make a phone call.'

She went reluctantly, Chief promising to call her later. He got in his car and drove to the Passover marshal's office. Red Mayer, the oldest one of the team, was behind the desk.

'Hey, Chief. What's happening?'

'Need to ask you a question, Red.'

'What's that?'

'Where's the nearest FBI field office?'

Mayer stared at him. 'What d'you want with the Feds?'

'Oh, nothing much. Just need to know, is all.'

'You ain't starting any of that Indian shit, are ya, Chief. We got enough trouble in Idaho.'

Chief grinned. 'Red, those days are over.'

'I know about you, buddy. Wounded Knee and all that.'

'History, Red. But I do need to talk to the Feds.'

'You a narc, Chief?'

'Red, if I was a narc I'd know where they're at, now wouldn't I.'

'OK. Just kidding.' Mayer scratched his chin. 'It's Salt Lake, I think. They got a resident agent's office in Pocatello, but Salt Lake's the field office.'

'Thanks.' Chief turned to go.

'Anything I ought to know about, Chief? I am the law round here.'

Chief winked at him. 'Naw, just gotta check in, is all.'

He walked back out to his car, stopped at the payphone by the laundromat and called the field office in Salt Lake City.

'FBI,' the voice answered.

'I'm calling you from Passover, Idaho. I think your undercover agent's in trouble.'

542

At his cabin, Chief took his high-tension hunting bow from the wall and his quiver full of arrows.

☆

Yves Mercier called Swann at three o'clock in the morning and told him the E-fit was ready. Swann ordered a cab and they drove to Mercier's office.

'The picture looks pretty good,' he said. 'The waiter has an eye for the ladies.' He took a printed computer sheet from his drawer and slid it across the desk.

For a long time Swann stared at it, eyes bunched at the corners. 'That's Pia,' he said.

# 27

Wilson and Johnson were considering the box. It was almost thirteen hours now since they had received the initial call. Wilson was tired, aware of every breath, the bomb suit over the charcoal restricting every move he made; his arms felt like lead, hands heavy, the blood full in the veins. Johnson had the salt of his sweat in his eyes and he stared with his head cocked to one side. He touched the box with his shoulder, recoiled and reached for his Fuller's Earth. Wilson had a small hand-held drill ready and was adjusting the bit in the chuck.

'Drill a little hole,' he said, kneeling down and indicating the middle of the box with his fingertip. 'Put in a fibre-optic torch and take a look. We need to see how much time we have.' He handed Johnson the drill.

Four TPUs linked to thirty-five tubes of metal and thirty-five detonators pressed into shaped Semtex charges. God only knew the potency of what was in the liquid. Wilson thought about the blood vessels expanding and the pressure on the brain that the scientists from Porton Down had told him about. Not that it would matter to him. Semtex exploding at seven thousand metres per second, he would know nothing about the disaster that followed. He shook his head, trying to clear the thoughts and the heat from his face. He blinked hard and watched as Johnson drilled the hole for the fibre-optic probe.

Wilson concentrated on the box then: two microswitch booby traps, the first a flat button placed behind the flap of the hasp on the front. From his tool case, he took a set of feeler gauges and selected the thinnest sliver of metal. He opened it, pressed the others against his palm and lay flat with his eye close to the hasp. The respirator was in the way, jutting out from his chin to butt against the wood. Johnson was through the skin of the box with the drill and selected the slim flexible tube with the camera built into the end. The monitor was set up next to them, battery-fed and with the screen open like a lap-top computer. He inserted the torch. Wilson waited, watching, feeler gauge in his rubbered palm, as Johnson fiddled with the probe.

Down in the underpass, the rest of the explosives team, together with Webb and Cregan, waited.

'Putting in the torch,' Johnson's hollow voice crackled over the radio. 'Gently, gently.' Talking to himself now. Then silence.

Upstairs, Johnson stared wide-eyed at the monitor. 'Jesus Christ, Tug. We've got eleven minutes.'

'What?' Wilson shifted himself round and peered hard through his goggles. Johnson had the probe over the top of one of the TPUs where the clock and mini-alarm setting were displayed. The time showed 6:49 in red digits, the ten-day decade switch was at zero and the alarm set to 7:00.

In the underpass, Webb squirmed in his seat and lifted the radio from its housing. 'Command Control from incident control point.' Christine Harris patched him through.

'Colson, Webb. What's happening?'

'Got a fibre-optic torch in the box, sir. There's eleven minutes left on the timer.'

'Jesus Christ. Is that all?'

'That's all. The lid's not open yet and there's two microswitches to get by.'

Upstairs, Wilson had the feeler gauge and was feeding it behind the fixing hasp that kept the lid down. Johnson was totally impotent. He had secured the torch and watched as the minutes were ticking away from them. He flicked his gaze from Wilson's hand to the monitor and back again. His body was soaking, the sweat dribbling off him, throat so dry he could barely swallow. All he wanted to do was rip off his face mask and drink.

Wilson had the feeler gauge behind the hasp now and his tongue traced the line of his lips, as he manoeuvred the blade between the button microswitch and the slim piece of metal that held it. He made it, and pressed the switch harder against the plastic housing, keeping it down. Johnson moved now. From his pocket, he took a small pair of metal cutters and a roll of thin black DPM tape. He snipped the lock off and set the cutters on the floor, then gingerly lifted away the hasp. The hinges were stiff: he got it to a right angle and then changed position and lifted it till it was vertical. Wilson still kept the pressure on the feeler gauge, pressing the button in place. Johnson fiddled with the tape, unrolling a short stretch with difficulty – no dexterity in the cumbersome NBC gloves. He cut the strip and then placed it as tightly as he could across the metal gauge. Taking two shorter strips, he fixed those over the ends of the first piece.

'OK?' Wilson said.

'I think so.'

'You better be fucking sure.'

Johnson fixed a fourth piece of tape and then two more. Then he took the metal cutters and snipped the gauge off at the stem. Wilson no longer had pressure on it. The tape held.

'One,' Wilson said. 'How much time do we have?'

'Nine minutes.'

Now they had to deal with the other microswitch, which Boese had placed at the back. Wilson scanned the lid where it fitted to the rim of the box. Already, the release of the fixing hasp had allowed the tiniest of cracks to appear and weaken the pressure on the second microswitch. He looked at the other side of the box then.

'Oh fuck,' he said.

'What?' Johnson stared at him. 'What, Tug? What?'

'There's a third microswitch. Bastard set a third. We missed it on the X-ray.'

Johnson looked where his partner pointed and spied the final booby trap. 'We can do it,' he said. 'Same thing.'

'Feeler gauges won't be heavy enough.' Wilson took a deep breath. 'Not enough vertical pressure.' He glanced at his tool kit and the time fell away on the clock. 'Metal rule,' he said. 'We need two of them.'

'We'll have to do it in unison, one either side of the box.'

Wilson nodded, the collar of the NBC hood scratching at the skin of his neck. 'What about when we get the lid open? We'll both be holding rules. That's if we can slide them in in the first place.'

'We need a third body up here. Right now.' Johnson spoke into the radio.

'On my way.' Hewitt's voice in his ear.

☆

Swann was absolutely silent on the 6 a.m. flight from Orly to Southampton. He sat by the window, staring through the tiny porthole of glass at clouds that lay like rumpled smoke below them. Byrne shifted in the seat next to him. Swann was shell-shocked, the knot in his gut gnawing at him like stomach cramps. Pia was Joanne Taylor, and probably Brigitte Hammani. The irony was that it made a terrible sense. He now knew where the leak was in the Branch, the slippage of information that had bothered him right through this investigation; the loose tongue was his own.

Two days before they hit Queen's House Mews, he remembered, Pia had wanted to see him the following night and he said he was going to be busy.

'IRA?' she had asked.

'No. Somebody else.'

That was all she needed to know. Three words. He had let the odd thing slip during the investigation, you always did. Names weren't mentioned, but if it wasn't PIRA, then who was it? It didn't take a genius from where she was sitting. No wonder Boese kept so well ahead of the game. And Jakob Salvesen, the billionaire psycho from America. He must be one of her clients. International private banker, the perfect, perfect cover. Byrne's theory about the Storm Crow putting himself on the market, what better way to study it than with someone whose clients are the richest people in the world.

Byrne touched him lightly on the shoulder. 'How you doing, buddy?'

'What do you think?'

'Rough on you, huh.'

Swann shook his head. 'You know, I asked the girl to marry me the other day.'

'What did she say?'

'She said that if she could marry anyone, it'd be me. But she couldn't get married. Now I know why.' He stared at the seatback in front of him and another thought struck him. 'Nobody delivered that feather to my flat, Louis. It was there all the time.'

Swann had phoned the command control unit from Orly Airport and spoken to DI Clements. Clements told him what was happening in the City.

'Listen, Guv,' Swann said. 'Any chance of a chopper from Southampton? I've found Joanne Taylor.'

'You've done what?'

'I know who she is. I need to speak to Colson and Garrod as soon as I get back.'

'I'll sort something out for you, Jack.'

The helicopter was waiting for them after they cleared customs. Forty-five minutes later, they landed on Shepherd's Bush common and Swann took Byrne to one side. 'Not a word, Louis – to anyone. Not till I've spoken to the senior officers.'

'Whatever you say, Jack. This is your deal.'

Garrod and Colson were listening to the reports coming back from the render safe team, when Swann and Byrne climbed the stairs to the operations room. Clements tapped Swann on the shoulder.

'Old man's free, Jack.'

'You better hear this too, Guv.'

The four of them sat down. Garrod pressed his glasses higher up the bridge of his nose and looked at him. 'The DI says you've identified Joanne Taylor.'

'Yes, sir. I have.' He paused. 'Byrne thinks she's also Brigitte Hammani.'

'So tell us, Jack. Who is she?'

Swann let go a short breath and looked from one to the other of them. 'There was a leak from the department, sir. Not intentional and it was minor, but there was a leak.'

Garrod frowned at him. 'Go on.'

'Me, sir.'

'You?' Clements stared at him. 'What're you on about, Jack?'

'Joanne Taylor is Pia Grava, my girlfriend.'

Garrod stared at him for a moment. 'You better explain,' he said.

'The Sunday night before we raided Queen's House Mews, she asked if she could see me the following night. I said, no, because we were going to be busy. She asked me if it was the IRA and I said, "No. Somebody else." That's all I told her, but it was all she needed to know. She's seen me after SO19 raids before. She knows the drill, roughly the timing, etc. All she had to do was tip off Boese.'

'What happened in Paris?' Colson asked him.

'I found out that Jake Salvesen had dinner with a girl with short dark hair. She'd had dinner with him before. The waiter from the restaurant gave an E-fit description to Yves Mercier's man.' He unfolded it and then took the photo of Pia he carried with him from his wallet, and laid them both on the desk.

'I went back to the waiter, sir, and showed him this picture. He ID'd her straight away, and so did a cleaner from the hotel where Salvesen was staying. Pia and Salvesen spent the night together.'

For a moment, nobody said anything. Swann looked at the floor between his feet. 'But how the hell does she know Salvesen?' Colson asked, staring at the pictures.

'He's her client. He must be. She's an international private banker with Luxembourg Directe.' Swann sat forward. 'Think about it, sir. Louis Byrne told us the Storm Crow was in it for the money. He actively marketed himself. What better way to do it than have a private banker in your pocket. She's got access to the richest individuals in the world.' He made an openhanded gesture. 'The rest of it fits – the way she looks, her age. So she wore a blonde wig and changed the colour of her eyes with contact lenses. She told me she was half Israeli and half Italian. Her parents are both dead, but she's got good clients in Israel. Storm Crow plucked her out of that situation in Tel Aviv and has used her ever since.'

He sat back then, falling silent. Three grave faces stared at him. 'I knew there'd been a leak. I just didn't think it was me.'

'Forget about that, Jack,' Colson told him. 'What d'you want to do now?'

'Do a covert on her office while the cordons are in. Check out her dealings with Salvesen. Everything in the UK has been paid for by international money order or cashing accounts at banks. I think by starting with Salvesen, I can trace it through one of the discretionary trusts she'll run for him. That's how she does her business, sir, acting for clients as a trustee through Bermuda or the Cayman Islands.' He thought for a moment. 'I know her mobile phone number. I want to get the subscriber info' and see who she's called.'

'Cairns?'

'And Ingram, maybe. If those numbers are there, then we've got her and both of them.'

'OK, Jack. You'll have to suit up.'

'Where's Webb?'

'Still in the City with Phil Cregan and the ATOs. They wanted his input on the TPUs.'

Swann stood up. 'Can I take Tania Briggs? She's as good a burglar as Webb.'

'Take whoever you want.'

Outside, Louis Byrne was waiting for him. He laid a hand on his shoulder. 'I know you're feeling like shit because you got fucked over, Jack. But don't blame yourself for anything else.'

Swann looked at him out of the corner of his eye. 'I'm not.'

☆

Harrison was six hundred yards into the hill now, on the downward sweep of the Bloodline, Heckler & Koch MP5 slung over one shoulder. Way back up the drift, he could see the approach of flashlights. He had killed Wingo and he had killed Tyler Oldfield. It occurred to him then that if the tapes had worked, he didn't need any of them alive. That both thrilled and chilled him in the same moment. To kill again in war; one on one, and down here under the earth, where last time he'd got it wrong. He could smell the dry heat of the tunnels, his own sweat and the stench of rotting rice.

The flashlights came nearer and he squatted on the floor with his gun across his knees, his own flashlight extinguished and clipped on his belt. The mine was damp. He was lucky it wasn't still frozen. Behind him was the shaft to the oldest, meanest tunnel under the mountain. Devil's Breath, the very lowest drift where two stopes had been split by a pillar of rock. The stopes had hardly been worked because a combination of silicon dust and methane gas had forced the men out. Harrison was going to get at least one of them down there. That was his way out. At the back of the Devil's Breath shaft was a patch of inky black water. Danny Dugger had shown him late last summer. There, the tunnel roof dipped to the surface, so the tunnel looked blocked. Danny had dived in, no warning, not removing his clothes – just upped and dove. Harrison had stared at the water, waiting for him to come up, but he didn't. In the end, he panicked and went in after him. The water was freezing and so black you could see nothing. He had come up after a few frantic moments of searching and found Danny shining a light on his face. They were the other side of the rock wall. Heaven's Gate, Danny told him; a natural rising shaft with a rope cable and a two-foot hole at the top of the mountain.

Jesse's men moved cautiously, given away by their

flashlights. Harrison squatted cross-legged and waited like the VietCong he used to hunt, the damp running off the rib walls behind him. An entry team of three, that meant others to follow and guards placed at the portal. He could no longer hear them talking over the radio, so he discarded the headset. They moved in a line, one behind the other. He could not tell who was in front but the beams from their flashlights played over the walls and refracted in water that spilled down the sides. Harrison rose and went deeper.

They still had not got as far as the Widow-maker shaft and Harrison was almost at the twin stopes on his right that contained the Doghouse, a sealed room where men went to protect themselves against sudden leakage of gas or a roof fall. The lights moved again and they split up as he hoped they would. Star Raise climbed above their heads and the iron rung ladder was still good. Harrison could see one man make his way up by the bobbing of his flashlight. A second peeled off left into the forked drift which followed the adit vein, and that left just one in the Bloodline. Harrison knew that within a few paces he would come to the Widow-maker. He watched him from his hiding place close to the stope wall and saw the light disappear.

At the ladder he shouldered his MP5. He didn't use the flashlight, feeling his way to the rungs. Whoever was down there was using his light and Harrison would see him long before he was seen. He climbed down carefully, silently, with the stealth he had learned in Cu-Chi. He could hear nothing, see nothing. He climbed lower and lower and dropped off the last rung on to the tunnel floor. He could see the flashlight bobbing ahead of him now, and he started down the tunnel towards it. Closer and closer, soft-soled boots making no sound on the rock floor. The light bobbed again. He heard somebody cough and then the trickle of dust and rock from above. The light was turned on the ceiling and Harrison stopped. From somewhere high above them, he heard the dull boom of gunshot. Somebody up there was spooked.

Now the light came back towards him much more quickly; whoever it was had also heard the shot and was heading for the raise. Harrison stood about ten paces outside the beam and pulled the pin from a stun grenade. The hairs lifted on the back of his neck and the smell of loose soil and human sweat stood out in his nostrils. He tossed the grenade up the tunnel.

He heard the scream as it went off. Slusher. Nine explosions in about twelve seconds, none of them fatal, but smoke and fire and a noise that boomed and echoed in the enclosed space of the tunnel. Harrison watched as he hopped and jumped and bounced off the walls, the grenade spitting at his feet like a firecracker. Then Slusher realized he was all right and started firing indiscriminately. Harrison leaned against the shallow stope wall and lifted the MP5. He saw Jakob Salvesen's face, hate in his eyes and the thin set of his mouth. He saw the silent faces gathered in the mock courtroom and felt the anger rise in his chest. Slusher stopped firing and picked up his fallen flashlight.

'Hey, Slusher,' Harrison called. 'Switch the damn light off.'

The light died instantly. Harrison pressed the torch on the end of his gun barrel and Slusher was framed in its sights. He shot him three times.

☆

Wilson and Johnson squatted in their own sweat, either side of the wooden box that housed the four timing and power units. Major Hewitt was at that moment climbing the stairs to get to them and they had seven minutes on the clock. They worked simultaneously, so, so slowly. The lid had to remain pressed low enough to keep the micro-switches down. Wilson looked sideways at his partner, twisting his head so he could see him properly through the eyeholes in his respirator. 'We've got to do this at exactly the same time, same speed, everything. If we don't, it's over.'

'I know.' Johnson was breathing hard. Wilson looked over his shoulder then, as Hewitt moved between them.

'Microswitches.' Wilson nodded to the drawings spread out on the floor. 'Bastard placed a third one. Got the one on the hasp, these two we need to do at the same time. He's set them right at the back. We're going to slide metal rules under the rim of the box and over the switches to keep them down. Then you open the box. We can maybe secure the switches with tape, but it takes time.' He glanced at the clock registering on the monitor. 'And we don't have much of that.'

Hewitt nodded and watched as the two warrant officers slid the rules under the lid, one hand on the rule, free hands used to keep the lid steady. The slightest judder could bounce it just a fraction and a fraction was all the booby traps needed.

'He is one nasty fucking bastard.' Wilson felt the pain in his eyes and cursed the suit and the mask and this job all over again. He watched Johnson's hands. Johnson watched his, as they worked the metal rules under the top of the box, like slicing open an envelope between them. Hewitt kept his hands off the lid, kneeling, breathing hard through the mask. He rested his hands on his thighs; tool kit by his side. Under six minutes now; he could feel the tension in his bowels.

Wilson reached the corner of the box first and waited. Johnson was with him and they glanced at one another, then eased the rules right up to the microswitches. Both paused a millimetre or so away from the depressed switch itself. Now they had to slide the rule over the switch while easing the pressure a little on the lid.

'You two OK?' Hewitt's voice was higher pitched than he would've liked. Wilson nodded, glanced at Johnson who also nodded. They began to ease the rules on to the switches, keeping the pressure down, forcing the blades up and over each switch. Wilson's stuck and he knew he was going to have to raise the lid a fraction more.

'Stuck,' he muttered.

'I'm there.'

Wilson nodded, heart in his mouth, and eased the pressure on the lid. He felt the switch give a tiny bit and his eyes balled, then the rule was in place and he pressed it home for all he was worth. 'Got it,' he said. 'OK, you can lift the lid.'

Hewitt used both hands, being careful not to catch any wires. He eased it up and back and it locked itself on a chain by the hinge. Still he held it, glancing from Johnson to Wilson and then back at the box. He saw four grey and black plastic boxes, all with liquid-crystal display clocks mounted on them and the ten-day decade switches. The switches were all at zero. The alarm clocks were set to go off at 7:00 and 6:55 was now displayed on each face. He saw that each TPU was separately armed with a mercury tilt switch. He checked the wiring, the configuration of the circuitry, and decided that the tilt switches were not for additional safety arming, but booby traps. Once those last five minutes had ticked down, the device *would* go off. Four car batteries feeding the power. Dual integrated circuits on each TPU, red and green wiring. The wires were tied together, then attached with feeders to the separate detonator wiring and fed out through the back of the box. Four and a half minutes.

Both Wilson and Johnson, still holding the rules over

the microswitches, stared into the mass of wiring, battery and circuitry. 'Batteries booby-trapped?' Johnson said.

Hewitt had his head bent, peering closely at them. You could not tell just by looking at them. They might have false bottoms, with separate Semtex charges rolled flat and taped inside. He could see now that they were armed with collapsing circuits, again not definitively evident from the X-rays. If he moved them or cut the wires, they could set the charges off. He looked at the wiring running from the batteries to the TPUs, then at the wiring going from the TPUs to the scaffolding pipes. Under four minutes and four of them to disarm.

Hewitt looked again at the batteries. The wires were finished by a little metal O-ring and screwed into the terminal heads. 'I'll have to disconnect them at source,' he said, and reached behind him for his tool kit. Selecting a screwdriver, he eased it over the lead terminal and gently fitted it into the screw head. There were eight in all and three and a half minutes on the clock. He finished the first one, prised it away and twisted the wire back over itself. Then he worked on the second. All the time, Johnson and Wilson held their rules in place and watched him. Hewitt gripped his tongue between his teeth and finished number two. Six to go, three minutes left.

Sweat rolled off him. For a moment, his mask was so restricting he could not breathe and had to think about the depth of each breath. His hand wavered and the head of the screwdriver lost the thread and slithered across the terminal.

'Keep it going, sir. You're doing great.' Wilson was helpless, both hands on the rule, keeping the balance and pressure down on the microswitch. Hewitt worked on. Two batteries free now, wires twisted away with no power running to the TPU. Two minutes on the clock. He worked on, again losing the connection between screwdriver and head. He swore under his breath, caught the screw head again and twisted. Three done and only one to go. A minute on the clock. He was soaking inside the suit. He started on the last battery. Johnson stared at his black rubber hands. The first screw was rusty and old and the screw driver slipped yet again.

'Fuck it.' Hewitt set it once more, twisted and it gave. He sighed, and both Wilson and Johnson heard the long wheezy breath through the respirator. The clock ticked down. First screw out, thirty seconds left. All at once Hewitt was weary, his eyelids were heavy: he blinked hard to see straight, turning his head to one side. The final screw; fitting the head in and turning; turning, turning. Loose, the clock ticking down, only seconds to go. The screw came free and the red digital display died on the face of the final clock.

Wilson let go the rule and rocked back on his heels, punching his fist in the air. He slapped his commanding officer on the back and hugged Johnson. 'Oh, Jesus,' he said. 'Thank you, fucking God.'

Hewitt was grinning like a Cheshire cat. 'That was closer than I would've liked.' He looked at the pipes. 'And we've still got thirty-five dets to render safe.' He pressed the transmitter button on his radio.

'Incident control point from Hewitt.'

'Go ahead, sir.'

'IED neutralized. Repeat IED is neutralized. You can tell the scientists to come up.'

☆

Harrison moved back to the ladder. The stun grenades would bring down part of the ceiling. He could already feel the trembling in the earth. They wouldn't need to drag Slusher out to bury him. His mind was cold now, no anger, no rage, just a chilled calculation: ten men had been hunting him and three of them were dead. He climbed back to the Bloodline. Caution when he reached the top; he might meet Jesse or Drake. He paused just before he reached floor level, keeping his head well down. Suddenly a shot rang out and he felt the bullet zing past his shoulder. He ducked, then flipped himself up and rolled along the floor of the tunnel. Another shot and another, bullets bouncing off the stone all around him. He couldn't tell where they were coming from and he pressed himself up against the ribs. Breathing hard now, the adrenalin suddenly high, he peered into the gloom.

It had to be Jesse: he must've got to the top of the shaft before him and sound had given him away. That made Jesse good. Drake he could take as he had taken Slusher and Wingo, but Jesse was a soldier by profession. The mines would not faze him. He sat against the damp wall and listened. He had trained himself to listen to the minutest sound underground, when all about you was darkness. Water dripped, rolling off the walls with the sound of a loose faucet. He did not move, breathed in silence, clutching the carbine across his lap. Then he heard it, the faintest of noises, somebody moving towards him. Backing away, he raised the carbine. He knew that was Jesse Tate out there and there was only one place he could take him.

☆

Swann and Tania Briggs were driven down past the common at Shepherd's Bush and along Holland Park Avenue. London was deserted. After the hubbub of the command control point the streets of the capital were like a ghost town. Swann felt a stone in the pit of his stomach. He was constricted in full NBC gear, rubber-encased fingers resting in his lap. The overboots were laced tight and cumbersome over his shoes. Already he could feel the perspiration trickling into his groin. Next to him Tania sat in silence, the second time she had been 'suited and booted' because of Ismael Boese. She thought back to the workshop at Healey Hall Farm: Bruno Kuhlmann's naked and bloated corpse, the blood in his eyes from the pressure that had built up in his brain. She could see again the way he clutched that length of scaffolding pipe, a silent omen of what was to come. She glanced at Swann, not being able to see his eyes, as he sat with his face towards the floor. 'You OK, Jack?' Her voice was muffled, strange in her ears, like on tape. Swann lifted his head. 'You really sure about this?'

'She was ID'd twice, Tania.'

Tania looked away again. 'I don't understand it.'

'I'm looking for a few answers myself.'

They were driven through Notting Hill and on to Bayswater, where the buildings were large and expensive. Earlier that morning a group of looters had smashed premises in Kensington High Street, followed by a second group in Oxford Street. The line had been broken a handful of times, but the army presence was massive and the looters were spotted from the air and picked up.

The United States Embassy, spread eagle on the roof, was silent and grey and empty. Even the grass in the park seemed to have stopped growing. The truck drove round the square and pulled up outside Luxembourg Directe. Swann had been here many times, met in the hall by the frock-coated commissionaire then escorted up three flights of stairs to Pia Grava's office. Pia, the dark-haired beauty he had met at Jimmy Pierce's leaving do. Since then a fixture in his life, the woman he talked to, shared a bed with, the woman he told all his fears.

Tania stood on the pavement with her tool bag. 'You want me to do a window or the door?' she asked.

'Better be the door.'

'Alarm?'

'Let it ring.'

'I can probably shut it off from inside.'

'Let's just get on with it, Tania.'

He sat on the kerbside, craving a cigarette, and listened to the silence of the streets. A few minutes later, he heard the bell start ringing and looked round. Tania was standing there with her arm wide and the oak front door standing open. Swann got up, and they went into the marble-floored hallway.

'Jesus, what a place,' Tania said.

'Loads of them like this round here. Some are permanently empty.' Swann stood with one hand on the bottom of the banister and looked up.

'Sort the alarm if you can. It'd be nice if they don't know that we've been here.'

'I can turn it off, but not reset it.'

'That'll do. Third floor, when you're done.'

He climbed the steps on his own, rubber boots making a soft sort of squelching sound on the stone. He took in everything he saw, as if he was seeing it for the first and last time: the pictures of some Luxembourg dignitaries, the wall covering, the velvet curtains on each of the landing windows. On the third floor he paused outside the suite of offices and caught his breath. It was not that warm a day, but the heat in the suit was stifling. Inside, he saw her desk, the smooth-polished wood and the high-backed leather chair. At that moment, he thought of her sitting in Amersham, glued to the news like everyone else in the country, the children playing on the floor or reading upstairs somewhere. Thank God Caroline was there. He had not spoken to Pia since he got back from Paris. He would have to play a part for a while.

He sat in her chair and looked at the silent computer screen. Her desk diary lay on the leather-bordered blotter, and he began flicking through the pages. Paris, he noted the entry a few weeks ago. It didn't say who she was seeing. He looked further back and found an entry which said Nevada. Then one for New York and one more for Baltimore. Nowhere was Salvesen's name mentioned.

He sat where he was for a moment and thought. He could not access her computer without some technical people to get over the password, but there must be paper files. They had evacuated as quickly as everyone else and he doubted they would have shipped much paper. The filing cabinet was locked, but it only took him a few minutes to pick it and he slid the drawers open. He shuffled through the papers, looking for a file under S, but found nothing. Then he saw one marked 'BVI trusts'. He slipped it from its holder and set it on the table. Tania appeared in the doorway and Swann jumped. He had not even heard the alarm stop ringing.

'Find anything?' she asked him.

'Still looking.' He opened the file and began to turn the pages. He didn't understand much of it, trustees and bankers and companies all over the place. Then he found what he was looking for and lifted the single sheet of paper. A letter from Jakob Salvesen, thanking Pia for the property investments she had made on his behalf and confirming a meeting in Paris.

He switched on the photocopier and as it warmed up he selected more correspondence, stuff from Bermuda and the Cayman Islands, money shifting here, there and everywhere. He noted some cash transactions, one of them for £18,200. It rang a bell and he looked at it more closely. Just a note on a sheet of paper, handwritten in pencil. Then he realized, it was the full six months' rent on the property in Queen's House Mews. He photocopied everything in the file and replaced it in exactly the order he found it. Tania did the copying while he passed her the sheets and collected the fresh ones. When they were done, he closed the drawer and it locked.

He tried the top drawer of her desk. It was locked. He watched while Tania picked it. She was so much better than he was; had a good tutor in Webb. She stood back then while Swann looked through the drawers. Everything was typically Pia: orderly, in its rightful place, barely a crease in any of the pages. He found a bundle of cellphone bills all clipped together. Maybe he would not have to request subscriber information after all. One by one he went through them and Tania copied the ones he selected. He scanned the numbers, but none stood out. There were a lot of international calls; a lot of calls to mobiles. He copied them all and replaced them in the drawer.

☆

Chief watched Salvesen walk away from the entrance to Magdalena with a hunting rifle in his hand. Another armed man was with him, two more seemed to be guarding the portal. Chief eased back the bowstring and set an arrow in place. He had parked the car on the dirt road and hiked the rest of the way. Despite his size he was an Indian, and had forgotten none of his ancestors' silence. He moved up to the saddle, skirting his prey in a circle. He would let them get only as far as the top. He moved more quickly now; they were making a lot of noise and were talking. At the saddle, he settled himself behind a rock and waited. It was dark, but the moon was high and the two men stood out clearly against the skyline. Chief rose up from behind the rock like some great black shadow and levelled his bow at Salvesen's chest.

'Stand still,' he said.

The other man lifted his gun and Chief shot him

through the chest. He grunted and stumbled back, the gun clattering away from him. He lifted both hands, then fell to his knees, before toppling on to his belly. Salvesen shot Chief in the left shoulder. Chief felt it shatter and gasped. He dropped his bow, staggered but did not fall. His left arm hung limply at his side and he looked at the blood spilling in a dark swathe over his jacket. His eyes dimmed, then focused and then he thinned them to all but nothing and stared at Jake Salvesen. And then he began to snarl, starting low in his chest, rising in pitch until it exploded in a roar like a grizzly. He took two loping strides. Salvesen raised the gun and fired a second time. The gun jammed, spat flame, and he dropped it. Chief was in his face, four inches taller. He reached out with his right hand and gripped Salvesen round the throat. For a moment he tensed, looked in his eyes and then lifted him clear off the ground. He held him, one-handed, a two-hundred-pound man with his feet flailing beneath him.

Chief was squeezing the life out of him. Salvesen's eyes bulged red in their sockets and then Chief dropped him. Salvesen crashed to the ground with a cry. Chief stepped over him, grabbed him by his hair and dragged him through scrub and rock and finally threw him against a boulder. Quivering now, he bent for the dead man's gun and cocked it, one-handed. Salvesen was breathing hard, holding his hands to his throat. Chief held the gun at waist height, then dropped to a sitting position, all the strength gone out of him.

☆

In the EOD lorry, Webb listened to Major Hewitt and momentarily closed his eyes. He picked up the radio to Colson. 'IED is neutralized, sir.'

'I heard, George. It's bloody excellent news.'

'Is Swann there?'

'No, he's up at Grosvenor Square.'

'Is he. What for?'

'I'll tell you when you get back. But we've found Brigitte Hammani.'

Together with the men from Porton Down, Webb went upstairs and found the EOD operators carefully dismantling the pipes. 'We decided to take out all the explosives here,' Hewitt told the duty officer from Porton Down. 'I want this fully rendered safe before we leave.'

'That might disturb the solution.'

'I don't think so. The inner seal looked pretty stable in the X-ray pictures. I think it's best. Then the pipes are all yours.'

'OK.'

They took apart the bottom seal on the pipes and withdrew the detonators first. Each one had its wires clipped and then twisted together and set to one side. Then the Semtex was scraped out. Webb organized it all into separate nylon evidence bags. The Porton Down men were busy with the dirty room.

At the BBC building in White City, the Antiterrorist Branch were in high spirits. Garrod sat smiling at his desk and Colson took a bottle of whisky from his bag and poured them each a large measure.

'Give a shot to the boys and girls, Bill,' Garrod told him. 'They deserve it.' He picked up the phone and dialled the direct line to the Prime Minister.

'John Garrod, sir,' he said. 'The bomb is rendered safe.'

'Excellent, Commander. That is wonderful news. Congratulations.'

'Under a minute to spare,' Garrod went on. 'The EOD operators did a brilliant job.'

'I'm sure they did. Please pass on my appreciation to their commanding officer. I shall speak to him myself as soon as I get the chance. When can we get back to normal?'

'Now, sir. IED's safe. The Porton Down men are conducting their tests, but so far there's been all but negative contamination.'

'Oh, that's wonderful news. Well done, Mr Garrod. The nation can be proud of you.'

'They're taking the explosives out of each tube now, sir. Should take about half an hour. Then we'll airlift the pipes to Porton Down for analysis. You can bring the people back.'

Garrod hung up and went out into the other room. The team were in uproar. Colson had dished out the Scotch and everyone was backslapping and hugging one another. Louis Byrne shook hands with them all and everyone wanted to kiss Cheyenne. Only Swann sat on his own, reading through some papers. Colson went over and handed him a drink.

'Jack?'

'Sir.' Swann looked up.

'Are you OK?'

'Fine.' He held up a sheet of paper. 'Record of Pia Grava's mobile phone calls,' he said. He pointed to one he had marked with a highlighter pen. 'That's Tommy Cairns' mobile. And there's this number too, 0385 902754. I've tried it, but it's switched off.'

Colson looked him in the eye then and laid a hand on his shoulder. 'I'm sorry, Jack,' he said.

'Yes, sir. So am I.'

☆

Harrison backed up the tunnel, keeping his gun high, careful where he placed his feet. Gunfire, ripping through his ears, the muzzle flash half blinding him. He dropped to one knee and returned fire. 'Missed me again, Jesse,' he yelled.

Jesse shot into the darkness again. Harrison was flat on the floor now and the shell pinged off the walls. He was at the lip of the shaft leading down to the Devil's Breath. He slung the carbine across his chest and gripped the iron rungs of the ladder. Now he was descending, quickly, aware of his heartbeat, the gun bouncing against his ribs. Above him, he saw the sudden beam of a flashlight. Instinctively, he fired, then dropped to the floor, squatted and turned 180 degrees. He could not smell gas in the air. He was glad: if Jesse started shooting in air contaminated by methane, he would kill the both of them.

He moved up the tunnel, one hundred feet, two half-cut stopes and the water. Beyond it, Heaven's Gate and the surface. He heard Jesse coming after him, his breathing slightly heavy now. Harrison wondered if he had hit him. He was using the flashlight intermittently, to get a handle on the path ahead and move on. Again he heard the thin voice of that VC calling out his name. Again in his mind he loosed off six shots instead of three, and bit down on his lip. He was almost to the water and he knelt against the tunnel wall. Jesse moved towards him. Harrison could not see him. All at once the flashlight was in his eyes and shots rang out. He leapt back and spun, lost his grip on the MP5 and rolled over backwards. He came to rest with one foot in the water. Jesse was still firing, round after round into the darkness. Harrison had both hands over his ears and slipped into the water. The shock nearly stopped his heart, freezing the blood in his veins. He almost surfaced again, but then he dived, kicked with his feet, three, four times – and then he surfaced. He was on the other side of the wall and he pulled himself out directly below the shaft that lifted to the top of the hillside.

On the other side of the rock, Jesse shone his light into the black of the water and frowned. The roof dipped right to the surface here, effectively the end of the tunnel. All that looked back was the reflected beam of the flashlight. He bent and studied the water line on the floor, but he could tell nothing from it. Harrison was gone. Standing, he thought for a moment, then, shining his flashlight back along the tunnel, he spotted the fallen MP5. He muttered something to himself and turned back to the water. Again he shone his flashlight, then levelled his Casull and fired six rounds into the darkness.

On the other side of the wall, Harrison heard the sudden muffled thuds. Six shots. He knew what Jesse was doing. Slowly he stood up, shook himself down and unclipped the flashlight from his belt. He took his Glock, worked the mechanism and then he slipped back into the water. This time he did not feel the cold, his mind was sharp and clear and he dived beneath the surface, brushing the top of his head against the underside of the roof. He swam deep, then breathed on the other side. All was blackness. He could hear Jesse retreating along the tunnel. He glided to the edge of the water and lifted himself gently so he was resting his arms and chest on the floor, the rest of him still in the water. Glock in his right hand now, flashlight in his left. He sucked a breath, flicked on the flashlight and framed Jesse in the sudden pool of light. Jesse half turned and Harrison drew his lips over his gums.

'Lights out, motherfucker.' He fired three times. Jesse buckled, dropped the pistol and fell against the wall. Momentarily he looked back, eyes pinched in the light that played over his face. Then he slipped down the wall and his head lolled to one side.

Harrison dragged himself back into the tunnel and crouched, still shining the beam over Jesse's fallen body. He stood up and walked towards him, aware of a tingling sensation; partly the cold and partly the exorcism of the past in his veins.

'Three shots, Johnny,' he whispered to himself. 'Just the three shots.'

Jesse was dead, slumped there on the floor. Harrison was desperately cold. Drake was back there somewhere, but he was suddenly tired of killing. He turned back to the water and dived beneath the surface. This time he came up spluttering, hauled himself out and immediately started up the incline, pulling on the tattered rope cable, feet slipping and sliding on the grease of the wall. He came out on the top of the hill and heard himself whistling 'Dixie'.

Chief heard Harrison as he sat on the ground at the top of the saddle, the rifle still pointed at Salvesen. He could feel himself getting weaker and he watched the sky for helicopters. The Feds ought to be here by now. He looked across the rise to the pinnacle of the hill and saw the small figure framed against the skyline. He moved the gun towards him.

Harrison shook himself and slapped his arms. Then he took the flashlight from his belt and played it across the hill to get his bearings. He didn't recognize where he was and then he saw Chief pointing a gun at him.

'Jesus Christ. Chief?'

'Yo.' Chief's voice was low and weary. Harrison sprinted across the hillside to get to him. He saw the blood seeping through Chief's jacket.

'What the fuck happened?'

Chief said nothing, but waggled the rifle at the boulder across from him. Harrison shone the torch into Salvesen's eyes.

For a moment, he forgot he was a law-enforcement officer. This man had tried to hang him, would've succeeded, had it on video tape even. Video tape. He smiled suddenly then. It didn't matter if the T-17 had failed him. He turned to Chief again.

'You OK, buddy? We need to get you down.'

'I'm OK. Bleeding's stopped, I think. Your friends should be on their way.'

'Friends?'

Chief shook his head at him then. 'Harrison, I knew you were FBI a long time ago. Don't you know I can smell 'em?' His breathing grew suddenly heavier. 'Little T saw Tate come get you. I figured the shit was hitting the fan, so I called your buddies in Salt Lake. Fuck, they're taking their time.' His head lolled again, then he looked up. 'Found that cooler of yours last year. You walked right by me one night in the rain.'

Harrison stared at him for a moment, then he saw the dead man from Salvesen's compound with an arrow broken under him. Chief looked slantedly at him. 'Figured you needed some help.' He breathed heavily again. 'What happened down there, anyways?'

Harrison glanced at Salvesen. 'Oh, nothing much. Wingo's dead. Oldfield's dead. Slusher's dead.' He paused then. 'Oh, and I put Jesse's lights out too.' He took the gun from his belt. In the distance he could hear a helicopter approaching. He walked over to where Salvesen was sitting. 'It's all on video tape, Jake. Vanity, it always gets you in the end.'

Salvesen stared at him then, beaten about the eyes. Harrison looked him over. 'Unhurt, huh? That was remiss of me.' He bent to his haunches and glanced at Chief. 'Can you walk, buddy?'

As if in answer, Chief got to his feet. Harrison nodded, then looked back at Salvesen. 'Seems like the situation's changed, Jake.'

Salvesen did not reply.

'Thing of it is, I don't need you alive. I got your camera

footage and my own audio tape.' He pressed his face in close then. 'You see, I wired up your courtroom.'

Salvesen licked white spittle from the line of his lip.

'Tell you what though, eh – we could make us a deal. You tell me how you knew I was out here and I'll just arrest you.'

'You think I'm gonna tell you anything?'

Harrison sighed and looked back at Chief for a second. 'Don't tempt me, Jake,' he said. 'I killed four men already today, a fifth ain't gonna make no difference.' He threw out a hand. 'I mean just look at this mess. We got your buddy lying dead there and Chief with a great big hole in him. Fuck, alls I gotta do is shoot you and the party's complete.' He unwound his wire garrotte from his pocket and flexed it in front of Salvesen's face. Then he moved behind him and slipped it round his throat. He pulled it tight, not enough to cut him, but almost. Salvesen stiffened, lifting his chin suddenly high.

'Now tell me, Jake. Who was it that burned me?'

'You can go to hell.'

Harrison looked at Chief who still rocked on his heels. 'Shoot him for me, buddy. Would you?'

'Pleasure.' Chief aimed the rifle, one-handed.

'OK.' Salvesen choked on the word. 'I got a visit from a fella down in Hagerman. John Henry Mackey.'

Harrison tweaked the garrotte that little bit tighter. 'And how come he knew?'

'He got a phone call.'

'From who?'

'I don't know.'

'Chief.'

'No. Wait.' Salvesen lifted his hands. 'The call came from the Storm Crow.'

# 28

George Webb dressed again after decontamination and felt the fresh air on his face. He could not help but smile. The city had been so silent, so incredibly still and now the people were streaming back in their droves. No sooner had the helicopter taken off for Porton Down, loaded with the sealed scaffolding pipes, than the Prime Minister went on television before flying to Rome for an EU summit meeting, and the City reopened. Effectively one day's trading had been lost; but the economic effects had still reverberated round the world. SO13 moved back to the Yard and Colson called a briefing. Webb met Tania and she told him about Swann's discovery in Paris. Webb found him talking on the telephone to his kids. He put the phone down, let go a sigh and placed both hands on the back of his head.

'You OK, mate?' Webb asked him.

Swann flared his nostrils. 'I got stitched up, Webby. It's how Boese stayed ahead of the game.'

'Pia.'

Swann nodded. 'Joanne Taylor, and Byrne thinks she's Brigitte Hammani too. Jakob Salvesen is one of her clients.'

'She's in banking. Could be just a coincidence.'

'No.' Swann showed him the cellphone bills. 'Made one mistake,' he said. 'She phoned Tommy Cairns from her mobile.'

Webb sat on the edge of the desk and studied the sheet of paper. 'Where is she now?'

'Your place still, with the kids.'

'She know anything?'

'No. The DSU's getting a warrant. We're going to nick her as soon as she's back in the office.'

Clements came in then and gestured to them. 'Meeting upstairs, lads.'

Colson stood at the front of the conference room with a smile on his face. 'All I can say is a big thank you to everyone,' he said. At the back of the room a mobile phone sounded and Louis Byrne got up and went outside. Colson turned to Webb and Christine Harris.

'I want to thank you two particularly for manning the ops room and spending so long in those suits. George, a special thanks for your input with 11 EOD.' He looked round and spotted Phil Cregan, sitting with his arms folded by the window. 'And you, Phil.' He paused again. 'The scaffolding pipes are at Porton Down right now. We should have some form of analysis soon.'

The door opened then and Byrne came back into the room. 'Jakob Salvesen's been arrested,' he said. 'He's being held in the Blaine County jail in Idaho.' He told them what the leg-att had just told him, Harrison's ordeal, the video tapes and the book of Revelation. 'I'm sorry,' he said. 'But we've got our fair share of psychos back home. US-funded terrorism on UK soil. I'm sorry.'

'Louis,' Webb said. 'We've had US-funded terrorism on UK soil for years.'

Colson stood up again. 'Stranger than fiction,' he muttered. 'But then most terrorism has its basis in land or religion, or both for that matter. Anyway, there's been a few other developments while the army were busy in the city. The Action 2000 crew are still in custody, and we've got enough evidence to put the Cairns brothers away. I'm not so sure about James Ingram – he's saying nothing. It'll depend on what Cairns says when he realizes he's going to be gone for a while.' He paused then and rubbed his lip with a thumbnail. 'Boese, Tal-Salem and Pier-Luigi Ramas are still at large. But at least we stopped them. There is something else, though.' He looked at Swann then. 'Do you want to tell them, Jack?'

Swann sucked at his teeth. 'Joanne Taylor,' he said. 'Possibly alias Brigitte Hammani. I found her in Paris. She's living right here in London, working as an international private banker. Her name is Pia Grava.'

Everyone stared at him; some of them knew, some of them did not. The silence was total save the buzz of the computers next door. Swann looked at the floor.

'The reason Boese stayed ahead of the game was probably down to me.' He stood up then. 'There I was squawking about leaks and moles and stuff and it was me all the time.' He flapped his arm at his side. 'You have my apologies.'

'I need to make something clear,' Colson said. 'Jack did not – I repeat, did not – leak any sensitive information. We all know what it's like with our partners, they guess most of what's going on. Pia or Brigitte Hammani, as we think she is, really wanted to know – so anything Jack muttered, she seized upon. They've been together for eighteen months now and nobody can blame him.' He looked at Swann then. 'You're an excellent copper, Jack. And nobody will ever blame you. If it wasn't for your initial vigilance we'd never have latched on to Boese.'

Swann looked between his feet. 'Anyway,' he said, 'we're scooping her up as soon as she gets back to her desk.' He looked back at Colson. 'I want to be there, sir.'

'Are you sure?'

'Positive.'

'OK. But you can't interview her, Jack. Someone else will have to do that.'

Swann stared at him.

'You know I can't allow it. Personal involvement.'

'I'm going to want to speak to her at some point.'

'Nobody said you couldn't, just not in an interview.' He looked at Louis Byrne. 'I guess you'll have a few questions to ask her too.'

☆

Pia brought the children back to Swann's flat. She took him in her arms and he held her, nothing showing on his face, but breaking to pieces inside. She kissed him again and again. 'I'm so glad you're all right, Jack. So glad.'

Outside, the streets were teeming with people, London back to normal, as if nothing whatever had happened. As Swann was trying to keep his demeanour and body language easy, the doorbell sounded. Charlotte stuck her head out of the window and squealed with delight. 'Daddy, Mummy's here.'

Rachael came upstairs. She looked weary, smiled at Pia, then took Swann to one side.

'Can I take them home with me?'

'For now or for good?'

She looked at him then. 'I've got my last few bits next month, but my parents are coming down from Suffolk.'

Swann forced the lump down in his throat. 'I've had them almost a year, Rachael.'

'I know. It's longer than I imagined, Jack. I'm sorry.'

'I'm not. I want to keep them.'

Twisted silence. She looked him in the eye and he looked away. Pia was making the girls laugh in the living room.

'Jack, you're not going to start fighting me for them, are you?' Rachael said. 'Please tell me you're not.'

Swann bit his lip. 'I don't want to lose them.'

'You won't lose them. We'll just go back to how it was.' She touched his arm. 'Please don't fight me, Jack. You've got Pia. Your lives can get back to normal.'

Swann looked right through her, not seeing anything. 'I won't fight you,' he said.

☆

Harrison sat in Jakob Salvesen's office with Bob Jackson and Max Scheller. Chief was in the Westlake Memorial Hospital having his shoulder repaired. Harrison had just left him. Stony-faced, the three of them watched the video tape from Salvesen's mock courtroom. Earlier, Harrison had shown them the armoury and gallows, and FBI agents were swarming all over the compound. The county sheriff had instructed the Fire and Rescue Service, under the guidance of Danny Dugger, to recover Tate's and Slusher's bodies from the Magdalena mine. Wingo's had been brought in already, as had Tyler Oldfield's, and the man Chief had shot. Salvesen was in custody. The rest of those who'd been in the 'common law' courtroom were taken by the FBI Hostage Rescue Team.

Jackson's face was thin and drawn as he watched Salvesen's rhetoric. Harrison said nothing, just sat in his chair with an ankle across his knee and smoked. The tape got to the bit where he threw the chair and disappeared underground. He got up and switched off the TV, then stood with his back to the set.

'Un-fucking-believable,' Scheller said.

'Wanted to do it for a long time.' Harrison crushed his cigarette against the hearth. 'They've bragged about it on the web sites. Posse wanted to do it years ago. Somebody'll try again.'

Scheller looked at him with admiration in his eyes. 'You got four of them, Johnny.'

Harrison made a face. 'I got burned, Max.'

Scheller was silent. Next to him Jackson was silent. 'The deal worked out, JB,' Scheller said. 'Scotland Yard disabled the bomb and we've got Jake Salvesen in custody.' He nodded to the video tape. 'Put this on the six o'clock news and the Bureau's image will catapult.' He looked at Jackson. 'What do you think, Bob?'

Jackson nodded. 'Kinda evens things up after Waco and Ruby Ridge.'

'Somebody burned my fucking ass.' Harrison's voice started low and rose as he ground out the words. 'Somebody on the inside.' He looked from one to the other of them. 'Who had access to the product?'

Jackson dragged fingers over his face. 'Fucking everyone, John. There's us here, the back-up team in Salt Lake. Then there's D.C. You got the Domestic Terrorism Ops Unit, that's what forty guys from unit chief down. You got the lab technicians and the Analytical Unit, that's another forty.' He made a hopeless gesture with his hands. 'Then you got the leg-att, the FEST and Scotland fucking Yard.'

Harrison kicked his toe against the hearth. 'Drive me back to my trailer, Max. I need to get my stuff.'

They left Jackson at the compound with the rest of the team and Scheller drove him into town. Harrison hadn't phoned Guffy or anybody else. His cover was blown and everyone in Passover would know that he had lied to them for all but two years. He sat silently in the car, window rolled down, a cigarette between his blackened fingers.

'What about the Indian?' Scheller said.

'What about him?'

'Maybe it was him.'

'You kidding me, Max? Chief got Salvesen for us.'

Scheller made a face. 'I heard he was at Wounded Knee with Banks and Means.'

'We fucked up at Wounded Knee, Max. You know it as well as I do.' He flicked ash out of the window. 'Anyway, why would Chief wanna burn me?'

'He called us out.'

'Which clears him.'

'Does it?' Scheller made a face. 'People do weird things, John.'

'Listen.' Harrison grabbed a handful of Scheller's jacket. 'He got shot for his trouble.'

'Hey.' Scheller shook off his grip. 'You're the one with a hair up your ass.'

Scheller drove him into town, slowly, twenty-five-mile-an-hour speed limit. Most people were home from work. Joe's club was busy, as was the Silver Dollar. FBI agents were everywhere and you could smell the tension and distrust in the air. They were almost at Joe's club when Harrison said: 'Drop me off here, Max.'

Scheller looked at him. 'Forget it, JB. Just get your gear and get out. There's nothing for you here.'

'Stop the fucking car.'

Scheller shook his head and pulled over. Harrison opened the door and climbed out. He caught a glimpse of his features in the door mirror, a blackened mark on the side of his head where the filth of the mine still stuck. He'd yet to take a shower or change his clothes.

Scheller drove off and Harrison stood for a moment outside the laundromat. Two other agents were watching from a parked sedan across the street. Harrison took another cigarette and flipped his Zippo, then he crossed the side street and walked into the Silver Dollar. The conversation dribbled to nothing. Harrison stood in the doorway, the cigarette clamped so hard between his teeth he almost bit through it. Everyone was there: Danny sitting at the far end of the bar, Monty, Cecil from Galveston Bay, Randy Miller and Sandy; Junior and Smitty, Wayne Olson, Colin, Kevin; Greg Gibson standing next to them, with Chris Shea and Mike and Billy. Fathead held a can of Coors in his hand. Cody was sitting with Terri, and Tracey Farrow and his brothers looked across the bar at him. Right at the far end, with Tracy, sat Lisa Guffy.

Harrison made his way towards her and the men parted in front of him. Charlie Love stared at him, but when Harrison caught his eye he looked away. Nobody looked him in the eye and nobody said anything. 'Guffy,' he said quietly. She looked up, narrowed her eyes and then slapped him hard across the face. She did not say anything, lips compressed to white, her whole body shaking. Harrison took it, didn't flinch, eyes not wavering from hers.

'Guffy,' he said again.

'Get-out-of-my-face.'

He stepped back and turned to the bar. Vicki folded her arms. 'Gimme a Bud, Vicki.' She nodded to the sign above her head: 'We reserve the right to refuse service to anyone.'

Harrison bunched his lips, sucked on his cigarette and crushed it under his thumbnail. He turned then, walked through the people who used to be his friends and stepped outside. Across the road in Joe's club, the crowd on the stoop stared at him. From his jeans pocket he took a pinch of chew and placed it under his lip. He sucked and spat, then walked down to his trailer.

Inside, he threw his clothes into a suitcase and grabbed a beer from the fridge. Scheller sat on the couch and watched him. 'Fucked you over, huh?'

Harrison looked at him. 'Nobody fucked me over, Max.

It was the other way round.' He picked up the keys to his truck. 'See you in Salt Lake.'

Outside, he threw his case into the back of the truck and got in. He fired her up, clanked in reverse and backed out. Little T stared at him from the stoop of his trailer. Harrison turned the truck round and drove down to the entrance. Danny Dugger stood in the middle of the road; a slight, hunched figure with his hands in his jeans pockets, jacket zipped up to the neck. Harrison stopped the truck in front of him. Danny looked left and right and moved over to the driver's door. Harrison rolled the window down. Danny sniffed, wiped his moustache with his fingers, then looked up out of clear blue eyes. He offered his right hand and Harrison clasped it firmly. 'Good luck,' Danny said, then turned and walked away.

Harrison drove the hour and a half to Hagerman in the southern part of the state. Down by the Snake River Dam, in a sun-filled valley surrounded by flat-topped bluffs. Farming country, flatter and hotter than Passover. He parked the truck outside the Angler bar and stepped inside. It was dark and cool and a number of men sat at the rail watching basketball on the TV. Two Mexicans shot a game of pool, one with a pockmarked face and a straw cowboy hat. He squinted briefly at Harrison, who walked the length of the bar, his gun hidden in the waistband of his jeans, and set himself on a vinyl-topped stool. The bartender served him a beer and a shot of Jagermeister, which he downed in one. She handed him his change.

'John Mackey drink here?' he asked her.

'John Henry? Ever' night.'

'What time?'

'Pretty soon. You a friend of his?'

'Kinda. Do me a favour, hon'. Would you? When he gets here, let me know.'

She drew up her face. 'You're his friend and you don't know what he looks like?'

'Only spoke on the telephone.'

She went to serve somebody else. Harrison lit a cigarette and nursed his beer for a half-hour or so. He could still feel Guffy's palm on his face. No more than he expected. But for a while there, you hoped they would understand. But how could they, when he'd told them a bunch of lies for two solid years. It was bitter though and the feeling of loss was intense. Ironic really. He'd got back a piece of himself stolen in the tunnels of Cu-Chi, almost thirty years ago; and yet in doing so, he had lost everything else. UCA, he told himself. Never a-fucking-gain.

Mackey came in at seven-thirty. The bartender was as good as her word and pointed him out to Harrison. He was a surly-looking big man, with black hair and a dusty red baseball hat. He bought a bottle of Bud and started talking to the man on the bar stool next to him. Harrison listened in.

'Fucking FBI busted Jake Salvesen,' Mackey was saying. 'Sonofabitch Feds. Can't leave a man alone.'

Harrison smiled to himself and drank. A few minutes later, Mackey slid off his bar stool and hitched up his pants, then he made his way to the men's room at the back of the bar. Harrison followed him. There were only two rest rooms – men's and women's – one pan in each, with no separate urinal. Harrison glanced back to the bar, then jerked open the men's room door. Mackey jumped, dick in his hand, and sprayed piss all over the cistern. Harrison closed the door and leaned on it.

'What the fuck – you goddamn fucking faggot.'

'Shut up.' Harrison pulled the Glock from his waistband and Mackey's mouth fell open. His piss dried up and he stood there holding his dick, with his pants around his ankles. Harrison worked a round into the breech, then very deliberately he pointed the gun at Mackey's privates.

'Who the fuck are you?'

Harrison pulled his shield from his shirt pocket and flapped it under his nose. 'I'm a sonofabitch Fed.' He stepped right up to him then and pressed the gun against the soft flesh at the base of Mackey's throat. 'You told Jake Salvesen that I was watching his compound. That really pissed me off.' Mackey's eyes were balling now and he was backed up against the wall. 'I wanna know exactly how you knew.'

☆

Swann and Clements drove along Upper Grosvenor Street and parked on double yellow lines. McCulloch and Tania Briggs pulled up behind them in the second car, placed the Met warrant book on the dashboard and got out. Swann stood on the pavement and tugged at the cuffs of his suit. He could feel the knot in his gut and the loneliness was just about unbearable. This morning, he had taken the girls to school himself. This afternoon, their mother would collect them and they would go home with her. McCulloch looked across the roof of the car at him.

'Jack, you don't have to do this. Why don't you fuck off and get drunk?'

Swann shook his head. 'I do have to do it, Macca. But thanks all the same.'

Inside, Bailey, the commissionaire, looked up, saw Swann and smiled. 'Mr Swann,' he said. 'How are you?'

'Just fine, Harry. Is Pia in?'

'I'll buzz her for you.'

Swann shook his head, laying a hand across Bailey's arm. 'Official, Harry. We'll make our own way up.'

He led the way; wide stone stairs spiralling up to the third floor. Clements walked alongside him, with Tania and McCulloch behind. Swann was aware of the sound of his footsteps, exactly how many he took before they met with the carpeted landing. He paused, glanced at the others, then opened the door to Pia's office. Debbie, her secretary, was sitting at her desk, with Pia across from her on the telephone. Her eyes lit up when she saw Swann and then darkened again as the others followed him in.

'Hi, Jack,' Debbie said. 'I didn't know you were here.'

Swann did not say anything. He stood to one side and looked at Pia. He had never seen her looking so beautiful. She put the phone down and stood up. Tania moved across the room to her, with Clements and McCulloch.

'Jack,' Pia said. 'What's going on?'

Clements showed her his warrant card. 'Brigitte Hammani,' he said. Pia flinched, the shock standing out in her eyes. Swann looked away: for a moment he had still hoped, but the recoil, the recognition there in her face. He wondered how long it had been since anyone had called her that. 'I'm Detective Inspector Clements,' the DI went on, 'Antiterrorist Branch. I have a warrant for your arrest.'

Pia sat down, opened her mouth and then closed it again. She looked across at Swann and he looked right back. Tania moved to her side of the desk. 'Stand up, please,' she said. Pia didn't move. She was still staring at Swann, something broken up in her eyes. 'Stand up,' Tania repeated, and this time Pia did get up. Debbie was still sitting in her chair, staring open-mouthed.

Paul Ellis, the banking director, walked across the landing and Swann moved out into the hall. From the corner of his eye, he could see Tania putting handcuffs on the woman he had slept with for the past eighteen months.

'Jack,' Ellis said. 'What the hell's going on?'

'Pia's under arrest, Paul. Conspiracy to cause explosions.'

Ellis stared at him. 'What're you talking about? She's a banker.'

'No, she's not. She's a terrorist.'

Clements sat one side of her, with Tania Briggs on the other. McCulloch drove the DI's car and Swann drove on his own. They took her straight to Paddington Green where Webb and the FBI team were waiting. She was stripped and searched and given a paper suit to wear and then she was locked in a cell. Swann went over the road for a drink. He sat on his own, chain-smoking. The barman polished glasses. Swann looked at his watch and thought about his children. Rachael would be picking them up pretty soon and tonight he would be in the flat on his own. His hand shook as he lit yet another cigarette, then he felt somebody behind him and looked round at George Webb.

'Guinness,' Webb said to the barman and sat down next to him. He sighed heavily. 'I don't know what to say, Jack.'

'Don't worry. I don't either.'

'I haven't told Caroline yet.'

'No?'

'I'll tell her tonight.'

'What's happening over the road?'

'Getting ready to interview her.'

'Who's doing it?'

'Clements and Louis Byrne.'

'Has she asked for a lawyer?'

'Not yet.'

Swann drank the last of his beer. 'I want to watch,' he said.

He was sitting in the anteroom, looking through the two-way mirror as Pia was brought in. Brigitte, her name was Brigitte. He must stop thinking of her as Pia. Byrne and Clements were already there and both of them got up as she was brought to the table. She looked very small in the oversized paper suit and Swann could see from her eyes that she had been crying. She looked long and hard at the mirror as if she knew he was there.

'This is a preliminary interview,' Clements told her, 'and we won't be taping it. If you want legal representation at this stage, you're entitled to it.'

They had taken everything from her desk, and established that on the occasions Joanne Taylor was active, Pia was not in the office.

She sat now, mouselike almost, with her hands in her lap. 'Do you want a solicitor present?' Clements asked her.

She shook her head. 'Can I smoke please?'

Swann watched as Clements took a packet of cigarettes from his pocket and gave them to her. She lit one with wavering hands and puffed nervously towards the ceiling.

'I want to talk to Jack Swann,' she said.

Clements shook his head. 'You need to talk to us first.'

Byrne leaned across the table then. 'My name's Louis Byrne,' he said. 'I'm a supervisory special agent with the FBI, International Terrorism Operations Unit. You *are* Brigitte Hammani, aren't you?'

Pia was staring at him, a strange light in her eyes, as if she were unsure of something.

'Yes,' she said, 'I am.'

Swann could see the tension slip from Clements's shoulders as he realized that he was going to get the information he wanted. There was a resignation about the set of her body, something like relief almost. Swann frowned and rested his chin on his fist.

'I was in Israel in 1989,' Byrne said. 'Tell me about the

fourth of July, when Welford-Jennings's car was attacked.'

Again she stared at him.

'Said Rabi,' he went on. 'Yasser Arafat's Fatah. Rabi was out on a limb. So, I believe, were you.'

She looked at the floor then and drew fiercely on the cigarette.

'Storm Crow,' Clements said. 'Ismael Boese.'

She looked up again.

'You know the name?'

'I never knew names.'

'But you did work with the terrorist known as the Storm Crow.'

'Yes.'

'What did you do exactly?'

'I co-ordinated things for him.'

'Why?'

'Because I had to.' She looked at Byrne then. 'You were in Tel Aviv?'

'Not on the fourth. I was in Athens, working with the legal attaché. I was dispatched to Tel Aviv from there.' He sat further forward in his chair. 'What happened afterwards?'

She looked beyond them both then and straight into Jack Swann's eyes. 'Said got killed. I never saw it. We ran, he one way, me another.' She paused and lit another cigarette. 'I didn't go to my flat. The Fatah were deciding whether to punish Said for things he had said. I was his girlfriend, they might look for me too.' She sucked hard on the cigarette, drawing her cheeks into hollows. Swann was listening intently.

Byrne shifted in his seat. 'What happened?'

'I went to the home of a friend. I stayed two days, then went to Bethlehem to a small hotel I know.'

'And?'

'Somebody telephoned me. Said he was a friend. He told me that Said had been working for him.' She frowned then. 'I didn't understand. I thought he was Mossad or maybe Fatah looking for a betrayal. Said never said anything about working for anyone else. He wanted to prove his worth to Arafat.'

Clements pushed the ashtray closer to her. Her hands were shaking and ash was spilling on to the table. 'Go on,' Byrne said. 'What happened then?'

'I listened. I was frightened, but what could I do? This man knew exactly where I was and how I had got there. He told me to listen to the television news and then he would call me back. I did watch the news and they said the attack on the American was claimed by the Storm Crow. I had never heard of him.' She paused again. 'He called me back. He told me he had a passport and plane tickets.'

'And did he?'

She nodded. 'The tickets came three days later. There was money and an Israeli passport with my picture in it. It said I was a banker.'

'Where did you go?'

'Italy first. A hotel was provided for me and then I received another call. This time I had to go to London. When I got there, I was to check into a guesthouse and wait till he contacted me again.' She made a face. 'Money was provided for food and lodging and clothes. Good clothes. I received another phone call and another passport. Italian this time; the name was Pia Grava. He told me that my parents were dead and that I was half Jewish and half Italian. He told me to find work. He also told me that the Fatah, the Israeli Secret Service and the FBI were looking for me. If I did as I was told and worked well, then he would keep me safe. But if I didn't, he would give me up to whoever caught me first.'

'He owned your life,' Clements said.

She nodded. 'From then until now.'

'What happened – how did you get into the bank?'

'I'm not stupid. I studied hard in the Middle East. But he sent me documents for qualifications that I did not have and I got a job with a bank. They put me on a management training programme and I went to college in England and then in the United States. I gained a degree in economics and then an MBA. He told me exactly what he wanted from me. I needed to get work with one of the private banking facilities. He didn't tell me why, but he said, with my background, my looks and my qualifications, I could make it work.' She shrugged her shoulders. 'I did make it work. Ask Jack Swann. I earned a lot of money.'

'But he owned your life,' Byrne said quietly.

She looked down again, stubbed out the cigarette and reached for another. 'He owned me, yes. I had to do what he told me, although sometimes he would not contact me for months. It was always the same though, he reminded me that he watched me always and with one phone call I would be visited by Mossad or the Palestinians.'

'So he effectively blackmailed you,' Clements said. 'For nearly ten years.'

'Yes.'

Byrne sat back and crossed his legs. Swann watched from behind the mirror. 'What do you know about him?'

'Nothing. Only what he does.'

'D'you have any Mexican clients?'

She looked at him strangely again. 'I don't personally, but the bank does, yes.'

'Who?'

'Roberon Manuel Ortega, for one.'

'Ortega banks with you?'

'In Bermuda.' She smiled then. 'The bank haven't got a clue what he really does.'

Byrne looked at Clements. 'The Ortega Querrer cartel,' he said. 'Fort Bliss.'

He looked back at Pia once more. 'Jakob Salvesen. He was your client?'

'The biggest.' She drew harshly again on the cigarette. 'The Storm Crow wanted Salvesen. I didn't know what he knew about him but I was instructed to get him as a client.'

'How did you do that?'

'First of all the Storm Crow attacked a bank in Bilbao and then killed a man called Alessandro Peroni in Paris. He was a European currency adviser. Storm Crow had researched Salvesen and knew he was concerned about the United States of Europe and the rise of the Antichrist. He was mad, of course, but convincing. Storm Crow committed those two acts to put himself on the market. I then made sure I was invited to the same parties Salvesen was. That's how the business works. In order to get the job in the first place, I had to convince Paul Ellis that I could bring people to him. I had a false background and Storm Crow gave me targets to get, so I got them.'

'How did you do that?' Clements asked her.

'How do you think, Inspector?'

Swann looked at the space between his feet and shook his head. The door opened behind him and Webb came in with Logan. She laid a hand on his shoulder.

In the interview room, Clements was speaking. 'So he used you to get to wealthy clients, clients who might have work for him. Is that it?'

She nodded.

'Ortega?' Byrne asked her. 'The drug-runner?'

'Not directly through me but yes, the same principle.'

'And Salvesen?'

'Definitely Salvesen.'

'How much did Salvesen pay?' Clements asked her.

She crushed out her cigarette. 'Ten million dollars.'

Both Byrne and Clements watched her. 'You arranged it?' Byrne asked.

'Yes I did. It was paid in cash.'

'How?'

'Salvesen gave it to me, then I took it to a dead drop and left it.'

'Where?'

'The Virginia City overlook in Nevada.'

Pia sat back then and looked through the glass at Swann. 'You know something,' she said. 'I'm glad you caught me. I was sick and tired of this. I'd rather spend the rest of my life in prison than be party to any more. Who caught me – Jack?'

Clements nodded.

'Paris, was it? He told me he was going to Paris.'

'You had a meeting with Salvesen.'

She nodded.

'You used Swann to get information for Storm Crow. Is that right?' Byrne asked her.

She nodded. 'He needed insurance. He always does. There's always a policeman or government official some-where. Jack didn't know I was doing it.'

'He chose Swann specifically?' Clements asked.

'Yes.'

'Why?'

'Because he was just divorced, a bit fragile, and Storm Crow knew he had a weakness.'

'Weakness?' Byrne said.

'Yes. In 1993, Jack killed his climbing partner in the Himalayas. He's never got over it.'

Swann felt the hairs rise on his cheeks. He got up,

pushed past Webb and went out into the corridor. He left Paddington Green and caught a tube train home. When he got there, he locked the door and sat in his living room with a bottle of beer and a cigarette. He felt as though somebody had taken hold of him by the scruff of the neck, shovelled out all that he was, then dumped it on the pavement for everyone to look at. The flat was empty, the children gone, and Pia Grava was Brigitte Hammani, a terrorist. The Storm Crow had singled out his life and ruined it. Boese's face, the first time they had met, stuck in his mind like an open wound.

But something still nagged at him. Boese had not been in Israel in 1989, or if he had they didn't know about it. But Boese had been in Queen's House Mews. Boese had been in Northumberland, and in Liddesdale Tower. What Pia had just described was the most cynical, systematic piece of planning he had ever heard. And the bottom line was profit. Somebody, somewhere, was pulling the strings and it was not Ismael Boese.

☆

Harrison was in Salt Lake City, at the FBI field office with Bob Jackson, his supervisor. Tom Kovalski was due in from D.C. later that morning. Harrison sat at a desk and leafed through the information he had gathered from the Strategic Intelligence Operations Center in D.C. He wanted to know exactly who had had access to his product, he wanted all the names and he made no bones about why.

'JB, Kovalski isn't gonna thank you for this,' Jackson told him.

'Hey, Bob.' Harrison looked up at him. 'Remember that video tape we watched? That was me in there.'

'I know that.' Jackson leaned his fists on the table. 'But

what're you gonna prove – and how're you gonna prove it?'

Harrison sat back and sighed. There were upwards of a hundred different people who had access to the product. 'I owe this to myself, Bob,' he said. 'And the Bureau owes it to me.'

He returned to his work, evidence copies laid out before him. Mackey, the militia man in Hagerman, had told him about the phone call and the message for Jake Salvesen. He said he knew no more than that and Harrison believed him. He had requested his phone records, however, to check the incoming calls. He knew the date and he knew roughly the time. Salvesen himself was being shipped from Blaine County to a holding centre there in Salt Lake so that the Bureau could begin their interrogation. That was partly why Kovalski was coming over. Salvesen had been arming and training the militia, not for a march on D.C., but in readiness for when the European Antichrist invaded or whatever the hell he thought was going to happen. But that still left a well-trained and heavily armed bunch of private armies all over the country.

Harrison stared at the photos in front of him. The compromise had corresponded with him getting inside Salvesen's office, so something he had filmed was the key to that timing. Somebody saw something they didn't want anyone else to see. By the time the FBI Hostage Rescue Team got inside the compound, the contents of Salvesen's drawers were gone.

He flicked through the pictures of the maps and the books and the Bible texts and then he stopped and considered the receipt from Paris. He knew now that Scotland Yard had picked up Brigitte Hammani because of it. He looked at it again; maybe that was it, just the receipt. But that only implicated Salvesen and Hammani.

He was about to discard it when he paused and looked more closely at the slip of paper poking out from underneath, handwritten bits of words. 'Ten, ction, aces'. He didn't know what it meant, but it was handwritten and he could tell from the shape of the letters that it was not Salvesen's hand.

Bob Jackson was back in his office when Harrison went looking for him. 'Who else was in the FEST that went over to England?' Harrison asked him.

'Why?'

'Because I need to know.'

Jackson steepled his fingers in front of him. 'Johnny, why don't you just sit and think about this for a few days, huh. We've got Jake Salvesen and the British rendered the bomb safe. You did a great job out there and you deserve a vacation. Why not get some rest?'

Harrison sat down opposite him. 'Bob, somebody tried to kill me.'

'I know that. But it could've been anyone. It could easily have been the Indian. You know he was at the Wounded Knee stand-off in 1972.'

Harrison shook his head. 'You know that doesn't make sense. Why would he compromise me, then call in the cavalry and *then* get himself shot?'

'I don't know. But he obviously knew who you were *and* what you were doing. How come he didn't mention it to you? From what you told us, you were friends.'

Harrison shook his head. 'Bob, you know it wasn't Chief.'

Jackson sighed. 'Listen, JB. I know how you feel, but don't go making waves, huh. If it is somebody on the inside, we'll get him in time and we'll get him quietly. We've had enough bad publicity in recent years, what with Oklahoma and Richard Jewel. This is a great victory for us and we can show the public just what some of these militia guys are really like. Washington is not gonna like a UCA running around with a hair up his ass.'

Harrison looked across the desk at him. 'I want Tom Kovalski to know how I feel, Bob. If you don't tell him, I will.'

# 29

Swann couldn't sleep properly and was at the Yard by 6 a.m. Byrne was there already and Swann was surprised to see him so early, sitting at the allotted desk in the squad room, his mobile phone in front of him.

'Hotel beds not suit you, Louis?' he said.

Byrne pushed his chair back. 'Get up at five when I'm working, Jack. Habit from my service days. I work in the hotel or at the embassy before I come in here.'

They were the only two in the squad room. Swann sat down at his own desk and looked through a few papers. An IRA trial was coming up and he was due at the Old Bailey to give evidence.

'I gotta message for you, Jack,' Byrne said, and Swann glanced over to him again.

'Who from?'

'Pia.'

'You mean Brigitte Hammani.'

'Right.'

'What'd she say?'

'She asked me to tell you that she was sorry.'

Swann stared at him. 'Thanks, Louis. But you know what – I really don't want to hear it.'

At the morning briefing later, Colson was speaking about the arrest of Brigitte Hammani. 'She was interviewed informally yesterday,' he said. 'Her full statement will be made today, but she is being very co-operative.'

He looked at Clements. 'Relieved almost. Wasn't that how you put it, Dave?'

'How it felt to me.'

'She admitted to being Joanne Taylor,' Colson went on. 'She also told us she was the woman who met Bruno Kuhlmann in Northumberland and liaised with Action 2000.' He paused. 'So we have a partial result at least. We've got the Cairns brothers and maybe James Ingram.'

'But not the guy we really want,' Swann said.

Colson glanced at him and shook his head. 'Hammani told us she had meetings with a man in Westminster Cathedral. Sometimes he dressed as a Greek Orthodox priest.'

'Boese,' Byrne cut in. 'And Storm Crow. Favoured disguise. They're one and the same person.'

Swann looked sideways at him then. 'I don't think so, Louis. What we were told yesterday, the planning, the patience of it all. That tells me someone else is behind this. Boese's just the man on the ground.'

'Profile, Jack. Background.'

Swann shrugged. 'Means he's a good man on the ground, that's all.'

Colson cut in on them: 'We won't know till we catch him, but I have to agree with Louis. My guess *is* Boese. Anyway, we've asked for CCTV tapes from the cathedral, but they wipe them every week. According to Hammani, the first meeting took place months ago.'

'Does she think Boese's the Storm Crow?' Webb asked him.

Clements answered for him. 'She doesn't know, George. The bottom line is no one does for sure, except Boese himself. She says she spoke on the telephone with someone, starting when she was in Israel. Recently, he's always used a mobile. She believes some of the calls came from the States, which puts Boese back in the frame.'

Colson nodded. 'What we can confirm for sure is Louis's theory that he's in this for the money. Hammani was effectively his researcher. He created an education, put her through college and made sure she got into banking. He then used her to pick up on some of the world's more unsavoury but wealthy individuals. That's how he established his reputation, cold cunning and calculating.'

'A strategist and a planner,' Swann said. 'In my experience, those guys tend to be REMFs.'

Rear echelon motherfuckers. Colson's features darkened, but Swann ignored him.

'When did Napoleon or Hitler actually pick up a gun and fight anyone?' he went on. 'They sat in their bunkers and planned what to do. What you've just described, sir, is serious strategic planning. I listened in to that interview yesterday. She talked about the Storm Crow claiming he'd recruited Said Rabi for the attack on the ambassador's car. Does that sound like Boese? Boese doesn't recruit, he's on the ground. Action man. I reckon somebody else recruited Rabi and that same person recruited Ismael Boese.'

'Hang on, Jack,' McCulloch said. 'You're saying that Boese's too much of a doer to have planned all this. I don't agree. He could easily have done it in advance. Let's face it, most of the donkey work was done by your ex-girlfriend.'

Swann stared at him.

'Sorry, man. I didn't mean it to sound like that.' He made a gesture with the flat of his hand. 'But, what better place to orchestrate things than at ground level. Carlos did it all the time.'

'Yeah and Carlos got caught.'

'Given up, Jack. Political will rather than police work.'

Colson looked at the rest of them. 'At the moment, it's immaterial. He's not here to ask.'

After the meeting, Swann drove to Paddington Green. He was not completely sure that was where he was going until he drove up to the gates. The security doors were opened and he parked. Downstairs, the custody sergeant met him.

'Hey, Jack. How's it going?'

'Not too bad. I want to see Brigitte Hammani.'

'Interview?'

Swann shook his head. 'Five minutes in the cell with her, that's all.'

The sergeant made a face. 'I shouldn't do it really.'

'Pete, she all but lived with me for eighteen months. Give me a break, eh?'

'OK, Jack. Only five minutes, though.'

Swann's heart was beating hard as the sergeant unlocked the metal door. Pia looked up from where she was lying on the bench with her back to them. She blinked a few times, then sat up with a jerk.

For a few moments they just looked at one another. She sat on the bench, no make-up, dark circles dragging under her eyes. Her hair was mussed on her head and the paper suit rustled as she moved. She looked at him and tears started to glisten. 'How are you, Jack?'

'How d'you think I am?'

She rubbed her eyes with stiff fingers. 'I was nineteen years old,' she said. 'You don't know anything at nineteen.'

'Why didn't you give yourself up there and then?'

'They would've killed me. If the Americans or Mossad didn't, then my own people would. The Fatah were the most deadly faction of the PLO even after it was unified. They'd've pegged me as an informer and made an example, even in jail. They've cut open pregnant women before now.'

'You were a terrorist, Pia. Your choice, long before the Storm Crow picked you up.'

'Was I?' Furrows cut in her brow. 'Maybe I was. Two Israeli soldiers smashed both my brother's arms. What does that make them?'

Swann just stared at her. 'You'll do thirty years, Pia. You'll be sixty before you get out.' He moved a little closer to her then. 'Why did you use me?'

She looked at the floor.

'Because I was weak. Isn't that what you said?'

'You're not weak, Jack. You had a weakness is what I said, a vulnerability.'

'Something to be exploited.'

'His idea.'

'But you did the exploiting.'

'What else could I do?' She lifted her hands. 'He owned me body and soul. Have you any idea what that feels like?'

'I know just what it feels like.' Swann said it viciously. For a few moments neither of them spoke, a cold metallic silence in the cell. 'I left you alone with my kids. I trusted you. Christ. I can't believe I did that.'

'Did I ever do anything to harm your kids?'

'You were a good actor, Pia. I'll give you that.'

She got up off the bench and moved towards him, but he backed away.

'Don't touch me.' He held up his hands, palm outwards. 'Please, do not touch me.'

She sat back on the bench. 'I wasn't acting, Jack. In the beginning maybe, but not later. In the end I loved you.'

'Bullshit, Pia. You wouldn't know love if it smacked you in the eye. You manipulated and used me. You set this whole thing up, a chemical bomb in London, for pity's sake. Millions of people could've died.'

'I did love you, Jack. You *know* I did.' She wrung her hands helplessly. 'Jesus Christ, the amount of times I nearly told you. You have no idea how sick of it I was.' She stood up again. 'I listened to you, Jack. In Scotland, remember? Your dreams, your fears, your pain.' Her eyes flashed then. 'You can think what else you like, but you *know* I loved you.'

Swann leaned on the door. 'What did he think, Pia, that you could get information from me – get to me because I was vulnerable? Fucked-up Jack Swann who killed his climbing partner.' He shook his head very bitterly. 'You know how that makes me feel?'

'There's no point in talking about this, Jack. You won't ever believe me, so what is the point.'

'You're right,' he said. 'There is no point.'

'Then why did you come to see me?'

'I want to ask you a question.' He moved closer to her then, hands in his jacket pockets. 'Is Ismael Boese the Storm Crow?'

'I don't know.'

'You spoke to him, Storm Crow, I mean?'

'Yes.'

'Face to face?'

'Somebody sat in front of me, always disguised. I was never allowed to look at his face.'

'Westminster Cathedral?'

She nodded.

'His voice, Pia. The same voice on the telephone?'

'I don't know.'

'Then think?'

She lifted her hands. 'I don't know, Jack. People sound different on the phone.'

He thought for a moment. 'Louis Byrne. Have you ever met him before?'

'No.'

'Spoken to him?'

'No.'

'Are you sure? Your face yesterday – you looked as though you recognized his voice.'

'Did I? I don't remember.'

Swann breathed out audibly and leaned against the wall. 'How did the crystal get over here – the pirillium derivative?'

'I don't know. That was nothing to do with me. I just had to do my end. Get the accommodation and drivers.'

'Why was Jean-Marie Mace killed?'

'A marker, same as the Soho bomb and Northumberland.'

'Europe. The federalization, trying to give us an idea what he was playing at?'

'I suppose so. I was never told the *whys* of anything.'

The sergeant opened the cell door then and Swann looked one last time at Pia. He felt the frustration and anger all over again.

'Goodbye, Pia,' he said.

She stared at him, her eyes suddenly soft. But she did not say anything.

Back at the Yard, the squad room was in a state of excitement. Swann cornered McCulloch. 'What gives?' he said.

'Word just came in from Porton Down. The scaffolding pipes were full of water.'

'*Just* water?'

'Yes.'

'What about the PINS analysis? EOD diagnostics found positive traces.'

'In the plastic container, yes. They only had time to

601

test four of the pipes, Jack. Porton Down checked the rest. No trace.'

Swann scratched his head. 'I don't get it,' he said.

'It's good news, Flash. Means he can't quite do what he wanted us to think he could.'

'That, or he didn't have to. The city was still evacuated, wasn't it.'

☆

Ismael Boese sat in the lounge of the Mount Pleasant Hotel in Hammersmith. He was watching Sky News on television. The commander of the Antiterrorist Branch was giving a press conference, talking about the operation to liberate the city and of how a major catastrophe had been averted. He relayed the information they had received from Porton Down: the thirty-five mortars contained nothing but water. Boese's eyes were dark. Fool, he thought. You stupid, stupid fool.

Pier-Luigi Ramas got on the tube train for Heathrow, carrying a small leather suitcase, and a lightweight travel bag. In the bag was a Ruger 9mm handgun. His flight was due to leave in just over two hours. He hadn't wanted to loiter in the country like this. As far as he was concerned, the job was more than done and he longed to get home. Tal-Salem did not seem overly bothered and Boese had insisted. Still, he had checked this morning and all of his money was safely accounted for. Yesterday, Boese phoned to tell him it was time to go. Women were waiting in Rome and he was itching to get away.

☆

Christine Harris was manning the base in the operations room, when a call came up from the central command complex.

'SO12.'

'We've just received an anonymous tip-off. Pier-Luigi Ramas is on a tube train bound for Heathrow.'

☆

Jakob Salvesen was brought to the interview room in chains and guarded by four FBI agents. He still bore the mark of Harrison's garrotte on his neck. Kovalski, Jackson and Harrison were going to interrogate him. Kovalski had arrived on a flight from D.C. via Cincinnati and Harrison had spoken briefly to him and Jackson before they went down.

'You did one helluva job, John,' Kovalski told him.

'Would've been easier if I didn't get burned.'

Kovalski looked at him then with concern evident in his eyes. 'You found out how?'

'I'm looking, Tom. I'm looking. Interviewed a militia man in Hagerman. He got a call which may've come from the Storm Crow. It was after I sent in the stuff I got from Salvesen's office.'

Kovalski tapped a tooth with his forefinger. 'Somebody on the inside.'

'Had to be.'

'A lot of people saw that product, John. Myself included.'

'I know it.'

'What d'you wanna do?'

Harrison glanced at Jackson then, who frowned. Harrison knew there was no way he could find out for sure, let alone prove anything. 'I guess we took out Jake,' he said wearily.

Kovalski nodded. 'Yeah, but if there's a bad guy about, I want him.'

'You and me both.'

'But quietly. There's no point in raising a stink when over one hundred people had access to that product.'

'I know.' Harrison blew out his cheeks. 'What we got is good, Tom. I know that. Might turn a few people off the militia.'

'It's what we needed. If Salvesen had been trying to get them all together, we'd have a hell of a problem. Right now, we need every weapon possible we can use against them. I'd appreciate it if you kept your suspicions between us for the time being. You know how things get leaked.'

Harrison pulled a face. 'No kidding. Remember the Palestinian internment saga?'

'Oh God. Don't remind me of that.' He looked Harrison in the eye then. 'You know me, John. This won't get whitewashed. I want to see you in D.C. We'll talk about it then.'

They went down to see Salvesen. He sat in the chains with his hair tousled, looking old but still defiant. When he saw Harrison, his face turned lobster red. 'I'm gonna have your balls,' he said, touching his neck. 'You nearly cut my throat.'

'You know what, Jake,' Kovalski said. 'There's those that wished he had.'

Salvesen sat more upright in his chair. 'Where's my attorney?' he demanded.

'On his way. Who made the pirillium derivative?'

Salvesen sneered. 'You think I'm going to speak to *you*? I claim the Fifth Amendment.'

'Abel Manley?' Kovalski said.

'I claim the Fifth Amendment.'

'He was in your compound. We've got photographs. You knew him from the sixties Minutemen. He was a chemist like Robert DePugh.'

'I claim the Fifth, sir. Did you not hear me?'

'Fine.' Kovalski leaned his forearms on the table. 'We got you, Jake. Whether you claim the Fifth or not.'

Salvesen smiled, the same light in his eyes that Harrison had witnessed in his courtroom.

'For now, maybe,' he said quietly. But I don't recognize your authority. You see, I only serve one master.'

'And you did that by trying to bomb London.'

'London, Frankfurt. Wherever. You fools. Don't you realize that I'm the patriot here? I'm the one on the side of righteousness.' He shook his head. 'Can't you see you're just puppets. The world is changing as we speak and you cannot see it. The Beast is alive and well and living in Western Europe. It takes a God-fearing *American* to stop him.'

'The beast?'

'The Abomination that causes desolation. The number of his name – Six Six Six.' Salvesen's eyes were shining. 'You ought to thank me. I've made a noise out there and people will begin to listen. When there are sixteen nations in the European Union, you *will* see him rise. Then you'll come to me.'

☆

On the fifteenth floor at Scotland Yard, a sterile arrest team was being dispatched to Heathrow. SO19 had been tasked and armed-response vehicles were heading for the airport.

On the tube train Ramas read the newspaper. When he got to the airport and quartered it, he would dump the gun in the toilets and move through to the departure gate. Just an hour or so more and he would be home free at last. He closed his eyes for a moment, then glanced up at the route-planner on the wall above the far window. They had just left Hounslow West, the next stop was Hatton Cross. He was due to get off at Terminal 2. The train thundered into Hatton Cross station and the doors opened. Two black women with children got off. Ramas looked again at the route-planner. Then two uniformed police officers got on, and both of them had MP5 carbines strapped across their chests. Ramas felt the ball of tension curl in his gut.

He sat where he was, the paper lifted to his face. The policemen stood by the door, each one leaning against the glass partition, facing one another. Ramas was three seats down; he could feel the blood at his temples. His hands were shaking just a fraction and he closed his eyes to calm down. The train pulled into Terminal 4. He would get off here and get back on when they'd gone. Picking up his bags, he moved down to the exit. He waited, the light came on and he pressed the button to open the doors. On the platform, he walked towards the exit. When he got there, he glanced over his shoulder. The two police officers were following.

Now his heart was beating; he could feel their eyes on his bag. He shouldered it, slipped one hand inside and gripped the butt of the gun. He needed the escalator or lift to take him up to the terminal. Two people were waiting by the lift with luggage trolleys. Ramas took the escalator, and behind him the police officers followed. Upstairs, he came out by the café and hesitated. Three more armed officers were standing in front of him, two of them had a sheet of paper in their hands. He ducked left and walked briskly. One of the officers glanced at him, then at the paper and back at his face once more. Ramas dropped his bag and came up pointing the gun.

He looked left and right, then ran for the exit. He could hear sirens outside. His heart was jumping in his chest, and he looked around for a hostage. Nobody close enough. The automatic doors opened and he rushed outside. As he hit the pavement he stopped. Two marked police cars drew up with a terrible screeching of brakes. Ramas stared, looked for a way of escape, but there was nowhere he could go.

'Armed police. You in the black. Stand still.' He looked up. Two officers were out of the first car, pistols drawn, using the doors as cover. Behind him, the others came out of the terminal. He thought of Boese and he thought of Tal-Salem. Betrayal. Again the man at the car shouted. 'Drop the weapon. Now.'

Ramas half turned and stared into the eyes of the uniformed officer nearest the terminal door. Young face, young eyes, more than a little bit frightened. Slowly, he levelled the gun. Bullets hit him, back and front. He forced the cry away, body jerking, arms flailing, the gun spinning into the air. He didn't hear it land; concentrating on keeping his feet, hands to the holes in his chest. A bloodied hole in one hand, another in his elbow. He retched and blood spilled on to the pavement. For a moment he looked at it, globs of saliva dyeing the red to pink. He fell then, forward on to his knees, one hand on the cold concrete. Gently, he lowered himself and twisted on to his back. He was aware of the life leaking out of him and the last thing he saw was the barrel of an MP5 pointing down at his face.

☆

Julian Moore of MI5 was sitting at his desk scanning a copy of the *International Herald Tribune*. This was technical intelligence, the art of finding what did not appear to be there. The phone rang on the desk and leisurely he picked it up.

'Julian Moore.'

'This is the duty officer at GCHQ. Operation Ding Dong, you gave us a tracker a year ago. It's just been activated.'

☆

Harrison sat in his hotel room with the caller information on John Henry Mackey in his hand. He had one number ringed, a payphone in London. In his other hand he held the telephone. 'Listen, Mackey. Don't fuck with me. I'll have your ass in chains so fucking fast, you won't know what day it is. Who do you know in London?'

'I don't know no one. I ain't never been there. I ain't never called there. I ain't never even spoke with nobody from London. You got that, Fed? I don't know nobody.'

'If I find out you're lying to me, I'll kill you myself. Even if I gotta come to jail to get you.'

'Do what you gotta do, asshole.' Mackey hung up the phone.

The call had come from London. That cleared everyone on this side of the ocean. Harrison stared at the names of the Foreign Emergency Search Team. Graham Ketner from the CIA. Bob Hicks, State Department. The other three were FBI. He had not known about the guy from the Weapons of Mass Destruction Unit. Logan he knew, ASAC with Tom Kovalski. And, of course, 'Lucky' Louis Byrne. He pursed his lips and lit another cigarette. He didn't know the guy from the Company, or Hicks for that matter. Cheyenne, he had met a couple of times, but not Larry Thomas. He laid the paper down and placed his hands behind his head. 'Lucky' Louis Byrne, the original Storm Crow hunter. Everyone knew that was his particular *bête noire*.

He closed his eyes then and thought instead about the people of Passover. Scheller had constantly warned him about going native. Not that there was any need. He had been a UCA twice before and he had never gone native. But he thought about Guffy and how warm her bed had been. He was forty-eight years old, battered about the face and heart, and he was alone again once more. He opened his eyes then and the thought of somebody on the inside compromising him pushed in on everything else. A death sentence, passed by someone reputedly on your own side. He picked up the papers and flicked through them over again. He sucked hard on his cigarette. What about the Englishman who'd been screwing Brigitte Hammani? They said it was down to him that Boese had stayed so far ahead of the game. Jack Swann. Who was Jack Swann and what did he know?

☆

'Get a helicopter up, Jack. We need to follow the car.' There was urgency in Colson's voice and Swann picked up the telephone.

'We need SO19 over here now.' Colson looked at Webb, who picked up the other extension. He got Sergeant Graves from blue team.

'Hello, Nick,' he said, looking at the CAD in front of him. 'Remember Queen's House Mews?'

'How could I forget?'

'How'd you like another go at him?'

They briefed en route: three Gunships, a Range Rover and two Vauxhall Omegas, unmarked cars driven by SO13 officers with three firearms officers in each of them, everyone in plainclothes. Colson and Swann sat in the back of the control car, with Graves in the front passenger seat. The Gunships were currently behind them. Graves was in communication with the aircraft overhead, which was tracking the movements of the Mondeo.

'Why go back to it after a year?' Swann was saying. 'It doesn't make any sense.'

Graves looked over his shoulder at him. 'We need eyeball.'

Colson nodded and got on the radio. 'Four/two from Colson. Come in.'

'Four/two, receiving,' the response crackled back.

'We need eyeball. Get up to him pronto.'

He put the radio down. Graves was scratching his bald head and scouring the map on his lap. They were driving quickly with no lights or sirens, making their way through the traffic and out of London.

'He's heading for the M1,' Graves said.

Webb was in another of the surveillance cars, ten in all, travelling in convoy away from the Yard in the direction of Hendon and the bottom of the M1 motorway. He was echoing the thoughts of Jack Swann. 'Why go back, Macca?' Byrne was sitting in the back seat with Cheyenne. 'He's been the consummate professional,' Webb went on. 'He must know we flagged the car. Jesus, why not just steal another one?'

'We don't know that it's him,' Byrne said.

Webb glanced over his shoulder. 'Ramas is dead. It's either Boese or Tal-Salem.'

'Or a car thief.' Cheyenne lifted her eyebrows.

McCulloch looked round at her. 'Well, if it is – he's going to get one hell of a shock when we catch up with him.'

The helicopter reported that the Mondeo had hit the bottom of the M1 and was travelling north. Graves spoke to the three Gunships. 'We follow at distance for the time being,' he said. 'Let's see where he goes.' He thought for a moment. 'Luton Airport, maybe. If he turns off, we take him.'

They were still waiting for the motorcyclist to try to establish the identity of the driver. He was well ahead of them now, and every now and then he would check in to confirm the location of the target. Just south of Luton, he called in. 'Control from four/two.'

Graves lifted the microphone. 'Go ahead, four/two.'

'Contact. Blue Mondeo ahead, middle lane.' He read out the index number.

'Confirmed,' Graves said. 'Can you give us eyeball ID?'

'Affirmative.'

The communication broke and Swann sat in the back staring out of the window. He was praying this was Boese. He really wanted to see him again.

'Control from four/two.'

'Go ahead, four/two.'

'Eyeball contact. Single occupant. IC3 male, short dark hair. Target confirmed.'

Swann looked at Graves. 'Let's take the fucker, Nick.'

Graves pondered for a moment, then spoke into the radio. 'Central command from Bronze Commander Graves, SO19.'

'Go ahead,' the response came back from the sixteenth floor at the Yard.

'Rolling take-out confirmed. SO19 will call the attack. Three Gunships, repeat three Gunships. Contact local forces along the route given by fixed-wing spotters. I want the entrances blocked on to the M1 carriageway travelling north. Junctions fourteen, fifteen and sixteen.'

'Confirmed.'

Graves looked over his shoulder at Colson. 'I want the surveillance cars to fall back behind us, sit in the three lanes and slow everyone down, one-hundred-yard intervals, eighty, seventy, sixty, down to forty mph.'

Colson nodded. 'It's your call, Nick.'

He relayed the information to the ten surveillance cars and then Graves nodded to the driver. 'Sirens and blue lights,' he said. Let's catch the bastard up.'

They were twenty miles back, so they could afford to hit the lights. All cars corresponded and the convoy hit the outside lane with sirens wailing and stick-on blue lights flashing. Everybody moved out of their way and within a short while they were only five miles behind the target. The motorcyclist had pulled off at the services, re-entered the traffic and was now one hundred yards behind the Mondeo. The helicopter flew overhead. Boese was moving north, still with no sign of turning off the motorway. He had already passed junction thirteen and was travelling at seventy miles an hour in the middle lane. Swann could feel the tension beginning to rise. He thought of his children back with their mother and of Pia Grava in the cells at Paddington Green.

The convoy got closer and closer. Three miles behind Boese, they eased back on their speed and switched off sirens and lights. Further up the motorway, the local traffic officers were setting rolling roadblocks at the entrance to the access roads. Nobody would be joining the carriageway north until the surveillance cars were beyond them. People would get irate, drivers always did, but the designated cars would hog the three lanes and gradually slow their speed to forty. That way, a gap would open between the assault cars and those following, allowing enough time for Graves to put the attack in and stop Boese's Mondeo. They got further and further north, and gradually the traffic eased behind the Gunships. A sterile arrest car joined them, with three SO13 officers on board. They wanted Boese clean and uncontaminated.

Graves was constantly on the radio, controlling the movement of vehicles. The lead Gunship, the black Range Rover, now had the target in sight. They passed the motorcyclist on the left and he nodded to them. Above them, the helicopter confirmed everything. The traffic continued ahead, but behind them the road was empty. Graves wanted five miles between the Gunships and the surveillance cars to stop one almighty pile-up. That would give the attack team seven and a half minutes to complete the arrest and get any damaged vehicles to the side of the road. The surveillance cars called in their positions and the helicopter monitored the distance.

When they hit the five-mile mark, the call came in to Graves.

'Confirmed,' Graves said. 'Attack cars, one, two and three. Move up.'

The Range Rover accelerated ahead of them. Boese was now in the outside lane doing eighty-five miles an hour. He was talking on a mobile phone. The Range Rover came alongside him, the driver keeping his eyes forward. If Boese looked left, the driver did not notice. He accelerated hard and pulled out into the outside lane, perhaps twenty yards ahead. The second car pulled alongside and the third entered the outside lane behind the Mondeo. The lead Range Rover slowed just a fraction and a gap opened between the attack team and the traffic travelling in front. Boese was boxed in.

Graves watched, eyes sharp, microphone to his lips. 'Stand by,' he murmured. 'Stand by. Stand by.' His eyes flicked ahead, then briefly over his shoulder, only empty tarmac behind them. 'Stand by. Stand by.' He paused. Then, 'ATTACK.'

Simultaneously, the drivers of the three Gunships hit their brakes. The Mondeo braked and ploughed into the back of the Range Rover. The inside Omega pulled hard right and forced Boese into the central reservation. The last one braked and brushed the Mondeo's bumper. Within seconds, nine armed officers hit the tarmac. Boese watched them coming: no means of escape, the driver's door was all but against the crash barrier. Nine MP5 carbines were levelled at his windows. Slowly, he raised his hands.

Swann was out of the car. The SFOs had Boese prostrate on the tarmac now, his discarded mobile phone lying beside him. They searched him and found nothing. Then they twisted plasti-cuffs over his wrists and dragged him to his feet. Jack Swann stood facing him. He had his own mobile in his hand and he pressed in the number on Pia's bill: 0385 902754. He stared in Boese's eyes. Boese stared back. On the tarmac, the phone started ringing.

☆

Tom Kovalski found Harrison in the parking lot outside the field office in Salt Lake City, packing his gear into the back of his truck.

'Johnny Buck,' he called, and Harrison looked up, a Marlboro sticking out of his mouth.

'Louis Byrne just called me from the leg-att's office in London.'

'Yeah?'

'Scotland Yard arrested the Storm Crow.'

Harrison sucked on the cigarette and let smoke drift from his nostrils. 'No kidding,' he said.

Kovalski shook his hand. 'It's a great day, John,' he said. 'A really great day.'

'Yeah. Right.'

'Another thing I wanted to tell you. Louis Freeh wants to see you when we get back to D.C. He heard what a great job you did in Idaho.'

Harrison smiled then. 'The director? No shit.' He ran his fingers over the doorhandle of his truck. 'D'you think he'll mind waiting for a little bit? I'm gonna take some time off, Tom,' he said. 'Get my head together.'

'Good idea. You deserve it. Where you gonna go?'

'Passover, Idaho.'

Kovalski looked at him then, with his head slightly to one side. 'That a good idea?'

'I don't know yet. I had a bit of a life there, Tom. I wanna see if I can get some of it back.'

'Never go back, John. You know the game.'

'Normally I do.' Harrison flipped away his cigarette. 'This time it's different, though.'

Kovalski nodded. 'OK. When you get done, call me in Washington. Let me know when you're coming in.'

Harrison drove back to Idaho: it took him five hours; dark when he got there. He cruised slowly through Passover, but nobody was on the street. He drove three miles further and passed the airport in Westlake where Salvesen had flown in all the militia leaders. Salvesen was in chains now and he would stay that way. He thought about his face though, when they had tried to interrogate him. *The Abomination that causes desolation, the Beast. When there are sixteen nations in the European Union, you will see him rise.* Israel reformed as a nation. The age of the Gentiles over in 1967. All would come to pass within one generation. He felt a shiver trickle down his spine. What if Salvesen was right?

He stopped the truck in Westlake and lit a cigarette. Cars and motorcycles were parked up outside the hotel and from the look of things it was busy. Harrison sat a while in the darkness, and the sheriff passed him on his way south. He could see Danny Dugger's battered truck and he thought about Magdalena's tunnels. There, he had killed Jesse Tate, and got back what he lost.

The hotel bar was crowded and noisy. Nobody noticed him at first. Sula-Mae was bartending. Harrison slipped on to a stool and gradually the noise subsided. Lisa Guffy was sitting with her home girl round the other side. Their eyes met and she looked away. Harrison sat there looking at the bar top, and then a bottle of Bud was set down in front of him. He looked up into Sula's brown eyes. 'Buck seventy-five,' she said.

He felt in his pocket for dollars and caught sight of Don, the owner, watching him from his seat by the tape machine. He had not put Frank Sinatra on yet, but he would. Harrison sipped the beer and lit a Merit. He watched Guffy and she ignored him. Cecil moved alongside him, dark-eyed man and gentle. 'So you're a Fed, Harrison,' he said.

'Yes, Cecil. I am.'

Cecil scraped fingers over his moustache. Harrison moved his shoulders.

'I'm sorry I lied to you, man. But there was no other way. Jake Salvesen tried to bomb London. Somebody had to get him.'

Cecil looked thoughtful for a moment, finished his drink and glanced sideways at him.

'You wanna shot?' he said.

Cecil bought him a Jack Daniel's and he knocked it back, the liquor harsh in his throat. Still he looked at Guffy and still she ignored him. Tracy was talking to her and motioning in his direction. Harrison caught Danny Dugger's eye and Danny inclined his head. He looked up and found Chief towering above him, left arm in a sling. 'Never thought we'd see you again,' he said.

'Got business to finish up. How's the shoulder?'

'It'll work.'

Harrison finished his beer and bought another one. Sula-Mae served him without speaking. Nobody else spoke to him. Cecil went off to play pool with Jimmy the Limey, who eyed Harrison cautiously. He nursed his beer, smoked another cigarette and thought about pulling out. He knew where he was going, but didn't want to go alone. He felt somebody move alongside him and smelled Guffy's perfume. Very slowly he looked up.

'You came back,' she said quietly.

'I did.'

'Why?'

'Things to say.'

'So say them.'

People were watching them now. Harrison straightened

on his stool. Wayne Olson vacated his and Guffy sat down next to him.

'I only ever lied to you about what I did,' he told her.

Lisa lit a cigarette and blew smoke at the ceiling. 'What does that mean?'

'Exactly what it says. Everything else I said was true.'

'Everything?'

He looked in her eyes. 'You think I'd drive for five hours back to a town full of people who hate me, if it wasn't?'

She looked away. Harrison could feel himself trembling.

'What you gonna do now?' she asked him.

'Go back to D.C. and finish up. Then I guess they'll assign me to another field office.'

'Where?'

He shrugged. 'New Orleans, New Mexico, maybe. I don't know, honey. I'll have to wait and see.'

'You going right away?'

'No,' he said. 'I'm due some vacation time.'

'What you gonna do with it?'

'I'm gonna drive to Marquette and fish the big lake.' He paused then and put out his cigarette. 'You wanna come with me, Miss Lady Mam?'

For a moment she sat very still, staring into space across the bar. Then she slipped her hand into his where it rested in his lap. She looked him hard in the eyes. 'You fuck me over again, Harrison – I'll kill you.'

☆

The S013 team were in Los Remos with the Americans. Beer was flowing. Boese was in custody and in the morning Swann was going to interview him. Everyone was in high spirits. The press knew nothing yet. The commander was keeping it quiet until they had the results of the swabbing and fibres. He was going to savour the moment, before personally calling the Prime Minister in Rome.

The moment was bittersweet for Swann; he wondered if the word had got round to Pia yet that Storm Crow was in custody. Or at least Boese was. The others, Webb included, reckoned they had their man. Swann harboured doubts. But hell, he might as well enjoy it along with everyone else, and he was looking forward to tomorrow. Byrne put an arm round his shoulders. 'Quiet, Jack. I thought this'd be your night?'

'Yeah, well. You know how it is, Louis.'

'Listen, you're a good police officer. You got chewed a bit. It happens.'

Swann took out his cigarettes. He caught Cheyenne's pretty, black eyes and she smiled at him. Byrne slapped him on the back and accepted another beer from Webb.

Cheyenne came over to Swann. 'You know, honey,' she said. 'You look like the little boy lost.'

Swann laughed then. 'Really?'

'I guess it's mixed feelings for you tonight.'

'I'm a bit pissed off, Chey. But I'll get over it.'

'Let me buy you a shot.' She bought him a single malt and he sipped it. 'When're you going back to the States?' he asked her.

'Couple of days.' She touched his arm. 'You ever get over there, you give me a call, y'hear.'

Swann nodded. 'You think Boese's the man?'

'Yes, I do. He's very bright, Jack. You've said that yourself. He hung out with Carlos. He must've learned something.'

'We don't know that was Boese for definite.'

'We're pretty sure. Louis's checked him out with the Jonathan Institute. He's pretty certain.'

Swann looked up then and caught Byrne's eye. For a while they looked at one another. Neither of them smiled.

☆

The following morning, Swann and Clements wheeled Ismael Boese into the interview room at Paddington Green. Ramas was dead, the foot soldiers were in custody, only Tal-Salem was at large. Boese, dressed in a paper suit and somebody else's shoes, was seated across the table from them. He said nothing, merely folded his arms and looked directly between them. His face showed no hint of emotion, but his eyes were dark and strong. He looked like a man totally at peace with himself. Since he had been arrested on the M1 motorway the previous afternoon, he had not said a single word.

'You're allowed to make a phone call,' Swann said to him. 'Do you want to call a solicitor or shall we appoint one for you?'

'I have one.' His voice was soft and firm.

'James Ingram's in custody.'

Boese looked at him. 'I have one,' he repeated.

Swann got a telephone and plugged it in. 'What's the number?'

'0181 405 1719.'

'Name of the firm?'

'Reeves & Company.'

'Solicitor's name?'

'Reeves.'

Swann picked up the *Yellow Pages* and looked under 'Solicitors'. He found Reeves & Co, checked the number and dialled.

☆

Mr Reeves lay in the corner of his office with a bullet hole in his head. Twenty minutes earlier, Tal-Salem had walked into the outer office and quietly locked the door.

'Excuse me,' the middle-aged receptionist said. 'What do you think you're doing?'

Tal-Salem turned and screwed the silencer into the barrel of his Beretta. He put a finger to his lips and smiled, then beckoned for her to get up. Her face had drained of all colour – wan and pale despite the layers of make-up. She was shaking and her red mouth wavered as she spoke. 'What – what do you want? We don't keep any money here.'

Tal-Salem pointed to Reeves's nameplate on the door. 'I have an appointment,' he said.

She showed him in and Reeves looked up from across the desk; a bald-headed man of about forty, large spectacles sitting low on his nose. He half rose and Tal-Salem shot him. The receptionist fainted and he had to slap hard to wake her.

Now he sat across Reeves's desk, with her in Reeves's chair, and he rested his gun hand on his thigh. The telephone rang and he motioned to it. 'Normal,' he said, 'or I'll shoot you.'

She picked it up with a hand that trembled. 'Reeves & Company,' she said.

Swann glanced at Boese. 'This is Detective Sergeant Swann of the Antiterrorist Branch, Metropolitan Police. We have a client of yours in custody, one Ismael Boese. He would like to speak to Mr Reeves.'

'One moment, please.' The receptionist handed the phone to Tal-Salem.

'Reeves here,' he said.

'Paddington Green police station. I have Ismael Boese for you.'

'Put him on.'

Swann passed the phone across to Boese.

Boese took it and raised it slowly to his ear. He stared at Swann, eyes penetrating, deep and suddenly very dark. 'Go to work,' he said, and put the phone down.

Swann stared at him, sweat on the palms of his hands. For the first time since this investigation began, he believed he was looking at the Storm Crow.

Tal-Salem put the phone down, sighed, then shot the receptionist in the middle of the forehead. For a second she stared at him in surprise, and then slumped back in the chair. He laid the gun on the desk, picked up the phone and dialled.

☆

Giancarlo Pasquali sat in his tiny Rome apartment and looked at his watch. The phone rang on the table.

'*Si?*'

'OK.'

'OK? *Si. Ciao.*' Pasquali put the phone down again, scratched his head and smiled. He opened his wallet, ran a finger over the crisp, stuffed notes and put it back in his pocket. Downstairs, he got into his ageing diesel taxi and headed down to St Peter's Square. He hummed as he drove, thinking this was the easiest money he had ever earned.

☆

In London, Tal-Salem sat on the desk and looked at the two dead bodies. He took a pre-rolled joint from his shirt pocket, lit it and drew the smoke in deeply. He thought about poor Pasquali and the second tank under the diesel one in his cab. He looked at his watch and smiled. In about ten minutes' time, the aerosol would start to work.

☆

Pasquali got to a set of red lights and let the engine idle. A man tied his dog to a lamppost and went into a kiosk for cigarettes. Thick, black fumes coughed from Pasquali's exhaust pipe. The man came out of the kiosk. The lights were green, but the taxi wasn't moving. He moved over to it: car drivers backed up behind were honking their horns as only frustrated Romans can do. The driver was rigid in the seat, vomit on his chest, eyes balling and very, very red. His whole body was shaking. The man stared, then suddenly he coughed, coughed again and looked at the blood in his hand.

☆

John Garrod sat at his desk and swivelled back and forth in his chair. He had just come off the phone to the Prime Minister, who was at the Capitol Chambers in Rome. He allowed himself a smile of self-congratulation and glanced at the American-Indian pictures that hung on the walls of his office. One of them caught his eye: the thin-lipped Apache, Geronimo. Master of illusion.

☆

Tony Blair came off the telephone and walked back into the council chamber. They had broken for coffee, and the other fourteen heads of Europe were standing and chatting together. It was in this very room that, forty-one years previously, the original six nations had signed the Treaty of Rome. Blair cleared his throat. 'Gentlemen,' he said. 'I have an announcement to make. The British government is delighted to be able to tell you that not only did our security forces successfully disable the chemical threat in London, but I have just been informed by the commander of the Antiterrorist Branch, that yesterday we apprehended Ismael Boese.' He smiled widely. 'The Storm Crow is in custody.'

They burst into applause and one by one they shook his hand. He moved to the window and allowed himself a moment of quiet contemplation. Chancellor Kohl stepped alongside and patted him on the back. 'Congratulations,' he said.

'Thank you.' The Prime Minister looked out of the window. Storm clouds were gathering over the city.